DRAGON'S CROWN

Book 4 of the Blood of the Covenants Series

Leah E. Welker

LIGHTBOUND MEDIA

CONTENTS

Key Terms & Translations   XI

The Six Realms   XIII

1. Tears   13

2. Awake   37

3. Oaths   46

4. Apologies   60

5. Spring   68

6. Morning   91

7. Pinprick   97

8. Bloodline   110

9. Lovely   121

10. Wing   142

11. Acceptance   158

12. Stars   171

13. Earrings   184

14. Flight   196

15. Sign   207

16. Beginning   219

17.	Belief	234
18.	Spirit	244
19.	Fever	246
20.	Prayer	254
21.	Family	259
22.	Allegiance	272
23.	Arrangements	283
24.	Emotions	297
25.	Production	311
26.	Breakthroughs	325
27.	Hunt	338
28.	Anger	353
29.	Formalities	364
30.	Hope	381
31.	Fear	395
32.	Wyrms	414
33.	Advice	424
34.	Realization	441
35.	Incursion	454
36.	After	462
37.	Rosin	477
38.	Searching	488
39.	Finding	509
40.	Need	527
41.	Shadow	541
42.	Glimmer	553

43. Tear   568

44. Negotiation   588

45. Relations   603

46. Secret   622

47. Siege   636

48. Weapons   648

49. Instincts   655

50. Purpose   660

About the Author   674

To Mom.

You told me when I was a girl that you didn't want to be a queen.

Somehow, you've shown me a hundred ways to be one, anyway.

Yes fire, light, air, birds, wax, the sun's own height
I draw from now, but every image breaks.
Only a child's simplicity can handle
Such moments when the hottest fire feels cool,
And every breath is like a sudden homage
To peace that penetrates and is not feared.

Elizabeth Jennings

KEY TERMS & TRANSLATIONS

Races

draká ("druh-KAH"): the original "dragons."

amá ("ah-MAH"): human(s); the sentient inhabitants of Earth.

dramá ("druh-MAH"): the race that emerged from the combination of draká and humans.

Blood Manifestations

drakón ("drah-KOHN"): dramá chosen to have far greater magic and gain a drakáform.

amón ("ah-MOHN"): dramá who are not chosen, yet still have the Blood of the Covenants and cannot accurately be called "human."

Distances

Rough equivalents

ild: inch.

foot: literal translation.

erd: yard (only a couple dramá feet).

ald: 100 dramá feet.

eld: half an English Imperial mile.

elden: an English Imperial mile.

Time

dek: Roughly 1 minute, made of 56 moments.

deken: Roughly 1 hour, made of 56 dek.

day: 28 deken.

THE SIX REALMS

Sun	Planet	Capital	Clan	Color	Specialty
Kaldrir	Ythra	Crownhold	Sunfilled	Gold	Central governance, priesthood, guarding Tree, maintaining sungates
Kyalid	Ekrel	Krevenyir	Battleblood	Violet	Battle, smithing, exploring, peacekeeping
Ashga	Oshal	Rosin	Starkissed	Sapphire	Magic, scholarship, diplomacy, artistry
Olmen	Romskal	Palla	Strongshield	Scarlet	Civil service, law, administration
Winalken	Yonvey	Remik	Brightflare	Orange	Tinkering, financing, mining, farming
Yedrik	Ykran	Danyeth	Peacegrowth	Emerald	Healing, farming, conserving

PROLOGUE

KORINTH

KORIBEN SUNFILLED, THE DRAKÓN King of the Six Realms, was dying.

One would not know it from looking at him as he strode into his study, where Korinth Starkissed, his leftwing and thus chief adviser, waited for him. The King's step was firm, and his shoulders straight. Even his golden eyes no longer had the haunted look that had filled them the first few days after his father's death.

But Kor, having been not just the young King's leftwing but also one of his closest friends for six years, knew better. The look that had replaced the haunting in the King's eyes wasn't a sign of healing but hardening...

...and what lay below the brittle crust was dangerous.

The Ben that Kor had known before *had* been prone to pushing himself to the breaking point, but at least then Ben would eat and sleep with some regularity, would laugh and smile and find the fun in life. Now, the King's dinner rested uneaten on a tray on his desk, and the mug of tsha that an attendant had made to tempt him to drink *something* was now cold. Though the King's movements were firm, and his healing energy prevented any shadows from forming beneath his eyes, Flame only knew how he was still going, because Kor knew from the stack of reviewed and completed paperwork that the King hadn't slept a wink the previous night.

The King couldn't have done it today, since he had been gone dealing with a rock wyrm hunt all day—which he had insisted on leading himself, and both his leftwing and rightwing had reluctantly agreed, hoping the exertion would do him some good.

Kor's faint hopes of that were dashed when he saw the King was still as hard and emotionless as ever.

Kor could not remember the last time he had seen his friend so much as smile.

Not for a month, at least. Not since the Battle of the Solstice, which had taken both the new King's father and his love from him in one day. Losing the former had been an unavoidable tragedy, since Kavarian had, in their darkest hour, given his life to save them all. Losing the latter....

One might argue that Sarah's forced departure had been avoidable. It was the King himself who had pushed her back into her own Realm and locked her out of all Six of his own for the past month, who even now had the power to let her back in, if he were so inclined.

Kor knew better. He of all people knew just how much the King's actions had been an inevitable consequence of his inability to bear being responsible for the death of yet one more person he loved.

Let alone Sarah.

Of all people, Kor should have known just what Ben would have done to Sarah after losing his father. The King's leftwing blamed only himself for not having prevented the King in time.

But blame...did not fix things. And things *had* to be fixed—now. Before that crust broke and they all found out what was underneath.

"Ah, Kor," the King said briskly as he came in. He ran his hands through his golden hair in a businesslike fashion to dry the last of the moisture from his shower. Kor noted that he had even taken the time to shave again, so his evening stubble was gone. "Good, you're already here."

Kor took a deep breath...and decided on a soft beginning. "How was the hunt?"

The King snorted as he pulled back his chair and sat in it. "As if you don't already know."

It was true. As not just the King's adviser but also spymaster, it was Kor's job to know everything of import that was going on in the Six Realms. Moreover, the King's rightwing, Yvera Battleblood, had reported in on the results of their experiment as soon as she had a private moment to give Kor advanced warning.

All the same, Kor said, "Indulge me."

The King rolled his eyes but complied as he dug for whatever document he had intended to discuss with his leftwing. "Young thing—caught up to it eld away from Perkan Hold. I almost felt sorry for the torched asher."

"That's not how Yvera tells it," Kor murmured. "She says you fought it with a savagery bordering on pleasure. You disturbed even her."

Given the rightwing's long-established proclivity for battle, that meant something.

"Yes, well, it *was* a rock wyrm," the King said dismissively, having found the report he wanted. "Now, about the crop yields—"

"Ben," Kor said, putting his hands on the desk and leaning in.

The King finally met his gaze, golden eyes hard. "What?"

"What if it *hadn't* been a rock wyrm?"

"What do you mean?"

"What if it had been something with reason, that was willing to negotiate? Abide by our laws? What if it had been one of our *people*?"

That would have meant something to the Ben that Kor once knew. The Heir that had given excruciating, excessive effort to control, to hiding who he was and just what he could do. To being something that his people did not have to fear.

The hardened King only raised an eyebrow. "Negotiate? It was heading for a hold. Beast or dramá, its intent would have been clear enough. I said that I *almost* felt sorry for it, but I didn't. It deserved every torched bit of its ashen grave."

And there was the problem. The Ben that Kor had known was dying, being replaced day by day over the past month with this *thing* that sat in front of him. This merciless, cold, savage thing that was everything Kavarian had eschewed and everything Ben had always been in horror of becoming.

Before.

Kor could only hope he wasn't too late to save his friend.

"Ben," Kor said, hardening himself. "This has to stop. *Now*."

The King folded his arms and leaned back in his chair. If he was surprised at the turn this conversation had taken, he didn't show it. Of course, he hardly ever showed emotion any longer. Long gone was the near-crystal-clear transparency that had plagued Ben's expressions. Even without the concealment of his former beard, not a single self-conscious blush had been seen on his face in a month. A thing of the past was his complete inability to deceive. This King had the face and voice of stone.

"What does?" he said.

"*This*," Kor said, rising to gesture to the King with both hands. "This hell-in-life that you are putting yourself through, this misery you are punishing yourself with that is turning you into a monster. It must end, and it must end *now*."

The King merely snorted. "Or what? You'll slap another ministerial order in my face? We've got bigger problems than bickering among ourselves right now, Kor."

Kor gritted his teeth. "Precisely. Which means you have to bring Sarah back. *Now*."

For perhaps the first time that Kor had seen in a month, the King's golden eyes glowed briefly with soulflare.

His response was short but ice-cold. "No."

Kor had expected this. He had prepared himself long and hard for this conversation, with both word and magic. There was a reason he had shielded himself—subtly, hopefully enough that the King hadn't noticed—before the King returned. Just in case this hard thing he had become turned...violent.

Kor almost hoped he would. Almost hoped that the first and hopefully only time that the King would break would be in private, and just with him. Then Kor could contain the disaster, at the least; at the most, if the King hurt him, then Kor might just be able to break through to Ben.

"Ben," Kor said. "All our greatest problems point to Sarah's absence. The decrease in crop yields just being the latest. The high numbers of consumed, this new fever—"

"All precisely why...the Queen of Ice must not return."

Flame help us, Kor thought. *He can't even say her name. Only her title.*

"No, Ben, that is precisely why we need her. She is perhaps the only one—"

"No," the King said.

Even the ice in his voice was disappearing now as his normal emotionless tone returned. Kor's flameheart sank at that sign of the rigidness of the King's control. He had an even tighter leash on Ben than Kor had feared.

The King tapped the report. "These are *our* problems, and we will solve them ourselves."

"We're not *meant* to, Ben. Why can't you see that? Why can't you see how dangerous a line you are walking with the Trees?"

The King's eyes narrowed. "What?"

Kor took a deep breath for calm. The King could—and hopefully would—lose his temper in this conversation, but Kor could not. *He* had to maintain control, and he had to not let his terror at their situation and of his friend show.

"Ben, by shutting Sarah out...surely you can see you are on the verge of breaking the Covenants. That *you both* just renewed."

The First Covenant, the Covenant of the Gates, was the basis for their sun-gates that were the lifeblood of their Six Realms. The Second Covenant, the Covenant of Power, was the reason their people, the dramá, were dual-natured beings capable of even somewhat surviving the Devourer's invasions—the first a thousand years ago, the second the month before.

But just as they had needed Sarah, the newly invested Queen of Ice, to survive the Second Invasion, they needed her perhaps even more desperately now to survive what came after.

Kor wasn't devout, not like Ben was—or had been. Kor accepted the reality of Trees because he had seen and heard Them with his own eyes, but that didn't mean he always trusted Their intentions. Immortal beings with supposedly infinite wisdom and knowledge who used such advantages in ways Kor did not understand made him...nervous.

Yet Kor had made the Covenants his life's study, perhaps for that reason. He, of all people, could recognize the signs of their weakening. *Again.* It would be the most tragic of ironies if the redemption that the peoples of Ice and Flame had waited nearly a thousand years for was ruined by one of the two people who had redeemed them.

Kor was shocked the Trees of Ice and Flame had shown the King of Flame even this much mercy so far. Perhaps it had been for Kavarian's sake, or perhaps They truly had compassion somewhere in Their immortal souls, as the High Priestess always insisted, and had given the newly invested King a grace period in which to mourn.

Though he had done very little mourning to speak of, his clean-shaven face and maroon clothing besides. Even on the former King's burning day, the new one didn't shed a single tear as far as Kor had seen and had gotten right back into the cleanup efforts the moment the ceremony was over.

The King just stared at Kor for a long moment. Kor held his breath, wondering if this would be it—the breakthrough.

But the King just looked back down at the report and said, "Well, then, the Trees can find some other torched idiot to renew them."

Kor stood there, stunned speechless. A month ago, he would have laughed in the face of anyone who had told him that one day, he would show more reverence for the will of the Trees than Ben did. Then again, a month ago...Ben had still been alive.

"Ben," Kor said, swallowing. With a chill, he realized it was time for his final argument. Already. "Your father...wouldn't have wanted this for you."

The King stilled, but it was only for a moment. When he looked up to meet Kor's eyes, the golds were as hard as ever. "Really? Then he should have thought twice before giving me his torched crown. Let alone before giving me life."

For the second time in as many dek, Kor stood there, stunned speechless. It was not a familiar feeling for the brilliant leftwing.

That, along with this terrible evidence of the utter loss of his friend, terrified him.

"Ben," Kor said with another difficult swallow. "Don't make me declare you unworthy. Don't make me take the crown from you."

Because he could. As the secret Tolsyon heir of the Starkissed leader who had helped Sarah's clan escape centuries before at the first breaking of the Covenants, Kor had the right. And the King knew it.

The King slowly raised his head again. Not only did his eyes soulflare, but his lips—for the very first time in at least a month—turned into a smile. But it was the kind of smile that sent a chill down Kor's spine.

"Do it," the King said. With *anticipation*.

Kor's flameheart sputtered, nearly going out.

"Ben," he gasped. "I—I don't *want* to."

Kor as King would not be ideal in the best of circumstances, let alone the dire straits they were in now. Leave aside that the Covenants would probably have to be renewed *anyway* for a Starkissed King to take over, given how closely the current ones were bound around the Sunfilled clan.

Kor could not be the King the people needed. The King Ben had been meant to become. If Kor were King of the Six Realms....

He realized with horror why this new "Ben"—this hard, calculating, ruthless thing—was so chillingly familiar to him. It was the kind of King that he, Korinth Starkissed, would become, if he were forced to assume the crown. And that would be with none of the heavy tragedies that had weighed on Ben's soul until they drowned him.

With the final cap in Kor's existential terror for himself and the Realms, he realized that the failsafe the Tree had made inside him...was no failsafe at all. The Realms would hardly be better off with *him* at the helm than this...stone.

The stone that watched Kor with eyes as sharp as a hawk's, and when Kor only remained frozen, the soulflare left his eyes and his wintry smile died.

The King folded his arms as he leaned back. "Well, that was a disappointment. I thought you really were going to do it that time. But then, I suppose I should have known you were bluffing. You never did have the courage to challenge me, did you?"

I might have, once, Kor thought dully. Back when Kor had first made the threat, when he was reeling from heartbreak and desire for Sarah and fury at

Ben for having everything he had never known he wanted and yet throwing it all away.

Would things have been better if he *had* taken Ben's place as Heir back then? Would Kavarian have survived, choosing not to sacrifice himself if Kor had been in danger instead of his own son? Would Sarah never have put herself in danger to save *him*, and instead saved herself and her strength for the shields that defended her, Kavarian, and the Tree? Would Ben have come to his senses then and reclaimed his birthright? Would everyone be happy and hard at work saving the Realms if Kor...had been the one to die instead?

Oh, yes. Kor blamed no one more than himself for the dire straits they were now in.

But self-blame, as the King was demonstrating more powerfully than anyone right now...didn't fix things.

"Listen, Kor," the King said with a wave of his hand. "I have work to do. If you're just going to rehash old, empty threats instead of advising me like you're supposed to, then you're dismissed for the evening. Go drink something strong enough to put the fire back in your blood and come prepared to be my leftwing in the morning."

He...has become me, Kor realized with numb horror. *The worst version of me. And I, the useless, torched idiot I am right now...have become him.*

At Ben's very worst, most useless, most guilt-ridden, most terrified state.

Good for nothing but to dully obey, turning on his heel and leaving the room. Letting the door softly slip shut behind him.

Of course...he was still *Kor* enough that the moment he was free to think...his formidable mind once again bent itself to the problem in front of him. As insurmountable as it now seemed.

He always *had* done his most brilliant thinking under pressure.

Yvera found him some time later sitting on a couch in the King's reception room, deep in thought.

"How did it go?" she asked warily. But even she seemed to be able to guess the answer from Kor's meditative expression and the King's closed study door.

"Poorly," Kor said. "In every sense. He didn't even lose his temper. Not once."

Yvera cursed and folded her arms, expression grim. "Well, that does it. There's only one thing for it now, isn't there?"

Kor blinked at her in surprise.

"What?" Yvera said flatly. "It's obvious: we find some way to get Sarah back. *Without* Ben."

When Kor only smiled thinly at her, she huffed. "You think I'm *that* much of a dimtorch?"

"Oh, no. I just didn't expect you to think objectively enough at this point to accept that was what Ben needed."

Yvera's own desire for her lifelong friend, former Heir, and current King was well known to everyone...except perhaps the King himself. Although Kor had an inkling that even *he* had figured out as much by now and had perhaps when he had still been Ben.

"At this point, I would bring him a torched ugle if that's what it would take to get him to snap out of this," Yvera grumbled. "Flame only knows why he needs *Sarah* so torching badly, but if she's it, then she's what he gets."

"Succinctly, if not elegantly, put," Kor agreed. "The problem, dear rightwing, is not knowing *what* he needs but *how* to get him it. Unless you have somehow gained authority over gates since last we spoke?"

"'Course not," Yvera said with a scowl.

"You see the problem, then? Ben needs Sarah but refuses to let her in. Ben is the only one who *can* let her in. If Ben were in the state to let her in, he wouldn't need her so desperately. That's called a *paradox*, Yv. An unsolvable contradiction."

"Don't give me that ashdust, Kor. You wouldn't have had that look on your face when I came in if you were giving up. So, what's the plan?"

Kor smiled slowly. Silently, using his inner voice, he said, *Do I take it that means you're in?*

Hellwinds, yes, Yvera replied. *This has to stop. Now.*

Wondrous Flame, Kor thought in dry amusement. He and Yvera rarely saw eye to eye enough to act in unison against Ben, but they had before—for his own good, of course. But only on momentary, ad hoc occasions. This would be the first and hopefully only time the King's wings would have to *conspire* against him.

Very well, Kor said, amusement dying as grimness took over again. Even Yvera would be aware of the legal gray area they were now entering. *This is going to require subtlety, artifice, illusion, and quite a bit of—*

A crash from the King's study. Of an unusual and dangerous enough nature for the soundproofing charms to let the noise through to them.

Yvera, having been the King's primary bodyguard for most of the past six years, didn't even stop to ask who might have been in there with him or what important meeting she might be interrupting. She simply acted—rushing to the door so fast she almost became a violet-haired blur. She thrust the door open with one hand, the gem on the door flaring in recognition of her clearance to enter, and with the other hand drew her claymore from her back.

"Ben!" she cried as she rushed in.

Kor was only a couple of seconds behind her, sapphire magic swirling around his hands, ready to be released.

The scene they found was rather anticlimactic. The King's food tray had somehow been knocked to the ground, as had his chair, and the reason for both accidents became clear as they rounded the King's desk and came upon him lying there, blinking blurrily up at them in a daze.

"Ben?" Yvera said uncertainly. "Are you alright?"

At the sound of her voice, his eyes finally cleared. Then widened in horror.

"*Sarah,*" Ben gasped.

Then disappeared. There one moment, gone the next.

"*Hellfrost!*" Yvera swore, clenching her free hand. "Why would he *do* that, *now*?!"

"That" meaning surging to a sungate, as only the Monarchs and Heirs of Flame had the power and authority to do. Anyone could *walk* through sungates to reach their intended destination, but Royals could simply pull themselves through the fabric of reality to go straight to one sungate and then through the entire network, in the blink of an eye.

Which, in Yvera's mind, meant that Ben could have been anywhere across the Six Realms by now, with no way for them to follow or know where he had gone.

Kor knew better, and he slowly smiled.

"Calm down, Yv," he said, holding up a hand. "This is a *good* thing. A very good thing."

"What in the torched blazes are you—"

"Didn't you see it?" Kor asked, meeting her gaze. "In his eyes? *Think. Remember.*"

Yvera scowled, but he could see her reliving the moment. Then growing still.

Kor could not resist stating it all the same. He nearly shook with relief now, and he subtly put his hand on the desk for support as he bent to lift the chair off the floor. "That wasn't 'the King' just now, Yvera. Those were *Ben's* eyes. Since Ben hasn't been alive, much less able to say Sarah's name, in a month now, where do you think he's gone?"

"I get it," Yvera said from between clenched teeth. "He's gone after her. But what in the Flame's name changed his mind about her now?"

Kor picked up one of the broken pieces of the shattered mug and sniffed. "Dreamhaze. Did you...?"

"Don't look at me," Yvera snapped. "*I* didn't drug him this time."

"Well, whoever did, it appears that the King drank it and fell asleep at his desk after I left, and when he woke up, he was Ben. So, whatever he dreamed in the meantime is the answer to the question *why*."

Kor scowled.

"What?" Yvera asked. "You just said this was good. That he's gone to Sarah. That's what we wanted all along, Kor. So what now?"

"'What now,' indeed," Kor said distastefully. "It appears, dear rightwing, that for once, the Tree has done our work for us."

And I am not certain how I feel about that. At all.

Because what could the Tree have told Ben that would bring him back to life? That would persuade him to allow *Sarah* back into that life?

Kor could only think of one reason, the clue being the horror in Ben's eyes as he gasped Sarah's name.

Sarah...was in danger.

I...am a torched idiot, Kor thought.

He dropped the shard and ran.

Chapter One

TEARS

Sarah

As was typical nowadays, I was the last of my family to wake up. That wasn't laziness. I was just the most affected now by the ebb and flow of power that was the day and night cycle, with my zenith being reached after all the others had gone to bed.

Technically, if I was careful to spend all my power as it grew, I could fall asleep at a somewhat normal time, but as we all settled into our new routines, and the full realization sunk into our minds that we had complete command of our schedules, I found the motivation to hold to my former one decrease with each day.

Besides, I found those quiet nighttime hours of wandering my hold increasingly bittersweet. Healthy or not, in the soft stillness after everyone had gone to bed, I found myself able to remember...and imagine. I could remember a time when it was just me and my drakón in this hold—and imagine that at any moment, I would hear Ben singing as he cooked us dinner in the kitchen; or smell his warm, desert scent as I passed through the training room; or see him as he stepped out of his bedroom, smiling as brilliantly as the sun at me, ready for another day.

I had always known during those twelve days I was with him that I would one day look back and wish I could live it all again—no matter how terrifying or strenuous those days had been.

I just didn't know how *much*. Could not have known, until I felt the never-ending ache for myself. Felt my iceheart crack as Ben walked away and disappeared...and the full horror of what he had done to shut me out sunk in.

That crack hadn't yet healed.

As was also typical, my dream and my first conscious thoughts as I woke up were of Ben—reliving a memory. As I woke, my lips burned with that memory, but my cheeks were already wet, my eyes already knowing what I would see when they opened.

My cracked iceheart, which would have already been weak from the high sun somewhere overhead, pulsed against all odds to keep power and (somehow) blood circulating through my body. Even though sometimes I wondered why it even tried.

Waking up was the hardest part of my day. Finding a reason to get out of bed was the second.

As always, the thought of how my family needed me was what finally gave me the strength to roll over, push myself up, and clamber out of my ocean of a bed.

A couple of my lights roused themselves enough to emerge from their glowing stone nests in the walls. During the day, those nests just looked like glowing white convex circles the size of small plates set into the stone walls of the mountain hold. One might, as I first did, mistake the nests for mere wall-mounted lights. Inside, though, perhaps dozens of living white orbs of light slumbered away—or whatever it was they usually preferred to do during the day. At night, they came out and maintained this magical place that was now my Earth-born American family's last remaining sanctuary in the universe.

They made an exception to their work/rest schedule for me, the Queen of Ice and (for lack of better phrasing) ruler of this snowy, mountainous world. I didn't know how they worked out who would serve the day shift with me, but every afternoon when I woke up, a couple of lights would sleepily drift themselves down to be of service to me.

I tried the first few days to tell them to just rest, but that only offended them. For featureless orbs of light so bright that I couldn't look directly into their centers to see what, if anything, was in there, they could make their feelings and intentions known surprisingly well through just a hum or a movement.

My efforts at dissuading them had been half-hearted to begin with. Their presence was absurdly comforting to me, and sometimes only the thought of their tender greeting awaiting me was the extra push I needed to rise.

They didn't disappoint this morning. The two orbs roused themselves enough to brush gently against my cheeks, magically drying the tear streaks there, and gave me a few comforting spins around my body, which I'd gathered was their equivalent to a hug. No matter how many days came and went just like this, they never judged; they never became awkward, not knowing what to do or say; they never whispered behind my back, wondering what to do about me. They never spoke about Ben in grim or angry tones, stopping the moment I came into the room.

They were simply always, always loving. Simply *there*.

Oh, how I needed just that.

"Thank you," I whispered hoarsely to them, as I did every day.

Then I pushed myself off the bed and stumbled my way into my private bathroom. That luxury had been the clincher that had made me finally claim this elaborate suite, fit for the queen I'd never thought I'd be, as my own. Having my own bathroom, along with all the usual perks, meant that no one had to see the tears that kept flowing, and would until I was done with my long, cold shower.

The cold shower was a new thing for me, but I'd quickly figured out after my transformation into the Queen of Ice that hot showers were about as uncomfortable as cold ones used to be. (Go figure.) The icy water—maybe coming straight from a glacier atop this mountain we were in—was like a shot of coffee straight into my veins, and not from adrenaline or shock.

My body now *needed* to be cold to feel well, energized, alive—and that counted double in the afternoon. My power had passed its lowest point of the day at noon and was rising again, but on its own, it was still only enough to sustain life. In an emergency, I could maybe do some magic, but I was learning there was a greater cost for exerting myself now.

More than ever, I appreciated how often my drakón had, without complaint, exerted their power and strength at night to protect me. Especially Ben.

I'd learned that if I had to be active at this time, I had to find sources of energy from other places, just as the drakón did at night. Food was the only one I'd found so far that we had in common, and I'd get to that soon. But I drew the line when my lights started bringing me breakfast in bed. First off, it was freaking out my family (at least the older ones) to see lights carrying the food items one by one through the halls, like a solemn parade of small, floating mice who had raided the pantry, and the first few days were rough enough of an adjustment for my parents and older siblings as it was.

Second, I needed the motivation to leave my room.

But to work myself up to that, I needed another, more rapid source of energy first: cold. So, the first hurdle was to get my sluggish body to my gorgeous, huge, black and silver bathroom, stumble into the shower inlaid with black and silver tiles in elaborate swirls, and slap my finger on the darkest blue crystal in the circle to indicate the coldest setting. Then stand there as that glacial meltwater drenched me.

After about fifteen minutes of that, I felt alive again. Not that I wanted to be, but I had enough energy to remember why I had to be. And I'd finally stopped crying.

Reluctantly, I tapped the crystal again to turn off the water and stepped out onto the spongy bath mat worthy of memory foam.

Dad, in his search through the archivals, had recently discovered a tidbit that the comfy substance that made up our best mattresses and cushions was, shockingly, a kind of cultivated fungus. Perfectly safe and in a latent state, as the writers had emphatically assured us. But of course, Rachel now thought they were gross and had swapped her mattress for one of the feather-stuffed ones, and the twins had insisted on sacrificing one cushion to dissection, in the noble name of "science." Despite my repeated reminders that there were no supermarkets for us anymore where we could simply buy replacements for such things.

That stark reality was a constant, sobering cloud over the heads of us older Linds. We still *technically* had one functioning moongate, which led back to

Earth. But that Earth location, being somewhere deep under the ice pack in the middle of Northeast Greenland National Park, wasn't exactly accessible to a Walmart. Even if it were, we had good reason to believe that half of us were presumed dead and the other half were wanted criminals blamed for the devastating fire that had burned to rubble at least three of the houses on our Pennsylvanian cul-de-sac.

Almost all meaningful ties with the world we had come from were now severed, with abrupt and chilling finality. As were our ties with the Six Realms...for the foreseeable future. So, for now, we had to assume that we were on our own, dependent on our Moontouched forebears who had, through some kind of precognitive power, foreseen our need and built this place for us nearly a thousand years ago.

That was the reason I had to keep functioning, moving, living. I had dragged my family into this mess, and I had to find our way out of it.

Our situation wasn't bad—currently. Mom and Dad estimated we had enough food in the cold storage room to last us a year. But since we intended to live longer than that, our greatest task began the day we realized we couldn't even rely on dramá help any longer: learning how to survive.

I had faith—still a funny concept to me, but I didn't have a better word for it—that it was possible. Our ancestors would not have so carefully prepared this place for us without making it self-sustaining, and we had good reasons by now to believe that was the case.

Besides, the Tree of Ice told me not to fear for my family. So, as difficult as that was to do emotionally, intellectually, I knew enough about Trees by now to trust Them when They said things would be fine.

That didn't mean I could just lie around all day in misery. Not only was that not the person I wanted to be, but the promise of my family being fine was most likely contingent on each of us doing our part. Especially me.

So, after drying myself off, putting on my bathrobe, and washing out my mouth with a tablet soaked in a cup of water that Dad had determined would *hopefully* be enough to prevent tooth decay, I forced myself to leave my nice, dark, cool bathroom and reenter my warmer bedroom.

The warmth was a feature, not a flaw. I'd hazarded a guess why the first time I'd come across this bedroom and had confirmed it the first time I'd tried to sleep in it. It was the same concept as with normal humans, but in reverse: the warmth was a signal to my rewired body that it was time to *rest*. Otherwise, I might never be able to sleep at night at all.

Still, it meant that I hurried into the clothes my lights had laid out for me now: underwear the breathability, support, and fit of which had been unattainable for me on Earth; a soft, white long-sleeved shirt with silver lining and a V-neck; comfy and formfitting yet durable black pants with a line of silver down the outer seams; breathable, soft black socks; and leather boots.

Typical of the usual outfit, right down to the colors—as if the lights expected me, now that I was transformed into a Moontouched in the fullest sense, to adopt the drakón practice of color-matching to one's hair and eyes. I supposed I was lucky that the lights even allowed my pants to be black to break up the white and silver, which otherwise might have made me look like a ghost, my light-brown skin besides.

Then, taking a deep breath for courage, I strode around the rim of my sunken seating area and to the bedroom door. Which, we had soon discovered after my family got here, only I could open—or my lights, if I asked them to. Unlike my drakón, my family handled most of the doors in the hold just fine without me. They were Moontouched too, and this hold had been made for them as much as for me...but this room remained solely mine.

That gave me far more relief than it probably should have.

Partly because it meant no one in my family could disturb me without badgering a light into delivering a message. Partly because, being the third child of eight, I had spent much of my life wearing hand-me-downs, sharing bedrooms, and fighting tooth and nail for a bit of privacy, let alone peace and quiet. Finally, as the most altruistic of the three oldest children, I'd taken on more responsibility than I should have by the time the Tree whisked me away to the Six Realms a month and a half ago.

My family learned just how much I had always done for them and rallied and adapted with a unity that had surprised me when I returned but probably shouldn't have. After all, we Linds, on top of being a large family, had also stood out like a sore thumb for moving frequently, and we'd learned long ago to stick together.

After I brought them here and we began settling into our new life, I'd had to resist the surprisingly powerful urge to fall back into normal patterns of housework and childcare, but Dad, Mom, and even Michael all put their feet down. Things were different now, they said. Mom and Dad, not torn this way and that by their demanding careers, had more time, and each of us now had a role to play for our survival. Mine was a different one entirely.

My bedroom had provided a necessary physical separation between me and my former responsibilities, as well as a literal symbol of how my role and place in my family had changed. I was meant to serve, not rule over them, yes. But I had finally learned that I did that best by giving myself the space, time, and resources I needed to do so.

I opened the door with just a touch, making the white outline flare and the door swing inward. Then I walked confidently through the dark to the other side of the passage I called the Outer Rim, since it went all the way around our leaf-shaped hold. Now that my power was in full blossom, the moonstone streaks in the stone walls began to glow with white light the moment I entered the passage, but I didn't even need the light to find the glowing door on the opposite wall, which again, I only had to touch to push open.

The passage beyond was dark but short, since it was only a connector that went between the two bedrooms on either side. When I emerged through the last door, I stepped into what we had begun to call the dormitory. Even though this hold wasn't a school, we couldn't think of a better word for the collection of bedrooms and bunkrooms in this area; besides, Noah and Jonah thought it was awesome, said it made them feel like they were at Hogwarts.

That wasn't the first time the littles had compared our hold to a castle, and it wasn't the last. I did nothing to dispel that illusion and actually did quite a bit to encourage it. The more we could get the littles to think of this as one great, magical adventure, the better.

Considering they were now taking magic lessons from me, Hogwarts wasn't as much of a stretch as you might think. Although soon, those littles might be teaching *me*. They were adapting the most quickly to our new way of life by far.

As a case in point, I had to throw up a shield of silver magic in front of my face as half a meat-and-cheese sandwich came flying at me along with a burst of frigid wind as I entered the kitchen-dining area.

"Noah!" Laura said firmly, pointing to the bread and fixings now scattered over the floor. "You know the rules: *no magic at the table*. You go clean that up. *Now*. And if you don't want to eat the other half, then you can just go hungry until dinner."

Noah sulkily got off the bench where he, Laura, and the other two littles were eating. Abby was contentedly munching away, ignoring the ruckus with a ladylike air. Jonah smirked and took a large bite of his own sandwich. Since it was his *first* bite, I knew better than to think him innocent. No doubt he had been just as repulsed as his twin at first; Noah, as usual, had just been the first and loudest to make his feelings known.

"I miss PB&J," Noah muttered.

I would have soothed and distracted. In fact, in the first place, I would have cut the sandwiches into fun shapes and cajoled the twins into eating them.

Laura, on the other hand, had cut them into triangles, and now she only snorted as she tucked an escaped white curl back behind her ear and broke up more bread for her one-year-old, Tommie. "Tough luck, kid. This castle ain't stocked with peanut butter."

Sometimes, in our previous life, I had wondered why Michael's wife had decided to be a teacher. She wasn't the sweet, nurturing type. But after a month of her handling the bulk of the littles' education, I realized why: she was incredible with kids, in her *own* way.

I also realized that my way had been spoiling the littles rotten. In just a month, she had done wonders with them, so much so that I had a hard time believing she wasn't a young, grumpy Ms. Frizzle whose hair had turned prematurely white and eyes silver in a mad science experiment. I no longer argued with her methods if they got these kinds of results.

"How can a *castle* not have *peanut butter*?" Noah whined.

Laura just laughed. "I think you can figure that one out yourself by now, mister."

"I know. Because they didn't have *peanuts*," Jonah said smugly. "Just like they didn't have toothpaste, and spaghetti, and—"

"Good deduction, Jonah, but I think we get the picture," I said, eying Noah's glare and feeling the power building up around him again.

It was a good thing the littles weren't capable of much yet. Brief spurts of mostly harmless magic were all they could manage, even after a month of practice. They grasped the theory, at least in its simplest form of bringing up magic and coaxing it into the form one desired, with an intuitiveness that put the rest of us to shame, but they still didn't have the *umph* to match their ambitions.

And thank Ice for that, or something much more deadly than a sandwich might have come flying at me.

"Having lunch this late again?" I asked Laura sympathetically after I reached her.

She grimaced. "Maria said they didn't get up until past nine. Tommie didn't wake until ten."

We shared a grim look at that. No one had changed so drastically and rapidly as I had, but the littles were on the trajectory to follow suit, at least in their sleep schedules. The adults still resisted. Even Rachel, who had been a party girl and night owl, now resolutely went to bed only a few hours after dinner. Which probably explained why she went around looking like a grouchy zombie most of the time now. (Albeit a gorgeous one, because how could Rachel be anything but?)

Our mental health would be better if we could just adapt as quickly and eagerly as the littles did to both our new surroundings and changing bodies, but adults weren't as moldable as children.

Probably another reason the Tree had chosen me out of all the Linds to become her Monarch. I was young enough in both body and mind to change, yet old enough to make the conscious choice to.

"Maria left porridge in the fridge for you again," Laura said, turning back to monitoring Tommie to make sure he was putting more food in his mouth than onto the floor. "I'd have made you a sandwich, but I didn't know when you'd be up."

"Thanks, and no worries," I said as I went to the "fridge," which was more like a magic ice chest set to refrigerator temperature. Really, we were lucky to have even that much, since the chest had been a mystery to my drakón when the four of us were originally exploring my hold; it wasn't normal dramá technology.

Once I'd eaten my porridge and washed my dishes, I walked out of the kitchen and into the Inner Rim to make my rounds.

I STARTED AS I always did (and always ended): with the Ythra moongate. Opening it in the morning and closing it before I went to sleep had become as ingrained a ritual as brushing my teeth had once been, and I let myself think about what I was doing about that much, lest memory creep in and overtake me.

Yet I didn't delegate this duty to anyone else, even though Rachel, as our Heir, could open moongates just as I could. But despite the pain, I couldn't have borne giving it up to her. Not only would she rather slam the door in Ben's face than let him in, it didn't feel right. Opening the door in invitation was my right and duty as Queen of Ice. Even if right now and perhaps forever...that door led to nowhere.

I only allowed myself one moment to stop in front of those arched double doors that glowed with the Sunfilled crest: a three-pronged crown circling a sun. I took a deep breath to brace myself and then hurriedly walked forward and placed my hands on the doors. They took their price in power from me—so slight compared to my reserves that I hardly noticed it anymore, even in broad daylight, even though the first time the price had knocked me unconscious. The white outline of the arch and the crest flared in unison, and the gray stone doors began to swing inward. With practiced ease, I stepped back to make room for them.

Every time, I tried to keep myself from hoping. But every time, I did.

And every day, that hope was crushed as I saw the thick solidity of the ice and the warping of the circular chamber and passage beyond. My gate was still only a wall: a glorified, unbreakable window into another world.

A window too filled with disappointment and pain for me to linger in front of. I turned on my heel and began striding to my next destination, fighting tears and a hard lump in my throat all the way.

A small door and a set of winding stairs led down from the balcony of the Inner Rim and into the innermost chamber, which was also the largest of the hold: the garden. Many gardens had a fountain. No gardens I had ever seen, except this one, had a glacial waterfall cascading from a hole in the ceiling that was covered in mirrors to reflect the distant sunlight and make the whole central chamber appear as if it were in broad daylight. (The helping lights cleaned and maintained those, thank Ice.)

The sunlight and mist from the waterfall, and no doubt the helping hand of the lights, was the reason a jungle of a garden had flourished for nearly a thousand years below. At long last, that garden had a gardener.

If anyone was nearly as excited with her new lot in life as the littles were, it was Mom. She had missed her calling by becoming a linguistics professor, but I understood why she didn't take an agrarian path. Though there was little enough money to be had in linguistics, I presumed there was even less to be made in puttering around one's own garden—unless someone also put a lot of effort into marketing themselves, I supposed, and Mom was far too shy to have done something like that.

I'd always known she'd had a green thumb. She'd done her best in the scant energy and time she'd had leftover to make whatever yard we'd owned look good and keep up at least a tiny *huerta*. But now she could not only putter to her heart's content, she could see it as her solemn duty to provide for her family. I didn't think I had ever seen her so happy. If there was one thing we had gained from our forced removal from Earth, then I supposed this was it: to give Mom the job of her dreams.

For a bit, I just wandered the garden, breathing it in. This was the one sanctuary of peace I had in our hold which had the least memories of the Time Before, which was why I always came here second; although I carefully avoided the stony rim of the pond that lay beneath the waterfall.

I found Mom and twelve-year-old Lizzy crouched gingerly among giant leaves of some squash-like plant, tying up other, smaller vines to a trellis.

Mom's brown eyes brightened when she spotted me. "Sarah! How did you sleep?"

Although Mom was one of the most sympathetic of my family to my new-found nocturnality, at the basis of that sympathy was the assumption that I was just going through a difficult time and would get back on track eventually. Which was about as comforting to me as Rachel's teasing or Michael's indifference.

"Fine," I said with a valiant effort at a smile.

As "fine" as my new normal ever was.

"So, how goes it?" I asked quickly.

"Beautifully," Mom beamed. "These ukka are coming right along."

She pointed to the indigo gourds that were growing beneath the leaves. "If Jake's understood the stones right, some should be ready to harvest."

I held back a sigh. "The stones are called archivals, Mom."

She'd made it sound as if Dad was consulting tossed bones like some village shaman. Of course, in Mom's mind, that could be the same thing as what he was really doing. It was remarkable that she could be so *happy* with her current lot in life and yet find it so difficult to wrap her otherwise very intelligent mind around just why and how our lives had changed. When it didn't come to her garden.

"Right, archives," Mom said as she turned back to winding twine around her precious...whatever they were called.

Lizzy smiled and shrugged behind Mom's back at me.

"Jake says they can be boiled and mashed like potatoes, except with far higher concentrations of nutrients," Mom went on. "I'm thinking of trying it out for dinner tonight."

"You'll...make something else to go with it, right?" Lizzy asked, eyeing the gourds.

Mom huffed, blowing some of her brown hair that had escaped her braid and sun hat out of her face. "Of course I will. Do you think I would just make mashed potatoes for dinner, Lizzy?"

"They're quite good," I told Lizzy before my preservative instincts could catch up with my mouth. "Especially the way Ben—"

I stopped as my brain blue-screened and had to reboot. Meanwhile, Mom and Lizzy shared a tight look.

I cleared the lump that had reformed in my throat and blinked rapidly. "I mean, the way I had them."

"Yes, I'm sure they are," Mom said quickly.

"Well, looks like you've got everything in hand," I said, still blinking as I turned hastily away. "I have to...go check on the others."

"Take me with you!" Lizzy mock pleaded. Although it was more plea than mock, and Mom knew it.

"Oh, come on, Lizzy. You've only been helping me for an hour, and you've only got another one to go...."

I gratefully let their voices fade into the thunder of the waterfall as I made my quick exit out of the garden. Which was a shame. Normally, I could glean a bit more serenity from the garden before I had to move on.

So, I switched up the order of things and went to the place that had the second-least number of memories. I would need all the fortifying I could get before the now-final stop.

The library was blessedly cool and dark, both things I desperately needed right now, and standing in front of one of the twelve-foot rectangular blocks of black stone was *my* rock, in the metaphorical sense.

Dad scrolled through the small area of glowing white text on the stone in front of him, but he spotted me soon after I entered the open doors and gave me a small smile.

"Sarah. You're up a bit earlier than usual."

Of all people except Abby, the youngest, Dad had taken my changes—and the changes in himself, manifested most blatantly in the white hair and silver eyes he'd gained—the most naturally. But then, Dad took everything in stride. Not even the need to swiftly evacuate his family from our home and leave behind practically everything to take us across the world to Greenland had done more than ruffle his feathers a bit. At least on the outside.

But I knew Dad's extraordinary acceptance of who we were and especially who I was now went deeper than his always placid exterior. As usual, I couldn't help but come up to him and hug him in wordless thanks for it.

I also thanked the Tree for giving me that kind of miracle. Dad still hadn't described in detail the dream he'd had of Her while I was gone that had prepared him to be the mastermind of our evacuation and Greenland expedition and the bulwark I needed right now, nor had I asked him to. But it must have been one hell of a dream.

"Actually," I said sheepishly as I pulled away from him, "I'm just getting to you early."

"Have something you want to talk about?" Dad asked. Somehow, he walked that fine line between being present and not seeming too interested or sympathetic.

Dad was the only Lind that I felt comfortable talking to about Ben, when I could manage that much, or couldn't help myself. Not only had he got to know Ben the best of all of them, he didn't judge him, not even for our current isolation. He was the only adult that had accepted my explanations for Ben's behavior—and the only adult besides me who continued to hope circumstances would change.

Sometimes I wondered if Dad's hope could better be called *knowledge*, and the question was always at the tip of my tongue whenever I was around him. I never asked it and didn't think I ever would. I didn't think I could bear to hear the answer, whatever it was.

"No," I said with a sigh and a wave of my hand. "Just...the usual. No change there."

"Nothing has to change for you to talk to me, Sarah," Dad said mildly, but he looked back at the text to give me some relief from his penetrating eyes, which were even more unnerving these days for their new silver color. "I'm always here to listen."

"And that matters."

So dang much.

"So, thank you. But...not now."

I took a deep breath, then made my voice more cheerful. "Anyway, any amazing new discoveries today?"

His lips twitched by the narrowest of margins, which was Dad's equivalent to a chuckle. "There's always something new to discover, though I'm not sure any of today's finds could be called 'amazing.' I found some new recipes for Maria to try."

In a strange turn of events, Mom was now our chief cook as well as gardener. We used to have a meal rotation from Dad down to Lizzy, and Mom's night was usually something quick and simple. I never thought I'd see the day when she would shove everyone else aside and take command of the kitchen, much less to such masterful effect. But then, she'd never had this kind of time and energy on her hands before—or the excuse to experiment with her labors in the garden.

"She'll be happy about that," I said quickly, trying very hard not to think about mashed ukka right now. "Anything else?"

"Some more instructions for the smithy."

I chuckled. "Enough that you'll finally let David try his hand at it?"

Dad's lips twitched again. "Not yet. I want to make sure *I* have a grasp of all the mechanics first, and to do that, I think I'm going to need language mastery."

That was the catch to our efforts at accessing the stores of knowledge our Moontouched ancestors had left for us in these stone slabs. At first, when it was just my drakón and me here, the archivals had shown a welcome message in English for me, but that was it. Or, at least, that was all I'd had the time and desire to discover, although there might have been more for *me* there if I had bothered.

The only one who had, Kor, hadn't been able to bring up anything, much less in his own rune-like script and language, Drona. Then again, he was Starkissed and probably barred from our Moontouched archivals for that reason.

Whereas when Dad had tried accessing the archivals for the first time, he'd encountered a flood of indecipherable information. His first challenge had been figuring out how it was all accessed, organized, and indexed, which had taken him several days of intense intellectual labor given the formidable foreign language, script, and technology barriers. His second challenge was to decrypt Drona.

Even though our ancestors had provided the first welcome message in English, they hadn't seemed to have the resources, time, or inclination to give us much more than that in our own alphabet and language. They gave Dad a few side-by-side texts to get him started, but there their generosity in providing for us ended, and Dad was left on his own.

The magic that my drakón had cast on all of us to understand their language was no help here. The magic required a live speaker whose mind acted as the dual-language dictionary. Thus, written Drona was still a mystery.

Fortunately, we could not have had a more intelligent or determined puzzle solver working to crack the Drona code. The irony wasn't lost on us that the linguist in the family was happily working away in the garden and kitchen, and only allowed herself to be dragged into the dark library when she had to be, and the engineering professor was left to use our Rosetta Stones to decipher the mysteries of our new existence. Then again, if you thought about it, that wasn't so surprising. Mom could help Dad out with basic concepts of language, but from there, the task was more about problem solving, pattern discerning, and memory more than anything, and Dad was the perfect person to do just that.

So, Dad spent his days learning to read Drona. Every day, he found some tidbit to help us, but every day, he insisted that there was far more for him to discover.

Right now, Dad scrolled through some more runes, which were still a near-indecipherable blur to me, and then noted a translation on the black stone tablet in his hands using an identical stone stylus. Dad had found those in a compartment in the library that had glowed and unlocked for him only a day into his work, and I, having seen a particular drakón use something similar, could give him enough information to figure them out. Now Dad used the magical stone tablet—which, as far as I could understand, was a mini personal archival—with the ease that he had used his electronic one back on Earth.

A similar compartment with another tablet-stylus set had appeared for me next to his, so I technically had one too, and Dad had even shown me how to use it. I hadn't had the occasion to record much on it to feel confident; I had this vague sense that as soon as I set the tablet down and let the text I had just written fade, the text would just disappear into the ether, forever irretrievable. Even though Dad assured me it would still be there and that he could help me find it if I couldn't remember how to myself.

Although that very concept had started appealing to me, and in the past week or so, I'd begun writing on it every night whatever I thought or felt, using it as a diary to capture and then dispose of my feelings into the void. The practice had been surprisingly cathartic. Even the few times I'd written hypothetical letters to Ben and always ended up sobbing my way through and for minutes after. I'd always slept better on those nights and woken up feeling...not quite like the crack in my iceheart had healed, but as if the rawness of it had softened, and my strength to bear it become greater.

Maybe I should try that again tonight. Although I flinched away from the thought of the pain I would have to first go through to get that reward in the end.

To distract myself, I asked Dad some questions, as usual, about the runes, and he in turn asked me about the probable pronunciations of the words, since I had heard the most Drona by far. He notated my suggestions and one insight I'd had into a possible translation.

Then I had to admit to myself that I had better let Dad get back to his primarily solitary work, and I resigned myself to my final stop.

The training room: A long rectangular stone room with huge, overlapping silver circles on the floor and right wall, and an excessive display of weaponry at the far short end. Three tiered benches like bleachers took up the left wall.

A too-familiar sight, with too many memories. The one saving grace I had in this room was that it looked quite different than it had in the Time Before with all the equipment that was now set up on either side of the entrance and everywhere else the silver circles had left room, now making this room look like some hybrid between an oddly marked basketball court and a gym.

Dad wasn't the only one to discover compartments that opened for him. This was Michael's domain, and as soon as my older brother had entered the training room for the first time, the wall above the bleachers began to glow with doors, and when he opened them, all this other equipment lay inside. Michael and David, the two rightwings of our fledgling clan, spent days figuring out how to put the more elaborate equipment (such as the monkey bars) together and organizing the more obvious (such as the dumbbells) into a useful, efficient setup.

But as soon as they were done, Michael offered entirely different classes than his wife was teaching the littles, ones which were mandatory for all older Linds: physical fitness and self-defense training.

His latest victim was Rachel, who seemed to be taking out her angst at the world right now by punching a dummy while Michael watched and occasionally corrected her form. Michael nodded a greeting to me but kept his focus on Rachel. He'd soon discovered that one-on-one sessions with us were more effective than group ones, given our various sizes, ages, and strengths, so we each had a slot with him at least several times a week, but more for the six of us Royals and wings, whom we guessed were the most likely to need to fight. Fight what or when, we didn't know. The Tree only told us to be prepared.

That, for once, was good enough for Michael.

My slot with him would come later, when I had more energy and power. I was about as eager for it as I would have been for a tooth extraction, but I knew too well by now how necessary it was. I, of all the Linds, had to be ready to protect my family, and so I would be.

I watched Rachel with envy. She had a confidence and ferocity about her that I despaired of matching. Let alone having that now-sculpted body; it had already been curvaceous, and now it was even more so, and tight and lean in all the best areas. One of the greatest injustices of my life was that I could somehow have the same genes as her and yet be...me.

More muscular now, true, and with a running speed and stamina that no one in my family could match. But still as skinny as a twig—slimmer than ever, in fact, even though I was now heavier with that muscle weight and an additional inch I'd somehow gained in just a month. Though I was lean, my muscles weren't *defined* like hers were.

I sighed.

"Hey, Sarah," David said cheerfully, fanning himself with a towel.

He'd been at one of the weight machines when I'd come in, doing his own exercises. Michael coached us one on one, but of course he also gave us homework he expected us to do on our own, and that was what I was here to do now.

"Hey, David," I said with a wan smile.

Speaking of getting sculpted, my sixteen-year-old brother was another prime example of the unfairness of my genetic makeup, or at least how unevenly our magic was enhancing our physiques. David hadn't even been *fit* a month before. He had been lean, but that was just from his teenage metabolism, because his primary occupation before this had been tinkering with our cars, playing video games, and watching YouTube videos—usually ones about cars or video games. He would get out and run around with a frisbee or football with his friends once in a while, but that was the extent of his physical activity.

Now he looked like he was on the football team. Good thing there weren't any girls around he wasn't related to anymore, or they'd be all over him, white hair and silver eyes notwithstanding. Or...maybe even because of that, too; I had to admit that on him, and Rachel, the combination with our tan skin looked exotic.

And, of course, David now ate three times as much as everyone. He was single-handedly making Mom reevaluate our original estimate of how long our food stores would last us. Thus, one of his primary responsibilities when he wasn't doing rightwing stuff or helping Dad and Lizzy figure out the crafting area was to help Mom in the garden.

Speaking of which....

"It's all yours," David said with a grin and a pat on my shoulder as he left. "I'm off to get dirty."

"Have fun," I said with mock enthusiasm.

"I'll try," he said over his shoulder with heroic stoicism.

With nothing left for it, and with Michael eying me pointedly, I sighed and went over to my cubby, where I kept my personal equipment and where I'd stashed my sneakers, since I didn't trust my lights to not make them disappear like snobby butlers if I kept them in my room. I took deep breaths for steadiness as I slipped off my boots and laced the sneakers on.

I used to enjoy running. I was on the track team in high school, and I did well. Now I was the fastest in our family, so no one understood what made me so reluctant now. They also didn't understand why I insisted on running in the Outer Rim, not believing my half-truths that it was because I found the darkness and moonstone energizing. I hadn't even told Dad why yet. This memory, I would probably take to my grave.

Unless things changed.

I stretched for a bit, then trudged up the bleachers to the secret access door that only appeared when one of us Moontouched came near. I put my hand on the door, and it swung inward, allowing me to step inside and close the door behind me, enclosing me in comforting darkness. I sighed, half in relief, half in reluctance.

Even in the darkness of the Outer Rim, where no memories lay in wait for me, tears stung my eyes as I began to run.

As hard as they were to start, I always felt better after my runs. Although I needed yet another cold shower to reenergize after my one-on-one with Michael, which had included a lot of heavy magical work to push the boundaries of what we had discovered we could do, including trying out both our transformative forms. Doing starform during the day did me in, but Michael kept insisting that practicing when it was more difficult was necessary to build up endurance.

Besides, we never knew *what* time of day we might need to use our greatest weapons.

After I was done with my shower and felt somewhat human again (even though that was a relative term for us nowadays), I helped Laura with the littles for a bit until Lizzy came in from her own shower to take over. Which meant I had just enough time for one of my most important tasks of the day before dinner: visiting the Tree of Ice.

At the northern point of our hold was the largest moongate of them all, emblazoned simply but clearly with a large white tree. It was the only moongate that still worked, and when I opened the doors, I saw the proper fragile-looking ice curtain there, which allowed me to step through, parting like cold water around me that didn't leave any trace behind. The doors slowly swung shut behind me.

Even though I now walked on Earth's soil, it didn't feel like it. I had entered an enormous underground rotunda capped with a dark dome lit with thousands of white stars. I was pretty sure by now that they gradually shifted over time, perhaps reflecting the sky above.

Beyond the rotunda was a short but large and tall passage that led to enormous double doors, this time with the tree represented in silver filigree over its surface. Those doors, too, opened at my touch, revealing the enormous ice cavern beyond.

The Tree of Ice sat atop a steep, frosted hill broken up by enormous roots, some of which were thicker around than a large man. The Tree Herself was perhaps a hundred feet thick and more than a hundred tall, so high so that I had to crane my neck while at the base of the hill to see Her canopy of ice leaves that spread under the thick ice dome overhead. Frosted stone steps set into the hill led up to the Tree's base, which I now climbed, my breath only mildly puffing out in front of me.

It should have come in great clouds; in fact, I should have been freezing in this wintery room without so much as a coat on me. But I now ran a temperature perhaps ten degrees cooler than the average human, and the cold outside me, instead of being painful, felt invigorating. Especially *this* cold—the cold of my Tree.

At the top of the steps was a stone circle set into the hill, with a retaining wall around its perimeter. In the center of that circle was a well that could have led into the void for all I knew, since I couldn't see anything past the darkness ten or twenty feet below. I'd dropped things down it (because the Tree told me to, not because I was being curious or disrespectful) without hearing any of them touch the bottom.

And that was all.

Only the first time I had come had the Tree's icy avatar been there to greet me already. I'd gathered enough about Trees by now, though, to understand that was normal; They weren't supposed to be at our beck and call, not even for their chosen Monarchs.

Besides, I found I appreciated the mental preparation of standing there in meditative silence, just closing my eyes or keeping them open with a relaxed gaze, just breathing in that cold, crystalline air and feeling my iceheart pulse with Her light.

Most times, that was all. She had seldom come to speak with me over this past month, and our meetings were usually short and to the point when She did: usually to give me one piece of instruction or answer one urgent question. When I came asking about our food stores, for example, She only appeared just long enough to smile and assure me that if we were diligent, we would be provided for. Then She had blown away just as swiftly, as if She had been merely a winter wind.

Yet Her very first instruction to me as Her Queen when I finally roused myself enough from my misery to come visit Her two days after the battle was that I was to come to Her every evening thereafter, no matter if She had anything to say or I had anything to ask. She didn't say why, and I didn't ask for a reason. By then, I hadn't needed to.

When a Tree asks you to do something, you had better do it. Not because They were some vengeful, controlling being; rather because whatever They asked you to do usually meant the difference between life or death.

So, every day, I came. And every day, no matter whether I spent that entire fifteen minutes or so simply standing there in silence or not, I walked away more still, more settled. Somehow strong enough to get through another day.

That day, I slowly walked the dozen steps to the well at the center of the circle, settled into my stance, let my eyes slowly drift closed, and just breathed.

The air was cold and fresh in my nostrils. The latter should have been impossible, considering how deep underground (or under-ice) we were, but then again, this was a magical being the likes of which put the most powerful mortal to shame.

There also was a slight breeze against my skin, also impossible yet there all the same. The only sound was of that draft tinkling the ice leaves hundreds of feet overhead like distant, angelic wind chimes.

As I often did to pass the time, I imagined roots growing down from my feet into that frosted earth below the stone, settling me in, growing myself into my own sort of tree—tall and strong. I even held out my hands as low branches.

Just as I was imagining leaves sprouting from my imaginary boughs, a now-familiar voice whispered in my mind.

Welcome, My daughter of Ice.

My eyes snapped open, but no avatar stood across the well from me, nor anywhere I looked around that circle. I didn't bother looking more. She had done that before—speaking to me only mind to mind.

"Thank you, my Lady," I answered quietly. "What is it you wish to say to me?"

You and your family have done well in following My instructions thus far. I commend you. Encourage them to continue when you return, and I will keep all My promises regarding their safety and prosperity. But now I have a different work for you, My Right Hand.

I started. "And what is that?"

When the King of Flame calls for you, go with him and aid him.

I froze.

I had never asked the Tree about Ben. She had never mentioned him.

Until now.

My iceheart trembled, the fracture inside it threatening to widen.

"My...Lady?" I asked, voice cracking.

Go with him and aid him, the Tree merely repeated, voice as soft as falling snow. *For now, your wings will remain with your family to continue aiding them and growing into their roles. When the Golden King comes for you, you will go and travel with him alone, until you receive further instruction from Me.*

I had to suppress a pained laugh.

"My Lady," I said, working excruciatingly hard to both be respectful and not think too hard about what I was saying. "It has been a month, and he has...shown no sign of doing any such thing."

This time We have given you both for rest and for mourning has and must come to an end. My Sister, His Tree, has sent him, and he is coming.

The breath rushed from my lungs. "*When?*"

The Tree of Ice's simple answer sent a fire through my blood—and that wasn't a good thing.

Now.

Chapter Two

AWAKE

Koriben

I jolted awake from my dream with a force that sent me and the tray on my desk tumbling, all of us falling to the ground with a clatter and a breathless *umph* from me.

I was so dazed and disoriented that, by the time I realized where and when I was and lifted my head, Kor and Yvera stood over me—Kor with his hands swirling with sapphire power and Yvera with her claymore in hand.

"Ben?" Yvera asked hesitantly.

The Tree's voice echoed in my mind, yanking me back for a single moment into the dream.

Go to her, now. *Before it is too late.*

"Sarah," I gasped, the name feeling like it was yanking itself from the depths of my restored flameheart to spill from my lips.

For the first time in too long.

And then I surged.

So far, being King had one singular perk: surging was now so *easy* that even though I had started in a prostrate position, when I emerged from the Library daygate a split second later, I came out walking upright, and in only another second had broken into a run, heedless of the stares I collected from patrons along the way.

If only some torched *idiot* (me) hadn't closed the gate that led to Sarah's hold, I could have surged straight there. As it was, this was the closest I could get.

Flame Above and Below, if Sarah died because of *me*...because of all I had done to *keep* her from dying because of me...

...I didn't think my flameheart could keep burning.

Of course, she might not be in immediate danger. The Tree's warning had been vague about that, and probably deliberately. I didn't even resent the Tree for that ambiguity. I knew I deserved every bit of that lightning bolt to my soul to get me moving, breathing, *living* again.

But as long as there was a *chance* that inaction now could cost her life, I had to act as if it did.

I bolted into the Covenantal History section, down the side, turned the corner, and dashed to the back of the Shrine of the Covenants, the Tree's golden eyes in the statue depicting Her seeming to flash at me as I passed.

Sorry, I told her with a wince.

I would give Her a proper apology later for my inexcusable behavior this past month, the full horror of which was only just now sinking in. I felt as if I were only just waking from a heavy nightmare that had begun the moment I realized my father was gone until the moment my dream of the Tree ended just dek ago, and my head was spinning as it fast forwarded through everything that had happened in that month with rapidly increasing dismay.

But right now, I was doing exactly what She had told me to, so I presumed that would be a sufficient atonement for the moment.

I slapped my hand to the wall at the back, praying with all my might that only my touch was all that was needed this time. It had been enough the one time I'd had to lead my wings through to the gate the long way, since they couldn't surge with me without Sarah to lash us together.

But I didn't know if I had ruined this door too. Which would be the tragedy to cap them all, since the only person who could help me open it if it were now locked was now trapped behind ice inside.

But the doors and the symbol of the sun all flared to life with golden light.

Thank the Flame, I thought, sagging with relief as the doors swung inward.

I only gave myself that one second of weakness, though. The moment the gap was wide enough for me, I dashed inside, then spent a few precious seconds closing the doors behind me to make sure no one went poking their noses where they shouldn't. The moment they were shut, I ran down the short passage to the next round chamber, giving the glowing gold streaks in the walls only just enough time to light the way ahead of me.

A small, freestanding stone arch was in the middle of the chamber. It should have had flames licking the side closest to me, but of course I'd gotten rid of those. So now there was only the semi-translucent sheet of solid ice that represented Sarah's half.

To my shock, I didn't see blackness beyond the ice, as I had expected to. I had expected to be pounding on her closed half of the gate, either metaphorically or literally as the magic allowed. But from the distorted light and shapes I saw beyond, it appeared...open.

I would ponder the miracle of *why* Sarah hadn't shut me out as thoroughly as I had her, *later*.

Now, without hesitation, I pulled my ceremonial knife out of the ether with my left hand. I didn't know if blood was required to undo what I had done and reopen the gate, but I wasn't about to waste time with half measures.

Saying a quick, silent prayer to the Tree of Flame first to forgive my unworthiness, I slit my right hand, allowed the golden blood to drip as close to inside the arch as I could with the ice in the way, and said the words of the First Covenant once again, just as I had done to activate the gate the first time—with the only difference being my title, which I had to say past a lump in my throat.

"By the power invested in me by the Tree of Flame, as the Golden King, I now invoke the First Covenant and swear by my blood that I and my people shall uphold its terms, for as long as the Flame above and Below may give us Their light."

Don't make her pay for my mistakes, please. Please, please let that be enough.

For a terrible moment, I thought it wasn't.

Then I felt such a sharp drain of energy that I sagged and had to throw out my hands to brace myself against the two sides of the arch. Still, it didn't knock me unconscious as it had the first time, so perhaps I *hadn't* torched the very Covenant I and Sarah had renewed by doing this the first time.

Flames surged up from the ground and all sides of the arch to lick across the ice before covering it completely. I felt the skin on my right palm crawl and sting as the slice healed—the last sign of the Tree's acceptance.

Thank you, thank you, I mentally gasped.

Now, for the final test. Was Sarah's half *truly* open?

Inhaling sharply in half hope, half dread, I slowly reached my hand through the curtain of flame...and through the curtain of ice.

I let out the breath. Trembling slightly, I stepped through...

...and into Sarah's hold.

Before I had time to even look for Sarah, I heard a little girl's delighted shriek. "Ben!"

I glanced sharply to my left to see Sarah's youngest sibling running as fast as her little legs could carry her to me.

"Abby," I said with my best attempt at a smile.

It was as if my lips were having to remember how to move that way. Really, I was shocked that I could manage that much, *and* that I had even remembered the little girl's name. I was certain I'd forgotten the names of most of Sarah's family, which I was sure wouldn't help my probably now abysmal relationships with them at all.

With this one apparently being an exception.

Abby jumped at me, so I didn't know what else I could have done except catch her and lift her up with another smile. She looked so much like a hatchling version of Sarah, with her tan skin and Sarah's formerly dark hair and eyes, that she wrenched my flameheart.

"I *told* them you'd be back," she declared loftily. "I told them."

"Well, then, that just proves you're smarter than all of us," I said with an even weaker smile.

I hadn't forgotten how she had called me the King of Flame while I was still only the Heir. Perhaps the ominous nature of that introduction was the reason I still remembered her name.

"Now, since you're so smart, I don't suppose you can tell me where your sist—"

"Well, well, well," a voice drawled, one that made me freeze. "Look what the monster cat dragged in. It's *his royal majesty.*"

Sarah's older sister strolled toward me.

Of all the people I had hoped to encounter, she had been the last—and she did *not* look pleased.

"Er, hi, Rachel," I said, feeling my cheeks go red as I hastily but carefully set Abby down. "Could you...um...point me in Sarah's direction?"

"That's it?" Rachel said flatly, putting her hands on her full hips as she came to a halt six feet from me. "You *break my sister's heart* and *trap* us here, and all you can say is 'Hi, Rachel' and 'Where's Sarah'?"

I winced. So, it was about as bad as I had feared, minus the open gate and Abby's welcome. "I am *sorry.* More than I can say, especially right now, because I *have* to find Sarah."

"'Have to,' my ass," Rachel snapped, shoving her finger in my direction. "You're lucky Michael hasn't heard you're back, mister, or you'd be so riddled with ice darts right now, you'd be a gold and blue porcupine."

The likelihood of becoming whatever a porcupine was might be increasing, though, as other members of Sarah's family began poking their heads out of arches and making their way toward us, with most of the older ones showing varying hard or sober expressions. But when my gaze darted around them, none of them were Sarah.

"*Please*, Rachel," I begged. "Where is Sarah? I swear, I will make it up to all of you somehow, but she could be in danger—"

"In danger?" Rachel seemed even more inflamed by the idea. "The greatest danger she's been in for the past month is dying from boredom and starvation, because of *you*, you—"

Her eyes darted to Abby and to her mother, who had just reached her.

"—pig," Rachel finished sullenly.

I didn't know what a pig was, but I presumed it was something unflattering—but also far milder an insult than the one she had been intending.

"Rachel," Sarah's mother murmured. "We don't have a right to stop him from talking to Sarah, if that's what she wants."

Though her eyes were worried when she looked back at me.

"We have *every* right," Rachel raged, looking at her mother while she gestured to me. "Who is going to protect Sarah from him if *we* don't?"

"Please," I said, holding my hands out to all of them in a plea. "I just want to make sure Sarah is safe. I know it's hard to believe now, but that's all I've *ever* wanted to do. And right now, she could be in trouble. So will you *please* either tell me where she is or take me to her?"

Sarah's mother cast Rachel a meaningful look, and I held my breath.

I released it when Rachel threw up her hands in defeat.

"Fine, *fine*." She pointed her finger at me, eyes blazing silver. "But you had better *grovel* for her, you hear me? I want *groveling*."

"I will grovel from now until eternity if that's what it takes, I swear," I said fervently.

"And if you break her heart again, I will shoot a shard through your stinkin' fire heart *myself*."

"Rachel!" her mother said, aghast.

"Agreed," I said swiftly, hiding my inner flinch.

Not because of my reluctance to accept Rachel's help in ending my life in that scenario but because of the repeated reminder of how much pain I had inflicted. Knowingly, which made it even more monstrous, especially with the stark knowledge I had now that it had all been in vain.

Rachel huffed, as if she hadn't quite expected me to concede—or to believe I meant it when I did.

"Fine. Follow me," she said with an impatient gesture, turning to the north and making her way through the gathered Linds.

I made my own way with just a bit of unease, still not sure whether any of them would start pulling out one of those deadly guns of theirs and start shooting. I deserved it, but I needed to make sure Sarah was alright first before I could let them have some payback, if that was what they still wanted. Still, even then, I couldn't let them kill me.

Because, at least according to the Tree, I was now the only one who could save their sister from what was coming for her.

"Could we, er, walk a bit faster?" I dared to ask when we'd cleared the group of them.

Rachel continued to stroll along the Rim as casually as if she were browsing the Grand Market at Crownhold and her sister's life wasn't on the line.

"Sarah waited one month for you to come back. One *miserable* month. You can wait a few minutes to see her again."

I flinched. "Rachel, punish me all you like later. If she's in danger...."

"What's stopping you from pushing her away like this again?" Rachel snapped. "Until the *next* time she's 'in danger'?"

I flinched again, flameheart sputtering. It was a fair question, but the answer delved too deeply into things I barely had the courage to tell Sarah, let alone *this* sister.

"Because I can't anymore," I said heavily.

"What do you mean, you *can't*? If you were capable of it once—"

Presumably, that meant she didn't know about the first time if she thought I had only done it once. Which again, like that open door, shocked me. Why hadn't Sarah told them? Railed about me at them?

"—then you sure as hell are capable of doing it again."

"Rachel, I only did that because I was worried I would get Sarah hurt or killed."

"So?" she demanded. "What's keeping you from thinking that way again?"

"Because the Tree said I couldn't, that's why," I snapped.

She eyed me sidelong, her look incredulous. "Your Flame Tree *told* you that you couldn't break up with my sister again?"

"Essentially," I said grimly.

I couldn't push Sarah away again, not even for her own good. Because the alternative was unthinkable.

"And that's it?" Rachel said dubiously.

"That's it," I said, giving her a hard look. "As the Heir of Ice, you should know enough about Trees by now to know that much."

"Hey, I've only had the job for a month," she grumbled. To my surprise, she looked away. "Besides, Sarah's been the one doing most of the talking to Her, anyway. Speaking of which...."

She stopped in front of the northernmost and largest moongate and gestured to it grandly. "Here you go, your majesty. As agreed, I led you to Sarah."

My flameheart sputtered with dread as I looked at the white tree on those doors. "Sarah...is communing with your Tree?"

"Is that a problem?" Rachel asked innocently.

"No," I lied—and, as usual, poorly.

It would be hard enough to face my *own* Tree right now. Let alone Sarah's.

But with Rachel still looking at me with a growing smirk on her face, I said, "It's just that I...can't open that."

I gestured to the gate.

"Oh," Rachel said with wide eyes. "Such a shame. If only the *Heir of Ice* were standing right here to open it for you."

I gritted my teeth. Even if I hadn't had a leftwing who was the expert in manipulation, I had dealt with Rachel's type all too often as Heir. That was why my flameheart had sunk so low after realizing she would be my access to Sarah.

I knew the couple of promises she had extracted from me had been too easy.

"What do you want?"

She smirked. "I knew you had a few brain cells knocking around in that blond head of yours. I want my stuff back."

I blinked. "Your...stuff?"

"Yes, *my* stuff," Rachel huffed, pointing to the ground. "Out with it, now. Those bags of things you 'carried' for us for our flight to Greenland."

"*Oh,*" I said sheepishly. "*That* stuff."

I...had completely forgotten I still had that. Obviously.

I hurriedly brought the large bags out of my ether storage and dumped them on the floor where Rachel had pointed.

"There, are we good?"

"Wait one second," Rachel said with a suspicious glare in my direction as she dug through one bag.

I gritted my teeth again. "Rachel, if Sarah is hurt because of you...."

"She's *fine*, you nitwit. Hold your horses. Aha!"

She triumphantly pulled out a clear box with trays and drawers full of colorful glass bottles, brushes, and various other instruments that I only could vaguely guess the purpose of. But I assumed they all had something to do with beautification.

"Oh, how I missed you!" she squealed to it, hugging it tightly to her chest.

I looked at the bags and then at her with a raised eyebrow. "I thought your father told you to only pack cold-weather gear and food in there."

"He said to pack 'essentials,'" Rachel said innocently, holding up the box. "And trust me, these are essential."

I could only shake my head at her. "And just *how* are you related to Sarah again?"

She rolled her eyes and flipped her long white braid back over her shoulder. "I ask myself that question every day, trust me. Now, I suppose you've kept up your end of the bargain, so as a proper Lind, I should keep mine."

She carefully set her precious box down and walked over to the gate, putting her hands on the doors. The lines and white tree flared, and the doors began to open.

"Thank you," I said fervently, and before she could change her mind, I slipped through the doors the moment I could.

Sarah was almost within reach now. Her star had not yet returned to my mind and might not for deken or days longer. But as soon as I had determined she was safe, I would beg for her forgiveness as long as it took until it was back.

Little did Rachel realize how much I had *already* intended to grovel. And more.

Whatever it took for her to let me save her.

Because the Tree had promised. She had *promised*. If I did what She asked, Sarah would be safe.

The Tree had finally given Her word to protect not just someone I loved but the most precious one I had left.

And I was damn well going to hold Her to it.

Chapter Three

OATHS

SARAH

WHEN THE TREE MEANT *now*, She meant *now*.

The moment She said the word, I heard the double doors to Her cavern swing open behind me.

I froze.

You could have given me a bit *more warning!* I thought to the Tree, not caring how irreverent that was.

My iceheart was pulsing double-time. My entire focus, all my senses strained to detect what was behind me. And yet, I still *could not move.*

Not until I heard his tentative whisper in my mind.

Sarah?

So quiet. So lost. So uncertain.

So much like *me.*

Then, I felt a tentative pull return to my heart. Like an offer. A hand reaching out.

I turned stiffly and staggered across the circle to the top of the steps, hardly daring to look down—and yet, unable to stop myself.

There he was, standing at the bottom of the hill, looking up. His eyes widened when they caught sight of me, but he otherwise froze. That made two of us, just standing there, both of us too overcome for a moment to do anything at all.

He was...Ice help me, he was everything I had remembered and ached for from the depths of my soul, from his absurdly tall height and heavy musculature to his golden, shoulder-length hair and chiseled jaw. And those eyes...I could tell even from this distance from the glow within them that those eyes were the soft twin suns that the real one above could never replace in my soul.

Yet there were two monumental differences that I noticed even through the tangled flood of emotion I felt the moment I saw him.

One, instead of his customary gold, plain clothing, he was dressed in maroon, and of a finer cut, material, and ornamentation than I was used to seeing on him. Even his brown boots looked fancier, polished and with nary a scuff mark to be seen.

Two....

"You shaved," I gasped, taking an unconscious step down.

He blinked up at me, as if he were just as staggered as I was in this moment.

"I'm...in mourning?" he said dazedly, his voice lifting at the end as if he wasn't quite certain that was the case.

I inhaled sharply from horror at what I'd done, for another reason entirely, and I took another few steps closer. "Oh. Oh, Ben. I am so—"

The daze in his eyes abruptly cleared.

"Don't you *dare* say sorry," he growled. He ran a hand through his hair, looking down. Pain lanced across his face, sharp as a knife, and he closed his eyes for a moment.

Tears came to my eyes as I, too, remembered and mourned. Though an even greater emotion rose within me than the sorrow I felt for the man I'd come to think of as a second father: the bone-deep ache to wrap my arms around his son and shield him from any further suffering.

Ben had already borne so much. How much more could any person even endure?

I began walking at a slow yet steady pace down the steps to him.

Ben opened his eyes, but he kept them on the ground. His voice came out as a rasp. "Sarah, I...I am the one who should be saying sorry. No, I am the one who should be *begging*."

Then, to my amazement, he sank down onto one knee, bowing his head to me. "Though I know what I did to you was unforgivable, and I am asking far too late...here I am, begging for your forgiveness. Whatever you want, whatever you ask of me to atone, I will do it. I am yours to command."

That shocking plea nearly broke me. If I had been the Sarah he first met, especially the one without the crown I now bore with all the weight of duty, it no doubt would have. But I wasn't.

He had already broken me once, in another way, and endangered my family besides. I hadn't blamed him for it. I didn't know why, but I didn't. I always *understood why*.

Yet that didn't mean I should let him fully back in, not in the way most of my heart was yearning to, almost screaming at me to. Not in the way I knew he was meaning, from the way he was intangibly reaching for me, the promise of the connection between us blossoming into full flower. It hung invisibly between us in the air, undeniably sweet, tender, and everything I had once held—and even *more*.

I would decide whether it would survive the frost.

Me...and my Tree. Because this wasn't entirely my decision anymore, just as my life was not mine.

Silence fell between us as I stared at Ben, frozen in agony. Long enough that he slowly tensed, though he still did not lift his head.

"*Please*, Sarah," he gasped, tears in his voice.

My eyes overflowed again. As the icy rivulets fell down my cheeks, I took one more step down.

Please, I begged my Tree in turn.

In the very next moment, peace filled me—as sure and still as the dawn rising over the pure snow, flooding the world with sparkling light. I gasped with the joy and relief and *rightness* of it.

Ben raised his head in alarm, just in time to see me disappear.

I surged to him, my gate, my sun. Surged in a silver blur until I smacked into his chest not a second later, throwing him so off balance from my impact and his surprise that he tumbled backward and me on top of him. Just in time, I summoned a blast of air that cushioned his head against the hard, cold stone floor. That was the only thought I took for his comfort, though, as I pulled myself up to his face and crushed my lips to his.

Then felt the smoothness and jerked away with a jolt as I remembered what it meant. He was in mourning, for Ice's sake. What was I thinking?

Ben blinked at me rapidly. Before I could fear I'd made a complete mistake in launching myself at him like this, I saw his eyes were glowing gold, even through his utter shock. His face started turning that adorable red I loved so much, with so much more skin exposed to reveal it.

Then he grabbed the back of my neck and pulled me back down to him.

Oh, it had been too long. *Far* too long since I'd felt his burning lips move against mine. Since I'd felt the heat of his skin, his heart of flame pulsing against my own heart of ice. Felt his strong arms capture my back, felt his healing, life-giving magic sink into and through me.

How he could concentrate on kissing *and* healing me simultaneously, I had no idea. I was going mad just *feeling* both at the same time. His was the only warmth I now craved, and now I needed *more*. The magic, magnetic pull I'd felt from him before was now fully restored and stronger than ever. I had to spend precious brainpower to resist the tug to go all the way into him, into his heart, as we discovered I could in the battle to defend his Tree and Realms.

Not that I was thinking about any of that, or of the practical reasons why I shouldn't supercharge Ben like that here and now. I couldn't even remember my own name, let alone his state of mourning, which was already forgotten once again. I only resisted because I wanted to feel him like *this*, as *me*.

And I wanted to feel more.

Without breaking the kiss, I rose onto all fours, bunched his shirt in my fists, and tugged upward.

Ben stilled, perhaps from the shock of the cold. "Sarah," he said with a short, tense laugh, breaking away.

What? I said silently, so I could immediately return my lips to his.

To my shock, he broke away again, withdrawing his hands to put them on my shoulders and keep me away. His eyes burned with desire, but his face was growing red again. "It's not that I don't want to, Sarah, but *this* isn't the place."

His eyes darted behind me.

I blinked rapidly, sense and memory only returning in a slow trickle. Something was familiar about those lines, but weren't they normally mine? "What...."

Then it all came back: where, when, what. Most especially, what I had been trying to do.

I gasped, falling sideways onto my rear. "Sorry! So sorry!"

"Don't apologize to *me*," he said with a shaky smile as he propped himself up into a sitting position. "I'm just as guilty as you are in that. It's just, the Trees are mad enough at me as it is. I'd rather not further aggravate yours."

Again, that nervous dart of his eyes, this time without me in the way, up toward the Tree.

"Why would the Trees be mad at you?" I asked, nonplussed.

"Who *isn't* mad at me right now?" Ben muttered. Then his eyes fell on me and widened. "As a matter of fact, why aren't *you*?"

I stilled, at a loss for words to explain the agonizing transformation I had just undergone, the peace and surety I'd felt.

He shook his head, pain lancing across his face. "After what I did to you...I expected to be begging from now until eternity. And I would have. As much as I hoped, I didn't think you would actually...."

That was when I realized my iceheart was not just healed—I couldn't find even a scar. None of the terrible, unbearable pain from before remained, and even the memory of it was already fading like a bad dream.

I didn't know what Ben saw in my expression, but he must have read wrong, because he sighed. He climbed to his feet and pulled me to my own. Then, to my shock, he kneeled down on one knee in front of me once again. "Sarah—"

"Ben, stop," I said in mild alarm, my cheeks warming—as much as they ever did nowadays. "You've already—"

"No, let me finish," he said firmly. "I need to do this, fully and properly this time, and not just because I promised Rachel I would grovel from now until eternity. I need to do this for you, and for your Tree, and for mine, and for all the people I have hurt and endangered because of my selfishness. So, allow me now to formally offer my deepest apologies for what I did and put you through, from the depths of my soul. You cannot know how sorry I am now for what I did to us both."

"You weren't selfish, Ben," I whispered, touching his face. His smooth, clean-shaven face. He was still my Ben, but his bare cheeks looked wrong somehow. "I know why you did it. You were protecting me."

"No," he said grimly. "I was protecting myself. I finally see that now. *I* made everyone else suffer, especially you, because *I* was the one who couldn't bear seeing you get hurt, much less because of me."

"And that only makes sense," I said gently, bringing my other hand to frame his face. "In that case, I'm just as selfish."

He smiled thinly. "Are you about to shut me out of your life and Realm? You have an odd way of doing that, seeing as you left the door open for me."

I warmed again. "That's...different. *You* aren't in danger here."

He just continued to smile thinly.

"It's different," I insisted. "I haven't.... Gosh, Ben, how are you even *functioning* right now?"

His smile faded. "I...wasn't, really. Not until today. Not until this deken, in fact. I just...."

At the devastation that overtook his face, I couldn't resist any longer. I stepped into him and threw my arms around him, holding him tight. And just in time, it seemed, because I felt him begin to tremble.

"Flame, Sarah," he gasped, pulling me to him. "Avva...Avva is...."

"Yes," I whispered.

"Flame," Ben repeated thickly, wrapping his arms even tighter.

Then he began to sob, convulsions overtaking him, so that he had to sit back. I moved with him to sit in his lap and let him hold me as he truly allowed himself to mourn.

Perhaps for the first time.

ABOUT A QUARTER HOUR later, Ben had stilled. I could have sat there forever with him, but I was worried about his temperature. He didn't even have a coat.

"Ben," I murmured. "You're getting cold."

"Give me another dek," he croaked.

"Of course." But I also reached my hand up over his heart and sent him a trickle of energy.

"Sarah—"

"Ben, it's *night* and I'm near my Tree. I've got bucketloads to spare right now."

He shivered, but it seemed to be the good kind of shiver from the soft moan that accompanied it. "Flame, I'd forgotten how that feels."

"Good, I take it?" I said in surprise. He hadn't ever described how my shared power felt to him, other than to imply that it was far more potent for him relative to the amount I'd given.

Ben held me tighter for a moment.

"You can have no idea," he rasped.

Well, his flameheart was getting warmer, which was what I cared about most. Still, I was anxious to get him back to relative warmth.

"Ready to go into the other room, at least? You don't have to go back into the hold just yet, but...."

"Ah, yes, that's alright," Ben said with relief. "Sorry, I'm just not...quite...."

"I understand," I said gently, turning and climbing out of his lap.

My iceheart pulsed at how reluctantly he let me go, and at how he smiled, if weakly, when I took his hand to help him balance as he stood. I would never be able to describe to him what a relief it was that he was finally letting me help him.

He started when we both fully stood next to each other. "You've grown, haven't you?"

"An inch," I said smugly. Not that being roughly five-foot-seven (we hadn't exactly packed a tape measure as an "essential" item in our escape from home) was a whole lot different from being five-foot-six, but it still was *one* inch closer to Ben's seven-foot-five....

"Wait," I said, narrowing my eyes at him. "Did you grow too?"

"An ild," Ben said sheepishly, hand on his neck. "It...happens, sometimes—after investment. Especially if the new Monarch..."

He took a deep breath, but the pain that crossed his face wasn't as raw as it had been before. "...is young."

As we both had been.

I played up my disappointment as a distraction for him. "Dang it."

"What?" he asked in surprise.

I scowled. "I was hoping I'd caught up to you at least a *little* bit."

He laughed at that until tears ran again from his eyes and we had walked hand in hand out of the ice cavern. He wiped the corners with his free hand and breathed deeply as the doors slowly swung shut behind us.

"Been a while?" I said gently. I realized I had said much the same thing the day after we'd met, when he'd laughed a bit like that.

"Sarah, I can't even tell you what the past month has been like," Ben said with a tremendous sigh. "I feel like I'm waking from a blurry nightmare."

I hesitated. "Kind of...like when you went berserk?"

"If only," he said grimly. "Unfortunately, I was in far too much control for that."

Since he didn't seem to want to go into it, and I didn't see a reason to press him, I asked the question that had been burning in my mind ever since he had first said my name in the ice cavern. "What...woke you up?"

"What do you think?" he said with another sigh, looking down at me. "The Tree."

"Ah," I said in a neutral tone. "That's what you meant by the Trees being mad at you."

He grimaced. "Yes.... She...had words for me. Strong ones."

He paused in the center of the rotunda and faced me. "We...need to talk about that, actually."

My iceheart sped. "Oh? What did She say?"

Ben hesitated, rubbing his neck with his free hand and looking at me anxiously. It was a look I knew well by now: it meant that he had something he *had* to say or show me but was certain I wouldn't like it.

My iceheart pulses came even faster, and if I had still been capable of sweating, then my palms would probably have become clammy. Still, hopefully I hid my inner reaction behind a sigh and a patient look.

"Ben, whatever it is, just tell me."

He took a deep breath. "I...that is, you...we...."

"Ben?" I asked, trying very hard to keep the nervousness from my voice. But I couldn't help but clench his hand tightly. I reminded myself of the Tree's assurance—and command.

Sure enough, I felt the faintest whisper in my mind, the brush of a winter wind: *Trust.*

Ben was beet red now. At least, I was pretty sure that was the right color in the cold white lighting of the stars above and moonstone streaks in the columns and walls.

He finally blurted, "I need you to come take a blood registration."

I blinked at him. That was...nothing like what I had been fearing. Or what I had been...hoping.

"A...*what?*"

"A blood registration," he said, letting out a heavy breath. "In practice, just prick your finger, give the blood register a few drops, let it recreate your bloodline from that."

"Oooh," I said, shoulders probably visibly sagging from relief. "You mean a *DNA* test."

"A what?" Ben said blankly.

"Earthren term. This is about those genealogical charts—bloodtrees, right?"

During Kor's elaborate explanation of where the Moontouched had actually gone (most of them secretly dispersing across the Six Realms rather than going back to Earth as they had previously thought) he had drawn some charts to represent Moontouched ancestry.

"Basically," Ben said with a bit of relief. "A blood*tree* is just a shorthand depiction of a blood*line*. And it's the line—the full, elaborate thing—that I need to ask you for. I mean, as a favor, one Monarch to another, if you're at all willing."

"What do you need that for?" I asked curiously.

"Lots of reasons," he said, coloring a bit again. "Although not the typical one. Blood registration is mandatory for all dramá, but that obviously doesn't apply to you. You're not one of my subjects or bound by our laws...entirely. But...when you enter my Realms, you kind of are. It's a whole legal gray area that Kor has been debating back and forth with our lawyers almost nonstop since...well, since we've had the luxury for such things."

"What is a blood registration *typically* for?" I asked.

Ben shrugged helplessly, clearly struggling to put into words what was a fact of life to him. "It's...the official record of a dramá's existence. Everyone is registered at their birth. Everyone. It shows that they...belong."

"Oh," I said slowly, understanding finally dawning. "You mean it's like receiving *citizenship*."

Except in a far more literal, visceral sense. Even Kor had had a hard time grasping the concept of driver's licenses, but they made *babies* take a DNA test to receive citizenship?

Then again, with blood—let alone clan and ancestry—being such a fundamental part of their society, I supposed I could see why they wouldn't see it as an infringement of the infant's rights or privacy. To them, it would be just the same as a birth certificate.

"What?" Ben asked blankly.

I hesitated, thinking of how to explain *my* concept that I took for granted. "Citizenship...means you have proof that you were born in or legally accepted by a certain...er...realm."

Sovereign countries had been a foreign concept to Ben as well, as I'd found out when I'd tried to explain to him the necessity of passports to get to Greenland.

"I...guess? But this is more about belonging to the dramá, not a realm or clan—at least the first time. All blood registration is done at Crownhold, and that's where the bloodline is archived, too."

"I think I've got that part," I said, before he could start getting too far into the weeds.

I'd long since figured out that the Realms were kind of like states, except ruled by Lords and Ladies chosen by offshoots of the Tree of Flame, and Crownhold was like Washington, D.C., the seat of the central government. So, it made sense that blood registration, which I thought of as like citizenship, was done at the central and not realm level.

"You're basically saying that I, as the Queen of Ice, am in a legal gray area by entering your Realms, because I technically aren't on the records and aren't bound by your laws. But, to make the lawyers happy, you and Kor have worked out a compromise wherein I take this blood test for you and at least put myself down on the books."

He let out a breath of relief, and his shoulders relaxed. "Essentially, yes. Sorry. I know I explained horribly, as usual—"

"No, Ben, you did fine, as usual. Is there anything else I should know before I make this decision?"

He sighed. "It isn't just the lawyers who want your blood registration. The Archivists Guild has been hounding me, too, simply because you're the first Moontouched in...a long time. They are dying to get ahold of your bloodline for study."

I figured it would come to something like this. I'd already learned that dramá had a much different idea of the right to privacy than my society did.

"Who would have access to my bloodline? Would it be made completely public?"

Ben grimaced. "In theory, that's up to you. You can restrict it to just the Archivists Guild and the Crown, if that's what you want. But since you're a Monarch and...well, the first Monarch of Ice that we know of, let alone a Moontouched...you're going to be flooded with researchers' requests for access, anyway."

I sighed and nodded. A Monarch's life truly wasn't their own—in ways I kept discovering.

"Even if you made it 'public,' no one could just come in and take a look," Ben added quickly. "They would still have to submit a justification, their access would be supervised, and their names notated in a register. You would just be able to let the blood archivists handle all that without bothering you."

That made the public option more tempting. And I found the level of care they still took with the record comforting.

I took a deep breath. I had always known what I would probably choose in the end, because this was Ben asking. But I still needed one more bit of clarification first.

"I take it that the reason you are asking at all...is that you intend to let me back in. For good, this time."

He flinched. I hated to pain him with the reminder, but I also needed to know where we now stood with each other.

And the likelihood of something like that happening again.

"Sarah...." he said tightly. He clenched my hand in his and, with his other, tentatively reached up. When I stepped forward in acceptance, he cupped my face in his large, warm hand. "When I said I was sorry, that meant that I was swearing to *never* make that kind of mistake ever again."

My iceheart pulsed, and I swallowed. Ben took his promises seriously. His very name meant *Oathbinder* in his tongue, and we had good reason to suppose by now that name choice was deliberate on his parents' part.

I hated to push, but...I deserved this much. My *family*, my people, deserved this much. "You...swear?"

His only answer was to let go of me with both hands, step back, and bring out a gold and alabaster knife. I inhaled sharply as I recognized it: it was the same one he had used to create our shared gate and give my family their translation magic. Besides, it was elaborate enough that I knew it wasn't meant for combat.

"Ben," I said, shaking my head and reaching for him. "That's not what I was asking. You don't have to swear a *blood oath* for this."

I hadn't seen one sworn before, but I knew this was the beginning.

I also knew a blood oath *couldn't* be broken. Ever.

"No, Sarah, I think I do," Ben said grimly as he summoned a ball of golden fire in his palm and released it to hang in the air. "I have a lot to make up for—to you, to your family, to the Trees, to everyone. But most of all, I don't want to leave you with a shred of doubt any longer."

Without giving me time to protest further, he slit the palm of his right hand and held his dripping gold blood over the flame.

"I, Koriben Sunfilled, King of Flame, do swear by my blood and the Flame to never bar the gates of the Six Realms to the people of Ice ever again, unless the Tree should permit."

He took a deep breath and met my gaze. "And I swear to always respect the choice of Sarah Moontouched, the Queen of Ice, to remain at my side, should she desire it, from this time forth. Thus I vow."

I couldn't breathe.

Ben clenched his fist and sent a few last drops into the fire. I gasped as the flame surged around his hand, but it disappeared a moment later, and his skin looked unharmed.

Still, I rushed forward, taking that hand in my own. "Did it burn you? Are you still bleeding? Do you need some energy from me to heal it?"

"No, no, and no," Ben chuckled wearily. He opened that hand to show me the palm. Which was perfectly whole, without even a bloodstain remaining.

"See? When the Tree accepts the oath, She sends the flame into the blood, and the fire heals the cut behind it."

I stared up at him, then at the blood vessel visible in his perfect forearm. "That fireball...just went into your *blood*?"

"What do you think gives the blood oath its power?" Ben asked with a thin smile.

Well, I had thought that was the *blood*, obviously. It still was, I supposed. It was just the fire...*in* the blood. And the blood in the fire. My head hurt trying to wrap itself around that concept.

"You *sure* you're OK?" I asked, swallowing. I traced that precious blood vessel with one finger while I still cradled his hand in my other.

His fingers curled reflexively in response to that touch.

"Well," he said, clearing his throat. "I wouldn't recommend *you* trying to swear a blood oath with fire, but yes, I'm sure *I'm* perfectly fine."

I glanced up at him and found his eyes glowing slightly.

For the second and even greater time, it hit me what he had just done. He had taken away his choice, at least in creating distance between us...to give me mine. No matter what came, no matter what happened...he couldn't shut me out again. Ever.

"Ben...." I whispered. My eyes prickled.

"It was necessary, Sarah," he said quietly. "I won't let myself hurt you like that again. If there ever comes a time when...."

He took a shaking breath. "Well. I...will just have to face the pain if it comes to that. Because that is *my* pain to bear. Not yours. From now on...you decide. You decide what risk you endure, what pain you bear, what life you want."

The tears overflowed now. "You didn't have to do it to that extreme. But...now that it's done, I suppose all I can say is...thank you."

He smiled slightly. "It's only what you deserved. From the very beginning. I've just been a torched idiot to take this long to see that."

"Ben," I said quietly. "Don't you ever talk that way about yourself again. You have had to endure more pain than I can even imagine. The reason you're still standing here, with me, now, is a miracle. You are *not* an idiot. You are a miracle."

His smile widened, and his eyes burned brighter. "And if *you're* the reason I'm standing here with even half my sanity, then what does that make you?"

I laughed shakily, tears still flowing. "Happy. *Very* happy."

"Good," he said. Then, with no other warning, he pulled me up and kissed me fiercely.

CHAPTER FOUR

APOLOGIES

KORIBEN

"So," I asked Sarah after we parted. "What's your answer about the blood registration?"

I tried to keep my voice casual, but my flameheart pulsed more quickly in hope and fear of her answer. One significant thing rode on her decision that I had deliberately avoided telling her—but that one thing was the real reason I was pressing the blood registration on her now at all. Lawyers and blood archivists could continue banging on my door for all I cared. I'd held them off for this long and would have for months longer for her sake if they were my only concerns.

But the Tree hadn't given me months. In fact, She'd given me only *one*. And blood registration was the first step—or obstacle, to be more precise—to doing what She had told me to do.

"Oh, that," Sarah said with a blink and a laugh. "Sure, I'll do it. Seems the least I can do for a lifetime visa to the Six Realms."

"A what?" I asked, but I couldn't suppress a grin of relief.

She would do it. *Thank the Flame.* Knowing her love of privacy and reluctance to involve herself in Crown affairs, I had been almost certain she would at least hesitate, if not refuse, that I would have to start giving her more information than I thought was wise at this point to persuade her. But for some miraculous reason, only the basics had done the trick. I could kiss her again from sheer gratitude, but I didn't want to let on just how much this meant to me.

She smiled. "Think of it like a pass—permission to enter a Realm, so to speak."

I snorted. "You got *that* from the Trees. I was the only—"

At her pointed look, I rethought my word choice. "—person stubborn enough to risk Their wrath to even temporarily deny that. Blood registration just smooths some ruffled feathers, that's all."

And removed an annoying legal impediment that she didn't need to concern herself with right now. Especially since everyone knew it was only a formality in her case. We couldn't *possibly* be so closely related as to cause an issue. But if I was going to do things by the book for her now....

"Well, then, I'll smooth those feathers for you," Sarah said easily. "Just say the word, and I'll donate blood and change my citizenship status for you, anytime."

I kissed her briefly and said, "Thank you."

Reluctantly, I slowly set her down. "Well...it's probably about time I faced your family."

"You didn't before?" Sarah asked in amusement. "To get here?"

"Well, some of them," I said uncomfortably. "Rachel, obviously, because she opened the gate for me."

Sarah winced. "I hope...she wasn't too...."

"Oh, she was mad, alright," I said, "but no more than I deserved."

"Ben," Sarah began, but I cut her off.

"Sarah, just because you can somehow forgive me, just like that, doesn't mean you should have. Or that anyone else can and should. They deserve an apology from me. How else are we going to move forward from here?"

She sighed and nodded. "You're right. But you can make that *one* apology, and no groveling is required."

I grinned at her. "But I promised Rachel—"

"You've done enough of that, promise kept." She turned and marched toward the moongate. "Come on, before I can change my mind about this and you get yourself too worked up again. Then you and I can go back to Crownhold."

"What?" I said, freezing mid-step to follow her.

She turned in surprise. "Ben, I just said I'd come."

Oh, right. That's what she meant. I relaxed.

"Sarah, it's night, at least a couple deken after sunset. The blood archives will be closed and not open for registrations until dawn tomorrow. I'll come back for you then."

Sarah sighed. "OK, first off, my sleep schedule has...changed a bit in a month. I pretty much have to sleep in until past noon."

I blinked at that, but I supposed that made sense. After all, *I* hated being awake at the lowest point of *my* power. Still, I was sharply disappointed at that first sign of how little time we might typically have to spend together.

"Alright...I'll come after noon."

The archivists would probably appreciate the extra time to prepare for such a momentous registration, anyway.

"Second, my Tree also gave *me* a message. Just in the normal, talking way. She said that when you came, I was supposed to go with you."

I stilled. "She...did? Did she say...why? Or for how long?"

"No. But She was adamant. She even said I was supposed to leave my wings, so they could keep helping my family."

My head spun. "What?"

Sarah's voice took on a solemn tone, and I knew at once that she was quoting her Tree, word for word. The Tree's words impressed themselves like runes etched in stone in the minds of Her Monarchs. "'*When the Golden King comes for you, you will go and travel with him alone, until you receive further instruction from Me.*'"

Go...and even travel.

Just what were the Trees up to? *Beyond* what my Tree had told me?

"And She *didn't* say why?"

"She said twice that I was supposed to 'aid' you," Sarah said with a shrug. "Anything come to mind that needs aiding?"

"Oh," I said, flameheart suddenly sinking in understanding. All those dangerous, unsolvable problems that kept piling up, the ones Kor insisted we needed *Sarah* for...

...and I had just sworn a blood oath to not keep her away, even for her own good.

I silently cursed. I knew I had done the right thing, but Flame.... This was going to be hard, and a lot sooner than I had thought.

"I take it you now have an idea of what we're supposed to be doing," Sarah said, studying my expression.

"One thing at a time," I said grimly, taking her hand. "First things first, facing your family."

THAT PART WENT MUCH better than I had been expecting. Sarah wasn't the only Lind who was too good.

True, Michael glared daggers at me when he entered the gathering hall where Sarah's family was congregating. But I was used to murderous glares; after all, my own rightwing and lifelong friend, Yvera, was the expert at them.

It probably also helped that the initial shock of my arrival was over, with word no doubt already having long since spread to anyone else who hadn't seen me come in. Sarah's father, Jake, even greeted us in front of the moongate and clasped arms with me. If he was upset with me, he certainly didn't show it, but I didn't let that put me off my guard. I knew by now how well Jake could hide his feelings. Still, his quiet offer of his condolences to me for Avva's passing gave me pause—and made my eyes sting.

Fortunately, Sarah took over from there, saving me from having to reply as she asked her father to call everyone into the assembly room and then led me there herself. This entire process began to feel familiar, as I'm sure it did to Sarah too, especially when she led me to the head of the room, just as she had when we had first arrived at her Earth home.

Rachel seemed over the worst of her pique; she sat down without so much as looking at me and began applying another coat of color to her nails from one of the tiny bottles that had been in her kit. David came up to me with a smile and clasped arms, and he too kindly offered condolences. At least this time I managed a simple thanks and kept the stinging in my eyes from getting to the danger zone.

Sarah's youngling sister didn't look directly at me as she sat down, as if not knowing how she was supposed to feel or behave. Sarah's hatchling brothers cast me curious looks but otherwise ignored me and chatted among themselves and to their mother, but Abby waved. Sarah's mother cast me a troubled look, but that seemed somewhat lessened when she saw Sarah standing next to me, at ease and confidently holding my hand. Sarah had refused to relinquish it, even though I'd self-consciously tried to pull away after Michael's pointed glare at that contact. Last came Sarah's sister-in-law, with her hatchling in tow. She gave me another glare, nearly as hot as her husband's.

Once she had sat down next to Michael, Sarah looked at me to begin.

Remember, she said. *One apology, so make it count.*

My lips twitched in a humorless and momentary smile as I met her gaze. Then I took a deep breath and looked at the assembled Linds.

"Thank you all for coming to hear me. I won't keep you long from your beds or work. I simply wanted to offer a deep and sincere apology to you all. Now I recognize something of the strain I must have put you all under. You are only here because of me, because you sacrificed everything to accept the call of the Tree of Ice and come to the aid of my people. You depended on me and my people for support, support which I refused and then left you in doubt."

I swallowed. This much *had* occurred to me during that nightmarish month, but in the mind of the hard *thing* I had become, it did not matter so much as keeping Sarah safe. I even thought I was doing them a favor by cutting them off completely from my Realms and our problems. After all, what if this new, deadly fever had spread among *them*?

I didn't let myself focus on the fact that Sarah would brave that fever now. There was nothing I could do about that if Sarah chose to come, and I still had to get through this trial first.

"I won't offer excuses. There are none for my behavior."

"Ben," Sarah murmured.

"There are none," I repeated, not taking my eyes off her family. In fact, I met the eyes of their father, whose cool, unreadable silvers only looked calmly back into mine. "So, in recognizing that, and the pain and difficulty you needlessly faced because of me, I offer my deepest regret. Moreover, I swear to you that nothing of the kind will ever happen again so long as I am King of Flame."

I paused for a moment. "Your daughter, sister, and Queen already witnessed me swear a blood oath to that effect, but I repeat the words of it again: 'I, Koriben Sunfilled, King of Flame, do swear by my blood and the Flame to never bar the gates of the Six Realms to the people of Ice ever again, unless the Tree should permit.'"

"He really did seal that oath with his blood," Sarah said to them seriously. Her eyes landed on Michael, whose hard expression remained unmoved. "He literally *can't* do that again, even if he wanted to."

I looked at Jake, Sarah's leftwing. "Before I leave, give me a list of any-thing—*anything*—you require, and I'll see that it gets to you by dawn."

"We don't need bribes," Michael snapped.

"It's not a bribe. It's compensation, and not nearly enough for what I have done and what you have sacrificed. My Realms still stand because of all of you. I could empty the Crown's treasury for you, and it still would not repay what you have lost and we gained—and that is even before the aid Sarah is about to give."

"What?" Michael demanded, glancing at Sarah.

Sarah met his gaze. "The Tree of Ice told me to go with him for the time being. He needs my help with the work of recovery, since the time after a Devourer invasion is almost as dangerous as the invasion itself."

Of course she had already figured out the why herself.

"No," Michael said flatly. "No way in—"

Sarah only raised an eyebrow. "I'm going, Michael."

"And you think *I* want to be dragged along with you to help this selfish jerk?"

"Well, it's a good thing the Tree said you're staying, isn't it?" she said dryly. She looked more apologetic when she turned to her father. "All of you. The Tree made it clear that I was supposed to go alone, that even my wings needed to stay to continue learning and helping our family."

Michael swore. "You think that makes me feel *better*?"

"You don't like it, go ask the Tree," Sarah said dismissively.

I was a bit in awe of her now. Long gone was the timid young woman I'd first found who couldn't say no, as was the one who had trembled to stand up to this very brother.

I took a deep breath. "There could be a good reason that the Tree has commanded only Sarah to go with me, and to not immediately return."

Sarah looked up at me in surprise. I looked back at her with pain lancing through my flameheart, knowing what I was about to say wouldn't stop her. "There's a new plague, started soon after the Battle of the Solstice. They're calling it brightfever."

She would soon see why.

"Oh," Sarah said as understanding slowly dawned. But my flameheart wavered as I saw the evidence I knew I would in her eyes: she was merely thoughtful, realizing why the Tree was minimizing the risk to her family. She would still come, by herself.

"Better and better," Michael said, throwing up his hands. He pointed accusingly at me. "You claim to love her, yet you're asking her to risk her life to help you, *again*?"

I answered as evenly as I could with how raw a nerve he was striking. "I wasn't the one to ask. Not even my Tree did. *Yours* gave the command, and if that is what Sarah is determined to do, I can't make the mistake of stopping her. Not again."

"Michael, even *if* I catch this fever, I'll receive the best care there is," Sarah said calmly. "Ben isn't about to let me die if there's anything that can be done to prevent it."

Michael snorted. "*Other* than letting you stay where it's safer."

Yes, I thought in despair. *Other than that.*

That, I no longer had a choice in.

"Sarah," her mother asked, face troubled as she looked between the two of us. "You'll...be careful, won't you?"

"I'll make sure of it, ma'am," I said with a thin smile for her and a pointed look at Sarah, which she returned with a thin smile of her own.

I returned my gaze to the others and said soberly, "I'll protect her with my blood and my life. I swear it."

Chapter Five

SPRING

Sarah

While Dad and Mom worked out a list with Ben, which he transcribed onto his own tablet, I went to go pack.

I had little that I cared to bring. Since I figured most of my needs would be provided for (in excess), and most of my sentimental belongings had been left behind then burned to a crisp in our home on Earth or dropped down the well at the Tree's request, I only packed the kinds of things that I didn't want to have to ask for, such as the period underwear, toiletries kit, and hairbrush that Svyer, Ben's cousin and my first real friend in the Six Realms, had gathered and organized for me.

Those few things fit into just one of the large duffel-like bags she had put all my new stuff in, with plenty of room to spare. In fact, I might have been able to fit them in the brown leather backpack she had also given me, but I wanted to have somewhere else to put those things so I could use the backpack for emergency supplies or day trips, as I had before.

I kept hoping I would get the ability that drakón did to store things in the ether, but no such luck so far. Probably because that ability of theirs was connected somehow to their transformation into dragons; every time they either put something in or drew something out of their ether storage (or "hoard," to use the slang term), they had to at least change a little, but the shift was typically so slight, I hardly noticed.

I had gained a lot of power and some impressive abilities since I first came to the Six Realms and my magic began to wake, but even after a month of straining, I hadn't been able to so much as make a scale appear. It could well be that I was never meant to become a drakón. After all, my limited understanding was that normally happened at one's formal presentation before the Tree, and I had already been presented *and* invested with Her power as Her Queen. If not even I could change into a dragon now, then perhaps the Moontouched truly were meant to be something else, something new.

I was still disappointed, not to mention saddened, by the differences that remained—and in some cases were growing—between Ben and me.

I finished packing hastily, aware that the longer I took, the more time Ben had to agonize and Michael had to torture him further. Then I slung the duffel over my arm, left my room, and reentered the dormitory.

I stopped by Rachel's room, where she was, as I had expected, finishing a pedicure.

"Let me guess," I said dryly. "You snuck that stuff into the bags Ben carried for us, and then right after he got here, you demanded he give it all back."

"For your information," Rachel said, completely unruffled, "I *first* gave him flack for your sake, since I knew you would never."

"Rachel...."

I sighed, leaving it at that. What was done was done, and I knew there wasn't anything I could say that would make her feel bad for it.

She ignored that while she continued focusing on painting her big toe sapphire. "I have my priorities in the right order: sisters first, boys second."

"Really?" I said incredulously. "*That's* been your motto our entire lives, when no boy before Ben would look at me twice because of you?"

And even Ben might have never if you had been around at the beginning, my most doubting inner voice said bitterly.

Her eyes were uncharacteristically serious when she looked up at me. "None of the boys you were interested in would have been any good for you, Sarah. They would have just broken your heart. I knew that. Believe it or not, I was protecting you."

I blinked as I rapidly thought through my admittedly short list of crush-es—and realized with no small amount of surprise that she was probably right.

Rachel snorted, looking more herself as she refocused on the next toe. "I had my doubts about Ben, too, and obviously he *did* break your heart, at least once. But he's slowly getting back into my good graces."

I rolled my eyes. "Probably in no small part by restoring your beauty stash."

"Not *just* that," Rachel said with a smirk. "Man, that guy knows how to admit when he's wrong. Do you know how hot that is?"

"Hands off," I snapped, temper flaring.

"Oh, don't you worry," she said, smirk deepening. "I'm not going through this effort for *Ben*. He's all yours, clearly. Nope, I have an entirely different dragon in mind right now."

Only now did the sapphire color she'd chosen register in my brain. And I moaned. "Rachel, Kor is...."

Her eyes got a dreamy look that suddenly had me truly worried. "Incredibly hot, magical, and brilliant?"

"*Kor*," I said emphatically. "Trust me, you do *not* know that guy like I do."

"Really?" she said with a slow smile. "Then do tell: just how good of a kisser is he?"

"It doesn't matter how good—" I began hotly, then froze as I realized my mistake. Rachel's smirk only deepened.

I darted surreptitious glances around but saw (thank goodness) that no one else was in the dormitory right now. I stepped into her room and whispered fiercely, "How did you know Kor kissed me?"

Rachel rolled her eyes. "Sarah, Sarah. This is *my* realm of expertise. I know what you sometimes think of my intelligence, but I am *not* an idiot. Or blind, for that matter. I saw how he looked at you, and how Ben and Kor behaved toward each other. You three had 'love triangle' written all over you like neon lights."

She traced a triangle in the air as she said the word in demonstration.

"OK, first off, Kor doesn't love me," I said flatly. "He was just...being Kor. Plus, Ben was going through...a rough patch, and Kor was giving me an option, out of duty."

Because of a certain Tree mandate, which I had carefully not mentioned to anyone in my family, that I, as the Queen of Ice, had to marry the King of Flame. And Kor, though not technically *King*, secretly had the potential to become such if needed.

"Duty," Rachel repeated dryly, giving me a look that, strangely enough, Kor was singularly good at: the one that said, *Are you really* that *much of an idiot?*

"OK, maybe it wasn't *entirely* out of duty," I grumbled. "But see, that's exactly the thing I'm trying to warn you about, Rachel. Kor may not be allowed to seek for power, because...reasons—"

I was *not* about to tell her that Kor was the Tolsyon heir and what that entailed.

"—but he is most definitely *attracted* to it."

Rachel only gave a feral smile. "Excellent."

"Aaagh," I cried. "Why can't you see that's a bad thing? You're the *Heir of Ice.*"

She shook her head at me. "Duh. That's one of my best advantages right now."

"Which means," I said through gritted teeth. "You should be on your guard *against* charming, manipulative guys like Kor who might be interested in you only because of that fact."

"Oh, I don't think it's *just* because of that."

"OK, you know what? Fine," I said, throwing up my free hand. "Fine. I delivered my warning. Now I'm washing my hands of this. Go let him break your heart if that's what you want."

She smirked. "I'm hurt. You really think I can't take care of myself when it comes to boys?"

Despite my declaration, I couldn't help one last warning. "Trust me, Kor is not like any boy you have ever dated before."

And her list was *long*.

She smiled slowly. "That's what I'm counting on."

"I'm washing my hands of this," I repeated, shaking my head as I made to leave.

Then I stopped and sighed as I remembered my original reason for coming to talk to her, and I turned.

"You realize that, with me gone, you're the Royal in charge, right?"

"What?" Rachel said, head jerking up and eyes widening for the first time.

"Yup. You're in charge of the moongates, making sure everyone has what they need, talking to the Tree—"

"To the...Tree?" she said hesitantly. "Are you...sure?"

I softened. Perhaps I hadn't done as good of a job at mentoring my Heir as I should have this past month. As in, mentoring her at all.

No matter how weird the thought was, with her being my older sister, and, well...Rachel.

"Rachel, the Tree chose you. And Trees don't make mistakes. That means She believes in you *and* wants you to come visit Her. She may not always talk to you or appear in front of you if you do, but I've found that I've learned something every time, anyway."

"But...do I have to go *every* day?" she said fretfully.

I tried not to stare. I didn't think I'd ever seen my normally spunky, confident sister this nervous before. Except, of course...when she was chosen.

Why hadn't I thought more about that moment?

"Ask Her how often you should come," I said gently. "It could be different for you. But whatever She says, it would be best to do it. For all our sakes."

When Rachel still hesitated, I dropped my bag at her doorstep and went over to put a gentle hand on her shoulder and give it a squeeze. "I'm sorry I didn't do a better job of getting you used to the Tree. That was my bad. But She's good. Trust me. She's *good*. And She loves you."

Rachel snorted mildly at that.

"Really," I said, somewhat surprised by her denial. "Couldn't you feel that, before?"

She didn't meet my eyes. "I don't know *what* I felt."

Something the old King's leftwing, Eskala, once told me came back to me. *There is no way to convince someone that they are worthy of love. They must first decide that for themselves.*

Had I felt that love from the Tree and understood it for what it was because I was *ready* for it?

But then why...would Rachel not be?

"Maybe visiting Her more will help you understand," I said slowly. "But even if not...it's important, Rachel. I know you can do this. We're counting on you to."

"Alright," she said heavily, shoulders sagging. "I'll...go see what She has to say, if anything...tomorrow."

"Thank you," I said simply, giving her shoulder another squeeze. "Love you, Rachel."

"Love you too," she said, meeting my eyes with a wan smile.

As I picked up my bag and walked out of the room, Rachel called after me with some of her normal cheek, "Tell Kor hi for me!"

"I'm staying *out* of this," I called back to her.

Way, way out.

GOODBYES WITH THE REST of my family were short and simple. Most of them had congregated to see me off by the Ythra moongate, where Ben stood waiting, trying hard not to look uncomfortable and maybe succeeding with about half of them.

He immediately reached for my bag once I came up to him.

"You know, I *can* carry this much myself," I said with a grin.

"Of course you can," Ben agreed with an answering smile—as he still took the bag from my hand. "But if I carry it, it's not in the way."

From the way his eyes momentarily glowed, I understood what he meant by that.

"Well," I said solemnly, "I suppose I can't argue with that logic."

Then before I could get too stirred up myself, I hurriedly turned my focus to saying goodbye to everyone else.

Hugs and brief "love yous" and "see you laters" all around. It felt like they were dropping me off at the airport, if with a bit more worry in the adults' eyes than normal. Fortunately, the littles seemed oblivious. Mom had to call the twins over to give me a hug, since they were busy chasing each other around the Inner Rim.

That complete loop had been an Icesend in working out their boyish energy, especially since we didn't have a yard or park anymore.

When Mom asked about Rachel, I assured her we'd already said our goodbye. Then I turned briskly to Ben and said, "Ready?"

"Ready."

Without further ado, I walked through the ice—which was, at long last, back to being a curtain. Amazing how quickly one's life could be turned upside down...and then righted again, just like that.

Except...not quite. There was one wrong that could never be righted.

This time as I entered Crownhold, the remarkable man I thought of as "the King," King Kavarian, would not be there to greet me. Though my devastation was nothing compared to Ben's, I'd come to love him in my own way, and I felt that ache for a moment as I stood in the round, roughly carved chamber, remembering.

I looked at the spot where he had stood, watching over Ben and me as we recovered from the creation of the gate behind me and the renewal of the First Covenant.

Ben put his hand on my shoulder.

"I'm sorry," he said quietly. "Again."

"What are you talking about?" I said, wiping my eyes hastily. "He was *your* father."

"But I know you loved him, too. I didn't even let you come to his burning. He...." Ben swallowed and continued hoarsely. "He would have wanted you there."

"I'm sure he understands why I wasn't," I said quietly, putting my hand over his. "And I'm sure he's happy that I'm here now, with you."

Strange. A month and a half ago, if you had asked me if I believed in an afterlife, I would have said I wasn't sure. But now....

The thought that the King no longer existed, in some form...was impossible. In fact, I almost *could* feel him, right there, in that moment. And another, less familiar presence besides....

I remembered the first time I had met the King in person. How, while he was hugging me, he said he could feel Ben's mother there. And in that moment, I'd felt a touch on my shoulder and a kiss on the back of my head, and an overwhelming love that had filled me to the brim.

That's what I felt now. Love.

It was as crushing as one of the King's bear hugs and as tender as a mother's touch. It was almost too much to contain.

Ben inhaled sharply, and his grip on my shoulder tightened, so I knew he felt something too. But neither of us said anything, lest words disturbed the sacredness of that moment. I didn't even dare look to the right or left, because I was almost certain that if I did, I would see *something* and catch a glimpse that would make them have to leave.

So, we both just stood there, silent and still, as the seconds slipped away....

And so...all too soon...did the feeling.

"Well," I finally whispered, throat tight with tears.

Ben wordlessly handed me a handkerchief. From the streaks I saw on his own cheeks when I glanced at him, I was surprised he didn't need one himself.

"Thanks," I said with a tight chuckle. "It seems to be our day for these, isn't it?"

"Yes," he rasped.

I blew my nose as quickly and tidily as I could and then stuffed the handkerchief in a pocket. Meanwhile, Ben didn't move, not even to wipe his tears.

"You...OK?" I asked tentatively, putting my hand in his.

He looked down at me with a weak smile. "No. Not in the least. But...."

His voice took on a tone of numb surprise as he looked back at the spot where his father had stood. "I think I will be, someday. The pain won't ever leave, but...."

"You'll grow strong enough to bear it," I whispered.

He looked back at me in surprise.

I shrugged sheepishly. "I know it's not even close to being the same thing. But that's how I felt, before you came back."

His eyes tightened. "Sarah...."

"Don't say it," I said, giving his hand a squeeze. "You've already apologized more than enough. Besides, that's all gone for me now. Iceheart, good as new. I told you it wasn't nearly the same thing."

If only I could give him back his father so easily.

"I just meant to say that...I think I understand what you mean."

He sighed. His grip on my hand tightened, and we looked at that spot for a few more moments.

"Well," Ben said eventually with a shaky chuckle. "This wasn't at all how I was intending to spend our few moments alone."

I laughed. "I'm OK with what we got instead. There'll be time for...other things later."

"I was hoping you'd say that."

He clenched my hand again and looked down at me with a smile. "Well, you ready to face *my* wings now?"

I chuckled. "Somehow, I don't think this part is going to be as bad for me as facing my family was for you."

Ben winced. "You might be surprised. I may...have left them in something of a lurch."

"What?" I asked, startled.

"After I woke up from the dream, I surged away without giving them any explanation," Ben said ruefully. "They both were calling me, a *lot*, until I called Yv back while I was waiting for you to pack. So, they know we're alright now. But just fair warning...."

I sighed. "Yvera might be in a mood. I see."

"Kor...might be too," Ben said, not meeting my eyes.

Huh. That was new. Normally, Yvera was the one to lose her temper at Ben's endangerment of his own life.

"Alright, then," I said, taking his hand. "Let's go smooth some *more* feathers."

I unfurled a bit of my power from where it emerged in the darkness deep within me and used it to tie Ben and me together.

"Lashed?" he asked.

I gathered he could feel *something* of what I did, but he always checked to make sure we were good to go, and for good reason. Interstellar travel wasn't something to take chances with.

"Yup," I said with a stoic face. "Take us away."

I had not missed *this* part. Surging in Ben's way normally felt like becoming pulverized into a cannonball of light and shot through the void of space before being spat out on the other side. Often forcefully enough to send us stumbling or even falling into each other.

Ben just grinned. "This is about to be a lot more comfortable than before. Trust me."

Before I could ask why, or even do anything more than blink, our surroundings just...swapped. No crushing force, no mind-boggling speed, no tripping on our way out. We simply were standing in one place in one moment...and then standing in another in the next.

I gaped as I stared around at the simple sitting room I had only seen once before, and then it had been full of people and goings on.

"What? But—how—"

Then I was being crushed in a tight hug by a familiar dark-blue-haired, dark-skinned, sapphire-clothed drakón.

"Hi...Kor," I said, a bit breathlessly.

Without saying anything in reply, Kor abruptly released me and rounded on Ben, sapphire eyes flashing. "Don't you *ever* scare me like that again."

I blinked. It was just as Ben had hinted: in a strange reversal of typical roles, Yvera was standing back, looking relatively calm (that glare was her normal expression—I would have been worried if she hadn't been doing that much), and Kor was the one furious with Ben.

"Sorry," Ben said, but to my surprise, he didn't look as sorry as I might have expected. He also clenched my hand, which he had never relinquished, not even during the hug. "Like I told Yv, the Tree wasn't specific on timing."

"About what?" I asked in surprise.

"That you would be in danger if I didn't let you back in." Ben was a terrible liar, so the honesty in his voice and expression meant something, but there was also something telling about the way he wouldn't meet my eyes.

Before I could press for details, Kor said hotly, "And yet, even though you couldn't spend the few seconds it would have taken to explain that, you spent the same amount to shut the door in our faces so we couldn't follow."

"Door?" I asked in confusion.

"The door at the back of the shrine," Kor snapped in answer, eyes still not leaving Ben. "Only you and Ben can open it, thus only you and Ben can access the crowngate beyond it. Not that either of you even *needs* to open the door to get to it, since you both can surge straight to it now that it's active again."

Oh. Now I realized *why* Kor and Yvera had to resort to just calling Ben until he answered. When they had tried to follow him...they couldn't even get past the Shrine of the Covenants.

Then something else about what Kor had said struck me.

"*Crowngate?*"

He sighed, but the worst of his temper seemed to die. He folded his arms and smirked tiredly at me. "Well, yes. You took your time picking a name for it, so I picked one for you. Do you disagree with it?"

"No," I grumbled. It was a good name, I had to admit. It was a gate defined more by Ben's and my shared custody of it than anything else.

Still, it grated that, once again, Kor was right on.

"What was I supposed to do, Kor?" Ben said. "Leave the door open for just *anyone* to come by and go through the gate?"

Kor clenched his jaw. "What you *should have done* is take us with you."

"And what if those few seconds made the difference—"

"And what if our *help* made the difference in saving Sarah's life?" Kor interrupted. "And those of her family? Flame, Ben. *Think.* A danger to her would have been a danger to all of them, and we can't afford to lose a single one of them. They are the future of the Moontouched clan. They are *our* future."

Finally, I understood with a chill why Kor was the furious one this time. Yvera cared about only one thing: Ben. Yvera had found out at least minutes ago that Ben was not just safe but that there had never been a danger to him; ergo, Yvera was now relatively calm. But Kor, who always saw the big picture, had understood more deeply than anyone what truly was at stake.

"I...." Ben began, but he was deflating. Besides, his eyes darted to mine. He could hardly say in front of me that I was more important than my family. I knew that *he* knew that I wasn't...in his head.

"I...am sorry," he said with a sigh, sounding much more sincere this time. "That was yet another of my mistakes, I see that now."

"Good," Kor huffed.

"Well," I said dryly. "Does anyone *else* want to have a go at Ben tonight? Yv, how about you?"

"Nah, I'm good for now," Yvera said, with a smirk from where she was leaning her over-six-foot, lean and muscled body against the far wall. "I'll just hit him extra hard next practice session."

Ben groaned.

I said, "Great, now that's settled, Ben's not allowed to apologize for *anything else* tonight. Understood?"

A slow smirk overtook Kor's lips. "Are you so sure you want to give him a pass as wide as that?"

"He's earned it," I said firmly.

"Has he now?" Kor said dryly, smile vanishing.

"Speaking of things I'm doing to redeem myself," Ben said hastily, "I have a list of supplies for Sarah's family that I need you to pass along, Kor. I promised I'd get them delivered by dawn."

Kor rolled his eyes as he took out his tablet. "Of course you did. Here, give it to me, and you can get Sarah settled in one of the guest rooms for tonight, at least."

"At least?" I asked in puzzlement as Ben brought out his own tablet and pulled up the list he'd transcribed.

Kor smirked at me as Ben touched their tablets together, and the same gold-runed list appeared on the surface of Kor's tablet. "What, you think we'd let someone of *your* stature and independence be a lowly guest in the King's Wing for longer than that? What kind of message would that send?"

"One I don't really care about?" I grumbled.

"It's a good thing you have me to think of such things, then," Kor said with a long-suffering sigh. "And it's a very good thing, given Ben's short notice in bringing you here, that your wing only requires a few finishing touches. Give me a day or two to hurry the work crew along and round up a sufficient staff and guard, and you should be able to move right in."

"My *wing*?" I choked.

"But of course," Kor said innocently as he scanned the list on his tablet. "By the Tree's decree, all the rulers of the clans require a wing in Crownhold where they can stay while here and still hold independent dominion. Even the Moontouched had one before they disbanded, and it's been left symbolically empty and carefully maintained ever since."

"Primarily by the Starkissed," Ben said dryly. "With a good chunk of funding from the Crown. But the Starkissed couldn't abide simply handing it over to you as it was, even though it was in a perfectly serviceable state. No, as soon as word got out about your actual title, they had to *renovate*."

"Renovate," I repeated, and glared at Kor. I knew who would have been the real mastermind behind this "Starkissed" initiative.

"Well, obviously," Kor said, looking up from his tablet at me with a smirk. "You're not a Lady, Sarah. You don't just need independent quarters. You need quarters to reflect your equality, not vassalhood, to the Golden King."

"And you agreed to this?" I asked Ben incredulously.

I knew the mistake I had made as soon as pain lanced across Ben's face. Even Kor's smirk faded.

"Avva gave his seal to the funding request," Ben said quietly. "It was one of his last acts before he went to the Temple of Flame."

Ah, and of course Ben wouldn't have rescinded it. I supposed even I couldn't argue with it now, either.

But dang it, Avva, I thought at him.

I was startled to feel the faintest trace of warm amusement for a moment, as brief as a flicker of flame.

"Go on, you two," Kor said with a shake of his head at our silence. He waved his hand as he wandered in the direction behind us. When I turned, I saw the daygate (essentially, a smaller, shorter-range version of a sungate) we must have come through set into the wall.

"I've got work to do, clearly," he finished dismissively, right before strolling through as casually as if he were going through a doorway.

Figures the King of Flame would have a daygate—which were supposed to be so costly that they were rare outside of Crownhold—right in his living room.

Although, come to think of it, this room was probably more like a reception area. It had a welcoming but neutral tone to its scarce décor and furnishings, the latter of which were primarily a few benches and couches along the walls.

"Isn't that kind of...risky?" I asked, eyeing the daygate. "Having that thing right in your quarters?"

"It would be," Ben said with a thin smile. "Except I have to permit people through that one. Like opening a door for them. Even Kor and Yvera have to 'knock' every time."

"It gets annoying, trust me," Yvera said with a grimace.

And she was the one normally obsessive about Ben's safety. As part of her job and for...personal reasons. But seeing as she was one of the biggest reasons Ben was still alive right now, I had long since forgiven her for those.

She continued, "Especially if he's sleeping. Then we just have to go the long way."

She gestured at the normal door that was right next to the daygate.

"So long," Ben said, rolling his eyes. "There's only another daygate, what, an eld from here?"

"Yes," Yvera said with a grimace. "But at night, when you're *supposed* to be sleeping, that one's no help."

"Wait," I said as understanding dawned. "That one...is still going. Even though it's night here."

"It's unique, that's for sure," Ben said with a shrug. "We don't know exactly why. Kor's theory is that it's because of its centuries-long proximity to the Monarchs. As if so much of our power has sunk into it by now that it can remain lit even at night, and even take us to an inactive gate."

"Which is what Kor must have done," I mused.

"Or not," Ben said with another shrug. "He could have gone to Yonvey to submit the requisition order for all we know. I *did* say I wanted the supplies by dawn, so he might have done the clerks the courtesy of going somewhere where it's day right now."

"Oh," I said, suddenly feeling better. Perhaps our order wouldn't be as much of a burden as I thought it would be for Ben's people to fulfill.

"Speaking of day, night, and when you should be sleeping, Ben," Yvera said pointedly. "Right now *is* night, deken after sunset, and you *should* be in bed, especially after the day we've had—even before all this ashdust."

"What kind of day?" I asked...and grew suspicious at Ben's annoyed and slightly alarmed look at Yvera.

"We hunted down a rock wyrm," Yvera said, blithely ignoring his glare.

My iceheart chilled further. "*What?*"

I'd only gathered bits and pieces of what those monsters were and how dangerous, but since I'd run through one of their miles-long tunnels myself and had seen how grim just the mention of them made Ben, I had some ideas.

"A young, small one," Ben said hastily. "Barely big enough to carve a tunnel tall enough for me to not have to stoop. And we caught up to it eld away from the hold."

Even so, a wyrm that could bore a tunnel of *Ben's* height, through solid rock....

"And you did that *before* coming to me and going through all of that?" I demanded. "Ben, how are you even standing right now?"

Oh, you don't even know the half of it, Yvera said darkly. To my shock, she said it silently, just to me.

She'd never been…buddy-buddy with me. For obvious reasons. In fact, until just recently, I was convinced that the only kind of relationship she would ever want to have with me was the assassin-victim, executioner-criminal kind.

"I'm *fine*," Ben said, but even if I hadn't seen the weariness that was now sinking over him, Yvera's snort would have betrayed his lie.

"Ben," I snapped. "You have to stop doing this to yourself. Go to bed. Now. I'm sure Yvera knows her way around enough to show me to a room."

Ben shot a glare at Yvera, who just folded her arms and looked back at him coolly. I could see a quick, silent conversation pass between them, the result of which made Ben's shoulders sag.

He sighed. "Alright."

Ignoring our audience, Ben ducked down to give me a slow and sweet kiss. One that had part of me regretting sending him away—as perhaps was his intent. But that knowledge of his unsubtle ploy and my consciousness of his exhaustion made me hold firm, so that when he pulled away, all he saw was my small smirk.

"Nice try, your majesty, but *goodnight*."

The mocking use of a royal style had a bit less punch to it, seeing as dramá had no such thing. What I'd said was essentially meaningless to him.

He sighed heavily, but this time in defeat. "I suppose I'll see you…tomorrow, at around noon?"

"Around," I said with a grimace. "Maybe later, maybe sooner. Don't know how far off Crownhold is from my hold."

"A couple deken ahead, I think."

I shrugged. "Then we'll see when I'm able to get moving again."

Although I had a feeling doing so would be much easier than it had been before. And, in fact, sleeping in would be out of the question. The moment I woke and realized where I was…and who was waiting for me….

I could almost feel the glow of that moment now. It made me ache to fall asleep at a *normal* time so we could have that reunion all the sooner.

Ben nodded. "I won't give the blood archivists a specific time, then. They'll fuss about that, but they can just deal."

"Oh, we're doing her blood registration *tomorrow*, are we?" Yvera asked, raising a violet eyebrow. The one with a scar.

I'd wondered about that one. I'd seen some other scars on drakón, too, so their self-healing wasn't infallible. It made me wonder what sort of wounds they could not completely heal—and what creature or person had gotten close enough to *Yvera*, the deadliest person I knew next to Ben.

"Might as well not put it off," Ben said, but his face began pinking under Yvera's skeptical look, making me suddenly wonder if there was more to this blood registration thing than Ben was letting on.

"Ben," I began slowly.

"Safe sleep, warm dreams!" Ben said hastily, backing away and waving his hand in farewell before pushing open a door that revealed a short hallway and letting it swing shut behind him.

After I heard yet another door close, I looked at Yvera. If she seemed to be in a communicative mood, I might as well ask. "What the heck was that about?"

"Ben being Ben," Yvera said, rolling her eyes as she pushed off from the wall. "But thank the Flame for that."

"What do you mean by that?" I asked, blinking.

"Ask Kor," Yvera said dryly. "I promised Ben not to tell in exchange for him getting his torched ass to bed. Come on. Let's find you a room."

Without slowing her long, graceful stride one bit for me, she walked across the room and pushed open the door next to the daygate. As she did so, the clear gem on it flashed violet for one second before fading again. I assumed that indicated some kind of authorization. Which I probably did not have.

I hastily followed Yvera before I was left behind and stuck spending the night in Ben's reception area. I could see Yvera doing just that sort of thing to me.

WE WALKED DOWN A wide hall with a few other doors along the side and then entered a central chamber that was much larger and more elaborate than the simple quarters we had left. It reminded me of the central court of the King's Wing in Olsdak, if less exotic and overdone: an enormous, raised stone firepit in the center the size of an ornamental fountain, still crackling away; cream and brown tile, polished marble columns, smooth and curvaceous arches, banners and tapestries; and, of course, gold. Everywhere. Gold sconces, gold gilding and filigree, gold embroidery on the seat cushions of the benches along the walls, gold statues in the alcoves.

Even at this hour, the court saw activity, with people in familiar gold uniforms coming and going across the court and through the various corridors that branched off like spokes on a wheel. Yvera must have been a familiar sight, but everyone who looked my way stopped almost in mid-stride and stared.

I wished I could say it was just because of the white hair, but that was only the dead giveaway as to who I must be, and anyone who had the right to be in here could put two and two together immediately.

I was fortunately distracted from such unwelcome attention by the emergence of a familiar small, slight figure with brown hair in a wispy bun and tired blue eyes, dressed in a gold uniform with an orange border at the collar.

"Eskala!" I said in delight, striding to meet her halfway.

"Hello, dear," she said in her warm, aunt-like fashion, taking both of my hands in hers. "I cannot tell you how good it is to see you."

The meaningful look in her eyes told me she truly couldn't. Not now, in public.

"Yvera, thank you for your help, dear, but I can show her to a room," Eskala said kindly as she put an arm around me. "I am certain you are nearly as tired as Koriben is by now."

"Torch right," Yvera said with a yawn and a careless wave to me as she turned away.

Still, even that much of a farewell came as a surprise to me.

"Did you bring anything with you, Sarah dear?" Eskala asked, looking around.

"Oh, dang it. Yv, Ben still has my stuff."

"Of course he does, the idiot," Yvera sighed. "I'll go—"

"That won't be necessary, Rightwing Yvera," Eskala said with a pointed look, perhaps to remind her of where they were—and of how the rightwing of the King should be speaking of him, at least in public.

She waved over one of the uniformed people who had followed her but had kept a respectful distance for our greeting. "Korren, would you please go ask the King for the Queen of Ice's belongings? Quickly?"

She added in a dry whisper, "*Before* we have to wake him up?"

"Right away, leftwing," Korren said with a smile before hurrying in the direction we had come from.

"Leftwing?" I whispered curiously.

"It seems I got my wish," Eskala said in a low voice. She waved to Yvera as the young woman shrugged and walked away. "Korinth made me *his* leftwing."

The heaviness in her eyes made it clear that was a wish she would have much preferred hadn't been granted. At least...not so soon.

I sighed as she led me arm in arm in a different direction. "Eskala...I don't know what the proper thing in Drona is to say to someone who has lost someone close to them, so hopefully the English will be good enough: I am so sorry for your loss."

"Thank you, dear," Eskala said with another thin smile. "I will not say it has been easy to lose Kavarian. He was my dearest friend. But...I was perhaps the best prepared of anyone for his passing."

I looked at her as understanding dawned.

"You knew," I whispered. "What he had to do...what he gave up for Ben."

In order to have a son and give the Sunfilled clan a long-awaited Heir, the old King and Queen had agreed with the Tree to give part of their flame-hearts—their very life force—to Ben. The resulting shortening of their lives was the reason Ben's mother had died six years ago...and why Ben's father *had* been dying, until I had brought him a token of peace from the Tree of Ice that restored him. The fact that he still died filled me with the greatest sense of failure I had ever felt, and I couldn't imagine what Ben must still be enduring.

Eskala blinked at me, then a sharp understanding came to her own eyes. "Koriben told you?"

I swallowed. "Just before he...pushed me away. In explanation."

"Ah, I see," she said, her eyes veiled.

We entered a short corridor with a few doors, and Eskala gestured with a stronger attempt at a smile. "Well, my dear, you have your choice tonight, since we have no distinguished guests at the moment that don't have their own quarters already in Crownhold."

"Speaking of quarters," I said dryly as I went up to one at random and touched the doorgem. It took a spark of power from me and lit with a brilliant white light. This time, the light remained, marking the room as mine and giving only me access. "What's this I hear about me needing my own? Much less an entire *renovated* wing?"

I touched the gold panel, felt the spark of recognition that authorized me to open it, pushed the handle-free door open, and politely held it open for Eskala. I had a feeling that she had things to discuss with me.

She smiled gratefully and followed me inside.

"Oh, don't be upset with Korinth. He has good justifications for what he's done to arrange quarters befitting your station. If he has had a bit of pleasure in some of the details, well—he's had scarce few pleasures over this past month."

Figures she would know just what to say to make me unable to protest the excess.

Although I couldn't see why this room wasn't excessive enough. Golden drapes, cream and brown furs, plush rugs, light wood furnishings—and this was just a sitting room. Through an open door, I caught a glimpse of an equally opulent bedroom, and through another, a personal bathroom—which, I was coming to learn from the dramá communal style of living, was a true luxury.

Eskala sighed as she sat on one of the couches arranged around the firepit in the center. "I know what you are thinking, Sarah dear, but you truly can't stay here. Too many factions will already try to write you off as no more than Koriben's consort at best or a weak-minded puppet of the Golden Crown at worst. Now that you have returned and will be staying for a time, you must assert your independence as publicly and swiftly as may be—for the good of your clan and Realm now and the precedent you set for future generations."

"I thought you *wanted* me to marry Ben," I said with a sigh of my own as I sat down on the couch perpendicular to hers.

"I do," Eskala said, lips twitching. "As does anyone else who has your and Ben's best interests and the good of the Realms at heart. But that is just yet another reason to stress your equality and independence."

She paused thoughtfully as she crossed her legs. "Or perhaps *interdependence* is a better word in this case, since if there is one lesson Koriben's...stubbornness has taught us forcefully over this past month, it is how closely the survival of both our peoples still depends on each other, just as much as ever."

I swallowed. "My Tree told me to go with Ben. To aid him. But She didn't say with what, and Ben didn't say either. Other than to warn me there was a new fever."

"Yes, that is one of our most worrisome troubles right now, particularly since this new, magic-resistant disease has hit Ykran the hardest."

I struggled for a moment to remember, then inhaled. "That's the Peacegrowth Realm, isn't it?"

The Peacegrowth clan was the source of the dramá's most powerful healers.

"Indeed," Eskala said, blue eyes deep with meaning. She rested her arm on the armrest and her chin in her hand. "Interesting, isn't it?"

I swallowed. "You don't think the fever is natural, do you?"

"No, I do not. The Devourer has many weapons at its disposal, and despite the devastation we dealt to its legions on the Battle of the Solstice, it no doubt reserved some of its most cunning servants and powerful magic workers for this very eventuality. Solim being among them."

Kor's psychopathic, power-hungry older brother who plotted to murder Ben six years ago in revenge for Ben's picking Kor as his leftwing instead of him. Then, when Kor had turned his brother in, Solim escaped and went to the Devourer, who changed him into the worst sort of monster there was: a lish. The lish that was responsible for Svyer's current catatonic state and, quite possibly, the destruction of my home and deaths of unknown numbers of my neighbors. And that didn't even include his many attempts to kill Ben, Kor, me, or all of us at once.

"So it begins," I said quietly. "The battle after the battle."

Eskala smiled thinly. "As good a way to put it as any."

She allowed silence to fall for a moment as her gaze became distant. Then she shook herself and refocused on me. "But I didn't come to lay all our burdens on your shoulders. Believe it or not, I truly *did* come to greet you and sincerely offer my gratitude that you agreed to come. I do not know what finally brought Koriben to his senses this evening, but it could not have been a moment too soon."

"Ben said he had a dream of the Tree of Flame," I said carefully. I didn't know how much I should reveal of his own affairs to even Eskala, but I figured at least that much was safe, since it was what he had told his own wings—and was practically all *I* knew.

"So Korinth said. I am not asking for details since that is not my place...but it must have been a dream of some significance to do even partially what no one and nothing else had accomplished for a month, let alone six years."

"What do you mean?" I asked, troubled.

Eskala sighed. "Koriben's needless guilt for what he sees as his role in his parents' passing has long had undue influence over him, but it was a guilt Kavarian could never shake from him—the latest result of which you just suffered from."

"That's what you meant," I murmured. "About how Ben thought himself unworthy of love."

"Yes," Eskala said with another sigh. "I wish I could be confident that his readmittance of you signals he has at last begun to allow others to love him again, but his self-loathing is so entrenched.... I...do not want to give you false hope, Sarah."

I took a deep breath. Perhaps she, of all people, could tell me if Ben had gone too far. "He swore a blood oath, Eskala."

She started, looking back at me with wide eyes. She leaned forward intently. "What?"

"He did it before I could stop him. He swore to never bar the people of Ice ever again...and to always respect my choice to be at his side."

The old King's leftwing leaned back, looking nearly as stunned as she had been when I had helped Ben both surge with someone else and straight to me for the first time.

"Flame Above and Below," Eskala said faintly, touching her forehead. "A *blood oath*? And you are certain that was the wording?"

I thought carefully, and then nodded. "Yes."

"What did the Tree *say* to him?" Eskala murmured to herself, her gaze distant.

"Should Ben have done that?" I asked uneasily.

She turned her attention back to me with some difficulty. "I truly do not know. But that he was even willing to says something quite significant about his sudden change of heart and mind. It gives me hope that this won't pass like an early winter thaw. Perhaps...spring is truly here to stay."

I hesitated, wondering if sharing this was going too far. But I didn't know who else I could better rely on to know and care for Ben in the same way as her, and thus give me the context I needed. She had once said that she thought of Ben as a son, and my gut believed her.

"He...mourned, Eskala. When he first came to me. He held me and let himself mourn. Then later, he said that he thought he might one day be able to bear the pain."

I drew the line there. I didn't think I would ever tell anyone what Ben and I had felt standing in that chamber together.

Eskala shook her head in quiet wonder. "Perhaps it *is* spring. And not a moment too soon."

Chapter Six

MORNING

Koriben

I THOUGHT FOR CERTAIN that I would hardly be able to sleep a wink, but my body had other plans. I was dead to the world from nearly the moment my head hit my pillow to when I heard a familiar voice repeatedly call me by name and title.

Both of which still sounded horribly wrong when said together like that.

"King Koriben? King Koriben!"

"What?" I asked hoarsely, blinking through the crust over my eyes to see my chief secretary, Olsan, a stiff old Strongshield amón who had served my father before me and probably deserved a few medals for how he had kept me from single-handedly smashing the Realms to smithereens from sheer ineptitude this past month.

A much younger, Brightflare drakón staffer in gold uniform stood beside him nervously, not directly meeting my eyes—and clearly trying not to stare at the disaster that was my bedroom, either. Which didn't leave him many places to rest his gaze, so he was staring fixedly at a corner of the room.

"The order you requested on behalf of the Moontouched clan is ready, my King," Olsan said stiffly, with a firm look. "But *this* good man requires your aid in opening the shrine door in order to deliver it by dawn, as you stipulated."

I jerked awake at that, startled at the deken. I could feel our sun, Kaldrir, just below the horizon. How had I managed to sleep until nearly *dawn*?

"Yes, yes, of course," I gasped, blinking at the staffer. "Sorry, so sorry, don't know what got into me."

As I scrambled out of bed to put a maroon shirt and a pair of boots on, I couldn't help but notice the equal parts puzzlement and relief that mingled on the staffer's face, and it took me a few moments to understand why. When I did, I inwardly groaned.

I had *so* much to make up for. To everyone.

"Sorry, Olsan. I know that I'll probably be late for that meeting with Minister—"

"Not to worry, my King," Olsan said emotionlessly. "I have cleared your schedule for the day and made your excuses."

I blinked at him as I pulled my second boot on. "Wait, *what*? The entire day?"

"In order to properly greet and settle in the Queen of Ice, of course."

"But she probably won't even be awake until after noon," I said in bafflement.

Shut up, my smarter side said sharply. I should *not* be arguing with the miracle of being able to miss my morning slate of meetings, for any reason. Particularly the first one that had been on the docket with Treasury Minister Thirra Brightflare.

"Leftwing Korinth's orders," Olsan said, and then I knew that was that. Even though Olsan assisted *me*, we both knew the one he truly answered to was Kor.

He continued, "Leftwing Korinth also asked me to inform you that he has made the necessary arrangements for the Queen's blood registration this afternoon. The blood archivists will be prepared and expecting you for whenever the Queen is ready."

Well, Kor had been busy. I supposed I owed him, again, for saving me the trouble of making the request myself. He'd probably delivered it in a much better fashion than I would have, too, hopefully making them happier than they otherwise would have been with the vague timeframe.

But...wait a dek. How had Kor known I wanted to do the blood registration today? And *when*?

I'd have to ponder that along the way, because dawn was coming. I didn't expect Jake and certainly not Rachel to be waiting at the gate for the delivery right at dawn, particularly because I was fairly sure Crownhold was a few deken ahead in daylight than Sarah's hold, but it was the principle of the thing. I wasn't about to let my people's efforts to keep *my* promise overnight go to waste.

"When you return, I recommend you make use of your free morning to make yourself a bit more...presentable," Olsan said, eyeing my rumpled appearance. "Leftwing Korinth also recommends you cook yourself breakfast, so I have canceled your morning delivery."

Which forced me to cook something, since I had long ago eaten anything preprepared either in my kitchen or in my ether storage. As Kor had no doubt guessed.

"If you need me," Olsan concluded as he turned to leave, "I shall be in my office. Enjoy your morning, my King."

The implication of *while it lasts* hung in the air as Olsan left, leaving me with the staffer, who, judging from his renewed stiffness, was nervous again.

I sighed, managed to smile at him, and gestured for him to lead the way. "Come on. Let's get this order delivered."

I COULDN'T REMEMBER THE last time I had been able to take my time with my morning preparations for the day. Even before...before, when I'd traveled across the Realms with Sarah to find and unlock her moongates, or even before when I had been searching for *her*, I had rarely had that kind of luxury.

Or rather, I had rarely felt like I could afford or deserve it. Even before Sarah arrived, I had always felt the flame of the timekeeper candle burning ever lower, with Avva's life slipping away with every second. Unable to face the guilt, and even deeper, the terror of what would happen when that candle burned out, I had pushed myself and my wings hard over that year of searching. If we weren't actively looking for the Earthren that the Tree had promised to send, then we were tackling some dangerous task that only the Heir and his wings could be trusted with. We were constantly rushing, fighting, and collapsing in an endless exhaustive cycle.

I knew at the time how cruel I was being to my wings, let alone how dangerously close I was to breaking under the strain. Everyone who cared about me warned me of the consequences of what I was doing, no one more piercingly yet lovingly than Avva. And yet I couldn't bear the thought of standing still. Not just at the thought of perhaps those few seconds of rest making the difference that cost Avva's life. I saw now that I simply couldn't bear to face the silence...and what it might bring.

Even after Avva's death, I didn't stop. If anything, I dug deeper into that worst part of myself, until it became all I was: the never-ending work, the demands and expectations of my people, the duty I was born to. I had thought it was all I had left to cling to. After all, it was the only reason my flameheart was still pulsing after Avva's had stopped.

Wasn't it?

And yet, living only for duty had gradually crushed the life out of me and made me into something hard, dark, and bitter. Something that my people had good reason to fear.

By giving everything that was left of me to serve and protect them, I had failed them.

It was a lesson Avva had tried to hammer into my thick skull many times, one that I *thought* I had learned soon after I became Heir and had to start learning the balance between the demands of others and my own needs. But the start of Avva's fading had thrown me off balance again, and worse than ever. I then began my slow spiral downward that had ended with the inevitable crash and burn, the fires of which had scorched everyone around me.

And none more horribly than Sarah.

That she could somehow forgive me made it even more necessary to make certain that *never* happened again. I had begun yesterday with making the blood oaths to protect her from the return of that aspect of my nature in the most thorough way possible.

As I stood numbly in my water-room after returning from the crown-gate, I realized I had the chance to take the next step now.

So, I did something that I hadn't allowed myself to do in I couldn't even remember how long: after I showered to get clean first, I took a bath. A *long, hot* bath, so hot the temperature would probably have scalded an amá, let alone a child of Ice like Sarah. So long that I fell asleep again as I lounged back in that steaming hot spring water and jerked awake perhaps dek later.

But Flame, when I finally clambered out, I felt more alive than I had in....

My water-room was so full of steam by then that I had to use an already-damp towel to wipe down the mirror to shave. But, after I applied the oil to the stubble on my cheeks, I simply stood there for a dek, holding the razor in my hand. Hesitating for a reason I couldn't at first name.

When I looked up to meet my own eyes in the mirror, it hit me, and I staggered back from the familiarity I saw there.

My eyes, softened and rested as they were now...looked like Avva's.

Suddenly, my beardless face looked *wrong*.

But...I was in mourning. This was all *for* Avva, after all. This was only what he would have expected of me....

Or...would he?

After feeling him and Avvi so strongly yesterday...I wasn't sure anymore.

My answer came to me as I met those eyes again, and his voice spoke in my mind with piercing clarity and loving gentleness.

Who are you mourning, son?

I reeled back and gasped, but the face in the mirror—still *my face*—stayed in place and smiled softly at me.

Until it blurred a moment later, as if in a wave of fog, and when it returned, I was in the correct spot, staring back at myself with shock.

I knew at once what he had meant. I'd had a year and a month to mourn, to resign myself to what was perhaps always meant to be. And yet, for a year and a month, I had refused to do so, just as I had refused to accept the will of the Tree and even my father. Not primarily for my love for Avva, who, I knew in the depths of my flameheart, had longed to move on.

It had been from fear. From my terror that I wasn't strong enough to bear his loss, too, and all that would come after.

Now it had come. And yet I still stood. As did the Realms...for the moment.

Though I ached, with all my soul, to have his arms crush me into him, I knew now that he wasn't gone. Hadn't ever truly left me.

Who was I mourning?

Avva....

Or the loss of the boy I had once been? And the man I now had to be?

The one I knew now...I *could* one day be?

If I began today.

CHAPTER SEVEN

PINPRICK

SARAH

SURE ENOUGH, THE MOMENT I stirred and realized I wasn't in my own bed, the moment memory came rushing back, adrenaline chased away any possibility of more sleep—even though I could feel my power was still waning, meaning it was before noon.

Sighing as I resigned myself to the inevitable, I dragged myself out of bed and to the bathroom...or water-room, as I think the dramá called them in Drona. My hope that they had truly cold water for the shower was faint.

And quickly dashed. Even the coldest setting felt only lukewarm on my cool skin. I almost got more refreshment from getting wet and then standing to the side to let the moisture evaporate from my skin.

I missed home already, but I still didn't regret coming here, even for a moment. What I lacked in cold, I gained in anticipation. After all, I could feel the pull beckon me, seeming to get stronger with every passing second.

I'd been careful to not get my hair wet so that the rest of my morning prep would go faster. Still, I fussed a bit more than necessary in front of the mirror, regretting for the first time both the loss of my light helpers and that I didn't own, and therefore couldn't have packed, makeup or anything along those lines more than a hairbrush and hair ties. So, I carefully braided my hair back, wincing at the inferior job I'd done, but deciding it was good enough. After all, Ben's opinion was the only one that *truly* mattered, and he had seen me in pretty much every messed up, frazzled, and exhausted state there was by now.

I thought that was that, but then I heard a knock on my door, and when I opened it, two familiar faces greeted me. Both dark-skinned young women were a little older than me, and their sisterly resemblance was obvious now, even though one was a tall, blue-haired and -eyed drakón and the other was a black-haired and hazel-eyed amón.

"Fenra, Vadya," I greeted in surprise. "Er, hello. Can I help you?"

Vadya, the amón, laughed. "What a funny question, since we're obviously here to help *you*."

I blinked. "For *what*?" I asked, iceheart beginning to pulse in dread.

The last time those two Starkissed sisters, who had been the heads of my staff during my stay in Olsdak, had that mischievous gleam in their eyes, they'd whisked me away to get me ready for the Moonfair, and I was pretty sure they had either cast some kind of spell on or drugged me to put me into a compliant, blissed daze the entire time.

"For your blood registration!" Fenra said with a wink, pushing her way inside before I could protest and wrapping her arm around mine to pull me back to the bathroom. Vadya was only a beat behind her and soon had my other arm, trapping me between them.

"Who told—" I began, then groaned. "*Kor*."

He checked in on me briefly last night. At the time, he hadn't reacted much to my mention that Ben had asked me to do the blood registration thing today. He'd just grunted and became thoughtful, then went away soon after that, muttering about yet more things he had to do.

Apparently arranging for these two to ambush me being among them.

"What else?" Vadya said innocently as Fenra brought forth and then set a high stool in front of the mirror and plopped me down on it. "You didn't expect us to leave you to fend for yourself in prepping for such a momentous occasion, did you?"

"Actually, I kind of—"

"Of course not," Fenra said cheerfully, beginning at once to undo the hard but admittedly disappointing work I'd put into my braid. "The blood registration of the Queen of Ice? The first Moontouched in over eight hundred years? The blood archivists are beside themselves. They might be insulted if you went like this."

"Really?" I said uneasily, my cheeks warming.

"Trust us," Vadya said sympathetically, patting my shoulder. Then she took over my hair so Fenra, the drakón with the ether storage, could start pulling out instruments of beautification and scatter them over my bathroom counter left and right. "This is a big day for everyone, nearly as big as your announcement on the day of the Solstice. This is the day you officially become one of *us*."

I swallowed. That implication of my decision to register hadn't occurred to me until just now. But what else had I expected? Even if nothing inside me changed, even if I never became a drakón, the act meant being numbered among the dramá of the Six Realms, from this day forward.

Vadya continued blithely, "You show respect for that, for the archivists, and for the Golden Crown by letting us help you with this small but significant part of it."

These dramá were certainly learning how to get me to comply—and that was seriously annoying.

Yet I didn't see what I could do about it now. It wasn't as if I hadn't just been feeling my own regrets about how woefully plain I was looking today.

"Fine," I huffed, resigned to my doom...and to my grudging gratitude for their help.

"We'll try to make this as painless as possible, we promise," Fenra said with a wink.

"Don't you dare drug me again," I said, waving my finger at them in the mirror.

"Would you rather suffer?" Vadya asked innocently.

"Well...no...but...."

"Don't worry," Fenra said with a chuckle as she began to help Vadya with my hair again. "We don't have the time for that. Somehow, the King has figured out you're awake, and that means Kor estimates we have about half a deken before he gets impatient enough to come knocking. And we want you to be clear-headed and ready by the time he does."

"Let's see if we can do enough in that time to stun him, now, shall we?" Vadya mock whispered to me.

My iceheart pulsed. Stunning Ben...was a very appealing idea.

Man, these two dramá were good at their jobs, and I couldn't even hate them for it.

"You two wouldn't happen to be related to Kor by any chance, would you?" I asked suspiciously.

"First cousins, actually," Vadya said, eyes wide in an all-too-familiar expression of innocence, despite the hazel of her eyes. "On his mother's side. How could you guess?"

My answer was dry. "Just a hunch."

AROUND HALF AN HOUR later, I was in a snow-white, A-line dress with a thick, silver-embroidered bodice; W-neckline that speared up in the center to end just below my collarbone and crested above my shoulders in a silver mantle; and flutter sleeves that blended with the white cape that draped around me. A stiff necklace made of a silver band with delicate branching leaves and clusters of diamond blossoms curled around my neck and splayed across my collarbones, and matching cuffs were on my ears.

The sisters had teased an incredible amount of volume and curls into my hair, and other than pulling it back enough to display my ears and leaving a few elegant curls to artfully frame my face, they had left that wild white mane to tumble freely where it would. They had stained my lips a dark, dark red and done their smoky magic from last time around my eyes, and, I swear, made my eyelashes—the only hairs on my body that had remained black after my transformation—*grow*. And curl as they did so.

I felt both amazing and self-conscious, certain that this time, my helpers had gone too far. Ben hadn't made this registration seem like it would be *this* big of a deal. If white and silver hadn't been my colors—and the dramá didn't likely have a different traditional color for brides—I would have been convinced that this was all an elaborate setup for a surprise wedding.

Nor did I feel better when Ben knocked on the door, as predicted. I knew it was him from the approaching pull, and besides, I heard him speaking to someone outside the door just before I answered.

Stun him, we did, enough that he stopped in mid-sentence to Kor when the door opened and he caught sight of me, and his jaw simply stayed open, no words coming out. Enough that Vadya and Fenra slipped back into the bathroom to clean up, seemingly without him noticing, somehow combining a beam and a smirk as they traded triumphant looks with each other.

I wasn't much better off.

Ben usually had a simple style: typically, a plain, long-sleeved shirt tucked into a belt and breeches and simple leather boots. The shirt and breeches had almost exclusively been gold-colored in the Time Before but yesterday had been maroon for the first time I had ever seen. The dramá color of mourning, I guessed, since I knew better than to think he had simply felt like a different color that day.

He wasn't dressed in either today.

Today...he was in black.

Gosh, how I loved him in black.

Gold made its appearance, of course, in the edging and flame-shaped embroidery of his high-collared coat, deep V-neck shirt that hinted at his significant musculature, and breeches. Even his boots were dyed black and had gold filigree in flames that wrapped around their entirety.

All of that, combined with his clean, tousled gold hair and the gold scruff on his cheeks....

All I could do was stare.

Long enough that Yvera cleared her throat—and ignored Kor's elbow into her side. After all, she was wearing her usual violet scale-plate armor.

That was enough to snap me out of the worst of the trance, although I wasn't sure what to do with my eyes, or hands, after that.

I cleared my throat. "Well...you look very nice. But you failed to mention in your description of this registration that it was a black-tie event."

"Kor's idea," Ben said tightly, still staring.

And did Kor arrange for a priest, too? I thought.

"Blood registrations aren't typically huge fanfares, true," Kor said smoothly. I noticed he was in his own fancy, silken, sapphire apparel; in his case, though, the coat was knee length and split in the back down the lower half. "But that's because they are for infants, and even children of Monarchs aren't guaranteed to become anyone special. You aren't some nobody infant, Sarah. Besides, this is your first public act since your presentation at the Solstice, and the significance of what you are doing by registering can't be overstated."

At my mutinous expression, Kor sighed. "Remember, this is a rite of power, one requiring your *blood*. It will bind you to our people more literally than you seem to realize. The Blood of the Covenants—it's already in your veins. What is in your blood is what qualifies you to belong among us, indisputably. But when you give us your blood, you become one of ours. It's your token, your oath, and your seal, all in one act."

"You're not exactly making me feel more comfortable about all of this," I snapped.

A bit of alarm entered Ben's eyes, and he shot Kor a glare. He took my hand and clenched it. "Everything is going to be fine, Sarah. Really, there's hardly any ceremony to it at all."

"And it's too late to back out now," Kor said cheerfully. "Not without losing face, both for both the White and Gold Crowns."

"Alright, fine," I said as I stepped out of my room and let the door swing shut behind me. "Let's just get this over with."

Before my iceheart could give out and I lost what little breakfast I'd nibbled in between my helpers' ministrations.

"Lash us, then?" Ben said with a faint smile.

I sighed. "Gather in."

Not strictly necessary, but it helped, especially with my power in limited supply right now.

Without an argument from even Yvera, the three drakón gathered tight around me, and I spun my power around us all.

"Ready," I told Ben when I had us secure.

He nodded. The world shifted, growing dark and cool. But before I could seriously wonder if this was some prelude to yet another new kind of surging, I realized we were simply *there*, and where we were was dark and cool. In fact, this was....

"The Library?" I asked in confusion.

There were the monoliths of archivals, in rows like the dark tombstones of giants; the cathedral-like ceiling lost to darkness; and the huge causeway in the center, big enough for even a smallish drakón fully transformed to walk down.

Ben began leading the way, but he gestured for me to walk beside him, so I quickened my pace to catch up, and he did his best after to match my own. "The blood archivists *are* archivists, after all. Storing information just as valuable as what's in these stones."

"I suppose that makes sense."

I'd just expected something a bit more like a hospital or a lab. They were going to extract blood from me, weren't they? Just a few drops, sure, but still.

In stark contrast to the last time we'd passed through the Library, we went straight down the center aisle, and instead of trying to hide me from view, Ben's wings walked casually behind the two of us, and Ben did his best to act just as casually as we walked side by side. He might have fooled the Library patrons who turned and looked—and then usually stared—but I knew from the curl of his fingers and the tightness in his neck that he disliked the attention nearly as much as I did.

And, for once, they weren't even staring at him as much as they were at me—this relatively small, white-haired, silver-eyed creature who practically glowed in the perpetual twilight of that cavernous room like she was from another planet.

Because, well...I was.

If word hadn't already spread across Crownhold and thus the Six Realms that I had returned, then it was most certainly spreading like wildfire now.

I focused very hard on staring straight ahead.

Fortunately, not long after, Ben led us down a perpendicular "road" and out of view of the main thoroughfare. But though this side road was not as densely populated, it was more brightly lit. The source of the light soon became obvious from the giant open doors at the end, where sunlight streamed down into the chamber beyond.

My eyes were drawn more to the doors than to what lay in the sunlit chamber, even though with them open and us coming on them straight on, I couldn't see what was on their longest surface: just their edges, which were mighty enough, perhaps the thickest wood objects I had ever seen.

Then it occurred to me: to my sixth sense, the doors hummed with power, making it clear that they were there for more than just show or as a physical deterrent. In fact, the magic in those doors felt...unusually deep. Ancient, even for this place.

There's quite a lot of magic in those doors, I silently told the drakón. One of the many things I'd made sure to master in our month apart was how to selectively project my inner voice. Of course, practicing on my family necessitated revealing the ability to them, and now almost everyone down to Abby had found their own and started using it, sometimes to bothersome effect.

The twins were getting more enigmatic and mischievous than ever, and Mom sometimes cast me a glare when they were clearly at it with each other.

Of course there is, Kor answered. *If you were to ask someone where the most heavily guarded treasures in the Six Realms were kept, the simple-minded might say the Treasury. Let them keep thinking that. Here, in the Hall of Blood, is where our greatest treasures are stored, behind some of the most ancient and powerful of our magics.*

I supposed that made sense, too. Even I knew by now that blood was the most potent piece of someone that could be used for magical purposes, for good or ill. If someone as twisted as Solim got ahold of enough of my Monarch's blood—or Ben's, too, I realized, now that he was King—he could use it to open a darkgate large enough to allow the Devourer to enter and consume a world.

Yet it was the old King's blood, freely and entirely given to his Tree, that had saved us all in the Battle of the Solstice. That offering gave the Tree the power to close the dark gates and strengthen the rest of Her defenders to scatter the consumed army. If the King hadn't sacrificed himself, Ben and I would have died, and my stolen blood would have perhaps been the catalyst for the end of their worlds.

So, for good...or ill.

Either way, probably any collection of blood would need the most painstaking of protections to not pose a catastrophic risk to the Six Realms.

That Kor had called the chamber we were approaching the "Hall of Blood" might have been disturbing, but there simply wasn't a good translation of the term he'd used into English. As far as I was aware, English only had one word for blood, but Kor had used a word in Drona with a much different connotation.

It was like...the life force of the universe, of all living things, but the force that tied us together, traced the paths between us through the ages. Maybe a more literal translation to English would have been "the Hall of the Records of Life," but that was a bit more of a mouthful.

The "DNA Hall" just didn't have the same ring. It made it sound like the lab I had been expecting, but I was coming to realize that we were approaching something that had much more of the feel of the...sacred.

It was a bit of the same thrum of power and deep-seated stillness I was coming to associate with my Tree.

It was a good thing our approach allowed our eyes to gradually adjust to the sunlight, otherwise I might have been nearly blinded when we finally passed through the doors and entered the vast chamber.

It was a perfect half-circle, with the wall we had come through being the flat portion. The other curved wall rose up in a dome, with the top third being entirely made of curved panes of glass or crystal that was nearly as clear, allowing the early afternoon sun to come through and make all that lay below glow with warmth and light. To add to the dazzling effect, the tiles below our feet were a metallic gold that radiated out from us in another half-circle and then waved in static rays beyond: a sun.

Now I could see that almost the entire length of the round wall had drawers from the floor to the average eye-level of a drakón. At first, I thought that each of those drawers had a glowing gem for a handle, but when we got closer to the far wall and the next set of doors, I discovered that each "gem" was a clear glass panel, and the glow came from within.

"That's where the svyenyir are stored," Kor said, following my gaze. "Come on, I'll have them show you."

"Ugh, Kor," Yvera groaned.

Before I could say a word, Kor was already turning toward one of the workers, who was opening a drawer a few dozen feet from us.

"Keeper Valis," Kor said with a charming smile as he approached her. "We're here with the Queen of Ice for her blood registration, and she has never seen a svyenyir before. Would you mind showing her?"

If I awed or baffled the keeper, she didn't show it. To my intense relief, the matronly, gray-haired woman in a gold robe bordered in green merely smiled at me warmly.

"Of course. Come have a look, my dear," she said, beckoning me to cross the last few feet to her. "After all, you should have some idea of what we will do with your blood after we collect it."

I approached and peered into the drawer she was holding open.

At first, it looked like someone's marble collection. It was about a dozen glass orbs, each one nestled in its own velvet-lined square. The orbs were about the size of marbles, but the colors in them weren't frozen. They moved inside, swirling with glowing, colorful energy; the many colors of light that spilled out to the edges of the box made it seem like there was a turning kaleidoscope inside.

"The blood is collected through a needle," Valis explained reverently. "That needle is attached to one of these orbs—an empty one, carefully crafted and magically prepared for that purpose. The blood flows down the needle and into the orb. The blood remains in the orb, but the orb acts as a prism of energy and light, pouring out a magic so thick it acts like ink onto the Reading Pool, where, on the surface of the water, the colors are transformed into patterns that we can study and record."

Her finger hovered over one orb, a dark, burned orange. "The color is that of the person's soulcolor. This one is Brightflare, obviously, but the exact shade and tint can vary tremendously within the clan's own hue."

"Can you distinguish the orbs of two people who are closely related?" I asked curiously.

"A layperson might not," Valis answered with approval. "That is why we Keepers of the Blood dedicate our lives to studying the different colors and the patterns they form in the Reading Pool. We take our sacred duties of interpretation seriously, and if there is any doubt, we take time to ponder and deliberate with each other before giving our consensus. But with practice, most keepers can immediately distinguish the colors, even if they are close together. There always is a difference, because each person's color, though they may technically be lumped into a broad category, will be unique to the person, and range the entire spectrum of possibility that isn't even visible to the naked eye. Even Koriben has a slightly different shade of gold than his father does; it may take special tools and vast experience to see the difference, but the difference is there, nonetheless."

My eyes darted to Ben at the woman's casual mention of the old King, let alone in the present tense, but though Ben's eyes were heavy, he didn't look as bad as I had feared, and he managed a thin smile at my glance.

"Interpretation seems like a very...involved science," I said politely.

"It is an art we have spent nearly a thousand years perfecting," Valis chuckled, pushing the drawer closed. "And there still is so much to learn. But don't worry—no one is going to ask you to be a keeper anytime soon. Your calling is clearly elsewhere, and I take no offense from that. But here, let me show you one more thing before you tire of my girlish enthusiasm—and Aldresh puts me on latrine duty for the next sevenday for holding you up this long. You see these squares?"

She touched the small glass panel on the front of the drawer. "These are to let in the sunlight. These orbs obtain their energy from the sun. Most of the time we store them in secure vaults, which necessarily means away from sunlight, so to keep them from losing their power entirely, and thus the precious information they contain, we rotate them back out here for recharging. You can't see it from here, but the tops of these shelves are glass. We put the dimmest orbs in the lower shelves to slowly acclimate them back to the light, and then we slowly rotate them upwards until they are at the top, where they remain until they are fully charged."

"But these are private records that you are storing out in the open," I said in surprise. "What's keeping some person from just coming in and...."

"Our most sacred duty, even more important than interpreting, is protecting these records," Valis said with a nod. "Though these seem like they are out in the open, many layers of security are between them and someone intending to tamper with them. The doors you passed through when you came in are one of them. I think you'd be surprised at how effective they are at deterring those who do not belong.

"As is the magic in the floor," she said, pointing to the elaborate tile work beneath our feet. "The orbs are never labeled by name, only by number, so you would have to have access to our records to find the one you wished to tamper with. The last protection I'll mention now—although it's by no means the last—is that only a keeper can open these drawers. There is a reason Korinth asked me to show the svyenyir to you. You see there is no handle. They open to our touch, but not to any of the uninitiated."

She rubbed her hands together briskly. "Now, I am glad for your sake that you stopped to learn a bit more before engaging in one of the most sacred of our rites, but I've held you up long enough. I hope to meet you again someday, Queen Sarah. Come back if you ever have questions or simply need to see a smiling face. Flame only knows you might see little of those."

She did indeed smile warmly at me and even patted my shoulder as she passed by.

"Can we go now?" Yvera said irritably. "I feel like I'm back in primary."

"This is Sarah's Blood Day, Yv," Kor scolded. "Let her actually learn to appreciate what that means."

"Babies don't appreciate what that means, yet they're brought here all the time for registration," Yvera said dismissively.

Kor gave me a sigh and a shrug in apology. I looked at Ben, and at my inclined head, he led the way again. I followed him, and Ben once again fell into step beside me. Which was a nice gesture, considering how much shorter he had to make his stride to match mine. It eased a bit of the fluttery nervousness that was once again increasing in my belly.

Although it made it hard to resist reaching my hand out for his. From the way his hand kept drifting to and brushing against mine, I guessed he felt the same. But even though he normally was much more comfortable with PDA than I was, still he resisted, and I found that fact significant. Either the occasion was too solemn or...now was not the time to show a greater connection between us than people would already assume.

Everyone was making such a big deal out of this pinprick that it was really starting to feel more than just a pinprick to me too. Which was ridiculous. The only reason I was doing this was to check a box for Ben so I could keep the peace and help him save the worlds. I didn't actually care about the results. Or about that mesmerizing orb that was hereafter going to carry my genetic information and be ensconced in the archives of the Hall of Blood for the rest of eternity.

Although, when I put it like that....

CHAPTER EIGHT

BLOODLINE

KORIBEN

BECAUSE I KNEW SARAH, I could tell she was nervous from the soberness of her expression, the fixed nature of her gaze, and her slow walk toward the next set of doors, which were smaller versions of the previous. Hopefully anyone else who saw her would think she was merely being dignified. She certainly looked that—as regal as the Queen she used to insist she wasn't worthy of being.

I had little hope that I was concealing my own nervousness so well, even though I knew it was needless. Or...should be. And yet....

Surely, with the will of the Trees being so clear and adamant, nothing would come up in the results that would present an impediment. Right?

And yet.

The doors to the Registration Hall were currently closed and had been since noon. Kor said they had reserved the entire afternoon for us, just in case. They of all people knew how important it was that we have privacy for this blood registration, and their reasons had nothing to do with Sarah's preferences and everything to do with protecting her and the precious knowledge contained within her blood.

When we approached, the guards on either side nodded to us and placed their hands in unison on the trunk of the golden tree inlaid on the surface of the doors. All the golden gemstones that formed the leaves flared, and the doors swung inward, allowing us to enter.

The hall beyond was a long triangle ending in a floor-to-ceiling point of clear, highly reinforced crystal. Angled views of the desert could be seen beyond—since this room rested at one edge of the enormous sandstone cliffs that sheltered Crownhold—but the most important use for the prism wasn't for the view: it was to allow pure, natural light to filter into the hall for the best reading possible.

The center of the room was a pool of water that mirrored the shape of the room: a long triangle that ended in a point. That point contained another crystal prism that sunk below the surface of the water and rose above it for about my height to end in yet another triangular point, this one tall and sharp as a needle at the tip. For obvious reasons.

A semicircular stone dais, with steps on either side, was at the far end of the pool and gave comfortable access to the tip of the crystal. That was where Keeper Aldresh stood. His hard, clean-shaven face was as stern as always, his long golden hair braided traditionally, with two on each side and the rest tied back in a loose single braid. He was dressed in the gold robe that indicated his calling as a blood archivist and the red stole with a gold border that showed his status as their head.

So, it was as I'd feared ever since Keeper Valis had let his name slip: Aldresh would be overseeing this registration himself. That only made sense, if you thought just about rank and the momentousness of the occasion.

It was just that Aldresh, as one of the staunchest leaders of the faction that aptly called themselves the Traditionalists...wasn't my biggest fan. More precisely, he hadn't been Avva's, but since he correctly guessed that I fully intended to follow in Avva's footsteps to the best of my ability, he had extended that dislike to me as soon as I became Heir.

I didn't think he'd throw Sarah's registration out of spite. Even he respected his calling and thus would respect the importance of this moment too much for that. Besides, there were too many witnesses—blood keepers sitting and standing everywhere in the pews on either side of the room that represented all clans, ranks, and schools of thought.

No, we could trust that nothing would interfere with both the ceremony and the purity of the results; even Kor seemed to think so from the grim look we briefly exchanged.

My worst concern right now was that Aldresh would not be kind to Sarah, who was not just the culmination but the living embodiment of all the changes over Avva's decades of rule that Aldresh had fought so hard against.

Sarah had once implied to me that I had never had a need to protect her from my own people, that she had been treated so well by us, she assumed all of us were ready to welcome her with open arms. Well, she was about to find out the hard truth about that for herself. Aldresh wouldn't have been able to remain as head keeper in such a holy place if he had as much darkness in his heart as to intend her harm, but I knew he would have much preferred she had never existed to begin with.

More than ever, I longed to grab Sarah's hand and pull her close to me, to shield her from Aldresh's hard golden gaze as he watched her approach. But now, more than ever, I could do no such thing. Sarah *had* to show her independence from me now, of all times.

Moreover, we couldn't legally be in a relationship until we'd taken care of this blasted formality. As Aldresh himself had taken pains to remind me over this past month.

Maybe we should have surprised them anyway, I silently muttered to Kor. *Then Aldresh might have been busy.*

Then he would have had our hides to record future bloodlines on, Kor said dryly.

Probably only a slight exaggeration. From what Kor had warned me, Aldresh was torched mad at us as it was for only having given him and his people less than a day's notice. But seeing as the archivists were the one of the factions hounding me the most to get her registered, I couldn't win.

Welcome to being me, as King.

I stopped reluctantly at the steps, and Sarah paused too, looking up at me in confusion.

Go ahead, I encouraged, trying to keep my anxiety from my face and inner voice. *This moment is just for you.*

And, traditionally, parents, since they had to hold the infant, but I didn't mention that—or that it would send entirely the wrong message if I stood in for one of them. It was bad enough that I and my wings were the closest people she had to accompany her here at all.

It killed me to see Sarah climbing the steps to face Aldresh on her own, but when she reached the top, she met his hard gaze with surprising equanimity—in fact, with even a slight lift in her dainty chin.

"Queen Sarah Moontouched," Aldresh said coldly. "You have come to the Hall of Blood this day to be registered. Is that correct?"

Quite an adaptation from the usual phrasing, but then, a version technically existed for adult registrations. They were rare, but occasionally some dramá in some backwater settlement was discovered to not have been registered and was brought here to rectify that omission.

"Correct," Sarah said coolly.

Contrary to what I had expected, Aldresh's coldness seemed to set Sarah at ease. Her shoulders were now relaxed, her face calm, her gaze direct. I didn't know if I had ever seen her more…queenly.

Flame, if I didn't get a chance to kiss her before she changed out of all that regal glory, I was going to be mad. The only reason I didn't do it right when she answered her door was because I was afraid to mess it all up before the ceremony.

Well, that, and I didn't recover in time.

Aldresh spoke so slowly and solemnly, his distaste was clear. "Then offer your blood to the light and Flame, and take your place among us."

He gestured to the sharp, pointed crystal.

Sarah turned with an elegant sweep of her cape and approached it.

Just a few drops, right? Her inner voice was tense, so she wasn't as calm as she appeared, after all.

Right, I said quickly. *Just prick your finger and then hold it there for a few seconds.*

She raised her finger to the tip. Just before pressing it down, she joked nervously, *If I collapse into eternal slumber, wake me up with a kiss, alright?*

Wait, WHAT— I began in pure alarm, but Sarah had already pressed her finger down.

The moment she did, I felt a surge of power explode outward and the crystal flared so brightly it blinded us all. I knew it wasn't just me with my proximity, because as I lowered my raised hands and blinked my vision clear, I saw keepers across the room doing the same thing—so shocked that they were breaking their infamous composure and protocol by looking at each other and whispering.

I was ridiculously relieved to see that Sarah was still standing—a bit dazed but otherwise looking none the worse as she continued to hold her finger over the point. I had no idea why she'd scared me with something about collapsing at a time like this. Was that something humans just *did* after they only bled a few drops? Then why didn't she say anything about that *before*?

I anxiously eyed the silver blood dripping down the hollow straw inside the crystal and into the svyenyir placed inside.

That's enough, I told Sarah the moment the stream hit the crystal orb.

Technically, it was Aldresh's job to tell her when to remove her finger, but he was taking his sweet time doing that, and I would not push Sarah's luck a moment further than necessary.

Fortunately for protocol's sake, just about the time Sarah lifted her finger, Aldresh said, "That is sufficient. You may remove your finger and step back."

Sarah did so, turning gracefully to him for further instructions. I watched Aldresh like a hawk as he came forward to offer a handkerchief to her for her to wipe away her remaining blood and then healed the prick on her finger.

Which was why I missed the glowing stream of colors as they first spilled down from the svyenyir and into the Reading Pool, where, on the surface, they began to form her bloodline.

I did have to step aside for the readers, who began pacing up and down the pool's length as it formed, watching with barely suppressed excitement.

Blood readers were supposed to be inscrutable, to reveal nothing of what they felt or saw lest they give parents and family members inaccurate impressions about the results. Not that anything in the typical bloodline was a *surprise* to anyone anymore, since everything past the infant's own trunk should be identical to the parents' bloodlines. The greatest drama that usually resulted in this century was the revelation of a different father than the one that was expected, but with the practice of blood registration so ingrained, mothers normally knew better than to conceal such information until this moment.

I could understand the readers' excitement in this case. Practically everything in this bloodline would be entirely new, making this the reading of their lifetime. That was also why there were so many of them: at least a dozen, though I hadn't bothered to make an exact count because most of my attention was still on Aldresh and Sarah. Only two were *required*, and usually only four were present as they were available.

At last, Aldresh told Sarah that she could go down, so she did, and I met her at the bottom of the steps with a smile. My hand burned more than ever to take hers, but even though I'd glanced enough at her bloodline to know that nothing of the first few branches of hers looked anything like mine (*thank the Flame*), I decided not to push it just yet with Aldresh still watching disapprovingly. Not that I cared in the least about the old stump's opinion, but he wasn't the only one who shouldn't muddy the waters of this ceremony with personal feelings.

I wasn't a blood reader. Therefore, this formality wasn't satisfied until the readers independently declared that there was no blood impediment to a union. They all would have guessed what *I* was most interested to hear and would include that note somehow in their preliminary conclusions.

In a hopefully discreet fashion. But discretion, like inscrutability, were two of the qualities you counted on blood readers to exemplify.

Kor was watching the bloodline unfold with just as much interest as the blood readers themselves, if not more, and I was certain he could give Sarah and me any other details we could care to know later.

So this is a bloodline, Sarah said, her inner voice tinged with awe as she came to the edge of the pool.

The magic in the svyenyir and prism had translated the information in her blood into visual form, spilling across the surface of the water like oil-based ink that stayed unnaturally static despite the occasional ripple across the water.

It began with a snow-white trunk that sprung straight from the crystal base.

That represents you, I said to her, pointing. *That's your unique soulcolor.*

People would know from the gesture that I was silently explaining things to her, but unlike in other situations in which the obvious use of inner voices would be rude, inner voices were actually polite and expected right now to not break the readers' concentration.

Ideally, in their minds, we would restrain ourselves from interpreting and discussing the results at all, but almost nobody held themselves to that purported standard, and blood archivists didn't even bother to enforce it. As long as we were quiet and unobtrusive, they would leave us alone.

Not much of a "color," is it? she jokingly replied.

It's identifying enough. See how it's different from your parents', even to the naked eye?

I gestured to the two branches coming off the trunk. Significantly, both were white as well, although one had a cream tone and the other a blue. Perhaps that wasn't such a surprise, seeing as they both had been presented before the Tree of Ice and formally adopted into the Moontouched clan, so even if their soulcolors had not been white before, they would have been by now.

What was *truly* significant were the branches that came next.

Wait, Ben, Sarah said slowly, her sharp mind already catching on to the implication without even being told. *Both of my parents...have a white branch as well.*

Yes, I agreed. *Which means you have Moontouched ancestry on both sides—from your mother and your father.*

Sarah stared at the evidence of that, stunned for a moment. Her eyes continued to trace the branches as they formed over and over again, the tree growing ever wider as the generations went on and on. And the bloodline was *still* forming, since it was only right now about one third of the way across that fan-shaped pool.

Most of the branches were some variation of brown, which perhaps represented pure humans. No doubt the blood readers and Kor would give us their theories about that later. There still were at least two white Moontouched branches for each generation, one for each side, but fascinatingly, there were sometimes *more*.

And that wasn't the only clan represented. Five generations back, a faint blue Starkissed emerged. Then another two generations, an orange Brightflare. Then a green Peacegrowth, then a red Strongshield.

That, in and of itself, would not have been surprising in a typical bloodline. The clans had mingled and intermarried so much over the centuries that probably the only reason they were still distinct entities was our soulcolors showing us as being one or another.

The shock in Sarah's case was that she was from *Earth*. Where, as far as I understood from what she'd told me, dramá had ceased to be such almost as soon as they returned and mingled with humanity again. Then what was the cause for these flares of color, clearly indicating a belonging to a clan, the active presence of the Blood?

I knew from Kor's eyes, which were glowing now from the intentness of his fascination, that he was wondering much the same thing—and probably had a few theories by now as to why.

With the revelation of a Battleblood perhaps fourteen or more generations back, almost *all* the clans were represented.

All except Sunfilled...

...but that one came just a bit later.

At its revelation, a reader broke her composure and gasped, pointing, and half a dozen of her fellows rushed over.

At this point, I wasn't worried. That lone gold branch had to have been over twenty generations back. If Aldresh tried declaring an impediment from *that*, he'd look like a torched fool. Practically all the dramá could claim that close of a relation to each other, let alone me.

Still, surrounded by all that brown...it was surprising, and that was no doubt what was getting the normally unflappable readers so worked up.

That's a Sunfilled, Sarah said, her eyes resting on the branch. She looked up at me, eyes wide. *Why?*

Good question, I said with a shrug.

That was the question that was no doubt on everyone's mind now. Especially Aldresh's, who watched with hard eyes from his superior vantage point up on the dais.

The fact that the bloodline was *still* unfolding meant that we hadn't yet reached the time of the first swearing of the Covenants, where all bloodlines ended. Even though amá and draká had both existed and had forbears before then, the magic that revealed our bloodlines to us depended on the Blood of the Covenants in our veins. Where that Blood ended, so did our ability to trace the line.

We hadn't even reached the Moontouched departure, where at least part of the bloodline should start becoming familiar to well-studied and experienced readers such as these. At *some* point, at least one of Sarah's ancestors must have come directly from the Six Realms, and they all waited with breathless anticipation for that connection.

When at last it arrived, the white branch shining nearly as brightly as Sarah's own, there was another collective gasp and rushing to the spot. Even Kor stood on tiptoes while leaning precariously far to the side over the pool, craning to get a glimpse. I felt a twinge of sympathy for him because of his shorter-than-average height, at least for a drakón. He had to keep his distance, though, or risk being thrown out. He wasn't a reader.

Even though he'd researched enough bloodlines by this point, he practically was one.

Which was how he could say silently—and privately, just to me—with excitement filling his inner voice, *Ben...I think that's Lady Serona.*

I stilled, inhaling sharply.

What? I demanded with a glance at him, ignoring Sarah's questioning look for the moment.

I'm almost sure of it, Kor said eagerly. *Flame knows I've studied her bloodline enough by now. The mate is Moryan, has to be. See that blue tinge?*

Moryan, Serona's husband, had had a Starkissed father—Lord Tolsyon's brother, in fact—but at Moryan's presentation and on becoming drakón, he had sworn himself to the clan of his Moontouched mother. Not an uncommon practice in dramá society (children could choose to join any, but traditionally chose their mother's), but the trace of his mixed heritage was clear from his soulcolor.

I struggled to keep my face composed. *But we don't have any record of Lady Serona having a child.... Do we?*

We didn't, Kor said. Even with his head turned from me to keep his gaze fixed on the furthest reaches of the bloodline, I knew his eyes would be burning. *Until now.*

If you're right, I said pointedly.

I wouldn't have told you if I wasn't almost certain it was her.

And yet he had told just me, not Sarah, which meant he wanted to be *certain* before the grand reveal to her.

When Sarah got impatient enough to ask me what the matter was, I simply said, *They've discovered where you tie in. Your Moontouched ancestor that left the Six Realms.*

Do they know who that is? she asked, eyes widening.

Honestly, I answered, *No, not yet.*

Both because of the uncertainty...and because we truly didn't know the name of the child, who might have been smuggled in secret to Earth by their father. If Kor was right...the child's mother never made it to Earth herself.

The bloodline ended only a few generations back from there, but that would be enough to definitively prove the identity of those two connecting branches that Kor was so certain were the final Lady and consort of the Moontouched clan.

If—as Avva, Kor, and I did—you recognized that woman as being their Lady, even though she was amón and therefore never lived to be confirmed by the Crownsmeet as such.

Someone like Aldresh...might not. As his stonelike expression hinted as he watched the subdued hubbub unfold.

He glanced at me, and then, seeing me watching, held my gaze. I stared back at him, calm but unyielding. I would not be cowed like a hatchling. We both knew that nothing had interfered in the proceedings. Not only were there too many witnesses and precautions in place to prevent such a thing, the magic in the air hummed pure and clear, the presence of the Tree palpable. Perhaps more than one Tree, at that.

If he found the results...inconvenient, that was his problem.

What? Sarah asked soberly, looking between the two of us.

Nothing, I said as I deliberately and blatantly took her hand, still not breaking Aldresh's gaze. *Nothing at all.*

Chapter Nine

LOVELY

Sarah

When the elaborate tree reached the ends of the pool and stopped, a couple gold-robed archivists who had remained at the pointed head of the pool produced an enormous scroll of a thick, hide-like substance wrapped around a wooden rod that was as long as Ben was tall. They held it between them while a third archivist hooked the end on a ring at the very tip of the pool and then unrolled the scroll as they walked along the pool's length. When necessary, they twisted the rod and increased its length even further so that they could keep holding the ends over the water on either side.

When they finally reached the end of the pool, the third archivist at the head of it carefully unhooked the tip, and all three of them in unison lowered the entire triangular sheet with excruciating care to the surface of the water.

"They'll leave that there for a quarter deken," Kor explained to me in a low voice. "Let the magic seep into it. Then we'll have a readily accessible record. Well, more accessible than using the svyenyir and a reading pool every time."

"Do they make a scroll for *every* bloodline?" I asked, eying the massive size of it now and remembering how thick and heavy the thing had been rolled up.

"Flame, no," Kor said with a muted laugh. "But for ones as important as this? That they *know* are going to be consulted and debated for years to come? They make the effort."

Lovely, I thought.

Meanwhile, it looked like the debating had already begun. The archivists who had been studying the bloodline as it had unfurled now huddled together at the end of the room, conferring with each other in agitated whispers and scribbling things down on various tablets or drawing bloodtrees out with styluses on smooth, blank sections of walls that seemed to be for that purpose.

Ben sighed as he followed my gaze. He looked at Kor. "They're not going to give us the official report for *months*, are they?"

"Probably not," Kor whispered with a grin. "But then, you knew that coming into this. It's a good thing we gleaned the most important bits for ourselves."

He tapped the side of his head meaningfully.

"Which are?" I asked curiously.

"Well, like I said, you have Moontouched ancestry on both sides," Ben said hastily.

That *was* interesting, I admitted. Although what were the odds that Mom and Dad, both Moontouched descendants, would come together like that?

"And?" I prompted. Because Kor had used the plural, *bits*.

Ben looked at Kor, a question in his eyes.

A discussion for when we have some privacy, I think, Kor said, looking behind Ben and me.

We both turned, having to pivot as one to avoid breaking our grip on each other, to see the stern-looking Sunfilled man who had instructed me on the dais approaching us.

"King Koriben," he greeted, his voice and eyes lacking in warmth.

My already poor opinion of him went downright sour.

I felt confident using Ben as the same gauge of character that some people used dogs. Anyone who didn't like dogs—as in, *truly* didn't like dogs, not just being afraid of them—and dogs didn't like *them* was probably someone who couldn't be trusted.

Anyone who disliked my golden-hearted Ben so thoroughly was probably worse than even that.

"Head Keeper Aldresh," Ben responded coolly, clenching my hand. "Thank you for your assistance, and that of your people, this afternoon."

"We live to serve the Realms," Aldresh answered, though his voice was dry and eyes pointed. As if he were accusing Ben of not doing the same.

Man, was I starting to hate this guy.

Then his eyes fell on our joined hands, and I remembered how Ben had taken mine in his so deliberately while Aldresh was watching before.

I could read between the lines here. Clearly not *everyone* in the Six Realms was pressuring Ben and me to get together, but the evidence of that didn't reassure me as much as I thought it might.

Aldresh said, "I trust you to keep what you have seen confidential, as is required by law. And to not do anything...unseemly...until the results are officially disseminated."

I had no idea what he meant by that last bit, but from Ben's subtle stiffening, Ben did.

Kor must have as well, but he was the picture of polite innocence. "Oh, don't worry, Keeper Aldresh. I imagine it should only take about ten more dek for the blood ink to be fixed to the hide, don't you?"

Aldresh looked at Kor in consternation, but Kor only looked back with the same wide-eyed innocence. "It was truly wise of you to so quickly create such a definitive and publicly accessible record that will be immediately available to anyone with any right to access it to verify that all is in order for certain other events to follow. Why, in fact, I'll be much surprised if the Queen's bloodline isn't on display in the Curing Room within the deken for all your archivists to study and interested parties to petition for a viewing."

Aldresh was going red, but it wasn't Ben's adorably self-conscious kind of coloring. "The report—"

"Should, of course, take all the months that might be needed to provide a thorough and supported assessment," Kor agreed, nodding eagerly. As if he and the keeper were on the same page. "But a preliminary assessment on one particular question is no doubt readily and indisputably available to anyone remotely familiar with bloodlines. Why, you could spare the least experienced of your readers to do the comparison and have the definitive answer within dek, I am certain."

What the heck was Kor talking about?

I had no idea, but I focused my energy on appearing as calm and knowledgeable as I could. Ben tried to appear to be doing the same, although he had an easier time with the knowledgeable part, since his lips kept twitching as if tempted to break into a grin.

That, I could understand. Most of the time, Kor was obnoxious with how overwhelmingly *right* he was. If he was focusing his obnoxiousness on someone who *deserved* it...I found it rather enjoyable to watch.

"Now, I am certain you have crucial duties that we have taken you from for too long," Kor concluded with a deep nod of respect. "And I have matters that need the King and Queen's urgent attention. So, we shall take our leave of your Hall and allow you to reopen as soon as may be for the normal course of registrations, shall we?"

Without waiting for the keeper's reply, Kor nodded to Ben and me and gestured ahead. "If you will lead the way, King Koriben, Queen Sarah?"

"Of course," Ben said, lips twitching, but he looked at me.

"Yes, let's be going," I said with all the dignity I could muster. I smiled sweetly at the keeper. "Urgent matters and all that. It was lovely to meet you, sir. Have a good day."

Then I led Ben forward, and Kor and Yvera followed.

Fortunately, it wasn't that hard for me to retrace our steps through the hall with the pool and the chamber full of the blood marbles (the formal term for which I had already forgotten) and back into the dark library.

We entered the welcoming, quiet darkness and slipped down a side aisle not a moment too soon, because the moment we were out of sight and hearing, Ben and I both broke down into laughter so hard that tears came to our eyes.

"Did I miss something?" Yvera asked Kor with a raised eyebrow. She had been so bored with the entire proceeding that she had kept back far enough to not have heard our conversation with Keeper Aldresh.

"The dignity of their station finally became too much for them, the poor souls," Kor answered Yvera sympathetically.

That only sent us into further peals of laughter. As we recovered, I clutched my side from pain as Ben gasped and wiped his eyes.

"Oh, the look on that stump's face. Kor, you were torching brilliant. I owe you a bottle of Kallin Red for this."

"Well, I'll certainly take you up on that," Kor said with a slow grin. "I can't claim all the credit, though. Sarah was the icing on the cake."

I was a little in awe of my gall, now that I looked back. But in the moment, and even now, I knew the keeper had deserved it, and that had made my facetiousness easy.

"Speaking of which," Ben said. With no other warning, he scooped me up and pressed his lips to mine, his kiss surprisingly hungry and demanding, considering our audience.

When Yvera cleared her throat, I pulled away, cheeks burning.

"You were magnificent," Ben said, eyes glowing. "The entire time, not just then."

Hmm, Kor sent to me. *It's almost as if* looking *like a queen helped you act like one.*

Dang it. I hated how right he was. As usual.

"Alright, I'm done standing around being an ornament," Yvera snapped.

"Feel free to go start hitting something, Yvera," Kor said with a snort.

She scowled. "I wish. Actually, I have less appealing things to be doing. Like finalizing preparations."

"For?" I asked intently as Ben set me down. More because Ben had gone tense than anything.

"Ben and I have a review of the Warflight this afternoon."

"I thought you'd cleared my schedule," Ben said to Kor.

"Of everything that was in *my* power to clear," Kor replied with an eye roll. "If you want out of the review, talk to your rightwing."

At Ben's plaintive look, Yvera just snorted. "Duty is duty, Ben. We have responsibilities now, remember? And it's more important than ever to get this one out of the way now, before you sweep us away on another mad tour of the Realms."

"What mad tour?" I asked, nonplussed.

Ben started going red, and Kor chuckled.

Not here, he told me but included the other two, glancing around meaningfully.

"Really?" Yvera said in exasperation. "You seriously didn't tell her any—ugh, that's it, I'm out. *I* have things to do to keep *your* blasted Realms safe."

And she marched off to the main library thoroughfare. Ben sighed but let her go.

Then he looked wearily at Kor. "Your office, then?"

"Probably the best place," Kor agreed.

"I still think it's hilarious that you have an *office*," I teased as Kor started leading us down one of the paths lining the library wall. "That sounds so official."

"Technically, it's my *old* office, thank you very much," Kor said with a smirk back at me. "But seeing as how there's no Heir leftwing right now, no one's bothered to kick me out. And it's in the Library, *and* nearby, which makes it convenient for us right now."

And because it's your office, it's safe from eavesdroppers, I thought.

Instead, I said in the same teasing tone, "Of course your office would be in the *Library*."

"Of course. That makes it convenient for *me*." He sighed heavily. "I'm going to go through withdrawals when they give me my eviction notice."

"Oh, please," Ben said with a chuckle. "If the administrative *suite* you've been given here as the King's leftwing isn't enough, you'll find another dark hole in here somewhere to burrow down in, and you know it."

"Yes, but I like *this* spot," Kor said with a pout. "It's so...private."

He gestured ahead of us, and I saw what he meant.

This had to be the darkest, quietest part of the Library. It was practically cave-like, with only the occasional glowing stone to light the path, and some of those were even flickering.

There was no one in sight.

"The philosophy section," Kor said with the contented sigh that people normally reserved for saying the word *home*.

"Not a glorified subject in the Six Realms, eh?" I asked as we stopped in front of a few doors. Kor put his hand on the touchplate of one while sadly shaking his head.

"No, alas—the unenlightened fools. Oh, well, that makes it all the easier for me to crush them beneath the weight of my brilliance."

As he spoke, the gem on the door glowed in acceptance of his identity, and I heard a click as the door unlocked. I was half-expecting the hinges to creak, but neither was I surprised when the door swung open in perfect silence. This was Kor's office, after all. Though I'd gathered he wasn't the most dedicated cleaner, one of his priorities was discretion.

The office, though, did not disappoint. As I entered first, I saw it was exactly the sort of chaotic mess of shelves, papers, scrolls, tablets, and books that I would have expected. There were a few dedicated walking paths between the stacks, and at the far end of the small room there was *probably* a desk underneath the biggest pile, but other than that....

When Ben had said Kor would find a new place to "burrow," he had meant it literally.

As Ben and I finished shuffling around the stacks to find a place to stand—a hard task for someone as big as Ben, who, try as he might, still knocked over one stack in the process—Kor closed the door behind him with a glare at me.

"I have a *system*," he said, pointing a finger at me.

"I didn't say anything," I said with a straight face.

"You didn't have to. I'm telling you, I *do*," he said sternly. "So, wipe that smirk out of your eyes, and let's get down to business, shall we?"

I was sure the smirk did, indeed, leave my eyes as I sobered. We all did—Ben especially as he straightened from restacking what he'd knocked over.

"Business. Right," I said.

"Which I will let Kor explain," Ben said awkwardly. "I need to go help Yvera get ready. I only came along to say goodbye."

"Wait, what?" I asked, feeling like he'd just pulled a rug out from underneath me. Which, in this kind of space, would have been disastrous.

"Just for the afternoon!" Ben said quickly, and I breathed a subtle sigh of relief. "I'll be right back, as soon as I can—as soon as Yv lets me go, anyway—and then we can...um...."

"Do something unseemly?" Kor suggested with a smirk.

"Excuse me?" I said with a blink.

Ben wasn't making me feel any more comfortable from the way he was turning bright red and glaring at his leftwing. "Kor...."

Kor rolled his eyes. "Oh, don't worry. I know you're trying to do things 'properly,' so I'll have a signed and notarized letter from the Hall of Blood in my hand by sunset. In fact, I'll be much surprised if our allies in there aren't already drafting it as we speak."

"*What* are you guys *talking* about?" I demanded, feeling lost now. It almost seemed as if the translation magic was malfunctioning, giving me the surface meaning of their words but nothing of the depth needed for understanding.

"Nothing," Ben said hastily, but with all the tightness in his voice and discomfiture in his expression that said the exact opposite. "Just...administrative stuff. Very boring. Not important at all."

"Ben, you're doing a terrible job of explaining things to her, as per usual," Kor said with a dramatic sigh as he passed between us.

He put a hand on my shoulder. "Sarah, why don't we let Ben go do his Kingly thing of talking to a bunch of people with pointy weapons and you and I have a nice chat to catch up?"

I blinked at him. "To...catch up."

"Of course," Kor said with a firm nod. But his eyes seemed to be trying to tell me something different. I noticed his back was turned toward Ben, even as he addressed him next.

"Isn't that right, Ben?"

Ben looked just as confused as I felt. "You...."

"Right, Ben?" Kor said intently, turning to give his friend and King a meaningful look.

"Right," Ben said tightly. His face was turning red again. "Um. Catching up."

"Really?" I said dryly.

Kor looked back at me. "Really."

Switching to his inner voice, he said, *Don't drag this out, Sarah. We're not going to get anywhere productive until he's gone. Trust me on this one.*

Trust you? I asked dryly.

Ouch. But fair. But also, totally unfair. You have no idea what I've suffered for you two. Just please *take my word for it that he's going to make a hopeless mess of this if we let him stay. So, say goodbye and let him go—for now. We have things to discuss. And I'm serious about that part.*

Judging from Ben's growing scowl, he'd guessed by now that we were silently communicating.

"Alright," I said slowly, keeping my eyes on Ben. "I guess we can...chat."

"Excellent," Kor said, patting my shoulder. "Let me go find the papers we need to discuss first while you two wrap up. They're here...somewhere. So, just fair warning...this might take a while."

"But—" I said in confusion, a bit surprised Kor was going to metaphorically shove me at Ben after all of *that*.

And then Kor did so in more than metaphor. It was a subtle nudge in the back in passing, so quick that Ben might not have seen, but it was still most definitely a shove. Then Kor turned his back to us as he began studiously shuffling around in the papers on his desk.

I had little choice but to look back at Ben, with my only comfort being that he looked perhaps twice as uncomfortable as I did.

"Well," I said, mouth dry, trying not to feel like this was a bigger deal than it seemed. "I guess...this is goodbye. Again."

"For a bit," Ben said quickly, and then winced. "I mean...that is...thank you."

"For what?" I asked, still feeling disoriented.

He sighed, hand on his neck. He finally made himself meet my gaze, and his golden eyes were heart-meltingly soft. All my confusion and discomfiture disappeared.

I saw there the truth he couldn't say, the truth I had known would be there and felt ashamed I had even momentarily forgotten: That he was in pain, greater pain than I could imagine. That he was doing what he felt was right by me. That I *mattered* to him, deeply.

"For...what you just did, with the blood registration and for...talking to Kor while I'm gone. And...everything. Just...thank you. For more than you will ever know."

I stared at him. *More than you will ever know.*

It could be just a coincidence. And yet...that phrasing was far too close to the dream I'd had for comfort.

Ben was going red again as I said nothing, did nothing but stare at him. He began looking as if he was afraid he'd said too much, even though all he'd done was *thank* me.

"Anyway, I have to...go. Yvera...waiting...get ready...." he stammered, stumbling backward to the door. He swore as his uncharacteristic clumsiness took down stack after stack, and he fell into Kor's office door.

He took one last look at me, swallowed, and then said, "Love—I mean, lovely to see you again."

And then he darted out and slammed the door shut behind him.

I STARED AT THE door for one full second.

And then I said dazedly to the room at large, "What...the heck...was that?"

"That, my dear Sarah," Kor drawled, "is a 'heck' of an improvement on what I've had to deal with for the past month."

I turned haltingly to face him and saw him looking over his shoulder at the door. He scrutinized the knocked over mess with a sigh and then turned back to the map he'd been studying, muttering something about how long that was going to take to organize again.

"That...was an *improvement*?" I demanded.

"Of course," Kor said with a snort. "Why, he practically looks like a person again. Red-faced and stumbling and stuttering and all."

He abruptly threw the map down on his desk in a sudden burst of aggravation. "Do you have *any* idea how carefully I cultivated Ben to become King, Sarah? Yet in the course of one sevenday—no, one *day*—he turns into a walking, breathing...block. A living stone. This is the first day—the *first day*—that he's acted even remotely like himself again since...."

The tirade died, and Kor leaned back against the desk, putting a hand to his forehead.

I swallowed. "Since his father died," I whispered.

"That was a bad day," Kor said with a deep sigh, folding his arms as he looked at the floor. Or...what little of it there was visible. "Even though I know now that Ben was bracing himself for his father's death for a while, it still came as a devastating blow. But that wasn't the moment he broke."

"What?" The word was barely more than a whisper.

"You were there, right after," Kor said heavily, looking at me. "You saw. He was...in a bad place. Then he shut you out, and like a fool, I didn't stop him in time."

"What happened?" I asked with a pounding heart, taking a few tentative steps along the path between us.

"I told you," Kor said with a tired shrug. For the first time, I noticed the shadows under his eyes, the way his curls were unusually tousled and probably unwashed. It had clearly been a long month for him too. "He turned to stone."

I smiled shakily. "I...have a hard time imagining that."

Kor huffed a dry, humorless laugh. "You'd think, wouldn't you, from what you knew of him before? Ben was...Ben. Too soft, too idealistic, too ready to laugh or tease.... But it's true. It was like he just...died inside. And all we were dealing with was a shell of him."

I swallowed. "It was inevitable his father's death...and everything that followed...would...change him...."

"True enough," Kor said with a weary nod. "But I think what we saw *today* was what this 'new' Ben is going to be like. It's as if he just...woke up."

There was a long moment—maybe a minute, actually—while Kor just stared into space, and I worked up the courage to ask the crucial question.

"Then why all of...that?"

I waved my hand behind me.

Kor laughed with more genuine humor. "The reason for all *that*, especially at the end, should have been obvious."

The reminder of Ben's behavior at the *end*, especially his words....

I had known for what felt like ages by now that Ben loved me, but I had known just as long, thanks to Kor and Eskala, how deep his inhibitions were against allowing me to love him in return—against being able to allow anything permanent between us. Yet here I was again, allowed back into his life, with him having sworn a blood oath to never push me away again, with my Tree having given me peace that all would be well.

Could Eskala be right? Was Ben...ready?

I bit my lip. "Kor...I want to know what you think of something, but you have to *swear* not to laugh or tell me I'm crazy. I just want one response from you: whether you think what I remember was a dream or a real memory."

"What?" he asked, eyes lighting up with curiosity. In my experience, there was nothing Kor loved more than a good secret.

"Uh-uh," I said firmly. "Not until you swear."

He rolled his eyes. "I swear not to laugh or tell you you're crazy, *just* whether I think what you said was a dream or a memory. Did that cover it?"

"I'm going to hold you to it," I warned him. "The second you start laughing at me...."

"Yes, yes, I get it," he said impatiently. "Now, what's this all about?"

I hesitated. But I was fit to burst to talk to *someone*, and Kor was the only person who might understand and maybe, just maybe, have the answer.

"Do you remember...toward the end of the battle? Just before...." I swallowed. "Ben's father...."

"I remember," Kor said, dark eyes even darker than normal. "That vorpex had you and Ben pinned under Ben's shield, right?"

His sobriety helped, made me feel less silly about the situation. Especially when I relived that tension. The fear. The near certainty that at any moment, that giant insect that I glimpsed through my cracked eyelashes would break through the golden barrier and spear us both through in one stab. And being unable to rouse myself to do anything about it.

I shook just remembering. I hadn't talked to anyone about this yet, for many reasons. None the least of which being that I didn't want to worry my family, and my drakón had been here on Ythra—and had seen or gone through worse.

Kor must have seen something of the tension in me, because his face softened. For all his fastidiousness about maintaining some mad method of organization, he shoved aside a pile of papers on his desk and patted the clear space beside him in invitation.

I let out a breath of relief and crossed the space to him. I sat in that spot, which put our heads nearly level, with him leaning against the desk and me sitting. He put an arm around my shoulders. I hesitated a moment, then leaned against him.

"That must have been terrifying," Kor said quietly.

"It was," I said with a shaky breath. "But...I wasn't conscious of much at that moment. I was only just waking up from overtaxing myself, and I was kind of fading in and out. I gathered that Ben and I were in mortal danger, but I just couldn't move or get myself to fully wake up. It felt like a nightmare, except the scary part was the real part, if that makes sense."

"It does."

I took another deep breath. "That's why I thought I dreamed this next bit, you know? Because it was just as I was fading out again, and I thought...I thought my mind made it up to comfort myself."

"What happened?" Kor asked.

Not *What do you think happened?*

"Remember that you promised not to laugh," I whispered.

"Sarah," he said with a heavy sigh. "No matter what you say, if you say you saw a rainbow field full of giant, fluffy contonies made of spun sugar, I will not laugh."

I gave a short, tense laugh, which he'd no doubt intended. Then sobered.

"Nothing like that," I said quietly, hands twisting in my lap.

I took a deep breath...and said my secret burden out loud. "All I did was dream that Ben finally told me he loved me."

Kor was true to his word. Far from laughing, he became still. "He...told you that? In...so many words?"

"I don't *know* if he did or *not*," I said emphatically. "That's the whole problem."

But I already felt a dozen times better. The release...it was incredible.

"Sarah, tell me *exactly* what he did and said," Kor said intently. "Tell me every *single* detail that you can remember."

"OK...." I said hesitantly, but I obliged him by closing my eyes and trying to relive that moment. That wasn't as hard as I expected. It had, after all, been the single moment of comfort amidst the life-threatening danger, the moment that had seemed to make our death in the next few seconds bearable.

"We were lying on the ground together," I said. "We'd fallen in some crevice or another, and I think with Ben's shield right over us, there wasn't much room. He was on top of me. Trying to shield me with his body, too, I think."

I didn't say what we both knew: that Ben's body alone would have been useless against that creature's spears.

"I don't think he knew I was conscious sometimes," I continued quietly. "I didn't have the energy to keep my eyes open, let alone to tell him. He kept saying my name, pleading for me to wake up, but he didn't sound like he thought I would."

Even if he'd known I was alive, he'd probably thought I wouldn't get the chance to open my eyes again. I had feared the same thing, after all.

"And then he...got quiet for a moment. Then he said, 'I love you, my star—more than you will ever know.'"

"Did he use those exact words? In Drona?" Kor asked intently, naming the lingua franca of the Six Realms and the only language I was familiar with enough to use myself.

I blinked. "No...actually.... Now that you mention it, he used something else for that last bit, something I didn't recognize. I understood, obviously, but I can't quite remember the exact words.... I think...there was a 'hadran' or something?"

"*Hadran avi'yen shen,*" Kor repeated softly in an unfamiliar language. *More than you will ever know.*

"That's it," I breathed. "That's the words he used. I couldn't remember them in the original language.... What was he speaking?"

"Vardak," Kor answered quietly.

"Why?"

"Because that was his mother's first tongue. It was what Kavarian would always say to her."

My heart thudded. My head spun dizzily, bad enough that I put it in my hands. "So...that means...."

"You made me swear to give you only one answer. Well, here it is: that wasn't a dream, Sarah."

"I...think I need to sit on the ground right now," I said unsteadily, and I slid off the desk and onto the floor.

I could hardly believe it. I had been *certain* that I'd made the whole thing up. Oh, I'd hoped. When I saw Ben again, I'd hoped with all my might that he'd bring it up. But he didn't, and I became sure I'd made it up. Besides, he was *grieving*. He'd been beside himself. That hadn't been the time to bring something like that up, even if I'd been one-hundred-percent certain.

Then...he'd sent me home. And shut me out.

"That *gadlek*," Kor swore, his fury cracking through the silence like a whip.

I looked up at him in shock. I wasn't sure what a *gadlek* was—my normally helpful translation magic didn't give me a meaning for it—and I wasn't going to ask.

"What was that for?" I demanded.

"You have *no idea*," Kor said, steaming. "No idea what I have gone through to—and then the only moment he—gah! He's lucky he's probably halfway across Crownhold, surrounded by elite right now, or I'd...."

"*You'd* try to wring the neck of your King? In front of everybody?"

"Don't tempt me," Kor said with narrowed eyes at his office door.

"Kor...."

I didn't believe he meant it. My drakón traded death threats with surprising frequency, and I knew by now that they were steadfast friends. But I seldom saw Kor get this angry, and I didn't doubt that he could hurt Ben if he wanted to. As the Tolsyon heir, he could surge to nothing, which meant he became invisible and incorporeal—unstoppable, unless the Tree revoked his birthright before he could misuse it.

"Oh, don't worry," Kor grumbled, folding his arms. "I've put far too much work into Ben to kill him off now."

"Well, good," I said dryly. "Because I'm rather fond of him."

Kor looked down at me with a tired smirk. "I don't see why, after all the grief he's given you."

"He always had his reasons," I answered quietly. "Speaking of which, though...what do you think I should be reasonably expecting from him right now?"

"What do you mean?"

I took a deep breath. "I mean...I know it's one thing for him to admit that he loves me when he thought we were about to die and I couldn't hear, and it's quite another for him to do so now. Which he hasn't yet. Even though in some ways, things are better than ever."

The blood oath, for example.

"Then he does things like...that." I waved at the door. "Can you understand why I'm a bit...confused?"

Kor sighed. "Yes. Which was why I wanted to talk to you, because he's doing a torched job of this as usual. In this case, I think 'that' is simply because he's being...well, Ben. His hopeless, awkward, noble self. Rather than for any more serious reason."

I blinked. "And by that, you mean...."

Kor slowly smirked again. "I mean, Sarah, that I am ninety-five percent certain he is going to offer you an earring tonight."

I just stared at him, frozen.

His smirk widened. "Allow me to explain. An offering of an *earring* means—"

"I know what it means!" I spluttered. I stood up so that I could be more level with him. "But what in the Seven Realms has you thinking that Ben is going to *propose* to me *tonight*?"

"Sarah, Sarah. Why else would Ben's very *first* request of you after you were reunited be for blood registration?"

I gritted my teeth. "I don't know. And you *know* I don't know this part."

Because this wasn't about smoothing feathers anymore. If it ever had been.

"Understandably, since it has to do with a certain little law that almost no one knew of or cared about except blood archivists, until you came along: whoever intends to marry into the Golden Crown must have a blood registration on record so the archivists may confirm that the two potential partners aren't so closely related as to preclude a union."

Kor winked. "The law came from a time when there were fewer of us to go around."

I stared at him again, hardly daring to breathe. When I managed to speak, my voice was shaky. "You're saying...that the very first thing Ben asked me for after he came back...was for me to remove a legal impediment to marriage?"

"It would seem so. The timing is rather telling, isn't it?"

The way Ben had blushed when Yvera asked why we were doing my blood registration *today*...and, when I'd begun to question him, ran from the room.

Just as he had done...from Kor's office. After almost accidentally telling me he loved me.

If Kor was right...Ben wasn't pushing me away again. He was doing his very hardest to not fall over himself in his haste to propose.

The greatest reason he hadn't yet being that, until just half an hour ago, he legally *couldn't*.

I dazedly backed up to the desk and sat on its surface, needing to get off my feet again.

I gave Kor a pleading look, swallowing. "You're sure?"

"Well, ninety-five percent sure," Kor said with a shrug. "But really, Sarah. I don't know what the Tree said to make him allow you back into his life, but once so thoroughly convinced he had to, what did you *think* he was going to do?"

"I...I don't know," I said numbly. "I didn't let myself think about it. At all."

Kor sighed and put his arm around my shoulders again. "Yeah, I can see why. Then allow me to clarify: this was what everyone *else* knew was coming as soon as you returned. Even Yvera. Because this is *Ben*."

"It's a bit...fast for marriage, don't you think?" I said with a wan smile.

Kor raised an eyebrow. "You're the Queen of Ice. He's the King of Flame. Those titles come with a bit more responsibility, not to mention scrutiny and expectation, when it comes to relationships. Add on top of that Ben's own principles, and what else could you expect?"

I took a deep breath. "I...see. I guess."

"You don't have to tell him yes. You can tell him no, or not yet, and he would respect that. But, as you've just seen, he won't be able to keep himself from at least asking for much longer."

I nodded to show I understood.

Kor grimaced. "You should know that even a 'not yet'...would be problematic. You two have made no secret of how you feel physically about each other, and now more than ever, both of you are seen as the literal Moondaughter and Heir of the Sun. I've been able to explain away your absence with some drivel about period of mourning, respecting Kavarian's passing and Ben's ascension, establishing your own Realm, et cetera. But now that you're back...."

"I understand," I said with a sigh.

After all, I had made my decision about Ben before I even made the one about becoming the Queen of Ice, since Eskala had told me they were one and the same in the mind of the Trees. I knew what I wanted, what I would *always* want—knew it now, more than ever.

I'd had a month to contemplate life without Ben, and that was a month too long.

But let's just say it was a good thing that Kor had given me some time to know what was on Ben's mind, hours before I would have to give an answer. Ben's one-eighty would have been dizzying for anyone, but I particularly needed time to adjust and process.

Although now that I thought back through the past night and day and all of Ben's tells...perhaps I *should* have seen this coming.

"*This* is what that guy meant about doing something 'unseemly'?" I said in exasperation.

Kor rolled his eyes. "Head Keeper Aldresh is a Traditionalist, down to the core. He honestly thinks it would be uncouth for the two of you to be betrothed, let alone married, before the full official report. But seeing as anyone with *eyes* could tell for themselves that you and Ben aren't remotely related, I'm not worried about that kind of fallout. Still, just to be *sure*, I'll get that signed and notarized letter stating as much for Ben, since he's fussing about doing things properly right now."

"Properly," I repeated. "Which is why he didn't even *talk* to me about this until he knew he could *legally* propose."

"Precisely," Kor said with a tired smirk. "Like I said, that's Ben for you."

I sighed and nodded. It was indeed. Ben's sense of honor and duty was one of the things I liked most about him. Even though at times like these, it could be bothersome.

Kor brightened. "But, as a pleasant distraction from your impending life-altering decision, want to know the most significant thing I gleaned from your bloodline?"

I raised an eyebrow. I had a feeling I had little choice in hearing it, given how eager he was. "Sure."

"Oh, this will mean something to you, trust me," Kor grinned. He leaned in, eyes gleaming. "I am almost certain...that you are a direct descendant of the last Lady Moontouched."

I became still and stared at him once more. "What? You mean the one who was...killed?"

Kor's smile faded. "Yes. Lady Serona."

I swallowed. "You sure?"

"Like I said, almost certain. I would recognize her bloodline anywhere. Have probably seen it in my *sleep*."

"So...she had a kid. Before."

"So it seems," Kor said, eyes burning with his excitement. "But we'd had no record of one before this. So, she and her husband, the man who led away the Moontouched after her assassination, must have kept the child a secret. And he, being drakón, must have taken the child to Earth."

"Instead of hiding in the Six Realms like the amón did," I mused.

"Indeed. Which led, eventually...to you. Poetic, don't you think? The blood of the Lady who was rejected and killed for being amón, returned to restore her clan in glory as the Queen of Ice."

"I suppose that's one word for it," I said, but my stomach churned. Every time I thought I understood the weight of expectation and destiny placed on me.... "What do you think she would think of her descendant marrying the King of Flame, though?"

"As his equal, not his consort?" Kor shrugged. "Particularly *this* King of Flame? She would probably be happy for you, if that was what you wanted."

That made me feel the teensiest bit better.

"Oh, so you're caring about what *I* want, versus the 'good of the Realms,' are you?" I teased.

Then regretted it at once as I remembered Kor's offer, and Rachel's theory as to why he'd made it.

Fortunately, Kor only smirked. "Of course I am. I just so happen to be one of the few to see that they are the same thing."

He slipped off his desk and stretched. "Well, now that you know how thoroughly the Moontouched wing is your birthright...are you ready to settle in?"

"It's done then, is it?" I said with a sigh.

"It's close enough," Kor said with a wink. "If you *do* decide to wear a gold earring after tonight, then it's all the more important to get you entrenched as soon as possible."

I sighed again but slipped off the desk as well and nodded. "Might as well, I suppose."

Secretly, though, I was relieved. Kor's complete casualness after my careless slip had set me at ease.

Rachel didn't know what she was talking about.

CHAPTER TEN

WING

SARAH

WITHOUT BEN TO SURGE us, Kor had to lead me around the old-fashioned dramá way: by walking to a daygate. So, we went back the way we came to the Library's daygate, with Kor not seeming the least bit bothered as he asked me details about my family, how they were settling in, and how the past month had been generally. He seemed to know without being told that it had been a hard month for us all, so he focused on neutral details, such as Mom's ukka or Dad's progress in learning to read Drona.

He sighed at that last bit. "I'll think on how we can help him. Unfortunately, we simply don't have something in your language for him to compare ours to."

"Still, just a dictionary of some sort might be useful, even if he has to translate the definitions as well as the words. Or a grammar."

"He asked for copies of those very things in his list, which I made sure he received."

"Oh, good," I said sheepishly. Figures Dad would have thought of asking for something like that.

"I also gave him one of my scales, with pictographic instructions on how to use it."

"You did?" I said with some relief.

"Yes. So, assuming scales *work* again between our Realms now that Ben has restored the crowngate—"

Kor rolled his eyes.

So, it hadn't just been me. The scale Kor had given me *hadn't* worked while Ben had shut us out. I wondered if he realized the effects of his impulsive act would be so far-reaching. I also wondered how many times Kor had tried to call me before giving up.

I'd tried nearly every day for a couple of weeks until I couldn't bear the disappointment any longer.

"—he can consult me occasionally. I won't always have time right when he calls, but I'll answer when I can."

"Kor, that alone could make all the difference. Thank you!"

"Well, I have some sympathy for him, after all," Kor replied wearily. "I know what it's like to be suddenly made a leftwing with no idea how to do your job but knowing the fate of the Realms hangs in the balance while you figure it out. At least *I* had Eskala."

"Sounds like you still do, in fact."

"Yes, and thank the Flame for that. She's probably the only thing keeping me sane right now."

"I'm sorry, Kor," I said quietly.

He flapped a hand. "Things will get better...eventually. Especially now that you are here. Busier, in some ways. But in better ways, I hope."

And you still think this is the time for things like engagements? I said.

Kor smirked tiredly. *Yours? I do. That part can't come soon enough.*

Out loud, he said with a grimace. "There's...reasons on top of Ben's own why this shouldn't wait."

I swallowed but nodded to show I understood. *Just when are you going to explain your grand theory about why the fate of the Realms hinges on Ben and me?*

"All in good time."

After a pause, Kor smirked. "Oh, by the way, speaking of scales, I even badgered Yvera into giving up one of her own."

I stared at him. "You didn't. For *who*?"

"Why, for your rightwings, of course. But she would only surrender one, so they're going to have to decide between the two of them who gets it. And I think we both know who that will be."

"David," I said with a sigh.

Kor was already familiar enough with Michael's growing grudge against drakón and the Six Realms, not to mention his obstinate pride, to guess that he would refuse to accept something that stank of drakón help and magic—even though, as *my* rightwing, the responsibility should fall to him.

"Probably for the best," I said morosely. "David will put up with Yvera better."

"Perhaps even have the gall to call her," Kor said with a chuckle, shaking his head. "I still can't believe he dared ask *Yvera* to perform the translation ritual for him."

"The even greater miracle: instead of killing him, she *did* it," I said, shaking my own head in awe.

"Yvera isn't as stonehearted as she likes to appear," Kor said with a knowing glint in his eyes. "Especially, it seems, with sunny, guileless, handsome young men who aren't easily scared off."

My jaw dropped. "You're...you're kidding, right? *Yvera* and *David*?"

Kor shrugged. "It's a long stretch to think anyone would willingly put up with Yvera, I know. But as for the enigma of Yvera's surprising tolerance for him, I have since realized that there *is* a resemblance between your younger brother and a certain Golden Heir we once knew. Especially before the weight of the Realms really started sinking into his shoulders."

I stared at Kor as much as I dared while still walking down the main Library thoroughfare and avoiding passersby. At least Kor was distracting me remarkably well from all the stares I was getting myself.

"I can't see it," I said finally, my brain having officially given up trying to form the picture.

Kor chuckled. "Like I said, it's a long stretch. Nor is it one I am necessarily recommending, especially given his age. He's, what—sixteen summers?"

"Almost seventeen," I said grudgingly. If we were counting years as summers, and if we had kept track of the days properly, his birthday was next week.

"Still, that's four fewer than Yvera, and in her immature mind, that might be an insurmountable number. But my suspicion of Yvera having at least a subconscious soft spot for David did give me the scant hope that the effort of prying a scale from her *might* not be in vain. Otherwise, I might not have bothered."

Now that I looked back...David *had* seemed to have a bit of a thing for Yvera. Approaching her to ask for her to do the translation ritual for him, for starters; nothing short of pure, reckless, boyish infatuation could have motivated him to risk his life like that. How could I have been so stressed and distracted to not have seen that? Then after, he *had* been the most helpful family member in getting her through the craziness of Earth air travel. Yvera had never seemed to scare him away, no matter how much she glared or snapped at him.

Fortunately, I was distracted from such disturbing thoughts by our arrival at the Library daygate.

I slowed my steps as we approached the freestanding arch filled with fire. "How...do you do this, exactly?"

Kor blinked at me, then chuckled. "Oh, right. You haven't had to do it on your own, have you?"

I shook my head. Before, I'd always either been riding on Ben's back as he flew through in dragon form, and the magic had seemed to consider us one entity in that case, or I had been surging with him, during which my lashing kept us together and he did the "driving."

"Well, you still won't have to, because I'm going to need to take you to the right daygate. Someone usually has to lead you through the first time to a gate that's new to you. After that, though, you picture your destination firmly in your mind as you walk through, and then you walk out there."

"That's it?" I asked dubiously as Kor led me to the side of the gate.

Kor smirked. "Not quite." He pointed to the external side of the arch, which had a glowing yellow gem at about shoulder height to me. "Touch that."

I sighed. "You know, it's a good thing for you that I trust you by now."

As Kor laughed, I reached out to touch it and wasn't even surprised when I felt a spark of power, like static electricity, leap from me and into the gem.

"That bonded yourself to the gate," Kor said. "To keep the explanation simple, let's just say that now a part of yourself is a part of this gate, and whenever you want to return to the Library gate, you're reaching for that part of yourself to pull you back here."

I shook my head in wonder. "So, all those times that you three were flying through all those sungates...you had already been there and bonded to them already?"

"Correct. Yvera and I are unusual in that way, though. Most people don't have so many gates under their belts, but part of our initiation in becoming Ben's wings was being taken on a whirlwind tour to *every* sun- and daygate there was, just so we could always be ready to serve with him wherever we were needed."

"What about Ben? Did he do that when he became Heir?"

"In a manner of speaking," Kor said with a chuckle. "The Golden Royals are the exception to the normal rule—they bond to all the gates at their investment, just as part of who they are."

"Oh, that's right," I said. "They see them in their mind's eye."

The old King had even "seen" when a new one had become available—the crowngate in the Library.

Which was currently close enough that even I, who had to be near my gates to sense them at all, could feel the magnetic pull from it and could have surged there if needed. But once I stepped through that gate with Kor, I might not, and that potential loss of a tether made me unreasonably anxious for a moment.

And yet, now I had a tie to this daygate. All I had to do to get back home if I had to was enter another daygate (or a sungate if I was too far away for the short-range version), come through to the Library one, and surge to mine.

Assuming the Library daygate was active, of course.

I sighed at the complexity of it all, and at my own silly self for needing that kind of security blanket.

"Ready, then?" Kor asked, holding out his hand.

I looked at it skeptically, making him roll his eyes. "We need to be in contact with each other to stay together, Sarah. This is perfectly normal. No one is going to think anything of it. Unless, of course, you continue just standing there, making this awkward."

"Fine," I said with a sigh, slipping my hand in his.

He smirked and pulled us through the back side of the gate.

There was the sensation I had not missed: the squeezing, stretching, cannonballing through nothingness and stumbling out the other side. Except, of course, Kor strolled out as casually as you please, keeping me upright with his grip on me.

He grinned. "You'll get used to it."

"*How?*" I choked.

"Try keeping the sensation of walking in your mind as you go through. It helps your feet get the right idea as you come out. Otherwise, the magic just has to *shove* you."

I didn't know how it was possible to keep the sensation of *anything* in one's head while undergoing the transition between gates. I supposed that was even more reason to surge with Ben whenever I could, now that it was so seamless for him.

"I like my gates better," I muttered as I pulled my hand from his.

"Well, if you figure out how to *make* one, do share. In the meantime, this will be your next best thing." Kor pointed to the daygate we'd just walked out of. "May I present the daygate of the Moontouched Wing. Rather ironic, I know, but it's the best that we of the Golden Crown can do."

"This is the Moontouched Wing?" I asked curiously, looking around. It was a vast hall, of the scale that humans of Earth almost never built to, but it didn't strike me as the grandeur I had been bracing for.

"Of course not," Kor said dismissively. He pointed behind us. "The entrance to the wing is there. But since this is a *public* daygate, it's out in the public corridor."

I turned and saw something much more along the lines I had been expecting: a huge, imposing entry framed with carved columns of trees—the leaves of which were mostly stone, but some were glowing white crystal—and massive double doors with only a small inset wicket gate currently open.

Two drakón guards stood by the gate—no surprise there. The shocker was in their uniforms: They wore their scale-plate in their own colors, of course (no getting around that, since they supplied their own scales), but they had formal *white* and *silver* one-shoulder capes over the top with matching scabbards holding the knives and swords at their waists and silver-colored spears with white-dyed shafts in their hands.

"Like the uniforms?" Kor asked. "I certainly hope so, because they're in public use now. I would have consulted you on the design, of course—had you been available."

"Well, I like the restraint, at least," I said dryly. With Kor as the designer, it could have been worse. Not garish, but certainly more extravagant.

"I thought you might," he said with a wink. "Now, are you going to touch this gatestone so we can go inside, or are you going to gawk here all day?"

I sighed and touched the gold gem at the side of the gate, then Kor led me to the wing.

I felt a shiver of power as we approached the gate, which probably meant we had crossed a protective ward. My gut told me those glowing white gems above weren't just for show, nor were the silver rings in the floor.

Good, you're paying more attention, Kor said silently, noticing where my eyes went.

I'm not oblivious, I answered, but we were approaching the guards, who saluted with their hands over their hearts and deep nods to me.

"Queen Sarah," the Brightflare drakón said with a warm smile. "Welcome home to your Wing of Ice."

"Thank you." I didn't know whether it was proper or not, but I placed my own hand over my heart and nodded back. No one seemed startled or offended by that, thank goodness.

She paused for a moment, as if hearing something we didn't, then nodded to us. "You are cleared to enter. Please proceed."

I gathered there was a lot more ensuring the security of my wing than what appeared on the surface, but again, I was grateful to Kor for the subtlety.

"Thank you," I said, nodding to both again, and I walked through the wicket gate.

The main court did not disappoint. It was everything I would have expected of Kor and his clan and more.

To my intense relief, I saw it wasn't searingly bright. I'd been subconsciously bracing myself for blinding whiteness everywhere, when in reality I needed the cool and the dark nowadays to feel restful and at home. Not that it was a gloomy cavern, either. But the Starkissed had somehow plastered over or covered the natural sandstone of Crownhold with various shades of cool, soothing gray on the lower hard surfaces, and the ceiling was a remarkably good replica of the dome over the rotunda at the Temple of Ice: an unnaturally dark backdrop with glowing stars, planets, and galaxies.

Other light sources were provided by the softly glowing white convex circles on each of the seven mighty pillars. As I walked slowly into the center of the court, I saw some pillars had just one circle, others had two, with one even having three, each of varying sizes.

"We had to estimate the phases of your Realm's moons, of course," Kor said, gesturing to the pillar directly across from the entrance gate, with two circles on its surface. "I made my best guesses, which will do in the meantime, but eventually the chief architect will want a study to be done to fine-tune the accuracy."

"Hopefully not anytime soon," I said in mild alarm, thinking of dramá invading my family's sanctuary just to do a moon study.

"No, of course not. I can put her off for a few months, at least, with excuses about the fever and your clan still settling in. I'm just giving you fair warning that she *will* see it done at some point. This may surprise you, but we Starkissed are a bit...perfectionist."

"No, really?" I said with mock surprise.

"It's true," Kor said with a stoic expression. "It's both a burden and a blessing, I assure you."

I noticed the placement of the pillars, which were spaced evenly around the rim of the dome, and I pointed. "A seven-pointed star, I'm assuming."

Unlike in the Oculus in my hold, the shape was made more than obvious by the silver-bordered triangles inlaid into the polished floor connecting into the center, each triangle alternating between black and white for shading. The floor surrounding the star was a polished gray.

Kor grinned and pointed above at the dome. "And the dark moon."

Which together made the Moontouched emblem.

"Speaking of whom...." Kor said as an elderly, brown-skinned amón woman with black hair streaked with white and dressed in a blue robe and dress strode quickly toward us, while several other similarly, if less elaborately, attired assistants trailed behind.

"Queen Sarah," Kor said genially, speaking to me but gesturing to the woman. "May I present the illustrious and brilliant Madam Gwinra, chief architect of your Wing's renovation and previously its chief custodian. In fact, she comes from a long line of Starkissed custodians who have carefully and faithfully maintained your hold to await your clan's return."

"Korinth, you young rascal," Gwinra said with a scowl and a shaking finger. "Flattery will not get you back into my good graces."

She smoothed her expression to something more polite as she turned to me and placed her hand over her heart. "Forgive our belated welcome, Queen Sarah. And our terrible state of unreadiness for your arrival."

"Everything looks beautiful," I said in surprise. "Far better than I could have imagined."

"You are gracious," Gwinra said wryly. "But this court alone has scarcely had the dust of its construction cleaned away and its workers vacated not a deken ago and has yet to be properly furnished. Your wing is not even fit to be seen, let alone by *you*, but the King's leftwing—"

She shot another glare at Kor.

"—insisted that you had to take residence *today*."

With surprising frankness, Kor said, "Would you rather the Queen have stayed in the King's Wing?"

The woman snorted. "Of course not. But I would *rather* have been given more than a night and a half-day's notice to prepare for her."

Kor opened his mouth, but I cut him off.

"Blame me for that. I am afraid my Tree's command for me to press my hospitality on you was rather sudden. Please do not blame Korinth or the King for my presumptuousness."

My frequent reading of Jane Austen novels was paying off in unexpected ways, making all the teasing I'd had to endure from my two older siblings worth it. Especially when Kor blinked at me with barely concealed surprise.

I could only hope that the translation magic transferred my English formality properly into Drona.

From the older woman's somewhat mollified expression, I hoped it had. "Well, is that how things stand?"

She looked at Kor for confirmation, and he nodded. "The Tree of Flame commanded the Queen's immediate return as well."

Gwinra huffed as she placed her hands on her hips. "I suppose there's no arguing with Trees, especially in combination, now, is there?"

"I understand my wing is not in the state you had envisioned for me," I continued soothingly. "I will therefore withhold any judgment of its current state, and of course I won't be bringing the rest of my clan until you deem it is ready for them, too."

"Or opening it to the public?" she demanded.

"Not a moment before you give the word," I said solemnly.

"Well," she said slowly, lowering her hands back to her sides. "Well, I suppose that is the best we can expect, given the circumstances. Of course, if the Trees say you have to be here, you shouldn't be staying anywhere *else*. We'll just have to make do. And you'll have to put up with the work going on around you for some time to come. We've managed to adequately stock your suite for the time being, but finishing and furnishing the rest of your wing might take another sevenday or two more."

"Of course. Do whatever is required to fulfill your vision, and take all the time you need."

"The Queen might also be staying in her wing very little over the next month, giving you more flexibility to work," Kor supplied. "Necessary *travels* might take her and the King away from Crownhold for sevendays."

I had no idea what the emphasis on the word *travels* had been for, but no one else seemed to think it strange.

In fact, Gwinra's lips twitched for the first time in something approaching a smile. "So, it's to be a grand tour, is it?"

Grand tour? I asked Kor silently. That harkened back to something Yvera had said, but I didn't have time to think on it.

Kor ignored me, merely smiling politely at the architect. "Perhaps."

"Yes, yes, I can see for myself that nothing is final yet," she said with a flap of her hand. "Keep your Crown secrets, then, as poorly guarded as this one is."

To everyone except me, apparently.

"Then with your permission, may I usher the Queen to her suite? She would no doubt appreciate some peace and quiet before the next portion of her day begins."

Heck, yes, I sent to Kor with intense longing.

"Of course, proceed," Gwinra said with a wave. "Welcome to your wing, Queen Sarah, such as it is now. When it is ready, I will give you a proper welcome and tour, but in the meantime, I need to be about the business of bringing that day to fruition. Korinth knows his way and is more than a sufficient escort. Ice go with you."

"And Flame go with you," I said, placing my hand over my heart as she did.

To my gratitude, she and her assistants left, walking toward one of the four main spokes off the central court.

Well, that went better than I had anticipated, Kor said cheekily as he began guiding me in the opposite direction across the court. *I knew you had untapped potential as a leader, but I hadn't expected to elicit* that *much yet.*

I fiddled self-consciously with the folds of my dress, glad that no one was around to notice. *Once I understood what her concerns were, the proper things to say seemed rather obvious.*

Ah, but as if that weren't impressive enough, it's also the way you said what had to be said that smoothed her ruffled feathers. Those things take sharp observation, empathy, quick thinking, and intuition, and not very many people have that innate combination, Sarah.

He made it sound like what I had done was easy. Just because that was the way I was built didn't make it without cost. There was a good reason I *needed* solitude right now—needed to be away from even Kor's eyes and expectations.

Or rather, especially his.

As if to hammer in the point, he continued, *We'll make a Queen of you yet.*

I thought I already was *one,* I said dryly.

Whether or not I liked it, I'd sworn myself to this life a month ago.

He smirked at me. *That's the spirit.*

My suite didn't disappoint either, and now I could see what Gwinra had meant about the rest of the wing being bare, if this was what she had called "adequately stocked."

Vadya and Fenra met me there, and even if their black and white uniforms with blue trims at the collars weren't hints enough, Kor formally confirmed their status as my new heads of staff. I might have resented my utter lack of choice in their appointment, except...who else would I have picked? At least I *knew* these troublemakers. And trusted them.

Mostly. Sort of.

At least they won points in my book for shooing away Kor and giving me the tour of the suite themselves. Though that wasn't leaving me in solitude, at least it was a break from Kor.

The theme of sophisticated, soothing gray with white and black accents continued—gray for the walls, at least part of the floor, and any stone features; white for the upholstery, banners, streamers; and black for the dark ceiling, which was studded with more stars. I had seen by now that not *all* the ceilings in my wing were enchanted to look like the night sky, but the ones in the central court and my suite were.

Like Ben, I had a reception area, although mine was much less spartan and, in fact, wouldn't have looked out of place as the reception of a high-brow spa, minus a desk. Though most spas didn't have a daygate set into the wall next to the door.

"Is that...what I think it is?" I said, pointing to the arch. It was inactive, flames nonexistent, and made of gray stone instead of sandstone, and the gems set into either side were clear instead of golden, but it otherwise looked identical in construction to Ben's own.

"It's a daygate alright," Vadya answered. "Or it will be, once Ben finally gets around to activating it. He wasn't...er...available, before."

Meaning he wasn't in the right frame of mind, most likely. That additional reminder of how the past month had been perhaps even harder for him than it had been for me saddened me.

"Then how come there's an active one outside the wing?" I asked.

"*That's* an old one, from ages ago," Fenra said dismissively. "Put in after the Moontouched left, yes, but the custodian at the time insisted it should still get one, just like all the others."

"Especially given how far away and deep the Moontouched Wing was compared with everything else at the time," Vadya added. "Made the custodian's life much easier after that."

"Deep?" I said in confusion.

"Well, yeah. It's on one of the lowest levels of Crownhold—below the ground level, even. Originally, that was seen as a snub to the Moontouched, but Kor says it's an advantage to you. Its remoteness makes it easier to secure, and the air is naturally cooler than on any other level. In fact, in the renovation, they found a spring with the coldest water available in Crownhold."

So *that's* why I'd gradually felt more comfortable the longer I was here. Well, other than the relative privacy and slow lowering of the distant, unseen sun. I was relieved to hear about the possibility of cool water, too. I didn't let my hopes get too high—this still couldn't possibly be glacial meltwater—but that was more than I had expected.

Also, I really wasn't used to thinking of a city in terms of *levels*.

I was surprised I wasn't feeling claustrophobic, but the dark sky, to me, created a sense of spaciousness, openness, and it helped that the court and all the halls I had seen branching off were immense. In my suite, potted plants and mosses of all sizes were everywhere: in nooks set into the wall, in giant, gray ceramic pots in the corners, in an entire wall just of vines. I was serious about the reception having the vibe of a spa: there was even a trickling fountain in a corner running in a stream down the length of the rest of that wall.

A question that should have occurred to me a long time ago, given how much time I'd spent in underground drakón holds by now, came to mind. "What do you guys do for air?"

"Spells, partly, which are carefully maintained, and alarms sound if they run out of power or if the air becomes impure or unideal. The rest of it is a combination of plants and air shafts." Vadya pointed to the ceiling. "You can't see them here because of the enchantment, obviously, but look for them along the corners of the walls anywhere else in a hold, and you'll see them."

"All the systems are designed to be redundant, in case any one or more should fail," Fenra added.

I imagined there were still substantial risks to living as they did, but there were risks to any kind of habitation. I had enough fatalistic calm that this was my lot in life now to accept that. I knew all too well that the risks of living outside the sanctuaries they had carved out for themselves were far greater than living within. Especially at night, when their power faded and their—now *our*—enemies reigned supreme.

I had a study off the reception room with a large gray desk, a cozy seating nook around a bed of moss and ferns, and a waterfall trickling down the entire length of the roughly carved wall at the far, short end of the rectangular room. The only current sign of any sort of "studying" aid to be had was the tablet and stylus waiting for me on the desk—which made me realize something about the wall opposite the waterfall.

"Is that...an archival?" I asked, pointing.

The dark, smooth black stone appeared to be the same type as the monoliths I was used to, even if I had always seen them as freestanding before.

"Yes, your personal one," Vadya said. "It was Kor's idea to incorporate it into your study itself, instead of tucking it out of the way somewhere where it was less convenient. He also said, with it being just for your use, there was no need to make it accessible from both sides, so it could simply be...a wall. Rather genius of him, don't you think?"

"Yes," I admitted grudgingly.

I pointed to the large, shiny black oval stone set into the wall opposite the seating area. "What's this for, then?"

If I had been on Earth, I might have said it was an oddly shaped, inset TV.

"Ah, that was also Kor's idea, one he said he got from your world—your birth world, I mean—Earth. He thought you might find its smoothness and placement convenient for your ice communication magic."

Dang it, he was right again. I could already see myself lounging on that couch while talking to my family. Or anyone, really. It looked comfortable enough for casual chats and yet dignified enough for calls with world leaders.

I was seeing why he had been put out about being kicked out of my tour of my suite. I was going to have to thank him later for all the little innovations he had incorporated to make my life better, let alone to accommodate my needs and my magic that were so different from theirs.

And somehow, I would have to give my thanks without clenched teeth. He deserved sincere gratitude...but the fact that he always did, and always *knew* he did, made it harder for me to express.

Fortunately, there wasn't as much of a call for innovation in the next two rooms: the bedroom and private bath. Although there was more than enough opulence in each. Again, the bed was excessively big...for just me. But I was finally coming to understand why that might be a necessity anyway...and, dang it, feel some gratitude for that much again. Even if I was just as hot and embarrassed as I was grateful.

As for the "bath"...I'd seen swimming pools that large. Small ones, true. But none with an entire curtain of water continuously running around its circular rim, complete with tree-columns and glowing strips of crystal for mood lighting.

There was one benefit to the bath's excessive design, though.

"That might make it harder to bathe me," I said to the sisters with a smirk, pointing to the water curtain.

"Oh, don't worry," Fenra assured me earnestly, pointing to the far end. "That's what that one is for."

That was when I noticed there was a second, smaller, raised pool at the head of the first one, overlapping it slightly. Not only would the raised height make it more convenient for attendants, but there was also a lip for the bather to recline, counters against the wall on either side like wings, and a wide rim around the pool suitable for placing all sorts of objects. There were even circular indents that were probably meant to be more than just decorative—perhaps for placing the candles or incense they might have drugged me with before, for example.

Dang it.

"We'll make good use of that later," Vadya said with a wink. "After we've given you a chance to rest, of course."

"What, why?" I asked in alarm.

Silly question. I couldn't believe I had even momentarily forgotten, since I remembered almost as soon as the words left my lips.

"Oh, no particular reason," Vadya said with wide, earnest eyes. "Kor just thought that you and the King might like to make dinner together—and enjoy a nice, quiet, uneventful evening afterward."

As if Ben and I had ever had an evening that could be remotely called uneventful over the entire course of time we'd known each other. As blissful as that sounded right about now, I knew that wouldn't be the case tonight, not even in the best-case scenario.

"Ah," I said. "Right. Well."

Maybe I would accept their help again after all.

CHAPTER ELEVEN

ACCEPTANCE

KORIBEN

I HADN'T EVER BEEN inside the Moontouched Wing, even before the renovation.

The Golden Crown had been traditionally barred from setting foot inside ever since the Moontouched departure, when Lord Tolsyon Starkissed had taken it upon himself to appoint and fund its first custodian. Even after the renewal of the Covenants, Avva's seal on the funding request, and Sarah's public introduction at the Battle of the Solstice, I had been kept out of the details of the renovation and had never been invited to tour its progress, even though Kor had immersed himself in all of it.

The Starkissed either blatantly ignored the fact that Kor was technically a member of the Golden Crown or justified the combination of his clanship and position as making him the perfect bridge between interests now.

I never asked whether my exclusion was out of respect for tradition or for other reasons, and I hadn't ever cared to. For that month, I was more than happy to have nothing to do with any of it and would have fought them tooth and claw if they'd tried to drag me inside, as Kor would have warned them.

In sharp contrast, I now hurried through my shower and change of clothing as quickly as was advisable, as impatient to get there as I'd been determined at just this time yesterday to avoid it. I knew the moment I walked through my daygate back into my quarters that was where Sarah must have been, even before

Kor caught up to me; her star in my mind's eye was too low and far away to have been anywhere in the King's Wing.

Despite my haste, I took enough care to put back on the black clothing Kor had given me that morning, remembering both Sarah's favorable reaction this morning and her shy compliment to me when I'd worn the color at the Moonfair. How Kor had figured out her preference when he'd arranged for my outfit this morning, I had no idea.

Or maybe it had just been a complete coincidence, and Kor was trying to start a new Royal trend. I had to admit that my black against her white had made us less of an eyesore standing together than gold against white would have been—not to mention mitigated to some extent the way I caught the eye more than she did, given my height and notoriety. The black pulled me somewhat into the background, the white bringing her into the foreground, visually rebalancing us.

Figures that Kor would think of details like that. Hating attention myself, I was far from being resentful at my leftwing's subtle attempt to lessen some of it on me. Having more attention on *Sarah* made me nervous for other reasons, but I could hardly do her status justice, let alone respect her as a person and the incredible young woman she was, by trying to hide her any longer—not even for the sake of protecting her.

I just reminded myself for the thousandth time of the Tree's promise.

She had *promised*.

So, I had better keep working on my end of the bargain.

Kor was waiting for me again as I hurried out into my sitting room.

"Good," he said in satisfaction as he saw my clothing. "I was hoping you'd have the good sense to put that back on. Though you can lose the dress coat."

"You sure?" I asked dubiously, but Kor was already pulling it off me.

"Of course I'm sure. It's too formal, and it's ollik wool besides. You're making dinner with her, for Flame's sake."

"Not just dinner," I grumbled, hoping we could leave it at that. But I knew better than to think Kor hadn't guessed precisely what I had in mind as the primary goal for tonight, especially when he told me *his* idea of how I should get to that point.

And torch it, I hated that I hadn't thought of anything better.

"Fine, take the coat with you and put it on later," Kor said, handing it back to me. "But lose it for now. You don't want to make Sarah nervous at first greeting. Attracted, yes, but not nervous."

"You're being awfully...helpful about this," I said suspiciously as he re-parted and arranged my hair.

Had his feelings for Sarah lessened to that degree? Last night, his anger at me and his warmth toward Sarah hadn't seemed to imply that to me.

Kor snorted as he straightened my shirt and briskly stepped back to examine me up and down. "Ben, I'll always love Sarah. But thanks to a certain sister of hers, my *romantic* interests have shifted quite a bit over this past month. And unlike you, *I* know how to court a woman, and that effort began today."

"Wait, what?" I said, blinking.

Then it hit me—the only sister he could be talking about. "*Rachel*?"

I'd seen how he'd eyed her while we met and traveled with Sarah's family on Earth, but that had hardly been surprising given how heavily Rachel had flirted with *him*. I'd expected him to indulge himself if given the chance and had prepared to prevent him if I could for both Rachel's and Sarah's sake, but otherwise I had thought nothing of it.

"Yes, Rachel," Kor said, abandoning his examination to smirk at me. "I honestly don't know why you sound so disturbed. She's a lovely creature, is she not?"

"She's *Rachel*," I said, flabbergasted—and slightly nauseated, to be honest.

Lovely, she was, but in the way that the exotic deathflower was—right before it injected you with its stunning venom, swallowed you whole, and slowly digested you in its acid for the next sevenday. Then *maybe*, if you were lucky, it would spit out enough identifiable parts of you that one day someone would discover what a sorry fool you were for getting too close.

"Well, yes, not an ideal match for *you*, obviously," Kor said, his smirk deepening at my expression. "Aren't you glad now that Sarah took up the mantle of Queen instead of leaving it to her?"

I froze in horror at that thought for one moment. Considering the Tree of Ice had made Rachel Her Heir, odds were good that she would have become Queen if Sarah had rejected her birthright, as Sarah had claimed so many times that she would do when the time of choice arrived.

If I had been forced to marry *Rachel*....

Nope. I would not think about that. Nope. There was no point in torturing myself in that way when that possibility was long and safely gone.

And thank the Flame, Ice, and Creators for that.

Still, even if I couldn't remotely understand the appeal Rachel had for Kor, I didn't want to argue him out of it. If anyone could survive that deathflower, it was probably him, and the longer she could keep him occupied, the more secure I could be of Sarah. Though I felt a twinge of guilt at not interfering for Sarah's sake, considering how I knew she felt about the two of them getting involved.

So, I made a token effort. Also, I was morbidly curious.

"How in the Flame's name did you begin to court her *today*?"

Kor winked. "I may have slipped a few extra things into the order you had delivered to them at dawn this morning. Including a package containing one of my scales, addressed to her."

"In Drona?" I said, grudgingly impressed. He really *was* way better at this than I was.

"Oh, no. She showed me how to write her name in their script while we were sitting together in one of those 'airplanes.'"

And Kor still remembered how to do it. Technically, Sarah had shown me how her name was written, but I couldn't have reproduced it if her life had depended on it.

I...should do something about that. Not that her life would ever *actually* depend on it—but I couldn't let Kor show me up in every way.

"So...you're just going to talk to her, by scale?" I asked sternly. "Because you know we can't risk—"

"Oh, I'm certain I'm more conscientious of the risks of contamination than you are," Kor said dryly. "After all, *I* was the one who instructed the delivery be sanitized, and *I* checked in with Jake this afternoon with the scale I had given *him* to make certain no one in his family had developed symptoms, given how you'd burst in on them last night with probably nary a care for what you might have been carrying with you."

"Oh," I said, face heating. "Er. Good. Thank you. For that. I...am assuming all is well?"

"Fortunately, for the sake of Sarah's good opinion of you, yes. And to answer your other question, yes, the only contact Rachel and I are going to have is by scale for now, for her safety. So you can stop feeling obligated for Sarah's sake to protect her from my...physical charm."

I rolled my eyes. "As significant as that is, we both know your mind is your most formidable asset, Kor."

"True," he said with his signature smirk. "But it's not as if you have any right to interfere."

I hesitated. But I had reached the end of both my authority and my desire to stick my nose into this business. I was catching the whiff of a deathflower's scent from even doing this much.

"Alright, fine. But if you hurt Sarah's sister, I'll be obligated to kill you to save my own skin. You realize that, right?"

"That's assuming Sarah doesn't go straight for me herself."

"But then you'd rat on me with your dying breath, and Sarah would come for me next. That's what I mean by me having to kill you to save my own life: I'm going to have to get to you first."

"Ah, I see," Kor said with a nod. "A sound strategy, and as such, I accept that. Especially since I have no intention of hurting Rachel."

At my disbelieving snort, he said with surprising soberness, "Truly, I don't, Ben. Even *if* she wasn't already unlike any other young woman I'd ever met, she's the Heir of Ice. You think I would risk alienating her?"

"You seemed to have no qualms about doing that to Sarah."

Kor huffed and waved dismissively. "I was never in danger of doing that with Sarah. Sarah only ever had eyes for you, and any obnoxiousness on my part was deliberately calculated to keep it that way."

"Really?" I asked—gratified, surprised, and discomforted by turns.

Kor rolled his eyes. "Really, Ben, even now you have *no* idea what I have done for the two of you. Speaking of which, do you have a set of earrings?"

I stilled. "Er...."

In my defense, I had not truly, up to this day, expected to need any. Let alone on such short notice. Although...perhaps I could have used my morning off a bit more productively. Yet even if I had, I doubted I could have obtained such a thing as discreetly as Kor no doubt had.

Kor raised an eyebrow while producing a small black box in his hand and holding it out to me. "You'd be lost without me. You know that, right?"

I snatched the box and said, "Oh, trust me, I know."

KOR LET SARAH KNOW I was coming, so she was waiting for me at the entrance to her wing when I walked out of the daygate. The sight of her promptly distracted me from my irritation at having to use Kor as the messenger, since I still hadn't given Sarah another of my scales after she'd had to give up the first one.

Though this morning's apparel was good enough for *me* to reuse, either Sarah's attendants or she herself had decided a change was in order. She now wore a one-piece suit made of white, shimmering silk that draped and hugged her slight body to perfection, aided by a silver girdle with an inset diamond around her waist and a halter top that wrapped around her neck, leaving her shoulders and the outer edges of her collarbones tantalizingly bare.

I wasn't allowed to risk ollik wool while cooking, but she was allowed to wear that?

Not that I was complaining.... Especially since I hadn't seen this much of her skin since the day she first arrived, when she was wearing those ridiculously short trousers and that sleeveless shirt.

As usual, I didn't know whether to curse Kor or thank him—especially as I felt the first premonition at how difficult it was going to be to keep my newest resolution tonight.

Sarah's brightened expression and brilliant smile at the sight of me helped soothe my nerves as always and brought an answering smile to my own lips.

"You look incredible," I said as I approached, and when I reached her, I ducked down and kissed her, heedless of the scant passerby and the guards in front of her gate. To my surprise, she lingered in that kiss, not seeming to mind. I hoped that meant the start of a trend.

"You don't look too bad yourself," she said with a grin as I finally pulled away, running a hand down my sleeve appreciatively with unusual boldness.

Well, I guess I knew what color I was wearing from now until the rest of eternity, traditions be torched. After all, I'd already worn these clothes in front of Aldresh himself—let alone at a blood registration, and only a month after Avva's death. There were many reasons Aldresh had been in a foul mood, but the unconventional color of my clothing at such a significant moment had definitely been one of them. At the time, I'd regretted letting Kor talk me into pushing the dress code boundaries for how it might have worsened how Aldresh had treated Sarah, but now I couldn't have cared less what Aldresh and the other Traditionalists thought.

The Realms weren't so fragile that they would shatter if I started wearing primarily black instead of gold, if that was what gave Sarah pleasure and me comfort. I was already appreciating how much more muted the color was than my usual gold; its understated nature conversely gave me a surprising boost of confidence. And Avva himself had told me I should throw off the trappings of mourning for him, so who else's opinion should I care about?

Sarah wrapped her arm around mine—so unconsciously my flameheart surged—and led me to the wicket gate. "So, have you honestly not been inside before?"

"Not at all. I think that might have been the first time I've ever come through that daygate, in fact."

"Well, hopefully the architect will forgive me for breaking with tradition today," she said, but she seemed unbothered by the risk she was taking.

I chuckled at her echo of my thoughts about clothing. "I think people have accepted by now that I would start to visit, now that the Moontouched Queen has taken up residence and can invite me in herself."

"I mostly was referring to the fact that I promised her I wouldn't bring the rest of my family or the public in before it was ready. But I said nothing about you, so I don't feel too bad about that."

She paused in front of the gate to wait for her guards' nod of permission, which they gave with scarcely maintained professionalism, with little they could do about the light in their eyes as they rested on the pair of us.

Kor and Yvera had handpicked the members of her currently small but formidable guard from a pool of volunteers among my own elites, and they had clearly chosen well. Open-minded Alvi and warmhearted Yervik were just the two I would have wanted to witness this moment.

"King Koriben," Alvi greeted. "Welcome to the Wing of Ice. You are cleared to enter."

Yervik couldn't help a mischievous addition. "With the Queen's permission, of course."

Sarah, seemingly sensing she was among friends, paused thoughtfully. "Hmm. I don't know.... He takes up a lot of space, after all, and it's not like I have much room...."

"Sarah," I said in mock protest while the guards finally broke into laughter.

Inside, I was more than amused. I was becoming intoxicated with this new, confident side of her. Much more of this, and I might accidentally propose in front of everyone, and then I *knew* I would have pushed my luck too far and wouldn't like the answer I'd get.

"I *suppose* I'll let you in," she said with a wide grin up at me. "Seeing as I don't have anyone else to cook me dinner."

I smiled crookedly. "I'm so glad to be of *some* use to you."

She laughed as she waved to the guards with her free hand and led me inside.

"I'm impressed," I said, looking around at the central court. Because Kor wasn't there, I could be sincere.

"It's nice, isn't it? My suite is even nicer, since they apparently furnished it first."

"Makes sense that Kor would have them prioritize that first. Just...in case."

In case Kor was ever suddenly successful in convincing me to let her back in. I was coming to learn that he had made a lot of quiet preparations like that for her return, including making the preliminary arrangements for her guard and staff and ordering the beginnings of her wardrobe. Yet more things I would owe him for from now until forever.

"That's what I figured," Sarah said easily. If her thoughts had turned as sober as mine had, she didn't show it.

She glanced at me and asked, "How was your review?"

I sighed. "Good, if...painful."

"In what way?" she asked quietly.

I grimaced. "We...didn't just lose Avva at the Battle of the Solstice."

Though today there were no gaps left in the ranks of the assembled members of the Warflight, the lesser numbers and tribute the speaker had paid to them made their absences still stark.

"How many?" Sarah asked quietly.

Too many.

"Not as many as we might have if it hadn't been for you," I said with a tight smile. "Only perhaps an eighth of the Warflight."

Still, it was the most devastating loss we had ever received at one time since the First Invasion. On the other hand, that loss was *nothing* compared to the devastation of the First Invasion, which our historians estimated had taken over half the draká's warriors and a quarter of their civilians. And that was just from the battle itself, to say nothing of the numbers they had lost to disease, famine, and sacrifice to make the first sungate to Earth.

Yet Sarah's face fell, and her echo of my words was a whisper. "An eighth...."

"You prevented it from being far more," I repeated, quietly yet insistently. "The surge of energy you gave them to heal and carry on came at a critical point that saved hundreds of lives, Sarah."

That gift—coming at the risk of her own safety, along with her brave speech and willingness to risk the battle alongside us to begin with—had won her the loyalty of the Warflight at large. Even their subset of the Traditionalist faction had been the least resistant of the whole to the idea of her return.

"I'm glad," she said, not meeting my eyes. "But in the moment, I was mostly thinking about you. That's why I did it, you know. I suddenly understood that you would die, and I...."

Her eyes blinked rapidly.

My chest tightened in an excruciating mix of warmth and pain and fear. I had guessed that was why she had left the protection of the Temple of Flame and its shields, as soon as I had seen her bright star in the sky—no, as soon as I had felt her strength pour into me. That guess, after all, was one reason I had locked her out. I couldn't bear the thought that *she* had nearly died to save me, too. Much less that she might try something like that again.

The thought that she still could was agony to me now. Only the Tree's promise and my subsequent blood oaths were keeping me grounded, making me face my pain and fear instead of flinching away as I always had before.

She looked up at me, eyes glistening. "Does that make me a monster?"

Even though I didn't understand at first what she meant, I wanted to answer with an immediate and emphatic negative, no matter what. But I knew that wouldn't comfort her, wouldn't help me understand her.

Instead, I asked softly, "What does?"

"That I was only thinking of you. That I only found the strength to do the impossible because of you. When if I had only done it before...instead of standing around like a stupid, useless *symbol....*"

I stilled and brought her to a halt. I was grateful for her sake that there was currently no one in the central court of this sparsely populated wing now.

With astonishing equanimity and firmness, I said slowly, "Sarah, Avva's death was *not* your fault."

The tears were flowing down her cheeks now. "I failed him, Ben. I failed you, I failed him—"

"Absolutely not," I said flatly as I kneeled and put my hands on her shoulders. "Sarah...."

I swallowed and forced myself to say the truth I had always known but never let myself see.

"There was, perhaps, no way we could have won that night without Avva's sacrifice. Not in any meaningful way. Not while still having enough left to survive the after."

"Ben, *I* was supposed to be the difference. Not him."

"Not just you. Never just you. All of us."

"What do you mean?" she whispered brokenly.

"The Tree of Ice said you had to return after your investment to help the King of Flame, remember? And so, you did. You helped him in the moment his people—in the moment that *I*—needed you most, doing for them and for me what he could not do. Then, after you saved me, I saved you. Then he saved us all. All of us—all three of us and everyone else that gave their lives or survived that night—were needed to ensure that something worth living for was left when it was over."

She stared at me for a long moment, face tight with pain, tears still pouring down. I brushed some of those tears with the back of one hand, then left my hand to cup her face. I wanted to pull her in, but some instinct kept me holding her at arm's reach, where she could look at my face and into my eyes.

She swallowed thickly. "How can you be so accepting? How can you *forgive* me?"

I smiled thinly. "The answer to the latter is quite easy: because there's nothing for me to forgive. You never failed either of us, Sarah. And if you could ask Avva that question now, I *know* he would say the same thing."

A smile flicked over her lips as briefly as a snowflake. "And the first question?"

My own smile, even as thin as it had been, faded as well. "I'm not. Not in my flameheart, not yet. But I still know what I know now. And...I can now start to face that knowledge...because of you."

"Me?" Sarah said wetly.

I brought my other hand up to the other side of her face. "You, my star. *You* were what *I* had to have left at the end, to make my life worth living. To give it meaning. I miss my father more than I can say—before this day, more than I thought I could bear. But if you had sacrificed yourself to give me him instead...well, my people might still have him as their King. But I don't think there would have been enough left of me to be their Heir. If that makes *me* a monster, well...I guess that's the way it has to be. Because that's the way it is."

"Then I guess that makes two of us," she said with a tremulous smile. "Two monsters."

"What a pair we make, then."

She laughed thickly and threw her arms around me, and I held her tight.

The thought of bringing the earrings out now occurred to me, but I dismissed it almost as quickly as it came. This moment was about loss and healing for both of us. Since I was doing everything I could now to make up for my botched courtship of her, I wanted that moment to be one of unadulterated joy.

Assuming...she was ready to accept one from me, of course. If not, well...all the better to wait.

So, I just held her until she pulled away to blow her nose with the handkerchief I offered.

"How many of these do you have?" she teased weakly.

"I restocked this morning," I said with mock sobriety. "You know, just in case. Since even I seem to be in the habit of crying lately."

I'd used one as soon as I'd gotten a relatively private moment after the review. Yvera had been shocked and concerned until I'd reassured her I *wasn't* dying and recovered within a few moments, as I'd promised I would.

"Now, come on," I said with a smile as I stood and put a hand at her back. "I haven't forgotten your main reason for letting me in, so let's get some food inside us, shall we?"

Yet another reason to delay offering an earring: I wouldn't want her decision influenced by an empty stomach.

"Oh, that sounds amazing," Sarah said, following me with relief. And to *my* relief, she wound her arm around mine again. "I can't tell you how much I've missed your cooking. We're doing a valiant job of it, but with everything we have to work with being so unfamiliar, we could use a few pointers from you."

I chuckled. "Well then, I'd better get started with you."

Chapter Twelve

STARS

Sarah

"Man, that was good," I sighed as I stood with difficulty. It was a shame this girdle didn't look adjustable. At least the apron I'd found had kept me from staining the soft, white silk.

"Oh, no you don't," Ben said, snatching the dishes I'd collected with a grin.

"You cooked!" I protested. "So I clean up. That's the deal."

"But you helped," Ben said easily, carrying the dishes to the huge sink.

I rolled my eyes. "Yes, I 'helped.' So much."

Ben had broken in my sparkling new kitchen with style, making twice as much food as we could eat in half the time it would have taken any less of an expert chef. Even though I didn't understand half of what he was talking about as he explained what he was doing, I was too happy to spoil the moment by slowing him down to elaborate. I mostly just tried to stay out of his way, mix the things he told me to mix, and chop the things he told me to chop (though he usually took over that bit eventually as well when he needed what I had before I could finish at my much slower pace).

"You did, though," Ben said with a chuckle. "So cleanup shouldn't all be on you, even under normal circumstances. But in these I called in a favor or two, and someone will come by to do the cleaning for us. *We* need to get going."

"What?" I asked in surprise. "Where?"

"You'll see." He chuckled, pulling his matching black dress coat out of the ether and slipping it on. He tugged at my apron. "You won't need that where we're going. But it will be cooler. Think you'll need a coat?"

"Most likely not," I said, pulling the apron off. "Not if that's the way you're going."

Although I was still baffled at where this could be.

"First off, let's see if we can activate that daygate of yours, shall we? Then I could bring you straight back here."

Without waiting for my reply, he strode out of the kitchen, and I trailed behind.

"The tricky part about this one," Ben said as I caught up, "is that we need to make it another one like mine—one that's only conditionally open. After researching how they did mine all those centuries ago, Kor came up with something that we could try."

"We?"

"Right, because that's the second tricky part. It's going to be *my* kind of gate, but we need it to imprint on you and your Heirs after you. If what Kor suggested doesn't work for that, I can always deactivate the gate once we get back, for your safety, and we can try something else another time."

We reached my reception room and the inactivated gate there, which Ben went to immediately with a businesslike air.

"How is this going to work?" I asked warily.

I remembered the last time I had seen him activate a gate all too well, particularly the part in which Ben had sliced his hand open to provide the necessary blood. Except he hadn't told me that all he had needed was a few drops, so when he'd brought out the knife, my mind had gone to his story about draká having to sacrifice their own lives to power the first gate, and he'd given me a momentary heart attack at the thought that he was about to do the same.

Ben looked at my expression and said soberly, "Now, I know this isn't going to be pleasant for you, Sarah, but, unfortunately, I think Kor is on to something when he says that the one who probably needs to contribute the blood this time is...you."

"*Me*?" I said with a blink.

Ben grimaced. "Yes. The magic needs to latch on to *you*, and only you—and your blood to come after you. I'll attempt to provide the power needed, but the blood...."

"Oh, I see," I said, nodding. "I suppose that makes sense."

"It does?" Ben said in surprise. "I mean, you're fine with that?"

I shrugged. "Well, I can't say I'm thrilled, but if I'd thought about it, I would have realized that it was only a matter of time before I needed to use my blood in some ritual or another. In fact, it's kind of surprising that this is the first time."

"You've only been among us for a month and a half," he reminded me. "And your power has had to grow during that time."

"Have I really?" I said with a sigh. "It feels like a lifetime already. Several lifetimes, actually."

"Tell me about it," Ben said with an echoing sigh.

I squared my shoulders. "Alright. What do I need to do?"

"You're *honestly* fine with this?" Ben asked dubiously.

"Well, yeah," I said. "Like I said. It makes sense. And it's healed after, right? No big deal."

"Right, it's just...*you* have always made a big deal about it before."

I sighed again. "That's because I was still getting used to the idea. Only a month and a half, remember? And because...well, it was *you* bleeding, Ben. For me. It's different in my head if I'm to bleed for me."

"Oh," Ben said, coloring a bit. "I guess...that makes sense."

With a flash of insight, I grinned. "And maybe explains why *you* are suddenly so reluctant to go through with this?"

"It's just a bit of blood," he retorted. But he seemed to be scolding himself, not me.

I just kept grinning as I came up to him. "Right. So, how do I do this?"

Ben grimaced, but he brought out his knife and handed it hilt first to me. "Just as you saw me do it before. Hold this in your left hand, use it to cut open your right—*not deeply*. Just enough to bleed, remember? Besides, you still need the use of your muscles to make the fist. Then hold your hand in the archway and repeat the words I give you. Meanwhile..."

He put his hands on either side of the arch, over the two clear gems there. "...I'll be like this, and hopefully that will be enough to make the magic take most of the power from me, not you."

I tried very hard not to think about the last time I had seen him stretch his arms to touch both sides of a gate like that. I reminded myself that this time, he was trying to *open* a gate. For me.

I stepped into the space remaining between him and the arch—and tried not to shiver at his coat brushing my back and his heat enveloping me even through the inches between us.

"Right here, like this?"

"Right," he said. "Remember: *not deep*. Or so help me, Sarah...."

I chuckled tensely as I held the blade over my right palm. For all the ceremonial dagger's beauty, I could already feel that it was razor sharp.

"I'll be careful, I promise."

I took a deep breath, and—trying very hard not to tense or flinch, more for Ben's sake than my own—I gently sliced a line across my palm, following one of the grooves that was already there.

The cut burned, but not as much as I'd expected it to. I didn't even have the urge to flinch. In fact, I stared in some fascination at the cool silver blood that pooled inside the slice. This was the first time I had seen more than a pinprick of it. I hadn't even seen the blood that had gone down the crystal for my registration. Then, I had mostly been looking away, as I had when donating blood before.

"Sarah," Ben said tensely, sounding far more uncomfortable than I felt. "Don't make yourself have to do this twice."

"Oh, right," I said sheepishly.

I held my hand inside the empty gate and allowed the blood to trickle in drops down the stone floor. Then I repeated the words that Ben silently gave me.

"By the power lent to me by the King of Flame, invested in him by the Tree of Flame, as the White Queen, I now invoke the First Covenant, and swear by my blood that I and my people shall uphold its terms for as long as the Flame Above and Below may give us Their light. Moreover, I ask that this gate belong only to me and to the White Monarchs after me, from this time forth and forever after."

The moment I clenched my fist, I felt a large drain of power. Still, that was nothing compared to what Ben felt. He gasped and buckled, nearly falling into me as his arms strained on either side to keep himself upright. Only just now, I realized how unideal a time it was for him to be exerting himself so much: if I was any judge of night and day now, it should have been sunset.

Before I could say anything, though, white flames with silver edges shot up from the floor of the arch and filled its entire space within a second. The flash of fire and heat made me instinctively recoil and stumble back into Ben.

He chuckled tiredly and pushed back from the arch, standing upright. "Well, that seems to have made a gate, at least. But just to be sure...."

He took my right hand in his own, turning the palm up.

The slice was gone, and so was any trace of blood.

He sighed. "Your hand is so cold, even more than usual. It worries me, even though I know it shouldn't."

That explained why his hand felt like it was burning hot—but in a good way. Only he could give me warmth that felt as good as warmth once did.

I laughed to hide how that warmth was spreading all over me at his touch and concern. "Yeah, if I ever start feeling hot to you, that's the point when I officially give you permission to panic."

He looked up from my hand to meet my eyes. "Let's pray that day never comes, shall we?"

Belatedly, I remembered the new fever...and how he might be thinking of me catching it, as I had the darkfever the day after I arrived.

"I'll be fine, Ben," I murmured. "The Tree wouldn't have told me to come and help you just to have me die from fever."

He flinched but sighed again and nodded. "I wouldn't put it past Her, if that was what was needed for the good of all, but in this case, I think you are right. I think She has other things in mind for you."

"Oh, really?" I said, curious more at the source of his conviction than dis-agreeing with him. "Like what?"

"Oh, other things," Ben said vaguely, looking away.

Back at the gate. Then back at me with a grin. "Well, do you want to try out this newest creation of ours?"

I looked back at the gate, the colors finally sinking in. "It's *white*."

"The flames are, yes," Ben said. Then he pointed. "But the gems…"

"…are gold," I finished in awe. "Just like all the others."

"And I can see it, just like all my gates. Can you feel it as if it's one of yours?"

"No," I said, shaking my head. "Not at all. No pull, nothing."

"Then, for lack of a better term for the moment, it really is a *day*gate," Ben mused. "And yet, unlike any daygate my people have ever made before."

Once again, we had created something new. Not something quite as symbol-ically significant as the crowngate, I thought, but still something miraculous. Something that was wholly *Ben's*, powered by his magic, his Tree, his ritual…yet given to me.

That made it more personally significant in my mind, and only the fact that the crowngate was the one that could take me back to my family and hold made the crowngate more precious. If only slightly.

"Time for the most important test," Ben said. "Is it a free gate, or a restricted one? And if restricted, is it yours to open?"

"How are we going to test that?"

He shrugged. "I'll go through and try to come back. Then you see if you have to let me back in."

"What will it feel like?"

"You'll know, don't worry. But it will feel something like a call scale does. Like someone you know is calling your name."

Then, before I could ask just *how* I was then supposed to let him back in, Ben strolled through the gate.

Dang it!

Before I could truly worry that he had stepped through a defective gate and was thrown into the nether regions of space and swiftly dying, I felt something.

Just as he said—it felt like someone was trying to get my attention, to ask me for something—and I *knew* that someone was Ben.

Just as instinctively, I gave him that indescribable thing he was asking for, with no more thought required than would have been necessary for me to open a physical door for him, and a moment later, he walked through, grinning from ear to ear at me.

"It worked, didn't it? I couldn't come through, not until I knocked and you let me in."

"Seems so," I said with intense relief. Mostly just because the gate had worked at all.

Ben was clearly excited for another reason, enough so that he pulled me up into a hug. "Sarah, I don't think you realize how incredible this is. Or how much relief it gives me. Now you have a sanctuary in *my* world that only you can access so easily."

"Oh," I said, blinking.

Well, when he put it like that....

He sat me down, still grinning. "Now all you need is access to a sun- or daygate, and you can come straight here, with no one the wiser. And no one else can use the gate without you letting them in. Not even me."

To me, that spelled *privacy*. To Ben, that spelled *safety*. Which, to me, were essentially the same thing.

I couldn't help teasing him. "Aren't you just the least bit concerned that you just gave me the key to one of your own gates?"

He smiled thinly. "Sarah, if you ever shut *me* out, then I'll have probably deserved it and then some."

I felt a chill, and my teasing smile faded. "Ben, that wasn't what I—"

"I know," he said, waving away my concern with a strengthening smile. "But it's true, nonetheless. You have every right to a space here that you can completely call your own, where I can only enter if you want me there."

"I'll always want you here," I said firmly.

His eyes warmed, and he chuckled as he put a hand on my shoulder. "Don't speak so hastily. If you stick with me, I'm sure I'll one day make you mad enough that you'll need your own space, at least for a bit. You've always needed your own space, to some extent."

That...was true. The fact that he had already seen and put into words what I was only just discovering as one of my basic needs made my eyes sting.

"That doesn't mean I don't want you in it, Ben. Right now, especially."

"I know," he said, smiling gently. "That just makes it a greater honor to be there."

Not knowing what else to do or say, I just hugged him, and he, seeming to understand, just held me.

"Now," he said after a few moments, stepping away to smile at me again.

Although he kept his hands on my shoulders, and man, was I grateful to the tailor of this jumpsuit for the direct skin-to-skin contact there.

"You ready to go?" he asked.

"I...guess?"

He was making me nervous. I was glad that sweaty palms were a thing of the past for me when he took my hand.

"Then lash us, please."

I did, winding my power around both of us, and particularly our joined hands. When I was done, I nodded to Ben.

Once again, the world around me only...shifted. As if *it* had moved, and not me. And then we were standing in front of a different daygate, except this one was unlit, banked for the night.

"Man, that's so much nicer with you," I said with a sigh of gratitude.

"Happy to be of service, ma'am," Ben said with a wink.

"Where are we?" I asked curiously, looking around. This wasn't the kind of place I had expected him to take me. It was small and dark, for one thing, with the only light coming from the top of the stairs circling the round, narrow space.

"You'll see," Ben said, beginning to lead me to the stairs. He paused abruptly on the first step. "Oh, er, I suppose this is a bit late to ask, but...are you afraid of heights?"

"Ben," I said in amusement. "You had me ride on your back, repeatedly, while you flew hundreds of feet above the ground as a dragon, and you never once asked me that question."

"Right, sorry," he said, flush apparent even in the darkness as my eyes adjusted. "But I still know that this might be different from riding on my back, secure in a saddle and everything. So...are you?"

"No more than the average person."

Perhaps even less, now that I had come fully into my power—though he didn't know that yet, and I was still waiting for the right moment to show him.

Showing him was really the only way to tell him.

"Well, good," he said, relief in his voice, even though his flush was still creeping. "But, er, if you ever get uncomfortable at any point, just let me know, and I can surge us away, immediately."

"Will do. Now, let's see whatever there is to be seen here."

I began climbing the stairs, tugging Ben along with me. His nerves had brushed away my own.

We emerged onto a circular landing that was open to the air. The sky was a breathtaking blend of the faintest pink and gold in the distance and a darkening blue, with a few of the brightest stars visible even now. Even if Ben hadn't already hinted that we would be up high, I would have known that from the complete lack of anything else visible from the center of the landing but sky.

Still holding Ben's hand, I walked to the stone barrier that ran along the rim of the space and cautiously peered out and down.

We were in a tower that protruded out of the highest peak in a range of desert mountains. The tan, craggy slopes had the appearance of mud dumped over wrinkles in a scrunched bedsheet and left to crack and toughen into hide. Even without a single plant or creature to be seen in that alien landscape, it was breathtakingly beautiful. There was something about all those thousands of folds and cracks, laid bare, with never an end of shapes and lines for the eye to follow. Especially now, with the last light of the sun fading and plunging us into a world of indigo and starlight above and baked rock beneath.

"This is the Crownspire," Ben said quietly, clenching my hand. "As you might have guessed, Crownhold is below all of that."

He gestured out at the mountainous desert expanse.

"Ben," I breathed, at a loss for words.

I felt the significance of the timing just as much as the view. I was reminded of the first time my power started waking, when Ben and I stood and watched the moonrise in front of the one window in my hold as the sun faded on the other side of the mountain. That was the moment Ben explained to me how his heart was a literal fire and had brought my hands to his chest to feel the warmth of it—and to feel how it weakened with the passing of the sunlight.

All to give me context for how afraid he was for me that, instead of fading as he was, I was increasing...and, in the severity of my waking power, growing cold as ice with it.

I hadn't ever had so strong of a reaction again. My temperature was much more stable now from day to night, and my skin didn't start glowing at the slightest surge of emotion just because the sun went down. Still, from that moment on, I had never been the same.

Nor had been my relationship with Ben.

"Are you...comfortable right now?" I asked, looking up at him. "With the sun gone?"

Being so high, out in the open like this....

Though he hadn't told me so in as many words, I had gathered that my drakón felt a kind of existential dread at the departure of the sun, and now with my own life force so closely tied to the diurnal cycle, I understood why.

He smiled slightly as he looked back down at me. "Sarah, I don't need a sun when I have my star."

My iceheart thudded, and I looked away quickly.

"Speaking of stars," he said more casually. He pointed. "Do you see that bright one there? The one that's at the tip of that line, and then the triangle?"

He traced the shapes as he spoke of them.

"Yes," I said, a curious lift to my voice.

"The whole thing is called Korrien's Spear, named after the first Sunfilled King. Who was born human."

"Really?" I said, gaping at him.

"Really," Ben said, grinning. "He was one of the seven humans who swore the Second Covenant and became the first drakón, creating our race, the dramá. His counterpart, the draká who swore with him, became his Heir. Back then, they ruled much more like equals, to fully represent the interests of both their races. When the two races truly became one, the Royal roles became more like they are now, like with..."

He swallowed and took a deep breath before continuing. "...Avva and me."

He cleared his throat. "Anyway, after Korrien, things worked out for a time, but after only a few generations...the lines between drakón and amón hardened again. Maybe if the drakón had never forgotten who truly had held the Crown and the key to their salvation in the beginning, the Moontouched never would have had to leave."

"Ben," I said heavily.

"Let me finish, Sarah," he said with a smile, giving my hand a squeeze. "It was the humans who left everything behind to save the draká, to change for them, to help them become something new. The draká, as large and dangerous as they were, would have died out without them. Just as I and so many more of my people would have died without you."

I swallowed at the sudden turn.

Ben pointed at the constellation again. "That's called *Korrien's* Spear for a reason. Because according to legend, that tip, that star...is Sekinek."

I inhaled sharply, eyes fixed on that point of light against the darkening sky. "You mean...*my* sun?"

"The sun you were born under, yes," Ben answered quietly. "The sun you gave up...because of me."

I met his eyes. "Not *just* because of you, Ben."

He looked back at the stars. "True, but even for the part that wasn't for me, I'll always be in your debt. You were—and still are—what my people need to survive...and what I need for life to be worth living. I tried for too many days

and nights to convince myself otherwise because I thought I couldn't bear
the pain if anything happened to you, as something was likely to if I let you
try to help me as you were meant to. But by depriving myself of my star, by
ignoring the place you were meant to have in my life, I became something
far worse than the Queen who let Lady Serona die."

"Ben—"

"I did, Sarah," Ben said implacably, looking back down at me. His
eyes were dark. "I'm not trying to apologize again. I'm simply stating
the facts: I was becoming...something that should never have a crown, let
alone be trusted with the power I have been given. If I had not woken up
and changed course after the Tree gave me Her warning, She would have
revoked my birthright and given it to another."

I inhaled again. "She...said that?"

"Yes."

Ben paused a moment and took a deep breath. "Perhaps I shouldn't have
brought up that last bit now. I'm not saying you have to.... I'm saying that
I think I've learned my lesson. So, you can do whatever you want to, Sarah.
Go wherever you want to, be...with whoever you want to be with. Return
to Earth if you think that is best. But if what you want is to be with me...for
the rest of our lives, and beyond...then that is what I want too."

He smiled thinly. "As you've already heard, I've sworn to never push you
away again."

I blinked at him through the tears stinging my eyes. I smiled tremulously.
"Does...that mean I'm allowed to tell you I love you now?"

"Flame, yes," Ben said immediately and emphatically. "I am doing my
torched best not to fall over from fear that you'll reject me right now, and
that would help quite a lot."

I laughed wetly. "I love you."

What an exquisite relief it was to finally say those words and know he
would accept them.

"Oh, *gosh*, how I love you, my sun," I said.

He scooped me up and crushed my cold lips to his burning ones, my wet cheeks brushing against his prickly jaw.

And so fire and ice melded into one.

Chapter Thirteen

EARRINGS

Koriben

WHEN WE FINALLY HAD to part for air, Sarah teased, *Did you just not have time to shave this morning?*

What? I said dazedly, blinking at her. Then I noticed the redness on her cheeks, and my flameheart thudded in horror. *Oh, so sorry. I didn't even think about that when I decided.... Did that hurt, just now?*

I set her down hastily and kneeled in front of her, tracing the tips of my fingers over her raw, cold skin and sending healing energy into her.

I groaned. "Sarah, I am so—"

"Don't you dare," she said breathlessly, grinning. "I'll...take another kiss like that...anytime."

She seemed to mean it. Her eyes were still burning with soulflare, and she looked about ready to duck in again for another round even as I finished healing.

Then her smile faded as my words must have sunk in. "Wait...decided.... Ben, are you not...."

I smiled thinly as I lowered my hands. "I'll mourn Avva until the day I pass through the Flame to rejoin him. But, given that kind of timeline, it seemed a bit pointless to continue making a show of it. Especially since...I know now that's not what Avva wants."

I flushed. "Although, I didn't think about you.... I can shave again, if you prefer."

Traditions be torched again. I might as well break all the rules that weren't rules.

"No!" Sarah said quickly.

"Are you sure?" I asked. "I remember most Earthren men I saw shaved, so if that really looks better to you, and makes you more comfortable...."

She laughed. "I never really thought I'd go for a guy with a beard, I'll admit, but on you, it looks...right. *This* clean-shaven nonsense—"

She cupped my cheeks in her hands with a grin. "—looked *wrong*. But I wasn't going to say anything because, you know, mourning."

I blinked at her. "You...*like* me with a beard?"

"Yup," she said appreciatively, brushing her thumbs over my skin. "Especially the way you trimmed it, kept it from getting bushy, you know? Although, I have to admit, the next best thing is this stubble you have going on. You have *no* idea how attractive it is right now. The only downside is the scratchiness, or I'd keep you this way forever."

"Right," I said, forcing my face to be stern and not show how my flameheart was roaring right now from her words or the look in her eyes. "Sarah, there's no way I'm going to risk doing that to you again every time I kiss you."

And I was going to want to kiss her *a lot*.

She sighed regretfully. "I figured you'd say that. So, my vote is that you keep growing it out until it's not scratchy."

I finally allowed myself a sigh of relief. "Oh, good. Because shaving every day was a *pain*."

Quite literally. Having been so out of practice, it took me days to get to the point where I didn't cut myself or irritate my skin.

Sarah smiled crookedly. "How do you think I felt, shaving elsewhere? Well...that is, before...."

"You stopped, didn't you?" I said, holding up her arm in both of my hands and noticing for the first time that the soft hairs that had been there before...were gone.

"Is that normal?" Sarah asked. "It happened to all of us—well, all of us that changed, that is. Me, Dad, Michael, David, Laura.... Rachel was beside herself with glee when we figured it out."

She would, I thought with an inner eye roll. But I kept my face calm for Sarah as I let go of her arm.

"Yes, that's normal upon becoming, at least for us. All drakón stop growing hair anywhere but on their heads. It's a sign, just as the color of the hair we have left, of what we gave up, what we gained, and what we owe our people and our Tree because of who we are now."

I smiled. "Plus, it might look rather strange to have hair in all those different colors all over us. The Tree didn't want us to look like beasts."

Sarah chuckled, then held up my own arm. "So *that's* why you never had hair here. Or...."

Her eyes darted to my chest and then away, her cool cheeks increasing in temperature by a few degrees.

"Yes," I said, smiling a bit more broadly. "That's why."

My smile faded. I couldn't believe I was going to bring up my leftwing at a time like this, but for the sake of fully explaining things to her....

"That's also why Kor *can't* grow facial hair. It's a further extension of that transformation. Because, traditionally, Kings have always grown a beard as a token of their...lingering humanity, so to speak. As a mixed symbol of both Kingship and solidarity with the amón."

"Ah, I see," Sarah said, with a casualness that eased the tightness in my flameheart. "And so, the Tolsyon heir isn't allowed to appear kingly."

"Right." I smiled. "The male ones, at least."

"Well, then, I guess that makes sense why I like you with a beard," she said with a returning smile.

I chuckled. "I still would have shaved it for you if that's what you wanted."

She pressed her lips to mine—briefly, careful not to move too much to avoid brushing my stubble. I forced myself to hold still until she pulled away.

"That's terribly sweet of you, sweeter than I deserve. But no. You do what you want, Ben. Clean-shaven or bearded, I'll take you."

My flameheart *burned* to hear her say that, even so casually.

I cleared my throat. "Since you brought that up, perhaps we should clarify something."

I switched the knee I was kneeling on but stayed down, because that's what made the most sense logistically for this next part. Then I brought out the black box that Kor had given me and handed it to Sarah.

Even with all she had done and told me so far, my flameheart still pounded as she grew still, took it from me, and opened it.

"Earrings," she said quietly. Then looked up at me solemnly.

Belatedly, I realized she might not know what that meant. "That, er, means—that is—"

She smiled gently. "I know what it means, Ben. And my answer, as before, is yes."

I swallowed. "Yes, as in...."

Just so we were on the same page.

She laughed quietly. "Yes, I'll marry you."

I froze, flameheart still for one eternal moment.

"Oh, good," I choked out finally. "That's...um...what I hoped you'd say."

"I should think so," she said with another laugh, throwing her arms around me and kissing me again.

Flame help me, I couldn't help but move to respond, but I pulled away as soon as the scratching of my skin against hers registered in my torched brain again.

"Hellwinds," I swore. "Sorry, Sarah."

This was going to be a rough few days. For us both.

"I'm fine, Ben," she chuckled, staying close and brushing her nose against mine. "So, what happens now? Do I put mine in, or do you?"

"Oh," I said, clearing my throat and letting her go. "Er, I do that. For you. And then you do mine."

As I took the box from her to pull out the smaller, silver earring, she fingered her earlobe regretfully. "Unfortunately, I think my piercings healed over at some point. Is that going to be a problem?"

"Wait, your what?"

"Oh, sorry," she said quickly upon seeing my baffled expression. "Earrings don't mean anything like that to Earthren—at least in my culture. Traditionally, girls have them most often, so my lobes were pierced when I was a baby."

"A baby?" I said in consternation. "Your parents did that to you? Before you had a *choice*?"

I had thought better of them.

She raised an eyebrow at me. "It's a Hispanic thing, and Grandmother insisted. It was Mom and Dad's compromise with her, which they started with Rachel, for not letting us be baptized as infants."

The term she had used to refer to her grandmother, *Abuela*, had a different flavor to it than the words she normally spoke in her tongue.

"Besides," Sarah went on. "Your parents pricked your finger on a needle to collect a bloodline full of personal details from you while you were a baby, without *your* choice. Then shared those personal details with the public, I'm sure."

"Well," I said awkwardly. "It wasn't like there was much of a secret there to begin with."

It would have caused a lot more trouble for me if they'd kept it private, since people would assume they were hiding something. My very birth, after a century of waiting, had been unexpected enough.

But I saw what she was saying, even before she sighed and pressed on.

"The point being, Ben, that both these things are cultural differences between us that are neither good nor bad. They simply *are*. I got piercings, no matter when, because that's just a thing that's done where I'm from, and I wore earrings frequently there because that's *normal* for girls to do. It meant absolutely nothing about my relationship status. We used rings for that."

"Rings? Like, finger rings?" I said, holding up my right hand. Where I now wore the golden seal of the Monarch: a three-pronged crown circling a tree with flames for leaves.

Sarah's eyes fell on the ring and sobered as she recognized it. "That was...."

I swallowed. "Avva's, yes."

The signet ring didn't even need to be refitted—it had slipped onto the middle finger of my right hand and stayed there perfectly, ever since Eskala took it from Avva's hand and placed it on mine just before his pyre was lit.

"Kor's wearing a ring now, too," Sarah murmured, eyes distant.

I tried not to let the fact that she'd noticed that detail bother me.

"Yes, because for us, rings mean *authority*. This is the signet ring of the Golden Monarch. Kor is wearing a ring now similar to the one Eskala had: the ring of the leftwing."

He'd required a new one entirely, of course.

"And Yvera is wearing Alyish's."

Which had needed refitting. Extensive refitting, in fact, but Yvera insisted that it be *his* ring. He was her great-grandfather.

"Knowing Kor," I said dryly, "I'm certain he has something in the works for you now. If only in the design stage."

"I can't take a ring from *Kor*," Sarah said, alarmed.

"What? Why—"

Oh. Right. Because taking a *ring* from him was like....

I gritted my teeth. "Well, there's an easy way around that. We just tell him to stop whatever he has going on and tell Eskala to handle it. With the help of *your* leftwing, if you'd like."

"Oh, that'll work," Sarah said with relief. "Sorry, I know it's silly, that it doesn't mean the same thing here...."

"It's not silly if it means something to you," I said firmly.

Particularly *that* kind of thing with *Kor*.

I groaned and stood. "Sorry, my knees need a break."

"Don't be sorry," Sarah said with a smile. "I'm not sure why you were still kneeling, anyway."

"Because how else are you going to reach my ear?" I said with a crooked smile.

"Oh, is that why?" she asked sheepishly. "I guess you have a point. Would you rather we sat on the ground, then? Or went somewhere more comfortable?"

"I like the idea of doing it out here, if you don't mind," I said, rubbing my neck.

This was where she had finally said yes. Also, I was expecting that if we had gone back down without the earrings in place, that meant she had rejected them.

"I don't," she said with a smile. "I like that too."

"Then sitting is probably a good idea," I said in relief.

I sat down cross-legged on the stone floor, and Sarah sat in the same way across from me, with her knees nearly touching mine. She would probably have to get up at some point to do my ear anyway, but hers was in easy enough reach for me now.

"How is this going to work if my ears are healed?" she asked, fingering her earlobe again.

I noticed that whoever had done her hair again had pulled it back nicely from her ears, just as before. Though this morning's efforts had been for the archivists' sake, to show them we had respected the law by not doing this before we had the results from her bloodline in hand.

"That doesn't matter," I said dismissively. "I would have had to make a new piercing anyway, because that's the whole point."

"What?" Sarah said, blinking.

I grimaced, realizing that whatever she had been told about earrings, this part hadn't been explained to her. "The earring needs to pierce you, become part of you, and take at least a drop of your blood. That's part of the binding ritual."

She blinked again. "Binding.... This is a *ritual*?"

Fortunately, she simply appeared surprised, not alarmed or disgusted.

"A very simple one," I said, cheeks growing hot. Then forced myself to be more honest. "Although powerful, all the same. It's like a blood oath, except not as...compulsive. It won't force you to do anything, because that defeats the point. But it signifies your choice—and *who* you've chosen—before the Tree and the Realms."

I took a deep breath, forcing myself to say the most significant thing, no matter if it made her reconsider. "And it does...change you, in a way."

"In what way?" Sarah asked. Still, her eyes were just curious. Sober, but not repulsed.

"It...especially the second time, at the heartbinding...it makes the two people of one blood."

Realizing how that could be misinterpreted, I grew even hotter and stammered. "I mean, partner blood, not...kin blood."

"I got what you meant by that," Sarah said with a chuckle. "So that's why you all call it that—a heartbinding? Because you symbolically share blood?"

"Not symbolically," I corrected hesitantly. "It's literal. In a way I don't really know how to explain, because we don't even understand it ourselves. I'm sorry."

"Alright, just tell me the details you know, then. Will my blood change color? Become a mix of gold or silver, for example?"

Her calm, and her use of the future tense *will*, gave me further hope.

"No, not like that," I said, chuckling in relief. "Although, if someone takes a blood registration *after* a heartbinding, the archivists have ways to detect the spouse's blood."

"Really?"

"Really," I said ruefully. "It's not usually visual to the naked eye, but something is there. That's why we think it's somehow literal. It doesn't overtake who a person is, what they had before. But it does...add to it in some way."

"Huh," Sarah mused. "Just like a relationship normally does."

"I...guess?"

As long as she seemed to understand the consequences, if she wanted to think of it in that way, I saw nothing wrong with that.

"Anything else I should know?" Sarah asked curiously.

I thought long and hard for a moment. "I...don't think so? I think the rest should be universal. A heartbinding is legally binding, things shared in common, complete and lifelong fidelity expected, all that stuff. Sound familiar to you?"

"Yes," she said firmly. "That's what I want and am offering."

"Good," I said, growing hot.

But that made one last thing occur to me. The darkest, heaviest thing.

I sighed. "Separation...is still possible with just a betrothal. Without *as much* difficulty, anyway. But after the heartbinding, it becomes...very difficult."

"I trust you on that," she said quietly. "And since I have absolutely no intention of separation, we can leave it at that."

"Are you sure?" I said heavily. "I want you to know everything—"

Sarah took my hand and looked into my eyes, her own wide, earnest, and clear. "I think I know all I need to about that, Ben. So, thank you. But I am sure."

"If you're sure...that's all I can think of."

"Alright then," she said with a firm nod, pulling her hair back even further. "Go ahead."

I blinked. Then my flameheart rose. "You're still...."

Sarah chuckled. "Ben, I didn't change my mind just because of a few extra details. You're worth more to me than that. You're worth everything."

I could have died content, right then and there...but then I would have died without giving Sarah my earring, and I couldn't have that.

Wordlessly, I took off the earring's cap, sanitized the tip with a drop of magic for good measure, and pressed the needle-sharp tip into my left pointer finger.

At Sarah's inhale, I explained, "First, it needs a drop of *my* blood."

That was what made it *mine* to give, after all. That was what made the previously dun and clear gem blossom with my soulcolor.

When the gold light had finished spreading through the whole gem, I reached forward, eyes still asking for permission. She gave it by turning her head toward me, showing the ear I had been reaching for: her left.

She shivered as I touched her earlobe, but when I hesitated, she chuckled. "Do you remember, a lifetime ago? When we first met, and you painted my ears with your blood to get me to understand you?"

"I remember," I said quietly as I leaned forward again.

"Your explanation to get me to let you probably took even longer than this last one did to let you give me an earring. Even though this time is much more significant."

"A language barrier will do that," I said, smiling humorlessly as I positioned the cushion behind her earlobe and the piercing earring—with the silver metal now stained with my blood—in front.

"Trust, too," she said. "The biggest difference now is that I trust you...and love you."

Flame, I didn't think I would ever get used to her saying those words. It made me ashamed that somehow, despite everything I felt for her, would do for her, I still couldn't seem to say them as easily as she did.

So far, she hadn't seemed bothered by that fact. Perhaps she understood it was the subtext to everything else I said and did. If not, somehow I would have to find the way to explain that to her, before she was hurt or doubted.

I took a deep breath. "Are you ready?"

"Yes," she said calmly.

Ever my valiant one, my *sera*.

"This will sting. I can't numb it for this. I'm so sorry."

She snorted. "Stop apologizing, Ben."

"So—" I cut myself off and sighed. "Here goes."

Sarah didn't even flinch.

I quickly set the cushion aside, screwed the cap over the needle, and sanitized the wound.

"I can't heal it more than making it clean," I said anxiously. "I'm so—argh, that's just the way it has to be. It has to heal on its own. And for you, that might take longer than for me."

I could hold back the healing from myself for a time, but there was little point to that, since the moment I lost concentration, my body would take my magic to heal me anyway.

"Or not," Sarah said easily, turning back to face me. "Seeing as you seem to heal me whether or not you think about it."

I blinked, then brightened. "True. As long as I'm not consciously trying, that's probably fine."

Sarah laughed and picked up the box. "So now I do that for you?"

"Yup. Now you get to stab *me*," I teased. "It's only fair."

Sarah rolled her eyes. "I'm not looking forward to that part, believe it or not. Just...start walking me through it, alright?"

So I did, explaining each step to her as she went through them. Sarah stared in awe as the clear gem set into the gold earring took to her soulcolor and flared a brilliant white, and then she fussed more than I did over the placement of the piercing over my left earlobe, trying to get it centered just so.

That made me anxious that I hadn't taken more care with hers. Oh, well, if she was going to be mad at me, I'd just have to find some way to make it up to her, because there was no taking it out and doing it over again, not unless she wanted to break the magic of what we were doing. Somehow, I didn't think she wanted to put us through that soulrending just for aesthetics.

There was a reason I'd wanted *Sarah* and not her sister.

I'll admit it: *I* flinched at that sting. Sarah's first tentative stab didn't help matters, making her have to press again before she broke all the way through.

"Sorry, sorry, sorry," Sarah babbled as she hovered over me. "What should I do? Does it still hurt?"

"It's fine, it's fine," I soothed her. "The sting's fading already. Just screw on the cap now."

I reached up and held the cap in her direction without moving my head. I'd titled my head much further to the side than she had to keep my hair from spilling over the area.

"How should I clean it?" she fussed as she screwed on the cap.

"No need. I'm drakón, remember? Any contamination that might have collected since I first sanitized the earrings, my blood would be killing it right now. I think the wound is almost healed, in fact."

"Oh, good," she breathed, brushing my hair aside to examine my earlobe even as I raised my head.

"It's fine, Sarah," I told her gently.

"It looks fine," she said, as if to herself. "It looks fine."

Her cool cheeks heated a few degrees, the temperature difference all the starker to my heatsense with her this close.

"What?" I asked curiously.

"Nothing," she said with a nervous chuckle, her fingers lingering in my hair. "It's just...it looks more than fine. That...that's *mine*, isn't it? My power, my blood. In *your* ear."

I understood what she meant now. I felt a flustered mix of awe and pleasure, and yes, even triumph, as I reached up and touched her own ear, which now had *my* gold soulcolor resting in it, gleaming bright and strong for all the world to see.

I pulled her into my lap and kissed her, trying not to let the possessive edge to my thoughts leak into the kiss or my embrace but probably failing. Still, she didn't seem to mind, because she clung to me in much the same way.

I thought my flameheart could burst with that one thought, that one word. *Mine.*

Chapter Fourteen

FLIGHT

Sarah

Ben abruptly broke off from me in a gasp. "Sarah!"

"What?" I said in a bewildered daze.

Then I realized *what*.

I was glowing. All over. My hair, my skin, my nails, and surely my eyes were all taking on a white, glowing sheen. And wisps of light like cold steam were trailing behind me, ready to take shape as soon as I focused enough.

Well, so much for no longer glowing at every major emotional spike. Although, in my defense, that had been quite a spike. I'd unconsciously begun bunching Ben's shirt in my hands again, tugging at his coat....

"Ah, dang it," I sighed. "This wasn't how I was planning on telling you."

"Telling me *what*?" Ben said, holding me back so he could look me up and down—but also holding me tight, as if afraid I was about to disappear.

He wasn't too far off, actually.

I smiled thinly. "I haven't let this past month go to waste. I've been...practicing. And I've discovered at least something of what *I'm* meant to be."

"Be...."

"You can become a draká. I...can become this."

"What...is this?" Ben said, his voice and face now awed.

I scooted off his lap and stood back so that he could appreciate the full effect, which was amplified by the white silk I was wearing. Good thing the cloth was thicker than it looked...and had *pants*. That would be important for the next part.

"I don't know what, exactly. We're calling this our lightform."

"We?" Ben said faintly, staring me up and down. I knew how he felt. This much radiance wasn't a sight for the faint of heart. The first time I saw Rachel manage it....

"My family and me. The changed ones, at least. The six of us. We all can do this now, to varying degrees. Some are brighter than others, though. Just like all drakón can become dragons, but of different sizes, I guess. But only Rachel and I can manage what comes after that."

"What?" Ben asked, staring into my eyes.

"You saw it for yourself," I said gently. "We call it the starform."

Technically, I had discovered both forms that night of the battle, when I followed my newly awakened instincts against all reason to try to save him. But Ben had probably been too far away and preoccupied fighting for his life to have seen the first.

"Star...." Ben said numbly, then swallowed. "When you became a star."

I nodded.

He inhaled. "You've managed to do that *again*?"

"Briefly," I said with a grimace. "Not nearly as long as the first time. Rachel has only managed a second or two. I think it's like your Royal half-form, for us. Except, it's at the end of the progression, so flipped for us. This half-form, the lightform, is what's easy to maintain once we get it going. What all six of us can do. And the end form, the starform, is what's hard, what only Rachel and I can do."

Ben just sat back and shook his head in wonder. "Sarah...I...I can't even describe...."

I smiled slowly. "How do you think I felt the first time I saw you as a draká?"

He laughed weakly. "You *ran* from me. Like I was your worst nightmare."

"Alright, good point," I said with a wince. "The *second* time, then. When I knew you weren't going to eat me. When I knew it was *you*. I think I felt just about what you look like you're feeling now."

Weak at the knees, almost dizzy with awe...and longing.

I could see that longing in his eyes now, clear as day.

He stood haltingly and hesitated with each step forward, as if he hardly dared approach.

"It's alright," I said quietly, holding my hand out. "It won't hurt you."

At least...I was seventy-five percent sure it wouldn't. The light hadn't hurt any of the rest of my unchanged family who had dared to touch us while we glowed like off-gassing fluorescent lightbulbs.

Ben slowly, carefully took my offered hand.

At his shudder, I grew alarmed and tried pulling away, but he held on tightly and said, "No, it's fine! It's just...Flame, it's like when you're giving me power, but *stronger*. I...I can't tell you how it feels."

Strange. None of my family had had that reaction. Of course, none of them were children of Flame...or had the connection with me that I had with Ben.

"Good?" I asked hesitantly.

"Good," Ben rasped, his eyes burning when they met mine. He gripped my hand tightly. "Very, very good. Flame, Sarah.... If I hadn't already proposed to you, I would have now. And if you'd said no, I probably would have asked again, anyway. I wouldn't have been able to help myself."

Oh. Well. That...made me hot all over. As hot as I ever got nowadays, anyway.

I brushed my hair behind my shoulder, unable to meet his eyes. "That's not even all I have to show you right now."

"What else could there *be*?" Ben said in bewilderment.

"That same night, I discovered something else I can do in this form. Though it took me a while to master all the applications."

I was still working on those, actually, but I wasn't about to make him anxious for me for what I was about to do by telling him that.

"What?"

I smiled. "You and I have something in common now. Now...I can fly."

Sort of. Like I said, I was still working on the *flying* aspect. But it was the application of my new surging ability that I was most eager to show him, so I was getting a little ahead of myself.

The look on Ben's face made it worth the risk, though—and worth every minute of strained practice to *hold* my shape instead of becoming a silver blur and *appearing* at my intended destination.

And in creating the wings.

I took a step back, letting go of his hand, and then I focused on the glowing effusions wisping off all parts of me but especially at my back.

I didn't know if this was what the magic I had been given was intended to do, but if not, then in wanting it so badly, I had *made* it that way. After all, there was no one around to tell me the rules—so I could make them myself. And yet, I had a few hints that I hadn't made these up.

At my call, the light coalesced at my back to burst out again into wings, each as long as I was tall. Wings in the roughest sense, since the light particles didn't stay in place and only vaguely formed featherlike shapes as they moved. But they were still unmistakably avian *wings*.

All...six of them.

Yes, not just one set, but three, all originating from a center point in my back so that they had to emerge and move at angles to avoid each other, with only the middle set coming out straight.

That excess had been entirely unintentional on my part and was one reason I suspected something else besides me had a hand in their formation. No matter how hard I tried, I could never produce just *one* pair. It was always all three pairs or nothing. Unlike with the rest of the changed members of my family: the four non-Royals could only produce one set and Rachel two.

Ben stared, frozen. "Wings. You...have wings."

They reflexively fluttered in my self-consciousness. That they responded to my emotions and instincts just like real limbs, and that I felt *some* ghostly sensation from them, was the second reason I felt like there was something more to their existence than mere wishing.

"Yeah, I know," I said sheepishly. "It's a bit much. Especially *six*."

It felt like I was showing off. Which...I guess I was, but not in *that* way. I would have been perfectly happy showing Ben just one, reasonable pair of wings. That was all most creatures needed, right? Except some bugs, I guess....

Now there was a lovely thought. Michael already teasingly called Rachel *dragonfly*. He'd restrained from giving me a nickname perhaps out of pity for my previously miserable state but also likely out of a lack of imagination.

"Sarah," Ben said. His eyes flashed, and his tone was almost angry. "They're *magnificent*."

My iceheart lifted. "You like them?"

"*Like*...." Ben shook his head. "I don't even.... Sarah, will you marry me?"

I burst into relieved laughter. "Ben, I already said yes."

In fact, I should have shown him this *before* I'd trapped him into an engagement—just so he knew what he was getting into. That's what I'd been intending to do before he sprung the question sooner than I had been expecting, and noble intentions had gone out the window with the rest of my senses. Fortunately for us both, any concerns about his continued willingness were apparently needless.

"Right," he said dazedly. "I knew that. Just making sure."

"The wings are mostly for show, I think," I said ruefully. "It's not like they're that practical, and I don't even need to bring them out to do this."

I looked at a space behind Ben and, as instinctively as taking a step forward, I surged there in a white-and-silver blur.

I turned in time to see Ben spinning in alarm, then gasping when he caught sight of me again. "Sarah! Don't *do* that to me!"

"Oops, sorry," I said sheepishly. I'd meant to surprise him, not give him a heart attack, but I should have known that's what would have happened.

"What did you *do*?"

"I surged, Ben. Except I don't have to surge to just a gate anymore. I can surge to...anywhere, basically."

Before I could clarify, he gasped, "*Anywhere*?"

"Anywhere I can currently *see*," I added hastily. "It's how I got through the Temple shields and into the sky to begin with, just before I entered starform. I just looked into the sky and...*willed* myself to be there. And once I got there, I just...floated."

I surged into the air to show him. When I resolidified not a second later, I was hovering with my feet dangling about ten feet above the center of the spire landing. Ben inhaled sharply and reached for me reflexively, but I could see him realize almost as soon as he did so that I *wasn't falling*.

I just...floated there, my wings flapping leisurely. Again, the wings weren't necessary. I had done this without them. But their presence and motion somehow helped my brain process and accept more easily the impossible thing I was doing by floating in midair. Especially in the beginning, they had given my screaming primal brain something to *do* besides flailing my limbs (which had only made Michael and David laugh uproariously at me).

Perhaps that was the whole point of the wings, in the end: to provide some *reason* other than the vaguest explanation of "magic." Minds needed some kind of anchor in the known to venture into the unknown.

Even when logically knowing that magic really *was* the only explanation in the end.

Ben's jaw dropped as his hands gradually lowered, and for once, he gazed *up* at me.

"You...you can just *stay* there?" he breathed.

"Yes," I said quietly.

Dragonfly wasn't *that* bad of a nickname, considering how we could just hover like this. Albeit more still than an insect could ever manage.

"For how *long*?"

I shrugged. "For as long as I can keep this form up. While I'm in lightform, I actually have to *focus* to stay on the ground, to move around as normal. My instincts keep telling me to just...go. Fly."

In the sense of surging. But I was working on slowing down the surging to where it *looked* and *felt* like flight. That was the trickiest part, the one I was still working on, because it went against the grain. It was slowing down what should be instantaneous, making hard what should be nearly effortless. I still wasn't sure it was a worthwhile endeavor, but I *wanted* to so badly, I was making it possible.

All in the subconscious hope—which I'd buried so deep over this past month of practice that I hadn't let myself think about it or put it into words—that one day, if Ben let me in again, we could do this together.

I had had far too many dreams about this moment.

I lowered myself back down to the ground, then approached Ben shyly.

"Ben," I said tentatively. "If I gave you enough power, do you think you could manage half-form right now?"

He stared at me.

"Sarah, you've been giving me power since the moment you started this." He waved at me vaguely. "I could manage *anything* right now, even draká-form."

"Oh, good," I said with relief. "That would probably be easier for you, wouldn't it?"

"Yes...." he said hesitantly. "But what do you have in mind?"

I took a deep breath. Then smiled up at him. "I want to try flying with you."

He blinked. "You want to *what*?"

"You fly in your way. I fly in mine. Together."

"Sarah, I...." He looked anxiously out at the desert, and his jaw clenched. "If you fell...."

"I won't fall," I said with perfect confidence. "As long as I'm in lightform, falling simply isn't possible."

"And how long can you maintain lightform?" Ben demanded.

"At least most of the night now."

I had been practicing, extending it as long as I could with each subsequent night. Just last night, I'd managed it for hours as I paced in my guest rooms, just to have something to do and to burn off energy as I waited for dawn and sleep to come.

Once I started getting tired, and definitely when dawn approached, the glow would dim, and I would know it was time to fix my feet firmly to the ground, but I wasn't going to mention that to Ben right now. Besides, Ben would need to go to bed himself long before then.

"Sarah...."

"It's perfectly safe, Ben. Just let me show you."

I took his hand and began tugging him to the edge of the landing. He followed the first few steps, perhaps without thinking, because as soon as understanding dawned, he dug in his heels and clenched my hand tightly, grabbing my arm with his other hand as well for good measure.

"Oh, no. No, you don't. No way in *hellwinds* am I letting you just walk off the *Crownspire*."

I sighed. "Ben, I'm telling you one more time that it's *safe*, that I'll be *fine*, that I can *do this*."

That would be his last warning before I took matters into my own hands.

Predictably, his jaw just clenched, and his eyes burned. "Sarah, it's not that I doubt how miraculous you are. I just can't let you *do* that. Not before...."

He trailed off as I started to grin. His eyes widened in horror, and he gripped me tighter.

In vain.

"Sarah, don't you dare—"

"Catch me," I said with a wink.

And I surged out of his grip and into the desert sky. Hundreds of feet away.

"SARAH!"

I turned in place to see Ben sprinting across the landing, changing and growing as he went, so that by the time he vaulted over the stone barrier, he only had a second or two to plummet—my iceheart pounding all the while—before his mighty wings came out and beat the air, and he was the giant golden dragon I knew and loved.

Who fixed me with his furious, golden serpentine eye as he flew to me.

Hellfrost, Sarah! he shouted at me with his inner voice, accompanied by an enormous, bestial snarl from his throat and smoke from his maw. *You swore to never do that to me again! You gave me your* oath.

It took me a moment to remember what oath he was referring to. Then I felt sheepish. As he circled me, I turned in place to keep his head in sight.

I did explain, I said. *Like I promised. It's not my fault you wouldn't listen. I* listened, *and I said* no. *Not until we tested this extensively* first.

I spread my hands in demonstration. *But I have* tested this, *Ben. What do you think my family and I have been* doing *for a month?*

Other than learning how to survive on our own, that is. But for all we knew, this could have been a part of doing just that.

But not in my Realms! What if the strength you felt before had to do with you being in your own, or near your gates, or...I don't know, anything! Anything could go wrong right now, Sarah. And if it did....

Well, I said with a shrug. *I guess we're testing it now.*

Then I surged another few hundred feet away again.

Sarah, he growled as he twisted in midair, spotted me, and came after me. *So help me, if you fall....*

Solemnly, I said, *Ben, I swear to you now that the* moment *I feel myself weaken, I will surge straight to you or to the ground, whichever is safest. But right now, I* am *fine.*

More than fine. Even despite his anger with me, or perhaps partly because of it, my iceheart was pulsing with an intoxicating thrill. This was more than the fulfillment of a dream. I felt light, buoyant, *powerful* in a way that the weight of my emotions had never let me feel over this past month of grim, dutiful practice. I was doing the same thing I had always done, and yet never had it been like this before. It was as if I had always drilled under a steady downpour before, and now the clouds had come out and I was playing in the sunshine.

I knew what the difference was. He had always been my sun.

With him, I felt like I could do anything.

Even if...right now he would much rather I didn't.

You'll surge straight *to me?* he demanded as he began circling me again. *You swear?*

Subconsciously, he was pulling me to him even now, trying to yank me inside his great heart, where, in his mind, I would finally be safe. But I could resist him, and I knew his words meant that the reality of how little he could do to stop me was finally sinking in.

The moment I feel myself weaken, I said soberly, carefully concealing the childish glee I was feeling at finally getting my wish.

Fine! We'll fly around for a few dek, if that's what will make you happy, and then you're coming straight back inside with me. Understood?

Understood.

Follow me, he grumbled, banking away. *We want to stay around Crownhold, and you don't know where the limits are.*

That was more than fine with me. I wasn't about to ruin this perfect night by endangering our lives. This flying thing not counting in that regard, obviously.

Jubilantly, I tested the fullest extent of my practiced "slow" surging to soar after him.

I still blurred, and glowed even brighter, but something recognizable as me zipped to and around Ben like an excited bee. I felt a bit like one of my helping lights as they greeted me. Ben, unused to such a thing, slowed in his flight and tried to track me by turning his great neck this way and that, but when I saw how that might cause trouble for his balance, I stopped spinning around him and flew level with his head.

I still slipped up sometimes and pulsed ahead instead of flowing in a continuous stream, but I was still "flying" far better than I had ever managed before.

Sarah, is that still you? Ben asked as he eyed me, his incredulous tone the only insight I had into what he was feeling. I wasn't a great reader of draconic expressions yet.

Still me, I reassured him. *Just like you're still you.*

Right, it's just you're so....

Awe was now tinging his voice again, so I didn't worry about his unfinished statement.

It took me a while to get used to you, too, I teased, lazily flipping onto my back as I flew next to him. Just because I could.

His response was dry. *Even now, I doubt I take your breath away in a good way.*

Actually...the best way.

I flew a wide circle over and under him, then another around him, examining him from every angle in a way I had never had the luxury to do before. His glistening wings; his ridge of spine spikes; his powerfully built yet lean, almost feline form; his crown of spiraling horns around his head....

You have three now, I said in surprise as I hovered over them. Then hastily clarified. *Horns, I mean. Three horns on each side.*

He used to have only two on each, for a total of four. I was positive.

Yes, he said softly. *Because now I'm the King of Flame.*

Just as I...had six wings, three for each side...because I was the Queen of Ice.

I had noticed that all the other dragons I had seen had only one set of horns, whereas Ben had had two, but I hadn't put the realization into words before this. Of course, I never saw his father as a dragon, either.

I'm sorry, I murmured.

You didn't know.

But I should have. If I'd been thinking, as I normally did, rather than being so drunk with the evening, the flight, and him, I would have figured out the reason for myself.

Oh, come on, Ben said, his voice still muted, but it was lighter now. *Don't get gloomy on me now. I was just getting used to this new side of you. I kind of like it.*

You do, do you?

I spun around his head a few times to tease him.

I do, he said, voice sobering as I came back to level with his eye. Which alone was as big as my torso, and I could see my glowing reflection in it.

In fact, I more than like it, he said, his inner voice a whisper. *I love it. I love you*—all *of you, my star.*

This form, especially as strongly as I was holding it now, wasn't very human, or even very solid. It didn't have a need for the basic reflexes of swallowing or crying. But that was what I would have done, had I been more human in that moment. As it was, my iceheart pulsed rapidly to hear him finally say those words when he knew I could hear them. I knew how difficult they were for him, and that made the gift of them priceless.

I reached out with what remained of my corporal arm and touched his scaled face. *And I love you, my sun.*

Chapter Fifteen

SIGN

Koriben

When Sarah said she was ready to go back, we both landed on one of the mountain peaks. I changed into amáform, and she let go of her lightform.

As I walked toward her, I was both relieved and disappointed to see her body solidify and her glow dim to nothing, restoring her to the Sarah I had known before.

On the one hand, I was almost weak with relief to have her back on solid ground and in a normal state.

On the other, she had been so…glorious. Something completely beyond my woefully inadequate ability to describe. I hated how little I had been able to convey to her what she had looked like, what she had done to me. I was fervently glad to see her gold-gem earring again as proof that I hadn't just hallucinated her acceptance of me.

She was *mine*. All of her. Every aspect of that magnificent being was mine. Or…soon would be. And couldn't be soon enough.

For so many reasons now.

I walked to her as quickly as I could without looking worried, eager to get her out of the open now that we were grounded—even though I was probably just being paranoid. Crownhold had a nauseating number of protections against darkrifts and consumed of all types, so the risk to Sarah, even on the ground, was minimal. Otherwise, I wouldn't have even brought her out into the open on the Crownspire, let alone flown with her like that.

Not that there was a whole lot I could have done to *stop* her, seeing as she could now surge out of reach, but if there had been a real risk to either of us, she *probably* would have listened to reason.

I hoped.

I held out my hand for hers as soon as she met me halfway, and she took it.

"Lash us, please."

She nodded firmly, seeming to understand the reason for my brisk attitude. "Lashed."

Immediately, I surged us straight to the daygate in her suite.

When we appeared in her reception room, I let out a breath of relief, and not just for being out of the open after nightfall. Here, at least, Sarah could only get so high off the ground before hitting the ceiling.

"How are you feeling?" I asked hesitantly, looking down at her.

"Tired," she said with a shrug. "The floating part is effortless, just a part of existing that way. So, I was never in danger of falling, like I told you. The constant surging, though.... That took something out of me."

I frowned. "Not to mention giving me all that power."

"I didn't give you anything directly, Ben," she said, eyes clear and earnest. "Whatever you got was a simple result of me *existing* that way."

"Really?" I asked, relieved and troubled, the latter simply because of all the unknowns. Every day with her felt like forging into unfamiliar territory, tonight being only the latest example—although perhaps one of the most spectacular.

She shrugged. "You just get passive energy from the sun, don't you?"

"I suppose," I mused.

Mindful of how tired we both were now, I led her to a couch and collapsed, and she snuggled delightfully close to me.

I put my arm around her. "I guess you weren't giving me energy directly in starform, were you?"

"Not consciously, no. I didn't know where you were, exactly."

"You gave it to *everyone*, then. Did you know that?"

"That's what Tyri said."

I shook my head. "Sarah, every time, you change everything. You just *flew*, and I just flew with you, *at night,* simply because you were glowing like a star next to me the entire time."

I smirked at her. It was time for a bit of payback. "You realize that probably everyone in Crownhold who is awake right now is talking about that, right?"

Her silver eyes went wide. "What?"

Maybe I should have tried that tack to begin with. Then maybe she would have come back right away.

"Sarah, we have lookouts. You may not have seen them, but they were there. I had a hellwind of a time explaining things to all of them *while* trying to keep an eye on you."

Which generally went something along the lines of, *Everything is fine, no need for alarm, the Queen is just stretching her wings....*

All six of them.

"Oh," she said numbly, her face frozen with horror.

I felt better now...but also guilty for doing this to her at the same time.

I clenched her hand. "You didn't show them much more than you already have at the battle, and no more than they would have inevitably found out soon enough. The most important thing right now is that you're safe."

I took her head in both hands and leaned in. "But don't you *dare* scare me like that again."

She came out of her shock at being a public spectacle to raise an eyebrow. "Were you really going to believe me any other way?"

I gritted my teeth. "You could have spared me the heart attack with a *few* more tests."

"I was going to—"

I let her go and leaned back. "That didn't involve stepping off the *Crownspire*. For Flame's sake, Sarah. That thing is eld high!"

She sighed. "Alright, maybe that was a bad first test, and maybe I *shouldn't* have given you a heart attack. I got excited and impatient. Sorry."

She got excited and impatient so seldom—my sober, thoughtful Sarah. I felt the guilt increase at deflating her like this. That flight, and the timing of it, had clearly *meant* something to her, something special.

"Agh, Sarah," I said, running a hand through my hair. "I'm...well, I won't say I'm sorry, because you *did* give me a torched heart attack. But...like I said. It's done, you're safe, you've proved your point, and...I'm glad we did it. That was probably the most fun I've had in...well, you can guess how long. And it clearly meant something to you. So...good."

She smiled tremulously. "So happy to give you both fear and fun in one night, your majesty."

Oh, you gave me far more than that, I thought, my eyes resting briefly on my earring in her ear. But I wasn't quite ready to get confessional again.

So, instead, I said, "Why do you keep calling me that?"

Though I could understand the two words individually, the intent of their combination didn't translate well, remaining hard for me to decipher.

Her tremulous smile strengthened into a smirk. "Because it doesn't mean anything to you, and I think that's funny."

"Agh, you...." I said, unable to come up with what to say next. So, I did the only logical thing and kissed her.

Once again forgetting about my scratchy face until the brushing sensation registered in my dimtorch brain and I tried pulling away. "Ah, torch it, sorry, Sar—"

She pressed in again, saying silently, *You can heal me later.*

She had other plans right now, and those became apparent when she pushed me back against the couch and shifted over me, her hands going to my coat, tugging.

I was immediately immersed in one of the hardest battles of my entire life. Harder even than the one I had fought when I realized how I was falling for her and had used all my reasoning, my care and concern for her as a friend, my duty as an Heir, and my reverence for my Tree to try to resist the pull of her gravity—and promptly lost all the same. But somehow, this time, I *had* to win.

For her.

Sarah, I tried desperately, barely even able to form the thought. That was not a promising beginning.

But it gained a surprising victory, because it made Sarah hesitate, then pull back. "Don't you...want to?" she asked, examining me.

Hellwinds, yes, I thought.

I swallowed. "Yes, yes, I do. Every bit as much as you, and probably more. But I *can't,* Sarah. I can't do that to you. Not like this, not yet."

I had known that nearly from the moment I had woken up and started running to save her. I had known then that I had lost any grace I might otherwise have had in this kind of situation. I had to do things *properly* for her, by every single letter in the book, or not at all.

The Tree hadn't told me that much. That, I had resolved on my own. This was *my* way to both do what the Tree had told me to do and do it in the way my conscience could sanction. In the way that was best for Sarah.

She blinked. Then got off me and sat back on her heels on the couch next to me. Her cool cheeks heated. Her eyes ducked, her shoulders hunched. "Oh. Sorry. I hadn't realized.... I thought that at least engaged people could...."

I took a deep breath, praying for stability...and the strength to not pull her back in, now with the *added* temptation of erasing that agonizing disappointment and embarrassment from her face.

"No, they—they often do. You're not wrong. About us—dramá. In general. But this is.... Argh, Sarah, this is just what I *have* to do."

Please don't ask why. Please.

In my head, I justified my secrecy about what the Tree had told me to do because I really *did* want to marry her for all the right reasons: I loved her—Flame, how I loved her—and knew I would want no one else to be by my side, forever. But if I told her the entirety of the Tree's commands, then she might find it impossible to understand that I was doing this *only* because I loved her.

Maybe, if I'd had a lifetime to soothe her feelings and bring her around, to court her *properly,* I might have found the courage to take that noblest of routes of complete transparency about everything.

But I didn't have a lifetime.

The Tree had given me one month to keep up my end of the bargain.

One.

And I wasn't about to risk the torched miracle of Sarah's willingness to, first, forgive me for shutting her out, and then, second, take my earring *after just one night*. Not by telling her everything now.

I *would* tell her. I'd kneel at her feet and explain and grovel from now until eternity—*again*.

After she had let me save her.

In that case, I knew what I had to do now to spare her as much hurt as possible then. To prove to her as much as was mortally possible that I did it all for her.

She raised her eyes finally to meet mine again, some of the heat leaving her face as she examined me, trying to understand.

I gulped, hoping she would see enough. But not too much.

"Is this a permission thing again?" she asked. "In case that wasn't clear, Ben, that was me giving you permission."

Gah, this would not be easy. But I held her future pain and reproof like a molten hot rod inside of me, scalding my unruly side into submission.

"I think even I understood that part, but thanks for the clarification. But no, that's not it. This is...about me, trying to do things the right way. For me, and especially for you."

She cocked her head. I was relieved to see that the more time passed, the more she seemed to just be puzzling me out instead of being hurt. "Is this against your religious code?"

"Not...specifically," I said uncomfortably. I was treading on dangerous ground here. "Fidelity *is* important to the Tree, though. She doesn't approve of us doing...that...unless we are committed. Fully."

"That makes sense to me. But isn't that what this is?" Sarah said, touching her earlobe.

And that was the thin crust I'd been trying to avoid. But I supposed I was the one who had led us right onto it.

"Yes, to some people.... But, Sarah...." I groaned. "After all I've done to you...it's not enough. Not to me."

She blinked. "Ben. You swore a *blood oath*."

"To not push you away *physically*. But what if I figured out some way to do it emotionally again, like the first time?"

I was just wildly throwing out excuses at this point, hoping one would stick, but apparently that one did, because Sarah's eyes grew heavy.

"Oh," she said quietly.

"Sarah, I have *no* intention of doing so," I said quickly. "I'm not even sure I can."

She was too much a part of the air I needed to breathe now—and her pain, while so visible in front of me, was too much for me to endure.

Which was part of the temptation right now.

I swallowed. "But I need some kind of sign between us that I will give *everything* to you. *After* I've promised everything to you, with the Tree and Realms as my witness. This...is that sign, I guess. I won't do that to you. Not before I've sworn everything to you."

She smiled thinly and shook her head. "I guess, knowing you...that makes sense."

"Does it?" I asked, blinking.

Was...that a good or a bad thing?

She chuckled wryly, and to my intense relief, she scooted back to and curled up against me, if this time with her knees to her chest. She ducked under my arm when I raised it and put it around her, and she laid her head trustingly on my chest.

"Yes. I knew what I was getting into when I fell in love with someone as noble as you."

So...good? Sort of?

Probably both good and bad.

I sighed and held her close, kissing the top of her head. "Sarah, trust me, I *want* to. Badly. But that's the entire torched problem. I want it too much. I'm terrified of hurting you because of that."

"I get it," she said, peace entering her voice. "This is what you need to do to make things right in your head, so I can wait. I wouldn't have you any other way than the way you are. Until then...this is enough."

"Oh," I said, overwhelmed by her goodness for a moment. "Well...thank you. For putting up with the way I am, that is."

"You're welcome. Besides," she said teasingly, "how long can it take to plan a heartbinding?"

I stilled.

"Well," I said guiltily, drawing out the word. "Now that you mention it...."

She craned her neck to look up at me.

"Ben," she said in a warning tone. "That was supposed to be a joke. What's the problem *now*?"

I sighed heavily. "If I had my way, we'd go to the Tree at first light. But...Kor is convinced that we need a grand tour first."

He'd spent a good portion of my morning presenting me with all the arguments, pretty much single-handedly retying all the knots in my muscles that had loosened from the bath. We'd been arguing about it right up until Sarah answered her door.

She blinked. "So *that's* what everyone kept hinting about? They all expected us to get engaged and then immediately go on this tour?"

"Probably," I muttered. I didn't know who else had hinted as much to her, but I knew that's what had been behind Yvera's impatient exclamation in front of Sarah before my rightwing had marched away to get ready for the review.

Sarah sighed. "What *is* a grand tour?"

"It's a trip the Monarch takes to visit all the capitals of the Realms. Usually after first being crowned or...becoming betrothed."

Sarah smiled crookedly as she began to see. "And you just did both."

"Right," I said dryly. "Which means I'm doomed by tradition to go now—and, with you *being* my betrothed, so are you. For that matter, you also just became a Monarch. Though the Six Realms aren't yours, this is as good a way to formally introduce you to all of them as any."

I took a deep breath and forced myself to say the words. Avoiding them now wouldn't make a difference in the end. "And...give you a chance to help as best you can along the way."

Her smile faded. "My Tree. Telling me to go and *travel* with you. To aid you."

"Right," I said heavily. "I'd say sorry, but I sure hope you had at least some idea of what you were getting into when you agreed to come with me, let alone marry me."

She grimaced. "You're right. It makes sense. We need to be out there, helping people. Them first, heartbinding second."

She sighed. "It had been nice to dream for a moment, though."

It had been. Even if my dreaming had been early this morning, before Kor had gotten to me. I'd wanted to strangle him by the time he'd convinced me of how logical the tour was, but it would take so much *time*....

Over half the twenty-seven days I had left—at least.

But no one would know that except me. So, at the risk of Sarah's life, I had to do my duty to my people first...and pray that the Tree had already factored that duty into Her deadline.

We became silent for a bit, each of us presumably lost in our sober thoughts at our impending duties. Hopefully hers didn't have the crushing edge of existential pressure that mine did, though.

Eventually, she looked up at me again. "You probably ought to be getting to bed soon, shouldn't you?"

It was as if her words had cast a spell, and suddenly I felt a tremendous weight of exhaustion sinking into me: from this day, as incredible as much of it had been, but also of the lingering burnout that I still hadn't had enough time to recover from.

Still, I grumbled like a hatchling and held her more tightly. "It's not fair. I only got half a day with you."

But even that was generous, considering I'd neglected nearly all my other duties to "settle in the Queen of Ice." Although, considering how urgent a task it had been for the sake of all our Realms to get her betrothed to me, I could argue that this had, in fact, been the most important thing I could have been doing with my day. That was no doubt how Kor had justified clearing my schedule for her—with no knowledge of Tree injunctions and deadlines.

"I'm feeling tired enough right now that I *might* be able to sleep," Sarah said, looking hopeful. "Then maybe I can get up earlier."

I looked at her sadly. "I hate to say it, but this tour is...not going to be good for your sleep schedule. I'll do my best to make them accommodate you, but I advise sleeping in while you can, just in case. Hopefully we'll have more time to spend together after...all this."

She smiled. "Because, obviously, we're not going to see each other on this grand tour we're going on together."

"Not as much as we'd like." I sighed. "Definitely not as much *alone* time as we'd like."

Although...maybe that lack was going to be a Flamesend, if this evening's temptations were just a taste of what was coming.

Sarah pulled away from me with an echoing sigh. "Well, go on. Get to bed and get some sleep."

"One more thing, first," I said, happy to have a legitimate excuse to linger a few dek longer. "I have something for you."

I pulled it out and proffered the small object to her.

She stared at it, then blinked rapidly, eyes glistening. "One of your scales."

"Of the same first set, as promised," I said quietly. "Primed and ready for you."

I had done *one* productive thing with my morning, at least. This business of using Kor as our messenger had to stop, as soon as possible.

"Thank you," she said thickly, taking it and then throwing her arms around me. "I know it's silly—"

"Alright," I said. "Let's agree on something. *I* try to stop apologizing excessively, and *you* try to stop thinking the way you feel about things is silly. Agreed?"

I had no idea *why* getting a twelve-summer scale from me meant so much to her, but I knew by now that it did from how emotional she had been about it the last time, and how reluctant she had been to give the first one up to the Tree of Ice. Just because I didn't understand didn't mean she should minimize the way she felt—especially when it came to the way she felt about me.

"Agreed," she said with a wet laugh as she pulled away. "Although I have a feeling we're going to have to keep reminding each other of that."

"That's what we're here for. And now, while we're on the subject of scales, here's your final present of the night."

"Another one—" she began in surprise, but then she stared as I held the much larger gold scale out to her. "Ben, thank you. But...why do I need two call scales from you?"

"This one isn't mine," I said softly.

She took the scale and looked between me and it in confusion. She must not have been seeing the difference in shape and color. The variations were slight, but they were there.

I took a deep breath. "This was...Avva's. The one he gave to me. And the one you first spoke to him on."

Her eyes widened and met mine. Then filled again. "Then why are you giving this to *me*?"

I smiled wanly. "Because something told me you might like it, to remember him by. Am I wrong?"

She shook her head and wiped her cheeks. "No," she said with a sniff. "You're not wrong. But Ben. He was your father...."

"As such, I have many other things to remember him by. You don't. Since I'm the one who kept you two apart for too long...I figured this was appropriate."

"Ben," Sarah said with a thick laugh. "You just said you would stop apologizing."

"This isn't an apology," I hedged. "It's...restoring balance to the universe."

She sighed and smiled at me. "Will it make you feel better if I take it?"

"Yes," I said earnestly as I handed her a handkerchief.

"Then I suppose I will, for *your* sake."

But I saw the way her fingers curled around the scale. I had just given her something she would treasure, and that made the sacrifice more than worth it.

A DEKEN OR SO later, I lay in bed, staring at my ceiling. As exhausted as I was, my mind kept spinning with the events of the day...and thinking about how nice it would be if Sarah were there now, for lots of reasons. My selfish side kicked myself for not letting her be.

Maybe it was time for some more dreamhaze....

Just then, I felt her calling me and shot upright. I pulled the paired scale out of the ether and tapped the glowing surface to answer it.

As soon as her face appeared on its surface, I said urgently, "What is it?"

"Nothing!" she said quickly. "Oh, are you...."

Her eyes darted to my rumpled hair and down to my bare shoulders, and no doubt took in the darkness of the room.

"I am so sorry," she said hastily, her cheeks darkening. "I was trying to catch you before you fell asleep."

I blinked blearily at her. "I wasn't asleep. Yet. So, what is it?"

She darkened further. "Alright, now I feel sill—"

"Sarah," I said sternly.

She sighed. "I just called...to make sure it worked...and to tell you I loved you again."

My flameheart burned in a way that really wasn't conducive to sleep.

I smiled thinly. With difficulty, but because she seemed to need it, I said, "I love you too, my star."

She smiled at me, her silver eyes glowing. My flameheart kept pulsing right along.

"I...should probably let you get back to trying to sleep now, shouldn't I?"

I hesitated. "If...I'm going to get *any* sleep tonight...then probably, yes."

"Right. Then...love you."

Her face faded, and the scale became just a scale. I thumped back onto the bed with a groan, convinced I was done for the night.

But strangely enough, I fell asleep not a few dek later.

With the scale that was connected to hers still in my hand.

Chapter Sixteen

BEGINNING

Sarah

Preparations to leave began as soon as I got up.

Well, knowing Kor, they probably had discreetly begun as soon as Ben let me back in, and began in open earnest as soon as Kor got word that Ben and I were officially engaged. I surmised as much as soon as I saw Kor come into my sitting room (where I was hiding from the bustle of my staff's hurried preparations to leave; considering how I had just moved in yesterday, and with hardly anything of my own, I thought it remarkable that so much work was required to move me).

Kor looked about as exhausted as a drakón ever did, what with their healing energy usually preventing shadows from forming beneath their eyes; still, his hair and clothes were untidy, and his eyelids and shoulders drooped.

The first words I said to him were, "Did you get *any* sleep last night?"

"Did *you*?" Kor retorted with his best attempt at his normal smirk.

I hesitated.

It had been a restless night. After calling Ben, I had killed an hour by testing out my new "TV" to call my family after it occurred to me that I had several updates for them of some significance. I made the ice on the other end appear in the kitchen, which I thought would be a more casual setting for them all to gather to than the meeting hall, and gather there they did once I caught Lizzy passing by and asked her to spread the word.

To my surprise, none of them appeared shocked that I was now engaged to Ben, let alone after only a day of being back with him in the Six Realms. Otherwise, their reactions were just what I would have expected. Abby clapped her hands and danced around in excitement, smugly telling all of us that she'd known it all along; the twins looked bored and just continued their poking war; Lizzy gave a troubled smile; David grinned and congratulated me; Rachel rolled her eyes as if to say, *well, duh*; Michael scowled but remained silent; Laura looked hard and disapproving; Mom gave much the same smile as Lizzy, if with a bit more forced cheer; and Dad gave his unreadable smile and simple congratulations.

He was the one to direct the conversation after that and ask me for the details—thankfully, only about what was coming next, letting me leave my night with Ben private. I didn't have much to share in that regard other than Ben and I would have to go on the tour first. Still, Mom was relieved to hear that we weren't eloping (at least not the next morning), and I did my best to assure her that we would do everything possible to make sure whoever wanted to could attend the ceremony safely.

After the call, I'd had little else to do but wander around. I'd even gone into the central court to practice surging, determined to build up my stamina for it even more now that I could fly with Ben. And, you know, for practical, life-saving reasons. Yup.

So much for going to bed early. Despite my exhaustion from surging more consistently than I'd ever had, for hours I simply couldn't let myself settle after the day and night I'd had. Besides, I was half afraid that if I went to sleep, I'd wake up without an earring. Even when I finally crawled into bed, every time I would wake and then start with alarm, I'd reach up to touch it just to make sure it was still there.

I finally answered Kor, "Not as much as I should have."

"Then that makes two of us," Kor said. "Three if you count Yvera. Probably only Ben got a good night's sleep last night."

"He did?" I asked, surprised and pleased.

Kor rolled his eyes. "Probably just from sheer exhaustion. He's...not let himself sleep much recently."

I sighed.

"Alright, enough doom and gloom," Kor said, crossing the last few steps to me with a grin. "Let me see it."

Knowing what he meant from where his gaze had gone, I turned my head to show off the earring, grinning even as my cheeks heated. Fortunately, my stylist this morning had styled my hair back again, and I was seeing why that trend had begun yesterday and would probably continue throughout the tour.

"Very good," Kor said clinically, fingers brushing my earlobe. I felt a bit of his power sink into my skin to examine the piercing. "It's already healed nicely—probably Ben's unconscious doing, I'm guessing?"

"Must be," I said with a shrug. "He didn't do it on purpose, as hard as that was for him."

And if there was one thing our separation over this past month had definitively proven, it was that my quick healing came from Ben, and Ben alone. Neither I nor anyone in my family had independently developed that ability, and I guessed we never would.

"And somehow Ben managed to get the placement of it right," Kor said. "Good enough, anyway."

"I think it's just fine," I retorted.

"You would, because you're biased right now. But as your friend, I'll be glad on your behalf that you won't have to give him grief about it in a year from now."

"*You're* just glad that it won't bother your OCD," I said with a smirk.

"My what?" he said in amusement.

"Er, perfectionism, sort of."

"Well, true enough, then."

"Ah, Kor," Vadya said hurriedly as she came out from my room. I had never seen the mischievous young woman in such a frazzled state as she had been this late morning. I gathered that, given their desire or perhaps even orders from Ben not to disturb me, I was probably one of the last of the travel party to begin preparations, and she was hurrying to catch up.

"Good, you're finally here," she said, then grabbed her cousin by the arm and whisked him away, leaving me alone again.

I was happy to be excluded from the whirlwind, but I hated feeling idle. So, with a sigh, I went to my study and called Dad to check in again. He was making some good progress with the grammar and dictionary that Kor had given him, which he was pleased about, and he had already had a brief conversation with Kor this morning about tour and wedding details, which made him more informed than I was.

"He said you were going to the Peacegrowth Realm first," Dad said when my cluelessness became apparent. His lips pressed into a thin line. "The one where this 'brightfever' is the most prevalent."

"Ah," I said.

That made sense to me from both an urgency and a traditional standpoint. Ykran was the last Realm the dramá had settled and thus came last in their symbolic hierarchy. The unintended consequences of having a hierarchy at all was one reason I thought the Tree of Ice had sent me there when sending me to the Six Realms, and it was the reason I had insisted we search for moongates in reverse order. Now, perhaps it was traditional to start a grand tour with Ykran, or Kor was using the same reasoning, or Ykran was simply where Ben and I were needed most.

I could understand why that would worry Dad.

"That means they need us there," I said gently.

"I know," he said with a small sigh. "But do you have any idea of how you can help? We aren't healers, like they are...."

"Not yet," I said with a grimace. "I'm just going to follow my instincts and trust the Tree again. She's the one who told me to help Ben's people, after all."

"Yes," Dad said, face and tone expressionless.

I could guess what was behind it. Miraculous dream or not, Dad was the most intellectual of all of us. I was surprised that he had always refrained from expressing doubts about the Tree and Her intentions, at least to me. Even though he had, without hesitation, thrown away everything to move our family to my hold and go with me to Greenland, I guessed that was probably more from simply accepting what was necessary for us to survive the danger I had brought on us all after my return and acting before it was too late.

He, of all of us, saw what needed to be done the most clearly and did it, regardless of how he felt. That didn't mean he didn't *feel*.

Now, especially, when things were more settled, the rest of his family was safe, and the odds of our long-term survival were going up, his freed-up mind could settle on worrying about me...and on questioning.

"Dad," I said hesitantly. "Have you ever...talked to the Tree? On your own, I mean?"

He raised an eyebrow. "That's a bit difficult for me to do, seeing as I can't open the moongate to Her."

That didn't sit right with me.

"Try. Maybe something has changed, or the rest of you could have grown stronger or something. Just try for me. And if you can't, get Rachel to let you in. I think you should have a talk with Her. On your own."

His lips pressed thin, but he nodded after a moment. "I think you are right. I'll try that."

"Thanks, Dad," I said with relief.

"No need to thank me. This is between me and Her, after all. Besides, there's no need for you to bear the weight of the worlds and our family all on your own, Sarah. I'm supposed to bear it with you—as your father *and* as your leftwing."

"True," I said ruefully.

I hesitated, then asked, "Dad, are you...*really* OK with me marrying Ben?"

He smiled thinly. "Are you? Are you *certain*, I mean?"

"Yes," I said with perfect surety. "He's what I want, Dad. And...this is the life I want. As hard as it is sometimes."

A lot of the time, actually, but Ben, the others of his people who were fast becoming friends and even family, and the wonders I had seen and even done all made the hard parts worth it.

"Then yes, I am OK with it," Dad said carefully. "I can't say that I won't worry. You're right: you've chosen a hard road. But...I think you've found as good a young man as you ever will to walk it with you."

My eyes stung. That compliment, as simple as it was on the surface, was probably the highest honor Dad could bestow on Ben...and thus, on my judgment. That last bit meant a great deal to me, more than I could say.

AN HOUR OR SO later, at someone's signal, Vadya led me through my daygate. She'd warned me what to expect at our destination, but it was still overwhelming.

The dramá in general weren't huge on ceremony, but when they wanted to make an impact, they did. If only because a good portion of them could become *dragons*.

That was what greeted me when Vadya led me to and then gestured at me to go through the largest, grandest hold entrance I had ever seen...

...and onto an enormous landing platform full of dragons. Dragons of all sizes, from that of a jumbo jet to a small propellor plane. And of all colors: red, blue, purple, green, orange, and gold, each in a different hue. All of them standing at attention and forming two lines across an empty aisle, with gold-uniformed amón filling in the gaps between them with their hands on their hearts.

And at the end, the largest and grandest of them all waited for me, slitted gold eyes piercing me even from this distance. Only in *this* form could Ben look so regally inscrutable. At least to me.

Trying my humanly best not to tremble under the weight of all those draconic stares, I walked through the arch. The moment I stepped into the sunlight, the two gold dragons at the front raised their throats in a roar. Fortunately, Vadya had warned me they would do that, and I had a bit of experience with drakón ceremonies by now, so I didn't *quite* die from a heart attack; in fact, I was rather proud that I didn't visibly flinch, although my fists did clench briefly. Hopefully nobody noticed.

I swiftly strode down the aisle, figuring that whatever pace I set would probably seem sedate to these long-legged people and look slow in comparison with those giants. Once I got close enough, Ben lowered himself to the ground, and platform workers rolled a set of stairs to his side and hooked the top to his saddle. I noticed even from a distance that it was a much larger, more ornate version than he had always used for me before, and that made me a bit sad. I hoped he'd kept it, and that we could use it again at some later point, when grandness wasn't necessary.

I never would have thought it, growing up moving so much and with such a large family, but it seemed I was becoming sentimental about things...or perhaps just things to do with the people I loved.

Yvera and Kor stood as draká on either side of Ben, so the humanlike figure to greet me at the end of the aisle was Eskala, and boy, was she a sight for sore eyes. I was afraid when she stopped me and took my hands that there would be some kind of speech, but she just kissed me on the cheek and began leading me to the stairs at Ben's side.

"I told you we would give you a proper welcome at Crownhold," she whispered to me with a dignified smile for the crowd. "Even if it is more of a send-off."

"As I said then, that was a promise you *really* didn't need to keep," I whispered back, hopefully maintaining my own gracious smile.

Behind us, the line broke up as dragons moved around, presumably getting into position for take-off. I noticed with a glance that most of them already had riders on board, who must have mounted before I came out.

"My dear, it is good that you do not *seek* honor for yourself," Eskala continued softly. "It is perhaps a trait for which your Tree chose you, as They often seem to choose the humblest among us. But especially now, you must learn to *accept* honor for the sake of your people, for that is the spirit in which the best of us are offering it. We do things like this not for you, but to atone for the past, acknowledge our need in the present, and pledge ourselves to the future."

That gave me pause. Not literally, because we continued toward the stairs. But I grew thoughtful, and when Eskala glanced at me, she gave me a quick smile of approval.

"Find that balance on this journey, Sarah. Do not drink in the honor, lest it corrupt you, but humbly accept the cup—for the sake of others. When the time comes, give it up freely, without a drop lost."

"I'll try," I said soberly.

"That's all the Tree asks of us," Eskala said with a final smile and a wave to the stairs as we stopped in front of them.

I hugged her, then turned and climbed.

An attendant awaited me at the top, helped me become familiar with the new saddle, and pointed out the compartments placed within easy reach with the things I would need when we landed. With Eskala's words fresh in my mind, I accepted the help without protest and warmly thanked the attendant when she was done. She grinned back at me and descended, and the staircase was soon rolled away.

Ready? Ben asked me.

Ready, I said.

I realized this was the first time I was riding on his back since discovering my inner voice in which I could really make use of it with him. Thank the Ice that I no longer had to use those signal flags to get his attention and give him simple one-word responses of *yes, no,* and *danger,* since I didn't know any of the more elaborate phrases that could be made with them. Although I noticed the flags were still stowed within reach, perhaps because that was simply the way things were done.

Ben rose carefully to his feet—more carefully than necessary, since I felt surprisingly secure and confident, even in this new saddle. Even though being on his back felt like riding a moving mountain.

I found, to my surprise, that I had missed this.

Even this next part.

Ben crouched low, with his great wings spread wide, and sprung into the air, wings pounding gusts of wind into the platform down below. Slowly, with mighty flaps and undulations of his body, we rose into the sky.

Ben circled higher and higher until we soared hundreds of feet above the ground. The necessity of such a height was to accommodate all the other drakón in our entourage, who formed circles of their own at lower levels, each lower circle wider and containing larger numbers. Using his inner voice but including me in many of the messages to show me what he was doing, Ben directed the drakón to break off in sets of two or three to go through the Crownhold sungate.

It was the largest sungate I had ever seen. I had caught glimpses of it as he and I had flown last night, though it had been banked for the night. Other than its size, it was identical from this distance to the other sungates I had seen: a stone arch hundreds of feet wide and even more tall, filled with an unbroken curtain of fire.

Ben continued directing the intermittent flow of dragons through the sungate, allowing time for them to get clear on the other side before sending on the next few. I enjoyed just sitting and listening to him. As awkward, self-conscious, and reluctant a leader as he sometimes was—or at least had been—he appeared to be in his element now. His directions were calm and authoritative, and he made a process that could have easily become chaotic and dangerous instead be methodical and orderly. And he made it sound easy.

True, this was a role for which he had trained his whole life, and he had probably led a flight of drakón through this kind of process many times. But many times by now, I had seen that Ben was a natural leader, especially in times of danger or strain. Perhaps that was because those were the times he stopped letting himself get in his own way, when he let his sound judgment and quick-thinking, strategic head rule over his oversized heart. Now, if only he could figure out how to do that in nonmartial settings....

I shook my head at myself. It wasn't my business to change Ben. He had enough people in his life trying to do that, for better or for worse. I'd figured out a long time ago that what he needed from me was unconditional friendship—to just be there for and accept him as he was. Just as that was what I needed most from him.

But I could hope for the best for him, and I could encourage or advise him if he asked me to. And right now, there was nothing stopping me from sitting back and admiring him. I was just glad he couldn't see my doting smile, or that might bring him right back into stumbling over himself again.

Finally, the last few drakón in the entourage went through, leaving only Ben and his two wings—from our flight, at least, though I saw other drakón standing ready below on the landing and others flying a mile-wide circle around us, all of them watching us closely. Traditionally, the highest-ranking member of a flight went through a sungate last to make sure their people got to safety before them, but Ben and I, being the Monarchs we were, had Blood that was too valuable to them and to the Devourer to leave unguarded all the same.

Probably yet another reason Ben and I would not be getting much privacy over these next few weeks. Gone were the days when we could fly around the Six Realms on our own, with just him and his wings to protect me. Now we *had* to have an entourage. Not because we were needy, pretentious dictators, but because we had to be protected for the good of all.

Because one day, our Blood might be needed to save them.

Kavarian had taught me that, with his last act—taught me once and for all what it meant to be a King or Queen.

I just prayed to the Trees and Creators that day would not come again. Not for Ben or me, at least.

But especially not Ben. I didn't think I could bear losing him in *any* way...but especially not in the way we had lost the King.

Ben, Yvera, and Kor lowered as they circled the sungate, with each circle lower and larger.

Going in, Ben said to me as they rounded the last time.

A bit unnecessary, but the first time he had brought me through a sungate—without sufficient warning or preparation—I had scolded him soundly. Even though he had taken me through plenty of sungates since then, this had been our first in a while, so perhaps he was remembering.

Ready, I told him, leaning into the saddle and gripping the handlebars there. I'd learned that the more I kept my body against and moving with his, the easier his maneuvers were on me.

When Ben came around to the front of the gate, he pulled in his own wings and dove, and his right- and leftwing on their respective sides of us followed suit.

As I felt the rush of the wind and the force of gravity dragging us back to the earth, and the wall of fire racing up to swallow us, I found myself smiling.

Even going through with Ben like this, without him *surging* us, was now easier, more instantaneous. I only barely registered a sensation of darkness and discomfort before we were shooting out the other side and Ben was snapping out his wings to slow our descent.

The Ykran capital of Danyeth was in an overgrown canyon of gray stone, which towered to dizzying heights and displayed fantastic, blocky basalt formations. Green moss, vines and even trees grew up and down the cliffs, and entire flocks of multicolored birds flitted to and fro between them, especially around the massive waterfall at the end of the canyon and over the roaring river that ran its length. Atop the cliffs, a massive forest stretched for miles, and the air was deliciously humid and cool to me after the baking heat outside Crownhold. I could even hear, if faintly from this height, the roar of the surf. That, and the hint of salt and seaweed in the air was explained as we turned in flight and I saw the canyon opened to the sea a mile or two down its length.

We had entered during a light drizzle that, despite its low volume, nevertheless had me damp and cold (in a good way) by the time Ben touched down on one of the landing circles that had been carved out from the forest at the lip of the canyon. There, the honor guard waited in formation once again, so it seemed we were going to do the same sort of ceremony in reverse. I noted with relief that they had dropped off their amón riders, who I hoped were inside and out of the wet.

At the other end of the aisle, underneath a large emerald canopy, a mixed group of amón and green-haired drakón waited, most of them wearing green uniforms aside from the most important-looking ones in the center. Behind the canopy was a structure that reminded me of a gray jungle temple, but I imagined that was just the primary entrance into the rest of the hold, which would be below our feet, and this was no ruin. From what I could see, the stone façade and columns were in good condition, despite the growth that ran rampant over every part, aside from the steps and walkways.

I was distracted from examining what lay ahead by the immediate concern of dismounting. This time, the landing workers brought a ladder, perhaps being easier to manage over the uneven surface of that circle. Two of them handled the ladder, propping it against Ben's side and one of them (gold uniform, the one who had helped me before) promptly began climbing, ensuring the ladder extended properly the rest of its length and hooking it to Ben's saddle once she reached the top. Then she came over to me. I had already unbuckled, so she began helping me with the protective equipment, apologizing for the necessity of putting it on out here, in the rain.

"Don't worry about it," I told her firmly. I understood immediately why it was best to be protected before even setting foot on the ground, and I had promised my parents I would be careful. Ben, who had turned his head to watch as best he could, had made his own promise to make sure I did.

My helper already had her own plague gear on, which looked a lot better and friendlier than I had expected: a hat with a short brim and a veil over all of that tucked beneath her collar and cloth gloves on her hands. All of which tingled to my sixth sense with magic, explaining why a veil that thin did her any good.

The cloth must have been spellweave and, because my helper was amón, the items must have received at least most of their power from the glowing gold gems set into the base of the hat and the clasps of the gloves. Those could have either been replaceable to aid in swapping them out for charged gems when the current ones ran out of power or could be built in and therefore had to be brought to a drakón for recharging.

My gear was fancier than the standard-issue fare she had. For one thing, no brimmed hat for me. She pulled up the hood of my tailored black travel robe and arranged the surprisingly stiff, white-ribboned hem of the hood (perhaps it contained a wire?) so that it overhung my face just so. Then she brought out my veil, the metallic hem of which attached as if by magnetism to the inner lining, further reinforcing my suspicion that there must have been some kind of bendable metal inside.

"I'm also attaching it by a few hooks," she explained as she continued to fiddle. "Just so it can't get yanked off."

She didn't specify how, but I wasn't so naive as to assume she only meant by accident. Though Ben and the Crown had done a remarkable job of sheltering me so far, I knew from Ben's dark hints that there *were* some elements among his people that wished me harm, simply for who I was.

Then she tucked the veil inside my robe.

"You'll have to keep that on until you get to your quarters," she said apologetically. "But the robe is spellweave too, and they tried to design it to be breathable and keep you cool."

Which explained why I hadn't felt *as* uncomfortable being out in the heat on Ythra as I might have been.

"Thank you," I said sincerely. "And please pass my thanks to the tailors."

She chuckled as she got out my gloves: white silk, of course. "I'll let them know. They'll appreciate hearing that."

She held the gloves out to me, then asked, "You think you can charge those? We would have ourselves, but Leftwing Korinth said it would look best if you did it yourself. Both symbolically and color-wise, you know."

Because no one else in the Six Realms could charge them with a white light.

I touched the gem clasps and gave them both spark. The power required was nothing to the reserves I had now, even during the day, yet the clear gems immediately lit with such a brilliant white light that my helper whistled quietly in spite of herself, then quickly apologized.

"Just, it's so amazing to see—coming from an amón, and all. Or someone that's not drakón, anyway."

"I know," I said with a simple smile. "No need to apologize."

"That one too," she said, tapping the gem clasp of my robe. "That one powers the robe and veil. Though it looks like it's been taking on some spark from you already."

I looked down in surprise to see that she was right. The clear gem was already glowing dimly.

"Ambient charging," she explained at my baffled expression. "Happens, sometimes, to uncharged gems that sit around folks as powerful as you. Still, better not let it run on only that much. Give it a good spark."

I did so, and she finally declared me ready. "Just try to avoid touching things or getting too close to people. The veil and gloves *should* protect you, but what with this fever being so new...well, no need to take unnecessary risks."

"Right," I agreed firmly.

She clambered down the ladder first, and once she was halfway down, I followed. Once I got clear of the bustle of the ladder removal, I hesitated, not sure what I should do next.

Just wait, Kor told me, coming up to me in humanform. As did Yvera. They were both wearing similar robes, veils, and gloves.

So, we're doing this part together, then? I asked him as I watched Ben change back out of the corner of my eye. Not *too* closely, though. It was usually better for my stomach if I only kept a vague sense of the progression when he was changing at a normal pace.

Together, Kor confirmed. *And in amáform, out of respect for you. That's why the Lord Peacegrowth is that way as well.*

Kor inclined his head subtly toward the emerald canopy. I cast a hopefully discreet glance in that direction and thought I finally identified the Lord with that hint. My guess was the tallest one, with short forest-green hair and beard, and matching formal robe, pants, and shirt. There was something familiar about that color, in fact....

Lord Fenrith, Kor said as Ben approached us, looking unusually sober underneath his hood and veil. *Ben's uncle.*

My eyes darted to Kor's and widened. *You mean....*

Svyer's father, he confirmed heavily.

No one had ever told me that Svyer was the daughter of the Peacegrowth *Lord*. But then, in their minds, that didn't matter as much. It didn't make Svyer the heir—which she probably wasn't, or they would have mentioned that much.

"Ready?" Ben said quietly when he reached us, smile half-hearted at best. Now I knew that wasn't because of the crowd and ceremony. This time.

Ben had always carried too much guilt for Svyer's fate, and I doubted the pain had lessened significantly over this past month while he'd had to heal from yet another tragedy.

I took his hand and clenched it in sympathy. He looked back down at me and gave a stronger smile and a clench of his own.

Before letting that smile fade. *I think...I can handle this, with you. But now is actually a good time for sobriety.*

I nodded. Sober, I could do.

Chapter Seventeen

BELIEF

Koriben

I WALKED TOWARD MY only uncle and living elder with a dim flameheart. Made all the dimmer by the fact that this was only the second time I was going to speak with him since Svyer's...condition, and the events that had led up to it.

I called him sometime in the whirlwind of those days just after to offer my deepest regret at failing his daughter so completely. An apology which, of course, being the brother of Avvi that he was, he had dismissed as being unnecessary even before I was finished. Somehow, the fact that he didn't blame me only made me blame myself more.

I should have done more than just call. Or call only once. Even if it had been one thing after another after that, with the final moongates, traveling on Earth to get Sarah to her Tree, bringing her back, the battle.... Avva....

I should have done more.

What right did I have to be *happy* right now? Not that I was right that second, but I was still walking hand in hand with Sarah. Even if our earrings weren't visible right now, all of them knew what she was to me. That was the reason they were standing out here in this miserable damp. They weren't just here to greet her as the Queen of Ice. They were here to meet *their* future Queen.

My Queen.

It seemed monstrous, on top of how thoroughly I had failed Fenrith, that the first time I had bothered to come to see him since he had lost his daughter was to present to him my betrothed.

Yet it was too late to fix that. I could have called him this morning. I thought about it, even. Then I didn't. Somehow, that had seemed even worse than showing up at his doorstep. Too little, too late.

I would have to do better from now on, if he still wanted contact at all. His miraculous understanding could have faded to bitterness over time. That would have only been mortal.

But from the softness in his emerald eyes as we approached, I doubted it.

I swallowed as Sarah and I walked under the canopy and stopped at a safe distance from the Lord and his consort, Lady Hilyan. Everyone within the tent was wearing protective clothing, were spaced apart, and had no doubt been confirmed to be fever-free before coming here, but I wasn't taking any chances.

Not with Sarah.

Sarah clenched my hand again. *I'm here. You can do this. I love you.*

Flame, I didn't deserve her—yet the Trees were sticking her with me anyway.

"King Koriben," Fenrith said quietly and gently. Being drakón, and as strong a healer as the Six Realms had ever seen, there wasn't a sign of age on his timeless face, even though he was just younger than Avva at one hundred and thirty-six. "I welcome you to Danyeth of Ykran."

I had been here plenty of times before, but this was my first time as King, so a bit more ceremony was required—especially for the sake of the tour. Fortunately, knowing Fenrith, it would be minimal.

"I thank you for your welcome, Lord Fenrith," I said as evenly as I could.

"What brings my King to my Realm on this day?"

The irony of him calling me his King. He should be standing in my place, Peacegrowth or not. He had led his clan with grace and skill for longer than Avva had led the Realms. I was just the gangly twenty-summer who scarcely knew what he was doing.

I took a deep breath. "I come to present my betrothed and your future Queen: Queen Sarah Moontouched of the Seventh Realm and Crown of Ice."

With permission now to do so, Fenrith turned his kindly eyes to Sarah.

"Be welcome to my Realm, Queen Sarah. I am Lord Fenrith Peace-growth. It is an honor to meet you at last."

"Thank you," Sarah said quietly. "It is an honor to meet you as well."

She could have ended it there, and I expected her to, so I wasn't prepared to stop her from breaking with ceremony by continuing.

"Your daughter was my first friend in the Six Realms and is one of the best souls I know. I am so sorry that she is...lost."

Others blinked and shifted at that raw admission, and pain flickered in Hilyan's eyes, but Fenrith only smiled slightly.

"I thank you for your kind words. She is lost now, as you say, but not lost forever. I have faith she will be returned to us."

I worked hard to control my expression, but I couldn't help at least a blink of surprise. What was the source of Fenrith's faith? Had his Tree told him something? Was *that* how he could forgive me?

Well, with us now officially off script, I might as well say what I'd been aching to all along.

"We do not come for celebrations or to force our hospitality on you. We know now is not the time for such things. Our Realms are still healing from the damage done by the Battles of the Solstice—"

Which had raged to varying extents across the Six Realms, not just at the Temple of Flame on Ythra, though that location had been the hardest hit by far. Still, I had seen the sad signs of battle as I had brought us in: scorch marks on the cliffs, toppled arches and columns, swaths of destroyed forest, broken vines and tree limbs everywhere.

Even the mighty Ronyan River had altered its banks, perhaps from the swell of bodies that might have once clogged it. Fenrith himself had fought in the battle to protect his Realm and Tree and taken a blow to one wing that had nearly ended his life. Thank the Flame he survived, and that no sign of his peril or pain was visible now.

"—and we have begun on this journey to aid them."

Far from being upset by the breach in protocol, Fenrith only smiled slightly again, and his emerald eyes glistened with approval.

"For that, we thank you. And thank the Trees for choosing our Monarchs so well."

I was stunned. This was Fenrith, so I knew he wasn't just giving some vain political flattery. He truly thought the Tree had chosen well. Well, that was self-evident in Sarah's case. But his eyes were on mine when he spoke.

Take heart, nephew, he told me silently. *You* are *Her chosen. For good reason.*

He didn't just forgive me.

He *believed* in me.

How?

When Fenrith led us inside, he guided us to the King's Wing, speaking quietly with Sarah along the way. Anchored primarily by Sarah's hand, I mostly just followed along in a daze—partly from the shock of Fenrith's words, partly from the pain of so many memories.

With Fenrith and Svyer being my only immediate kin, and this being Avvi's birth Realm, I had come here more often than to any other place in the Six Realms outside of Ythra, despite its infamous cool, damp weather. Or...I used to. Before Avvi....

There was yet another reason I had slowly pulled away from Svyer, and especially Fenrith, why I had been so terrible a nephew to him after Svyer's fate. He reminded me so much of Avvi.

But the sight of him now, and the memories washing over me of playing in that fountain with Svyer or sliding down the stone rim of those steps, or begging hotsweets from Avvi in that marketplace...didn't hurt as much as I had thought they would.

The power of that unconditional love and forgiveness, the difference it had wrought inside me was...incredible. Sarah's, his.... But perhaps most miraculous of all, that of my parents, sent to me from beyond the Flame itself.

I came to when Sarah asked Fenrith quietly, "May I see Svyer?"

My flameheart clenched. Despite the evidence I just had of somehow being able to bear the ghosts of my past, I wasn't sure I was ready to bear this latest and rawest one just yet. And yet, how could I do anything else?

"Of course you may," Fenrith replied with his usual gentle dignity, no sign of pain in his expression from the request. "Only send word when you wish to go, and I will bring you to her."

Sarah hesitated. I couldn't see her expression through her hood and veil from my vantage, but I knew from the clench of her hand and just knowing *her* what she would ask before she asked it.

"Would it be alright if I saw her now?"

"My dear," Hilyan said in surprise. "That is good of you, but don't you wish to at least be settled first? To rest or eat?"

Lady Hilyan was a good match for Fenrith; Flame knew he waited long enough for her. She was a tall, lithe, elegant Peacegrowth amón with chestnut hair and eyes very nearly the color of their beloved cliffs outside. She was from a remote region in the Athalin Jungle on Ykran—not too far from where the Tree had brought Sarah, actually—and was born nearly a century after her mate, explaining why they had only met and married thirty years ago and why Svyer was only a few summers older than me.

"Thank you, but no," Sarah said, voice steady and sure. "I have a feeling I need to see her now."

I clenched Sarah's hand in surprise.

A feeling? I asked her silently.

Yes. I just can't get her out of my head. And I don't think it's just because—

"Very well," Fenrith said, a little surprised. For the first time, his eyes tightened in pain, or perhaps concern. "Then this way."

He gestured down a different passage as we crossed the latest juncture, and we followed him to the Lord's Wing instead. Most of us, anyway.

I'm going to the King's Wing, Yvera sent me impatiently. *I have work to do.*

That's fine with me, I answered, and I just shook my head at Sarah's questioning look when Yvera split off.

I figured that now Yvera had seen me safely inside, her patience for ceremony and socializing was at an end. Being a showpiece was the aspect she liked least about being my rightwing, and her limited stamina for it was always near its limit now that I was King. I tried to let her go or off the hook entirely whenever I could.

Sarah gaped when we came to the Lord's Wing, and I could see why. Danyeth's interior had more vegetation everywhere than was usual, but the Lord's Wing was practically an indoor garden that people happened to live and work in.

No one had come further than the Danyeth Peacegrowth to figuring out how to cultivate life underground without compromising the security of a hold—perhaps inspired by their Tree, who was safely contained elsewhere within this capital city.

Huge slabs of clear, magically grown and strengthened crystal provided frequent skylights to allow the sunlight—as cool and scant as it was now—to filter down below, but to provide their beloved plants the rest of the energy they needed to flourish, gems the size of plates (also magically grown) cast golden light down, making the space feel bright and warm. The Peacegrowth sacrificed much of their own power to charge those gems, and they had had to master the tricky technique of spelling gems to display a desired spectrum rather than one's own soulcolor.

So life flourished, to fantastic effect. On either side of the paved paths were expansive, carefully nourished beds full of towering trees, thick undergrowth, and small creatures that could be permitted as part of the ecosystem. The trees often formed an arched canopy over our heads, and occasionally a root or vine crawled across our path. The caretakers did their best to encourage their growth elsewhere, but life will do what it wants in the end, and the caretakers generally let the most stubborn ones have at it. The only reason the walkway wasn't also littered with leaves and branches were powerful, invisible wards that made them slide to the side and fall into the beds instead.

Sarah's hood fell back enough for me to see her gape as she followed the unnatural path of a few leaves that did just that. I smiled at her but tugged her hood back down and forward with my free hand.

Just when we were approaching the Lord's suite, a green-clad staffer ran up to us, her eyes wide. "Lord Fenrith, thank Flame. She's fading—Svyer's fading."

"What?" Fenrith asked, face falling.

"No!" Hilyan choked out, and began to run, her mate only a heartbeat behind her.

And I was only one behind him.

No. No, no, no. Flame, don't do this to us now!

Yet I understood what was happening immediately. Solim had kept Svyer's spirit alive this long to use her against me again if he could. And if he couldn't....

To publicly ruin me—and Sarah. The timing could not be a coincidence. Svyer's final death, at the very start of the grand tour, which Sarah and I had begun to help our Realms heal....

Why had I not seen this coming?! Why had I been too absorbed in my guilt and misery to see the end that our arrival would likely bring on Svyer?

Yet the Tree had. And...had told Sarah.

Sarah had had a feeling, she said.

Why?

I froze in my tracks—as hard as it was to do, as much as my body screamed at me to keep moving—and looked back. Sarah sprinted toward me, doing her best to keep up. She was a remarkably fast runner for her size, but there was only so much she could do to keep up with people of our height and stamina, especially weighed down by her robe and encumbered by her veil.

I held my arms out, and she understood at once, reaching back for me. I scooped her up into my arms and bolted forward once more. We had already lost sight of the Lord and Lady, but I knew the way. Even after all these years, I knew this wing, particularly these rooms, almost as well as my own.

I burst into Syver's room, where her parents were bent over her on either side of her bed. Lord Fenrith had his hands on her shoulders and his eyes were closed in concentration; from the stirring of magic I felt emanating from him, I knew he was pouring power into her. But though a healer as powerful as he was could keep her body alive, as he had done for over a month, there was only so much he could do to maintain the connection between her body and spirit. And her *spirit* was the part we knew, loved, and needed.

And it was the spirit that was dying.

"*No*," Sarah sobbed when I set her down.

Hilyan, though tears were streaming down her face, turned to Sarah and held out her arm, and Sarah rushed to her side and accepted Svyer's hand that Hilyan offered her. Sarah clenched that hand and bowed over her friend for a moment, trembling with suppressed sobs.

Then she glanced back at me, eyes pleading.

I couldn't swallow through the thickness in my throat. *I can't do anything, Sarah. This isn't like when I brought back Kor. If I could have brought her back, I would have. But he's taken her too far away for me to feel her.*

Instead of tightening in despair, Sarah's eyes widened. *Then...how come I can?*

I inhaled sharply and approached her. "What?" I whispered out loud.

"I can feel her, Ben," Sarah said in distress. She held her free hand out for me, and I took it.

And then...I could too.

The thinnest of threads that held the essence of my cousin, going out into the ether.

Impossible.

But then, that was what Sarah had always done.

Hilyan gasped and gripped Sarah's shoulder. "Can you bring her back?"

Sarah looked at me, face hardening with that resolve I knew too well by now. "What do I need to do?"

My flameheart trembled, nearly going out with fear. "Sarah...to bring her back, you would have to go after her. *In spirit*. Near *Solim*. If he feels you there.... He could take you, too."

And with Sarah's spirit as his captive....

He *knew* I would do anything to get her back.

Anything.

Hilyan slowly shook her head, looking at Sarah, her face tightening in anguish. But her voice was surprisingly steady. "No, Sarah. Don't."

But Sarah's hard silver eyes never left mine.

"I have to do this, Ben."

I flinched. Those were the exact words I had given her when I'd told her I had to go after Solim, to do my duty as Heir to protect my people from him.

And she, understanding that, had let me go.

I let out a wordless exclamation of agony, but I ducked in and pressed my lips to hers. Only for a second, though. Every one mattered now.

"You had *better* come back to me," I growled when I pulled away just enough to meet her eyes.

She smiled thinly. "Of course I will. You're my gate."

Then, following her instincts, she closed her eyes.

Breathe, I told her, clenching her hand tightly. *Focus on your breath, on your heartbeat. Turn inward, find that quiet place inside. Then follow her.*

Sarah nodded. And breathed. And stilled.

I knew she was gone when she became so still that she was like a statue.

Kor came to my other side and gripped my shoulder, and when I looked at him, his eyes were burning with the force of his fear for her. He, more than anyone, knew what his brother was capable of, what kind of danger Sarah was going into. And he was the only one in that room who came even close to loving her as much as I did.

If he takes her, kill me, I told him. *Quickly.*

That was probably the safest measure in that scenario, for the good of the Realms. To keep me from doing something from berserker rage to those around us, and to prevent Solim from using Sarah to make me do something even more monstrous and destructive elsewhere.

Kor snorted. *No. Seeing as I would need* you *to get her back.*

Kor, you know I....

Regardless, that won't happen, Kor said, jaw set. *She's coming back.*

His lips twitched into the driest and most momentary of smiles. *Since when do I have more trust in the Trees than you do?*

Since now, apparently. Since the Tree asked my betrothed to risk her spirit venturing near a lish.

I'm doing all you asked! I raged at Her, not caring how irreverent I was being. *Everything you asked. And you promised to protect her. You* promised. *So bring her back to me.*

Or I didn't know if I would have the strength left to be Her King any longer.

Then a voice whispered back.

Look.

I looked at Sarah.

And to my shock, though a deken of daylight at least remained, she was glowing as brightly as she had last night. All the lights in the room had dimmed as they streamed to her in beams, and shadows lengthened and stretched toward her. Everyone but Kor, Hilyan, Fenrith and I were backing away from her and exclaiming.

And Sarah's wings gradually unfurled, like the blossoms of a flower.

Like a promise.

CHAPTER EIGHTEEN

SPIRIT

SARAH

IT WAS DISTURBINGLY EASY to find my way out of my own body—at least with the trail of Svyer's spirit to follow, and my urgent need to rush after it, before it faded entirely. Even now, I could feel it weakening, the connection withering and pulling away.

I surged after it. Not in any way I had before. I wasn't anything like I had been before, nor any*where* I had ever been or seen. All senses were cut off—no sight, no sound, no touch, no smell, no taste. Only my sense of self remained and plunged ahead through the void, and only my sixth sense and the feel for Svyer guided me.

I rushed through the void for what felt like an eternity, but it couldn't have been, because Svyer didn't have that long left.

Eventually, the speed of my surging overtook the speed of her withering, and I knew I was getting close.

My instincts slowed me then, as excruciating as it was to take the risk. I could feel another spirit nearby, one that was dark—the terrible kind of dark, not the natural kind of night. The kind that raged against light, that tried to *swallow* light when it could instead of giving way before it according to the order of things.

That darkness was stirring. Perhaps it had been waiting for me, perhaps it had merely caught a whiff of me on the winds of the ether. But its awareness of me was growing just as mine was of it, and now it was coming.

Sarah! Svyer screamed into the void. *Fly!*

I flew, like an arrow shot from a bow.

But straight toward her.

Using arms that weren't arms, I encircled her body that wasn't a body. Using power, I bound her to me even more tightly. Then, as dark arms closed around us both, I reached for my gate, my sun...

...and I wrenched both of us back to him in an instant.

But not...before the darkness brushed me.

And its touch was poison.

Chapter Nineteen

FEVER

Koriben

A BURST OF LIGHT blinded me, but through my hand in hers, I felt Sarah collapsing.

Crying out, I caught her clumsily and raised her up in my arms while blinking away the spots in my vision. Then I realized the darkness wasn't just me. All lights in the room had gone completely out. Even Sarah's glow had faded, leaving the only source of light coming in through the open door.

Though I could feel Sarah's spirit was back with us, the expected relief would not come. Her eyes were closed, her body limp, her skin pale yet warm—almost feverish.

And "almost feverish" for Sarah was....

No.

No, no, no....

"No," I sobbed out loud, holding her close as I bowed over her.

Kor threw up a ball of sapphire light and rounded in front of me. "What is it? How is she?"

"She's hot. Kor, she's *hot*."

He stilled, apart from the hand he placed on her forehead. Even through the veil and his thin gloves, he must have felt that heat, because his eyes widened. His power joined mine in racing through her, trying to combat the heat before it was too late.

"Let me see her," a gentle yet authoritative voice said, and Kor reluctantly stepped aside to make way for Fenrith.

I looked up at him desperately, I imagined with the same look Sarah gave me to ask me to save Svyer.

With about as much hope.

Fenrith touched her veil, and with my nod of permission, he untucked the lower portion and threw it all over the back of her head. Then he pulled off his gloves—his own skin was probably more sanitary at this point in any case—and placed his hands on either side of her neck.

As I felt his power sink into her, and he felt mine, he said, "Give me space, Koriben."

With excruciating reluctance, I withdrew my power and gave him free rein.

Kor and I waited tensely as he stood there for at least a dek, maybe two, emerald streams of light swirling around him slightly with the force of his power and concentration. Especially in the dim lighting, I could see the emerald soulflare leaking around the edges of his closed eyelids.

Then Fenrith's power retreated, and his soulflare dimmed. With Sarah none the cooler, and her skin still too pale, I knew what look would be in his eyes before he opened them.

Sorrow. Worry.

"I am sorry, Koriben. So sorry."

"No," I said thickly, shaking my head. "She just got here. She didn't have it before. It couldn't have progressed this quickly...."

Kor spoke quietly. "Unless...she got it straight from its source."

Its....

Solim.

Sarah had gotten away from him, miraculously...but not unscathed.

Even in defeat, that hellfrosted monster always found a way to win.

No! I cried in despair, flameheart shrinking to nothing more than a flickering candle flame, in danger of going out at any moment.

"What?" a voice croaked.

Perhaps the only voice that could have distracted me in that moment.

I looked to the side numbly. Svyer's eyes were open, blinking dazedly at us. But open.

And those emeralds I knew so well were flecked with silver.

OVER A MONTH AGO, as soon as Svyer's innocent, spiritless body had been brought home and to the Ykran Tree, the Tree had cleansed it of the consumption Solim had placed on Svyer without her knowledge. Then, even though her body was comatose for over a month, it had been well taken care of, tenderly administered to by every measure that a clan full of healers, herbalists, and apothecaries could devise.

So, after some hot broth, explanations, and her drakón energy speeding her recovery, it wasn't long before Svyer was determinedly stumbling around enough to take charge of Sarah's care, with no one able to dissuade her.

Not that anyone truly tried. I certainly didn't. I was too numb to do anything but stand around uselessly, or sit when Kor finally shoved me into a chair.

Nor did Fenrith, who just calmly did whatever his daughter asked him to do to assist her. Most everyone else was too awed or unnerved by the streaks of silver that were now in Svyer's emerald hair and eyes.

Not even Hilyan made more than a token protest to say that Svyer was still so weak. Wouldn't it be wiser for her to—

"Avvi, if I'm understanding all of you right now, I'm only here because of Sarah. That I owe her first my body, then my spirit. Is that right?"

The others had had to explain everything to her. At least currently, she appeared to remember little of the Moonfair and nothing of Solim.

Which, considering what he might have done to her...was perhaps a Flame-send.

"Yes," Hilyan said with a sigh, knowing where this would lead.

"Then I'm going to make her better," Svyer said, emerald-and-silver eyes flashing. "*Personally.*"

As she said, she oversaw everything that was done regarding Sarah's care after that. She even made them take over her bedroom as Sarah's own, since it was practically a healing room already, with all Svyer's personal effects long since cleared from every surface to make room for tools of healing.

The choice of location also had the practical application of reducing the fever's spread. Everyone who had been near Sarah was thoroughly examined and cleansed before being allowed to leave. Kor and I simply never left, though Yvera gave me hellwinds for it when she found out and called.

No matter how she blustered, I refused to leave, and I refused to let Yvera come to the Lord's Wing and risk exposure. Someone looked her over, just in case, but found nothing. If Kor's theory about where Sarah got the disease was true, which seemed increasingly likely, then Yvera wouldn't have been at risk to begin with, and with all the authority I could summon in this state, I intended to keep her that way.

Once Svyer and Fenrith got Sarah settled, Svyer finally allowed herself to sit and drink some strong tsha laced with sundew for energy recovery as her father explained to her all that they knew so far about the new fever—silently, perhaps trying to spare me.

Unfortunately, as King, I had already read too many reports on that very subject, and all the details came back to me with horrifying clarity now.

Brightfever had risen suddenly, mere days after the Solstice, originating on Ykran and becoming epidemic there before they had managed to largely contain it to their world. The disadvantage of the disease's origin was that it was attacking Peacegrowth, the clan with our best healers. The advantage was that those healers and even the common citizens knew how to fight such outbreaks and were selfless enough to do everything in their power both for the victims and to stop the spread. Any other world would have been far less prepared, and their heroic sacrifices to do their part may have saved the rest of the Realms.

Brightfever's progress was in three primary stages: first, a communicable stage with few symptoms which could last a few days; second, a swift descent over the course of a day through fever, paleness, and unconsciousness; and third, the victim's skin took on an unnatural glow.

When that happened, death was within deken.

If the fever was caught in the first stage, our healing magic could remove it. The other stages were bafflingly resistant to healing, the disease seemingly impervious to our efforts to purge it. Still, a victim had a three-quarters chance of survival...*if* they didn't reach unconsciousness.

I tried very, very hard not to remember the odds of survival then. Because Sarah....

No.

No, no, no.

It just couldn't be.

It couldn't.

I just kept staring at her lying in Svyer's bed, praying that at any moment, she would open her eyes, recovered from her exertion as she had all the other times she had performed miracles to save our lives. But she never did. Though she never sweated, she had all the other symptoms of advanced second-stage brightfever, and perhaps worse.

She was a child of Ice. Her body *had* to be far cooler than ours, cooler than an amón's, even a human's, to survive. Her iceheart's pulses weakened unusually quickly just from the sheer effort of combatting the heat of her body. Svyer had ordered ice to be brought in by the bagful, which we had arranged around her like heavy blankets, and that seemed to give her iceheart strength. But I feared how little time that relief might last...and, given how depleted the cold stores were, how much more ice we could find.

I was realizing with dawning horror just how perfectly this disease had been timed and crafted—for *her.*

Even the glow would have been a cruel irony, a mocking jab from Solim at Sarah's very nature.

Yet there was nothing I could do.

I had *tried* to heal her on my own, right at the beginning, as had Kor, even though we both knew it was too late for that. So had Fenrith, one of the most powerful and experienced healers of our time, with firsthand experience with this fever. All to no avail.

I felt so helpless, so defenseless, I couldn't even rage. No red overcame my vision, no fire entered my blood. I just sat there, frozen. It was as if Sarah's and my natures had been cruelly and lethally reversed, and the ice in my blood and the fire in hers were slowly killing us both.

"And riyadroot?" Svyer demanded out loud.

I numbly realized that at some point, she and her father had begun speaking audibly.

Fenrith shook his head. "Has too little effect to outweigh the risk. Generally, the outcomes are even worse."

Svyer cursed. "Not even mikan powder?"

"We could try it, but it usually only does any good at an earlier stage, and we are nearly out. For the Queen of Ice, we can find some."

"You are overlooking the fact that this is a magic-origin disease," Kor said grimly, standing near them with his arms folded. "And thus most likely requires a magic-origin cure."

"But it's magic *resistant*, Kor," Svyer snapped.

"Then it's not our magic she needs."

I was almost as surprised as everyone else to hear the words come out of my mouth. But as soon as I said them, I knew they were true.

I turned from staring at Sarah to see them all looking at me. "She needs her magic. The magic of Ice."

"But she is the only child of Ice *here*, Ben," Kor said.

As I saw a path forward for the very first time, I hardened with resolve. "There's still daylight. If I leave now, if I'm quick, I might be able to bring back Rachel—"

"No," Kor interrupted flatly. "Absolutely not."

I gritted my teeth. Did he care about Sarah or not? Or had his latest fancy gotten that deeply into his head?

"Think *logically*, Kor—"

"*I'm* the one thinking logically," Kor cried, pointing to himself. "Think, Ben. What will Solim do if he hears that we have brought the Queen *and* the Heir of Ice to one location—just before nightfall, no less? Are you really willing to risk a lish laying siege to Danyeth at night? *Without* Sarah to help you drive him off? Flame Above, Ben. He might even try coming with just her here."

"Why?" I demanded, tensing at the thought.

"Because I don't think the Devourer is exactly happy with him for killing off the Queen of Ice in petty revenge," Kor snapped. "But now that Sarah is *vulnerable*, and unable to help you, it might order Solim to risk his life trying to fetch her, so that perhaps it can have her Blood before she dies. Or maybe it will simply be satisfied with Solim taking you, as you try to defend Danyeth."

Torch it, he was right.

"Maybe," Svyer put in loudly, getting us both to look at her. "Maybe we don't need a complete child of Ice."

She held a silver strand of her hair to her eyes grimly. "Maybe we need *me*."

We stared at her.

"What? There must be a *reason* the Tree of Ice did this to me. Because I'm sure as hellwinds that it wasn't a lish. Do I feel consumed to you, Ben?"

Her consumption had been subtle last time, but still detectable to me. If only in my subconscious, because I had refused to face what it meant. No trace of Solim's scent or the sickness of consumption was on her now.

"No," I said definitively.

"But you've already examined her yourself, dear," Fenrith said. "You said it resisted you, too."

"Yes, but...." Her eyes drifted to me, and she grimaced. "Torch it, I didn't want to get Ben's hopes up, but...I felt some give, Avva. I felt like I could *do* something, if only with a bit more help."

The candle flame that my heart had become expanded dangerously, just as she had known it would. I gripped the sides of my chair and leaned forward breathlessly. "What?"

Svyer looked back at her father. "That's why I was trying to ask you about herbal remedies. That's my specialty. If there is some grand purpose in all this, if the Trees asked Sarah to risk her life to save me for a *reason*, then perhaps it's not just because of what I am now...but also what I know. What I'm good at."

"Perhaps," Fenrith agreed. "Then what do you suggest?"

"I don't *know*," Svyer groaned, running her hands through her hair. "I've asked you about everything I can think of. I think we need something new."

Something...new. Something as new as Sarah was.

I had begun to think the Tree had abandoned me. But if Svyer was right, if there was meaning to be found in this crucible....

The one thing the Tree had told me was to look. Look in time to see Sarah's wings unfold. Like a flower, I'd thought. But what an *odd* thing to think in such a moment. Like a....

Suddenly, a scent came to my mind. I shut my eyes to pinpoint the memory.

"Ben?" Svyer asked uncertainly.

"Quiet," I said, then added belatedly, "Please."

Then it came, with remarkable clarity. Sarah, standing on the bank of the small waterfall in her hold with me. I'd smelled many things that day in that garden, but one clear note had stood out: sharp and cool. Bunches of green leaves growing along the shadowy borders, the flowers of which were ice blue...and had six petals.

My eyes snapped open. "Kor. You said you gave a scale to Jake?"

"Yes, but we're not risking Rach—"

"If Svyer's right, if she can do this, we're not risking anyone," I said flatly. "Call Jake now and tell him I'll be at the crowngate in a moment...and that I need him to bring me some flowers."

CHAPTER TWENTY

PRAYER

KORIBEN

I PACED IN FRONT of the crowngate, cursing that I couldn't see through the flames to know what was happening on the other side. But *they* would see me through the ice and know I was there.

I just hoped they would follow Kor's instructions to the letter and not come out, no matter their concern for Sarah and probably their desire to rail at me. I had been thoroughly cleansed before I had left Svyer's room, but I still would not risk having any of their deaths on my conscience. Plus, I was certain that was the one thing Sarah would never forgive me for.

Thank the Flame, they didn't emerge. I didn't even see a hand come through the gate. The bag was tossed through the flames and fell at my feet with a thump, just as Kor had instructed.

I grabbed it and looked into the gate. "Thank you," I said fervently. "And I am so sorry. More than you'll ever know."

Then I surged back immediately, knowing I had only dek, perhaps seconds of daylight to spare. In fact, I felt the Danyeth sungate go out as I was racing over the welcoming court and down the steps to descend inside the hold, not even acknowledging the salutes of the guards as I passed.

I was equally heedless of all the other stares I collected from civilians as I sprinted through the rest of the hold and to the Lord's Wing. Kor had tried to quiet the witnesses of Sarah's retrieval of Svyer and subsequent illness, but the former event had been too momentous to conceal, given all Danyeth had done to keep their beloved Peacegrowth daughter alive. Word about what *Sarah* had sacrificed to do the same had followed right on the first's heels.

So, though I startled the people I raced past, I thought it was more from the suddenness of my approach rather than wonder at the reason. Once they recognized me and I saw understanding dawn on their faces, they swiftly moved aside. One of the older women even called after me, saying she had burned a leaf for Sarah.

I sure hoped *her* prayer counted for something, because I wasn't certain mine did anymore.

But I kept praying all the same.

What else could I do?

Other than run with my precious burden as fast as my legs could carry me.

The guards in front of the Lord's Wing waved me right on through, so I sprinted even faster the last few hundred erd to Svyer's room and burst inside. To my horror, I saw that Sarah's skin, already too pale, had taken on a luminescence that was obvious even in the restored lighting.

No!

Lungs heaving, flameheart pounding, I thrust the bag into Svyer's outstretched hands.

"Flame, Ben, how much did they give you?" Svyer said with a blink as she swiftly carried the armful over to a table she had set up for this purpose.

They might not have had many options for containers, I said silently to save my breath. I rose from my bent position over my legs and stumbled over to Sarah, folding my legs under me to collapse at the side of the bed and touch her hand.

Her feverish hand.

Tears stung my eyes as I immediately let go, lest my own heat do her more harm. Had it been just yesterday that I had said her cold skin worried me?

"That's not the only reason. Flame, look at all of this, Avva," Svyer said, gesturing to the bag she had just opened. "Get someone in here to find an isolated spot to plant the rest of this."

She scooped up the handful of plants she wanted—not doing things by half, the Linds had pulled up the entire things to their roots—and handed the bag to Fenrith, who went to the door and called over a staffer.

I knew they weren't just being fussy gardeners with offended sensibilities. If this plant had the power to cure brightfever....

Then each petal could be a life saved.

Which was...perhaps the very reason the Linds had torn them up by the roots to begin with. Either that, or they weren't taking chances with which part Svyer would need. For either of those reasons or both, I blessed them.

And I kept praying.

SVYER, HER FATHER, AND a couple volunteers worked with focused frenzy for several deken, testing every part of the plant for safety and efficacy against every measure available to us before debating on and then trying the application they thought to be the most likely cure. In the end, they used the hints the Tree had given me to make their decision.

They concentrated the oils from the petals, diluted them again in a solution, and then added that to a nasal diffuser: a vial with a pointed nozzle and an attached pump, similar to a perfume bottle but made for its sprayed contents to be inhaled. Then Svyer infused the oil solution with her own healing power, making the tinted vial glow with emerald light that silvered at the end of its spectrum.

Svyer slowly approached where I kept vigil beside Sarah.

"Ben," she murmured. "This is our best guess. At the very least, we're fairly sure it won't hurt her."

Unable to speak, I just nodded. It wasn't like we had much choice at this point. I'd long ago given in to holding her hand, just so I could feel her pulse as it weakened. Sarah's iceheart was failing, and she burned like a glowing white ember beside me.

I clenched that hot hand tightly as Svyer dabbed a few drops of diluted oil across Sarah's forehead. Then, on one of Sarah's rattling inhales, Svyer administered the diffused solution into her nose. The sharp, cool scent filled me from where I sat...and reminded me, painfully, of her own—especially with her power in full bloom.

Flame, if I never saw her standing gloriously in front of me ever again....

I kissed that hand and closed my eyes tightly as tears stung them.

Come back to me. You promised. You promised you would come back to me.

I heard Svyer shifting on the other side of the bed, and I felt her power sink into Sarah a moment later.

There *was* something different about it now. Something cooler, clearer, sharper. It cut through the heat in Sarah's blood as my power never had, no matter how I'd wasted my reserves away trying.

My flameheart flickered with hope. Dangerous hope.

Sarah's nasal passages cooled to my heatsense first, the inflammation dying wherever the scent from the oil traveled. The phenomenon spread to her lungs, then aided by Svyer, through her blood. Even the oil on her forehead appeared to be having some effect, the temperature there dropping so markedly that I could "see" the streaks where the oil had been applied with my heatsense alone.

"Uncle," I said urgently, opening my eyes. "Do you have more of that oil? The topical kind?"

He handed me the dropper vial without a word.

Heedless of the potential waste, I dribbled the oil all over one of my hands and then massaged it into Sarah's arms, her neck, her face. It was a lightweight oil that absorbed into Sarah's parched skin quickly, but it did *something* as it did so, cooling her wherever it touched, dimming the unnatural glow, and giving something to Svyer that she could use, like fuel to her cold fire that was steadily icing the fever out of every cell of Sarah's body, overtaking her like blessed winter frost.

The hope burned brighter, increasing with each measure of Sarah's decrease in heat and light.

Still, I held my breath, and didn't fully release it...

...until Svyer pulled away, a tired but triumphant smile on her lips. She sagged and sat down hastily on the bed, and Fenrith held her shoulder to steady her.

"Svyer," I said in a choked voice.

"It's gone, Ben," Svyer said with that exhausted smile. "She'll live."

I too sagged, but I rested my forehead on Sarah's pillow. Where I could hear her rasping breath even...and, through my touch at her hand again, feel her iceheart strengthen.

CHAPTER TWENTY-ONE

FAMILY

SARAH

I DRIFTED AWAKE, WARM and relaxed. Which was odd, considering those two things weren't often compatible for me anymore.

Unless....

Ben shifted in his sleep, pulling me closer. I knew it was him from just the feel and smell, but I got my confirmation as soon as my eyes shot open. Even in the darkness, I knew that chest I was pressed against, that arm that was slung around me and holding me there. Besides, I knew that muted almost-snore, which I found adorable.

I went stiff with surprise, but not anger. I was more than happy to discover myself where I was. Though I was also more than baffled to be there, considering Ben's latest resolution.

Then memory trickled back, and I understood. I had gone after Svyer, and the effort must have exhausted me so much I blacked out, and Ben, to help me recover as quickly as possible, had slept beside me, as I had done with him before.

My evidence in favor of this theory was the fact that he was still wearing a shirt, when I knew by blessedly unfortunate experience that he preferred to sleep without. Also, he was on top of the blankets in this enormous bed, and I was under.

His snores meant he was genuinely and soundly asleep, but I guessed he hadn't intended to be that way for long. Just as I, when I'd crawled in bed with him while he was in a "magically enhanced deep sleep" (*not* coma, per Kor), had fully intended to get out of bed before he woke up. Yet I could feel it was perhaps hours past dawn, indicating that he'd slept in much longer than he had intended. Now I, like he had before, had woken first.

Now that I was awake, I was wide awake. With it being so far past dawn, it wasn't with my usual Moontouched night buzz; it was simply restfulness and the shot of adrenaline I'd received upon discovering where I was. Rather, more accurately, who I was *with*, since I still didn't know *where* that was, and I didn't know how to figure that out without moving, pressed up as I was against Ben in the darkness.

No one could make rooms as cave dark and silent as the dramá could. No sunlight, no blinking smoke alarms or high-pitched electronic buzzing....

I debated intensely on whether to risk waking him by slipping away. On the one hand, I was anxious to discover if Svyer was alright. On the other, I was almost *certain* I had made it back with her spirit. With that near certainty, I didn't want to disturb the sleep that Ben must have desperately needed.

In the chance Svyer had *died*....

My eyes stung and throat tightened at that fear...but perhaps that was even more reason to let Ben sleep while he could. Perhaps he had collapsed with me from grief as well as the desire to help. Should I really risk disturbing his oblivion?

I was spared the agony of indecision by Ben's snores cutting off and his stirring, perhaps in response to my stiffness. I felt guilty, but I also let out a breath of relief.

Ben shifted, and I felt his breath brush my hair, so it seemed he could tell I was awake too.

"Hey," he greeted me, voice audibly tinged with embarrassment despite the sleep phlegm in his throat.

"Hey," I responded in amusement.

"I wasn't...er, you were...you needed...."

I wondered if he would stop being this adorably bashful after we actually started sleeping together, or if this was simply the way he was built.

"I get it," I said with a chuckle as he pulled away and started slapping around the wall for the gem that would turn on the others.

He found the gem "switch" a moment later, which mercifully made the lightgems *slowly* increase in luminosity to allow our eyes to adjust. Which showed me that, as I thought, he was still fully dressed in a formal shirt and pants—black with artful gold-embroidered swirls. I never saw what had been beneath his robe, but I guessed this was it.

To my pleasure, he slumped back down with a sleepy groan, rubbing his eyes. So maybe he wasn't *quite* ready to run from me. I scooted up the bed to place my head on the pillow so that our faces would be level.

He lowered his hand and blinked at me. "Oh. Sorry about that. I put you on the pillow first, honest."

"I believe you."

I could easily see why I had slipped down from a combination of him pulling me and me snuggling.

"How is Svyer?" I asked quietly.

His gold eyes tightened, which gave me a terrible jolt, but then he said, "Just fine. You brought her back. She's fully herself again."

I cupped his face. "Then why aren't you happy?"

His jaw clenched. "Because of what you put me through after."

I blinked. "What?"

He sighed, eyes drifting closed. "Flame, Sarah. Solim somehow gave you *brightfever.*"

I grew still. Then swiftly withdrew my hand.

"What?" I breathed. "And you *slept* with—"

"You don't have it *now*," Ben said as he cracked open his eyes again. "Through some torched miracle, and with a bit of help from the Trees, Svyer discovered the cure. In one night. So there. You're fine now."

That last part made more sense. I didn't *feel* sick.

But the rest of it....

"In *one night*? She discovered a cure to this plague that's been going across Ykran for a month, which all the best healers of the Realms couldn't stop, in one night?"

He glared at me. "It was that or lose you."

"What?" I whispered.

"Flame, Sarah," he said, closing his eyes again. But this time, he pulled me back in, resting my head against his neck.

He held me tightly, and more than sleep caught in his throat when he said, "I came within dek of losing you. You realize that? *Dek.*"

So, Ben *had* slept beside me partly from grief.

Just not the kind I'd thought.

"I'm sorry," I whispered.

"You'd better be," he muttered.

I laughed faintly. Since it wasn't comfortable to converse in the position I was in, I scooted back just enough to bring my head back to the pillow and meet his eyes. "I'm really not that interested in dying, you know."

"That's nice to hear. Considering how you keep doing this to me."

"Oh, and you've *never* given me a moment of worry," I said dryly.

He sighed. "Point taken. Sorry I'm in such a mood."

"I guess you've earned it, considering."

"But you've earned something too, considering you just single-handedly saved my cousin. Again." He grimaced. "I'm sounding torched ungrateful, aren't I?"

"Well, *technically*, we both did the first time. And the second. I surged back to you, just like you surged back to me."

"You did?" he asked in surprise.

"Yes," I said soberly. "It was how I got away from Solim so quickly. But...not fast enough, apparently."

Ben sighed again. "Sarah, you're a miracle. Don't listen to me complain. I clearly have unreasonable expectations of life."

I snorted. "Yes, truly unreasonable. Me *not dying*."

I regretted my flippancy when I saw him wince. For most people, that would have been funny. Not to Ben, who had already lost too much.

"I'm sorry," I said quietly.

He smiled thinly. To my regret, he let go and rolled away with a groan, sitting up with his back to me at the edge of the bed.

As he pulled on his socks and boots, which he'd carelessly discarded on the floor, I looked around to distract myself from my disappointment. The room was large and grand, but in a cozier, more practical sort of way that seemed to fit my feel for Peacegrowth sensibilities. All that gold mixed with the green, though....

"Where are we?" I asked.

"The Queen's suite," Ben said, though he stood hastily, and his cheeks pinked.

Which helped me put two and two together as I sat up. "You gave me your suite, didn't you?"

I was certain that the Peacegrowth clan hadn't carved out a new suite just for me—in the half-day of warning they had been given before we arrived.

"No, I gave you the *Monarch's* suite. Which I have never used, since I always stayed in the Heir's or a guest room before—and I am perfectly content staying there again."

"Ben," I said with a sigh.

"Kor supports me in this," Ben said. He was probably trying to be firm but was failing. "He says it would send the wrong message to put you in the Heir's suite or anywhere else. Your things are already here and unpacked, and your staff settled in, so...it's final."

"And what kind of message does it send if the King of Flame continues to act like he's the Heir?" I said in exasperation.

"Sleeping in my old room doesn't mean I'm acting like I'm the Heir."

"So, by that logic, *me* sleeping in the Heir's suite is meaningless, too."

He clenched his jaw. "Sarah, there's simply not going to be two suites befitting our station, here or in the other Realms. So, the only logical solution is—"

"—for you to stay here with me."

I hadn't even realized that was where I was going with this until I said it. Ben's jaw clenched.

"Look, Ben," I said with a sigh. "I'm not saying you should sleep in the same bed. But for Flame's sake, these Monarch suites are large enough for a *family*, let alone just the two of us. Sleep wherever you want—on a pallet, on the couch, on the floor—I don't care. But you going to the Heir's suite is nonsense."

"Sarah, I'm *trying* to do what's best for you—"

"You know what's best for me? Acting like you're my partner, *not* my Heir. You're concerned about appearances? What kind of message does it send to the Realms if I keep treating you like my inferior?"

I gripped my earring. "We're a *team* now, Ben, dang it. A *family*. So, we should start acting like one."

He still fumed silently for a second, and during that time, I had a glimmer of insight.

I took a deep breath to calm myself and then asked more gently, "Ben, how much does your reluctance have to do with wanting to do the right thing, and how much does it have to do with your discomfort with taking your father's place?"

He flinched, as I thought he might, but I also thought the blow had been needed. I could only hope I was right.

He turned away for a moment, folding his arms. I let him chew that over. I'd made my points; now was the time for his decision.

He looked back and sighed. "You're...right. Well, it's both reasons, but...it's more the second than I'd realized."

I got up and held out my arms. When he sighed again and held out his own, I went to him and hugged him, and he hugged me back tightly.

"I understand a bit how you feel," I said. "We have big shoes to fill, don't we? ... Er, that's an English phrase that means—"

"I think I understood what it means," Ben said with a rueful chuckle. "And yes, you're right. But it's not fair to you for me to make you fill them yourself. Even just symbolically."

I breathed a sigh of relief that he had finally got it.

Ben sighed too. "You realize it's not just the sleeping situation, right? We're going to have to share the water-rooms."

Which was the Drona term for the bathroom. His use of future tense signaling his resignation gave me even more relief.

I chuckled as I pulled back. "We can come up with a schedule or something. Shouldn't be too hard with our different sleep schedules. Er, today being an exception."

"Speaking of which," Ben said sheepishly. He held me by the shoulders and looked me up and down. "Here I am going on about my own torched problems again, and you just nearly died yesterday. How are *you* feeling?"

His power sunk into me, checking on my health for himself.

"Definitely *not* like I just nearly died yesterday," I said cheerfully. "I feel amazing, thanks to you and Svyer, most likely. And far more awake than I have any right to be at this time of day. I don't suppose you could sleep with me every night...."

I laughed at his glare. "Just kidding."

"I *knew* I was going to regret doing that," he muttered to himself as he let me go.

"I'll behave, Ben," I said earnestly. "Promise."

As hard as it was becoming to wait, I respected his need to do things this way. Now that he'd given in on the room situation, I had to respect it even more. That was the only fair thing for me to do for *him*.

He grunted. "It's not *your* behavior I'm worried about."

SOMEHOW, THE TWO OF us managed the dance that morning of changing and morning ablutions without *too* much awkwardness, which made me hopeful for the coming days.

If my small staff thought that dance strange—from what they could see of it as we each crossed the central sitting room to trade places—they were far too well-trained to show it...or to ask why Ben had suddenly decided to stay in my rooms after all. With surprising equanimity, I let them come to their own conclusions.

But then, I had basically *asked* for Ben to start gossip—for the sake of a unified front, but that was asking for people to make assumptions about us all the same. I supposed I had finally learned that people were going to talk no matter what we did, so I might as well make sure they were saying what I wanted them to.

How...Kor-like of me.

Would wonders never cease.

Fortunately, I got the bathroom second, because Fenra and another attendant came in to help me get ready, so my time took much longer. I was seeing why I had a staff at all, *other* than the fact that Royal attendants were trained to double as bodyguards—and why Ben, being male (and *Ben*) didn't seem to have nearly so many, though I saw a couple gold-uniformed males around by the time I emerged from the bathroom.

Though they all had noticed the way the winds were blowing and adapted quickly, I guessed that our respective attendants would have been much more disgruntled if *I* had decided to pick up and move in with *Ben*.

After I was ready, Vadya, who seemed in command of my schedule, suggested I call my family. When I blanched at the thought of telling them how I'd spent yesterday, she misinterpreted my troubled expression by saying that they had already been informed of my healing.

"They were informed I was *sick*?" I asked, horrified now.

"Of course," she said in surprise. "They helped with the cure, after all."

Ben, I silently growled. I didn't blame him for involving my family if that was necessary to save me, but I did for not mentioning as much. Fortunately for him, he was nowhere in sight, having probably disappeared to do kingly things.

"*Before* I call them, perhaps you had better explain to me everything that happened yesterday," I said grimly.

She did the best she could as a nonparticipant, then I went into the "consort's" study to use one of the walls to call them.

Dad was visibly relieved to see me up and well, which made me inwardly cringe with guilt. He immediately fetched Mom, who gave me a sound scolding accompanied by some tears. Even though I had done my best to keep my promise to be careful and knew I had only done what was necessary, I took it all without a single protest. It was the least I could do after worrying them like that.

Once Mom had her emotional purge, Dad managed to turn the conversation toward any updates about the flowers they had given Ben and how they were going to be used from now on. A good move, considering Mom brightened right away with interest, but unfortunately, I had nothing new to tell them and pointed them to Kor.

I'd been surprised at first to hear that those blue flowers from Mom's garden had been the source of the cure. Then, the more I thought about it, the more sense it made. The archivals had called them icemint and given instructions about making the leaves into a cold-brew tea, so we'd just shrugged and done that, thinking that was all there was to it.

Speaking of which, Mom promised, without prompting, to cultivate what they had left of it carefully and stop harvesting it for tea. I heartily agreed and thanked her, and that brought our conversation to a close—after Mom gave me one last scolding about being careful.

When I came back out of the study, I got a pleasant jolt: Svyer was sitting in my reception room, lounging on one couch and chatting with Fenra.

"Svyer!" I gasped, then ran to her.

She laughed and stood just in time for me to throw my arms around her, and she did the same, giving me a tight squeeze before letting me go to look me up and down. "Goodness, girl, for being at Flame's gate yesterday, you look *good*."

My cheeks warmed. I was getting used to having custom-designed clothing and beauty experts to help me every morning—and appreciating all the practical reasons for each.

Not that I was going to admit that to Kor.

"I could say the same about you, except...."

I stared openly at the silver in her hair. I knew better than to think it was tinsel when I looked into her eyes and saw the flecks there.

"Svyer," I said, aghast. "What did I *do* to you?"

She smiled easily. "I'm not entirely sure it was you—or just you, anyway. I think this might be a Tree thing."

"Why's that?"

"Because our coloring is a Tree thing to begin with," Fenra said casually, still lounging back. I noted again her dark sapphire hair and eyes. "Nothing *we* can do can change it, and that's the way it's meant to be. For drakón, it's our sign of our unwavering allegiance to our Trees. It's also why we can't change clans after we've made our choice...normally."

"Normally," I said faintly, turning my gaze back to Svyer's silver.

She just shrugged with an enigmatic smile. "I think it was necessary to find the cure. We needed something that hadn't existed before: a child of Flame with just a touch of...Ice."

"Vadya said you enchanted the oil," I said slowly.

"And healed you. It felt different when I did. There was something in me that hadn't been there before."

"Svyer...." I said sadly.

"Don't you dare say sorry," she said, wagging a finger at me. "I'm not the least bit sad about it. You saved my life, Sarah. *Twice.*"

Then she grinned broadly. "And gave me a healing edge not even my father has."

I finally put my finger on what was bothering me so much about how calmly Svyer was taking all of this.

My eyes darted to Fenra, our only audience at the moment. She got up and stretched casually. "Well, nice catching up, Svyer, but I'd better get back to work before my sister has my hide. She's gotten so *bossy* for some reason."

She winked at me as she strolled away.

"What's up?" Svyer asked me, raising an eyebrow.

"Svyer, how are you doing?" I asked quietly. "Mentally, I mean."

I could see for myself that she looked remarkably fine physically, considering she'd just been in a coma for over a month. But then, she *was* a drakón, and a daughter of the Peacegrowth Lord besides.

But how could she be acting as if nothing had ever happened to her?

She sobered. "Sarah...I...can't remember anything."

"What?" I asked with a blink.

She sighed. "It's...a common side-effect of innocent consumption. I can't re-member anything remotely related to it. Some more things about the Moonfair have come back to me than I had last night, but all of it's about you, or Ben, or things I did on my own. Neutral or happy things."

I tried not to stare. "Why would that be?"

She shrugged. "We don't know. It makes sense strategically for the Devourer, I guess. I can't tell you anything that might be of use."

She frowned at that.

I shook my head slightly. "How do you feel about that? Really?"

Her eyes soulflared.

"Honestly? *Mad.* I am furious that that—" She said a word that my blood provided no English equivalent for. "—used *me* to hurt you and Ben like that. I could kill him myself right now."

It seemed Solim was racking up quite the list of would-be executioners.

A thin smile flickered to my lips. "What? You haven't taken an oath as a healer to harm no one?"

"Flame no," Svyer said in consternation. "What kind of torched nonsense would that be? There's no point in healing somebody and then letting them die the next day because you won't lift a sword to defend them."

"I guess when you put it like that, that makes sense."

"Besides, I'm *drakón.* I may not be the deadliest drakón, but I'm still sup-posed to protect those less powerful than me."

"So, you're mad. Good. But...are you really OK otherwise?" I asked softly. "You don't have to talk to me, of course, but...."

She smiled thinly and gripped my shoulder. "Thank you, Sarah. I really *am* fine, otherwise. Trust me, though. You'll be one of the people I'll need if anything...more comes back."

I blinked rapidly. "Thank you. It's good to know that."

"Hey," she said with a grin. "You're my friend, too. I hope you know that."

I grinned back. "I do."

"Plus," she said with a wink, "you're about to become *family*. Now that Ben has *finally* gotten around to giving you that earring. Speaking of which!"

She took my chin in one hand to tilt my head to the side, examining the earring. "Very nice! Subtle, classic—no need for all that fanciness that people have gotten into lately. Ben even got it centered."

"Everyone seems surprised by that," I said with a grin.

Svyer rolled her eyes. "Well, it's Ben. Case in point: I can't believe it's been over a month for all of you, and yet he only gave that to you *two* days ago."

My face fell. "He was...busy for a while."

Svyer sighed. "By that, you mean he was being Ben."

"He was *mourning*, Svyer."

"From what I've heard, no, he wasn't. Am I surprised at what he did do? No. Do I blame him? No. I'm just torched mad at that hellfrosted monster for making it so I wasn't there for him, on top of everything—and that I wasn't there to talk some sense into him for your sake."

"I'm not sure even you could have," I mused, thinking of Eskala's words. "It seems only a sound scolding from the Tree could have woken him up like that."

Svyer shook her head. "You're probably right. What wouldn't I give to know just what She said to him to get him to do that."

For the first time, I realized Ben had never told me *exactly* what the Tree had said to him. Not that it had ever come up; I wasn't even sure whether it was appropriate for me to ask. Besides, there really could be nothing more to it than what he'd told me, and its purpose was served and past us now.

But...had Ben been *avoiding* talking about it? If so....

Before I could come to the end of that thought, the other study door opened and Ben walked out, followed by Kor.

"Svyer!" Ben said, grinning with delight, coming over to give her a one-armed hug.

There was something different about him now, something in his eyes. It was more obvious with his cousin miraculously restored and that tragedy, at least, no longer weighing on his soul, but I realized that the beginnings of it had started long before. Perhaps with the Tree's message on my mind, Eskala's words came back to me.

That maybe, just maybe, he had begun to allow others to love him again. Everyone, not just me.

Now, feeling more secure in the hope that spring was here to stay, I allowed myself to ask the same question Eskala had.

Why?

This went deeper than vague warnings and commands. You couldn't command someone to heal or scare someone into love.

Just *what* had the Tree told him?

Chapter Twenty-Two

ALLEGIANCE

Koriben

"Hey, you big lug," Svyer said, grinning at me as I let go of her. "I thought Kor was going to trap you in there forever."

I winced dramatically. "He might have, except I finally convinced him to let me have some breakfast."

"In my defense, he never said he hadn't eaten anything," Kor drawled.

Deliberately, because I'd been hoping to eat with Sarah. The timing of my bringing it up had been deliberate as well when I judged Sarah was waiting for me in the sitting room from how her star in my mind had lingered there.

Svyer chuckled. "Oh, then is this poor timing to invite you and Sarah to dinner with Avva, Avvi, and me?"

"Not at all."

I had only expected as much. Sarah and I were going to have to have at least a private dinner, if not a feast, with every Lord and Lady we visited. At least tonight I could look forward to. It would be more of a quiet family affair, both because that was Fenrith's style and because of the fever precluding large gatherings.

Cure or no, we hadn't yet produced enough of it, sufficiently tested its safety in all situations, and identified the most efficient application. We couldn't declare victory yet, and wouldn't be able to for sevendays or even months to come. Though Fenrith's best healers were now working nonstop to do just that.

The biggest question right now was whether Svyer's intervention was required. If Svyer had to personally enchant every vial of oil, that would be a major bottleneck to combatting the fever. If she had to heal every patient, then we would *have* to keep looking for another solution. But if this plant could work on its own, at least in most cases, then it would be a true cure.

The latest results that Kor had just given me this late morning were looking promising, especially for mid-to-late second-stage patients that had previously been unhealable. Something about that oil—inhaling its vapors or having it applied, or both—appeared to be the key unlocking the door for our healing power to do its work.

The Danyeth healers were beside themselves right now, and their cultivators were hard at work propagating the spare plants Svyer had given them as quickly as possible. Drakón cultivators could speed the growth and reproduction of plants far beyond their natural pace; doing so took a tremendous amount of energy from them, and they disliked forcing growth in general, but in crises like these, they were willing to make an exception. In fact, as soon as dawn had come, they had sent seeds through the sungate to across Ykran and even Yonvey—the Brightflare Realm and our greatest agricultural hub—for cultivators everywhere to do the same.

Once again, Sarah—with the help of her family—had changed everything. I felt more the torched fool than ever to have kept her back for this long. At the same time, with the cure having come nearly at the cost of her own life, as I had somehow *known* it might....

I had felt the burn of the oath in my blood as I held her in the darkness and contemplated how I could get her to go back—not to sever any ties between us, but to finally persuade her to stay where it was safe. But I knew from the Tree's warnings that wasn't possible anymore for her, and I knew I could never persuade my *sera*. Somehow, I would have to keep bearing that risk, holding more tightly than ever to the Tree's promise to protect her.

Were all the lives that had been lost from this fever on my conscience because I hadn't been able to bear that risk before? Did that make me a cold-blooded murderer?

"Well, good," Svyer said. Her sobering expression snapped my thoughts back into the present. "Because I have another invitation to deliver. Just in case no one has spoken to you about it yet, I want the two of you to come to my presentation."

My flameheart sank.

"Your what?" Sarah asked.

"I'm going before my Tree," Svyer said calmly. "Just as soon as the two of you are ready."

I looked at her, pained. "Is that necessary, Svyer? You've already been declared innocent and purged."

"While I was unconscious. Yes, no one is pounding on Avva's gates to force me to, but I *want* to do this, Ben. It feels...right. What I need."

You haven't remembered, have you? I asked silently, trying to hide the sudden clench I felt inside.

No, I haven't. That's not the reason.

Svyer's eyes were clear and honest, and I let out a hopefully subtle breath of relief. Although, from those silver flecks, I received my first inkling about what her true reason was, and I felt another kind of clench.

But...if this was what she wanted, needed....

She saw comprehension dawn in my eyes and nodded slowly. Then smiled. "Go have your breakfast with Sarah, and I'll come back for you two in half a deken. That is, if you're coming."

"Of course we are," Sarah said, taking my hand. She looked troubled as well, but not as if she had yet guessed what Svyer intended. "Or, at least, *I* am."

Svyer looked at me. Not in a challenge, but in question.

Gauging whether I would truly be alright.

I nodded. *It's your decision. It's not like you need my permission, you know that. Especially if this is the will of the Trees. But for what it's worth, I'll support this.*

Out loud, I said, "Of course I'm coming."

Svyer's eyes warmed in relief. I didn't think she would have let me stop her, but she hadn't wanted to create ill feelings between us, or between Sarah and me, either.

"Thanks, Ben," she said simply.

FORTUNATELY, KOR WAS THINKING ahead, as usual, because before we left, he had Vadya get out the prototypes of the protective gear he had commissioned for Sarah—this time, not to protect her from the fever, but rather the heat of a Tree of Flame.

Although the clothing looked very similar, and thus not out of place with our own veils and gloves. It might seem counterintuitive to put Sarah in a hooded robe that heavy and thick, but if it insulated her from the heat outside and kept her cool within, then it would serve its purpose. Given the time of day, Kor allowed me to charge the robe myself, reluctantly allowing me to make the gems glow gold instead of white.

"At least the gold doesn't clash with the black and white," Svyer pointed out to him with a grin, gesturing to the colors of Sarah's robe. "Now she just matches Ben more than ever."

Because of course I was also wearing black with gold accents again, having put on what my attendant had set out for me.

"Hmm, I wonder why I commissioned their wardrobe to be this way," Kor said with an answering smirk.

So, there was yet *another* reason Kor had persuaded me to buck tradition. Figured.

Svyer rolled her eyes. Without Solim's influence on her, she no longer seemed to have a fireball to throw at Kor. That didn't mean the two of them had ever been close, and probably never would be.

"Yes, yes, you're a genius. Can we go now?"

We met with Yvera in the central court, and with Lord Fenrith and Lady Hilyan outside the King's Wing, along with his wings, which finished out our small party. Even as momentous an occasion as this was, we had a legitimate excuse to keep the audience for Svyer's presentation small, and thank the Flame for that.

Just as before, Sarah examined our surroundings with interest as we walked through the hold. I tried imagining what it would be like to see Danyeth for the first time, especially without a fundamental understanding of how the Realms worked. I found it difficult, but I had a bit of personal experience to go by: I had found what little I had seen of Earth to be bewildering.

Sarah had done much better than I had in learning to navigate a new way of life, and her expression right now was one of interest and delight rather than what mine had probably been of bafflement and overwhelm.

Once, she asked me, *Have they made each section a different biome?*

Yes, I said, inwardly shaking my head in awe of her. *Each represents a different region on Ykran.*

Ah, that makes sense, Sarah said in satisfaction.

After a pause, she said with a contented sigh, *I like it here.*

I looked down at her in surprise. *Why in particular?*

Again, I tried to look at my second home with fresh eyes. I saw many things to like, but I wanted to know what exactly drew Sarah so that I could reproduce it for her if possible. I was all too aware of how much she had given up to be with me, in my worlds.

Sarah was silent for a moment. When she answered, her voice was thoughtful. *It doesn't feel like I'm underground. I feel like I can breathe more easily.*

I suddenly realized what she meant, and my flameheart sank.

No sections of Danyeth were as overwhelmingly full of life as the Lord's Wing, but plants had been brought in and cultivated as best as they could be from each region, and what the inhabitants couldn't reproduce in life, they did so in landscape tapestries, tile mosaics or murals in the floors and walls, and representative color schemes. No other capital city had tried as hard or as successfully to make one feel as if one weren't cloistered in a hold but rather out in the beauty of their world—minus all its dangers.

To most dramá, being inside a mountain's heart meant *safety*. Warmth. Community. Why hadn't I thought more about how Sarah, used to living out in the open, might feel the opposite?

Yet another example of what she had given up.

Why didn't you ever say anything? I asked, trying to hide my distress.

She must have heard the emotion anyway, because she glanced up at me in concern. *Ben, I didn't mean.... You people build your spaces so large and bright that most of the time, I don't think about it.*

Yet something had always been missing, even if she hadn't realized it or put it into words before. Only now did I understand why she had loved the garden in Olsdak so much, why it had given her something she had been lacking before. That thing I'd resolved to discover so that I could give it to her again.

Now that I knew what that thing was, my flameheart only sank. I didn't know how I was going to keep that promise. I couldn't replicate the Olsdak garden at Crownhold—not outdoors, at least. The scorching desert would make any effort unjustifiably laborious and expensive. And though the region around Crownhold was generally safe, I wasn't about to create a spot where the Devourer could count on Sarah appearing.

I need to talk to Kor, I thought grimly. *Perhaps it's not too late to make some adjustments to her wing.*

If so, I would do what it would take to persuade Gwinra. Surely if I made her see how necessary it was for the Queen's comfort, she would comply. However grudgingly.

We reached the Danyeth Temple soon after that, shifting my thoughts from gloom about Sarah to trepidation about Svyer.

I'd told Svyer that I supported this, which was true. I wasn't a jealous King begrudging her right to choose. But as her cousin and friend, I worried all the same. What if she was making a hasty decision? What if some physical or spiritual trauma was lingering, however unconsciously, that was driving her to do this before she'd fully thought things through, and one day she would regret her choice? Given the previous impossibility of what she was about to do, I doubted the Trees would let her take her choice back.

From Hilyan's stoic expression, I guessed she had similar worries, magnified by the feelings of a mother. If Fenrith did, he didn't show it. His eyes and smile radiated tranquility just as strongly as ever, especially with Svyer now restored. Just...as he had always had faith she would be.

Was I supposed to be taking more strength from the fulfillment of that sign he had been given than I had been?

Sarah's slowing steps, and her dragging at my hand, finally registered in my torched brain, and I shifted my focus once again back to her.

Are you alright? I asked.

Getting better, she said resolutely, lifting her chin and quickening her step. *The humidity was getting to me, but I think the robe has kicked into higher gear.*

The metaphor confused me a bit, but I thought I got the gist, especially from the flare of the gold gems that were the buttons of her robe. I made a stern mental note to myself to keep track of the power levels and recharge them as soon as they flagged.

I understood what she meant by the humidity. The cloying heat was increasing with each step we took down that bright central passage to the Temple Heart. It felt nice to me, apart from how my clothing began clinging to my skin as it dampened from the steam. As much as I normally enjoyed steam rooms, you weren't supposed to be *clothed* in them, for good reason. We were all going to have to change after we got back, but that was to be expected. The Peacegrowth clan had long ago accepted that as simply the price of visiting their Tree.

A price that the rest of us were paying with varying degrees of acceptance.

Gah, Yvera sent me. *I'm going to have to put my armor in a heat vent to get it dry now.*

You chose to wear it here, I replied. She had been to the Ykran Tree with me before; she would have known what she was getting into.

When we entered the Heart chamber, its fullest extent was lost to the waves of hot water vapors that glistened like fog under the light of the cracks in the earth above; that was where all the moisture came from. There was good reason for the temperate rainforest surrounding Danyeth: even when it wasn't raining, it was always damp.

That dampness, in combination with a Tree of Flame, created the steaming jungle that we had just entered.

More than just the steam obscured the extent and shape of the chamber. Thick vines covered the walls, and lesser trees of all varieties formed their own forest and canopy around us, twining their roots among the great ones of the Tree.

We approached Her along the only clear path. Here, perhaps at the Tree's command, the growth obediently stopped short of the gravel road and formed a natural, living barrier as all the roots, moss, and ferns combined and spread along its borders. Only straight ahead could we see Her mighty trunk that dwarfed all the others as a moon does the stars, and only through spots in the canopy could we catch sight of Her flickering emerald leaves of fire high above.

We climbed the steps to the dais set into the ground at Her base, with Her roots curving in a circle to form a natural retaining wall. We had the Heart to ourselves for now. Fenrith could have arranged that, but our solitude could also be coincidence. Daughter Trees in other Realms weren't visited as much as the Mother one on Ythra was, with the former rarely showing an avatar to anyone but Their Lords or Ladies outside of ceremonies and being considered by everyone else as extensions of the Mother.

The moist heat came off the Tree in waves. Sarah's movements were stiff, and her shoulders drooped, so as Svyer approached the shallow pit with the ritual flame in the center, I sent a prayer to the Tree for her sake that She would not take long to grant us an audience.

Svyer raised her hand over the flame. With her back to me, I couldn't be certain, but I imagined her eyes were closed as she spoke. I did so as well.

"My Lady of the Flame," she said reverently. "I, Svyer, your daughter, come before You seeking an audience."

My flameheart jolted with surprise, relief, and trepidation when a voice responded almost at once. A voice that sounded like sliding ash and crackling embers.

"Speak, Svyer. I am here."

My eyes shot open.

There indeed, on the other side of the fire, was the Ykran version of the fiery avatar most people knew as the Tree's sentient manifestation. She could appear in other forms, but those were private, subliminal messages used in personal audiences. In public, She most often appeared as this being, which had cracked, dark coal for a body, flickering flames to cover Her torso, pupilless embers for eyes, and flowing ash for hair that moved in a nonexistent wind. The flames and embers in this case were the same color as the emerald ones in the ritual fire.

Sarah stiffened in surprise, and I clenched her hand in comfort. This was the first time she was being presented before a Tree of Flame, let alone seeing Her avatar—and She was an intimidating sight indeed. Even I felt tempted to flinch, especially at my unworthiness to come before Her again.

Fortunately, She didn't so much as glance away from Svyer.

"My Lady," Svyer said calmly. "I thank you."

"*Speak,*" the Tree said.

"I have come to present myself before You after having been purified by You and now my spirit restored by the Queen behind me."

"*Again, I declare you innocent of your consumption, which I have long since purged, as you said. What more have you come here to ask of Me, child?*"

The Tree's voice was not scolding, no matter how it crackled by nature. It was patient and dignified, prompting Svyer to continue.

Svyer took a deep breath. "If it pleases You, my Lady...I wish to pledge myself to the Tree of Ice and Her Queen."

Sarah inhaled sharply. I clenched her hand, and when her head lifted to glance in alarm at me, I told her evenly, *This is her choice.*

Hopefully I hid my own doubts from my tone and expression. If Svyer would one day regret her choice, the Tree would know that and could refuse her now.

When the Tree's avatar turned Her head to look at my betrothed, I doubted She intended to.

"*Sarah, My Sister's Queen—come forward.*"

Sarah's eyes darted to mine one more time, and I let go of her hand and nodded encouragingly. Inside, I prayed again that the Tree would be swift for her sake. She was looking too dazed and exhausted for my comfort.

Sarah walked slowly to stand next to Svyer at the ritual fire.

"*You have heard My daughter's request. What say you?*"

Sarah glanced at Svyer.

Out loud, perhaps for the benefit of everyone, Svyer said, "This is what I want, Sarah. It's how I think I can do the most good—for you, for the Realms, and for myself. I want to help, and this is how."

Sarah swallowed and looked back at the Tree. "I say that this is her choice."

"*Well spoken,*" the Tree said quietly.

She looked back at Svyer. "*Are you certain, child? If you so desire, I can remove what has begun in you and restore you completely as a child of Flame. If you decide to retain your sliver of Ice now, it will remain forever.*"

"I am certain," Svyer answered. Her voice was calm, her back straight, her chin only lowered in deference.

Without changing Her emotionless expression, the Tree nodded. "*Then I now grant you leave to present yourself before My Sister, who will seal what has begun. You will keep your flameheart, for to take that from you now would kill you, and you will remain drakón, but you will become a child of Ice nonetheless, subject to My Sister and Her Queen.*"

Svyer bowed—an honor we only bestowed on our Tree. "Thank you, my Lady."

For the first time, the hint of a smile touched the Tree's lips. "*You have chosen well, My faithful daughter. Though I will miss you.*"

For the first time, a hint of emotion entered Svyer's voice. "And I will miss You."

The Tree's smile faded, and She nodded slowly. "*Go now. Take your Queen away, for she has endured My presence long enough.*"

Her eyes fell on Sarah, and I was shocked to see a bit of...humor in that normally emotionless face.

"I will, my Lady," Svyer said, putting a hand on Sarah's shoulder.

Then the Tree's avatar was gone. One moment there, only empty air in the next.

Svyer put an arm around Sarah and began to lead her back to the rest of us. I strode forward and scooped her up into my arms before she could stop me.

"I'm *fine*," Sarah protested, face darkening as her eyes darted to the group.

"Of course you are. And you'll be finer *faster* if you let me carry you," I said firmly as I swiftly led the way down the steps.

Sarah grumbled something so low, I didn't catch it, but she didn't tell me to put her down. I knew my gut was right when she let her head rest against me and her eyes drifted closed, too tired for the moment to put up a fight. I ached to use my power to make sure she was truly alright and didn't have a resurgence of the fever, but I didn't want to give her more heat.

"Sorry, Sarah," Svyer said as she kept pace with me. "You really did have to be there, though."

"I know," Sarah sighed. "Not your fault."

She cracked open her eyes to glare. "Except for getting it into your head to become one of my subjects."

"Technically," Svyer said with a grin, holding up silver strands of her hair. "I think *you* got it into my head first."

Chapter Twenty-Three

ARRANGEMENTS

Sarah

THE DINNER THAT EVENING became a bittersweet farewell for both Ben and me and for Svyer. After some discussion, Ben, Kor, Fenrith, and I thought it best to continue the tour, allowing Fenrith to focus his efforts on healing his people; Ben and I had already done for them what we could, and now we served them best by getting out of their way to let them do their jobs.

After even more discussion with Svyer, me, and my family, Svyer decided to stay with my family in our hold for the time being. That was where she felt she was meant to be and could do the most good, and that feeling had factored into her decision to become of Ice.

"They need one of us to be with them," Svyer insisted. "I can be their healer. I already have more experience healing humans than anyone besides Ben, and more healing knowledge and skill than him besides. No offense, cousin."

She added that last with a smirk at Ben.

"None taken," Ben said with a smile.

In fact, Ben seemed to be taking Svyer's shift in allegiance from him to me with surprising acceptance. Not that I thought him the petty, greedy type of leader, but this would change things between them. They would always be family, but Ben was no longer her Monarch, as he'd seemed destined to be their whole lives up to this point. Now...I was.

Yet Ben didn't seem to mind. The only negative emotion I caught from him was the slight tightening of his eyes in worry when he would look at Svyer when she wouldn't notice. I could understand that kind of worry—I felt it myself, but I knew I would only offend Svyer if I questioned her. She seemed resolute, and...her Tree said she had chosen well.

Though I was sad at the thought of Svyer picking up her life and moving to my Realm, for the relief alone I felt at the thought of my family having access to a healer, I could not thank her enough.

"And I can show them our way of life," Svyer continued thoughtfully. She looked at me. "Your family must have so many questions, just as you did in the beginning."

We'd met because I was standing helplessly in front of the two choices of water-room doors, not even knowing which one was for females, let alone how to use the facilities beyond. Svyer had taken me under her wing immediately, before ever knowing that I was different, and long before knowing what I was meant to become.

I chuckled in memory, and at the thought of all the questions my family would immediately have for her about the most basic of things. I hoped she was prepared to teach Mom how to cook everything that was in her garden.

"You have *no* idea. But, honestly," I said with a faint smile, "you might become Dad's multilingual dictionary more than anything, at least for a while. He's been struggling learning to read what's in our archivals, and you could be just the breakthrough he needs."

Svyer chuckled. "Well, my Vardak teacher would never have believed that *I* would become a language tutor, but I guess if that's what's needed the most at the moment, then that's what I'll be."

That settled, I just had to convince my family. I knew most of them would either accept her offer of help wholeheartedly or be neutral, and Svyer's warmth and goodness would soon win even the neutral ones over.

The only one I was worried about was Michael.

So, before bringing it up with the whole family, I went alone to my study and got him and Dad on a call first—ostensibly to discuss something with my wings.

Once they were both there, I presented Svyer's offer to them, and their reactions were just what I had expected: Dad grew thoughtful, and Michael swore.

"Hell no. No way are we allowing one of *those dragons* to *stay* here."

"She's not a dragon, Michael," I said firmly, overlooking the fact that I frequently slipped into that terminology in my own mind, particularly when they were in drakáform. "Her race is *dramá*, and her Blood manifestation is *drakón*. And for your purposes, most of the time, she's human."

That made one potential problem occur to me. I wondered if Svyer had thought about the fact that our hold didn't have any openings that led to the surface—that we were aware of, anyway—and we suspected the air outside might be suboptimal from the enchantments Kor had discerned on the window in the welcoming hall. Even if it was breathable after all, I doubted Svyer was going to become enough of Ice to make the frozen landscape outside pleasant for her. All that meant she wasn't going to be able to fly as a draká as much as she was used to—not until it was safe for her to come and go between our Realms without risking carrying brightfever to my family.

I sighed and made a note to talk to her about it. Right now, I had to focus on the conversation at hand.

"Michael, what are your objections?" Dad said, looking at him. "Be specific."

"We don't know her. We don't know if we can trust her. We can't just give her free access to...*everything*, much less our family."

"I know her, and I trust her," I said, trying to keep my temper in check. The very thought of *Svyer* intending harm on anyone (Solim aside) was unthinkable. "She saved my life, Michael. *Twice*."

First from darkfever when I first arrived in the Six Realms, and yesterday from brightfever.

"Yeah, well, from what I've heard, you saved hers, so you're even."

"It's not a matter of being even or owing anything. She's a *good* person. Like, truly good. She's offering to sacrifice her home, her people, and, to some extent, even her identity to help us."

"That's what's so fishy," Michael insisted, arms folded. "Why?"

I gritted my teeth, then took a few breaths. "Because we need the help, and that's what Svyer does. She helps people."

"We're doing just fine—"

"Michael," Dad said in warning. He would not allow his son to spout pure falsehoods, even to vent.

Michael just looked away, fuming.

I reminded myself of all the reasons Michael had for being difficult. He, just like all of us, had given up his own home, people, and identity—without as much choice as Svyer had in the matter. The one thing he had truly chosen was to become my rightwing, and that had required him to become something *not human*. Still, he did it, out of love for our family and particularly for me, and a sense of duty that was a fundamental part of him.

As much as he'd relished his newfound abilities as we'd practiced, I knew that what we were now still disturbed him at a deep level. On top of all those things, his pride, especially in taking care of our family, had taken beating after beating as I, his younger sister, braved dangers he wasn't allowed to protect me from, and he was forced to take what he saw as handouts for us to survive.

I sighed.

"Michael," I said slowly. "If the Tree said it was safe for you to let Svyer stay...would you let her?"

He clenched his jaw. "There you go about the Tree again. The Tree this, the Tree that. What does that *Tree* care about us? All it's done is bring us here, maybe to die. Certainly seems like it's trying to off *you*."

I winced at his use of *it*, more than at any other part of his irreverent speech. Good thing Ben wasn't in the room right then. But then, this was why I'd made sure of that.

I had been hoping to suggest that Michael talk to the Tree, as I had with Rachel and Dad. But...I didn't think he was ready for that, nor did he seem ready to even accept Her answer if someone else obtained it. I could *maybe* try ordering him, but that's not the way we had operated so far since I'd been invested as Queen. I didn't think he'd accept an order from me. In fact, I thought it would only make him more incensed and entrenched.

I needed some way to convince him that Svyer was trustworthy. That she would never....

I winced at the thought of asking her for this, on top of everything she had already offered, on top of what she had already sworn: at the Moonfair, she had sworn a blood oath not to harm me just to be let into the King's Wing to *see* me.

But if it would convince Michael....

"Michael, if she swore a blood oath, would that be enough?"

He met my eyes, expression skeptical. "That's that thing that Ben did? That promise they can't break, because of 'magic'?"

"Right."

He frowned. "What *exactly* stops them?"

"They swear over a fire, with their blood. And when they're done, that fire goes into the cut they made. Into their blood, Michael. That's what stops them. They...just can't break that kind of promise."

"What's it like when they try, anyway?"

I swallowed. "I don't know. But Svyer already swore one to not harm me, as part of being allowed to enter a secure place where I was staying once."

I wasn't about to go into why security measures had been so stringent. And even though I was tempted to mention as evidence of the efficacy of her oath that even Solim hadn't been able to force her to break it to harm me, I decided that wasn't wise to get into either. I trusted the Tree of Flame if She had said (twice) that Svyer was innocent and purged of the consumption, but Michael wouldn't.

Michael frowned. But when he glanced at Dad, and saw Dad's answer there, he grunted.

"Fine. *If* she'll swear this 'blood' oath to not hurt any of us or abuse our trust, and in front of me...then I suppose she can stay."

SVYER AGREED AND BRUSHED aside all my apologies.

"Sarah, it's only natural for them to have concerns. I'm a stranger, and a different race besides. Our peoples are naturally going to have challenges adjusting to each other. Flame only knows they did in the beginning. But that's exactly one of the reasons why I should do this. I need to show them that at least some of us mean well. I need to be the bridge for them, just like you are for us."

So Svyer followed me back into my study and, when I called Dad and Michael again, she swore the blood oath without hesitation, on Michael's terms. But first she answered Michael's questions about why she was doing this.

The longer they talked face to face, the more I could see Michael's resistance melting. He'd always had an instinctual feel for who was trustworthy and who wasn't; that was one thing that had made him a good cop. Not even he seemed able to convince himself Svyer was *un*trustworthy by the time she was done with her oath.

Not that he was happy; he still had his bruised pride to nurse. But he conceded with slightly more grace this time that she could come.

"Not that we have much room," he said inhospitably. "All the bedrooms we have are taken."

I'd already thought of this. Technically, there were four free bunks, two in the girls' room that Lizzy and Abby shared and two in the twins' room, but I could see why neither one was ideal for Svyer to share. So, I had already come up with a solution that I thought would be fair to Svyer and keep the peace in my family.

"Tell Rachel that if she gives up her room to Svyer, she can sleep in mine. I have a hunch the door will start opening for her, if that's what I want."

Michael's eyebrows went up, and he whistled.

"Are you sure, Sarah?" Dad asked quietly.

He knew at least something of how much that room had meant to me over this past month.

"Sarah," Svyer said hesitantly. "You don't have to do this."

I thought I did. Svyer was the daughter of a Lord. As little as that meant here, it still meant she had grown up in the Lord's Wing, and I doubted she had ever couch surfed in her life. Giving Svyer her own room was the least I could do to make sure she didn't instantly regret her decision to help my family.

"Yup," I said to Dad, hopefully showing nothing of my sadness. "I'm sure."

Michael grunted. "Well, you're going to make Rachel's day."

That was an understatement. Rachel had been green with envy when she'd seen my bedroom. It was a testament to how much she loved me and how good of a sister she was that she hadn't let that room drive a wedge between us.

Or...not a big one, anyway. Most of the time.

Alright, she had only brought it up at least once a day, but for her, that was generous. I could tell she was genuinely *trying* not to be bitter, and to me, that counted for something.

I felt a bit of a loss. This was tantamount to surrendering the room to her forever, because there wasn't any kicking Rachel out once she got entrenched; even if she were willing to leave, asking her to go back to her humdrum room after living like a princess for who knows how long would be too cruel.

On the other hand, it wasn't like I didn't have an excess of places to stay already, some of them even more elaborate. Leaving my room vacant while I traveled in luxury and my family squeezed to accommodate my friend would have been ridiculous, and certainly not the act of a leader who was supposed to be serving them.

Giving that room up to my Heir felt...right. Like this was yet another step toward becoming Ben's partner, just as he had surrendered his comfortable place as Heir for me. That rightness was one reason I was sure that the door would start opening for Rachel.

Perhaps it had been meant for *her* all along.

Everything was settled by the time Ben led me from the King's Wing to the Lord's Wing for dinner. Which was remarkably simple, just the five of us in their private family dining room, and felt remarkably natural, considering this was the first time I had sat down with anyone from his family for a meal. Boy, had I lucked out on the in-law front.

Neither of Svyer's parents seemed bitter that I was stealing their newly restored daughter. Lady Hilyan was sad, but whenever she would look at me, she would smile. And *all* Lord Fenrith did was smile. A calm, simple smile, but still powerful in how its tranquility seemed to permeate the room.

I studied him when I thought I could get away with it. He was the closest thing I'd had so far to guess what Ben's mother might have been like. If
his mother had been anything like his uncle, then I could see how the old
King might have fallen for her and fallen hard...and why both he and Ben had
mourned her so deeply.

Fenrith caught me studying him once, and his smile deepened and his eyes
glittered knowingly.

I knew he'd guessed what I was doing when he told me silently, *Nyethra would
have loved you, my dear. In fact, I am certain she does, from beyond the Flame.*

I looked away hastily, unable to tell him I already knew for myself that he was
right, as incredible as both that love and that knowledge were.

The time flew. We sat in our chairs long after we were done eating, just
talking. Svyer and her parents had many questions for me, and I greedily drank
in all the tidbits they gave me, particularly about Ben and Svyer growing up.
They made Ben blush more than once—especially Svyer, who relished tattling
on his exploits to me.

Apparently, he had been guilty of everything from petty theft (stealing freshly made hotsweets from Hilyan's kitchen) to disturbing the public peace by
turning a volpan (sounded like a hyper cross between a fox and a squirrel that
lived in the forest above) loose during a spring equinox ceremony.

That latter story took a while as Svyer delightedly recounted all the chaos that
had ensued as people had chased it, eventually running it up to the top tier of
an ornamental fountain, where it had clung, soaked and terrified, to the stone
topper—and how much trouble Ben had been in afterward.

"Uncle Kavarian was *mad*," she laughed. "I don't think I've ever seen him
that furious with Ben. He—"

Then she stopped, face falling as Ben flinched at her use of the present tense
and the reality that the old King was now gone dawned on her face anew. She,
of all of us, had had the least time to adjust to that fact, and the least closure to
deal with her grief.

As Svyer blinked back tears, Hilyan swiftly intervened with a different story.
By the time she was done, Svyer had recovered enough to recount the time soon

after Ben had become drakón that he had accidentally set a rare potted plant on fire, whose fumes had made everyone who inhaled it inebriated. He had got it so bad that he'd begun arguing with a tree. The normal, non-talking kind.

"You'd think you were trying to convince Sarah that I was a tiny, idiotic barbarian," Ben muttered after that one, glaring at her.

"But you *were*." Svyer grinned, shoving him fondly.

She winked at me. "I didn't always like him this much. A lot of the time, I thought he was a nuisance. I figured it was finally time for some payback."

Ben narrowed his eyes. "You know, you're almost making me glad that you didn't wake up until *after* she'd taken my earring."

Once again, I glanced in wonder at the white gem I could only just see glowing through his shoulder-length hair. It still came as a surprise, every time. Especially since this was Ben: the single earring gave him a kind of roguish air that was hilariously incongruous to me.

"Oh, there's a reason I've been saving these until now," Svyer said. "I want her as family too, you know."

Family, I thought in wonder again. These people were going to be my family. That day couldn't come soon enough.

Although Svyer was making me a little nervous to have kids. I knew plenty about raising and corralling little ones—the normal kind. Magic, as I was discovering with my youngest siblings, seemed to add a whole new level.

Hang on a sec, I thought with dawning bewilderment. *What kind of kids would Ben and I have?*

Should that question have occurred to me before now? Not that I was regretting my decision, but....

It needed pondering. I found myself wishing I could get Svyer alone before we parted ways so we could have yet another kind of talk that I only felt comfortable having with her.

Fortunately, that was probably a concern for years from now. Not only did I not feel ready, I couldn't imagine my overprotective Ben thinking it was safe to have kids yet. Not until we had gotten the Realms as stable as they were going to be. If even then.

Plenty of time to ponder, I told myself. *Plenty.*

BY THE TIME WE got back to the King's Wing, it was late—for Ben, at least. Even though we had woken up at the same time, I still had more rest than he had, and my power was waxing while his was waning. He was yawning most of the way, and I knew he was truly tired because he followed me automatically into the Monarch's suite and only realized where we were and what was coming next when I halted in the sitting room.

He froze for a moment, eyes glancing around sharply as if belatedly planning his defense strategy. Fortunately, there were currently no staff members around to witness his minor panic.

"What?" I teased. "You haven't actually decided where you're sleeping yet?"

"No," he growled, running a hand through his hair. He glared at me. "You're taking the bed."

"Agreed," I said. Even though I would feel ridiculous, when he needed the size of that thing far more than I did. But I would give him this.

It was worth it when his shoulders lowered slightly with that first battle won, and with an ease that visibly surprised him. Perhaps I should have held out as part of a negotiation strategy; that was something Rachel would have done. But that fact made me want to do it even less.

Besides, Ben had already conceded in what mattered most to me, in what was an emotionally and physically difficult thing for him. It was my turn now to give him whatever would make him comfortable doing that for me.

"There's always a couch," I said, gesturing to the ones around the sitting room. But hoped that wasn't what he was planning.

"Like that would be restful, with everyone coming and going at all deken." He raised an eyebrow at me. "Besides, isn't this about appearances?"

I grinned, glad he understood. "Yeah, it would look like I'd kicked you out."

It would be better to send him to the Heir's suite at that point.

His eyes rested darkly on the bedroom, having come to the same conclusion I had.

"There are couches in there, too," I said.

He sighed. "None of them would be comfortable, though."

Too short, too small.

He groaned. "Alright, I'll set up a pallet on the floor in there. Happy?"

"Thank you," I said simply, squeezing his hand. "I'll behave, promise. Besides, I'm not ready to go to bed yet, so you have it to yourself for the moment. I imagine you'll be out long before I turn in."

"Probably," he agreed with a sigh.

He let go of my hand. I was a bit surprised that was it, but then he said, "I'll come say goodnight after I've done my thing."

He gestured to the passage leading to the water-room. Or rather rooms, because the various functions were separated, which would make our dance to avoid awkwardness easier. Perhaps my joke that this suite could fit a family wasn't so far off—maybe it was meant to. After all, if a Monarch traveled with young children, where were they supposed to put them? Not the Heir's suite, especially if that spot was taken.

"Ah, makes sense," I told him. "Enjoy."

I knew how much the dramá liked their evening dose of warmth, and as I'd discovered this morning, there was even a sauna in that hallway.

He smiled. Then, seeming not able to resist, he ducked in and kissed me, slowly and sweetly.

Of course, someone chose that moment to walk in. I started, but Ben didn't let me go for another couple of seconds. When he pulled away, I saw Kor standing there, smirking. Ben just nodded to him in casual greeting.

"Need anything, Kor? I was about to head to bed...."

"Oh, no. Nothing that can't wait. Go on ahead."

Ben nodded again and then strode out of the room.

"Hi," I said to Kor, cheeks warm. I didn't know why I felt so awkward now, when we hadn't been caught doing anything more than we'd already done a dozen times in front of him by now. Yet there was something to his smile....

"I was wondering if he would bow out at the last dek," Kor said casually. "But I should have known I could count on you to seduce him into staying, just like you did this morning."

Now I understood what was behind that smile, and my cheeks heated even more.

Stiffly, I retorted, "I'll have you know I did no such thing. *Either* time."

"Sarah, Sarah." Kor chuckled. "Ben has had girls *try* to seduce him for years. It's your very lack of intending to do any such thing that he finds so seductive. I knew he would find you irresistible nearly the moment I saw you."

I blinked.

If Kor was on to something…that would explain some of Ben's reluctance to stay in the same room as me. My iceheart sank. I'd promised to behave…but was I doomed to tempt him either way?

Then something hit me.

"That fibber," I gasped. "Ben said you *supported* him staying in the Heir's suite."

Kor rolled his eyes. "That was true only so far as I said that, if he was going to *insist* on sleeping separately from you, then he had better take the Heir's suite and give you the Monarch's."

Oh. Well, that made me feel better. I couldn't remember Ben ever blatantly lying to me—at least, not in a way that was believable, so that almost amounted to honesty. So the evidence of at least a half-truth was comforting…and explained Ben's awkwardness when he'd tried convincing me of as much.

Kor said, "But thank the Flame you persuaded him otherwise."

I grew hot again at his renewed smirk. "You realize we're still not…."

Why was I even bothering to explain myself to him? Perhaps it had been his comments about my intentions. I didn't like the implication of me being manipulative.

"Oh, I don't care," Kor said dismissively. "Do—or don't do—whatever you like, so long as you keep Ben here. We *need* the two of you acting unitedly, as partners just as much as equals. It might be different if we had two Monarch's suites, but we don't. And maybe if how you two felt about each other wasn't such public knowledge, if you two weren't the Moondaughter and Golden Heir of legend, it might be different. But separate sleeping arrangements at this point will make it look like there's a schism between you, or that you're only marrying because of the politics, and we can't afford that right now."

So, my gut had been right. That was comforting.

Still, I raised an eyebrow at him. "You realize this might not have been an issue if *someone* had let us heartbind first?"

"The grand tour comes first," Kor said innocently. "The people have a right to meet their future Queen before everything is final."

My gut twisted. "Can they.... Is there a vote or something?"

"No," Kor said with comforting finality. "It's a symbolic gesture, that's all. You've already removed the only legal impediment with your blood registration. The only being that can deny your right to marry now is the Tree."

"Oh, right," I said, grimacing. "Because I'm technically underage by your law, right? I'm only eighteen, so I need my Tree's permission."

Kor grinned. "Well, that's another reason. But technically, even if you were nineteen summers, the Tree could refuse at the ceremony to allow you to heartbind. Just a precaution for the Monarch's heartbinding—that's not typical for everyone. But that's only happened once in public before, because every Monarch with half their wits about them now seeks the Tree's permission in private first. Fortunately for you, She's already given it. Seeing as how, according to Eskala, the Trees told Kavarian that you and Ben *had* to marry."

"Oh, so you know about that now, do you?" I said dryly.

"Privilege of being leftwing to the King," Kor said with a wink.

I narrowed my eyes. "Eskala also said when she told *me* that you had already guessed as much, without being told."

"But of course. It was a rather obvious conclusion, don't you think? King of Flame, Queen of Ice...."

I knew from the wide innocence in his eyes that there was far more to it than that. Besides, we'd already touched on this topic together more than once.

I sighed. "Kor, when are you going to tell me your grand theory?"

He slowly grinned. "At this point, why spoil the surprise?"

I groaned. "I had a feeling you might say that."

CHAPTER TWENTY-FOUR

EMOTIONS

KORIBEN

I WOKE AGAIN TO Sarah's scent swimming around me, and for a moment I froze at the thought that she had come to my pallet after all. But no, I felt I was alone the moment I reached my arm out, even as encumbered as I was by my cocoon of blankets. When I blinked my eyes open and propped myself up, I could see the shape of her on the bed, and finally identified her slow, quiet breath.

I let out a breath of my own as I brushed my hair back from my face with one hand—a sigh both of relief and disappointment.

Flame, this was going to be hard.

Not letting myself glance at her a second time, I got myself up, out the door, and to the water-room. Even though it was only dawn, and Sarah probably wouldn't be ready to leave for deken, it was time for me to get moving.

I had duties to attend to, as usual—even while traveling—and I wanted to speak with my uncle before Kor descended on me and the whirlwind of preparations to leave began.

As I'd hoped, by the time I reached the Lord's Wing, Fenrith was awake and working, and he quickly admitted me into his study after an attendant notified him I was there.

He offered me a cup of tsha, knowing well how Avvi had passed the fondness for it on to me, and we sat around his brazier.

"Now, what's troubling you, nephew?"

I smiled thinly as I avoided his too-gentle eyes. "It's sad that you can already tell that I haven't just come to spend some time with you before we leave."

"I'm not offended," he said, smiling. "In fact, I'm relieved. I saw the same look in your eyes last night, especially when you looked at me, but I feared you wouldn't come to speak with me about it."

I sipped my tsha to hide the cringe I felt inside, and to give me the courage to say what had to be said. "Yes, I...haven't let you help me much lately, have I? Not for years."

"You had your father," Fenrith said quietly. "And many others besides."

"You know that's not the reason. At least, I think you do. I *know* you know that's not the reason since Svyer...and Avva...."

I took a deep breath and set down my mug so that the liquid wouldn't betray the trembling in my hands.

"You're too good to not blame me, but let me apologize all the same. I was grieving, and then I was guilty, and then I was...not grieving. At least, not the way I should have been. But my inability to deal with my feelings was no excuse for my behavior. I'm sorry that I let all that get in the way of our closeness, Uncle."

He let silence fall between us for a moment as he pondered his reply. I was both relieved that he wasn't immediately dismissing my apology and tensing at what he might say. As I waited, I looked anywhere but at him.

"You are right," he said when he finally broke the silence with a gentle tone. "I did know why. I knew I reminded you too much of the mother you lost. The one you thought you had killed."

I inhaled sharply and looked at him. "You knew?"

His eyes were heavy. "Yes, I knew. Nyethra told me why she was fading. To ask me to look out for you, if you would let me. She knew how you would blame yourself."

I swallowed, and the space between my eyes ached from the force of the tears I was trying to suppress.

He examined me with eyes that saw too much, but somehow, this time, I met them.

"You know now, don't you?" he said quietly, relief growing in those emerald eyes. Her eyes. "You know she doesn't blame you. That she would make the same choice, again."

I finally lost the battle, and the tears spilled over. I let them fall as they would now. Perhaps they were needed. For my uncle. For Avvi. For myself.

"Yes," I said thickly. "I know. I can hardly believe it. I don't deserve it. But I know."

Fenrith smiled with a kindness that pierced my flameheart, and his eyes glistened. "Koriben, I hope that one day, you will have a child. Only then will you understand that you gave your mother everything she had left to want from life. That no matter how many more years she would have lived, they would have been meaningless without you. And your father felt the same."

I trembled, and the tears came hot and fast now. Fenrith handed me a handkerchief without a word, and I took it with a tremulous chuckle. It both helped me feel less ashamed and made my waterworks worse to see that he had his own streams going down his face and into his emerald beard now.

"So yes," he continued. "I knew why. I understood why, more than even you did. You were just a boy, Koriben. Just a boy. Though you have been forced to grow too quickly into a man, you still should have more compassion for yourself, for that very reason."

I looked away, vision blurry, but Fenrith persisted. "There is so much more of life that you have yet to experience, both its joys and its pains, and so much left to learn and become. We old things—your father, mother, and I—knew that too well. Do not compare the ways you have to cope with your grief and burdens to the ways they did, and I do. Koriben, considering all you were forced to endure and do, you have done *well*."

I shook my head tightly. Here, he was wrong. "You don't know everything. You don't know what I did, what I became. Especially this past month."

"Yet you woke up," Fenrith said softly. "You changed. And you are trying to make amends now. Nephew, that *matters*. More than the fact that you made mistakes. All mortals make mistakes."

I shook my head again. "You of all people should understand that when a Lord...when a King...makes mistakes like that...."

Fenrith smiled thinly. "Mortals are all the Tree has ever had to be Her Lords and Ladies, Kings and Queens. Did you honestly think to be better than us all?"

"No!" I exclaimed. "But you don't understand. Even though you *should*. How many of your people's lives were lost because I shut out Sarah? If I had just.... But now their deaths are on my head, and I'll never be rid of them."

I put my head into my hands, and my chest shook with suppressed sobs.

I felt his hand clench my shoulder.

"Koriben, has the Tree revoked you?"

I shook my head without lifting it. Then answered silently, not trusting my voice. *No. But She nearly did. She said if I didn't....*

"And so you did," Fenrith said with unusual firmness. "You changed course. Immediately, as I understand it. Is that correct?"

I didn't answer.

"Koriben, so long as the Tree retains you as Her vessel and so long as you are striving to do Her will with all your might, those deaths will *not* be on your head. If you broke under the weight She placed upon you for one month, then perhaps...it was what was meant to be."

I raised my head and blinked blearily at him. "You...can't be serious," I said breathlessly.

But his eyes and face *were*. "I am not saying that what you did was right or what the Trees would have asked you to do. But first, remember that this plague was not your doing: it was that of the enemy of us all, who struck when it *knew* you would be at your weakest. And the Tree, knowing all, knowing the Devourer's plans *and* your weakness, still chose you as Her King. That is why you must do all you can, but all life is ultimately in the Creators' hands. Not yours."

Seeing my continued stiffness, he clenched my shoulder. "Cease making simplistic assumptions about what might have been if you had acted differently. Has it occurred to you that if Sarah had not had that month to grow into her power and abilities, that she might never have been able to save Svyer? Or worse, that she might have been taken herself?"

I choked, as clear an answer as any to him that I had *not* thought of that.

Fenrith nodded. "If you had brought her right away, we may have lost the Queen of Ice and may never have found the cure that would save my people. Or we may have. But do not presume to *know*, Koriben. Any thousands of things could have been different if you had not shut her out, but you have no way of knowing how much would have been for good and how much for ill."

He finally let me go and leaned back with a sigh. "It does little good and much harm to ponder on what might have been. What is past is past. What is present is what matters. And it is in the present that you are doing remarkably well. Well enough that you still have the approval of the Tree, and you have my own. *I* am so very proud of you, Koriben. Proud to call you my nephew...and my King."

I slowly put my head in my hands again, feeling the heat and moisture of my fresh tears on my skin. It seemed I was doomed to be loved far more than I deserved.

But oh, how I needed that love. So much so that I couldn't shut it out any longer.

And oh, how it was changing me.

SARAH CAME WITH ME to help surge Svyer to the crowngate.

When we arrived, Sarah shook her head at Svyer and chuckled, then explained at our questioning looks, "It's still so odd—you're uprooting your whole life, and you aren't holding a bag or anything."

"That's the handy thing about being a drakón," Svyer said with a grin. "Thank goodness I get to keep that much, or Ben might have been staggering under the weight of all my stuff right now."

I rolled my eyes. "Because of course *I* would have been carrying it all."

"Of course! I need my hands free to say goodbye to Sarah, after all."

Sarah's face sobered. She rushed forward and gave Svyer a fierce hug with eyes clenched shut, and tears were in them as she pulled away.

"Hey," Svyer said gently, but she was blinking rapidly as well. "This isn't goodbye forever. Or even for a while. You have my scale now, and I'm sure you'll be able to go back and see me sometime soon."

"I know," Sarah said with a weak laugh, wiping her eyes. "It isn't just that. It's just.... Thank you. What you're doing...it means everything to me. You didn't have to do it. You didn't even have to switch realms and peoples to do it."

"I think I did," Svyer said with a small smile. "I think this was meant. After all, Ben may have been the one to find you, but I was the one to *find* you, if you know what I mean."

She winked at me, and Sarah laughed, with more ease this time.

"Svyer," I said with a grin. "You're making me jealous."

"So what?" She gave me a playful shove. "You're not my King anymore."

I winced dramatically. "Ouch. Love you too, cousin."

She laughed. "Love you too, Ben."

I sobered and made myself say the words, as difficult as they still were—and meet her eyes as I said them. Fenrith wasn't the only one I had to make amends to.

"I really do. I love you, Svyer."

Her eyes glistened, and she blinked and looked away, tucking her hair. She finally cleared her throat and said, "Well, now you're going to make *Sarah* jealous. So, I had better leave before I get you two in a fight or something."

"Not before giving me a hug, you don't," I said, pulling her in for a crushing one. She held me tightly in return.

Thank you, I told her silently. *For doing this for her.*

I'm doing it for me, too, she answered.

I saw that in her eyes as she pulled back. That anger and resolve. She may not remember everything, but she had guessed enough. Now she was going to do everything in her power to fight back against the evil that had done this to her—and this was how.

I nodded stiffly, showing I understood.

"Well," Svyer said, turning to the gate. "Think that thing is open on the other end yet?"

"There's one way to find out," Sarah said with a shrug. "Stick your hand through."

"This is still so weird," Svyer said idly as she did so. "A gate half fire, half ice? That only goes one place? I've got so much to catch up on."

Her hand went through, so she turned back and winked at the two of us. "So, I had better go get started."

Then she stepped the rest of the way through and disappeared into the flames.

Sarah sniffed, and I put a hand on her shoulder.

She'll be alright, I said silently, in case Svyer could still hear.

Just to myself, I thought, *Thanks to you.*

I know, Sarah said as she put her hand over mine. *I know. But Flame, I'm going to miss her.*

I sighed. *So am I.*

THE SKY OVER REMIK was a gorgeous, clear blue—a Flamesend after the gloom of Danyeth that we left behind. I wriggled in mid-flight to shake as much moisture off my scales as possible, luxuriating in the feeling of the Yonvey sun, Winalken, beginning to warm them.

Ben, Sarah protested, but there was a laughing edge to her voice.

Oops, sorry.

Bet she's not, Sarah said as Yvera pinwheeled, some of her spray landing on us.

No, she's most definitely not, I said ruefully.

Yvera hated Danyeth. Well...that was putting it a bit strongly, since she hated a lot of places, and Danyeth not more than most. Unlike the Brightflare capital we were now soaring above, which she despised with a burning passion. But for a couple blessed dek, she could bask in the sun and freedom, and so I let her do so without complaint.

Flying over Remik was a delight, after all. You could usually count on a good, warm air current, and—aside from the giant mound that formed the uppermost part of the warren and the wall that encircled and clear dome of energy that capped it—there was nothing in sight but rolling, cultivated plains, farmland, and grazing herds for elden.

This is a capital city? Sarah asked in amusement as we circled to wait for our turn to land.

My chest rumbled with a chuckle. *You should know by now that most of our structures are underground.*

Well, yes. But it's so...countrified on the outside.

It's nothing like that underneath, I said dryly.

If she loved Danyeth for its natural amenities, then she was going to have a hard time here. For the Brightflare, nature and its chaos stopped at their gates.

Well, at least it would only be a couple of days or so. Hopefully.

The landing cleared, and I and my wings descended and touched down. I lay on my stomach and allowed the landing crew to help Sarah down before changing back and walking to her. I couldn't help an answering smile when her eyes lit up at the sight of me approaching, or, when I reached her, resist stroking some windblown hair that had escaped from her braid out of her face.

Flame, she was beautiful.

I took her hand and gave it a squeeze. *You ready?*

As I'll ever be, Sarah said, eyeing the crowd gathered to greet us.

This ceremony will be easier, I reassured her.

Stiffer, sure. But about as long, and much less emotionally taxing. We had gotten the worst over first in that last regard.

I hoped.

Sarah and I walked toward the welcoming party, which stood spread out just outside the roped-off landing circle. About halfway there, we stopped to be cleansed and examined by a Brightflare drakón healer, as all the rest of our entourage were being as they passed that way toward the hold entrance in the mound ahead. We'd done the same ourselves before we left Danyeth, but Lady

Rowin's caution was understandable, especially given Sarah's recent illness and the size of our group.

Yvera was less understanding. *Flame forbid that we disrupt production with a plague.*

Yvera, I cautioned her.

Yes, yes, keep comments like that to myself or you. Why else do you think I did just that?

Just making sure.

Her adjustment to being the King's rightwing had been a hard one, and I had not previously been as there for her as I should have been, or as careful in...*channeling* her. Flame only knew how the two of us hadn't managed to start a war.

When the healer turned to her, Sarah shivered at the wave of power, still not used to the quick, tingling burn of purification. I clenched her hand in sympathy as soon as I was allowed to take it again. When we were both declared clean and free from the fever, the healer gestured for us to proceed, and I led her on.

Lady Rowin stood with her great-niece and Heir at the head of her small entourage—just her wings, whom I couldn't remember by name, and the few others she had thought could be spared from their duties for such a tiresome interruption of their work as this.

She was an imposing woman: tall (just half a foot shorter than me), with flame-orange hair only somewhat contained in a braid, skin that had seen a fair amount of sunlight, for a Brightflare (enough for even a drakón to tan), and a surprising amount of wrinkles, considering she hadn't yet reached a century. She was dressed as formally as Brightflare ever did in a durable orange shirt and breeches, a leather apron, and a belt with her finest tools. Finally, she had eyes of flames that could take your measure in an instant—and in my case, always found me lacking.

With this time being no exception. There would be no miraculous acceptance for me here, and right then, I was fine with that. I'd shed enough tears today.

I was less understanding when those hard eyes turned to Sarah, but my star stared back at her with an equanimity that made my flameheart burn, and I gave her hand another brief clench.

She's not as bad as she looks, I told her. *Just don't waste her time.*

And her Heir? Sarah asked skeptically. *I assume that's the young woman standing right next to her?*

Oh. Right. Kindra.

Well...visually, she was the younger image of her great-aunt, even despite the familial side-step and generational divide. In personality, she was softer. At least...she had been when we were classmates. In this case, that slight softening wasn't a good thing. It meant that her problem with me was for a more personal reason...which could be deduced from how she was glaring daggers at Sarah now.

I didn't figure out how to tactfully explain before we reached them, so I conveniently didn't.

Lady Rowin addressed me briskly. "Welcome, King Koriben, to Remik of Yonvey."

"I thank you for your welcome, Lady Rowin."

Just as on Ykran, she asked me why I was here, I introduced Sarah, and Rowin welcomed her. Though that welcome wasn't as warm as Lord Fenrith's had been, it wasn't as cold as it might have been, either. To my surprise, she still seemed to be weighing Sarah, and not necessarily finding her wanting. Yet.

Unlike Kindra, who, when the two of them were next introduced, was stiff with insincerity when she said she was honored to meet her. Sarah echoed her words in a dignified tone that made it clear to me and probably everyone that she wasn't fooled.

I was surprised when Rowin said that Kindra would escort us to the King's Wing while she returned to her duties. Rowin slipping away wasn't a wonder; I'd have been shocked if she had bothered to play hostess. But being the intelligent and capable leader she was, I would have expected her to have read the situation better than to give that duty to her Heir.

And yet, off she went, as did the rest of her entourage. Leaving us with Kindra.

Without a glance at me, she turned. "Follow me, please."

As soon as it looked like Kindra would not bother with conversation, Sarah spoke silently to me, as I'd thought she might.

Alright, what's the history between you?

History? I said, trying not to cringe.

You think I can't read what's going on here? Sarah said. *You two can't even look at each other.*

I glanced at her apprehensively.

She looked back at me and shook her head subtly, expression neutral. *I'm alright, Ben. I know you had a life before I came around. So just tell me and get it off your chest.*

I gritted my teeth. *It wasn't like that. I've told you—you're the first one I've ever....*

I sighed. *But Kindra...couldn't understand that. Flame, she's probably not failed in any other goal she's ever set in her life.*

I took a teensy bit of pride in that achievement...with what part of me that wasn't conflicted with guilt. Though even *I* knew that guilt was unnecessary.

Because I owed it to Sarah, though, I forced myself to elaborate. *We were classmates but never even friends. As far as I'm aware, I never once gave her a moment of encouragement. I tried very hard to be clear about how I felt, from the very first time she approached me. I'm almost positive that all I bruised was her pride.*

For Kindra, that was quite enough. Even so, I would have thought she would have moved on by now. That was years ago. And yet here she was, holding a grudge against Sarah as if they were rivals in secondary.

I see now, Sarah said calmly, examining Kindra's back. *Thank you for telling me.*

I'm sorry about her attitude toward you, I finished. *That's beneath her.*

Sarah's lips flickered with a brief, thin smile. *I can handle it. Not everyone has to love me, Ben. Or is going to be able to.*

I don't see why they wouldn't, I grumbled.

Her smile returned, stronger this time. *Hmm, maybe because I'm the one who finally won the kindest, handsomest young man in the Six Realms?*

Torch it. Now my cheeks were warming on top of everything. I sure hoped Kindra didn't look back in that moment and mistake the reason.

To distract myself, especially since we were entering the enormous arch set into the mound that led to the warren, I said, *Well, then it's a good thing we're not taking a tour of Earth, otherwise I might have had to spend much of my time in duels with the young men* you *disappointed.*

I had a hard time believing her implication that no one worthwhile had ever been interested in her. Surely, if we had grown up together there, some of them would have come out of the woodwork when I began to court her.

That's a thing? Sarah asked incredulously. *Boys dueling over a girl?*

It isn't just boys challenging boys, I said, surprised by her reaction. *Sometimes it's girls challenging girls, especially drakón girls.*

Those were some of the fiercest fights of all, and the most necessary for the good of everyone involved.

I continued. *Or any mix of genders, for any reason, really. Mostly just when we're young, though. When we're still learning control.*

The dueling ring just gave us a place—especially drakón in our difficult, volatile youth—to work things out in a civilized way, before our strength and power got someone actually hurt.

Just...when boys dueled each other, it tended to be about a girl.

It's not that way on Earth? I asked, puzzled.

No, Sarah said in consternation. *Not in my culture, at least.*

Then how do they work out those things? In a way that doesn't let them fester?

Sarah paused. *Well...I was about to say by talking or just getting over it, like civilized people, but...actually, I'm not so sure how often they do that. You're...right. They tend to fight anyway, except not in good ways.*

Her voice ended on a sober note that made me yearn to know the reason behind it, as her dark hints about her birth world often did. I wanted to understand what life had been like for her growing up—what dangers she must have faced, despite her insistence that her life on Earth had been safe. To me, her emotions and implications often seemed to contradict her words. I didn't think she was consciously lying to me, but I wondered how much her mind glossed over the peril she had been in, and it always made me ache that I had not been there to protect her.

But as usual, I didn't press her.

We don't duel as much anymore, I offered, trying to distract her now. To show that perhaps we weren't that different.

Though I'd had to dodge more than my fair share of challenges, and one or two because of Kindra, in fact. Not that I was afraid to fight any of the jilted would-be courters, but my consenting to a duel on those grounds was tantamount to consenting to the girl's attentions in the first place. In fact, I suspected Kindra of instigating one of those challenges herself for that very reason.

Usually, I was able to talk the boy down and convince him of my uninterest, especially over an *informal, private* fight to let him work out his angst.

That was what duels were all about, after all. To just let us fight it out, work that emotion out in a healthier way—so long as the combatants stuck to the rules—and then move on.

I continued, *It's a draká thing. Over the centuries, as we've become more amá, it's become less common.*

Although, for the first time, I wondered if that was a good thing. Our draká instincts needed tempering, but they were often simpler—healthier, some-times—than our overly complicated amá emotions. Which, on top of often being incomprehensible, didn't lay out a clear path forward.

Had our giving those instincts structure, rules, and ritual given us a necessary outlet for those emotions?

On the other hand, the thought of Kindra challenging Sarah....

No. That would be *wrong.* Sarah was different, human—not like us, as amá as we had become. Perhaps not all her people had figured out a way to work out their differences without duels, but Sarah had. Dragging her into a dueling ring would not only be unnecessary, it would be selfish—immoral, even.

No matter if Sarah could hold her own, it would force her to be something she was not, and perhaps was never meant to be.

CHAPTER TWENTY-FIVE

PRODUCTION

SARAH

BEN HAD GIVEN ME some things to think about, but I would have to ponder them later, because we were emerging into a large central chamber with such a commotion of movement, voices, and echoes that I brought my attention back to the present. Especially when I heard sounds I hadn't heard in what felt like an eternity: the metallic grinding and squeaking of machinery.

All around the rim of the room were stations of varying sizes with an assortment of cables, metal frames, and gears, and rising and sinking in their midst were *elevators*. True, they were the old-style lifts, most of them with barely even a railing to keep the passengers or contents inside, but the concept was solidly there.

Some of them, especially the largest ones, seemed designed to only accommodate freight, judging from the lifts' size and the carts they were raising and lowering. Those carts proceeded to and from the lifts in orderly lines, often coming and going through other entrances to this mound than the enormous one we had entered. Those paths were clearly designated in the tile borders laid into the stone underneath our feet, and the wheels had even worn grooves into the stone over time that further kept them in line.

Not a single beast of burden was in sight, meaning the dramá were pulling each handcart themselves. Neither were they straining, no matter how heavy the load looked. I found the explanation for their ease in the gems that glowed orange in the center of each wheel. Gems also appeared to power the lifts and the occasional small crane, flashing on the gears that they turned with each surge of energy required of them.

We were following another path, but one made for pedestrians—ones heading inward, because any others were walking the path to our left, as if we were jostling, mingling cars on a two-lane road. There seemed to be lanes even within that road, since the slower traffic stayed toward the center and the faster to the outer edges, where the fastest could occasionally step out of line to pass a group; but I noticed that those power walkers always swiftly got back in as soon as they could.

The space buzzed with the energy of a productive port combined with a bustling train station—somehow through its orderliness managing the flow of goods and people side by side without mishap. At least, I didn't see any accidents in the few minutes it took for Ben and me to cross the chamber and wait our turn in line for a passenger lift.

Ben caught me examining our surroundings and said dryly, *Welcome to Remik.*

He didn't sound thrilled to be here, but I guessed his reluctance was for a different reason than mine. All the dramá innovations fascinated me, but the echoing commotion, the constant movement out of the corners of my eyes, and the stares were eating away at my already limited energy. Especially since it appeared to be only an hour or two after sunrise here, further setting me back in my energy recovery. With my initial interest over, all I wanted to do was shut myself away somewhere dark and quiet, preferably in a bedroom where I could bury myself under the covers.

Not a promising beginning to the day.

Finally, our turn for the lift came and my drakón and I stepped on, along with Kindra and a bunch of others. Apparently not even rank afforded you personal space among the dramá—or at least not the Brightflare—because, though the people not in our entourage stared, they still piled on as many as could fit. The proximity just made their stares even more uncomfortable for me.

Ben did his best to shelter me by getting us into a corner, but he couldn't *hide* me without looking like that was what he was doing. At least his wings spread themselves casually in front of the two of us, and to my surprise, Yvera even took it on herself to glare at any gawkers, one by one, until they found something else to look at.

Thank you, I sent her, so grateful that I risked negating any good feeling she might have for me by acknowledging as much.

Not looking back at me, Yvera snorted. *Brightflare are ashers—especially Remik Brightflare. I don't need you as an excuse to scare them off.*

My lips twitched despite my discomfort, so I was glad her back was to me. *Right, my mistake.*

To my surprise, we sank only three levels or so before getting off and had to push our way past half the people on the lift to do so, because only Kindra and the people in our entourage got off. That reason was apparent when I looked down the short yet grand passage and saw an open gate with two sets of drakón I recognized as being our elites—two of mine, two of Ben's—guarding the way, closely examining everyone who passed through.

Wait, this is the King's Wing, already? I asked Ben in surprise as we passed them and our respective guards nodded to us. *That's the only thing on this level?*

In this section, Ben said. *The whole warren is like a root, and the wings of it are like the smaller roots that branch off the center. If we'd taken another lift but stepped off after the same amount of time, we would have ended up somewhere else.*

No wonder we had waited so long for *that* lift, when others had come up and down in the meantime.

Isn't it risky to have only one way in and out of this place?

Especially if that way was a lift.

Ben shook his head slightly. *There are other ways. Passages that lead to the surface and other sections of the warren. But for the King's Wing, the entrances to those passages are heavily guarded and meant to be used only in an emergency.*

Oh, that made sense. Make everyone come through one main entrance for security, have others for backup. After all, that was typical of Earth buildings, too.

"Well, here you are," Kindra said stiffly, waving her hand as we stopped in the central chamber. Which was large, but otherwise more utilitarian than any King's Wing I'd seen so far.

"We will allow you to become settled. In two deken, I will return with Lady Rowin to give you the tour."

Tour? As in, something separate from this "grand tour"?

I kept my confusion to myself as Ben only nodded to her. "Thank you, Heir Kindra."

"You are welcome," she said, not meeting his gaze. Then she swiftly turned and went back the way we had come.

Ben sighed, clenched my hand, and looked down at me wearily. "You look like you need a break even more than I do."

I echoed his sigh. "Heck, yes."

It had been a day—already.

"Come on," he said, pulling me onward. "Let's find some peace and quiet."

That sounded like heaven. The only thing that would make it better would be if....

Hmm, what are the odds of you snuggling with me when we get there?

Not even Ben's growing bristle could hide the pink that crept over his face. *Not a good idea.*

Oh, well. It had been worth a shot.

THIS "TOUR" APPARENTLY REFERRED to a tradition as part of the "grand tour" in which the insular Brightflare bestowed an honor they only ever gave to two people outside their clan: they took the newly crowned Monarch or betrothed consort (or both, in our case) through all of Remik, even the parts that no one else ever got to see. Or, at least, no one else did without swearing blood oaths. The Brightflare took their NDAs that seriously.

I wasn't sure what was so special about those places. They seemed to my inexperienced mind like all the other artisan shops, factory floors, and warehouses that we visited, which all blurred together as the hours dragged on. But I was told firmly every time we stepped inside one of those areas that I was to never tell a soul about what I had seen.

True, what the people were crafting inside was usually a bit more interesting: more powerful, more dangerous, more elaborate, and so on. Yet they were still things I had either seen all the time outside—like scale armor—or that were recognizable as being within the boundaries of the technology I had already seen, such as the black crystal hemisphere that projected what looked to me like a galaxy.

Over time, I gathered that it wasn't the things themselves that the Brightflare wanted to guard so carefully—after all, they were making them here in large quantities to sell them. It was the *methods* they wanted to protect. I supposed that made sense. Still, after the dozenth warning, I wanted to snap that I would have had no way to describe to anyone afterward how to make so much as a cartwheel, let alone a solarus. Through my sheer lack of any trade experience, their precious secrets were safe from me.

Ben's own interest was hit and miss. He tried to maintain a polite expression throughout, but I knew when he was actually engaged. He couldn't have cared less about the archival craft shop, but he looked like a kid in a candy store when we went through the magic-based weaponry smithy.

Yvera is dying *from jealousy right now,* Ben said, eyes glowing the slightest bit from his ardor as he took it all in. *She would kill to be allowed inside here.*

I...didn't ask whether he meant that literally. I didn't want to know.

I thought she hated all things Brightflare, I said in amusement. Though I wondered if I should be distracting Ben as he leaned over a mold that was currently being filled with molten metal.

I was staying clear back. I was wearing the heat-combatting robe again at Kor's suggestion, and now I saw why. So, I was fine right then. The heat of the forges was still nothing in comparison with the penetrating sauna-worthy humidity of the Ykran Tree's chamber, which had surpassed this prototype's capabilities to keep me cool. It was managing well now as long as I steered clear of the heat sources as best as I could, though I would probably have to ask Ben for a recharge after this.

She does, Ben said in amusement. *Particularly because they keep secrets like this from her. She could swear their blood oaths to not make any of the things herself, but that would defeat the point. Plus, she thinks Erdan should have gotten more of the profits from his contracts with them.*

Ah, Erdan would be her great-uncle, the retired legendary magicsmith that had designed my arm shields—well, shield in singular, now, since I had given up one of them to the Tree of Ice.

Did Erdan feel cheated?

Ashes, no, Ben said absently as he craned his neck to watch a smith pounding away at a rod as we passed. *He was content to make just enough profit to keep doing his thing. The only other thing he cared about was making sure the Bright-flare kept the methods secret and always built in his protections against abuse.*

I blinked. *Like what?*

Like the imprinting, which you already know about. But also, they're magic weapons, so they can detect emotions. A true magicsmith can teach the magic in them the difference between bloodthirst and protective rage, for example, and make it so it doesn't respond to the first. That's one reason magic-based weapons are so difficult to make.

Or why Erdan had *chosen* to make them so difficult to make, and had guarded the secrets of their manufacturing so closely, so the unscrupulous couldn't make them without those safeguards.

I watched those smiths from then on with far greater awe—still no comprehension, but much greater respect. I wondered about the gun I wore now out of habit, hidden (by chance, not choice) now by the folds of my robe. It had been in my hold when we found it, so it must have been made by my Moontouched ancestors centuries ago. Far ahead of their time, true, but not by Erdan. Did it have similar safeguards? If I were to try to misuse it, would it stop working?

I sure hoped so. That would make me feel a whole lot better about owning and using it from then on. Ever since I had used it to shoot a shard through the eye of an ice bear and then froze its brain until it exploded...I had felt a bit sick with the fear of what I could do with it. After that, only lots of talks with and gentle coaching from Michael got me through the first few target-practice sessions he'd asked of me.

He really was a nice guy, normally.

Most of the craftspeople on the tour ignored us, going about their business as if we weren't even there, but one time, an artisan stood outside her shop, looking toward us expectantly.

As we approached, Lady Rowin said while looking at me, "Here we have one of our latest developments, which I understand you are at least partly responsible for."

I pulled myself out of my overstimulated, exhausted daze and refocused with a jerk. In a second, I recognized the blond-haired, bespectacled young amón woman dressed in Strongshield red underneath her apron—who, I realized, was waiting for *me*.

"Alya!" I cried in delight.

"Hello, Queen Sarah," she said formally, nodding deeply and saluting with her hand over her heart. I knew not to take offense at her tone or expression. She, like many Strongshield I had met, was simply a serious person. If she hadn't wanted to see me, she wouldn't have been there.

My cheeks still grew warm at her greeting. The last time we'd met, she had known little more about me than my first name, that Ben was guarding and escorting me for unknown reasons, and that I had a "divergence," as she'd called it, that didn't allow me to feel the progress of the sun throughout the day and thus tell time indoors as almost all dramá could. She was smart enough that she had probably guessed I was human, and maybe Moontouched, but I doubted even she had supposed that I would become the Queen of Ice and Ben's betrothed.

OK...she might have guessed that last bit, too. Apparently, only Ben and I had been oblivious to how the other felt at that point.

Lady Rowin's lips twitched in something approaching a smile, and I tried not to stare. "Alya is the capable designer of the schematic for the 'watches' we have begun to manufacture here, and when she can be excused from her duties at Goldek Gate, she comes here to consult us on its development. She obtained a special leave of absence to be here today."

"Thank you," I told Alya, trying to sober my expression to more closely match hers.

She nodded again. "It was the least I could do for the Queen of Ice. And to keep a promise I made to you before."

I blanked. "Which was...?"

Her lips twitched, and she held out something to me. "A finished product—to replace that far inferior prototype I first gave you."

It was indeed a watch—which, to the dramá, was an entirely new concept, though Alya's innovation blended my Earthren ideas with their technology. At first glance, it appeared much the same as the prototype: a leather wristband attached to a round, dark crystal. But subtle improvements were obvious on just a second look. The notches that had been carved into the crystal were now painted silver, and the crystal's rims were now protected in a silver casing.

"It's beautiful," I said appreciatively.

Alya's lips twitched again. "It's far more than that. May I?"

She gestured at my wrist.

"Of course." I held it out and pulled the robe's sleeve back for her.

As she put it on, I said soberly, "I'm so sorry about the last one. I...had to give it up."

"No apologies needed. Leftwing Korinth already explained as much to me. I am honored that it was as much use as it was to you."

"He spoke to you about it?" I asked in surprise.

As I carefully avoided looking at Ben, I wondered how much detail Kor had included in his explanation. Did she know that my sacrifice of her gift to the Tree was one reason the old King had lived for one more day?

If she did, she didn't show it. "Yes, it came up when we were discussing the patent, which he personally reviewed and approved."

Ah, of course Kor did.

"Leftwing Korinth also connected me with Lady Rowin with a generous recommendation about its manufacturing potential."

"The device shows promise," Lady Rowin said, that flicker of a smile reaching her lips again. "For far more than Artificer Alya originally modestly proposed. This watch is more exact, convenient, and versatile than any other timekeeping device we have so far."

Suddenly, I understood. Ben had told me Lady Rowin wasn't as bad as she looked—so long as you didn't *waste her time*.

Alya and I had done far more than avoid that grievance. We had *given* her time. Or, at least, a way to measure and harness it more precisely than ever before. To a Brightflare, that must be gold.

Ben seemed to have come to the same conclusion. He had his very polite, kingly face on right now. "You don't mind that she released the schematic to the public after filing the patent?"

"Of course not. The device has value to us far above and beyond profit—direct profit, at least. The first few orders that will soon come out of this shop are for ourselves alone."

She gestured to the relatively small room beyond, where a dozen or so workers stood or sat around tables, working with magnifying lenses, carving tools, and many other instruments I didn't recognize on watches in every stage.

Lady Rowin, being drakón, brought out a watch with an orange casing and genuinely smiled for the first time. "I have one of the second-generation devices, of course, but I did not wish to wear it before now and spoil Alya's surprise."

"Lady Rowin also graciously agreed to keep the price low once it becomes available elsewhere," Alya added diplomatically. "So that it still should be affordable even to those who cannot make the watches themselves from the schematic."

"Of course, as the first manufacturer of the devices, the Brightflare are bound to make a tidy sum anyway," Ben said with a neutral smile, tone still carefully polite.

As kind as he was, Ben was no one's fool.

"That's business, Ben," Kindra snapped, directly addressing him for the first time. "It's what *really* makes *your* Realms run—"

"Kindra," Rowin said in a calm tone, only raising her eyebrow at her Heir. When she looked at Ben, it was with a thin smile. "I think he grasps the concept surprisingly well. You have grown up a bit, haven't you, Koriben?"

Ah, so that was why Ben kept pushing, at the risk of embarrassing Alya in front of her patron. He wanted *Rowin* to know he was no fool—and to warn her not to press Alya to go beyond her original, noble intentions. He was telling her he would be watching.

Ben mirrored her thin smile. "That tends to happen to boys after a few years, Lady Rowin."

Rowin rolled her eyes and smirked, breaking the tension in the air. "You would be surprised. Good to see that you are the exception to the rule."

She turned to the artificer. "Alya, why don't you come by the King's Wing later to show the Queen the improvements you've made since the prototype? We have brought the King and Queen a long way and still have more ground to cover before dinner."

I kept my expression polite, but inwardly, I groaned.

I COULDN'T EVER REMEMBER being more relieved to sit down in my life. Yet the day's trial wasn't over, because no sooner was the food served than Lady Rowin began discussing the state of her Realm.

So, it was to be a working dinner, and a serious one at that. Over the course of the tour, Ben had won enough of Lady Rowin's respect that she was being frank with him, listing both the good and the bad. From what I could discern, there was a fair amount of good, but the bad was significant.

Most worrisome seemed to be a new pestilence that was devastating their crop yields, particularly with their staple equivalent of wheat: olgum. Ben assured me they had grain storage that would be sufficient for months, so they weren't in immediate danger of starvation. The most concerning aspect was that the darkmold had begun—you guessed it—about a month ago, and now it was spreading to other crops besides olgum. If they didn't stop its progression and increase their yields, then famine could be just around the corner.

Ben was grim. "I think we can safely assume that the evidence points to sabotage, correct?"

"Correct," Rowin said evenly.

He took a deep breath. "Do you have reason to suppose it comes from among us?"

I looked at him in alarm, but I realized it was a theory that had to be addressed. The Devourer had consumed agents among the dramá—not many, because it was hard for them to hide what they were, especially if they were willing, but some. Enough perhaps to have started the pestilence.

Rowin's leftwing, a tan, brunette amón whose name I had already forgotten, answered. "Our analysts can't rule out the possibility, but they generally agree that not enough indicators point to internal sabotage. We've been sweeping settlements and surrounding areas for consumption, including using Leftwing Korinth's prototype, at every point where the darkmold is sighted."

She nodded at Kor, and he smiled charmingly back. He had joined us for the dinner, but Ben had made excuses for Yvera, saying she had rightwing business to attend to. Since Rowin's rightwing wasn't here either, no one seemed to take that amiss. Maybe everyone accepted that formal working dinners were something one simply could not ask rightwings to endure.

Lucky.

"So glad it's being put to good use," Kor said. "If you have any suggestions for its development, please send them my way."

"Certainly. Have you—"

Lady Rowin tapped her fork against the table. Her tone was mild, but firm. "You were discussing why internal sabotage is not our primary theory?"

"Right." The leftwing cleared her throat. "So far, our sweeps have found nothing that strikes us as indicative of dramá consumption. The sightings also first occur in the morning, meaning it is probably being spread at night. Finally, darkmold was discovered just yesterday morning, not two elden from Remik."

"Very close to the Yonvey Tree," Ben explained to me. He looked at Rowin. "Have you consulted Her?"

"Only every dawn," Rowin said dryly. "But until this one, She did not answer. That answer today was to consult with you."

Ben smiled. They had built enough of a rapport by now that he said boldly, "I'm certain that did not make you a very pleased Lady."

She chuckled, seemingly appreciating his cheek. "No, it most certainly did not. So, any insight thus far, O King?"

Ben only smiled again at the slightly mocking use of his title. "None so far, I'm afraid."

He looked at me. "Sarah, what about you?"

"Me?" I said before I could think better of it.

Kindra snorted, and Ben stiffened as if he wanted to scold her but resisted.

Yes, you, Kor said silently. Though his expression did not change, I could *hear* a sigh. *The Queen of Ice. Whom the Tree of Ice sent to help us.*

I'm torching tired, *alright?*

Even though night was falling, my head was in such a fog from such a long day of walking and overstimulation that I had barely been able to *follow* the conversation, let alone think of participating. Until now.

I said the first semi-intelligent thing that came to my head, even though it was a question. "What's being done to combat the pestilence itself?"

Rowin's leftwing answered, fortunately looking as if she thought that was a good question for me to have asked. I breathed an internal sigh of relief.

"We've been working with our Peacegrowth botanists that are based here on a treatment, but as you can probably guess, they've been preoccupied with the more urgent priority of finding a cure to brightfever. At least until two days ago. Now a few have refocused their efforts on the darkmold, but the rest of them are helping study the icemint plant you provided and recommending the best ways for the cultivators to grow them and the herbalists to harvest and use them. They've assured us they'll return their full attention to the darkmold in a sevenday or two."

Rowin grimaced at that. I gave her the benefit of the doubt and assumed that she was thinking of the famine that would result if this problem wasn't solved *yesterday*—and not about a loss in profits.

"Have they tried using the icemint to address the darkmold?" I asked curiously.

When everyone just looked at me, I tried to keep my composure. "Yes, I realize it might sound like a long shot that it would be the cure for the pestilence too. But it's worth looking into, isn't it? Especially if they're already studying the plant."

"True," Rowin's leftwing said slowly, then looked to her Lady.

"I don't see why not," she said with a shrug. "As she said, they're already studying it in depth. The catch with *that* being the cure is how little of it we have right now."

She looked at me. "I understand you don't have fields' worth of it back in your Realm, correct?"

I grimaced. "No, we don't. Just part of a garden's worth."

And I would rather that much be saved for my family, in case brightfever should come to them. Thank goodness for Svyer being with them.

"So, we would have to wait for sufficient quantities to be grown of *whatever* part of it we would need, which could take sevendays—and that is only if the part we need for the darkmold is one that is leftover after the healers have what they need for the brightfever cure."

All fair points, so I hesitated to add one more thing to support the icemint theory, lest it seem like I was pursuing it just because I'd thought of it.

Go on, Ben encouraged. He must have been able to tell I still had something to say.

I took a deep breath. "You're right. But just in case this is of help.... Svyer got the oil from the flowers, right?"

I looked at Ben for confirmation, and he nodded.

I continued. "That came as a surprise to me, because we used the *leaves* for tea—er, tsha, essentially. What if the leaves could be steeped in water, and the water be the treatment? That would increase the quantity of treatment you would have to work with, especially if you didn't need a high concentration."

Everyone just looked at me for a moment again.

Then Lady Rowin chuckled and looked at Ben. "Now, why did the Tree ask me to consult with *you*?"

Ben grinned. "Perhaps because I would inevitably consult with Sarah. Now do you see why I'm marrying her?"

My face warmed, but I kept my head up and shoulders down, and pointedly avoided looking Kindra's way—though I could *feel* the daggers now. Fortunately, thanks to Yvera, I was used to far worse. It also helped to look at Ben.

"You're going to be needed too. As I see it, we have two problems: the pestilence itself, and the cause—this saboteur. That one seems much more up your alley."

He leaned back with a grim expression. "I think you're right. So, I had better start doing my part, first thing tomorrow."

Chapter Twenty-Six

BREAKTHROUGHS

Koriben

Half a deken after dawn, Kor and I stood at the edge of a field of olgum as one of Rowin's Peacegrowth botanists showed us the latest example of the pestilence. Yvera stayed back on the road, still in drakáform as she oversaw my elites that had spread themselves around me in every direction, even in the field.

Flame, I missed the days when I could just fly out on my own, or with my wings if necessary. Not that I disliked any of my elites—some of them were my good friends, and I got along with or at least respected all the others. But the bother of such a large group and the restriction on my freedom of movement suffocated me if I let myself think about it for too long.

Right now, I tried to ignore all of them and pay attention to what the botanist was showing me.

"See here?" Edra said, holding out one of the lowest leaves of the stalk, which was covered in dark blotches. "It usually starts from the ground up, traveling up through the leaves..."

She rose from her crouch and pointed as she went. "...to the grain."

Which at the *moment* was clear from splotches, but the stalk was nowhere close to being harvestable, so there was little chance of saving the grain—if we couldn't find a cure.

"How long does that take?" I asked.

"Three to five days. But meanwhile, the darkmold works on the leaves."

Edra scraped one splotch on a higher leaf with her gloved finger, and the blotch removed—mostly. A stain still colored the leaf beneath.

"See, we can technically remove it in the early stage, but that's unfeasible to do at a large scale."

"Right," I said with a sigh.

"And at a later stage..." She crouched and scraped darkmold off one of the lower leaves. It came off, but there was a hole there instead. "...it's too late. That's the trick. It starts killing off the stalk long before it reaches the grain. Infecting the grain is only the final straw."

Her lips flickered in a brief smile at her unintentional pun, but not even that could keep back her grimness for long.

Kor looked thoughtfully at the ground. "Perhaps there really is something to Sarah's suggestion about a water infusion of icemint leaves. If it comes from the ground, then spreading the water there might address the darkmold at the source."

"Or allow the stalk to absorb something that lets it combat the disease," I mused. "In that case, the infusion could be added to the irrigation system."

Kor said, "I suppose if there's something to the theory, then the question is, is it a preventive measure or a cure?"

I eyed the field. "Let's pray it's both. As much of a torched miracle as that would be, I know. But Flame knows we need it."

"I'll burn a leaf to that," Edra said fervently. "Well, I'll just take my samples and then head back to the lab to figure that out, shall I?"

"Wait, didn't you say you brought a vial of the infusion with you? To test it in the field?"

"Several vials, actually," Edra said in surprise. "To test various concentrations. But I was going to let you move on and do that last."

I didn't know if what I felt was a gut instinct, a naive hope, or an impulse coming from the Tree, but I figured it wouldn't hurt to follow it. "Would you mind trying it in front of us? Just to indulge me."

She shrugged. "Alright, but please don't hold your breath. Even if the infusion will have some efficacy, these things take time to work."

"Of course."

Being amón, she pulled some supplies out of the shoulder bag at her side. She first set a marker into the ground in front of a stalk, then she colored around the leaf she chose with a wax pencil.

As she worked, she sighed. "If there is a saboteur, and they have any sort of intelligence, these field tests could be for nothing, since I might come back to the markers gone or the test subjects tampered with. But for the sake of thoroughness...."

"Discouraging, I know," Kor said sympathetically. "But you're right—you do what you must."

She stood and wrote a few things in a notebook. "Alright, time for testing vial one: the highest concentration."

She took out one vial from a pouch at her waist. Then she uncapped the vial, held a leaf out with one hand, and tipped the vial over the leaf with the other hand. The dropper seal gathered a droplet.

Contrary to her request, as that drop grew and fell, I held my breath...and prayed.

The drop disappeared into one splotch of darkmold. Edra was about to let go of the leaf, no doubt to move on to the next, but I held a hand out to stop her.

Flameheart pulsing, I said, "Wait, look."

The splotch of darkmold...was shrinking.

Shriveling to nothingness before our very eyes.

Edra stared as, a second later, it disappeared entirely. The stain remained, but the mold was most certainly gone.

"Impossible," she breathed.

Kor chuckled. "When it comes to Sarah, you'll learn to stop saying that word fairly quickly."

"But—but that's not the way a cure *works*. Particularly not without magical aid. We didn't do *anything* to this infusion."

Which was yet another sign of the promise of this cure. If the water had needed to be infused with power as well as the leaves, then we might never have been able to provide enough spark for the vats' worth that would be needed to overtake this darkmold.

"This is no normal disease," Kor said, smile fading. His eyes became hard. "It comes from the Devourer. Given the extremity of its origins, it seems the Trees have had mercy on us in giving us an extremity of a cure."

It seemed They had. As Edra continued to stare, I sent a very belated prayer of gratitude.

Perhaps the Flame was with me after all. At the very least, the Ice was with Sarah, and between the two of us, that might just be enough.

WE LEFT EDRA BABBLING about the results of the short-lived experiment to her team over scale, demonstrating the miracle for them as we walked back to Yvera.

Well, what now? my rightwing asked, hope clear in her voice as she gazed down at me.

I smiled thinly. *Now, we hunt.*

The miracle of a cure did us little good if we couldn't stop our saboteur. And as Sarah had said last night, this was *my* expertise.

Flame, I thought you'd never say that, the violet draká said with a savage grin, showing enormous teeth.

A farmer led us to the corner of the field where the darkmold had begun before spreading further, making it the most logical place we could think of for the saboteur to have done its work. The hunter over the case met us there.

Unlike with Rowin, I had already won Head Hunter Korith's respect a long time ago. We'd worked together many times while I was Heir on the worst of Yonvey's consumed cases.

That respect helped prevent the natural irritation he might have felt at my interloping. Which was good, because he was plenty irritated at the situation already.

"It's frustrating, Ben, I'll tell you," the Brightflare drakón said, folding his arms and scowling at the field.

Even though he was a few decades older than me, his informal, get-it-done nature meant he was one of the few of my elders that not only never used my title but also called me by my nickname.

"Every time I'm called in, we find *nothing*. No tracks, no scent, nada. Occasionally we can get a whiff of consumption, but that's it. Our analysts haven't even figured out a pattern to the infestations, other than that it happens at night, and usually starts at the corner of the field that's furthest from the settlement—the most isolated point."

He jerked his thumb behind him, where only regular plains rolled on.

I mused, "Perhaps that's another indicator that it's not a dramá."

As much as my training on objectivity told me not to cling to one theory, I couldn't help but *hope* our saboteur wasn't dramá. If they were, that would make our situation much more dire. Still, hopes aside, Rowin had assured me that they were protecting the grain stores with the most stringent measures possible. The last thing we could afford was to become so careless as to give the Devourer access to poison those, too. Because if it did, we were done.

Kor brought back some of that needed objectivity by adding darkly, "Or that's what they want us to believe."

"True," Korith agreed. "Yet the consumption we've always detected isn't dramá—its bestial."

My eyes flicked back to him. "Beast?"

Something about that word, combined with the faintest of scents in the air, stirred something inside my mind.

"So we think. The instruments aren't detecting the level of consumption necessary for sentients."

That was how we told the difference: generally—this new strain of consumption that had affected Svyer excepted—the more intelligence the life form had, the more the Devourer needed to consume of their life force before being able to control them. Hence, greater consumption detected, greater intelligence.

"Again," Kor told me, "that could be to throw us off. Just like when they used the scent of krathen on Sarah's things."

That memory didn't stir the rage it might have normally, because it sparked something quite different instead—giving me the final bridge I needed to put the clues together. The first set, anyway.

Yv, I said, speaking with my inner voice for the sake of a draká's poor hearing, but I projected it to Kor and Korith too. *Do you smell krathen?*

She had the best nose of all of us and was still in drakáform besides. Though she had carefully remained on the road to avoid trampling any clues that might have been lying around for us to find.

She inhaled deeply, nostrils flaring, eyes narrowing. *Now that you mention it, that's what it reminds me of. But it's not—not quite.*

"Krathen?" Korith said, sniffing the air. "Hmm...."

"Not krathen," I said, agreeing with Yvera. "But it's the closest thing I can think of, as faint as it is. Has it rained since the darkmold was discovered?"

"No, it hasn't. Which is torched lucky, since we're in the rainy season. Perhaps that's why I haven't smelled it before."

Korith scowled.

"There could have been many reasons why," I assured him. "The agent might simply have been more careless this time."

Certainly, they had risked more than on other occasions by infecting a field this close to the Yonvey Tree and Her capital defenders.

Kor said, "So, if we put that all together at face value, then we come up with something *like* krathen but not quite, something that only operates at night, something intelligent enough to follow commands but not so intelligent as to register much on our detection methods, something fast and stealthy that doesn't leave footprints or, most of the time, even a scent."

As Kor spoke, my eyes fell on the moon setting in the west. It was waning, having reached its peak a day or two ago....

A day or two....

Then, with Kor's reminder of Sarah and krathen, my mind made another connection.

My flameheart began pounding—both from a surge of adrenaline at the thought that we could *already* be on to something but also from a flare of rage and sorrow for Sarah.

"Ben, what is it?" Kor said sharply.

"Korith," I said slowly, eyes still on the moon. "Have your analysts determine if the timing of each infection correlates with the moon being at least visible above that location at the time."

It wouldn't be definitive proof, but with it being the rainy season over the Great Plains, at least, it might indicate we were on the right track.

Kor looked where I was looking, and as he remembered as well, his own eyes widened. Then narrowed dangerously, eyes soulflaring, his fists and jaw clenching.

That goshek, he fumed silently to me.

I assumed he meant his brother. The Devourer's evil was beyond epithets.

"Alright," Korith said slowly. "But care to share why?"

"The Devourer may have created...or perhaps *re*created a monster just for this. One perhaps native to Earth, whose powers depend on night and the moon."

"Native to" being a euphemistic way of saying that the Devourer may have used one of Sarah's birth people for this.

If I was right, then once again, either Solim or the Devourer itself had delivered Sarah a mocking blow.

She...was not going to like my theory. For many reasons.

I WAS RIGHT. I was glad that I had made sure Sarah was sitting down next to me first before I delivered the news, and that I'd done it in private, in our bedroom. She became as pale as she ever did, and her hands trembled in her lap.

"A *werewolf*? You're saying you think the Devourer is using a *werewolf* as its saboteur? And, to make it, it took a human and...."

She swallowed, looking like she was going to be sick.

Alarmed, I pulled her in closer to me with one arm and handed her a bowl with the other hand. I nearly trembled myself—but with fury. For my people who risked famine, for the human that perhaps was taken (or perhaps more than one). But, because she was the one closest to me, I raged most of all for Sarah.

After we had first encountered krathen, she had confessed that they were very similar to an Earthren monster she had previously hoped was only fiction—a monster that was her worst nightmare. She had faced down other dangers with astounding composure and courage, but the krathen had shaken her to her core. Either the Devourer had figured that out, or it had simply been lucky that one of the worst monsters it could create from humanity was the one Sarah feared the most.

Somehow, I doubted this was luck.

I gave Sarah time to recover before answering. Only when she stopped clenching her thighs and sunk back and into me did I speak.

"I don't know for sure, of course. It may not even be what you think of as a 'werewolf.' It might not even have been human—the Devourer could have used any number of things to make it, including a krathen. That would explain the smell."

"But that's not what you think it did," Sarah said hoarsely.

No, I didn't think it would just use a krathen, even though that would probably have been easier. Not when it could do this to Sarah.

I *hated* being its messenger—the one to make her feel these things. I wanted so badly to shelter her from all of this. But if we caught this thing, and I was right, she would find out through someone else at some point, and she would be rightly furious at me for not telling her everything. Our partnership demanded greater honesty than that. I needed to recognize her strength more than that.

"I am trying to prepare you for the worst," I said heavily, then attempted a weak smile. "So that when it turns out to be just an ugle that swallowed some krathen bones then learned how to fly, you can punch me in relief."

Sarah laughed tightly. Then sighed. "I know. And...thank you. For telling me. I can tell you would rather not have."

I winced. "I'm that obvious, am I?"

She smiled, snuggling into me further. "To me at least."

She was quiet for a bit, and I didn't disturb the silence, letting her get what she needed. I wasn't as big on quiet and certainly not on solitude as she was, but neither did they bother me with her. Even though I was used to going, doing, seeing, acting, Sarah made stillness, which normally might have been uncomfortable for me, seem restful.

I guess it wasn't true solitude with her by my side, in any case.

Sure enough, her breath slowed, and the slight trembling that had lingered entirely left. When she straightened away from me, her face and eyes were calm and ready.

My *sera*.

"What happens next?"

I sighed. "We tracked the scent as far as we could, which was only an eld or two. But then, by circling around that area, we found traces of a darkrift."

The tears in the universe's fabric that allowed the Devourer to slip its consumed through into our Realms.

"So that seems to further support the theory that this is an outside agent that the Devourer is moving around whenever it sees an opportunity—possibly somewhere with clear skies with the moon visible, if my other theory is correct."

Sarah's eyes tightened with worry. "So, you're going to have everyone keep an eye out for healthy fields with moon visibility tonight."

"Right," I said heavily. "Because this is Brightflare, they were already developing a device that produces a special ward to detect the opening of darkrifts. When I spoke to Lady Rowin, she ordered the analysts to figure out which places are most likely to be hit tonight given the new hints we've gleaned, and for the engineers to place them at those sites. Then we wait for one to trigger and go after it."

"'We' meaning me too, right?"

I tensed at once. "Absolutely not."

She only raised an eyebrow, unsurprised. "Ben, you're going after an unknown monster *at night*. You need me."

I gritted my teeth. "Be that as it may, we can't be risking *two* Monarchs at the same time. That could be exactly what the Devourer is hoping."

"By that logic, you shouldn't be risking yourself at all," Sarah said calmly.

"I'm the King!" I snapped. "I have *no* Heir yet to send in my place, Sarah. I can't just sit back and let my people go into danger without me."

"Precisely. Which is why you need me too, because the Devourer could be waiting to take you. But hopefully it would find that much more difficult if *I* was there to help you."

"Gah!" I cried, putting my head in my hands. Why did she have to be so right about this? Or so calm?

I looked back up at her, pained. "Sarah, you realize this *could* be everything from your worst nightmares, right? I'm not questioning your courage—you've proved yourself beyond question. But all of us have fears that can break us."

And mine was losing her.

"I know," Sarah said, swallowing. At least that much told me she was taking this seriously. "I know, Ben. I'm getting sick again at just the thought...."

Her hands trembled as they clenched in her lap. My flameheart sputtered, and I put my hand over both of hers and closed my fingers gently around them.

Perhaps I shouldn't have given her that strength, because she stilled, took a deep breath, and looked back at me. My flameheart lowered at the resolve I saw there.

"That's why I have to do this. Even if you catch this thing and nothing else happens tonight, if I hide, then the Devourer wins. I *have* to show it that it doesn't hold any power over me."

My gut twisted, but this time, I knew she was right...and my blood burned to remind me I could not stop her.

I pulled her all the way into my lap and held her, tightly enough that she probably found it harder to breathe.

Wetness stung my eyes and thickened my voice as I asked, "Why do you have to be so *sera*?"

So valiant.

"Because that's my name, silly," she answered.

But her voice trembled, and she buried herself in me all the same.

"I can't lose you either, you know," she whispered. "I love you. Flame and Ice, how I love you."

My flameheart lowered even further. I couldn't get the words past my throat. I felt them—to my core, I felt them. Every time, every day, even more. But every day, it got harder to say them.

Guessing at the reason behind my stiff silence, she said gently, "It's OK, Ben. I know you love me too, and you've said it enough. You don't have to say it when it's difficult, just because I do."

I clenched my teeth. "But I *should*. I should be able to, and I should. I don't want you to ever think I...."

"I don't doubt you. I never doubted you, from the moment I knew. You make it so *obvious*. It's in every time you look at me, or touch me, or protect me, or help me. I didn't doubt how you felt, even when you pushed me away. I knew that was why."

She was too good. That was exactly why she deserved more.

"*You* say it," I said in despair.

"I'm not saying it as a challenge or a request, Ben. I say it because I can't help it, because it just bubbles out of me, and I can't contain it. Don't compare what's *easy* for me to what's *hard* for you."

"It shouldn't *be* hard! My father told my mother what felt like every deken."

"And you've had to grow up a different way than he did. Didn't you?"

I sighed heavily and let that be my answer.

"Here's a thought," she said after a moment. "If you *have* to have a way to *say* it, who says you have to say it with words?"

"Sarah, that's not the point. I want to be able to *say* it."

"No, no," Sarah said, pushing away from me to meet my eyes. "There are other languages besides ones that use our voices, Ben. In my world, they had a sign language, a language that uses your hands."

She touched her chin with the tips of her fingers and brought her hand forward. "That's how you say *thank you*."

I blinked. That was like the hand signals that amón in the Warflight or hunter's corps used with drakón and each other in situations that required silence. Except those codes, to my knowledge, didn't have a way to say anything so courteous as *thank you*, let alone as sentimental as what I was looking for.

"Then how do you say...the other thing?"

"Unfortunately, that's all I've got," Sarah said sheepishly. "But that was just an example of what I meant. We could come up with something like that, or something...even simpler. Probably the simpler the better, I'm guessing. And subtle, so you could do it any time...."

Her eyes lit with an idea. "How about this? You do this all the time, already."

She grabbed my hand and gave it a squeeze.

"That's it?" I asked, troubled. "I could just do that by accident. How would you know...."

"OK, but what if you did it three times? One time for each word? In English it's three, I mean."

She squeezed my hand three times, very intentionally. "It's like a code, but with touch. If you do it three times, I'll *know*. Think that's doable?"

My flameheart rose. "I...think?"

"Only one way to find out."

She looked me in the eye and said with deliberate slowness, "I love you."

I swallowed. But I found my hand almost instinctively clenching hers three times, in the same rhythm.

A brilliant smile broke over her face. "There! How was that? Was that easier?"

"Yes," I said with numb surprise.

I found myself doing it again: three clenches. Then again. By that time, Sarah's eyes were shining with both soulflare and tears.

I knew it. Despite all her reassurances, I knew she needed the *words*. Not because she doubted, but simply because she needed them.

And now she had just given me the way to say them.

Just to make certain, though, I said, "That really is enough? That will mean the same thing to you?"

Sarah laughed wetly, wiping her eyes. "Ben, even when you use your voice, you use a different language than mine to tell me. Whatever way you can say it, it's all the same to me."

I looked directly into her eyes and clenched her hand three times, slowly.

I almost didn't finish the last before she pulled her hand away to throw her arms around my neck and head and press her lips to mine.

Chapter Twenty-Seven

HUNT

Sarah

It was amazing how different a place could be at a different time of day. When the sungate banked after the sun set, the reason for the foot and wagon traffic in the central surface chamber (which I'd begun to call "the train station" in my head) faded with it. The last people to wander in were the herders, having brought their livestock within the wall for the night. By the time everyone who would be participating in the night's events had gathered, we had the place almost entirely to ourselves.

Which was good, because there were quite a lot of us.

Ben, Yvera, Rowin, and Rowin's rightwing had spent almost the entire day planning and preparing for tonight. They had even used the lone daygate in Remik (in the Lady's Wing, of course—couldn't be wasting her time) to subtly bring in reinforcements one by one, making the ranks of Royal elites swell to nearly twice their usual number with the additions of the reserves and some of the Warflight. Even Alyish—the old King's rightwing who had become *Yvera's* rightwing just as Eskala had become Kor's leftwing—was here. He would once again be staying behind to act as our HQ commander so that Yvera could stay with Ben.

Centralizing their forces had been a gamble. They'd debated long and hard about distributing them across Yonvey so that there would be at least one team everywhere able to assist each settlement's normal guard in investigating any alerts from the sensors Rowin had her artificers plant. In the end, they decided they could go one more night without stopping the saboteur; the greater risk was losing Ben and me to the Devourer.

Now they were all here, ready to protect us...in the off chance that the saboteur struck within flight distance. Otherwise, if the alert went off elsewhere, it would alert the guard there as well, and they would know to keep as careful an eye out as they could from the safety of their posts so that we could at least hopefully glean more information.

But Ben had a gut feeling that the Devourer would strike close enough. The skies around Remik would once again be clear for elden (which I gathered was kind of like miles), and the Devourer was essentially challenging us to stop it. It *wanted* Ben and me to go after its agent. All of this screamed *trap*.

We just had to make sure we were ready to keep that trap from killing us. Or worse, extracting our Blood.

We *might* have had a bit more of an edge...if I hadn't insisted on flying with Ben above Crownhold, telling the Devourer almost everything I now could do. When Kor made the connection for me, I felt so terrible that he couldn't even be mad in the moment, though he said he could have strangled me when he'd heard what I'd done.

But as Kor went on to grudgingly say, technically, the Devourer could have extrapolated my forms and their abilities from the Battle of the Solstice. The only extra edge I had really gained since then was strength and familiarity with them.

The best edge we had *now* was how we were going to take advantage of what I could do, deliberately and in concert with all the gathered warriors.

That experimentation began as soon as we had the station to ourselves and I felt my lightform become accessible. Trying my best not to feel self-conscious and utterly failing, I activated the form and allowed myself to begin glowing and steaming like I was radioactive dry ice.

You'd think that's exactly what I'd become from everyone's expressions except Ben's. Even fully forewarned, many of them stepped back, shielded their eyes, or gaped—or did all of that at once. Lady Rowin whistled, and stoic Alyish blinked, expression blanking. Kindra paled, then hastily looked away. Even Kor stared.

Ben just grinned, gold eyes burning.

Go on, he encouraged with a nod upward. *Show them what you can* really *do.*

I glared at him. *Oh,* now *I'm allowed to fly around.*

I've had time to adjust to the idea, he said, unperturbed. *Plus, I'm* pretty *sure I could catch you if you fell in here.*

Thanks for that bit of reassurance.

Not that I feared falling. My nerves were coming from another source.

His expression sobered, but his eyes continued to burn. *I believe in you, Sarah.*

What else could I do after he said something like that?

I took a deep breath and thought, *Well, here goes nothing.*

"I'm going to fly," I warned the circle of people around me.

Then before I could chicken out, I flapped my six wings and slow-surged into the air. And by "slow" I mean I blurred into the center of the cavernous dome within a second, but it still had been slow enough that their eyes could follow me.

Now absolutely every gaze of the several hundred people in that station was fixed on me, and all echoes of conversation ceased for a few heart pulses.

Fantastic, I thought.

Flame, Sarah, Ben said as he looked up at me from the dozens of feet between us, with an edge to his voice that made my iceheart pulse for yet another reason.

Trying to sound blasé, I said, *Well, energy check?*

Oh, it's there.

Ben paused, looking at the others. After a few minutes of conferring, he said, *Yup, we're all feeling it. As long as you can keep that up, we've got enough spark for drakáform.*

Even with just lightform, I said in relief. *Good.*

Then we could proceed as planned. If I'd just been able to power Ben like this, then we wouldn't have called the night off altogether, but plan B would have been riskier.

Not that plan *A* made me feel warm and fuzzy, mind. Not when it still involved a Devourer trap baited with plague-carrying werewolves.

I tried very hard not to think about that fact. My iceheart already felt like it was going to pound its way out of my semi-corporal chest. I supposed one of the unexpected benefits to being this deep in this form was that my intestines weren't quite *there* enough to tie themselves into knots.

Ready for the next test? Ben asked.

I nodded. *Yes. You?*

Hang on a dek.

He spoke to the people around him, gesturing, and they began backing away from him. They passed the word on, because soon everyone within a two-hundred-foot radius of Ben began moving away.

Just in case, he told me as they went.

I understood. We hadn't tried this before while he was in amáform; if it *made* him transform, then we didn't want anyone anywhere near him.

Alright, Ben said when everyone was sufficiently clear. *Go ahead.*

This part made me nervous for yet another reason. On the one hand, I was ready to be out of view. On the other...it was a frightening thing, to give up your *self* to another. I didn't even remember anything from the first and only time I had done this. If I didn't trust Ben so completely....

I breathed in, unintentionally making my glow flare...

...and surged into his heart.

WE OPENED OUR EYES. We hadn't even remembered closing them, but closed they had been. Part of us was surprised at what we saw, even though we saw nothing unusual.

But there was so much more detail than we had ever seen before, and yet just as much as we had always seen. The *smells* coming into our nostrils: dust, oil, grease from the distant gears, metal, and, still lingering in the air, the molten undertone of dramá. Even the amón had that flavor, so different now to us than the neutrality of humans or the cool sharpness of Sarah.

Sarah.

We darted our eyes upward to where she had been, on reflex, but we knew even before we looked that she was no longer there. She had surged inside us....

Us.

We put our hand over our heart. Our...starheart. That's where she was, wasn't she?

Then where had *we* come from?

Ben? Yvera asked us tentatively.

That wasn't right. We weren't just Ben. Not anymore.

He was there, just as Sarah was. We both were.

We.

And we were glowing like a sun.

Every inch of us, of our skin, our nails, our hair. Far brighter and warmer than we had ever shone separately.

We were...glorious. We *felt* glorious. Ice and Flame, we felt *unstoppable.*

And yet...it was...becoming...harder...to be us.

The more we realized what had happened...was happening to us...the more we realized our separateness....

The more we unraveled.

Once begun...the unraveling quickened, and quickened, and quickened, until—

Sundering.

SARAH? SARAH!

Ben's alarm pierced through my unconsciousness and brought me to the surface. I groaned, my head pounding.

"Thank Flame," Ben gasped out loud, holding me tightly against him.

"Whah...." I mumbled, blinking my eyes open.

When I saw his worried face close to mine, and the train station ceiling above that, I finally remembered.

Not that I *understood.*

"What...*happened*?" I asked, dumbfounded.

"An excellent question," Kor said, bracing his hands on his thighs to bend over us.

Ben must have been sitting on the floor, because I could feel the warmth of his crossed legs underneath me as well. Fortunately, everyone else except Yvera seemed to be keeping their previous distant positions. Whether that was from respect, nervousness about what was going on, Yvera's glares, or sheer inertia, I didn't care—I was grateful.

Kor continued, "I gather that *wasn't* what happened last time you went into his flameheart?"

"No," Ben said tightly, then looked at me.

"Don't look at me," I protested, wincing as another lance of pain went through my head. "I don't remember *anything* from last time."

Ben immediately shifted to free a hand to place it on the side of my face. I sighed in relief as his healing energy sunk into me.

"But do you remember from this time?" Ben asked, eyes intent as they looked into mine.

"Yes," I said numbly. "But I don't *understand* it. I...I was you. Except, not you. Me-you."

"I think you mean *we* were *us*," Ben said grimly. "Somehow, we became one. Something new. Inside my body."

I blinked.

The only thing my bewildered brain could think to say was, "Man, you *smell* a lot more things than I do."

Ben laughed tensely and held me more tightly for a moment. "I'm drakón, Sarah."

"Interesting," Kor said clinically. "I'm going to hazard a guess that this time was different either because Ben was in a form you somewhat had in common or because now you two are partially heartbonded."

"What difference would *that* make?" I asked, baffled.

Kor smiled thinly. "This surging to each other is possible in the first place because of the bond between the two of you. Don't you think that *strengthening* that bond might do something?"

"Oh," I said grudgingly.

Now my cheeks were getting warm. Ben's weren't, oddly enough. Maybe he was still too shaken. I wondered what had made him so worried before I woke up—and, for that matter, why I'd *had* to wake up, when it seemed as if he hadn't.

Though Ben looked reluctant, he asked, "Think you can sit up on your own now?"

His eyes glanced toward the crowd. I didn't think the closeness was what he was worried about. I'd gathered by now that shows of strength were important to dramá. Besides that, we were supposed to be preparing to go into battle.

This test could have been better timed, both in terms of privacy and in the chosen moment. But then, we'd had no idea we'd do *that*. We were just trying to see if I could still impart energy to the entire group even while being inside Ben. The results from the Battle of the Solstice were inconclusive.

"Yes," I told Ben firmly. I could feel my physical strength and magic resurging.

Ben sat me up, and I scooted out of his lap and sat beside him.

Kor asked, "I assume that state wasn't easy to maintain?"

"No," Ben answered, shaking his head. "It wasn't...bad."

"Just so *weird*," I added. "And I think when the weirdness finally hit us...we broke apart."

"Well," Kor said cheerfully. "Ready to try surging into Ben while he's in drakáform?"

"No!" both of us said in unison.

Kor pouted. "Oh, come on. How else will we know—"

"Koriben," Alyish said grimly, coming up to us. "There's been an alert—at Roketh."

Ben was on his feet at once. "That's about seven elden away, right?"

I took Ben's offered hand and let him pull me up.

"Correct."

Ben looked at me, his face a grim mix of the King and Ben. "Can you do it, Sarah?"

I knew what he meant. We'd gone over this many times. I had to maintain lightform for seven elden, however long it took for them to deal with what we found when we got there, and seven elden back.

Though my iceheart was once again pulsing, intestines knotting, and bile rising, I knew in my bones and the quiet stillness deep within that this was what I was meant to do.

I nodded firmly. "I can."

Ben gave me three rapid clenches through our joined hands, then looked at Yvera. "Let's move."

ONLY A HANDFUL OF minutes later, we and the rest of the hunt team were soaring, racing against time to both catch the saboteur—*if* that was what had come through the darkrift—and outmaneuver any other surprises the Devourer might have planned.

I was in the saddle on Ben's back. Not because gravity had any hold on me right now, since I was shining like a second moon in my lightform to provide the energy he and the others needed to maintain their lethal drakáforms, but because it simply was the easiest way for me to stay close to Ben, relatively sheltered by his golden, scaly mass. He had been adamant about that, and I didn't argue with him.

Besides, it also saved me the energy of surging. Not that I would have been so foolish as to throw away energy on *slow*-surging right now, but even the instantaneous kind cost me something, and when it came to battle, the slightest bit of energy could be the difference between life and death.

And when it came to *my* energy, it could be the difference between any of their lives or deaths. Including Ben's.

This time, instead of leading the flight from the front, Ben was surrounded on all sides, including from above and below, as the flight skillfully flew in a dangerously tight formation around us. That formation served the dual purpose of sheltering us two Monarchs and giving the flight as direct access to my ambient energy as possible. Thus, my view of the dark landscape that rushed past beneath us was limited to what I could see around so many masses of scale and wing.

After a short eternity, someone mentally shouted to us all, *There! South by southeast.*

Second and third wing, Yvera said coolly from where she flew at the head. *Go.*

Two pairs of three dragons on the outermost parts of the formation broke off and soared into the night. I craned my neck to see what was going on, but even though we began to circle, I still couldn't see much or understand what I did see, besides flares of drakáflame lighting up the night.

It was a darkrift, alright, someone said. *What was left of it is torched now.*

Well, good to know the detection devices were working. But....

Did you see anything? Yvera demanded.

No—

Movement, due south. At the field.

Two, three, go! Yvera ordered sharply.

Those wings took off again, and at her lead, the flight broke from the circling pattern and flew straight for a bit before circling again.

Torched asher is fast!

It's in the field.

So, that meant there was only one so far. I felt a flicker of hope that the Devourer hadn't created an army of werewolves. Still, how long would it only be—

Darkrifts!

That was the last thing I understood before the chaos began. The Devourer's trap had sprung.

I thought, and sincerely hoped, that it was organized chaos. Yvera was shouting out orders right and left, the wings were obeying swiftly, and heart-stopping minutes went by without me hearing of a casualty amid all the shouted reports. But the main flight formation had broken up, and only four drakón remained with Ben—one for each side, one above, and one below. Even they had to give him a much wider berth to allow him room to maneuver as even he joined in the fight for our lives.

Flyers of all sorts flapped through the darkness toward us. After all, land-bound monsters would hardly be any threat to airborne drakón. But with flyers, the drakón were pushed to their limits to eliminate those swarms of smaller and more agile creatures and prevent them from getting at their most vulnerable points: their eyes and wings. The flyers I caught sufficient glimpses of ranged from arrel—grotesque stone humanoids with drakáwings—to giant dark eagles and vultures to flying serpents.

Drakáflame lit up the night like a near-constant firework show. Draká roars, bestial cries, and avian screeches echoed all around. Smoke and scorched flesh, earth, and plant matter filled my nostrils and coated the back of my throat and mouth. Even as only semi-corporal as I was, I was jerked every which way on the wildest rollercoaster ride of my life as Ben fought with all his might.

Yet all their efforts to protect me weren't enough to stop one arrel from finally grasping my arm.

Terror froze all cognitive function as I was immersed in the memory of the last time stony arms like that had grabbed and taken off with me. Forgotten was both my ability to surge away and Ben's stern orders that I surge inside him the very moment something like this happened.

I simply thrashed, wildly and dumbly, as the arrel pulled me out of my saddle—restraints somehow suddenly broken—and off Ben's back.

Somehow, Ben felt my absence at once and roared, twisting in the air.

SARAH, SURGE!

His shout was like a slap in my face, finally jerking me out of my stupor of terror. Still, I wasn't *entirely* functional yet. Ben had most likely meant for me to surge into *him*.

Instead, I surged *away*.

I rematerialized not a second later about a hundred feet away.

Then I had to immediately surge again as a draká tail—larger than a tree—swung toward me.

Then again, as a dark eagle swooped toward me.

By now, I was entirely outside of the fight, floating alone in the night air. For the moment.

Sarah, to ME*!* Ben roared.

By now, my brain had unfrozen enough to remember why that wasn't an ideal solution, even though I *longed* more than I could remember longing for anything to disappear inside him, hiding from all of this.

But....

Ben, we never found out if you could still give them energy if—

Torch it, to me, *Sarah!*

But if I did that, the others could die. Ben would be alright—he would be able to either fight his way out or surge us to safety. But if I couldn't still give the others energy through him, then his people...the ones who had followed us out here because they trusted me to give them the energy to keep them alive...might die.

We didn't know if I could consciously separate from Ben if I wasn't able to give them what they needed through him. *I* didn't know if Ben could—would—let me go.

I froze in indecision. What was I supposed to *do*?

SARAH!

The golden dragon had broken free of the fight and was flying straight for me, eyes burning.

Then I saw movement on the ground: a dark, shaggy creature racing down the road beneath me faster than it had any right to on all fours, given its roughly humanoid shape. Running away from the fight.

For the first time, fury burned in my blood.

I was *not* going to let this night be for naught.

Without thinking, my right hand went to the gun at my waist, and I activated the shield on my left arm, causing a concave circle to cover me from head to toe on that side.

Then surged straight down and into the path of the werewolf.

Though I shook with terror, I shot it, again and again, pouring power into the gun to give each shot sharpness, light, and accuracy.

Yet even those measures, combined with my month of practice, which had made my shots hit dead center before, were now all for naught, because they just hit a dark shield that only appeared with each impact.

The werewolf slowed, stopped a few dozen feet from me, and rose onto its unnatural hind legs. It was shaped much like a krathen—there was a good reason I had originally thought that was what those were. Yet it was more shadow than substance, its form as vague and darkly ephemeral as mine was brightly so now. And there was something familiar about those burning white eyes with dark centers....

By the time I realized why, it was too late.

A dark dome sprung into being around us, dampening Ben's roar of fear and rage to a disturbing degree. All sounds from the distant battle were either dampened or cut off entirely. I could see little beyond it, either—only vague shapes and shadows.

The primary illumination I now had to see the monster in front of me was my own radiance.

The monster...which turned into an even more disturbing kind before my eyes.

Becoming human—at least in shape. And too familiar, given his eerie resemblance to his younger brother, Kor.

The primary difference being the darkness that took the place of Kor's sapphire irises, causing iris and pupil to blend into a featureless dark circle.

"Solim," I said.

I did not know how, but my voice was steady, as was the hand still holding the gun pointed straight at him.

Inside, my instincts were at war.

Every sense of self-preservation told me to flee, to surge away, far away—to Ben if I could, but just *away* if I couldn't. I could feel Ben getting closer through the pull I always felt from him, and now ten times more strongly than usual as he pulled with all his might. Even without that pull, he would be here in seconds—it would almost be too easy.

Yet something else kept me rooted where I was. Something in the dark, restful silence inside of me that was the source of my power and the connection to my Tree. Some gut instinct told me I was here for a *reason*.

"Sarah," Solim responded, smiling politely. "How good to see you. Did you like the surprise we so carefully prepared for you?"

He gestured to himself.

I ignored his jab. I'd already faced and conquered that fear, with astonishing swiftness and ease. Part of that had to do with making the connection in my gut and my head that there were far worse things than werewolves; I'd already known that in theory, but now my whole being *knew* that. The other part of it was simply having a reason to confront the fear, and then realizing its power lay in the unknown—in not being certain I could face and defeat it. Now I *knew* that had this been any normal monster, I could have.

Now I knew that any ordinary monster was no match for me.

But Solim was no ordinary monster.

And yet...I stayed.

Because....

"So you were the saboteur all along," I said evenly.

The ground shook, and through the dark haze of the shield, I saw the golden blurs that explained why.

Solim ignored the gold draká behind him, even when his half of the dome lit up with golden tongues of flame.

"Yes." His polite smile stayed in place, as if we were discussing the weather.

But his dark eyes somehow glittered with a reverse light—corrupted darkness, the hunger of the void that could not be sated.

A flash of gold scales and ivory claws, a bang against the shield, again and again—still for naught. A pull growing all the stronger by the second. I was surprised his inner voice wasn't shouting away inside my head; the only reasons I could think of why not were, first, Ben thought I was past hearing, or, second, that he couldn't project it through the shield.

"Who else would the Devourer entrust with the darkest of its power?"

Solim held up a dark orb, one that seemed to bend the light that touched it, sucking it in. From the waves of deathly, nausea-inducing power I felt from it, I knew instinctively that *this* was the source, even before Solim spoke again.

He looked at the orb fondly. "With this, I will keep poisoning your fields every night, faster than you can heal them, until I bring your precious Realms to their knees from starvation. I think you know this, don't you?"

I did. That was why I was still there. Because if I surged to Ben and to safety now, Solim, the coward he was, would disappear, and this night would be for nothing. Because Solim would come again, and again, and each time, his poisons and his traps would be more costly.

Solim was still here because he thought he could take me while I was alone. I was still here because I had to use that arrogance to stop him. I felt that conviction all the way to the *true* darkness inside me, which waited to be unleashed.

"So *sera*," Solim said, that polite smile hardening to a smirk. No doubt he guessed why I was still here as well.

Now the only question remaining was to see who was delusional.

He didn't give me any more warning than that before he sent a wave of dark, nauseating power toward me. But I had been ready for him.

Technically, I had learned to do something else over this past month. I just hadn't expected it to be useful tonight.

Instantly, I created a solid dome of ice over and around me, entirely encasing myself. Not just ice alone: ice with every particle infused with my glowing power—magic given solid, brilliant form, a type of shield all my own.

One that Solim had not been prepared to break.

The dark wave crashed harmlessly over me, and the very second it dissipated, I heard a voice inside say, *Now.*

Without hesitation, I flexed that shield until it shattered, sending razor-sharp shards that were more magic than ice flying in all directions.

Ones that Solim had not been prepared to block.

When I caught sight of him next, he was standing still, eyes wide with shock as he stared down at himself—at the dozen shards of glowing shrapnel that had penetrated his flesh. And those were only the ones that had stuck. Gashes were everywhere, including one across his cheek. All his wounds were seeping black blood, coating his skin in horrifying rivulets.

But none of those injuries were as bad as what the cracked orb in his hands was doing to him. It spilled a liquid darker than ink with the viscosity of sap which stained his skin black, and that stain was creeping far more swiftly than the liquid itself down his hand to his arm.

He gurgled from the shard that had pierced his throat, and his eyes met mine, burning with dark fury.

I braced myself, ready to throw up another shield.

But in the next moment, he was gone.

And so was the dark dome.

All at once, I was surrounded by drakón in amáform, though some of them rushed away and changed into draká now that my light was restored to them. The dramá that remained encircled me and faced outward, prepared to repel any attackers with magic and steel rather than might and claw.

My eyes darted around in alarm. I saw no gold draká anywhere. Where was....

Two amáform drakón parted to let a tall one through, his gold eyes blazing at me.

"Sarah," he said in a quiet, deadly voice.

Uh-oh, I thought numbly.

Now I trembled—belatedly, from the peril I had just somehow miraculously survived, and in anticipation of the next. But this time, I had no defenses.

I'm dead.

Chapter Twenty-Eight

ANGER

Koriben

FLAME ONLY KNOWS HOW, but I managed to contain my fury.

Long enough, anyway.

Long enough to make sure Sarah wasn't hurt, then change and get her back on my back, with a sharp order to stay there—which she, thank Flame, readily agreed to.

Long enough to oversee the final elimination of the consumed that the Devourer had sent after us. It opened no more darkrifts, and within dek, we were once again flying, racing Sarah back to Remik before it changed its mind.

Long enough for Sarah to return to the King's Wing to rest while I saw that any lingering wounds among the flight were treated, and I debriefed with Alyish, Yvera, and Kor. Kor, who had stayed behind to assist Alyish, demanded what had happened under Solim's dark dome, and I couldn't tell him, because I had been too furious to ask Sarah, and she hadn't braved that fury to tell me.

"But, Ben," Kor said, staggered. "You realize what this means, right? Either Sarah drove off Solim *by herself*, or—"

I held up a hand and glared at him. "Not now, Kor. I can't take this right now."

Not the first scenario, nor the *or*. Nor any thought remotely approaching what might have happened instead.

Long enough to get away when I could and go down. But I didn't go to the King's suite, not right away. I was in no state to be around anyone, much less Sarah. I sent even Yvera away, though if I had been a tad less murderous, I might have kept her with me for this part.

Long enough to get to an empty training room.

To activate a dome.

And then to unleash my fury in its fullest—destroying, shattering, burning. Obliterating target after target after target with everything I had left in me.

Until I finally collapsed to my knees from exhaustion, muscles trembling with weakness, with absolutely no spark left to burn. Not without plunging myself into unconsciousness.

Not that oblivion wasn't tempting right now....

Only then, when I could no longer hurt so much as an insect, did I allow myself to think about what had happened. What had...nearly happened.

You promised me, I told the void. *You* promised.

No answer came. I hadn't expected one. After all, She had *technically* kept Her promise. Somehow, even though Sarah had been trapped with Solim, she now lived. Not only alive, but unharmed.

I still could not believe it.

How?

I knew Sarah was a miracle. I believed in that miracle perhaps more than I believed in anything else right now—as problematic as that blasphemy was.

Yet this....

This wasn't the miracle I wanted. This wasn't what I thought the Tree had meant when She said she would protect Sarah if I did what She asked. This wasn't *protecting* Sarah. This was *using* her, this was *endangering* her.

Throwing her in the ring with our most deadly enemy besides the Devourer itself, *where I could not help her.*

How close had I come to losing her?

How close did she come to....

While I could do nothing.

I trembled so badly that I sank to my side on the freshly scorched stone floor and curled up into a fetal position, and the tears burned hot through my sweat as they streaked down my face to the floor.

How could you do this to her? I raged.

This time, an answer came. But it was in the echo of my own voice, my much younger voice, swearing my oaths as newly invested drakón and Heir.

My life for the Realms, my life for my Tree.

My *life*, I shouted back. *Mine. Mine alone. Why won't you take* my *life instead?*

I almost wished She would, and do it now. Before I had to suffer another blow like that.

Again, a memory answered me. But this time, it *was* in the Tree's voice.

Because she needs you. And We need you both. Or all are lost.

I stilled.

The Trees...needed Sarah. Yes, They needed her to run risks, for the good of all. But They *needed her*.

Alive.

The Tree hadn't just made that promise to placate me, to bribe me into obedience.

The Trees needed her alive.

And so, They were going to do whatever it took to protect her—not for my sake, but for the good of the Realms. And whenever They asked her to risk herself, They would prepare for her deliverance.

For the good of all life.

Yes, the Tree whispered.

I gasped, and suddenly, for the first time since Sarah had been pulled from my back—no, perhaps from the time Sarah told me she was coming—I felt like I could truly *breathe* again.

In a way, nothing had changed. The Tree's promise still should have stood as it had before.

Yet everything had changed. Because if there was one thing I still doubted, it was about what the Tree was willing to make me suffer.

But I still believed—somehow—that everything She did was for the good of all.

So, if that good meant keeping *Sarah alive*....

Then, with that unexpected alignment between my belief and my hope, I could summon the courage to keep going.

For at least one more day.

To my surprise, Sarah was asleep by the time I came into our room—though she'd clearly not intended to be. She was curled up, fully dressed, on a couch, using an armrest as an uncomfortable-looking pillow.

I caught the swinging door to slow its closure, bringing it to a soundless stop. Then I walked as quietly as I could and stood over her, taking advantage of this rare opportunity to just look at her.

No sign of the peril that she had been in—that she had chosen—remained. She had showered, as I had, and her still-damp hair clung to and curled around her. She had changed into something comfortable but still not her normal night clothes. Her face was clear and calm.

Or it was when I first approached, but then her forehead furrowed, and she tensed. I thought she was just waking, but then she started shaking, and her fists clenched.

"No," she whimpered. "*No.*"

My flameheart sank. A nightmare.

I reached out to wake her, just as she gasped, "Ben, no!"

I inhaled, wondering if I should be the one to wake her right now, but my hand was already on her shoulder. She started, eyes flashing open, already glowing silver from her terror. I pulled my hand back and took a hasty step away.

"Sarah, I'm—"

"Ben?" she gasped, sitting up and looking around. "Oh, thank Flame."

She stumbled to me and threw her arms around me, clenching me tightly.

My flameheart rose a bit at that sign that I might not have been the monster in her nightmare.

"Bad dream?" I asked quietly.

"Yes," she said thickly. "He...he had you, and he was...."

I stilled. I didn't have to ask her who she meant. Or what he had been doing.

At least with that confirmation, I felt safe enough scooping her up, and when she went willingly and curled into me, I carried her back to the couch and sat down with her. And so, quite unexpectedly, I was the one comforting her, holding her as she cried her fill into my shirt, holding her as her tremors slowly stilled, simply holding her as the silence stretched on for dek.

Eventually, she craned her neck to look up at me.

"Sorry," she whispered.

My voice was surprisingly calm. "Do you understand the slightest bit of what you did to me?"

"I think so," she said, turning her head down again. "That's probably why I.... It was all I could think about, waiting for you to come back. Imagining what it would have been like if you...."

I sighed deeply. "You make it really hard for me to stay mad at you. You know that?"

Though I didn't have a good view of her face, I could hear the faint smile in her voice. "Is that why you aren't shouting at me right now?"

"That, and I already worked out my shouting in a training room. So, if you've been bracing yourself for a tirade, you can relax now."

I ached when she did indeed relax, losing any lingering tension as she sunk fully into me. I was fervently glad that I had not brought my fury down on her, to any degree. I might have shattered her, or truly made myself the monster of her nightmares.

Certainly I would not have been able to hold her now—and holding her was exactly what I needed to let go of the last of the night's agony, to allow her very aliveness and wellness still the last of my internal tremors and allow my soul to cleave together again.

"Why did you do it?"

I had to ask. Even though I knew the answer.

"I had to, Ben," she rasped. "He would have just run if we'd gone after him together. Because it was just me, I could get close enough to hurt him. I was the trap within the trap."

I inhaled. "You...you *hurt* him?"

"At least for a moment," she said dubiously. "He was covered in shards, some of them going in deep. One was in his *throat*."

She shuddered.

Of course Sarah could shudder at the horror of what she'd done to a monster like Solim.

"*How?*"

"I think I surprised him. The ice barrier I made, then exploded.... I don't think it was anything like he expected or guarded against. Somehow, the shards got through to him. Kor thinks so too."

"Does he?" I said tightly.

I knew I had no right to throw a fireball at Kor for going and getting the explanation from her before me. I was the one throwing fireballs in a training room while Sarah had nothing to do but wait for me to come back. And this was Kor's brother, after all.

Yet the acid that burned at me didn't answer to reason.

Fortunately, Sarah seemed to misinterpret the reason for the tension in my voice.

"Kor doesn't think I killed him...but we think I might just have bought us the time we need."

"What do you mean?" I said intently, distracted finally from less worthy emotions.

"Solim had this orb." Sarah shifted to form both of her hands into a ball. "About this size. Said it had the Devourer's power inside, that he had been using it to spread the pestilence. Well, one of my shards cracked it, and the stuff inside got on him. And it...."

Sarah's voice turned queasy. "It wasn't good, Ben. I don't know what it was, I don't know what it did to him. But it wasn't good."

I became still. I could hardly believe my ears.

"The source of the pestilence...is now damaged," I said faintly, "and Solim may have been hurt."

Perhaps in a way that even a lish could not recover from. His master's power wasn't the kind to be trifled with, nor the kind that could be healed from. It was the antithesis to life.

"Flame, Sarah," I said numbly. "Do you have any idea what you may have done for us?"

"I got lucky," she said quietly. "It was only because Solim was being so arrogant, careless. He'll be ready for me next time."

And there would be a next time. My flameheart shuddered, and I held her more tightly from the surety of that. But Flame willing, that next time would not be as soon as it otherwise might have been.

In asking Sarah to risk her life...had the Trees actually saved it?

She took a deep breath. "What I'm trying to say is...I know what kind of risk I took, and I'm sorry for the pain I caused you because of it. I'm not so foolish as to think the same thing will work twice. I can't make promises, because...because we both have to do what we have to do, but next time...I think I'll need you. With me."

I pressed my face into her hair and breathed her in. "I suppose that's the best I can ask for, isn't it?"

"I'm sorry it isn't more," she whispered.

My lips pulled into a thin smile. "Now who's apologizing too much?"

I tapped her back three times. She shifted to look up at me and smiled at me through the moisture in her eyes.

"I love you too, my sun."

I tapped her four times, hoping she would know what the last word was.

She laughed thickly. "No, you do *not*."

As I'd also hoped she would, she attempted to prove it by stretching up and kissing me.

No DARK RIFTS OPENED the next night—not any that our sensors detected, at any rate. No fields were infected the next morning.

We stayed another day for that reason alone, though we made good use of the time to rest and take care of business. Me more so than Sarah in that last regard, but she caught up with her family and spent time with Alya, learning what she could about Alya's craft just for the pleasure of it. That gave Alya the chance to pick Sarah's brain about recommendations for a third generation of watches.

Even Lady Rowin took time to speak with Sarah, wondering if she had any recommendations for an emergency dispersal of the icemint infusion—something that would work faster and more directly than injecting it into the irrigation system. As grateful as Rowin was to have a solution at all, she was eager to figure out if the late-stage infestations could be reversed in time to save the grain.

And Sarah did. I heard about it all later, of course, but it seemed Sarah had thought for a moment, then asked if we used anything like a "crop duster," and explained the concept when Lady Rowin just stared at her. Rowin caught on quickly, and that was when Sarah interrupted Kor and me to borrow Kor's scale that matched the one he'd given her father. From Sarah's brief explanation, Jake was something like an artificer, and once Sarah connected him with Lady Rowin, they became immersed in details. Kor had to track Rowin down deken later to get his scale back. She had long since passed it on to her own artificers, who were working with Jake on schematics.

Sarah's family also had an agricultural development. Apparently, on the day of the discovery of the cure and the hunt, a door had opened for Sarah's mother in their garden, and the passage beyond eventually led to a series of cavernous rooms with dirt floors. After a little exploration with Svyer and the light helpers, they uncovered skylights and figured out how to heat them to rid them of the snow and ice that had collected on top.

Which meant Sarah's family now had the means and space to grow more than just garden herbs and vegetables. Svyer requested a long list of seeds, Kor made the arrangements, and I took the large bags over, leaving them in front of the crowngate for them to collect when I was gone.

I used another of my breaks to track down Kindra. She was surprised to see me, but her face hardened when I asked to speak with her alone. When we stepped into her study and she closed the door, I said, "Alright, out with it."

"Out with what?" she said with a scowl and folded arms.

"What's this problem you have with me and Sarah?"

She huffed. "My 'problem,' Ben, was that I thought you were making the most common mistake of all time, except with far more dire consequences for the rest of us: letting your twitterpation make you marry someone that would let you let the Realms fall apart."

I'd prepared myself for something like this, so I could keep my temper in check—and catch a surprising key word. "Wait, was?"

She scowled at a corner of the room. "I...may have seen and heard some things since then that have made me...reevaluate my assessment."

"Oh?"

She glared at me. "Ben, I didn't *really* care that you didn't want to marry me. What I cared about was that you found a consort who would make up for your shortcomings. Which, at the time we were classmates, were significant. Now you seem to have...wised up a bit in the way of the worlds, and...you've also seemed to choose a consort who is more...sober than I had expected."

When I finally understood, my response was flat. "You thought I was enough of a torched idiot to fall for an empty-headed seductress."

"Oh, don't pretend you're immune to her pretty face," Kindra snapped. "I'm just thanking the Flame that the one you *did* finally lose your senses over so happens to be a tolerable choice for the Realms. By all rights, she should be dead right now, not having saved us from fever and famine. So, either she has a head on her shoulders and some spark inside her heart, or she's Tree-blessed—but probably a bit of both. And I guess both are what we need in a Queen right now. So, I suppose she'll have to do."

I glared at her. Ironic that in revealing there was no need for me to offer a challenge to her, she made me so *badly* want to drag her into the ring, anyway.

Sometimes being an adult was a pain.

I took a deep breath and let it out slowly before letting myself speak again. "So, that's it?"

"What's it?"

"You're good with Sarah?"

She scowled. "We're not going to become friends if that's what you—"

She stopped, then rolled her eyes. "Ben, you didn't *honestly* think I was going to challenge her, did you?"

I answered flatly, "With how immaturely you were behaving, the thought crossed my mind."

"Oh, so *I'm* the immature one now?" she snapped.

I didn't know what she meant by that, but I assumed it had something to do with me having never shown an interest in her.

"By taking your anger out on Sarah, yes. If you had a problem, your problem should have been with me, not her. As much as you're giving excuses about objectivity and 'the good of the Realms,' admit that deep down, this might just be about your pride being bruised that I chose her instead of you."

She clenched her jaw, and her orange eyes glowed. "You're full of yourself, Ben. Always have been."

That's when I finally knew I was right about the source of her bitterness—and that she had never truly seen or cared about *me* at all.

With surprising calm, I said, "Actually, no, I wasn't. It just goes to show how little you got to know me if you could think I was. If I'd been a bit more full of myself, I might have chosen you—or someone like you. Someone cunning and exacting who could have helped me run the Realms with the regimented order you envisioned, to lead the both of us on to glory and then ruin. Instead, I was a shy, mourning boy, too afraid to allow anyone close enough to care about me. I'll let you come to your own conclusions about the man and King I'm at least trying to be now."

I put my hand on her door. "Hate me however you like, I don't care. Just remember that your problem is with me, not Sarah. Keep it that way, and I don't think we'll have any problems. Go after her...and it's me you'll be facing in the ring."

I shoved the door open and then let it swing shut behind me as I strode out.

It was only after I'd left the Lady's Wing that I realized I didn't apologize to Kindra.

Not even once.

Chapter Twenty-Nine

FORMALITIES

Sarah

"Finally," Lady Rowin huffed mockingly as we said farewell on the landing circle. "I thought I would never drive you out."

"And here I was thinking we'd never be able to leave," Ben quipped with a smirk. "Rest assured, we won't hurry back."

I had a hard time suppressing an eye roll. I rarely approved of deprecating humor, but between Ben and Rowin, it seemed to be just what the two of them had needed to reset their working relationship. Even when the two of them were seriously discussing something as King and Lady, one of them would inevitably slip in a good-humored jab that would begin a bit of verbal sparring before they got back to the topic at hand.

I could see that Ben had needed someone like her: an elder who understood something of his position and could give him advice, yet who wasn't family and didn't love him—and didn't let him take himself too seriously.

It was a good thing I understood all that without being told. Otherwise, I would have been a bit jealous.

"*You* don't have to bother, but your sensible betrothed is welcome any time," Rowin said with a serious face. And a wink at me.

"Particularly if I bring my lucrative ideas with me," I said with a smile.

Rowin chuckled. "It's so good to know that we can all understand one another. Admit it, Koriben. You're going to miss being here after what is coming next for you."

Ben sighed, but perhaps because there were still others within earshot, he said nothing.

"Best of luck in Palla," Rowin said with her hand over her heart. "Flame go with you."

Flame knows, you're going to need it, she added dryly in her inner voice. I knew from the echo that it hadn't been to just me, but the thing about projected inner voices was that you couldn't tell how many others heard. I guessed at least Ben did, judging from his second sigh.

"Flame go with you, Lady Rowin, Heir Kindra."

"And Ice watch over you," I added, resting my eyes on Kindra to let her know I included her as well—and meant her no ill will.

Rowin looked at Kindra, but her Heir just turned and walked away without having said anything to either of us, having been stone-faced the entire farewell. Rowin just shrugged and let her go. Probably for the best.

The Lady then stepped back, which appeared to be a signal for us to depart. Ben smiled at me, gave my hand three quick clenches, and let go to put enough space between us to change.

Take care of him, Rowin sent to just me as we both watched him go. *Not that I'm attached, mind. But he's the only Royal we've got right now, and I'm not interested in the anarchy that could result if we lost him.*

My chest tightened, though I worked hard to keep my face neutral. *Well, I am attached, so I don't need another reason to watch out for him, thank you. I don't know if you've realized this, but I love him.*

Oh, I have. Thank the Flame that you do.

Out of the corner of my eye, I saw her turn and walk away. I didn't bother asking her what she meant by that. I was confident by now that she wasn't as unmoved by Ben as she made it seem, making her emphasis on "you" something of a puzzle to me.

Yet even if she had stayed and I had asked, I didn't think she would have answered.

THE LAST TIME I had been to Romskal, we had come to a desert mountain range. That's what I was expecting when we emerged from the sungate, even though that was a bit silly. After all, the Strongshield had an entire planet to spread out on, all to themselves; plus, Danyeth had been in a different biome than the jungle I'd first visited on Ykran.

I was still startled to see the forested valley spread below us between towering, white-capped peaks. The air was deliciously crisp, and I gathered from the snow caps and brown barrenness in the deciduous trees in the lowest regions that this place was either in its late fall or early spring.

Spring, Ben told me in answer to my question. *It's a shame that you couldn't see it in the summer.*

I imagine it must be beautiful, I said as we circled above the landing pad, waiting for it to clear.

Well, it is. But it's almost more of a shame just because you're never going to hear the end of them saying "if only you had come here in summer," until you're sick of it. Lord Kolwin is probably never going to forgive us for our timing.

Oh, well then, I said in amusement. *We'll just have to postpone our heartbinding until then to accommodate the Romskal seasons, now, won't we?*

Don't joke about things like that in front of him! Ben said in alarm. *Or any of them. They'll think you're serious and agree wholeheartedly, and* then *we're doomed.*

I concealed my growing amusement, making my voice serious. *Who said I was joking? It's just a few months. That's surely not an unreasonable expectation.*

Sarah.... Ben growled, turning his golden head to cast me a reptilian glare. *Don't you dare.*

Surprisingly, underneath his irritation at my teasing, I still sensed real...alarm.

Was he really that worried I'd try to put it off? If so, why? I could understand a delay being *undesirable* to him, but...worry?

Before I could probe deeper, Ben brought us in—which took me by surprise, since the landing pad wasn't as clear as I thought it should be. Then I realized why as Ben carefully touched down at the end, with Yvera and Kor skillfully landing in the very last possible spaces on either side of him.

Another aisle of dragons—this time primarily various shades of red—awaited us. The Peacegrowth had done the same thing to welcome us to Danyeth, but with their landing being on the flat top of a cliff rather than cut out of a mountainside, their drakón had had more room to spread themselves out. And Peacegrowth draká, I was gathering, were generally smaller and much less intimidating than their Strongshield counterparts. Not to mention more...alive. These draká were staying alarmingly still, almost like enormous, colorful statues. Even their eyes stared fixedly ahead, not looking toward Ben, his wings, or me.

I hadn't realized until that moment that there might be something worse than having those draconic stares *on* me.

Given the tight quarters, landing workers brought me a ladder versus a staircase. I was getting familiar enough with the routine to not need any help getting out of the saddle, across Ben's back, and down the ladder, which gave me a flicker of pride and relief. As soon as I was on the ground and the ladder was removed, Ben changed back and made his way to me, either seeing or guessing how unnerved this eerily still honor guard was making me.

Strongshield...are very formal, Ben said carefully as he took my hand and gave it three squeezes.

So I've gathered.

I knew that from when I'd encountered them the first time I came to their world.

Still, brace yourself, he said with a sigh as he turned us to face the large welcoming parting of amón and amáform drakón that awaited us at the end of the row, under the grand entrance to the hold—all of which was festooned with scarlet streamers, banners, and ribbons. They had even placed a rectangular rug that led the way all the way from us to them—having literally rolled out the red carpet.

This could take a while, Ben said grimly as we began walking down the aisle.

Is that what Rowin meant when she said we'd need all the luck we could get with them?

Partly, Ben said with another sigh. When I cast a glance at him, his expression was sober as his eyes rested on the central figure. *But...I am not the only new leader here.*

I tried to keep my eyes from darting too quickly back to the man I had noted as being the tip of the triangular formation of the welcoming party. This time, with Ben's hint and the reduced distance between us, I noticed the scarlet-haired man's youth.

He looks our age, I said, stunned.

He is—only nineteen summers, Ben said heavily.

When did he....

I realized a moment before Ben answered how loaded that answer could have been. *Same time as me. And...for the same reason. The last Lady....*

I inhaled sharply, eyes now riveted on the young man, standing tall and strong in his elaborate maroon robes and decorative side braid, with a handsome face that could have been carved from stone. And, I now noticed, he was clean-shaven.

He was in mourning. As were all the rest of his people behind him. I had never seen so much maroon and so many clean-shaven draká men in one place in all the time I had been among them.

Why didn't you tell me before? I demanded, aghast.

I.... Ben said, trailing off softly.

At once, I understood, and I gave his hand three squeezes.

Ben took a deep breath. *He wasn't a close relation to her—a distant cousin. From what I could tell, they didn't become much closer even after he became Heir. But the Strongshield are...traditional.*

Ah. I finally understood another part of Rowin's grim parting as I glanced at Ben again—at the beard he was regrowing and his black and gold clothing. As practical as she was, Rowin would not have minded Ben's lack of the trappings of mourning only one month after his father's death; in fact, she might have respected him for it. But I suspected this Lord Kolwin would be another matter entirely.

I also guessed the Strongshield had yet another, far deeper reason to disapprove of our timing than the seasons. Was that what had been behind Ben's alarm at my joking suggestion? That if I brought it up, if I showed the slightest willingness to give in, the Strongshield would push until we did? And once the date was under negotiation, they might not be satisfied with even a few months....

Ben clenched my hand tightly, seemingly thinking along the same lines. *Just, please. Don't even joke about postponing. Politely ignore anything they might say about it. Please.*

I will, don't worry, I soothed. *Sorry for the teasing. I see that was in poor taste now.*

You didn't know. Ben's voice was as relieved as it was ashamed. *Because I didn't tell you.*

Again, I understood why, but I resolved that from now on, I was going to be more proactive about preparing myself for what was coming next. I was sure that Vadya would have been more than willing to give me all the details, and the only reason she hadn't was that it probably hadn't occurred to her that I didn't know them; the tragic change in Strongshield's leadership would have been old news to her.

I could understand now, though, why she and my other attendants had taken particular care with my appearance and wardrobe this morning, dressing me in an elaborate white and black suit and train and pinning my hair down so tightly in an elaborate crown braid that not even the flight over had mussed it up significantly.

Ben and I came to that understanding just in time, because not a few moments later, Ben stopped us a respectful distance from Lord Kolwin.

Again, I was struck by his handsomeness, which, particularly with his carved features and side braid that went nearly to his waist, bordered on beauty. His scarlet eyes held no degree of softness, however; they took in the two of us with a severity that put Lady Rowin's estimating look to shame. I tried not to let the disturbing color of those spheres prejudice me against him, but the look they were giving us—particularly Ben—wasn't helping.

"King Koriben," Lord Kolwin said. I was surprised at how deep his voice was, considering his age and appearance. "I welcome you to Palla of Romskal."

"I thank you for your welcome, Lord Kolwin," Ben said formally, his expression unusually reserved.

"What brings my...King to my Realm on this day?"

Lord Kolwin's barest hint of emphasis on *King* carried a backhanded blow that made me stiffen, and Ben clenched my hand more tightly for a moment in response.

At the same time, Kor sent, *Calm, Sarah. Don't show emotion.*

Easier said than done, when someone had the audacity to verbally attack *Ben* upon greeting.

Without changing his expression, Ben said, "I come to present my betrothed and your future Queen: Queen Sarah Moontouched of the Seventh Realm and Crown of Ice."

Kolwin turned his formidable glare fully to me for the first time. I met his gaze without flinching, determined to not give in the slightest, no matter how those hard rubies unsettled me.

"Be welcome to my Realm, Queen Sarah," he said, the chill in his tone belying any such intention. "I am Lord Kolwin Strongshield."

"It is an honor to meet you, Lord Kolwin," I said coolly.

"And I you," he said. "I am particularly honored that you grace us with your presence so soon after your betrothal. And our loss."

Ben stiffened. I didn't need to glance at him to know that he too was struggling to control his expression now at the blatancy of Kolwin's critique.

I took a hopefully subtle deep breath, then said with all the quiet sincerity I could muster, "I mourn for your loss."

Now Ben wasn't the only one to stiffen. Many of the people close enough in Kolwin's entourage did, and Kolwin's own eyes tightened minutely.

Sarah, Kor said uneasily.

It seemed I had once again thrown us off script, but I strangely felt not a flicker of regret.

"Kind words," Kolwin murmured. "Spoken from lips that otherwise show no sign of mourning."

My iceheart and mind were racing now, but I continued to follow some impulse I couldn't explain.

"On the contrary," I said, gesturing to my black shirt and trousers. "Black, among my people, is the color of mourning."

Kolwin was startled enough to slightly raise one eyebrow. "As you perhaps have been informed, black among ours is the color of danger."

I hadn't been—directly. But my mind quickly went to the signal flags and finally made the obvious connection: the black flag *was* the signal for danger. Considering what color Solim's soul had turned after becoming a lish, I had an inkling why.

I *knew* I was now treading treacherous ground, even without the tightness of Ben's hand in mine, yet still I spoke before he could open his mouth to intervene.

"That combination seems appropriate for our time, doesn't it? These are times not just for mourning or gladness but also times of danger and struggle. Thus, the King and I have done our best to represent all facets of what now is and what we hope one day to be."

Which might have even been the truth. After all, I had never asked Kor or Vadya exactly why they had chosen these colors for us. Neither of those clever Starkissed would have been ignorant of the risks in dressing us in black, as I had been, and yet they had done it anyway.

I might have stumbled on why.

I seemed to have stunned everyone to silence. So, I continued following that feeling. "The King and I mourn your loss. We honor the sacrifice of your Lady and your devotion in remembering her. We mourn the loss of all the Seven Realms, for we *all* have lost much. And we honor that loss by continuing the fight. By serving our peoples. By showing the Devourer that it did not and *will not* win, not in any way. Not while we draw breath."

All eyes were riveted on me now, and silence reigned for the space of at least three breaths.

Broken when Kolwin suddenly chuckled. His expression didn't soften much. But the look in his eyes lost some of their coldness to speculation.

"The way of Trees truly is mysterious indeed, for Ice to have chosen a Queen such as you."

It sounded as backhanded a compliment as one could get. And yet it broke the tension in the air. Ben let out a breath of relief, and Kolwin's entourage relaxed.

"Duty takes on many guises, Lord Kolwin," Ben said quietly. "We have not forgotten ours. That is why we are here."

Kolwin's reply was dry. "I take such comfort from knowing that, among your *other* motivations, duty remains among them."

How in the worlds could this young man be nineteen years old? He sounded like he should be a hundred. Maybe that's what came of being the heir of such a serious clan.

"Trust us," Ben said with surprising frankness—and a gleam in his eyes. "If it hadn't been for *duty*, we would have been heartbound by now."

That would have elicited a round of chuckles from any other crowd, but I assumed the lip-twitching and huffs were the Strongshield equivalent. Fortunately, thanks to Dad, I was used to interpreting the minutest change of expression. He would have probably gotten along with the Strongshield splendidly.

Lord Kolwin was an even tougher customer: he only raised a slight eyebrow, and his eyes rested on our joined hands.

"Yes, your...devotion to each other precedes you."

I assumed that if he had been any less dignified, he might have used a word more like *twitterpation*. Or something even more disapproving.

Kor spoke up for the first time, with perfect ease and politeness. "Then hopefully their devotion to the Realms did as well. As you are no doubt aware, in the last few days alone, they have both proven the Queen's words many times over by risking their very lives for the good of the Realms."

"So I have heard," Kolwin admitted slowly. "I trust *that* 'devotion' holds. For Flame knows I and my people have need of it."

Ben's hand tightened around mine—the only outward sign he gave that belied the calm in his reply. "We will do whatever we can to aid you."

LORD KOLWIN SAID NO more about what he needed our help with. Instead, I got the feeling he steered us back into ceremonial waters by beginning a more elaborate welcome speech. Then Ben replied in kind with something much shorter and less rehearsed. To my surprise, we then exchanged gifts—which seemed like a very world-leader-like thing to do, when I thought about it, but we hadn't bothered with something like that before. Figures the first time would be with Lord Kolwin.

Kor handed me the "gift from the Moontouched clan" to present to Lord Kolwin: a white staff capped with a clear gem. If that fist-sized, spear-shaped stone was a diamond, it was the largest I had ever seen. I did my very best to keep my composure as I handed the staff over with both hands. That was perhaps one of the most surreal moments of my queenship yet.

Yes, here you go, have this priceless thingamajig that I just had lying around in my treasury somewhere, waiting to give out, because that's apparently what I do for a living now.

Thank goodness that wasn't actually the case.

Most of the time.

Little did I realize that experience was about to be capped by Lord Kolwin returning the favor by stiffly placing an elaborate, silver, ruby-studded necklace over my head, and I wore that Earthly fortune around my neck for the next hour or so while the Lord Strongshield finished the ceremony and led us inside on a tour.

The only mercy was that his version of a tour wasn't the Brightflare day-long kind. It was merely a roundabout way to the King's Wing to hit the highlights of the major areas, such as the central court and the commerce, artists', and warriors' wings.

The inside of Palla was as grand as I could have expected from our reception on the outside—not as decorative as the one Starkissed hold I'd seen, and definitely not as whimsical, but every bit its match in grandeur. Elaborate stone- and tile-work were everywhere, from the columns to the arches to the statues to the floors. The scale added to its austerity: every room we entered was massive, and every corridor spacious, and all brightly lit. Only scarlet tile-work and pottery and multicolored tapestries broke up the monotony of the polished stone, but each piece was so masterfully done, they only added to the intimidation factor.

I liked the "sand gardens," though. Occasionally, I would glimpse small side rooms filled with beds of sand raked in various patterns around pots of plants, sculptures, or unaltered boulders. Even though they had a museum-like air of untouchable order and deliberation, they still presented a tantalizing escape from the hardness of the rest of the surroundings. After the first couple, I kept an eye out for them, and tried to see each one as a sign of hope for my time here.

Finally, at long last, Lord Kolwin left Ben and me at the King's Wing, and as soon as he was gone, Ben whisked me to our room, sensing how close I was to being *done*.

"Thank Flame," I gasped as soon as he closed the door behind us. I yanked the necklace off my neck as quickly as I could while still handling it delicately and shoved it at Ben.

"Here, take this and make it disappear, *please*."

"What?" he said with a crooked grin as he took it from me. "You don't want to put it with your things so you can wear it whenever you like?"

I collapsed face first onto the bed with a groan. "Flame, no. I'll be perfectly content if I never see it again, thank you."

He sat next to me and rubbed my back, sending ripples of deliciously warm healing energy into my muscles.

His voice still held a trace of amusement. "I hate to say it, but you'll be expected to wear it to the feast tomorrow night."

"I was afraid you would say something like that."

I turned my head to the side, both to breathe more easily and to look at him. "Any idea what this grim thing he needs doing is?"

"I think I do," Ben said, sobering. "Romskal's desert regions have been having more trouble with sand wyrms lately."

I felt an internal shudder of premonition and pushed myself onto my elbows. "What?"

Ben's eyes were dark. "Sand wyrms are cousins of rock wyrms. They're both native to Romskal. The sand variety are bigger and nastier, but since they stick to *sand*, they've claimed fewer lives. Still, attacks have become more frequent over this past month."

I let out a heavy breath. "Of course they have. And let me guess: fighting wyrms is a Royal thing."

"It's an elite thing at least," Ben said carefully. "The Strongshield have whole flights that are dedicated to hunting them. But, proportionally, Strongshield also lost the most drakón and amón of all the clans in the Battle of the Solstice."

"They did?" I said soberly, sitting fully upright and tucking my legs into a crossed position.

"They contributed the most to the Warflight," Ben said heavily. "Lady Maya left her holds with minimal defenses—even Palla. Alyish couldn't dissuade her.... Perhaps she was intending to sacrifice herself all along."

"What?" I whispered, taking his hand. "Why?"

Ben wouldn't meet my gaze. His was far away. "She was old. Very old. Nearly two hundred. And...she was Strongshield, to the core. So...even though Romskal was left almost unguarded, it was the least affected by the battles across the Six Realms."

I swallowed. No wonder her people were honoring her so deeply.

I gripped Ben's hand more tightly. No matter her reasons, I knew this would be a sore subject for him. I crawled the short distance between us to put my arms around him, and he turned more fully toward me to wrap his own around me in return.

"Avva would never have left you if he'd had any other choice," I said quietly.

"I know," Ben said thickly, holding me close.

After a moment, he laughed tightly. "At the very least, I know he would never have left *you*. Do you know how much he wanted a daughter?"

"Ben, I'm being serious," I said with a sigh, pulling away to frame his face with my hands.

My thumbs brushed along his bristles, which were growing longer by the day. I marveled again at his willingness to move on even outwardly, when I knew his scars inside might take years to heal.

"So am I," Ben said with a thin smile. "At least about that last part. He waited a long time for you, Sarah."

"That doesn't mean he loved you any less," I said softly. "You were his *son*."

Ben sighed and closed his eyes. "I know. I know."

I let out a breath and rested against him again, letting him pull me in more tightly. I let him hold me like that as long as was comfortable, given the angle of our bodies, but eventually, I pulled away and sat back again.

"When are we leaving?"

Ben set his jaw. "*We* aren't leaving Romskal until the situation is under control. *I* will probably leave for the hunt with a good portion of my elites the day after tomorrow, after the feast."

I figured he would be difficult about this. "Ben—"

He held up his hand. "No, Sarah, listen to me. You have formidable abilities, but sand wyrms are unlike anything you have ever seen. They are so large and lethal, only a skilled team of draká stands a chance against them. That means we're going to be hunting the wyrms during the day, when we're at our strongest and have the best visibility—it would be madness to do otherwise. Besides, that's when they are the most active, anyway. So, in the daytime, any benefit you could have by being there with me would be negated by us having to protect you."

"You mean by you distracting yourself by fussing about me," I grumbled.

He smiled thinly. "That too. But do you *really* want my elites to hold back their strength and fire because there's an amón on my back?"

An amón who wouldn't be able to contribute much to that fight—not in broad daylight.

"It won't just be day, Sarah," Ben pressed on, perhaps seeing me begin to cave. He took my hand and squeezed it three times. "It's going to be in the desert. In the dunes along the equator, or just to the south of it. Which means it's going to be *hot*."

Which meant I *really* wouldn't have much power to contribute as everything I had went to maintaining my homeostasis. I really would just be a hindrance if I were with them. For the fighting, at least....

"But what will you be doing at night?" I demanded.

"We won't engage anytime close to sunset," Ben said firmly. "We'll either return here if we can get to a sungate in time, or we'll nightshelter at the closest hold. I won't take any needless risks with daylight or my safety in general—I promise, Sarah."

I didn't ask him to repeat that promise to me. I knew how seriously he took his oaths.

I still gave him a glare. "Why do I get the feeling that you prepared for this argument?"

He had countered my every protest with almost Kor-like foresight and skill, which was a bit disturbing. Although I supposed it would have been impossible for Kor to not have rubbed off on Ben at least a *little* over the course of his six years as Ben's leftwing, and Ben had had training in negotiation as part of being Heir, besides. When I thought about it that way, it was more of a wonder that I hadn't gotten the full brunt of his persuasive skills before this.

Then again, he'd never had logic so solidly on his side before.

Ben smiled crookedly, confirming my suspicions. "Because I did."

I groaned and fell back onto the bed. "*Fine*. You win this one, your majesty."

"Thank you," Ben said fervently. "I can't tell you how helpful it is going to be for me to know you're safe, Sarah."

He had kept his hold on my hand and gave it another three squeezes.

"Surely there's something else I can do to be helpful, *other* than sitting out of the hunt," I grumbled, glaring at the ceiling.

At Ben's silence, I glanced at him. He was looking away guiltily. "Ben...."

"Well," he said, rubbing his neck. "Since I'll be busy hunting, I won't be here to go through all the usual grand tour ceremonies that Strongshield always insists on, at least during the day...."

I used our joined hands as leverage to sit up again. "You have got to be kidding. You're going to go gallivanting off on a hunt and leave me behind to endure *ceremonies*?"

He winced. "Well, only one or two of those. And some feasts. And a performance or two. And a few...other things."

"Ben!"

"Look, Sarah, I'm not *trying* to get out of them."

At my glare, he sighed. "Alright, maybe I won't...mourn being able to miss one or two of them, but if circumstances were different, there would be no way I'd abandon you to suffer through them alone. I wouldn't do that to you, Sarah. And I'll do my best to be back every evening. I promise."

I huffed. "Like you're going to be in the most patient of moods by then after a long day of hunting."

"But I'll do it," he insisted. "I really am *not* trying to abandon you."

That was what finally convinced me: his clear determination to work double shifts every day to shoulder as much as he could of both his burden and mine.

I sighed. That was so...*Ben.*

"Alright, my initial grumpiness aside, I don't want you killing yourself over this, Ben. I can see that you've given me the lighter load after all. So let me handle the formalities and you handle the monsters. Deal?"

He grimaced. "I really should try to be here in the evenings, or Lord Kolwin might take my absences personally."

I rolled my eyes. "Really? He'll be offended if you can't make it to some feast because you're out in the field killing wyrms for him?"

"Maybe if we actually *get* a wyrm or two that day, I might have an excuse," Ben said with a sigh, running a hand through his hair. "But if we hunt all day with nothing to show for it...."

"I see," I said grimly. I clenched his hand. "Well, here's the new deal: I stay here where it's safe and keep Lord Kolwin as happy as I can, and you only show up when it's *convenient.* Don't burn yourself out again, Ben. Not now. Not over this."

"Well," Ben said, glancing away. "There's also the fact that I'll simply want to see you."

I frowned. That may be true, but there was something else. Something I'd said had made a momentary flicker of irritation pass over his face. I ran my words through my head again. Then sighed.

"Ben, you can't possibly be jealous of *Lord Kolwin*, can you?"

He shifted uncomfortably, still not meeting my gaze.

"Ben," I snapped. "Does this mean anything to you?"

I fingered his earring in my ear.

He groaned and clenched my other hand tightly. "Of course it does, Sarah. I'm *sorry*. Especially since I'm the one who's asking you to stay in the first place. I *know* what a torched idiot I'm being about this. Doesn't...mean my emotions listen to my head so easily."

I sighed. It wasn't like I didn't know how he felt—and by recent experience, too, what with encountering Kindra.

I smiled crookedly. "Especially when I use poor phrasing like 'keep him happy,' right?"

He smiled thinly as he finally met my eyes, clearly relieved at how I was taking this. "Or when he gives you fancy necklaces."

I snorted. Now I realized there might have been another reason behind Ben's amusement at my dismissiveness of the gift.

"I thought that was an entirely platonic gesture between leaders, or I wouldn't have taken it."

"It was," Ben grumbled. "I told you: I know I'm not being logical about this."

I smirked. "If it bothers you that much, you're welcome to give me all the fancy necklaces you want to make up for it."

He laughed. "And how often would you wear them if I did?"

"As seldom as possible," I said frankly. "But I would be *more* likely to wear them if they came from you."

He smirked, but his eyes were lighter. "That's what I thought."

I clenched his hand, sobering. "Thank you for telling me, Ben. Instead of letting this fester, I mean. Does it help a bit to talk about it? And to hear that I have zero interest in reneging on any of my promises to you, let alone for some stodgy jerk whose face would probably break if he genuinely smiled?"

Ben chuckled. "It does, actually. Especially hearing that last part. Even though I'll admit that's unfair. Kolwin isn't *that* bad, normally."

"Yeah, you're probably right," I allowed. "Grief added to the burden of new leadership doesn't bring out the best in people, as we both know for ourselves."

Ben sighed. "Yes, we do. Which is why I should make more allowances for him, too. It's just...well, he...has a bit of a reputation."

Both my eyebrows rose, and I grinned. "*Kolwin*? A lady's man?"

"No—exactly the opposite. He's known for being even more blatantly uninterested in courtship than I am. Well, er, than I *was*."

He flushed a bit as his eyes darted to me. "But that's apparently a part of his draw. Or so I'm told."

"Ah, I finally get it," I said with a chuckle. "Combine that kind of untouchability with that level of attractiveness.... Yeah, I can see how others might find that appealing."

"Oh, so you find him attractive, do you?"

I was relieved to see that Ben was confident enough by now to accompany that mild accusation with a crooked grin.

"I don't do you any favors by trying to hide the fact that I'm human, if you know what I mean. To me, I earn your trust by being upfront about it, just like this—to show you I have nothing to hide from you. Is it working?"

"It is," Ben said with a chuckle. "I...didn't expect that."

"And how about this?" I said, cupping his face again and leaning in. "As attractive as Lord Kolwin is, he holds *none* of the draw that you hold for me. None. I'm yours, Ben. Yesterday, today, forever."

Ben's eyes began to soulflare, and I felt the pull from him give a tug. "Hmm, yes, that *does* make me feel better. But you know what would cap it off?"

I laughed and pressed my lips to his.

Chapter Thirty

HOPE

Koriben

Sarah and I took full advantage of our brief reprieve to rest and settle in before the formalities began tomorrow. When I suggested she take a nap, she said she would if I did. Her silver eyes narrowed in concern, making me think she was already worried about me wearing myself out over the upcoming days of hunting by day and placating Kolwin and his people by night.

Just the thought of the days ahead of us made me tired. As much as the thought of spending so much time on Romskal killed me, I feared that between the sand wyrms and Strongshield's need for ceremony, we would be lucky if we got away before a sevenday. So, between my preemptive exhaustion and her concern, I agreed to pull out my pallet early and lie down.

I thought I would just relax a bit until she drifted off, mostly just to reassure her, but to my surprise, she was the one to shake me awake to say that dinner was served in the dining room. I was so disoriented for a few moments that she laughed.

I could get used to Sarah kissing me fully awake—and far sooner than I should, considering our heartbinding seemed to get further away by the day, torch it. I found it perilously difficult to not pull her down with me.

Fortunately, she drew back first, saying I'd better hurry up, since she was starving. So, trying to hide my flush of heat with a laugh, I pushed myself up and followed her.

Fortunately, the public dinner helped cool me off. Though we generally had a late breakfast or midday meal with just the two of us whenever she got up, Sarah and I had restarted a tradition of Avva's to open dinner whenever we could as a gathering time for my wings, the heads of our staffs, the officers of our elites, and a rotation of non-ranking members of both groups. When we didn't have to eat somewhere else than the King's Wing, we both felt ridiculous hogging the large dining rooms in each of the King's suites to ourselves; they were sized to entertain, after all.

Besides, we thought those dinners would help Sarah get familiar with the others in a relaxed setting. I already knew everyone, because in the case of my peers, if I hadn't grown up with them in Crownhold, I usually had taken a class or two with them or served with them; and, in the case of my elders, they had helped raise me. Sarah, obviously, didn't have the benefit of a lifetime of such experiences with them, but she expressed a desire early on to get to know the people who served with us as *people*, which I wholeheartedly supported. Which made me think of one way Avva had managed it, even with his busy schedule.

Actually, once I thought about it, the dinner tradition traced back to Avvi, in the end. Whether she'd had the time to cook the meal herself or not, she had always made dinner a time of gathering, and with seemingly effortless grace, she would make whoever she or Avva had gathered that evening feel like they belonged.

I wasn't the least bit surprised to discover that Sarah had the same knack, if in her more subdued style. She had a quiet watchfulness and subtle way of putting everyone around her at ease; even though this was our third night doing this, dinner already was a warm, laugh-filled, familial time—more so than I could remember it being in over a year.

Not since I'd learned Avva was dying and frantically began traveling the Realms searching for the one who could cure him. No doubt Avva had continued his dinners in my absence, but I hadn't let myself come home as often as I should have to bask in the warmth of them. I'd heard even those occasions had become rarer for him as his energy flagged and the need to hide his dimming flameheart became more urgent.

I hadn't had the heart—or soul—to start them on my own in the month after he was gone.

But all the warmth was back now, thanks to Sarah. She sat next to me, but she made sure someone different sat on her other side every night so that she could get to know them, and that was already a coveted seat as word spread both of her intent and of how worthwhile it was to get to know her in turn. She was already calling people by name, asking them about their days and duties, and listening with intoxicating intensity with those open, piercing eyes of hers that had drawn me in from the very beginning.

I was often distracted from my own conversations just from the sheer pleasure of watching her work her subtle magic. She caught me one time with a grin on my face, and she looked away with a flush that darkened her cheeks.

What? she asked me silently.

I just took her hand under the table and gave it three clenches.

I'd tried the night before, the second night, to explain to her the miracle she'd performed by bringing us together like this, but she wouldn't believe me. She thought of all of this as my idea to start with, and that if there was any extra credit to be given, it was to the cooks and the universal enjoyment of sharing good food. She couldn't seem to understand that it would never have worked if not for her.

As Heir and now King, I'd endured enough formal dinners and feasts to know that duty could bring people together, and the mortal need for food could make them stay, but neither of those things could make people *family*. But somehow, even as a stranger to our people and Realms, she was doing just that.

Case in point: when the meal ended, Sarah called the cooks into the room and everyone clapped, cheered, and toasted them with the last of the wine—or, in Sarah's and my case, water. It seemed we'd both inherited an inclination to sobriety from our parents, although I guessed hers had taught her more on principle and mine more on necessity.

The potent, volatile power that a Golden Royal bore wasn't something to be trifled with, even on the warmest of occasions. After three quarters of a century of Avva's rule, the tradition of Royal sobriety that he had reinstated was as cemented by now as any, so no one batted an eye when Sarah followed suit.

Vadya groaned contentedly with a hand over her stomach as she got up from the table. "It's a shame you two won't be available for a while after this."

"We won't?" Sarah asked, with more resignation than surprise.

"Unfortunately not," I answered with a sigh. "It's probably going to be public feasts or dinners with Lord Kolwin from now on."

Sarah echoed my sigh but caught Vadya's hand before she left. "Keep it going while we're gone. If the cooks are OK with it, that is. Use the dining room, invite whoever you want."

Vadya shrugged. "I'll talk to Merik," she said, mentioning her counterpart over my staff. "See what he thinks. Even if we do, it won't be the same without you two."

"Why?" Sarah asked in surprise. "That's two more seats available, and surely you all can have even more fun with it, with Ben and me gone."

Vadya cast me a smirk. Even though, as an amón, she didn't have an inner voice, her look spoke plainly enough: *She really doesn't get it, does she?*

No, she doesn't, I replied silently with a crooked smile.

Before Sarah could get too suspicious, Vadya looked back at her Queen with a mischievous gleam in her eyes. "Believe it or not, we actually *like* having you and Ben around. You're not half bad—for Royals, that is."

"Har har," Sarah said with a grin. "Consider dining room privileges revoked, then."

"Oof, there you go. Blowing what little progress you've made," Vadya said with a sad shake of her head. "Guess we'll just have to use this time to forgive you."

"Guess you will. Or, you know, sneak in here and use it behind our backs."

"Us?" Vadya demanded, putting a hand to her chest with an affronted look.

"What are we being accused of now?" Fenra asked with a grin, coming up to her sister and slinging her arm around her shoulders.

"Plotting to usurp the dining room like naughty hatchlings while our Monarchs are busy elsewhere."

"Pssh," Fenra said dismissively. "As if we'd do something like that. Now, their *bedroom*, on the other hand—"

"Don't start," Sarah said with a groan, holding up a hand. "I don't even want to know. Just as long as everything is cleaned up and in order by the time we get back, I don't want to know."

"Oh, *I* do," Kor said with a wide grin from across the table, propping his chin on the bridge he made with his hands. "Do tell."

"I believe that's our cue to leave," I said hastily.

I stood and took Sarah's hand, helping her up as well, and we made our exit while Vadya and Fenra playfully bickered about whether to include Kor in their plotting, considering whether they could trust him and if he would be of any use, since he'd likely have to attend any feast or dinner that would take Sarah and me away.

Sarah kept her composure until we were out in the hall, but as soon as we were clear, she laughed. For her peace of mind, I let her think the mischievous sisters were merely teasing, but I was fairly certain by that point that they would feel obligated to go through with something now, if only to maintain their reputation.

I made a mental note to use all the spells I knew to scan for traps (or other magical surprises) before I went to sleep every night. Since I was the first one to retire by a long shot, hopefully that would be enough to protect Sarah, too.

For now, though, I was wide awake from my poorly timed nap, but I didn't regret that disruption to my sleep schedule one bit. Sarah and I would have precious little time together over the coming days, even less than usual as I left at dawn every day and came back only around sunset—if at all.

Besides, there was something I had wanted to show her.

"Where are we going?" she asked curiously when I began leading her from the King's suite.

"If I told you, it wouldn't be a surprise, would it?" I said with a grin.

She rolled her eyes. "Notice you hadn't mentioned anything about a surprise."

"Because it's a surprise."

Sarah laughed. "Ben, I love you, but your surprise-giving needs a bit of work. For it to truly be a surprise, you need to go all in. As in, come up with some excuse for us to be heading this direction *without* using the word 'surprise.'"

I chuckled and squeezed her hand three times. "I'll try that when I'm giving you a *real* surprise. This was just something I thought you would like to see."

And it was something that I wanted her to see with me, so I could watch her reactions. So, perhaps this was a gift just as much for me as for her. She would have probably found the place on her own, or someone would have shown it to her. I was just being greedy—but I didn't think Sarah would mind.

We entered the central court of the King's wing and turned off onto a relatively small corridor.

"The healing ward?" Sarah asked curiously, obviously having become more familiar with the typical layout of Royal wings.

"Through there," I said, waving vaguely at a door we were just passing. "There are usually a few more things in this corridor, though. A few private meditation rooms, a massage room—"

"Massage?" Sarah said in surprise.

"Well, yes," I answered with a blink. "I guess, now that I think about it, massage as a form of healing *did* start with the Strongshield. But it caught on quickly, though, so it's been a standard part of a healing practice for a century or two."

I glanced at her, trying not to blush. "Er, if you're ever interested, you could ask Vadya who on your staff has training. At the very least, your personal healer should, but even amón attendants can receive training if they have an interest."

I carefully didn't mention that even *I* had been forced to undergo massage therapy training—despite my distinct *lack* of interest at the time—as part of my mandatory healing coursework. Even though my thinking had somewhat shifted since then, now was *not* the time.

Sarah's lips twitched for some reason. "Figures."

"What?" I asked, trying hard to hide my alarm and desperately hoping she hadn't seen the heat creeping into my face.

She shook her head and chuckled. "Nothing wrong. I'm just surprised I didn't think of it before. A massage-healing practice fits with what I know of you people."

I let out a hopefully subtle breath of relief.

She paused thoughtfully. "But not necessarily what I know of Strongshield, though."

"How do you think they manage such emotional control in front of others?" I said ruefully. "Don't think that the mask they show to the public is still glued to their faces in private. They're still mortal, needing mortal outlets. Speaking of which...."

We came to the end of the corridor, where only one door remained. I placed my hand on the plate, but it wasn't the kind of door that restricted access, so the gem didn't even glow in acknowledgement. Any spells within that wood were to maintain the homeostasis of the room inside.

I pushed and held it open, and Sarah inhaled in delight as she moved past me to enter.

It was a Strongshield sand garden. I'd seen Sarah wistfully eye the others we had passed and, putting it together with what I'd learned about her need for the outdoors, I'd resolved to show her this one as soon as possible. Particularly *this* one.

There was the look I'd been hoping for, the one of simple happiness lighting her up like a candle lit within. Although seeing it caused me nearly as much pain as it did pleasure, knowing how much more of this she deserved...and how little I could give it to her.

"I didn't see any of the others having plants," Sarah said softly, brushing her fingers along a frond that was within easy reach.

It was one of the many varieties of plant life that were the centerpieces of this garden, taking the usual places of Strongshield's favored art forms. Right now, with the sun set outside, the garden was in night mode, with only the lightgems along the walkway alight, casting much of the garden into peaceful shadow.

I followed her inside, allowing the door to swing shut behind us. I matched the volume of my answer to hers. "Most of them don't, given the effort needed to keep them alive and the space as orderly as the Strongshield would like. But they made an exception for this one."

"Why?" Sarah asked, glancing at me.

My chest constricted painfully. "Because of Avvi."

Sarah's face sobered, and I kicked myself for spoiling her enjoyment.

"Please don't...be sad," I said, swallowing. "I didn't bring you here to be sad."

"I'm not," she answered.

She turned away and began walking down the winding path through the small, cultivated grove. She ran her hand along the petals of a blossoming tree overhead.

"I'm actually...happy, in a way. I like thinking of her walking down this same way, enjoying it just like I am. I can almost picture her here."

She sighed. "Almost. I wish I could have *seen* her, at least once."

I wished she could have, too—desperately. I hadn't realized, before that moment, that Sarah wouldn't even have a face to put to her name, and that seemed like too cruel of an injustice to be borne.

Then I realized I might have something else to show her this evening after all. It was a more sober surprise than I'd intended, but I guessed I had already dampened the mood. And I couldn't think of a better place to show her here than Avvi's garden.

I caught Sarah's hand but didn't answer her questioning look. I only led her to a bench, where Avva and Avvi had no doubt sat before.

I brought out a large, thick, leather-bound bundle of papers with one hand and laid my other on the well-worn cover for a moment. As familiar a sight as the bundle was, it wasn't mine—or, at least, it hadn't been until...a month ago. Even then, I hadn't opened it, knowing what kinds of things I would find inside. But now...it was time.

Long past time.

"What is it?" Sarah asked quietly. I noticed she wasn't looking at my face—perhaps trying to be kind. She only looked at the bundle.

I swallowed and took a deep breath. "Avva...like me, didn't have much time for pastimes, but he was better at keeping them up than I was. He always loved to draw, even before he became Heir."

And there was no one he had liked to draw more than...Avvi.

Without any other explanation, I handed the portfolio to Sarah. She took it, opened the leather cover...and gasped at the first page.

The first drawing was more appropriate than even I had realized. Avvi could have been sitting on the bench across from us. There were the same trees bowing over her, if shorter, the same sand below, if in a different pattern....

I felt a chill go down my spine, though I tried to keep my expression still when Sarah glanced up at me. I let her think I'd known that would be the first sketch she would see, that it was the sketch itself that had made me sit us down here and bring the portfolio out in this moment. Even though it was the first time I had seen it, too.

Though, technically, it would not be the first time I had seen this scene.

"Is that...*you*?" Sarah asked, putting her finger on the child in Avvi's lap.

"It must be."

I recognized that untidy mop of short, loose curls from other sketches and portraits—and that same scowl at having to sit still for such a thing.

"How old were you?" Sarah said with a laugh in her voice.

I could see why. Somehow, Avva had captured even my wriggling impatience, and Avvi's own laugh in her eyes and parted, smiling lips. I could almost *hear* her warning Avva that he'd better get the initial sketch done quickly, before I escaped. Perhaps they had begun when I was sleeping, but that hadn't been the case by the end.

I turned the portfolio slightly in her lap to get a better glimpse of the date that Avva had noted in the interior bottom corner.

"It would have been before my second summer."

Sarah stared, riveted at the scene in front of her. Her fingers traced the lines, her face etched with longing. As if she wanted nearly as badly as I did to enter that moment again.

Her finger rested on Avvi. "She's beautiful," she whispered.

I didn't miss her use of the present tense. Which, in the moment, seemed...right. Besides, in whatever form she was in now, I knew that was still true.

"She is," I whispered back.

"You look like your dad," she added softly. "A *lot* like your dad. But there's something about her in you.... I think it's in the eyes. Not the color, obviously. But in the look."

"I had the same color, back then," I said quietly.

She glanced at me, startled. "What?"

"They used to be green," I said with a shrug. "Just like hers. Before."

"Oh," she whispered, looking into my eyes. "Right. Before...."

She looked back down at the page, her finger resting on the toddler there.

"How does that...work, exactly? If both the parents are...changed."

My flameheart thudded. Was she asking just from curiosity or...?

I tried to answer as casually as I could. "A child can inherit any of the characteristics of the parents—from before they became drakón or after. I just so happened to inherit both of theirs from after."

"So, your hair...."

"Was always this color," I said ruefully. "The combination made me look odd, to be honest."

Or so I'd always thought. In my young view of the world, colors that intense should have matched. Or perhaps the conflict on the outside merely reflected, to an embarrassing degree, the conflict I had felt within, from even before I became fully aware of the choice I would face.

When the time for my presentation before the Tree came, I knew full well the risk I took by choosing to become Sunfilled. Avva and Avvi never said a word or gave me a single look to persuade me either way, but I *knew*—how could I not have known?—what everyone but they were expecting me to choose and hoping I would then become. And at twelve summers, I was more than terrified of becoming Avva's Heir. I longed to choose Avvi's clan more than I had ever wanted anything else, to take on her hair as well as her eyes.

But I was self-aware enough by that point to know that want stemmed from fear, not desire. That choosing Peacegrowth would just be hiding, running. I knew that if I chose her clan just to disqualify myself from becoming the Sunfilled Heir, I would never be able to look in the mirror again, knowing that I had failed our people and become nothing more than a coward. So, I knew that to honor Avvi in truth, I had to give up the part of me that looked like her.

She had been sad when she had cupped my face to look into my golden eyes for the first time...but also proud.

It was a look that I had seen on her face often, and I hadn't understood until that moment why.

I returned to the present to see Sarah was looking at me speculatively.

"What?" I asked self-consciously, looking away.

"Do you have a color portrait from that time?"

"Somewhere, I'm sure," I said, taking the portfolio from her to flip through the pages. "Avva sometimes would go back and paint—"

I stopped at one such finished portrait...and felt an even greater chill.

It wasn't me. Or Avvi.

Sarah leaned over and inhaled. "That's...*me*."

In breathtaking detail. Just her, though, from the shoulders up, the background left blank. And the colors made it obvious that this sketch was from before Sarah's own transformation: there was her dark brown hair, her warm brown eyes. But the soft look in them had never changed, nor that small, kind smile.

"When...did he do this?" Sarah asked, fingering the number of pages between the first and this one. There weren't many.

I looked at the year and swallowed. "That same year."

Sarah stilled. "Then I...would have been less than one. Right? You're two years older than me?"

"If our years mean the same thing," I said numbly. "How...."

I turned the portfolio to read the small line he'd written near the spine.

"What does it say?" Sarah asked.

"'Where have I seen her?'" I quoted in a whisper. "Then there's a short-hand symbol that means 'connected to,' my name, and another question symbol."

I shook my head as I lowered the portfolio back to my lap, hopefully concealing the trembling in my hands. "What is he talking about?"

"Oh," Sarah whispered. I glanced at her in time to see her eyes widening.

"What?" I demanded.

She looked up at me, biting her lip briefly before answering. "Avva told me...the first time we spoke, when he asked to speak with me alone—you remember?"

"Yes," I said slowly.

I also remembered how I had paced in the hall outside, wondering what he could have to say to her that he didn't want me to hear.

Sarah took a deep breath. "He told me the Tree used avatars in the shape of women from his past. Except...for me."

I stared at her. "He *said* that? That the Tree used your form as an avatar?"

"Yes—sometimes, he said. He didn't say how often. Just sometimes. Is that...normal?"

I swallowed. "It's...normal for the Tree to use different personas with Her Monarchs. Only during their private audiences, though. Avva said that the persona She chose usually carried a message for him. But he said that She almost always used the form of women he knew."

Almost, I realized. He never said *always*. Only almost.

"What about for you?" Sarah asked tentatively.

I smiled thinly. "I...have not been Her King for long, and in that time...I haven't been a good servant. I've only visited Her once. With you and Svyer."

I tuned out Sarah's murmured assurance and turned the portfolio to read Avva's note again.

Where have I seen her? Connected to Koriben?

"Connected to...." I muttered. If Avva knew what Sarah looked like only because the Tree had used her form to speak with him, what would make him think she had any connection to me?

When I finally understood, I closed my eyes and sighed. "Of course. The Tree used your form...when Avva spoke to Her about *me*."

"Oh," Sarah said faintly. "Um.... I'm not sure how I feel about that."

Neither did I. But I set the portfolio back down with a rueful chuckle. Now I finally understood why Avva had kept this portfolio so private, only occasionally showing me a selected sketch or painting here and there. He wouldn't have wanted me glimpsing Sarah....

Not before I found her for myself.

I rubbed my forehead and said wearily, "That explains a lot, actually. He became attached to you so quickly...."

"That's actually why he told me that," Sarah said sheepishly. "To explain, at least in part, how he already loved me. He said he had waited for me for a long time. Longer than you had been searching for me."

"Years longer," I said, glancing at the date again. "If that was the first year he saw you. I know I just said a few deken ago that he had waited for a daughter, but I didn't know that he had waited for *you*."

I felt another stab of guilt for keeping the two of them apart for so long.

On impulse, I opened to a page toward the back of the portfolio and began skimming through the pages. Avva had kept many drawing pads, but this portfolio was where he stored his most treasured and polished sketches and paintings, at least during my lifetime. Which explained the rapid progress of the years, and how Avva's sketches of Avvi on these final pages were now less refined, more nostalgic. By that point, she had already passed on. His sketches of me from that time made my throat constrict nearly as much, so even though Sarah protested, I kept flipping quickly, skimming toward the end.

I was both anxious and afraid to know what his last sketch would be. I knew now that it would be a message of some kind for me. Avva had known he would be leaving; he had prepared as much as he could. He might have even guessed that no letter or note would have comforted me right after he was gone. So, knowing him, knowing me, he might have left something for me here, knowing that I would only open this when I was ready.

I turned the last page...and stared. Sarah's breath caught as well.

It was of the two of us: me and Sarah. We were the only figures clearly sketched, but there were enough hasty outlines for me to finally identify the time and place. There was the crowngate to the side of us, the round chamber with twining lines in the rock, and vaguely recognizable outlines of Kor, Yvera, Alyish, and Eskala.

Sarah was in my arms, and I was kissing her. I remembered the moment vividly: we had just recovered from the renewing of the First Covenant and realized what we had done, what we had made together. Sarah had said something that made me laugh, and I'd pulled her up for a kiss.

It had only been a moment, given our audience, but Avva had captured it perfectly: the relief, the joy, the wonder, the hope for the future.

That was his message to me.

My eyes burned and finally spilled over, blurring my view of the sketch in my lap.

"Avva...had a good memory, didn't he?" Sarah asked, cheeks warming.

"He did," I said thickly, turning my head to surreptitiously wipe my eyes. There was no way I was going to let a drop fall on his last gift to me. To us.

Sarah fidgeted. "He...was also a hopeless romantic, wasn't he?"

I laughed and kissed the top of her head. "I think I know what you mean, and the answer is yes. But I think he was far from being without hope."

And...I was starting to see why.

CHAPTER THIRTY-ONE

FEAR

SARAH

THE NEXT DAY ENDED our reprieve. When I woke up, Ben was long gone from not just our suite but the King's Wing entirely, having valiantly taken the first tranche of meetings and ceremonies with Lord Kolwin so I could sleep in. Even Kor and Yvera had gone with them, apparently so Lord Kolwin could officially discuss the sand wyrm situation with them and ask for Ben's help. Even though we knew that was what was coming all along, Strongshield had to be formal about it.

I used the time while they were gone to catch up with my family and Svyer. All of them had been working hard ever since discovering our new "fields," preparing the soil and brainstorming irrigation strategies.

When Dad could tear Svyer and Mom away from the gardening, the three of them made rapid strides in deciphering the information in the archivals and giving them a foundation in Drona. Svyer had taught them all the letters and vowel notations, correcting a few misunderstandings along the way. Dad said he'd taken to going through the dictionary with her page by page and noting the English equivalents next to each word.

At least in terms of word order, Drona's grammar wasn't terribly different from English's, as we'd already gleaned from having *listened* to it. That surface simplicity concealed the hardest difficulty for us to read or produce it ourselves: their more complex conjugations and declensions for person and gender. Ex-

cept, interestingly enough, in number. As I'd figured out almost immediately after Ben had extended the translation magic in his blood to me,
Drona didn't have a plural form and relied on context, an article (*a* or
the, for example), or a number to indicate more than one thing was being
discussed: one *drakón*, two *drakón*, many *drakón*, no *drakón*, and a *drakón*
were all simply *drakón*, so long as you were using the neuter form.

Dad became as animated as he ever did as he recounted his latest discoveries, and I loved listening to him, both to see him be so "excited"
and to glean what I could. In fact, I was a bit jealous as I listened to his
explanations of all the things he was formally learning that I'd had to pick
up as I went along and often hadn't put into words.

My vocabulary and even my pronunciation were solidifying by the day,
but those darn conjugations and declensions always eroded my confidence
in actually trying to speak full sentences. Mostly I just sprinkled in a simply
inflected noun here and there, especially for terms like *Tree* or *wing* that I'd
heard so often I thought about them primarily in Drona, even in my head.
Ben wasn't "the King" to me. He was "*eh'Vereth'ei*"—the male Monarch.
And I was "*eh'Vereth'ai.*"

Inflected terms like that came naturally to me now, since I'd heard
them put together like that hundreds of times. But I hadn't had time or
training to stop and dissect them into so many chunks of discrete meaning.
I'd started adding the articles *eh* (the) and *ah* (a) onto things purely by
instinct, since that was simple enough. But male and female (let alone
neuter) inflections still eluded me unless I'd heard the word used that way
enough—I didn't know how to add them properly on my own.

And that was only the *nouns* and *adjectives*. The *verbs*.... And even
numbers. Gosh, I must have heard them all by now, but I couldn't tell you
even the neuter numbers in order beyond five, let alone which versions to
use with which gender.

The more I thought about my limitations, the more they bothered me. They
were exactly what you would expect from having zero formal training and only

being immersed in the language for a few weeks. And yet, surely people expected more from me by now.

Especially me. As I listened to Dad, for the first time I realized that learning the language was only a matter of convenience for my family, especially now that our survival was more certain, and we had a dramá join our clan to teach us their way of life in person. For my clan, linguistic fluency was now more of an intellectual pursuit and backup measure rather than an urgent necessity.

But I was different. More deeply than ever, I was shaken by the fact that I had chosen to become not just the Queen of the Seventh Realm but *all* the Seven Realms.

All of them, I thought numbly.

I was intensely glad that I was alone in the consort's study, the door shut, Ben perhaps a mile or more away.

"Sarah?" Dad asked, looking up from his notes and seeing my expression—or perhaps it had been my silence that had tipped him off first.

"Dad," I said in a choked voice. "I'm not just going to be the Queen of Ice. I'm going to be *their* Queen."

Their Queen. That was what it meant to become Ben's consort.

"Yes, I gathered that," Dad said with infuriating calm. "Didn't you?"

"Well, theoretically, yes, but...." I swallowed. "But, Dad. I can't even speak Ben's—*my* people's—primary language. How am I going to *do* this?"

Dad paused, studying me, then sighed. "I was wondering when it would start hitting you."

I didn't answer. I didn't know how I'd avoided facing it until that moment—maybe it was the whirlwind of emotions and events since Ben had let me back in, not to mention the near-constant dangers we'd had to endure and recover from.

As odd as it may seem, I had somehow neglected to consider what the earring in my ear, this tour, the heartbinding *meant*—apart from being with Ben. I'd heard Ben ceremonially introduce me, but even in those moments, I had always been too occupied with the ceremony or charged circumstances to let that sink in. I hadn't really thought through my future beyond all of this.

Until now.

"Do you regret your decision, Sarah?" Dad asked evenly, with no apparent judgment.

I swallowed. "I...."

I took a few deep breaths, forcing back the urge to hyperventilate. I thought carefully about my answer, examining all my emotions. Introspection was my strength; even Dad had said so, when he had given his support for my decision to become Queen.

"No," I said finally, voice quiet. "I would make it again."

I didn't want to sound dramatic in front of Dad, but I would walk through fire to stay with Ben. The past month had taught me that. And the past two altogether had taught me that my place was here. My duty, my...people...were here. In all Seven Realms now. Why I'd been chosen with Ben to serve them *all*, I didn't know—but I would not abandon them or let another take my place at his side.

Dad nodded, as if he had been expecting that answer. I couldn't tell if he approved or not, and that might have been deliberate. His approval, though I craved it, would not get me through this panic I could still feel fluttering in my chest. Approval might only turn into pressure.

"You knew this would be a hard path," he said. "I hope you *also* knew that you would have no way of knowing just *how* hard it would be before you began walking it."

I took another deep breath. "Yes. I knew that. Knew that I couldn't know, I mean. But I'm feeling it, Dad. And this is just the beginning."

"Let's focus on the language for now. Though I'm sure that's not the only thing on your mind, that's what triggered this."

He paused just long enough to emphasize a break, then continued. "I'm glad you care about speaking the language of your new people, Sarah, but remember that you're at a significant advantage here: they *can* understand you when you speak English, and you *can* understand them when they speak Drona. Yes, you can't read or write it at the moment, but has that caused any issues so far?"

"No," I said slowly. "I have so many people around to help...and so much of what I've been asked to do so far just has to do with talking. But, Dad, I *should* be able to talk to them in their own language. What kind of Queen am I to them if I can't even do that?"

Dad's lips twitched. "History—human history, at least—is full of royals and nobles who had to marry foreign monarchs and couldn't speak the local language."

"Yeah, and how did that usually work out for them?" I snapped, knowing something of the answer. I'd had a historical fiction phase in middle school.

"The good ones learned," Dad said calmly. "And you will too. Again, at an enormous advantage, considering your ability to understand them."

"I don't need you to tell me how lucky I am, Dad," I groaned.

"Then what *do* you need, Sarah?"

His question wasn't facetious—it was serious, intent. Probing me into thinking again instead of panicking.

I took a few deep breaths again and thought. Hard.

What *did* I need? What would make this crushing sense of failure at least ease? Realistically, instead of asking for a miraculous brain dump of linguistic ability, more than I had *already* been magically given.

The answer hit me: it was, after all, about what had started this panic to begin with.

I met his eyes again. "I need lessons."

"ARE YOU SURE?" VADYA asked, unusually serious.

"I'm sure," I said firmly.

After my conversation with Dad, in which he had finally shown visible approval as I'd formed my plan, I had called Vadya into my study and given my request.

My chief of staff sighed. "I mean, Kor and I had talked about it, obviously. We were even planning on giving you some tutors after the grand tour, but I pushed back on doing it now. I thought it seemed like too much to ask of you during it. You've hardly had moments to breathe, let alone study. And you're learning so much every day as it is. About our culture, our food, our history, our clothing, our clans, our politics—just by doing all of this. Are you sure adding formal lessons on top of that won't backfire?"

I hesitated. I could see her point, and the past week or so had definitely felt like a crash course on all of those subjects combined. And I knew from being an AP student in high school the dangers of information overload.

I was also touched to see how much Vadya had been paying attention to what I could handle, and I appreciated all the informal lessons she had given me as we went along to keep me from making an egregious mistake. Her neglecting to tell me about the death of the Lady Strongshield had been an unusual oversight, not the rule.

But perhaps that was what had got me thinking about how I needed to take a more proactive role in my preparations to become Ben's partner. Vadya couldn't know everything I didn't know—and definitely not what I felt like I *needed* to know in order to feel ready for what was coming.

I took a deep breath.

"I think you were right, until a point. So thank you. I really appreciate you looking out for me. Now, though, I think I've reached a point where I have a little more brain power to spare, and the language barrier is getting at me."

"It's not much of a barrier," Vadya said in amusement. "We can understand you just fine. And we have other languages besides Drona, you know. That's just the most common. People are used to speaking in the one they're most comfortable with, even if someone replies in another."

"And what *good* kind of message could it send if I managed a speech in Drona? Or held up a short conversation with someone? Even if speaking English isn't as significant a negative as I can't help feeling it is, you can't tell me that speaking Drona wouldn't be a big positive."

I knew that all too well from personal experience. To my regret now, I had never properly learned Spanish, even though I'd seen what an impact that had had on my relationships with the older generations of Mom's family and even some of my cousins. Nothing Vadya could say could convince me that the language you spoke didn't matter, even *if* you could be mutually understood.

Vadya sighed again. "Sarah, you're being too hard on yourself. You've only been among us for what, about three sevendays? Total? Considering that, you've learned *so much*."

"I realize that. But I also know I could learn so much more, so much faster, with just a bit of help. You've done an amazing job of taking care of and preparing me, Vadya. This is not a criticism of your work. This is just me saying that I'm now ready for a bit more, and I think I need to begin with Drona. I can't think of a more obvious sign that I can show to everyone that I'm trying *hard* to prepare to be a good Queen than learning to speak your most common language."

Vadya shrugged. "Alright, then, if you feel that strongly about it. What kind of lessons are you thinking?"

I hesitated. "You know my schedule best, so I'll leave it to you to figure out how to work it in, and who to teach me, but I'm not asking for much. Just maybe an hour—er, I mean a deken—or less a day. Even a half deken would help me make a lot of progress, I'm sure."

"Sounds doable," she said with a thoughtful frown, eyes distant as she thought through the logistics.

I took a deep breath, and then the plunge: the commitment that I knew would make the biggest difference of all. "One more thing: I'll try to speak only in Drona from now on—at least in the King's Wing for now, until I get more confident. So, I'd appreciate it if you spread the word, so if I start saying even *less* than usual, people know why."

Vadya chuckled, her usual sparkle returning to her eyes. "Oh, I will do that. This ought to be interesting."

I suddenly wondered if I was going to regret this.

UNFORTUNATELY (OR FORTUNATELY, DEPENDING on your perspective), Vadya tested my new commitment almost immediately, because as soon as we were done with our discussion, she whisked me away to get ready for the evening feast.

She then required an unusual amount of verbal participation from me, nor would she take pointing for an answer. All the other attendants joined in as soon as she explained, with an enthusiasm that officially confirmed to me that a streak of mischief was a requirement for their job.

But they weren't without mercy, either, because after I would struggle in frustration for a few seconds to name a color, cloth, or style, they would explain the choices, enunciated clearly and slowly, so that I could finally mimic them and pass their test. And I mean *test*, because they usually went with whatever they wanted to put me in or do to me anyway, as usual.

Like I said: mischief.

But I had to admit that the result was, as always, impressive. The dress they had put me in had almost an empire waistline, bound by a wide black and silver girdle that blended with the black trim of the V-neck, high collar, and long sleeves; the latter opened into many effervescent layers at a diagonal that began near my outer shoulders and continued to my inner elbows, enveloping my forearms in billows of white, just like the many silver and white layers of the skirt.

As usual, they pulled my hair back to keep the gold-gem earring on prominent display, this time with two artfully loose Dutch braids that extended just past my ears to allow my hair to tumble freely down my back in carefully styled curls, with plenty of strands to frame my face. I wore the obligatory ruby necklace, which added the only bits of red on me besides my lip coloring. Speaking of which, the makeup job was masterful, as usual, giving my face maturity and nobility while still allowing me to recognize myself underneath. Internal grumbling aside, I was grateful for every bit of confidence that their hard work and artistry gave me every day, but especially on days like today.

Ben's reactions were a definite bonus, and he didn't disappoint today. Although I seemed to be losing the stun factor with him, he still grinned widely when I came out, his eyes glowing ever so slightly for a moment.

"Beautiful," he said simply, taking my hand and kissing it. From how his eyes lingered on my face, I had a feeling my hand wasn't his preference, but he also cast a glance at Vadya and Fenra hovering nearby as usual, perhaps to prevent such a move before he could mess me up.

Ben, I said teasingly. I spoke with an inner voice, partly for privacy, partly to cheat on my language commitment. *What's gotten into you? That was almost suave.*

He laughed in a way that further stirred the building heat in the pit of my stomach, especially as my eyes went back down to his long, black-and-gold, high-collared, buttoned coat that highlighted his broad shoulders and golden hair and beard so well.

He answered, *Apparently I'm not as hopeless as Kor says I am, then.*

"Ready?" he said out loud, winding my arm around his.

Because we were among friends right now, I groaned in answer.

"Oh, come on," Ben said with a chuckle as he began leading us out of our suite, Kor and Yvera following behind. "It won't be that bad."

I cast him a suspicious glance. *You're in a surprisingly good mood, considering how I know you don't like this stuff any more than I do.*

Am I? Ben said evasively, not meeting my eyes.

Now I was certain: he was definitely happy about *something*. Even though he tried to hide it under my scrutiny, he couldn't quite keep the smug smile off his face. Which was a sharp contrast to the *last* feast we'd gone to together. Although only "together," in the loosest sense, since, to disguise my presence, I'd gone with Kor....

That's when it hit me, and I inwardly groaned. Now that I looked back at the last few minutes, there had been something telling about how Ben had kept himself between Kor and me.

I said, *You're so smug because* this *time, I'm going with you. Aren't you?*

Ben hesitated a moment too long. Then finally had to admit in a mental mutter, *Maybe.*

I sighed. *Well, I suppose I owe you quite a lot of feasts to make up for that one.*

Oh, you do, Ben said seriously, but he smirked as he glanced at me. *A lifetime of them, actually.*

Fair, I agreed. *Although, for what it's worth, I honestly had no idea what going with Kor would signify. And if I'd had the option, I would have gone with you instead, without hesitation.*

Ben grinned again at that, his eyes glimmering for a moment. *And if I'd had the option, I would have asked you.*

Since it seemed he had finally forgiven me for that fiasco, I couldn't help teasing him again, just a little. *Would you have, though? I seem to recall that you hadn't even worked up the courage to kiss me yet.*

That wasn't about courage, he grumbled, flushing a bit as he avoided my eyes again. *That was about you giving me permission. Trust me, I would have kissed you* long *before that if I'd known you were interested.*

Hmm. Just how *much sooner?*

That adorable flush of his deepened. *You don't want to know.*

Oh, I think I do.

Regardless, I'm not going to tell you.

You realize the more you hide it, the more curious I get, right?

His gaze was fixed straight ahead now. *I don't care. I'm not telling. You can't make me.*

Not today, maybe, I said smugly. *But one of these days, I think I'll have the privacy and permission to manage it.*

His face was flaming now. *Sarah!*

But his inner voice, as strained as it was, lacked the forbidding force necessary to stop me. Especially since he hadn't asked me *not* to.

SURPRISINGLY, BEN WAS RIGHT: the feast wasn't too bad. Yes, the ceremonial introduction was painful. We entered through the grand doors at the end of the long hall, and everyone stood silently at their tables while Ben and I walked all the way down the center to the high table, but that was the worst bit, and at least I had Ben there for moral support. Though I drew far more looks than he did, perhaps since I was the newcomer here. Once we sat down and the short introductory speeches were out of the way, the inevitable clatter of eating began, and I could relax to an unexpected degree.

The fortunate bit about Strongshield's taciturn nature was that remarkably little conversation was expected of me—which was good, considering Ben and I were separated, seated on either side of Lord Kolwin, with Kolwin's wings on their respective sides on either side of us. Plus, even the Strongshield didn't overly complicate the process of eating; none of the dramá, as far as I had seen, had more than one type of each utensil, and only as many cups and goblets as was required for any different drinks they served as side dishes unto themselves, such as a kefir in the middle or a particularly flavorful tsha at the end.

After the meal came a few performances: slow, elegant dances with mesmerizing costumes and banners of glowing, shifting spellweave silks, a solo given by an elaborately dressed musician playing a large stringed instrument, and some storytelling and poetry recitation. When I could drive back the sleepiness from the full meal, I found I was actually enjoying myself—even if I would have much rather been seated in the back of the hall. Then again, I supposed I wouldn't have had such an unobstructed view.

When it was over, we didn't have to reverse our grand entrance, because the others began trickling out first, so Ben and I could slip away without fanfare, and no one so much as stopped us on our way out.

Then we were walking back to the King's Wing, with only Ben's wings and a few of our elites accompanying us. Kor walked at Ben's other side, and the two of them appeared to be silently conferring. Not about anything urgent or tragic, judging from Ben's calm expressions, so I imagined Kor was just reporting a few things and getting Ben's input on others before Ben left tomorrow.

Tomorrow.... The next time I woke up, Ben would be gone—not just across a hold, but across a world, perhaps having already been hunting for hours for one of the deadliest predators of the Six Realms.

All my relief at yet another royal duty done vanished, just like that, and anxiety once again began twisting my stomach. Tomorrow would feel like just another day on the job to Ben, but it would be far more than that to me. This would be the first time we would part ways with him *knowingly* going into danger—without me.

I wasn't under any illusions that I would be of help. His arguments had convinced me with disheartening thoroughness. Not only was I at a disadvantage by nature, I lacked Ben's lifetime of training. He was, essentially, a born-and-bred soldier and commander—a warrior King. I...wasn't. The way I had panicked during our hunt on Yonvey had hammered into me that even a month of growing and honing my skills didn't mean I was ready for combat yet. I still had *so much* to learn....

And so little time to learn it.

I sighed heavily. Not for the first time, I wondered why the Trees had chosen me as the Queen of their Realms. What advantages did I, an ignorant and untrained Earthren, have to offer in Their service? Language was only the beginning, the tip of the iceberg at what I had to learn and become to be worthy of the mantle.

Why....

A memory came to my mind, from when Ben was first teaching me how to fight. When I'd been discouraged at the disparity between us, he asked me if the Seven Realms needed two of him. I had jokingly said that I thought he was pretty great, and he'd smiled but rephrased his question.

Do you think the Tree of Ice needs an Heir like me?

I had reluctantly admitted that She must not have...because She hadn't chosen another like him.

She had chosen me.

And if She did not make mistakes, that must mean that the Trees didn't need a warrior Queen. At least not right away. No doubt I should learn to hold my own as soon as I could, but for now.... They must have something else in mind for me.

As grimly comforting as that realization was, it did little to release the knots in my stomach that were purely caused by fear for Ben. My frustration with myself at being able to do so little to help him in this situation was only a part of the much larger problem: that he had to go into danger at all. Tomorrow.

And not just tomorrow, or the next day, or the next. This was his life, his duty—especially until he had a capable Heir. Considering how it had taken seventy years after Kavarian had become King for Ben to become his Heir, another might not be chosen anytime soon.

How was I going to do this? I was still as determined as ever to try, but I simply didn't know *how*. How was I going to cope with the fact that Ben's duty so frequently involved putting himself in danger? Especially when there was little I could do to help him....

The more I thought about it, the more twisted the knots became, until it felt like my stomach was rising into my throat.

How? I kept repeating in my head, with no answer coming. *How?*

I must have kept most of my dread from my expression, because when we reached our suite, Ben kissed me like nothing was wrong before going to the water-room for his nighttime routine. I let Fenra lead me away into the dressing room to undo my hair and dress and give me something more comfortable to wear; if she noticed my deeper-than-usual reticence, she must have pinned it down to my language commitment or exhaustion. Whatever the reason, she didn't press me.

Even though Ben typically went to bed far sooner, we had taken to spending his final waking minutes cuddling on the couch, talking or silently decompressing from the day. Since we'd both come to look forward to that time so much, I knew that if I didn't come or say something, he would go looking for me to see what was wrong.

Otherwise, I would have been tempted to just avoid him that night. As hard as it would have been to not see him awake before he left, I knew I couldn't hold myself together much longer.

I vowed to myself that I would try. I would just stay silent and if Ben asked what was wrong, I would just say I was tired from the feast. I didn't want to distress or distract him tonight, didn't want him to lose sleep that might endanger him tomorrow, didn't want him to doubt my commitment to him or this path.

No matter how many doubts I had right then about how I would be strong enough to walk it.

I would just not think about any of it, as hard as I could, until he went to sleep. Then, in the solitary hours I would have before sleep took me too, I would work through this on my own, like a grown woman. I could handle this. I *would* handle this.

I would....

As soon as I pushed open the door and stepped in, I saw Ben was sprawled in the sitting nook, one leg resting on top of the other in a figure four, reading some papers as he waited for me.

In the same moment, he raised his head and smiled at me, and that was it. I'd like to say that I broke when his smile faded and his warm eyes tightened in concern.

But I knew that it truly was the second before that, the second he looked up and smiled, and I was suddenly devastated by the thought that I might not see that smile again.

That the next time I saw him, it could be with his lifeless body on a bier. Just like his father.

"Sarah," Ben said, shoving the papers aside as he stood. "What's wrong?"

Then I was sobbing, and Ben was scooping me up and crushing me to him. That, of course, only made me sob all the harder and cling to him as if I would never be able to let go.

"Sarah, what is it?" Ben said in alarm. "Did you hear something from your family? Is something wrong?"

The delicious warmth of his healing power sunk into me in another form of questioning, searching for any sign of hurt. Which, of course, made my mental anguish even *worse.*

"N-no," I choked. "N-nothing."

He let out a breath. He put an arm under my legs and swung them up, carrying me to the couch—all without ever breaking the power that flowed into me from the hand at my back. The amount of power he was spending on me right now was ridiculous, considering it was hours past sunset. I tried to summon the willpower to tell him to stop, but I couldn't quite manage it.

Though my pain was mental, it manifested in physical symptoms that he was diligently easing, now that his focus had turned from searching for a nonexistent injury. The tension in my muscles was melting, the knots in my intestines were being undone, the racing pulses of my iceheart were slowing. Everywhere, my fight-or-flight instincts were being overridden and told to *rest*. In spite of myself, my sobs were easing, even before Ben resettled onto the couch with me in his arms.

Finally, after a few moments, I managed between hiccups, "Ben...."

He only tightened his hold on me. "If you're going to tell me to stop, save your breath."

I decided saving my breath *was* wise. But fortunately, my vocal cords weren't the only way I had to talk to him.

I'll be OK now, I think. You really need to stop. You can't afford to burn yourself out the night before....

He let out a deep sigh. He pressed a kiss to the top of my head and spoke softly, no trace of judgment or exasperation in his voice. "Is that what this is about? The hunt starting tomorrow?"

That's what...started it. I just....

The tears started flowing hot and fast again, but at least my chest wasn't shaking with the heartrending sobs from before.

I...I can't lose you, Ben. I can't.

Not again. Not like that.

"You won't lose me tomorrow," Ben soothed softly. "Or the next day, or any of the days of this hunt. Not to a sand wyrm. You think Yvera would let me go if there was a chance of that? I'll be surrounded by elites, and every one of us has done this sort of thing before. We know how to do this, Sarah. Trust me."

I sighed, snuggling into him. *I know. But the fact that this is just...routine for you is what is terrifying me right now. That this should be normal...will be normal....*

That this would simply be my life from now on....

Ben let out another deep breath. "I...can see that now. Sorry I was such a dimtorch that I didn't realize how worried you were before."

You're not a dimtorch, I snapped, turning my head up to glare at what I could see of his face from this angle. *Stop calling yourself that.*

He smiled thinly as he offered me a handkerchief. "Sorry."

I groaned, took it, and turned my head back down to blow my nose. *It only just started getting bad as we were coming back, anyway. You noticed as soon as I came in that something was wrong, so give yourself more credit.*

His perceptiveness had been one reason I'd broken so hard, after all. That was my Ben: kind to a fault, and so full of love for me it was painful right now. Like holding on to the most exquisitely beautiful rose—one full of thorns that cut into my hand the more deeply the tighter I gripped it. Yet, no matter how it hurt me, I knew I could never let go. It was a part of me now, a part of my blood, my heart, my life.

"I don't know what to say," Ben said heavily. "Except that I know more of what you feel than you probably realize. In fact, to be honest...you've handled this much better than I have so far."

I huffed in disbelief.

"No, really, you have," Ben said grimly. "You *know* why I pushed you away, Sarah."

I stilled as I remembered.

His voice lowered. "And surely you know why I'm not letting you come tomorrow."

You have good reasons.

It was his turn to huff. "And that's the only reason I've finally convinced you to stay. That doesn't change the fact that I'd be in a worse state than you are now if you still insisted on coming."

I chuckled tightly. My voice had recovered enough by then that I said out loud, "Despite how 'safe' sand wyrm hunting is?"

"I never said it was 'safe,'" Ben grumbled. "Just that I and my *many* body-guards are equipped to deal with the dangers."

"And I'm not," I whispered.

"You can't be everything," Ben teased gently, tapping me on the arm three times. "For Flame's sake, Sarah, if I can't do this much, what am I even good for?"

"Excuse me," I said tartly. "I think you're good for a great deal more than wyrm-slaying, thank you very much. In fact, I wouldn't mind it if you weren't good for that at all. Then we wouldn't even be having this discussion."

He chuckled. "Good to know."

After a moment, he spoke again, the humor gone from his voice. "Really—this is what drakón are meant to do, Sarah. It's why the Tree made us the way we are."

That hit too close to my insecurities for comfort.

I whispered, "Then what did mine make *me* to do?"

"Oh, nothing much," Ben said dryly. "Only *everything else.*"

"And by that, you mean...?"

Ben sighed. "Sarah, when are you going to understand what a miracle you are? Who was it that figured out the solution to the pestilence?"

"Someone would have tried it—"

"The tisane? The crop dusting?"

"The Moontouched who told us about the icemint on the archival said it was for a tea. And I didn't even come up with the dusting mechanism itself. That was Dad and—"

"Sarah, you're still not getting it."

He held me back from him so our eyes could meet, and when I avoided his, he pulled out the arm he'd had under my legs and used that hand to force my chin up.

His gold eyes burned. "It all started with you, being you, when we needed *you.* And that was only *one* example. I could go on for deken, until *you* fell asleep, about all the ways you're already the Queen we desperately need. And every day, you prove that even more."

My eyes stung. How could he have known that was exactly what I'd needed to hear today?

Perhaps he hadn't. Perhaps there was something else at work here, giving him the words. Trees, as I was learning, worked in strange ways. Especially through Their chosen vessels.

I swallowed. "Then why do I feel so useless right now? Why can't I help you?"

He closed his eyes and sighed. "Have you thought about the fact that maybe there are some things you're *supposed* to rely on me for? Otherwise, why would you even need me?"

Was I not the only one having doubts about what worth I brought to the Realms? Or...to our relationship?

I reached up to cup his cheek, swallowing again. "I'll always need you, Ben. That's part of the problem. If you don't come back...."

He opened his eyes, smiling thinly. "I'll come back from this, Sarah. I promise."

My eyes stung again. "Don't...don't make promises to me. Not about that."

"No," he said with a strange calm. "I will, this time, about *that*. I can feel it this time, Sarah. I'm coming back to you."

I became still for a moment, searching his eyes. Then, when I couldn't see a trace of deception or disbelief in them, I sank back into him, almost trembling in relief. I didn't know why I believed in Ben's belief...but I did. Enough that, for the first time since the feast was over, I felt like I could truly breathe again.

Still, I knew this would only be a reprieve. I knew now that the dread would be back, and that, in fact, it would become my lifelong companion.

Which meant I had to learn ways to manage it on my own, when Ben wasn't there to hold me and still my body's panic with his healing, and no immortal promises of reassurance were forthcoming.

A face came to my mind, one I knew well, even though her curly hair was no longer the orangish-red I pictured. I was startled that I was thinking of Laura now of all times, but then a moment later, I realized why.

Laura...had married a police officer. Then nodded her acceptance when Michael had asked for her permission to become my rightwing. If there was anyone that would understand what I was going through right now...it would be her.

I hadn't had many heart-to-hearts with my prickly sister-in-law. Alright...make that none. I liked her well enough, and I thought she liked me too, in her own way. Or at least...she had before I'd decided to marry Ben. But even before she had a reason to question my life choices, she wasn't the type to just chat, let alone about emotional subjects.

Maybe...it was time we did.

Chapter Thirty-Two

WYRMS

Koriben

I ROSE A DEKEN before dawn, since I and the hunting team wanted to be at the sungate right as it relit to make as much use of daylight as possible. As usual, I dressed in the dark, careful not to wake Sarah, and once I was ready to leave, I paused at her bedside to look at her. One of the most bittersweet aspects of sharing a room was getting to see her asleep—to study her as much as I liked for a few moments and take comfort in her unguarded repose...and ache for the day that I could wake up to see her beside me.

Also as usual, I stayed there for a long moment, but this time, I was filled with more than the usual reluctance. Last night, before I'd gone to sleep, Sarah had made me promise to wake her before I left. Yet it seemed a shame to disturb the peace she seemed to have finally found in sleep; I wondered how much more rest she would get after I was gone.

But even if I hadn't *promised*, I knew I had to wake her. I knew Sarah would lose peace and rest anyway if she woke up to discover I'd ignored her wishes. In that scenario, even if I made it back tonight, she would be so furious with me, I might have to find somewhere else to sleep, and that wouldn't do. I was already becoming far more accustomed than was good for either of us to sleeping near her.

I gingerly sat on the edge of the bed, knowing by now that she was a deep enough sleeper that the movement alone wouldn't wake her. So, I savored a couple more seconds of gazing at her before reaching out and brushing hair away from her face.

She gasped and twitched awake.

"*Adelak*," I said soothingly, using the same word I'd first spoken to her face to face. In one word, it conveyed the sense of intending no harm and offering assurance that all was well. I cupped her face in my hand. "It's me."

Her eyes sought mine in the darkness but didn't quite find them. Belatedly, I remembered her weak darksight and nonexistent heatsense and realized I should have turned on a light before waking her. I'd been hoping to disturb her as little as possible, with the intent that she would fall asleep more quickly after I left. But I supposed the shot of adrenaline I'd given her by waking her in the darkness might have been worse.

She must have recognized enough of me, or my touch or voice, to relax back with a groan after only a moment.

"Sorry," I said sheepishly.

"Not your fault," she mumbled with her eyes closed. "I asked you to."

Sarah opened her eyes again, then pushed herself up and to me, throwing her arms around my neck and pressing the side of her face into my chest. I put my own arms around her and held her close but not too tight. I didn't want her to think I was desperate. Which I wasn't—I was as confident now that I would be fine as I had been last night—but I *was* already feeling the ache of the days and maybe nights I would spend apart from her, and that made me want to cling to her now.

Even as I thanked the Flame for the hundredth time that she had agreed to stay.

"Come back," Sarah whispered.

"I will," I said, rubbing comforting circles into her back.

She sighed. "I love you."

I yearned to be able to say those words out loud, but times like these made them stick harder than ever in my throat. So, feeling miserably inadequate, I tapped her on the back three times. Then added a fourth tap with slow emphasis.

Predictably, that made her chuckle and seek out my lips in the darkness for a kiss. As our mouths moved together, I felt an urge as powerful as it was dangerous to push her back down and join her on the bed, so I cut off far sooner than either of us would have liked and let her go.

She sighed again but sat back, seeming to understand. Still, her fingers reached up and tentatively traced my jaw in the darkness, sending a shiver of fire through to my skin with every brush against the hairs there. She swallowed, looking as if she wanted to say something more, but didn't. I knew how she felt. What more was there to be said that we hadn't said already?

Gently, I murmured, "Go back to sleep, Sarah."

"I'm not sure if I can," she said, but she sank back down and allowed me to pull the cover over her torso and under her lifted arm before she settled the arm back around the pillow she liked to hug close to her body.

"Try," I encouraged, lips twitching. "Flame knows you're going to need it."

Sarah groaned at the reminder of all the duties ahead of her today. I surprised myself by thinking wistfully of staying behind to face them with her. But no. I had my own duty.

I leaned down and kissed her forehead.

As I rose, I said, "I'll see you tonight, if I can..."

I wished I could do away with the caveat, but there were sadly too many circumstances that would make it more practical and right for me to stay away.

"...or I'll call if I can't."

"You'd better," she muttered, eyes drifting closed.

I chuckled. Flame, how good it felt to be wanted. I'd always been *needed*, often more so than I'd liked. But wanted, missed? In the way that she had made it clear she would want and miss me?

Never before her.

And that made me *need* her, in a way I'd never needed anything before.

LESS THAN A DEKEN later, the hunt team and I soared over the dunes of Romskal's Great Desert—the birthplace of wyrms. Or so the researchers told us. Wyrms had already spread to other parts of Romskal by the time we came to this Realm, and with the Devourer's help, they subsequently spread in varying degrees to the other five.

But this, the experts told us, was where it all began, and I had no reason to doubt them. I'd seen for myself that the Great Desert was the perfect breeding and sheltering ground for the creatures, and most of my sand wyrm hunts had been in some quadrant or other of this enormous sandy, rocky waste that spanned a quarter of Romskal's equator.

Whereas wyrm sightings elsewhere were still rare, hunts had to go on near constantly here to keep their numbers down to tolerable levels. Occasionally, a great hunt spanning the whole desert was needed to purge as many as possible.

That's what we were here to do, and that was why it was no doubt going to take us days to complete our task. We had hard, dangerous work ahead and a lot of ground to cover to do it.

Fortunately, wyrms weren't intelligent or communicative with their fellows, which meant we could use the same hunting tactics we had used for centuries without fail. Also fortunately, Sarah hadn't asked me to describe how a sand wyrm hunt worked, and I hadn't volunteered the information, for good reason.

Because it usually began with using me as bait.

Well, not just me, obviously, since hunts went on without me all the time. But when I was there, I was the bait by default, since the largest and most powerful drakón on the hunt usually served in that role—both because they had the highest odds of surviving and because they had the most draw. We didn't know for sure why that was, but wyrm researchers speculated that what wyrms sensed of us and what made us irresistible to them was the power of our flamehearts—so it made sense that the biggest flameheart would have the biggest pull.

Yet another reason I was glad Sarah hadn't insisted on coming. Even if I'd sheltered her from the danger and this baking heat within my heart, I didn't want to find out what kind of draw we might have *together*. As efficient as it would be to pull half the sand wyrms of the Great Desert to us at once, I shuddered at the apocalyptic image that thought evoked. Efficiency was meaningless if we couldn't handle the numbers we had summoned and thus became the hunted.

As it was, Royal hunts were always the largest, both to protect the Royal involved and to handle the numbers that a Royal alone could summon. Especially a King. Golden Queens were the most powerful, but Kings were the largest, and wyrms found that combination of power and size irresistible. Either that, or they had just enough intelligence to guess we males were the easier and more hot-blooded targets.

For now, I soared high above the rest of the flight, not wanting to lure in a sand wyrm before it was time to begin.

Ready, Ben? Yvera asked me as she flew point below me, inner voice coated with relish.

I was always amused at how, in any other instance, she was violently opposed to me putting myself in any sort of dangerous position, but when it came to wyrm hunts....

So eager to throw me to the wyrms, Yv? I teased, trying to hide how my stomach was clenching and flameheart was pounding.

No matter how many times I did this, it never got easier. In fact, it got a bit worse each time as my experiences of coming up close and personal with a sand wyrm's maw stacked up.

Yvera wasn't fooled by my lighthearted tone. Her violet head turned to the side to eye me above her, and she snorted a puff of smoke. *Oh, get down there, you big hatchling. You'll be fine.*

And I knew I would be. Probably.

That didn't mean it might not hurt first. Yet another detail I'd managed to conceal from Sarah.

At Yvera's signal, the flight diverged in two, leaving me room for a dive and removing any interference between the sand and my flameheart, which was helpfully pounding like a drum to summon the closest wyrm in.

We might not get a bite yet. It was early in the day, and we were on the outskirts of the dune sea. But, in case one happened to be near enough to be lured, it was time to begin.

I exhaled, mighty lungs emptying and buoyant air sacs shrinking, then pulled in my wings...and dove.

A half eld or so above the dunes, I snapped my wings out, pulled up, and flew level for a bit. Now I was a couple eld below the flight—close enough for them to reach me within seconds if any of them spotted the slightest sign of an incoming wyrm, but far enough away to hopefully make the wyrm think I was on my own.

A drakón with the largest flameheart they'd ever sensed, just out for a solitary, low-altitude jaunt across the deadliest desert in the Six Realms.

Like I said—wyrms weren't the most intelligent bunch. And, used to being the apex predator of their realm for the millennia before we came, they had almost no sense of self-preservation.

Rise, Yvera ordered me after a dek. The command meant no wyrm had been sighted, and I'd risked myself long enough. I beat my wings and began the long climb back to my former altitude, feeling a mixture of relief and resignation. Even if we didn't get a bite soon, I'd be exhausted by the time we finished the two long sides of our first search triangle of the day and reached our first resting place back at the edge of the Great Desert. Still, I'd rather keep climbing back up than remain within—

Up, Ben, up! Yvera said sharply, and only a second later, I saw the disturbed sand just ahead of me, rising and spilling down. As the rest of the flight dove for that spot, I swerved to the side and pounded upward, straining to rise as fast as my wings could manage. My flameheart, now my enemy, pounded from the exertion and fear, especially when I saw the size of that growing mound.

Torch it, it was going to be a big one.

And then hell itself exploded from the sand: a gaping maw almost large enough to swallow *me*, filled with rows upon rows of hard, jagged teeth. And, despite my swerve, it was right beneath me, having angled to follow me as it rose from the sand.

It was an incredibly good thing I had already been climbing, because I only evaded it by erd as it reached the apex of its lunge and fell back with a frustrated groan to the sand.

Hellfrost! I swore to myself, lungs heaving and wings and heart pounding as my designated bodyguards reached and flanked me, and the rest of the flight, including Yvera, launched themselves at the wyrm's exposed sides.

Now, the trickiest business was to sever its massive maw from the rest of its body. That alone wouldn't kill it, since whatever passed for its brain was deeper inside, but the limited decapitation would trap it, render it relatively helpless (though it could still crush one of us under its weight if we weren't careful), and leave it as easy prey for the rest of its kind, who were opportunistic cannibals. The first bait and kill in an area was the hardest. After that, it became easier to find and kill the others as they all mindlessly swarmed in to stupidly get their shot at the carcass. Sometimes they would even do our job for us as they squabbled, and the carcasses would stack, drawing in even more.

A first kill *this* big might help us clear the whole quadrant.

You alright, Ben? Ordran, my temporary rightwing and the permanent captain of my elites, asked.

Yes, fine, I snapped, adrenaline making my tone tense.

As fine as could be expected with almost just having become wyrm food.

Flame, I'd be lucky if I didn't have nightmares about that maw tonight. Or the hot, fetid stench of its breath....

I leveled off and circled the fight below. As the designated bait, I was expected to remain out of the fight for my safety and to keep watch for other incoming wyrms, but close enough that the current wyrm wouldn't give up hope of catching me. Now that it had a lock on me, it would stubbornly remain instead of fleeing, as any creature of sense would have the moment it realized that this was a trap.

The wyrm had already sunk its head back into the dunes to attempt another explosive dive and rise, but drakón were already tearing away at its scaly hide, exposing its more sensitive skin beneath. Unsurprisingly, Yvera was the first to draw blood, making the sand tremble under the wyrm's muffled roar.

Enraged now, the wyrm forgot about the dive and reared back up, aiming for Yvera, but she was gone, having taken off as soon as she made her mark. To give her and the others clawing at it a bit of extra time, I dove in, getting just close enough to recapture the wyrm's attention.

It swerved its eyeless head toward me as soon as it sensed me again, and an elite on the ground made another mark, then another did the same. The wyrm bugled in deafening fury, the punch of its breath making me gag. I breathed a maelstrom of flame down its throat in return, making it clamp the beaklike prongs of its outer mouth shut. Though I'd no doubt caused it significant pain, I knew better than to hope my fire had gotten far enough down its throat to get to its brain or hearts, and now it would be wary about opening up.

At least now, with its burned mouth and so many scales ripped free and blood dripping from three different points, the wyrm was incapable of the rapid dives and ascents that were one of its most dangerous attacks. And yet, it still did not flee, now more determined than ever to get a feast for its pains.

Then the longest, most dangerous part began: the deadly dance of drakón lunging in to swipe or bite at its sides, making each gash deeper and deeper, and then immediately rushing away before the wyrm could turn its maw on them or attempt to fall on and crush them.

Fortunately, its movements were slow enough they could anticipate its intent and, if they were careful, get clear in time—and anyone allowed on a wyrm hunt would *know* to be careful. Occasionally, the wyrm would dive under the sand to get a reprieve, but it would always emerge again, and its dives became less frequent the more injuries it sustained.

Wyrm kills were never a quick business: there was simply too much flesh to carve through, and too much care had to be taken to carve it. The process stretched on for what felt like eternity, but I could tell from the progress of Romskal's sun, Olmen, that just a deken passed before things changed. By then, the hunt party had split into shifts, with half in the air and half down below, swapping out as one half tired. The ones in the air doubled as scouts, and it was one of them who spotted the signs of another wyrm approaching.

Fly! she mentally shouted, accompanying the word with a roar of warning. *South by southeast!*

The elites on the ground all rose without question, darting up and away. The ones in the southeast left not a moment too soon as an only slightly smaller wyrm burst out of the sand and lunged, only just missing them. The second wyrm fell on its kin instead, maw closing on its flesh, which made the first wyrm roar and rear back to retaliate.

Well, that's lucky, Mitha, a cheerful and unusually large Starkissed, said as she rejoined us in the sky.

She meant that now our work was much simpler. All we had to do was circle at a safe altitude and wait for one of the wyrms to finish the other off, hopefully leaving the victor weakened enough for an easy kill. Even if the first wyrm wasn't already incensed, wyrms were highly territorial, and it wouldn't leave the newcomer's incursion unpunished. Or vice versa, if the first had been the interloper.

Only because all of us got away, Kordan, a blunt Battleblood, snapped.

That was the most perilous aspect about engaging a wyrm: the greatest threat wasn't the wyrm you could see, but the one you couldn't—the one who might yet be coming. Yet another reason to always be on the move if you were among the number on the ground.

I checked to make sure before I said that, Mitha said easily. *Who's taking bets on the winner? Mine is on the big guy.*

Ashdust, Remi, a Brightflare, said. *That one's cut to ribbons right now, and the second isn't that much smaller.*

Finally, now that we had the luxury for such questions, someone asked the one that had been on our minds.

What are two wyrms as big as those *doing this close to the edge of the dune sea?*

That sobering question made silence fall for a moment, until a Strongshield spoke. He was one of the few members of this hunt who weren't among my elites and instead had been sent with us by Lord Kolwin. *We told you they were becoming more aggressive of late.*

No kidding, if we lured two mature wyrms within elden, after only one bait dive. I began to feel exhausted for a different reason than I had expected by now—just at the thought of the days ahead. Perhaps they might be fewer, if we could lure them so easily, but they would be longer and more dangerous.

Torch it. Maybe I wouldn't be making it back to Sarah tonight after all.

And if she found out any of the details of my day, she would kill me.

Chapter Thirty-Three

ADVICE

Sarah

Almost the moment I'd woken up, Fenra whisked me away to get ready, hardly giving me time to even register that Ben was gone.

I'd gotten used to him being out of the room when I woke up, but the gravitational pull he had for me had almost always been there, comfortingly strong and close by. Now I could feel as well as know that he was half a world away, the connection between us thinned to a thread—a thread of something harder and more resilient than steel, but still far smaller than I liked.

Then Lord Kolwin came for me—in person, and all the way to the central court of the King's Wing to boot. I dreaded what kind of ceremonial torture he had in mind that would require him to be so proactive, but to my surprise, he led us and our small entourage of guards straight to the hold's healing ward, where he brought me to the bedsides of short-term and long-term patients alike.

I wouldn't say he became a different person, but he showed a far softer side than I had previously seen, especially when we had the excuse to leave our guards outside the room and converse with the patient privately. To my surprise, he knew every long-term patient by name, what their ailment was, and how they were being treated.

Few conditions were beyond the powers of drakón healers to swiftly mend, but I learned all about them that day. Some were comatose, their bodies healed but minds gone; some had chemical imbalances, malfunctioning nerves, genetic disorders, or other delicate conditions that the healers hadn't yet figured out how to safely fix, and therefore required frequent care to keep alive. Some were amputees, especially from the Battle of the Solstice, who were still learning how to adjust to their new life.

Those last ones put my heart through the wringer. Not one of them seemed to harbor the resentment toward me I might have expected. In fact, as far as I could tell, many of them were as grateful and awed to meet me as their Strongshield masks would allow them to appear to be. After the first one thanked me and said she wouldn't have survived if it hadn't been for my sudden influx of power, I had to bite my tongue to keep myself from crying.

After the third survivor, Lord Kolwin stopped in front of a painting outside the room and studied it for half a minute before I realized he was giving me a chance to compose myself.

Thank you, I told him silently after I was sure no more tears were going to spill.

His back remained to me, and for a moment, I feared that I'd offended him by addressing him privately. Then he answered, voice neutral. *One of the hardest parts of embracing our duties is accepting that we, as mortals, will never be enough. That for every life we save, we lose another. That for every person we help, we fail another. That is the burden we must bear: to remember our failures and frailties so that they may teach us how to better serve the ones we have left.*

Somehow, he had understood. Not just understood—he had felt and put to words this crushing weight I felt inside, and somehow hearing it named and shared made the weight lift enough to keep bearing it.

Why was he doing this? He didn't even seem to like me, or Ben.

Maybe his personal feelings had nothing to do with it. For better or for worse, I was his future Queen, and it was in his best interest to make sure I was a good one.

I hesitated, then dared ask, *Is that why you come here?*

Three seconds of silence.

Then he answered in the same neutral tone. *I wished to be a healer, once.*

His confession reminded me of Kor, who had once told me he'd wanted to be a historian and teacher. Here was yet another chosen of a Tree who had never wanted the mantle thrust on him.

Had any of us? Is that what *all* of us shared in common, in some way?

With only the slightest of pauses, Kolwin continued, still speaking tonelessly. *Now I serve my people in a different way.*

Is that why you brought me *here?* I asked quietly. *To serve them?*

I brought you here to teach you that there are more ways to serve our people than to fight for them. Leading a warflight into battle or on a hunt is the work of a day. Serving the remnants after is the true duty of a lifetime.

I inhaled. He couldn't have known the doubt that had always festered in my heart, could he? From the moment I learned what my Tree intended for me. The doubt ebbed and flowed, having periods of strength and weakness. But these past couple of days had made it rear its ugly head again, especially when I compared my abilities and preparation to Ben's.

Yet, without saying it directly, Kolwin was implying I had the potential to be as much use to the dramá as Ben was.

If I tried. If I would just stop looking inward, open my eyes, and *see* all the people I could help in a way Ben simply couldn't. Ben couldn't be everything; I'd told him that much myself. He was careful with the power the Tree of Flame had given him, but the Tree had made her Royals to be intimidating and dangerous by nature, as necessary but deadly as flame itself. One mortal could only do and be so much.

He couldn't be their protector and their comforter. Both of us were needed.

I...was needed. Here. Now.

As I was.

When would I finally accept that?

Kolwin gave me a few moments to process and turned to look at me. His expression was still unreadable as ever, his eyes lacking warmth. Yet an understanding passed between us: one Tree's reluctant chosen to another.

He inclined his head subtly, asking if I was ready to continue. I took a deep breath and nodded.

It was time to return to our duties.

My duties.

THE REST OF MY day was just as much of a whirlwind. Our visit to the healing ward took us until the late afternoon, when Kolwin returned me to the King's Wing and Vadya and Fenra got me ready for the night's feast. To my disappointment, Ben called and said he wouldn't be able to make it to a sungate before sunset here. They had stopped at a shelter, but he wasn't about to leave the hunt party to surge alone to a gate, since that would require them to cover even more distance early tomorrow to meet and guard him when he reemerged.

I didn't have time to press him for details about his day, since I had sent my helpers away in the middle of preparations, and they said they could only afford to give me a few dek. But I could tell Ben looked dirty and exhausted. When I asked him if he would have access to a bath, he just laughed tiredly as he ran his hand through his dusty hair.

"You remember the shelter we stayed at in the Wirthen Desert? It's like that."

Which meant it barely even had a privy, and certainly no room to himself. It looked like he'd stepped into a rough sandstone hallway just to have some space to talk to me.

I grimaced. "Hopefully it's safer for you tonight than that one was."

"It will be," Ben said firmly. "This is a shelter at the edge of the *Great* Desert. We have sensors galore to tell us if any rock wyrms or their tunnels are anywhere close."

I hesitated, not sure if I wanted to get into this in the minute remaining, but not sure if I could hold the question back. "And what would you be able to do if one of them went off?"

It would be night. They would be trapped, with nowhere safe to go and no means to get there, even if they did.

Ice and Flame, should I have gone with him, anyway? Even if it was just to protect him at night?

Ben's eyes darkened, but he shrugged. "We've all fought rock wyrms before, Sarah. I'll be fine."

He tugged his lips in an effort at a teasing smile. "Worry more about yourself. You're the one I'm leaving to go to a Strongshield feast on your own."

My reply was dry. "Truly a more dangerous prospect than sleeping in a nightshelter at the edge of a wyrm-infested desert."

Ben's expression was solemn, but he couldn't entirely hide the light dancing in his eyes. "Indeed."

His eyes turned wistful. "I really *would* rather be there to face it with you, Sarah."

I sighed. "I know."

If it weren't for the danger, though, part of me would have been glad to keep him away. With how tired he looked, I really didn't want him doing double shifts for me. I could handle this much now, I was sure. After all, this was *my* contribution.

That was all we got before there was a knock on the door again.

"Time's up," I sighed.

"Call me again after the feast," Ben urged.

I looked at him dubiously. "Are you sure? You look exhausted. Shouldn't you be in bed by then?"

"I can wait up."

"Ben...."

"Just call me. If I'm awake, I'll answer. If I'm too far gone, I won't."

I sighed and nodded. "Alright, I will. I love you, Ben."

Before he could struggle over trying to answer that, I ended the call.

As I'd thought, the feast wasn't so bad, with the lack of expected conversation and my mastery of dramá eating etiquette once again playing in my favor. The hardest part was staying awake through the night's entertainment—an epic poetry reading with musical accompaniment. Which was a shame, since that was the sort of thing I might have enjoyed after a less exhausting day and on an emptier stomach.

But my "day" still wasn't over even after. First, I tried calling Ben, and I was almost relieved when I didn't get an answer. But, with thoughts of rock wyrms on my mind, I went to ask Kor whether Ben's group was alright. Kor just laughed and said that he had heard from Yvera recently, that everything was fine, and Ben had simply collapsed into a bed and fallen asleep almost immediately, as I'd suspected he might.

Then, because I'd asked for it, I received my first formal lesson in Drona, which mostly consisted of meeting the tutor Vadya had brought in and making her familiar with my knowledge and gaps so far.

After *that*, Kor and Vadya had a few matters to bring to my attention, seeing as I was the Royal in charge right now—a reality of Ben being gone that hadn't sunk in until that moment.

"Are you serious?" I asked them. "You really want me to decide on something that I have almost no knowledge of whatsoever?"

Kor smirked. "That's why we have a recommendation, of course. But by law, a Royal must give their seal on certain things."

"I don't have a seal, though."

Wrong, of course, as I saw as soon as Kor produced a silver signet ring. It was much like Ben's, with the same three-pronged crown circling the tree, except my tree had prism-shaped shards for leaves instead of flames.

When I hesitated to take it, Kor rolled his eyes. "Oh, don't get your tail in a knot. Eskala designed it, with input from Vadya and your father. I'm just the delivery boy."

I flushed, wondering what Ben had told Kor.

"What's the fuss?" Vadya said, eyes bright with interest.

"Rings are like earrings to her," Kor said.

"Oooh," Vadya said with a wicked grin, eyes falling once again on the ring in Kor's hand. Mercifully, though, she plucked the ring from Kor and then handed it to me innocently. "Here, Queen Sarah. As your *chief of staff*, I have arranged a signet ring for you. Does it meet your expectations?"

I took it from her with mock solemnity. "Thank you, *Vadya*. It's lovely."

Kor rolled his eyes again, but seeing as he didn't have a hand in its creation either, I didn't think he would truly take offense. "There. *Now* you have a seal. How does it fit?"

I slipped it on my right index finger, the same position Ben's was in. "Perfect."

"Well," Kor said idly. "First try. Will you look at that."

I glanced at him suspiciously. He and Vadya were looking far too innocent. Perhaps Kor had more of a hand than he'd implied, if only when it came to sizing.

"Should I really be wearing this right now, though? I'm a Queen, but I'm not *your* Queen. Yet."

"True, so for now, that ring signifies your authority over the Seventh Realm alone. Which means you *can* and *should* wear it, but you shouldn't use it on any of our legal documents yet."

I rolled my eyes. "Then why are you giving it to me to do just that?"

"I'm not," Kor said with a smirk. "That's separate. You just mentioned you didn't have a ring, which reminded me to give it to you."

Sometimes, talking to Kor made my head hurt. "You *just said* that certain decisions require a royal seal."

Kor waved a hand. "I meant that in a general sense, a statement of fact to prepare you for the future. Tonight, I'm not bringing anything to you that requires a seal. Everything I want you to decide on is nothing that any lawyer has any standing to quibble over you deciding, seeing as you're Ben's betrothed and he left you in charge."

You'd think Ben would have mentioned that to me himself, but maybe that was just something I should have assumed.

I eyed Kor. "Then how important *are* these decisions, anyway?"

"Why, Queen Sarah," Vadya said with wide eyes. "It is absolutely essential that we decide the material for the table runners for your heartbinding feast—tonight."

I glared at the two of them. "Seriously? *That* is what you've come to talk to me about? *Table runners*?"

Kor raised an eyebrow. "Would you rather your first decision be about Warflight draft numbers? Treasury allocations? Case arbitration?"

I was seeing where the two of them were going with all of this. Kor always seemed to have more than one motive for doing what he did.

I grimaced. "No."

Kor looked into my eyes and smiled. "Trust me, Sarah, I tried to field most of the decisions that I could make myself or push off the ones that could wait for Ben. But you have to get used to making decisions. Taking over when the Monarch is off doing battle is one of the consort's primary duties. That's why I'm starting you out on trivial things like table runners."

Which was why I couldn't hate him. As much as he often tempted me to.

"We really *do* have to decide on the fabric, though," Vadya said, pulling out a booklet of swatches with a flourish. "To give the threadworkers a fair timeline. You don't want them to have to work overtime for *this*, do you?"

I sighed. "No, I don't."

"Wonderful! What do you think of this cream linen?"

AT LONG LAST, HOURS after sunset, I was finally alone in my study and able to do the one thing *I* had wanted to accomplish that day: call home and ask to speak with Laura.

During the day, I'd taken to making my ice spell connect with a wall in the library. That room was quiet while still being a public space, and I could often catch Dad. He was usually the one I needed to speak to, anyway, and if not, he was fine with passing along any messages or bringing people to me.

At night, I tried the kitchen, which was our usual gathering place; there, I could often catch someone or call out to see if anyone was in earshot. Since the kitchen was between the bathrooms and the bedrooms, if there was anyone awake, they could usually hear me.

The one thing I'd determined to never do was abuse my powers of icesight by creating ice in a bedroom. With cellphones or even call scales, the one you called had the option to decline the call if they didn't want to be seen or heard.

The people at the other end of my ice spell had no such option, at least as far as we were aware so far. So, unless I had a previous arrangement with someone, I stuck to public areas and stayed out of those where my family should expect to have some privacy.

Those were my rules for dealing with my family in my Realm. As for the Six Realms...I hadn't yet worked out my personal code of ethics. So far, I was just glad that Kor hadn't asked me to spy on anyone—although I was certain the thought had occurred to him. Perhaps he was simply being nice...but I thought it was more likely that not even he had entirely worked out the full legal and ethical ramifications of what I could do and was refraining from temptation until he was certain the negative repercussions were within tolerable parameters.

Tolerable to him, that is. Which was an entirely different ballpark than my own comfort zone.

I caught David in the kitchen—making himself yet another snack, since it seemed like the only time he wasn't eating nowadays was in his sleep. I made a note to myself to ask Ben if that was normal for adolescent drakón; we weren't drakón—we six altered Linds still didn't even have a name for what we were—but drakón were the closest analogies we had.

By now, all my family were familiar with my calls and comfortable with my rules, so when I called out to him, David looked up and greeted me like I'd just appeared on some smart screen and, when I made my request, cheerfully left the room to pass on my message to Laura, munching on his sandwich all the way.

If Laura seemed surprised that I'd requested to speak with her, she didn't show it. She came into the Oculus—the ice cave at the northernmost point of the main hold—where I'd told David I'd meet her, face hard and inscrutable. When she stopped in front of the wall of ice that displayed my image on it, she folded her arms.

"Thank you for coming," I said sincerely. "Especially so late. I know you must be tired, but this was the first time I've had a chance to call all day."

Laura shrugged. "This would have been my first chance to talk, anyway, since I just put Tommie to bed."

"I assume you just want me to get right to it so you can go to bed yourself."

Her lips finally twitched slightly—the closest thing to a smile I'd seen from her since I'd left with Ben. "Good to hear you're still smart in some ways, at least."

I sighed. With Laura, I'd found it was best to address the elephant in the room yourself, or she would do it for you. "You're referring to my decision to marry Ben. Which you don't approve of."

"I don't," Laura said bluntly. "I think you're making a hasty, emotional decision that you'll probably regret—especially considering how he treated you. It's a mistake that teenagers make all the time, but I expected better of you, honestly."

She hadn't said anything that I hadn't already expected, so it was refreshing to hear her finally say it out loud. Except for the next part.

"To me, you seemed to have the most sense of all your siblings."

My own lips twitched despite myself. "Even more than Michael?"

Laura snorted and almost smiled. "Definitely more than Michael. You've seen how often that guy lets his emotions rule his head."

"And yet you still married him," I said, rubbing my neck self-consciously. "That's...why I wanted to talk to you, actually."

Laura blinked. "You want to know why I married your brother?"

"Specifically, I want to know why you married a *cop*. Or, at the time, someone you knew wanted to be a cop."

Her eyes narrowed. "What brought this up?"

"To put it simply, Ben's job is dangerous," I said wearily, slumping in my desk chair. I'd made my ice screen appear in the wall just behind the desk, below the brackets that were made to hold a call scale for much the same purpose. I missed the comfort of my couch back in my wing on Ythra.

I continued, "I'm not having doubts about Ben. I know you don't approve, and I can see where you're coming from, but we don't need to get into that right now. I'm not here to make you think I made the right decision. Right now, I want to know how you cope...or used to cope...with the fact that your husband had a job that...."

I swallowed.

Laura cocked her head and studied me for a moment. "He was your brother. How did *you* cope?"

I sighed. "He was my big brother. He was *Michael*. Not even my overactive imagination made me think that anything could touch him. Now...now I know better. And you must have as well."

Laura huffed and folded her arms. She was silent for a few moments.

She began reluctantly. "One reason I'm mad at you right now is that I've been where you are, Sarah. And around the same age, too. Maybe part of me is hoping you won't make the same decision I did."

I blinked. "Are you saying...you regret...."

I knew things were tense sometimes between Laura and Michael, as things got between most couples occasionally. They both had forceful personalities and diverse ways of doing things. But I had seen nothing that made me think they weren't going to make it. Michael was still crazy about her and doted on his son, and Laura was as affectionate with him as she ever got toward anyone except Tommie.

"Regret is a strong word," Laura said carefully, meeting my eyes. "Notice I said I hoped you wouldn't make the same *decision*, not *mistake*. I don't...think it was a mistake for me to marry Michael. But there's no denying it had a significant impact on my life—much more than I'd thought it would. Marriage always does. It affects where we live, what we do for a living, who our friends are, and ultimately, who we become. And that's just under normal circumstances, let alone ours. If I hadn't married Michael, I wouldn't be *here*, trapped on some other planet, and my mother wouldn't think her son-in-law murdered her daughter and grandson."

I winced. During our first couple weeks or so of adjusting to our new lives, we'd tried using ice communication to reach out to a select few extended family members and friends to let them know what had really happened to us, with varying success. The worst reaction came from Laura's mother, who refused to believe, let alone listen, and convinced herself that the daughter she saw in the ice was just a product of her grief. Laura had quickly stopped trying for fear that her mom would put herself in a psych ward. Now she simply had to make herself content with watching her mother from afar.

Laura sighed. "I don't blame you for that anymore, Sarah. Or Michael. It...well, it simply *is* the way things are now, and blame won't give me...or my mom...peace. But...because I'm human, I can't stop myself from wondering *what if*. And I'm worried your what ifs will be even bigger than mine."

I swallowed. "What do you mean?"

Laura shook her head. "Sarah, you're thinking about marrying a *king*. A king who we ultimately depend on for our survival right now, as much as we would like otherwise. What happens to *us* if things go badly again? Or to you?"

I took a deep breath and suppressed my impulse to jump to Ben's defense. Laura needed to see that I was thinking about this logically, not emotionally. And the level-headed part of me could understand her worry.

"He swore a blood oath, Laura. He *can't* block us out again, which means no one can. And if you can't trust *him* anymore, then trust the many other friends I have on this side who will never let us starve so long as there is any way to reach us. Others just like Svyer—who is Ben's only cousin, remember. Ben is not about to let Svyer suffer, no matter what happens between the two of us."

Laura grimaced at that rebuttal. As I'd suspected, it seemed Svyer had already been a good ambassador for the dramá, making her way into even Laura's good graces.

"Alright. Forget survival then. Just think about yourself. Are you *really* sure, Sarah? Really? This is just so rushed. You're thinking about becoming a queen. I mean an *actual* queen, not just holding some kind of mystical position in our family. Have you really thought about what that means?"

"Trust me," I said dryly. "I've been thinking about it, with a new aspect coming up seemingly every day."

This wasn't supposed to be about my decision to marry Ben. But then, I guess it ultimately was. After all, the easiest solution to my dread was to simply walk away from him—to refuse that kind of life. It was eight days too late for that kind of withdrawal, though. In fact, more. I had put myself on this path the moment I'd chosen to accept the role that the Tree of Ice had in store for me.

First, I had to convince Laura of that.

"And you're still going through with this?" Laura demanded.

I took another deep breath. "Yes."

"Why?"

I paused. My intuition quieted all my gut responses and prompted me to return her question with one of my own. I asked it gently, taking care not to sound defensive. "Why did you decide to marry Michael? And why don't you regret it, even now?"

Laura folded her arms and frowned at the floor for a long moment. Finally, she sighed and said quietly, "I married him because I loved him, obviously. I couldn't imagine life without him."

Her lips twitched humorlessly. "Typical twitterpated nonsense. Like most people after the honeymoon phase, I can imagine it now. And so will you, trust me."

I didn't know about that. Laura's cynicism seemed very *her*, but I didn't think I was doomed to the same fate. At the least, I knew if I asked Michael the same question about whether he thought he could live without Laura, I'd get a quite different answer. And Mom was prone to smiling lovingly at Dad and wondering out loud what she would do without him.

"Yet you said that you still don't regret it."

Laura looked at me and slowly nodded. "No, I don't. Because the one thing I can't ever regret is Tommie. And that means I can't regret staying with his father. I never got to have a father around. Not a good one, anyway; even the jerks didn't stick around. I always promised myself I would make sure things were different for my children. Michael, for all his drama, is a good man and a good father. That alone makes him worth keeping around."

She smiled crookedly. "And, I guess, following him across the galaxy."

"And putting up with his dangerous job?" I prompted quietly, reminding her of the reason for my call.

Laura sighed. "Don't get me wrong—it made me mad, sometimes. Why would he *choose* a job that might take him away from us? Didn't he care how we would be hurt if he didn't come back? And that only got worse after I had

Tommie. But deep down, I always knew that Michael was a protector—of us, of you all, of his community. That's simply the way he *was*. And he wouldn't be happy, or the guy I loved, if he wasn't doing that."

And Ben wouldn't be the man I loved if he abandoned his duty—to his people, his Tree, or me. But I already understood that part. Knowing he couldn't make any other choice and still be *Ben* didn't make it easier for me to bear.

"But how did you *cope*?" I asked, chest tight.

Laura studied me for several moments, the longest ones yet. I waited as patiently as I could, taking advantage of the time to try to loosen the knot in my stomach.

Laura finally looked away. "You...really aren't going to leave him. Are you? You really know something of how hard it's going to be, in all the ways, and you still aren't going to change your mind."

I swallowed. "No. I'm not. This is where I'm meant to be, Laura. And who I'm meant to be with." I knew that to my core. "That's why I'm asking you for ways to help me bear it."

She huffed quietly, flicking her eyes back to mine. "Well. You're probably going to need that kind of stubbornness to make it, anyway."

She sighed. "I don't have a magical formula for you, Sarah. What worked for me might not work for you. But for what it's worth...I worked out a lot. When other things are outside my control, it helps to feel capable and powerful in that way, at least. And now, training with him, using these powers..."

She held up a pointer finger and idly watched as she summoned frost over the tip. "...means I can help him directly."

I nodded. "That makes sense."

She had also reminded me that I had been neglecting my own training. Yet another thing to add to my to-do list for my precious night hours. But if it helped me collapse into bed and sleep soundly at the end of it all.... That alone might make the effort worth it.

Still, I said, "But there're times—like right now—when I can't fight alongside him. When I have to stay behind."

Laura grimaced. "Tough break. Well...the more religious spouses in my support group prayed—a lot. Seems like the kind of thing you might try. Have you?"

I blinked. That...hadn't occurred to me, honestly. It wasn't something I was in the habit of doing growing up. I'd seen Abuela and Mom praying at their respective shrines to *La Virgen de Guadalupe*, but I'd stopped as soon as Mom had let me. Even now, when I was the chief servant of a demi-deity, it hadn't occurred to me as simply a way to stay sane. If I had thought about it, I might have assumed that if the Tree knew what was going to happen anyway and had nothing to say to me to alter the outcome, then what was the point?

Laura must have seen something in my face, because she shrugged. "I can't believe *I'm* the one explaining this to you, but from what they said, it was like a kind of meditation for them. It centered them, comforted them. You could always try meditation, or breathing exercises, instead."

"That...makes sense to me," I said, with a bit of surprise. "I'll try it."

"As for me...I just tried not to think about it too much. Focusing on what you can't control is a sure-fire way to go insane—and drive your guy insane while he's with you. So, I just tried to let it go, not sweat the small stuff, and be grateful for each day I got."

She chuckled dryly. "Sounds rather hippy of me, now that I say it out loud like that. But it made more logical sense in my head."

I nodded absently, taking mental notes.

Laura grimaced. "That probably wasn't much help. I'll be honest, I really wasn't a model example of a serene, supportive spouse."

"No," I said sincerely. "That...helped. It really did. The suggestions and...even just the talking."

Laura nodded, eyes softening. "That was another thing, I guess: I talked to other people in my situation. It helped. And...I'm glad to have done you the same favor. I guess we have even more in common now than I thought."

I smiled thinly at her, feeling warmth at the same realization. "I guess...we do."

I wouldn't have thought it, before. This was by far the longest conversation we'd ever had, let alone one so frank and sensitive.

Laura frowned, opened her mouth, closed it, and let out a huff.

"What is it?" I asked quietly.

She met my eyes again, lips pressed thin. "Answer me honestly, Sarah. No rose-colored glasses, alright?"

I nodded.

She hesitated a moment. "Is Ben...good? Truly good. Will he be that kind of husband and father for you that Michael is for me?"

I blinked, then chuckled nervously. "Father?"

Laura rolled her eyes. "You're telling me you've thought of everything else *but* that?"

I tucked a lock of hair behind my ear. "I mean...vaguely, I guess. Yes. But...that's just so far out there."

"But it's still something you need to think about," Laura said sternly. "I know you, Sarah. You're going to want kids *someday*. So if you don't think he's—"

I held up a hand. Then I paused just long enough that hopefully she would believe I'd taken the rose-colored glasses off. "He is, Laura. He's good. And he will *be* good. For all those things."

I still didn't want to repeat the word *father*. The word, in connection with Ben, was filling me with a fluttering mix of warmth and nervousness—and quite a bit of the latter. Though not because I had any doubts about Ben, rather because I had doubts about myself. Because if he was a *father*, that made me a *mother*.

And that thought was still beyond bizarre.

Laura studied me closely, then finally nodded. "OK. Good."

My lips twitched. "Does that mean you finally believe me?"

Laura smiled thinly. "I finally believe you're absolutely convinced of it. And, who knows? Maybe that will be enough. That's what a marriage ultimately comes down to, after all: commitment."

I sighed and shook my head with a smile of my own. "I wish you could have had a chance to really get to know him."

Laura shrugged, her smile turning into a smirk. "Well, it seems like he's sticking around for a bit, at least. Probably long enough for me to corner him and suss him out myself."

I laughed at the image. "Be nice when you do. He may seem big and tough, but he's a softie at heart."

Laura's smirk deepened. "Like a certain brother of yours?"

"A lot like."

If only Michael could see all the two of them had in common—he might finally find it in him to forgive Ben. But for now, I was grateful that Laura seemed much closer to doing so herself.

That was a miracle I had not expected at all. If nothing else came of this conversation than that, well...it had all been worth it.

Chapter Thirty-Four

REALIZATION

Sarah

Laura could have given me yet another suggestion: be busy. And, without consciously trying, that was exactly what I did during the following days and nights while Ben was gone. Every one of them was even more packed than the first.

My seven or so daylight hours were taken up by Lord Kolwin, who took me around Palla to visit with his people. For example, one day, he brought me to what seemed like it must have been every single school class in Palla, the students' ages spanning all the way from toddlers to teens just a few years younger than me. Another half-day was with the guard, touring the hold's defenses and watching a synchronized flyover.

I wasn't sure what the unifying factor was in all these visits. Other than his hint on the first day, Lord Kolwin never explained himself. In fact, he hardly spoke to me directly, saving most of his few words for the people he brought me to. I could only assume, then, that he was showing me how I could serve his people. If that was the case, I chose to be grateful rather than resentful for his unsolicited instruction.

After all, I hadn't previously had much chance to interact with the common dramá, and though I was utterly exhausted by the end of every day, I found myself enjoying being among them. Each day I grew more confident in my ability to interact with them, and some of my nebulous fear of being their Queen eased at coming to know just who "they" were.

Even knowing they must be on their best behavior, I couldn't help but be comforted by the welcome, interest, and kindness that was often evident even through their Strongshield masks, especially in the younger or the lonely. A few dramá were unfriendly, some even cold, but those few didn't bother me as much as I had expected compared with the roaring fire of warmth that the others were building inside me. It felt good to be about the work of serving them—even the ones who didn't want my help.

Every night was a feast, which marked the turning point of my "day." If I had the time, I tried to take a power nap right before my attendants needed to prepare me, but when I didn't, Vadya taught me various tricks to keep myself awake, such as lifting my legs subtly off the floor to keep me alert or pressing my tongue to the roof of my mouth to stave off a yawn.

After I got back to the King's Wing, my time was more flexible but still full. I usually got a few minutes to breathe and call my family, and then my language tutor came in. After the first night, Vadya added dance instruction after that, saying something vague about how I would need the skill soon. That enigmatic statement left me with a kaleidoscope of anxious butterflies in my stomach, but the butterflies provided a lot of motivation while working with my instructor, and I counted the vigorous dances as resuming some sort of cardio practice.

Too late, I regretted never taking up Latin dancing with Mom's side of the family, who frequently tried to drag me into a salsa or bachata at family events, but I'd resisted, never thinking dance was my thing. Besides, how was I supposed to compete with gorgeous, graceful *Rachel*? No, I much preferred busying myself on the sidelines with making sure everyone else was having a good time.

Yet here I was, without any excuses, being forced to learn—and in public, too. Most of the dramá dances required groups and music to function, so the instruction took place in the central court, and anyone who was still awake and energetic was encouraged to join in. Word spread rapidly, and every night my dance class became a party that went on long after I slipped away.

Only then was I finally left to my own devices, and I used those precious couple hours to unwind and work on my magic as best as I could manage in the privacy of my study, before finally getting ready for sleep and collapsing into bed.

Ben and the hunters made it back to Palla just before sunset on the third day of the hunt, and even then, they only managed it because a local team took over their watch on their prey and the hunters pushed themselves hard to make it to a sungate in time. But, as Kor told it, Ben was determined to spend the night in Palla and, more important, his elites were too. In fact, it was Yvera who insisted they return to rotate their elites for rested ones.

Lord Kolwin and I were just finishing up with the last class visit of the day when someone brought me word from Kor that they were on their way. Having overheard, Lord Kolwin dismissed me without making it seem like that was what he was doing, and I gratefully escaped and hurried with my guards to the King's Wing landing to meet him.

From where we waited in the shadow of the landing arch, the sungate was behind us and further up the mountain, out of sight. Our only indication of their arrival was the moment draká began filling the sky as they shot out of the gate and began to circle the mountain.

And still Ben's pull remained thin. I knew custom dictated he would be among the last to come through, but the wait was agony. I shifted from foot to foot, both from impatience and from the discomfort of having been on my feet all day.

My custom-made everyday shoes—a set of black leather flats that seemed to match most anything my attendants put me in—were exceedingly comfortable (there must have been something like mushroom foam underneath the soft leather insole), but even their comfort had been put to the test the past couple of days of walking, standing, and dancing.

Elites began landing, shifting, and wandering inside, all of them looking tired but whole, and most of them smiling, calling out to friends, or walking with arms casually slung around each other, cheerful at the promise of good showers and rest. Some of them, especially the ones I had eaten dinner with, waved at or greeted me, and I waved and smiled back as best as I could. I was happy to see them back safe and sound, but I was glad that none of them stopped to speak with me. My social energies were spent, and all my remaining attention was fixed on the pull.

Then the moment I'd been waiting for came: the pull swelled like a dam had broken and the river behind it had surged free, flooding me with the force of it. I gasped, and Petra, one of the two guards who lingered with me even now that we were in the King's wing, looked at me in concern, but I just shook my head and kept my gaze fixed on the sky.

A second later, the golden dragon soared into view, sweeping across the valley and followed closely by a familiar violet on his right and an unfamiliar scarlet on his left. He roared, perhaps to announce his presence, or perhaps as a signal that all had made it through—I wasn't sure. Whatever the cause, the sound sent a pleasant chill down my spine, and my lips pulled into a smile so wide it hurt. A draká from the hunt team stretched up his or her neck and roared in reply, as did another draká somewhere else on the mountain.

Even though the King's landing was smaller than the others, Ben's team had cleared it promptly after each had landed, and no honor guard waited for a welcoming ceremony, so after only one pass over the valley to get into position, Ben was able to lead his wings in for a swift landing. I raised my hand and narrowed my eyes to slits against the gusts of wind that the three sets of wings produced—especially Ben's—but I refused to shut them entirely.

Which was good, otherwise I might have lost sight of Ben. He changed back so swiftly that he was a golden behemoth touching down in one moment, and a golden-haired human running toward me in the next.

Laughing, I ran to meet him halfway, and he pulled me up and into a bone-crushing hug. He didn't say a word other than my name, but he didn't need to. I clutched him with all my might in return.

Time, which had dragged on with terrible sluggishness for the past half hour, once again sped up, and seemed to go twice as quickly as normal the whole time Ben was there. We only seemed to have moments to catch up and breathe before attendants came for me to get me ready. I tried to persuade Ben to stay back from the feast, but he was insistent. Fortunately, Lord Kolwin canceled the evening entertainment, otherwise Ben might have collapsed onto the table and started snoring. As it was, I had to keep mentally prodding him to stay awake, and we left as soon as we could.

Not much later, Ben really did fall asleep on our couch while he was waiting for me to change, and I had to prod him awake. The exhaustion must have been getting to his head, because he let me lead him to the bed instead of his pallet, and once he collapsed again, he pulled me with him. He sighed contentedly as he held me to him, his eyes drifted closed again, and in moments, he was out cold.

I would have much preferred to stay there, but I still had hours left before my bedtime, and I still had things to do. Besides, when Ben had agreed to sleep in the same room as me, I had promised I would behave, and that included protecting him from his own tired-drunk choices. So, reluctantly, I slipped away, but before I left, I folded the rest of the top blanket over him as a covering and turned out the lights.

When I came back hours later, he had hardly moved, and I knew from his heavy breathing that he was still deeply under. Smiling, I crawled into the pallet, which he'd left there from before the hunt. Even with him not having used it for days, it still smelled of him, a scent which always brought to my mind sunbaked stone and desert shrubs. I snuggled into it contentedly and fell asleep to that pungent warmth.

I WAS REWARDED FOR my trickery by being startled awake once again by Ben, this time as he carried me back to the bed. Once he noticed I was awake, he said, "Sarah, care to explain why you were on the *floor*?"

"You needed the bed more," I mumbled sleepily as he gently settled me on the bed and pulled the blanket over me.

He sighed. "I guess that might have been true, seeing as I spent almost all the time we would have had together *sleeping*. I'm sorry. That wasn't what I planned."

"S'kay," I said, eyes drifting closed.

Before I could drift under again, he kissed my forehead. "Flame watch over you, Sarah," he whispered, and drew back with another sigh.

My eyes shot open again. "Wait, you're leaving? Now?"

"It's almost dawn," he said sadly, brushing my hair out of my face.

I bit my tongue to hold back my protest. Instead, I pushed myself up and hugged him.

"Not much longer now," he said, wrapping his arms around me tightly. "Just a day or two more. Then I'll be back for good, I promise."

Until the next time, I thought, trying to swallow the lump in my throat.

Instead, I teased, "You'd better. I haven't been wearing my feet out in dance practice for nothing."

I had avoided mentioning the lessons on our calls, wanting to keep it a surprise, but I'd just decided to spring it early.

Ben stilled, then chuckled. "Have you, now? Well, then, I guess that gives me something to look forward to."

He pulled away and leaned down to kiss me, his lips warm and languid, with a suppressed undercurrent of need. Just when the need started to break free, igniting a fire inside me, Ben abruptly broke it off, kissed my forehead again, and stood. He pushed me gently back down.

"Back to sleep with you. Hopefully more soundly now that you're where you belong."

"I slept just fine, I'll have you know," I said with a thin smile, though I let him pull the blanket over me again and hand me a pillow to hold on to.

"Right. You're just saying that so I won't feel guilty. Well, I'm telling you now that it's a vain effort. I can assure you that my mother's spirit will haunt me from across the Flame for the entire day for letting you sleep on the floor."

I laughed. "Say hi to your mom for me, then."

"Go to sleep, Sarah," Ben said, shaking his head in the dark.

I didn't need a light to know that his lips were pulled into a smile that said the three words he couldn't speak out loud.

TIME ONCE AGAIN SLOWED to a crawl, with that day dragging on the slowest of all.

It didn't help that today was *portrait* day. Lord Kolwin had used my time productively so far, in my opinion, but either he couldn't put off the renowned portrait painters of Palla any longer or my sitting had been scheduled for that day all along. Or, for all I knew, the portraits could have been Kor's doing, since apparently they were being sent across the Six Realms before the heartbinding so that those who couldn't attend or couldn't meet me on the grand tour would at least know what their future Queen looked like.

So, I was surrounded on most sides by artists, all sketching and painting in various styles and methods—the most practical being the one who was making a very detailed monochrome sketch of me on a tablet so that the image could be passed from archival to archival with a simple touch.

Multiple colors, the artist told me, simply weren't possible in that medium, since the stylus wrote in one's soulcolor alone. She was a Starkissed, so her sketch was in a vibrant blue, but she was an expert at making that one hue and the darkness of the stone surface work for her. The stylus was still sensitive to pressure, angle, and timing, so she could still coax variety out of her line work, or so she said. I couldn't see what she was working on most of the time, but I was still glad she was sitting front and center to me, since with her swift, fluid movements, she was the most interesting for me to watch.

Her method impressed me. Hers was the quickest and most basic, but it was the one that would be passed on the most broadly because of the ease of copying. Still, it took the regular amount of time to take the sketch to begin with, and I spent most of my time stewing about the inefficiency of portrait painting and trying to think of a better method. Any flattery or interest I might have felt at being a subject for so many experts was lost in the day's lethargy, my self-consciousness, and a growing restlessness the source of which I couldn't name. Not even the soothing music or occasional storytelling could pull me out of today's funk. It was a good thing they didn't need me to smile.

All I could think was that I wanted to be somewhere, anywhere but there, *doing* something.

I should have known better than to make that kind of wish.

At long last, the day came to an end. I had never been so glad for my attendants to drag me away, though with how done up I already was and how little I'd been allowed to disturb their previous work, they had little to do other than carefully getting me into the night's dress, touching up my makeup, and resettling my hair. Ben once again called to let me know he wouldn't be making it back, which wasn't a surprise to me but was still a disappointment. By the time I got to the feast, my mood had turned downright dour, and Lord Kolwin wisely didn't engage me in even the limited conversation he had before.

Midway through the courses, he stiffened abruptly, locking eyes with a Strongshield guard who entered from the side. They silently communicated for half a minute, while Kolwin grew still and pale and my heart pounded. I bit my tongue to keep myself from asking what the matter was. I knew that would simply be distracting. Still, I clenched the napkin in my lap into a ball and didn't eat a bite more the entire time.

And prayed. With astonishing fervor.

Please let Ben be alright. Please. Please.

Surely if it had been about Ben, someone would have spoken with me first, right? Or with Kor, who was sitting nearby. He was outwardly calm but was watching Kolwin out of the corner of his eye like a hawk.

Kolwin broke eye contact with the guard and slowly stood. Strongshield feasts were already subdued affairs, but silence like a wet blanket fell as soon as people caught sight of their standing lord.

"My friends," he said once he had their attention. "I regret to say that we must bring this meal to a close. Please return to your homes as quickly as you can and do not leave. Members of the guard, report to your commanding officers. I thank you."

He nodded deeply to them and then turned to me. Without saying a word, he pulled out my chair, and a couple of my elites made their way out of the confused, rising crowd and rushed to me.

Kolwin spoke to them quietly, his voice barely audible over the growing chaos. "Take the Queen and follow Captain Jasan."

He gestured to the guard he had spoken with. "He will lead you to the saferoom. Do *not* return to the King's Wing. We believe it is heading there."

"It?" I demanded out loud.

"Understood," Petra said, subtly putting a hand at my back. "Queen Sarah, please come with us. Now."

I went along, but only because I figured I would be more likely to get answers once we were out of view. As soon as we slipped into the side passage and the rest of my elites surrounded me, I demanded, "What's going on?"

"What do you think?" Kor said, coming to my side. His face was chilling, his eyes hard. "There's only one thing that could make Lord Kolwin act the way he is now."

Danger. But not coming for Ben. For *us*.

Palla was under attack—or soon would be. And there was only one thing I knew of that could threaten a dramá hold like this.

Rock wyrm.

I dug in my heels, nearly causing the elites behind to run into Kor and me. Kor, however, seemed unsurprised, and he just grabbed me by the elbow and dragged me along.

"Not now, Sarah. We are getting you to safety, and that is *final*."

"But, Kor—it's night—I need to help—"

"You *help* by getting to safety. As soon as possible."

"Kor—"

"No, Sarah, you don't get it," Kor said, eyes blazing with soulflare when I looked at him. "Wyrms hunt for our *hearts*. The more powerful the heart, the greater the draw. Even if this wyrm isn't consumed, even if your heart is of ice, you have the most powerful heart in this hold, and we can't risk that it will head straight for *you*."

"Oh," I breathed, eyes widening as I realized.

"Saferooms are contained in the very center of holds for a reason," Kor said grimly. "You'll be obscured by all the hearts around you, and even if it senses you, it will know that no matter which way it comes at you, it will have to go through all of us first."

I looked back. "Will Lord Kolwin go there, too, then?"

As a Tree's chosen, surely he had the most powerful heart next to mine?

Kor's only answer was to clench his jaw.

"Kor," I snapped.

"He will not. He's leading the defense of his people."

Of course. Always in the service of his people—even at the risk to his own life. Just as his Lady did before him.

My iceheart seemed to freeze for one moment. Then I stopped again, jerking my arm away from Kor's grip.

My voice was filled with icy determination. "You mean *my* people."

"Sarah—"

I drew myself up to my full height and raised my chin. "By my authority as the King's betrothed and the one he left in command in his stead, I *order* you to include me in the defense of Palla."

My elites and Kor all stared at me. Then Petra rolled her eyes and looked at Kor, who looked fit to burst. "Did you really expect anything less?"

"Gah!" Kor cried, throwing up his hands. He glared daggers at me, and silently, he said, *Sarah...you realize that if you do this, Ben is going to kill* both *of us, don't you? As soon as he hears Palla is under threat of wyrm incursion, with no way for him to get here, he is going to combust. And that is if he assumes you're ensconced in a saferoom. If he hears you've gotten yourself involved...you may find your orders countermanded faster than you can blink.*

Then let's get this over with quickly, I replied grimly.

Out loud, I said, "I will follow the commanding officer's lead. I will stand where they want me to stand and stay back from the main fighting if that is best. But I order you to make me of some use in the defense—beyond hiding me away. I *will* be of service to my people, and I *will not* use them as a shield."

Kor let out a wordless exclamation of frustration and heaved a breath. He put his head in his hands for a moment, muttering under his breath something that sounded suspiciously like my older sister's name.

I blinked, but before I could ask him about it, Kor lowered his hands and looked at Petra, eyes hard but resigned. "Run ahead and get our orders from Rightwing Yermi. Tell her that the Queen...insists."

RIGHTWING YERMI SHOWED NO sign of consternation at the sudden change of plans when we reached her as she and Lord Kolwin supervised the militarization of the barren dead-end corridor near the King's Wing that they had chosen as the point to lure the rock wyrm to. The hold's guard were moving in a disciplined flurry, setting up barricades, tracing magic wards in every color of the rainbow and in a dizzying array of patterns, and readying gem-powered machines that looked like ballistae. This degree of preparation made my iceheart pound even faster.

Just how deadly was this thing?

Yermi's Strongshield mask held firmly in place as she nodded in acknowledgement to me, even as her Lord glared at me with more emotion than I had ever seen in his eyes.

I met his gaze calmly. That was the thing about teaching someone to lead—you couldn't expect them to always do it when you thought it was convenient and in the way you thought was best. As Kor had just discovered to his own dismay.

"Well," Yermi said pragmatically. "We can almost guarantee it will come this way now."

"There's no hope of intercepting it, then?" Kor asked.

"No," Yermi answered. "We discovered it too late, and it is moving too quickly."

She gestured to the flame table in front of them. I'd seen its like once before, in the command room of the Temple of Flame during the Battle of the Solstice. Except now, the flames that flickered above the bed of coals showed not a battlefield but a grid that I surmised must have been a map of the hold, and an enormous worm of flame that was winding its way toward us.

"What happened to the warning net?" Kor demanded.

"Nothing," Lord Kolwin said stiffly, his eyes like ruby flints. He gestured to the worm's path and the small points of light around it. "It followed a path through the blind spots perfectly. Some of which not even we knew of."

My iceheart chilled further, but I spoke with surprising calm. "That means it's consumed. Isn't it?"

"Almost certainly," Yermi confirmed.

Sent and guided by the Devourer, timed for when the dramá were weak and I was strong—and Ben could not reach me.

And you still think it's a good idea to be here, Kor silently muttered to me.

The Devourer wanted me to hide like a coward, I countered.

It wanted to discredit me in the eyes of the people. It wanted to torture my soul with the aftermath, knowing how doubt and self-blame would fester deep inside as I wondered what I might have done to prevent it.

As I visited with the broken survivors and wondered how many more I might have saved.

Well, I wasn't going to have any of that. I was Sarah Lind, the White Queen of Ice, leader of the restored Moontouched clan and the Seventh Realm, and betrothed of the King of Flame. Whatever came, I would face it alongside the people of the Six Realms.

My people.

Knowing I had given them my all.

I didn't realize I'd entered lightform until I saw the reactions of the people around me. Other than Kor, Kolwin, and Yermi, the people closest to me stepped back in shock. Then people further away either sensed the change in the atmosphere or saw the light, because they began to turn and look. For a moment, everyone stopped and stared, no matter what they were doing or what position they were in. For that single moment, a hush, a stillness, fell over the frantic preparations as the defenders looked at me in awe.

Just like when I had shone for all our elites in the central station of Remik. Yet this time, I did not mind. This wasn't about me, after all. This was about them.

This was about giving my all to *them*.

I had once seen the old King in all his regal glory, just before the battle that would claim his life, and realized that there was a time for concealing one's power and majesty, as one might close the shutters of a lantern when it was not needed, and there was a time for throwing off any semblance of concealment and shining as brightly as a star.

I was a lantern, that was all. A vessel. Just as Eskala had said, I gathered the glory not for myself but so that I could share it. I held the power of the Tree of Ice inside me so that I could use it on behalf of the people She had asked me to serve.

They were not staring at me. They were staring at a star.

They were staring at hope.

"Well," Yermi said mildly. "That could be useful. What else can you do?"

Chapter Thirty-Five

INCURSION

Sarah

Mere minutes later, we were ready. As ready as we were going to be, anyway.

Every member of the guard and my elites that could be spared for this conflict were in position behind barricades, controlling the ballistae, or in reserve in the back with us. Everyone was once again still and silent, but this time, they were all looking the opposite direction: at the dead end of the corridor, where we were now near certain the wyrm would emerge.

They had increased the odds by sending a magical field at an outward angle from the two corners of the dead end that passed through the rock beyond; I could see from their representations on the flame table that the two fields formed the sides of a funnel to guide the wyrm in. The fields couldn't stop the wyrm entirely, otherwise we wouldn't be having this problem; but wyrms disliked going through them, and they were apparently dumb enough to follow the path of least resistance so long as that path was still in the direction of their prey.

And so it was, with the cluster of defenders, Lord Kolwin, Kor—who, as the Tolsyon heir, was more powerful than anyone besides me knew—and me. Particularly me, since, besides my Queen status, I was now radiating power like there was no tomorrow. Ever since I had entered lightform, that ribbon of fire on the flame table had made a beeline for our position on the map, and it had redoubled its already furious pace.

It wasn't even going near the "bumpers" we'd made as it chewed straight through the rock for me. We had even tested its fixation on me (since Kor couldn't resist a bit of experimentation) by having me walk from one side of the corridor to the other. The only variations in that flame-ribbon's path had come from when it followed those movements, even as small as they were in the scale of things.

I watched that ribbon as it approached the grid. I could hear it, now: a terrible grinding and crushing that went on and on, like a constant cave collapse. I could even feel it: a low tremor in the ground. And I could see the dust sliding down the walls, chips of rock coming loose, cobwebs waving.

All of that...coming for me.

I stood in a wide-legged stance. Someone had gone for my gun and my shield and brought them to me, and I held the gun in my right hand and wore the shield on my left, ready to activate either at a moment's notice. They had also brought me more practical clothing: a shirt, pants, and boots.

They were better than a dress, even though they still looked pitiful against the scale armor that everyone else, even Kor, was now wearing. But I had left my Moontouched armor back in my hold and there was no time to go for it now; I would fix that gross strategic error later. For now, what I had would be good enough for what they needed me to do.

My iceheart pulsed like it was trying to make its way out of my chest. If I had still sweated, I would have been covered in a cold sheath of moisture. I could only barely suppress a tremble. Still I held my ground, and still I shone like a beacon on a hill, luring it in.

Come on, I told it. *Come for me. Ignore all the others. Come to me.*

It was seconds away now.

A crack appeared in the dead-end wall.

The grinding sound echoed down to us like the demons of hell were banging at the gates.

And then the wall exploded into a gaping maw of convulsing rings of teeth.

My iceheart stopped, and I froze.

Good thing that, this time, my panic incited the correct response. At least for the second it took for a blood-curdling shriek to echo down the corridor.

I had only one thought as I stared down the face of death: *If I survive, Ben is going to* kill *me.*

The next few seconds were a blur of ballista bolts, and that maw barreling down on us as it squeezed its flesh to fit into the corridor.

It was slightly too big, which Yermi had said would slow it down, since it wouldn't quite be able to grasp the edges of the corridor to gnaw away at them, so if it wanted to still follow the path of least resistance, the most direct path to me, then it would have to squeeze. And that squeezing and inching forward bought the defenders precious seconds to shoot a couple bolts each and then run.

Within moments, the wyrm's maw was a porcupine of bolts, and it shrieked in deafening rage and thrust its head from side to side as much as it could in the confined space. Yet another advantage of the corridor: it didn't have room or momentum to body slam.

The maw convulsed, cracking and breaking the bolts free from the hard flesh of its mouth. I knew better than to hope those bolts had done serious damage from their hurried explanations to me; the flesh there was too tough, the nerve endings and blood vessels too few. We would be lucky if some of the poison on their tips entered its bloodstream and caused it enough pain to slow it down. That was why the defenders abandoned the ballistae the moment the wyrm came close.

Surprisingly, the barricades were a more effective weapon. They were angled like the teeth of road traps that popped the tires of cars that ran into them, and once the wyrm pushed itself into them, their sharp edges were pushed deep beneath the wyrm's armored scales by its own momentum and strength. When the wyrm hit the first few, it let out another ear-splitting bellow.

But all this only slowed it down by mere seconds, and it was less than twenty before Kor grabbed my arm and pulled me further down the corridor.

The movement snapped me out of my initial mind block of terror, and I remembered what my role was here: giving the defenders energy, keeping the wyrm focused on me, and *staying out of reach*.

Because anything that came within reach of that maw....

As if in demonstration, the wyrm rolled over the fire table where we had just been standing, crushing it beneath its mass and sending hissing coals spilling everywhere before even those disappeared a moment later.

The defenders had all retreated by this point and switched tactics to what my formerly video-game-obsessed brother, David, would have called "kiting." The ones in front aimed bows, crossbows, spears, and even fireballs at the open maw, all while carefully backing up to stay ahead of the wyrm.

The ones just behind maintained several mobile layers of shields between us and the wyrm; I assumed those shields wouldn't be enough to stop the wyrm entirely, especially since they were permeable from at least this side to let the projectiles through, but the shields protected us from the occasional rebounding projectile, splintering bit of wood, or even crumbling stone, since it seemed the wyrm was straining the integrity of the corridor.

Further evidence that the corridor might not exist after this incursion came with the mighty cracking sounds that had no visible source but appeared to originate from beyond and behind the wyrm.

Lord Kolwin, Kor, and I stayed just behind the shielders—the tempting morsels that mustn't be kept *too* far from the wyrm, lest it swerve off and decide to attack the hold from a different angle.

Kolwin held a sword in one hand, scarlet eyes blazing with soulflare; if I hadn't gotten used to the color by now, I might have found the sight more than a little disturbing. Even as busy as she was shouting out commands and keeping track of everyone, Yermi often spared her Lord a glance, making me think she was worried he might decide to charge at any moment.

Though Kor didn't carry a weapon or a shield, he exuded a buildup of magic to my sixth sense like waves of heat off asphalt in summer, and his jaw clenched.

He glanced at me, eyes grim. "Well? Can you get a shard far enough in?"

Oh, right. My other job.

I raised my gun, taking tremendous care that my shot would not hit any of the people in front of me, and fired.

With excruciating focus, I directed the path of the ice shard straight into the mouth of the wyrm and down, down its throat, then stabbed it straight into the much softer flesh that waited there, embedding it deep within. Then, with the shard as my anchor, I flared out my magic to freeze all its flesh around the shard.

It was a technique I had used to bring down a bear the likes of which would have put the polar bears of earth to shame—with just one shot. But that shot had gone into its brain.

The wyrm bellowed and gnashed its many rows of teeth, and it put on a slight burst of speed, but it otherwise seemed unharmed.

"I hit it. And froze what I could. Did that do anything?" I asked tightly.

"Not what we were hoping for, at least," Kor said grimly. "Keep shooting, though. It's all any of us can do until we get lucky."

Meaning, until we hit its brain or several of its hearts. That was the real goal—the only way to stop the wyrm in its tracks. That's what all the ranged attackers were trying to do: to get shots in as far as they could beyond those many, many circular layers of teeth and deep within the much narrower cavity beyond.

I raised my gun again and fired it whenever I thought it was safe. With my strong magical connection between me and the shards, I could feel and guide them with far more surety than the others could with their various projectiles, and within a few minutes I had peppered the inside of the wyrm's throat with shards and frozen flesh. Targeting grew easier for me with each one as I felt my network of awareness grow, as if each one provided guiding lights in the dark.

Then, after icing the flesh around one embedded shot, I felt a difference. A greater heat, a spattering of liquid that began melting my shard and thawing the flesh much more quickly than normal. The wyrm bellowed furiously, solidifying my hope.

"Kor," I gasped, grabbing for him blindly with my left hand. I closed my eyes and focused with all my might on my shard. "I think...I think I scraped a heart."

Hot liquid of some kind was seeping around the shard, spilling forth into the wyrm's throat but melting the shard in the process.

"Shoot more there!" Kor urged. "Quickly, now!"

I raised the gun and shot three shards in quick succession, opening my eyes only long enough to make certain they went above the heads of the defenders and into the wyrm's mouth. As soon as they were out of sight, I closed my eyes and guided them in, plunging them into the flesh around the shard that was almost gone.

The wyrm *roared*. It thrashed in place, for the first time stopping entirely, if only for a single moment. Someone let out a whoop.

Then the wyrm closed its mouth.

"No!" Kolwin snarled.

The wyrm wriggled forward once again, but this time, its roughly cone-shaped chitinous front remained shut up.

"What's it doing?" I asked Kor frantically.

Kor groaned. "It feels threatened enough now that it's clammed up. It won't open unless...it knows it's going to get something for it."

Which meant people were going to have to get close. Close enough to....

Kor's grim explanation from before all this began echoed in my mind—how often it took someone going *inside* it to end it. And how that someone almost always died, even if their body was swiftly recovered. Even if someone somehow got past all those teeth in any state to do damage, the mucus lining of the wyrm's throat was acidic poison.

Kolwin began striding forward purposefully, heedless of his rightwing's exclamation. He shoved away the one guard who made a grab for him with enough force to send the person stumbling back. No one else dared hinder the Strongshield Lord who was determined that no one else make the ultimate sacrifice that day but him.

After all, the wyrm would no doubt open for him.

I clenched my jaw.

Oh, no you don't.

There was no way in hell I was going to let *another* Strongshield Noble die on my watch.

I could have frozen him. I felt the power and the knowledge inside me, building in my pulsing iceheart. If I could freeze *Michael* into immobility, who shared my power over ice, then I could stop Kolwin without doing him harm if I was careful.

But then what? *Someone* was going to have to make the wyrm expose itself again if we were going to end this. Was I going to allow someone else to throw themselves away?

No.

It would have to be me.

Especially since I was the one who had the greatest odds of survival.

I only had seconds to decide and then plan. Kolwin was pushing through the shields. The wyrm was turning its head down toward him....

I closed my eyes and gave my all into my lightform, becoming more than just a brightly glowing human...becoming something not human at all. My wings unfurled from my back, and I rose off the ground, as if gravity no longer tethered me to the floor.

"Sarah," Kor began in alarm, grabbing what remained of my corporal arm.

Without opening my eyes, lest I lose my focus on the three remaining shards inside the wyrm, I told Kor silently, *If this doesn't work...tell Ben I'm sorry.*

"NO—"

Kor's shout abruptly cut off as I surged into darkness, aiming for the area inside the wyrm where the last traces of my crystal shards lingered, the area I knew had at least one heart.

Then I burst through the last of my barriers, my first form flowed into the next, and I became pure *light*.

Light so brilliant and powerful, it burned.

I HELD STARFORM FOR as long as I could, with no way of knowing how long that was and only able to hope it was enough. I had turned up my radiation higher than ever before, high enough that my instincts told me my light could do damage, especially to flesh and organs so tender and exposed as the wyrm's were with me deep inside it. Yet without any of the five senses—no sight, sound, touch, taste, or smell—and only the vaguest sense of self, time became a slippery thing, as I knew from my practice sessions.

Then, before letting the form go, I surged back the way I'd come, following the same path, which I could feel still in the air with the only sense that remained to me: magic. A familiar source of power lay at the end of the trail, a friendly sapphire beacon to guide me home.

I materialized back into being and slammed into Kor, sending him flying backward. Fortunately, several people were just behind him and caught our fall. Also fortunately, I'd flowed back into human form as I emerged, so the only thing that hit Kor was my normal self—not the energy equivalent of a battering ram.

Unfortunately, I was utterly spent, and if Kor hadn't reflexively thrown his arms around me, even before the others pushed him fully back up, I might have slid off him and tumbled to the floor.

"Sarah," Kor gasped, half in relief, half in rage.

"Izzit dead?" I slurred, barely able to make my tongue function. My eyes slid closed, unable to stay open.

Please, please let it be dead.

Kor huffed as he pulled me up and into his arms. "It's dead, you torched fool. It's been still for over five dek. We've been trying to pry its mouth open to recover your hellfrosted remains."

I meant to say *Oh, good*, but it came out sounding more like, "Uhgud."

Then true oblivion claimed me.

Chapter Thirty-Six

AFTER

Koriben

THE MOMENT MY CLAWS hit the landing, I started changing back, and only seconds later, I was charging at Kor, who wearily awaited me near the arch into the King's Wing.

"Where is she?" I demanded. I could have asked him silently, but I needed to use my voice. Even if I had to use agonizing control to modulate the tone and volume, I needed *some* physical release for the tightly tangled bundle of energy and pain inside me.

"In your room, still sleeping," Kor said hoarsely, turning to stride with me through the arch. Judging from his bearing, voice, and rumpled appearance, he might have never gone to bed himself.

I felt some petty satisfaction from that. I hadn't gotten much sleep either, not after I was woken to be informed that Palla was facing a rock wyrm incursion.

And realized there was absolutely nothing I could do about it. Nothing I could have done to prevent the worst sort of consumed attack possible, the one that my people had nightmares over and burned leaves in prayer that it would never happen to their hold, never in their lifetime. Nothing to spare them the kind of bloodbath that could occur if the incursion wasn't carefully controlled, and even then....

Nothing I could have done to protect Sarah.

Kor could have, however. And far from getting her to safety, he had *let Sarah help*. He had let her....

He was lucky I wasn't strangling him right now. If she had been hurt.... Or....

Kor, however, had some practice in dealing with me in my near-berserk state. "And before you ask, *yes*, we checked on her, just before you arrived. I even sent Fenra in to check her vitals again. All is well. She is perfectly safe and whole. She is just sleeping it all off."

I let out a breath, getting a firmer grip on myself. "I still want to see her first."

"Understood."

I scowled at him sidelong. "I'm still thinking about killing you."

"And I'm thinking about letting you," Kor said grimly, pressing a hand to his forehead and closing his eyes for a moment. "You'd be doing me a favor by saving me from this headache that feels like it's splitting my skull in two."

I grunted. He'd known just what to say to make me keep him alive.

Kor lowered his hand and spoke quietly. "Truly, Ben...I'm sorry."

My remaining bit of sense that was trying desperately to keep the rest of me in line made me hold my tongue, since it knew that whatever I said now, I would regret when my blood finally cooled.

Kor continued. "She gave an order."

I snapped. At least I mitigated the damage by using my inner voice. *You could have called me to countermand it.*

As if starting a fight between our Royals was the wisest choice in that moment, Kor retorted. *And you* know *what Sarah would have done if you'd made us use force with her. With her short-surging ability, she would have gotten away from us in a blink and gone looking for the rock wyrm herself. At least by giving in once I saw she was that determined, we could keep her with us, as safe as we could.*

I glared at him. I could feel my eyes soulflaring by now. *And* you *should have known exactly what Sarah would have done when the wyrm closed up.*

She had.... Flame, I couldn't even think it, even now. Even knowing she was fine, even seeing her star in my mind's eye for myself, coming closer with each step I took.

Sacrifice was so often necessary to end a rock wyrm incursion that it was almost ingrained in us now. Even without the real historical tally, there were too many ballads and epics and books with heroes who did just that. If fear of an incursion was now ingrained in our psyche, then so was our resignation to the need for an offering to deliver us.

That's what we called them: *yven'roka*.

Blood offerings.

Sarah...had made herself a *yven'roka*.

She's alive, I chanted to myself, returning my focus to her star. *Alive, alive, alive.*

Yet no one lived after making themselves a blood offering. No one. The teeth, the acid, the internal collapse when the wyrm died.... We were lucky if we ever found remains.

She's alive!

Kor hesitated, then lowered his head and shoulders for a moment in defeat. *Yes. I should have. In that, I failed you both. You trusted me to keep her safe in your absence...and I failed.*

Kor admitted he was wrong so seldom that I couldn't continue to rail at him now. It would have been like continuing to strike at an opponent in a duel after they had surrendered. There was no satisfaction or honor, let alone humanity, in it.

Besides, we had stopped in front of Sarah's bedroom door. I needed my conscience clean and my temper cooled if I was going to enter.

I looked at Kor for a moment, jaw clenched.

"She's alive," I said in a low voice, still mindful of the ears around us but needing to speak those words out loud.

That was the closest I would come to accepting his apology.

Kor smiled thinly. "Sure you still don't want to kill me? I bet you'd make it cleaner than Rachel will."

I let out a hard laugh of surprise. I had almost forgotten about Kor's latest interest. "Oh, no. I think I'll leave you to her mercy."

This ought to be good. I felt lighter than I should have at the thought of Kor getting chewed out by that deathflower. What I would have given to watch that happen.

Kor sighed. "You're heartless."

"You're the one who decided to court *Rachel Lind*. I can't be held responsible for *that*."

"True," my leftwing said morosely. "At least she can't touch me right now."

"Yet," I said cheerfully. "If her behavior toward me is any indication, she seems like the type to hold grudges."

And exact calculated revenge. A good match for Kor, actually....

I shook my head, dispelling the thought. Surely I wasn't bearing Kor that much ill will, right?

Kor winced, as if imagining that revenge. Then he flapped his hand and began walking away. "Go on, Ben. Go see your betrothed's wellbeing for yourself."

I put my hand on the door, feeling it unlock for me, but hesitated. Then, sighing, I turned and called to my leftwing. "Kor?"

He turned back, raising an eyebrow.

I sighed again, gesturing with my head. "Go see a healer about that headache. And then get some rest. I can handle things for a few deken."

A slight smile touched Kor's lips, and he shook his head at me.

"What?"

"Nothing," Kor said out loud.

But as he turned away, he said silently, *There's a reason* you're *the one meant to be King, Ben.*

I blinked and watched him go for a moment, wondering where in the hell-winds that had come from. Kor never complimented me. Ever. And not once, over the course of his six years as my leftwing, did he ever express confidence in my ability to lead the Six Realms. In fact, he had frequently despaired out loud at my many inadequacies and acted as if he were the only thing standing between me and our utter ruin.

Yet he'd spoken just now as if he were repeating some well-established truth between us. It was baffling.

After a moment, I shrugged, let out a breath, and quietly pushed my way into the dark bedroom. I had better things to do than try to figure out the labyrinth that was Kor's mind.

I held the door to make certain it swung shut as silently as possible and felt the vibration of its locking mechanism before I let go. I stood in the darkness, letting my eyes adjust to the faintest traces of light. A better perception of the room came from my sense of smell and heat, and those both highlighted Sarah curled up in the middle of the bed at the far end of the room. Clearly she had been put there, since she preferred to sleep on the edge, and no one had given her a pillow to hold.

I sighed and carefully made my way to her bedside, inhaling her cool, clear scent with every breath. It was inordinately soothing, as if cleansing my lungs from a choking disease with every inhale. I felt tension leave my body with each step.

Sarah was alive, she was resting, she was well.

Still, once I reached her bedside, I battled with myself against touching her to be *sure*. To pour my power into her and know it in the most thorough way possible, then erase any last bruise or scar they might have missed—even though I knew I would find nothing. Sarah would have been given the best care before being brought here to rest.

Even if she wasn't the Queen of Ice, the Moondaughter, and my betrothed, now she was *yven'roka*, and *yven'roka* were honored beyond measure. Somehow I didn't think her miraculous survival would lessen the reverence people, especially the Strongshield, would inevitably hold for her—at least for a while. I inwardly laughed, thinking of the horror in Sarah's eyes once someone explained to her the veneration she had brought on herself. Perhaps if she had fully understood the social consequences of her choice, she wouldn't have made it.

My flameheart sank, all humor dying. No, she would have made the sacrifice even then. She was always my *sera*.

Which meant I shouldn't risk disturbing her. I had come the very moment I could, surging ahead of the hunt party to the sungate and then flying down to the King's landing, so it was only just after dawn here—in the middle of her sleep cycle after an exhausting night.

As I was standing there debating, Sarah stirred.

"Ben?" she mumbled, turning her head.

I let out a breath and sat down. "I'm here."

She relaxed, and I gently found and took her hand, threading my fingers through hers.

"I'm sorry," I murmured. "I didn't mean to wake you."

But I still took full advantage of both the contact and her wakefulness to send my power down her arm and into the rest of her body.

"Y'fine," she said, turning her head back to the pillow. "S'good you're back."

She stiffened abruptly, inhaling. She pushed herself up. "Oh, gosh. You're back. And you...."

Her shoulders hunched and head bowed. "You, er...must have heard about ...."

"Sarah, I'm the King," I said quietly. "They woke me to tell me."

Of course, by then, the wyrm had almost broken through and Sarah was already involved, so my immediate questions and demands concerning her safety came too late to extract her from the unfolding situation.

It had all been over for them in less than a deken, from start to finish. And each moment of my half-deken awareness of it had been agony.

She winced.

"I'm sorry," she said quietly, still looking down.

I lifted her chin, more for the contact than because I expected her to meet my eyes in the darkness. I tried to make my voice light but failed. "Enough to promise not to do that again?"

"No," she said heavily. "They're my people too, Ben."

I slowly lowered my hand. "I know."

She was a Queen, heart and soul. To all of us.

What would we do if we lost her?

I pulled her into me, wrapping her tightly in my arms, and buried my face in her hair, in her scent.

"I wasn't being suicidal, honest," she said earnestly. "I really thought I had a chance to get in and out without...."

"A chance," I repeated thickly.

"More than Lord Kolwin did."

I stiffened. I had already heard that the Strongshield Lord had been going for the wyrm before Sarah intervened, but I didn't like hearing from her that had been a deciding factor.

Sarah sighed. "That's not what I meant, Ben. That idiot was just going to throw his life away. I couldn't let him do that to his clan. Not again. They don't even have an Heir right now."

I forced myself to relax. More than just her reasoning, it soothed my feelings more than it should have to hear Sarah call Kolwin an idiot—and in Drona, too.

Our insults just sounded so much more forceful in her voice. And in this case, more satisfying.

I refocused. "Be that as it may, can you imagine how I felt when I heard you had offered yourself to a wyrm?"

My flameheart had gone out for the second it took for Yvera to slap me and say Sarah survived, and for me to come to my senses and see her star still glowing in my mind, half a world away. Only my duty to remain with my foster sister and team at the shelter until at least dawn had kept me from attempting to surge across the universe straight to her for the first time, and that duty had been a tenuous anchor at best.

Sarah cringed against me. "Yes," she said in a small voice.

But some of the pain still lingered, both from yesterday and from the much more distant past, so my voice was sharper than it should have been. "I'm not sure you can. Sarah, one of the blackest days of my life was the one incursion I've lived through. It was...it was not like what you experienced. It wasn't controlled, they didn't know until it broke through, they weren't prepared. Nearly fifty died before we finally ended it, and it took the life of the hold's captain to do it. Yvera still has scars...."

So many scars. And yet, she had refused to let the healers remove them all. They were her tribute to the captain who had saved her life...and, I think, a reminder to everyone that not even a wyrm had managed to kill her.

"Scars?" Sarah said faintly, sounding slightly nauseated. "How...."

A fair question, since Sarah would know by now that getting close enough for a wyrm to *scar* someone usually meant death.

I answered in a detached tone. "She was in its mouth when it finally died. She was torn to ribbons and bleeding out. I thought I'd lost her too, until we pried the mouth open and found her there."

Sobbing and still stabbing the wyrm's mouth, over and over. I'd had to crawl inside to coax her out, since she wouldn't believe it was dead.

"Ben...." Sarah said in horror, curling further against me. "I...."

I took a deep, steadying breath. Still, my voice shook when I spoke. "I...didn't mean to snap at you. But I owed you an explanation. Because even though I understand in my head why you did what you did, I'm still not...I'm going to need time, Sarah. I can't just get over this in a day. Because what you just went through was my hell, and what you just did is too much like how I nearly lost the closest thing I have to a sister."

"I see," she whispered. "Again...I'm sorry."

"I know," I said, trying to swallow the lump in my throat. I held her more tightly. "But please, for the love of the Flame, can you *not* risk your life for just a few days? I don't know how much more of this I can take."

"I'll try."

"No, I'm sorry, I need you to promise me. Give me just three days of peace, please. Three days of knowing you'll do what is safe, stay where it's safe, no matter what happens."

She hesitated.

I couldn't help it. I begged, my voice breaking. "Just three days. Please."

Surely the Trees could give us that much time to recover.

Please, give us that much.

Sarah slowly let out a breath. "Three days. I promise."

I sagged with relief. "Thank you."

Thank you.

I GAVE MYSELF A few more dek with Sarah, just until she settled back down and went back to sleep. Once she was deep enough under that I thought I could move without disturbing her, I forced myself to stand and leave the room, shutting the door quietly behind me.

I had work to do, starting with facing a dead rock wyrm—even though I would rather have done almost anything else. Even a Moonfair pageant sounded mildly tempting at this point.

An elite guided me to the scene. I'd already been told that the wyrm had emerged near the King's Wing, but the moment the guard opened the inset wicket gate for us—with the larger set kept shut as part of a heightened level of security—I caught a whiff of a wyrm's familiar stench, and I had to fight the impulse to retch as all the horror of Ilyam came flooding back. Again. It had been bad last night, as I paced to wait for the outcome, and after as I processed, but I'd managed to get a handle on it by dawn. Now my grip was slipping again.

Aside from the memories, the mere dek it took to walk from the King's gate to the corridor made my blood boil and my jaw clench. It was just another confirmation that this attack had been aimed at Sarah—to harm her mentally if not threaten her physically.

As much as I loathed to admit it, Sarah had probably done the best thing she could have for her own psychological wellbeing and public image. Far from being wracked with guilt and self-doubt, she could now rest knowing she had slain the Devourer's monster herself and, miraculously, not one life was lost. Whatever trauma might linger, we could help her work through.

And the Strongshield, far from being shaken by such a bold and direct attack on their capital, had proven themselves capable of its defense once again and found their future Queen to be a hero. Her survival would buoy their spirits even more: *this* time, there was no lingering tragedy, no cause to mourn. She lived on, and so would their hope for the future of the Realms. For the dramá, this had been an unalloyed triumph—all thanks to her.

The Devourer was always underestimating Sarah. I wished I could hope that trend would continue...but I knew from the Tree's warning to me that it would not. Not for much longer.

Flame, why was this tour taking so long? The Tree had given me a command, and Sarah's life depended on me fulfilling it. How it did, I didn't know, but I knew better than to doubt the Tree's word.

I had to carefully control my breathing as we came around the bend of the corridor and the wyrm came into view. I reminded myself of all the reasons that this time was different, but my body was still on the cusp of trembling. Not even a mindhealer's help, many talks with Avva, and a couple years had entirely healed me from Ilyam.

It's dead, Sarah's alive, and so is everyone else, I chanted to myself.

I forced myself to compartmentalize, to eye the wyrm as we approached as I would any other consumed beast and read the situation for myself.

"How far did it make it in?" I asked, my voice emotionless.

"Less than half an eld," Yeran, the elite accompanying me, answered. By coincidence, he was Strongshield himself, but he had been there last night as one of the elites that had volunteered to join Sarah's new guard.

"Not far," I said, nodding.

And they had managed to keep it in the corridor, too. Good. That was usually best. It meant the defenders had only one way to stop the wyrm—they had to get enough hits to enough vital organs far down its throat—but the close quarters also hampered the wyrm. It could only go forward; if it tried to dive back into the rock, it would expose a side for us to attempt to cut through before it could reemerge; and finally, it couldn't use its formidable mass as a weapon or swing around to attack from any angle.

In the Ilyam incursion, the wyrm had emerged, previously undetected, in a central court. That was one of the primary reasons so many died that day: the wyrm grabbed civilians right and left, with full freedom of movement, before they cleared the area and the guard swept in. Yvera and I came in dek after that, having rushed across the Realms with what handful of elites we could gather to answer their call for help. By then, blood and gore were everywhere.

I blinked, forcing myself back into the present with a savage mental jerk. I made myself look and see for myself that no bodies lay around, and even more telling, no scents of dramá blood or other bodily liquids hung in the air, which would have lingered long after the bodies had been removed.

I mentally measured the corridor and eyed the wyrm. It was already sagging, but I could picture what it had been like alive.

"The corridor was just the right size, wasn't it?" I asked as we slowed to a halt in front of the wyrm's protruding, beak-like mouth, which had been pried and permanently jacked open. Several guards and a zoologist were there, the former standing by to keep away unauthorized persons (mischievous children high on that list), the latter doing tests.

"Yes," Yeran said with a nod. "Just large enough that it chose to enter, but small enough to slow it down and keep it controlled."

"It was a good choice. But I'm almost surprised it went for it."

Wyrms were dumb, but not always *that* dumb, and considering this was most likely a consumed wyrm, the Devourer might have tried to give it a bit more direction. Then again, as far as we could tell, even the Devourer had only limited success controlling the creatures. Perhaps the lack of intelligence and high predatory drive made their overruling the Devourer's directives easier.

"Rightwing Yermi had doubts and was considering several access points, but when the Queen sent word she was coming, the rightwing committed most of her resources to this one. And she was right: the wyrm was already angling for Lord Kolwin, but once Queen Sarah arrived, it never deviated."

Of course it didn't, I thought darkly, bile rising again.

I crouched to get a different angle as I peered inside the mouth...and frowned. There didn't seem to be as much damage as I had been expecting. "It clammed up after less than half of an eld?"

"Queen Sarah's 'gun' was quite effective. She usually got past the innermost dental ring and, toward the end, hit at least one heart. That was when it closed."

I stood slowly. I phrased my next question carefully, mindful of what clan Yeran and the two nearby guards belonged to. I didn't want them to interpret my inquiry as a critique of their Lord.

Even though that's what it was.

"What options was Rightwing Yermi considering at that moment?"

There *were* other options besides sacrifice. They could have sent Sarah and Kolwin away, which might have baited the wyrm into diving and exposing a side. They could have continued to lure the wyrm forward; even closed up, with Sarah and Kolwin still within reach, it would have probably followed, and they could have gotten it to a more open area and exposed a side that way, or eventually baited it into opening again without immediate gratification in sight. Or they could have turned the full force of their firepower to trying to crack it open.

All those options weren't ideal. They all came with a loss of control, an introduction of unpredictability, and a greater risk of loss of life. But they were options.

"I did not give Rightwing Yermi a chance to execute another option."

I turned, hardening. I had been so distracted, I hadn't noticed Lord Kolwin himself coming up behind me. Either he had come to survey the scene again himself, or he had heard that I had arrived and was coming to meet me. A debriefing between us *was* inevitably on the docket for the morning, so perhaps I should be glad he showed up and allowed me to multitask.

But right now, he wasn't my favorite person in the Six Realms.

He met my hard gaze with his usual unreadable mask. Just looking at him, you would never have known that he fought in a wyrm incursion just last night. He was clean, his hair was perfectly brushed and braided, and he was back in his formal scarlet robes. Only a hint of weariness in his posture, of shadows beneath his eyes, suggested that perhaps he might not have gotten much more sleep than I had.

"Why?" I said coldly, folding my arms. I wasn't surprised that he so calmly and immediately took responsibility for the way things had gone last night, but I *was* even angrier with him for it.

Sarah had nearly died last night because he had forced her hand, and even now, he couldn't break that torched mask and show some shame and self-doubt.

I sensed the Strongshield guards stiffen at my tone. Yeran, next to me, remained still and unreadable. I sympathized with his position, caught as he was between two loyalties. Three, if you counted his latest allegiance to Sarah.

I was trying hard to not make this a fight, and I was reasonably sure of my control right now, but they all didn't know that. Golden Royals were notoriously unpredictable when it came to those who had harmed or endangered their loved ones, and I was young, known to be a bit hotheaded, and already had one berserk episode blackening my record. Not to mention a month of cold-hearted behavior that I would spend a long time making up for.

Kolwin's gaze finally dropped from mine. "Because I thought it was my duty to protect my people...and my Queen."

A careful choice of words. Not "the Queen of Ice" or "the Queen." Sarah technically wasn't *his* Queen yet. And yet that was what he had called her.

Whether or not he actually felt that way—which I highly doubted—it was a gesture of deference between us. Here, finally, with his averted gaze and acknowledgement of Sarah's future status, was the closest thing to an apology that I was going to get from the Strongshield Lord.

Or so I thought.

Yet, after only a pause, Kolwin lifted his eyes, which had tightened, and said in a quiet voice, "I did not expect her to offer herself in my place. Or I would never have made that mistake."

I was momentarily stunned. That was an apology, out there in the open, with witnesses. And torch it...I believed him. My gut said that this wasn't posturing; this wasn't just choosing the right words to soothe tensions with his King. I believed he was being real with me.

He truly *hadn't* anticipated the sequence of events that his determination to sacrifice himself would have triggered.

I let out an audible breath and unfolded my arms. The other Strongshield around us visibly relaxed. "Come with me. I've seen what I need to see, so let's take this discussion somewhere else."

"Then may my people begin removing the wyrm?" Kolwin asked, his cool mask sliding firmly into place again.

They had left it intact for me to examine, which had been another gesture of deference. Under normal circumstances, if I'd only heard about the incursion from Crownhold and the Crown hadn't been involved, I wouldn't have expected it. I would still have gotten there as soon as possible, but in that case, my presence would have only been to show my support as King and offer assistance in the recovery efforts.

The cleanup would take so long that every moment counted. By the end, not even preservative spells would keep this corridor from stinking to the frozen wastes of hell, and the corpse might lure in other wyrms besides. No doubt, with the sun up, people were already hard at work accessing and securing the tunnel from the other end. After completing their assessments, they would begin the demanding work of either collapsing or filling it in to remove that vulnerability as soon as possible, ideally before the end of the day.

"Of course," I said, waving a hand. "Thank you for leaving it for me, but please begin."

Kolwin nodded to one guard. "Tell my wings that they may proceed."

Both would be involved: the leftwing to oversee logistics, the rightwing over security. This wyrm would keep Palla busy for days to come.

"Yes, my Lord," the guard said, nodding.

I turned, and Kolwin followed me, walking at my side. Yeran followed behind at a respectful distance—far enough to allow us to speak without him hearing if we did so quietly but close enough to interfere if necessary. Or protect us from another threat, of course.

Regardless of the relative privacy, I expected Kolwin to retain his stony silence the entire way to my study, so I almost started when he spoke. And it was in a burst, too—muted, but still forceful, as if he couldn't contain the question any longer.

"Why did she do it?"

I glanced at him. With no one ahead of us and his back to those behind, Kolwin's mask had slipped again, even more so this time. A lost look had entered his eyes. For the first time, he looked younger than me, and perhaps even more vulnerable. As if his rigid exterior had only been a brittle crust this whole time.

I forced my expression to be blank and my tone neutral. Although I couldn't help a bit of a bite with my word choice. Besides, maybe he needed a bit of a metaphorical slap to knock himself out of whatever he had going on in his head. *I* usually did.

"Because she thought you could serve your people better alive and whole than as a corpse being slowly disintegrated in a wyrm's collapsed intestines."

Lord Kolwin glared at me. I guessed it was probably more for my crudeness than a sign of disagreement, but just in case, I thought I'd hammer in the point. Though I made my voice gentler.

"There has been enough death and sacrifice, don't you think? Sometimes the greater duty is to live on. As torched hard as that can be. Trust me, I know something of how hard that is. But it's true."

Kolwin looked away, jaw working.

My flameheart softened more than I thought it could toward this cold peer of mine. Perhaps we had more in common than I had realized.

Of course we did. A fool should have been able to see that. I, of all people, should have seen how close he was to the breaking point.

Yet he had hidden it so much better than I had.

"Lady Maya's sacrifice was not your fault," I said quietly. "You have nothing to atone for, you have nothing to prove. The Tree chose you to lead your people now, Kolwin. Have some faith in Her. And in yourself. You're strong enough to bear this. And you're good enough to lead them."

Kolwin was silent for a few long moments. When he spoke, his voice was almost inaudible. "Easier to say than to believe."

I sighed. "I know. Trust me, I *know*."

Chapter Thirty-Seven

ROSIN

Sarah

I COLLAPSED FACE FIRST onto the largest couch in my latest bedroom, this one in the opulent Starkissed capital of Rosin. It was only partway through my "day," and it had already been a long one.

I groaned into the cushion, then turned my head to speak. "I hate moving. Did I ever tell you how much I hate moving?"

"At least once," Ben chuckled, running a comforting hand down my back. At least, I was fairly sure he meant the touch to be comforting. I had to hold still to hide the warm tingles that it evoked.

Partly to distract me, partly to distract him, I said, "At least I don't have to do most of the packing and unpacking myself."

In fact, the packing had begun even before I'd woken up from my starform-induced exhaustion, and no sooner did I relinquish the bedroom than attendants swept in to continue their work in there. I was a bit startled at how abruptly we were leaving, but Vadya told me that Ben wanted to be gone as soon as may be. When I tracked him down, he said it was to allow the Strongshield to deal with the remnants of the wyrm and the tunnel it had created near the King's Wing without them having to worry about disturbing or endangering us. Which may have been true, but I thought he had other, deeper motivations as well.

Fortunately, he and Lord Kolwin had already concluded that another day of hunting was unnecessary, even before the incursion.

"But is that really all we need to do here?" I asked, blinking. I couldn't believe that I'd already been through all the necessary Strongshield traditions and ceremonies.

Ben huffed dismissively. "We dealt with their most urgent problems. I've spoken with Kolwin, and he takes no offense. He knows we have done enough."

We. I knew from the hard look he cast me that he was including me in the pronoun.

I stared at him for a moment. My heart pounded as it finally hit me. "Ben...I've killed a wyrm."

He smiled thinly. "You've done more than that, Sarah. You've killed a rock wyrm and *survived*."

"You've done that," I said with a blink.

He shook his head grimly. "Not like you did. Not in an incursion. And certainly not after having gone *inside* one. I can't really explain to you what that means, Sarah. Have you noticed a change in the way people are treating you?"

"A...bit," I said hesitantly. Vadya had given me a tight hug but otherwise tried to act as normal, so I'd just chalked it up to worry. But other people, elites and attendants...now that I thought about it, I'd been getting some strange looks.

"We have a word for people who offer themselves to wyrms to kill them," Ben said, eyes heavy. "*Yven'roka.*"

Blood offering.

"That's what you are to people now."

I choked. "But I didn't—"

"That's not a technicality anyone is going to care about, Sarah," Ben sighed. "You went in knowing you might not come out. Didn't you?"

I hesitated, not wanting to hurt him with the truth.

"Didn't you?" he asked quietly.

"Yes," I said softly, looking down. I knew that was a possibility. That's why I'd given Kor a message to give to Ben.

Ben let out a breath. When I looked back up at him, he was looking away. But he took my hand and clenched it. "That makes you a *yven'roka*. Except you are the only one who has ever lived."

And I'd thought I was useless.

Not that I thought my deed was something to celebrate, considering how I'd still ended a life, and I'd probably have nightmares for weeks about that maw alone....

In the moment, there had only been time to react. After I'd collapsed, I'd slept soundly from sheer exhaustion. Then the whirl of preparing to leave gave me another distraction. But tonight...I was worried about tonight.

Perhaps that was another reason Ben had wanted to get me away as soon as possible—to thoroughly remove me from everything to do with Palla and what I had endured there. I had to admit that it was a relief to leave it behind. There had been something cleansing about flying away on Ben's back, and even going through the burning sungate, as if the wind was blowing and the fire was burning those moments away. Something felt surreal about last night, now that I was so thoroughly detached from it all.

Had that all really happened?

As if thinking along the same lines, Ben's expression sobered, and his voice became soft. "How are you doing?"

I pushed myself up and curled in my legs to make room for him on the couch. He sat next to me and put his arm around my shoulders.

"I...am doing alright, I think. But I haven't really had time to process. And sometimes when I close my eyes...."

Teeth. So many teeth, reaching for me. Coming for *me*.

I flinched and curled into him.

"The smell often does it for me," Ben said quietly. "Every time I think I'm getting over it, then I smell...."

He covered his face with his free hand for a moment, and his arm tightened around me.

I felt a flicker of relief that he seemed willing to talk about it with me.

"Is that one of the reasons you wanted to leave?" I asked gently.

He lowered his hand and smiled at me thinly. "One of them. I was starting to smell it all the way to our suite. Not sure if that was just my imagination or not, but...."

"Did that make hunting harder for you?"

He'd done it nonstop for *days*.

"Not by much," Ben assured me. "Sand wyrms have a different scent. Cleaner, less...earthy. And the circumstances were completely different."

He paused, thinking, then spoke slowly. "I think it's because I'm out there hunting *them*. In a rock wyrm incursion...."

"It's the opposite," I said quietly.

I was beginning to understand why rock wyrm incursions struck such a deep chord in the dramá psyche. The dramá lived their lives in a continual cycle of power and weakness, freedom and enclosure. Every night, they came together deep in the heart of their underground shelters to weather the siege of night, and for the most part, it worked. There was only one monster who could penetrate their protections, coming into the one place they thought they could be *safe*, and so thoroughly and swiftly prove them wrong.

Ben had been through many terrible, bloody battles and lost many people in his life. But this one battle that still haunted him had been particularly costly, and it had taken the lives of people who otherwise would never have been in danger, who were safe one moment and gone the next. To a protector like Ben, that would be...as he had said to me, his hell.

Ben wouldn't have been able to let his guard down in Palla, I realized.

Not after its bubble of safety had been breached, and so near where we were staying, too. I could see the difference, now, from how he had been after I had woken up in Palla to now when he was finally lounging with me in Rosin. Before, there had been an undercurrent of tension in him, a watchfulness—the kind he exhibited outside, especially the closer the sun got to the horizon. He didn't even touch me more than a couple times, and for Ben, that was significant. Now, he held me to him, his legs were sprawled carelessly in front of him, he had slid down enough to rest his neck on the back of the couch, and his eyes were drifting lower.

"You wouldn't have been able to sleep there, would you?" I murmured.

He turned his head and looked into my eyes for a moment. His golden ones tightened at what he saw there; perhaps he could see how much I understood without being told. He looked away with a sigh.

"No," he answered simply. "Not really."

I cupped the side of his face with my hand and brushed my thumb along his cheek. "And you *need* sleep."

How much had he gotten last night, after they had woken him to tell him about the incursion? I didn't bother to ask, because I was fairly certain I knew the answer.

I felt the hairs of his beard and the muscles of his face move under my fingers to form a dry smile. "Flame, yes."

"Then you did the right thing," I concluded. "You're right. We did enough there."

And it wasn't like we had totally abandoned Palla. Ben had left almost a third of his elites there to bolster their security, and he had called for various specialists to come all the way from Crownhold to help in the cleanup and rebuilding.

He had done everything he reasonably could for them, and then he had taken me somewhere where he could feel safe again. I knew I was a crucial part of it, that it would never have worked if he had left me behind. The only reason he had stayed sane leaving me behind in Palla before was he had been confident as he could be that I would be safe there.

That safety had always been an illusion, as absolute safety always was, but it was the kind that the mortal mind needed; we *had* to ignore some dangers, to tell ourselves that we were secure in our own homes, otherwise we would go mad.

Then that illusion had shattered for Ben, at least in Palla, and he *had* to get me out.

I wasn't about to ask Ben what the risk of rock wyrm incursions were here, in the Starkissed island capital of Rosin, but I assumed it had to be even lower than usual for Ben to relax like this so soon after Palla.

I had seen evidence of a lesser threat from consumed on all fronts, actually.

Most holds I had been to—even the capitals—were built with security in mind. Outside structures were minimal, primarily limited to sungates and landing pads or strips, or the occasional wall, and the entrances into the hold usually had the thick, heavily reinforced gates that you could imagine outlasting a battering ram—and sometimes more than one set of those. Now that I was sensitive to it, I felt magic *saturating* me like a waterfall every time I went through one of those open archways. I hadn't been near a gate at night, but I could imagine the guardrooms that I passed during the day being full for the night shift, and I had seen enough of a war room to imagine each hold having a similar one, fully staffed with dramá keeping a careful eye on the night. I could see why consumed generally had no luck getting in.

Rosin reminded me of Olsdak, the first and only other Starkissed hold I had been to. Both of them were island mountains in the middle of a gorgeous turquoise sea, and both of them much more closely resembled a resort than a fortress. Outside structures abounded: winding mountain paths, gardens, fountains, pergolas, gazebos, and beach shelters, just to name a few. And whereas dramá rarely seemed to linger outside their holds without a productive purpose, here the mountain slopes, beaches, and waters were full of people seemingly just enjoying themselves, in draká or amáform, clothed or otherwise. (There was a reason I'd never cared to go down to the beach at Olsdak.)

I didn't know what made the difference in both places, but there must have been something significant to allow the dramá to feel like here, they could shed their armor and scales and simply *be*, remembering that life wasn't just a constant siege and could be bright and worth living.

In fact, the primary difference that I, as an outsider, could tell between Rosin and Olsdak was that Rosin was bigger, thus allowing the Starkissed more room for their grandiose whimsy. I wouldn't have thought it possible for them to have increased the level of opulence from the King's Wing of Olsdak, but they had. I should have known better than to underestimate the Starkissed by now.

Ben leaned his head on top of mine. "We should be safer here," he said, echoing my thoughts. His tone turned wry. "Even *you* should be able to stay out of trouble for a few days."

I really hoped he hadn't just jinxed me. I felt an urge to knock on some wood, but there wasn't any within reach, and I didn't want to leave Ben's side.

"What's the difference?" I asked, hoping going over the details would be soothing to him.

"Lots, fortunately. The biggest one is the water. Wyrms of all types *hate* water." I could hear a wry smile in his voice. "They won't go near or even under it. And Oshal is mostly ocean."

I chuckled. "So, not many wyrms on this planet, huh?"

"Normally, none. Even the Devourer seems to have given up trying to bring them here, since they go completely mad. They don't even try to eat us—they just flail around and scream until they eventually hit the water and drown themselves."

I could forgive a bit of dark humor in Ben's voice in this case. It faded as he continued.

"The water brings other dangers. There are natural predators here that can cause even a draká some trouble. But all Oshal holds have multiple rings of barriers out in the ocean that keep those at bay, and sensors to catch the ones that slip through darkrifts.

"Overall, though, the ocean keeps Oshal much safer than the other Realms. The Starkissed can guard most of the land against darkrifts, so the Devourer has to create them out in the ocean, and anything that can do well in the ocean can't get to us on land, especially not through the Starkissed protections. So, we stay out of the water at night and don't swim in the deep ocean, and we're usually fine."

"That makes sense," I said slowly. "So, what do the Starkissed need from us?"

Ben groaned, running a hand through his hair. "Just the usual grand tour stuff."

I blinked. "Really? That's it? No plagues needing curing, monsters needing fighting...."

"The Starkissed were among the least troubled by the last invasion," Ben said with a sigh. "For all the same reasons. The predator levels are unusually high, and they've had sightings of some new monsters, but their sea hunters and guard have things well in hand. And so far—Flame will it stay that way—no plagues or pestilences have broken out here. So, they really just want the usual. Thank the Flame, because that's quite bad enough."

I grinned and looked up at him. "Are we going to have to reenact another romance for them?"

He glared back down at me. "Don't give them ideas. It's bad enough that they're convinced you're *the* Moondaughter. We'll be lucky if they don't decide to rope us into a full-length production someday."

I laughed. "They're probably too smart for that. They know how hard it is to get you to participate in the pageant, and that's without you having to memorize *lines*."

Ben shuddered. "Let's hope."

"So, what *is* the usual?"

"Well, we've just gotten through the first thing, the welcoming," Ben said, plucking a petal from my hair with a smirk.

We'd done the usual welcome on the main landing, except this time was much more extravagant. For one thing, all the drakón had been in amáform. I'd had mixed feelings about that from the start. The crowds lined up on either side of the aisle were only a different kind of intimidating, but I had to admit that amáform allowed much more egalitarian access, and from how packed they were behind the ribbon barriers, it seemed plenty wanted to take part. But that meant a much more familiar and gut-clenching kind of uproar as everyone cheered, shot bursts of colorful, sparkling blue magic in every shade, and threw balls of flower petals above us that somehow stuck together until the apex and then exploded apart like floral grenades.

"I felt attacked," I complained, flicking another petal off my shoulder. "I think I'm going to be finding those things everywhere for days."

At least their version of throwable sparkles, unlike the insidious Earthren kind, seemed to go away on their own, winking out of existence like bubbles did. Otherwise, I would still be covered in them from head to toe.

Ben laughed at my complaint, as he had then at my barely concealed alarm in the moment.

It was a good thing I had already met the Lady Starkissed—a charming, intelligent woman who looked much more well-rested than the last time I'd seen her, although she was still surrounded by her three young children, the youngest two of whom broke all sense of protocol by running toward me with huge smiles and hugging me. Lady Winthra just laughed and hugged me herself when we finally reached her, so maybe there hadn't been much of a protocol to begin with. That was the one pleasant thing about the clan's unrestrained exuberance. That, and the unrelenting cacophony preventing a formal verbal exchange.

Our walk through the hold with the Lady was hardly any better. I'd expected relief from the crowds, but I was soon disappointed. They had lined the streets all the way to the King's Wing, turning our arrival into some kind of parade—never-ending rows of people waving, cheering, and tossing stuff at us. I tried to smile and wave back as best as I could, but the sheer numbers were staggering. I had asked Ben at one point if most of the Starkissed clan had shown up for this, and he had said yes, in a tone that made it clear he wasn't joking.

I'd had good reason to collapse the moment Ben managed to get us to our room.

Now, I asked, "Are the Starkissed normally this...?"

"Enthusiastic?" Ben said dryly.

I nodded.

"They always love a good party—and a chance to torture the Golden Heir and Monarch." Ben rolled his eyes, then sobered. "But...to answer your question, no. I don't think so. This is the first grand tour I've been on, obviously, but if the Starkissed don't like you, they find devious ways to let you *know*—without ever doing anything you can actually call them out on. Trust me, Sarah. They don't just like you—I think they couldn't have been happier if I'd chosen one of *them* as my consort. And that's saying something. Before you came along, they were always griping that they haven't had their share of the Crown in four generations. If I wasn't determined not to marry, I might have chosen one of them just to shut them up."

I grinned. "You, with a Starkissed? I can't picture it."

Ben smiled back at me and fingered my chin. "Well, obviously none of them were tempting enough to make me break my oath. Unlike you."

I grinned wider, iceheart pounding pleasantly at that look in his eyes.

Before I could get too warm, I looked away and thought back to my question and his answer.

"It's the Moondaughter thing, isn't it?"

Ben sighed. "I think so. Sorry. I don't think there's anything we can do to convince them otherwise. Trust me, right after the Moonfair, I tried. And that...was before the Solstice."

I shrugged, trying to avoid the heavy. "Good to know I'm among friends, at least."

I chuckled, remembering. "You know, the first time I met Lady Winthra, her older daughter asked me why I wasn't wearing your earring."

"Did she?" Ben said, flushing.

For all that people kept telling me Ben was interested in me, he had only just kissed me for the first time—and that was because our roles in the Moonfair pageant made him. Not that anything about his kiss felt *forced*....

"Mmhmm." Feeling unusually bold, I reached up and played with some of his hair, and his flush deepened. "She asked when we were heartbinding, and she was outraged when I told her we hadn't even discussed that yet."

Ben cleared his throat. "Er, well...I didn't think you were ready for that."

I sat back, grinning incredulously. "Wait, you honestly might have proposed at that point? If you knew I was interested?"

Svyer had said he was emotionally there, and I hadn't believed her.

"I might have." Ben grimaced. "In hindsight, it wouldn't have been a good idea, considering...what I put you through after that. But I'd known for days that if I was going to marry anyone, it would be you."

He sighed. "I was intending to court you, after...the Solstice and everything. Assuming I survived."

I sobered. I had been intending to avoid the heavy, but this hinted at something I hadn't realized had been a factor before in his behavior toward me back then, and I wanted to be sure.

"Is that...one reason you held back for so long?"

"Yes," he said heavily, looking at me. "I thought it wasn't fair to you, to ask you for anything before...before I knew I'd have something to give in return."

I swallowed, eyes stinging at the self-sacrifice behind those words. That was so...*him*. And I had come up with a thousand and one reasons he couldn't have been interested. I should have known him better.

I was also reminded of a hurt I never had the chance to express to him.

I shifted onto his lap and cupped his face in my hands. "You never told me. How much danger you would be in, I mean. In the battle. How little chance you might have...."

I had to come to that conclusion myself, long after we had been separated without even a goodbye, when it was almost too late to save him.

He closed his eyes and let out a breath. "What good would that have done? You had enough things to worry about—including your own survival."

He opened his eyes and smiled thinly. "Besides...I think I'd started to believe in miracles by then. I know I believed in you."

I sighed and sunk into him, tucking my head under his chin. "I suppose I'll have to forgive you. Seeing as the shock of me putting it all together is what made me finally break into lightform. You might not have gotten your 'miracle' otherwise."

He sighed and held me close. "And if I'd known it would 'shock' you into risking your life like that, I might have.... But we've been over this. The past...is in the past. It happened the way it did and...maybe for a reason. So, thank you for your forgiveness."

He attempted a lighter tone, which only fell a little flat. "And thank you especially for accepting my earring, even as late as I was in offering it. Hopefully little Asha is satisfied now."

I chuckled. "She seemed happy when she saw us together. Don't you think?"

"Hmm." Ben shifted his arm behind me and dipped me back to plant a kiss on my neck, just underneath his earring. "Not as happy as I am to be with you."

And then his lips traced to my mouth, and I forgot about everything else.

Chapter Thirty-Eight

SEARCHING

Koriben

THE STARKISSED—MERCILESS AS ALWAYS—DIDN'T even give us a full day to settle in and recover. Just that one blissful evening...which was way too short, considering I failed in my resolve to stay up past dinner. At least this time Sarah didn't manage to maneuver me onto the bed, mostly because when I fell asleep on the couch with her, and she woke me up to get me to lie down properly, I had enough sense to go straight to my pallet, fully dressed and all.

When I woke up deken later, she was gone.

Even before I opened my eyes, I reflexively looked, as usual, for her star in my mind's eye, the brightest point of light in my mental star chart of all my gates.

A jolt of adrenaline shot me awake when I saw her star was much further away than it had any right to be.

I bolted upright, twisting to look back and sparing only a glance at the bed to confirm that she wasn't there—and to see it was cold. If she had ever lain in it, it had been long ago, but I doubted she had. Her scent was faint and old, and only lingered around the couch where we had sat.

I threw off my blanket and pushed to my feet so quickly my head spun, and I had to grab onto a nearby chair for a painstaking moment to steady myself. Then I was out the door.

Kor and Vadya happened to be conversing in the central room.

"Where's Sarah?" I demanded, flameheart pulsing. "Is she alright?"

The only remotely legitimate explanation I could think of for why she would be elden from me just after dawn was that she had taken ill during the night and been rushed to a healer. But that still made no sense. We had healers aplenty in our entourage—some of the best in the Realms. Even if for some unfathomable reason one of our healers couldn't tend to her needs while someone else in Rosin could, a Rosin healer could have come and tended to her in the King's Wing healing ward. And why wouldn't anyone have woken me?!

The two Starkissed cousins turned and looked at me with infuriating calm.

"Sarah?" Kor repeated innocently.

My flameheart sputtered. *No.* Surely they knew *something.* Surely she couldn't have been....

"Sarah is gone," I choked. "Long gone, across Rosin at least, maybe even on another island. I don't think she even slept...."

Finally, their still too-calm, too-innocent expressions sunk into my brain. For all the adrenaline pumping through my veins, I still wasn't thinking straight.

"No," I moaned, putting my head in my hands. I nearly sagged with relief for a moment before fury replaced fear.

"You have got to be kidding," I growled, lowering my hands. "*Seriously*? The betrothal search? *Now*?"

Of all the stupid Starkissed notions of how to entertain themselves by torturing Golden Royals...*that* had been the one I was least prepared to just...*wake up* to.

Even though I should have known better. After all, I had only given the Starkissed three days. They clearly were determined to take advantage of every dek...and had some very well-placed allies to help them do so.

Why had I let Kor make his cousin the head of Sarah's staff? For that matter, why had I chosen a Starkissed as my leftwing in the first place? I must have been mad. Or an idiot.

Probably both.

"Or whenever you feel like getting started, King Koriben," Vadya said with wide-open eyes and a brilliant smile. "After all, Sarah won't even be awake for another few deken at least."

I folded my arms and glared daggers at the two of them. "She really *didn't* sleep here tonight, did she?"

"Of course not," Vadya said indulgently. "We wouldn't want to interrupt her sleep cycle, now, would we? So, we got her into position last night. Isn't it brilliant? She can sleep, and you can search—not a moment wasted."

They really *were* trying to pack in every dek, torch it. I was hoping to cut the tormenting down even more with Sarah's half-day availability, but I'd underestimated them.

"I can't believe Sarah went along with this."

"We were very...persuasive," Kor said, smirking.

I gave him a hard look. "You better not have forced her."

As aggravating as the thought was of Sarah willingly going along with this scheme, I preferred it to the thought of her being manipulated or forced into it. If Sarah woke up confused and frightened in a new place, without anyone having obtained her consent or at least explained things to her in advance....

I would wring Kor's neck. And find her a different head of staff.

Vadya put a hand to her chest, aghast. "What a hurtful accusation. Of course not. We *bribed* her, obviously."

I felt a flicker of relief, which I carefully didn't show. "With *what*?"

I was at a loss as to what Sarah would find motivating enough. Her natural resistance to such machinations was yet another reason this search had taken me by surprise. Of course, that was what I had counted on when it came to the Moonfair pageant, too, and look where that had led us.

"That's between us and the Queen," Vadya said primly. "Now, we'll be gracious and let you ready yourself before we inform the master of ceremonies that you're awake and she gets impatient and lights the candle for you. Just come back here once you wish to begin."

I suddenly realized why they had been standing in the central room, and why no one else was around. They had been *waiting* for me.

The games had begun.

I groaned and headed to the water-room. The sooner I got this over with, the sooner I could get Sarah back. Then at least I'd have an ally in this.

Unless they had managed to buy her out for the duration of our time enduring Starkissed "hospitality." Somehow, though, I doubted even Kor could find a great enough bribe to accomplish *that*.

THE STARKISSED WERE ROMANTICS. Plain and simple. What was never so plain nor simple was how they manifested that quality, because Starkissed never did anything halfway.

Their heartbinding ritual was the same short and simple ceremony as everyone else's. With a Tree's involvement, there wasn't much they could do to complicate it. *So*, over the centuries, they had created a number of elaborate rites to lead *up* to the heartbinding; not every couple underwent every one of them, but when it came to the Starkissed's hosting a Royal betrothed couple on a grand tour, they insisted on fitting in as many as possible.

One of their longest, most elaborate, and most entertaining heartbinding traditions (and thus one of their favorites) was the betrothed search.

It went like this: One of the couple (normally they drew lots for this, but when a Golden Royal was involved, it was always the Royal's betrothed) was carefully hidden somewhere in Rosin or in the surrounding smaller islands of the Rosin Archipelago, and the other had to find them by following an elaborate series of clues that would eventually lead them to the hiding place.

It was supposed to represent something, as all the heartbinding traditions did: in this case, probably something about journeys, effort, discoveries, and other symbolic nonsense. Honestly, I had never cared. Whenever I'd heard about the betrothed search, I had found it even more motivation to never marry. Now, with that resolve having evaporated in the last two months, I found myself abruptly facing a level of public humiliation I hadn't mentally prepared myself to endure.

It wasn't enough to make me jump through these hoops—they all had to *watch*.

You realize I can just surge to her at any moment, I mentally growled at Kor as we walked down the hall of suites to the central court of the King's Wing.

Normally, the King's Wing was closed to the public. Not this morning—from what I could smell, hear, and see at the end of the hall, thousands were lining its enormous rim to await the official start of the search. The only reason I wasn't chewing Kor out right now for allowing that massive security risk was because Sarah was elden away, hopefully in a secure location that only a very select few knew about, surrounded by her elite. Yvera, on my right, looked like she was sorely tempted to give Kor a piece of her mind and steel, anyway. After all, *I* was still here.

Then again, maybe she already had, since she could hardly have been kept in the dark about this. Kor would have needed her permission to open the gates to them in the first place, *and* her coordination of my elites to manage the crowd. That must have taken yet another monumental feat of coercion. I wondered just how long and carefully he had been planning this.

Yes, but that would be cheating, Kor responded to my statement, smirking. *And you know what the consequences of that will be.*

One other thing to know about the Starkissed was their unspoken, unwritten condition for their crucial support to the Golden Crown: that we would always go along with their "harmless" traditions.

As for the Starkissed's reasoning for this, various members of the clan had hinted to me at different times that we Sunfilled, especially us Royals, became too serious and overburdened with the cares of the Realms, and that they were doing their loyal duty in lightening our loads and livening up our lives while we were in their care. Avva's opinion, which he shared with me before my second Moonfair, was that we Royals tended to seem distant and unapproachable to the common people, and the Starkissed were helping humanize us with minimal loss of face, due to the nature of long-established ritual.

I was sure I knew the truth: the Starkissed lived to use us as entertainment.

Thus, cheating them of the best entertainment they'd had in decades, perhaps in their whole lives, by either refusing to play their games or using shortcuts would lead to pure, universal outrage. As much as my gut was twisting with dread and my flameheart pounding with fury, I didn't want to alienate the most magically powerful and culturally influential clan of the Six Realms this early into my reign. Not over this, at least. As Heir, I endured four Moonfairs (and suffered through the dread of another before I found a way out of it) to keep the peace, and I would not let all that suffering go to waste now.

I really don't like you right now, I told Kor.

I wasn't feeling friendly toward his entire clan, but him in particular. He wasn't just a convenient target for my angst. I knew my leftwing. I knew that he would have been intimately involved in the planning of every part of these three days.

I know, he said, unbothered. *But one of these days, you'll thank me.*

I highly doubted that, but before I could say so, we passed the elites guarding the end of the hallway and emerged into the central court, and a round of cheers broke out, echoing to almost deafening levels in that large space.

I forced myself to smile and walk calmly to the center of the court, where Lady Winthra, her wings, and the organizer of these events stood in front of the central fountain, all of whom were beaming innocently at me as if to say, *Isn't this fun?*

I really, really wanted to hit something right now. Preferably something wearing blue.

But that wouldn't help matters, so I made myself take deep breaths instead.

Focus on Sarah, I told myself. *Focus on getting her back....*

Then I could handle everything else the Starkissed could throw at me.

Just behind the Starkissed leaders was a rectangular plinth that rose about to my mid-thigh, on which sat a large oval brass bowl with steep sides. In the center of that bowl was a brass trunk that rose into a tree with seven main branches, each of which held a candle with fourteen gold rings painted onto the white wax and a small, pyramid-shaped pin stuck into each mark. The smallest pin was stuck into the uppermost ring, and the pins gradually increased in size all the way to the last at the bottom. Each pin was aesthetically placed at a different position around the candle, forming something that looked a bit like a pinecone. The entire setup of brass bowl, candleholder, and candles was covered in a wood-framed glass case to protect the flames from drafts and thus ensure a more even burn.

This was a timekeeping device. Nothing so efficient and practical as Sarah's watch, but certainly beautiful, even mesmerizing. Even the pins would add to the drama, since when a candle burned down to the ring the pin was in, the pin would drop into the bowl and let out a melodious chime. It was an eye- and ear-catching representation of the passage of time to add just another layer of excitement—for everyone else.

Yes, I was being *timed*.

Officially, there weren't any consequences if I didn't find Sarah by the time the last candle burned out at roughly this time tomorrow—but it wasn't a good look. People were guaranteed to illogically see the results of this as a measure of my devotion to Sarah at the least; betrothals had been broken off before based on search times or even on how well the searcher executed their tasks. I wasn't concerned about Sarah doing that, but I knew that our public unity lent us crucial influence with the people, and I didn't want to cost us any of it.

At the most, since I was the King, the people would see how well I did as a measure of my ability to lead our Six—soon to be Seven—Realms.

How they thought *that* was a fair conclusion, I had no idea, but it added yet another element of pressure that was turning my insides into knots. It was yet another reason I was determined not to let this search drag out the full time. Besides, I wasn't about to leave Sarah holed up somewhere on her own (even relatively speaking) for longer than I could help.

The sooner I found and brought Sarah back here to put out the latest candle, the better...for everyone.

I stopped about five feet from the Starkissed leaders and the plinth just behind them. My wings walked away, leaving me feeling exposed. But both Kor and Yvera had to have been involved in the planning, so if they took part, people would accuse me of cheating.

"King Koriben," Lady Winthra said warmly, sky-blue eyes sparkling. As usual, I was sure she knew exactly how I felt about all of this, which just seemed further proof in my mind of Starkissed sadism. "Flame be with you this bright morning."

"Flame be with you, Lady Winthra," I said evenly. It was the best tone I could manage.

"Are you ready?"

No, absolutely not, I thought, slightly nauseated.

"Yes, I am," I said firmly.

"Excellent," she said, and she took a lantern from her leftwing and a taper from her rightwing and approached me.

The lantern would have been lit from the fire of Oshal's Tree at dawn that very morning. I could tell the source of the flame by its blue tint, and fires lit by Tree flame only lasted until just before dawn the next day—yet another reason to not let this search drag on.

The Starkissed Lady handed the lantern and taper to me and nodded to me deeply, moving aside and gesturing to the candelabra. "Then light the first candle and let your search for your betrothed begin."

I walked up to the plinth, shifted the taper to the same hand as the lantern, and opened the door of the glass case. I opened the similar glass door of the lantern, took the taper back into my free hand, and then touched the taper to the blue flame flickering around the wick inside. Once the taper lit, I brought it out and into the case and, my hand surprisingly steady, touched the freshly burning tip to the first candle.

It lit, and the crowd cheered. The race was now on.

Lady Winthra's wings took the lantern and taper from me, and the Lady handed me a folded piece of paper.

"Flame go with you," she said, still smiling wickedly. "And may your flameheart guide you true."

I held the paper over the flame of the first candle, and words written in sapphire ink appeared on its surface. The crowd quieted so that I could read the words out loud, as custom demanded. I felt a surge of magic as someone—probably Kor—magically magnified my voice so that it echoed through the court, since I deliberately hadn't done so myself.

"*Under air, over stone, under flame, over leaf.*"

Speculative murmurs broke out among the crowd. I gazed down at the paper, focusing hard for one moment. Even with my guess only partly formed, my feet began carrying me to the King's landing, and it was surprisingly easy to ignore the cheers as I left. I was more conscious of the two people that moved to my sides: Ordran to my right and to my left a drakón woman in Starkissed uniform, meaning she was one of Lady Winthra's. No doubt she had been included as one of my two honorary wings for the day to be the storyteller to describe everything in detail to the Starkissed after the search was over. This was, after all, meant to be a spectacle.

She also would make sure I followed the rules: primarily, that I didn't get help from anyone or surge, either to the sungate or to Sarah. No hints, no shortcuts.

I ignored them both as I kept walking out onto the landing, thinking. From what I'd heard, the riddles for these searches generally had a theme, usually using clues that only the couple would know how to interpret. Or, more likely in my case, that Kor would know I knew, since I doubted Sarah had consented enough to compose these herself, as tradition normally dictated. She certainly wasn't the scribe: the message was in Drona, in our alphabet, and in Kor's impeccable handwriting.

I was right: this search literally had his hand all over it.

Under air, over stone. Well, that seemed to mean outside, obviously, and high up, possibly over the tree line. It was worth a look. It was even more worth getting away from that crowd and the eyes that would no doubt follow me all over inside Rosin proper. I'd probably have to go in there at *some* point, but I was grudgingly grateful to Kor for first giving me a chance to fly away from it all.

Though, as soon as I spread my wings, I was sorely tempted to just head for Sarah, especially when I got some height and started pinpointing where she could be. My eyes fell on one of the much smaller islands of the archipelago, near one tip of its roughly crescent shape.

There. Her star was somewhere in there. There wasn't much vegetation, mostly just a hunk of rock, so she had to be inside, in a shelter of some kind.

Knowing that both settled me and gave me a hard-to-ignore itch. She was right *there*....

I sighed and turned my attention to finding the next clue. I searched Rosin and the surrounding islands, eyes peeled for the slightest thing that reminded me of the riddle or seemed familiar or out of place.

Then my eyes fell on another of the rocky islands. After rising from the water at a typical slanted angle, it had an unusually flat top about half an eld up, almost as if someone had taken a giant blade and severed the rest off. It seemed almost like a mesa....

Memory struck me, and I flew straight there, Ordran and the Starkissed following.

Unlike the mesa from my memory, a garden had been constructed on its surface, so plenty of vegetation grew there. But before I could be disappointed, I noticed a statue with an offering bowl, already lit. Given the early deken, that was unusual.

I dove for the mesa and landed on the bare rocky portion that had been deliberately left uncultivated for just that purpose. Then I quickly changed so my bodyguards could follow. Ordran didn't bother to land or change; he continued circling overhead to keep watch, but the woman landed and trailed after me as I made my way to the statue holding the bowl.

It was a depiction of the Tree, of course, in one of her human avatars. Dried leaves or other objects were burned in the bowl as a prayer offering. This was an old and weathered shrine, covered in leafy vines at the base—mostly redleaf, popular both as a soporific tsha and as an offering. When used as the latter, the leaf represented wisdom, and the prayer was usually a question.

Well, that was certainly promising. Could it really be that easy?

I reached the shrine and began looking around.

Under flame....

I chuckled. I thought Kor had meant the sun, but perhaps he was being more literal than that. I ducked to look under the bowl.

Sure enough, a small wax-paper envelope was stuck to the back of one of the statue's hands. I plucked it off and looked at the seal. Then rolled my eyes.

Pressed into the silver wax was a seal much like mine, except instead of flames for leaves, this one had shards that were meant to be ice.

Kor had borrowed Sarah's new signet ring. Perhaps he'd even used it before giving it to her.

I cracked the envelope open and took out the slip of paper inside. It was blank. With little hope, I held it over the offering flame, but nothing happened.

"You have to bring it back to the candle," the Starkissed woman said with a smirk.

"I know," I said with a sigh. "But it was worth a try."

No shortcuts. And no avoiding a reappearance in front of everyone.

"Well, back we go," I said, unable to muster any enthusiasm. The woman laughed.

I CREATED A LITTLE stir when I strode back through the arch into the central court. Some spectators had left, but some had stayed. Those were sitting on the benches in the alcoves or on cushions on the floor and were settling in for the long wait. Some had even brought games. I wasn't sure whether to be flattered or annoyed at how many people thought it worthwhile to linger.

Yvera was probably fit to be tied. Sure enough, when I caught sight of her standing near the hall of Crown suites, she was glowering, eyeing the nearest group of card players balefully. A brave bunch, those.

The nearest people to the landing turned and exclaimed when they saw me, and a ripple effect went through the entire court. I'd only been gone less than ten dek, probably, and I could see that surprised many of them. More than a few coins changed hands, with quite a few scowls to go around.

I knew not to get smug. There were six more clues to figure out, counting the one in my hand.

Sure enough, when I reached the candelabra, I saw that the first notch in the first candle hadn't quite burned down, and the first pin hadn't yet dropped.

"Welcome back, O King," Lady Winthra said with a grin. "Good hunting?"

"Thank you, yes," I said briskly, opening the case with only enough care to try to not disturb the candle and holding the paper over the blue candle flame.

The next message faded into being, and I pulled the paper out and closed the case.

This time, resigned and mindful of Kor's careful eye on me, I cast the projection spell myself and read, "*Follow light in fields left fallow.*"

My feet once again began taking me to the landing as I pondered that paper and its message. The last clue's location had hints of the mesa in the middle of the Athalin Jungle where we had rested the day after we found Sarah.

This one....

Fallow fields.

I heard someone mutter the problem out loud to a friend as I passed. "We don't *have* any fallow fields."

Rosin didn't have the land to spare for it. After the beach, it was mostly slopes and cliffs, and the residents had dedicated any remotely suitable spaces to ornamental gardens, relying primarily on the subterranean fields (much like the ones that Sarah's family had discovered in their hold) that the Peacegrowth had helped them create to grow their local produce. Even those fields were never left to fallow but were manually replenished, given how precious space was.

"Where's he going?" someone else said just before I passed through the arch to the landing.

A fair question, since Rosin's underground farm would be accessed through the hold proper, and I was once again heading outside. But I had a feeling those fields weren't what Kor was referring to, from more than just the word *fallow.* Nothing about the subterranean fields sounded any horns of familiarity in my mind. Kor would have chosen clues and locations that would mean something to both Sarah and me but practically no one else.

Things like...

...the location of her moongates.

Of course! The fallow field on the rise where Sarah's Yonvey moongate was. And the mesa was where we discovered the Ykran gate.

I might have just discovered the theme, and the key to interpreting this clue.

What would be something *like* that field on Yonvey? It would be outside the main hold, for one, so my instincts had guided me true.

Then it struck me, and with my back now to everyone, but especially Kor, I risked rolling my eyes.

Kor had recently reported to me about a new Rosin project to recultivate a kelp forest that had been decimated when the local population of chipin had exploded and eaten most of it. Now that the locals had hunted the chipin down to reasonable numbers, they were risking a replanting, and so far the results were promising.

At the time, I was puzzled at why Kor was bringing it up. It was a locally funded and run movement, so the Crown had nothing to do with it. When I'd asked what he meant me to do with that information, he just shrugged and said he thought I could use some good news mixed in with all the dour things I had to know about or address. Though I'd been skeptical—I knew my leftwing better than that—I let it go.

That had been at least a sevenday ago, when we were back on Yonvey. Which meant Kor had been planning this search at least that long. Knowing him, most likely longer. Hence my eye roll.

That also explained why two other sets of feet beyond my original two body-guards were now following me. I cast a glance back and saw two more of my elites looking back at me, expressions professionally neutral.

I glanced at Ordran. "I'm likely going to be getting wet."

Ordran nodded, seeming unsurprised. He was good at keeping a straight face, but I knew him well, and years of formal and informal training as Heir had made me a good people reader.

Thinking I had received confirmation that I was on the right track, I continued after only a slight pause. "In case your orders weren't clear, I leave you in charge of directing the others in that scenario, since I imagine you know what I'm getting myself into better than I do."

Likely nothing deadly, and certainly nothing I couldn't handle...but they were there to keep things that way. After all, there was no reason to tempt the Devourer by leaving me exposed.

Ordran's lips twitched in a momentary smile. "Understood, sir."

I nodded and jogged forward, changing all the while, so that by the time I reached the edge of the landing, I was fully transformed and pushing off.

It took a dek or two of circling for me to identify where the kelp field was. Fortunately, the shallow waters around the archipelago were crystal clear, even as far out as I had to go to find the spikes of green sticking up through the sand. I circled for a bit, lowering with each pass as I examined the area. Other than the kelp, the only noticeable features were the large outcrops of pitted gray volcanic rock jutting through the sand, high enough in some places to have small caves and crevices—perfect hiding places for chipin. They might give me a bit of trouble, but I wasn't worried.

And then something flashed, glittering under the water. I couldn't make out the details, but there was something glowing down there—glowing *white*.

Follow light....

It seemed I had found what I was looking for. Now, to reach it.

I tucked my wings, filled my enormous lungs with air, and dove into the water.

Given how they were creatures of flame and air, draká were more suited to the water than they had a right to be. My vision underwater was crystal clear, aided by the same translucent lids that helped protect and lend a much greater range of focus to my eyes in flight.

The moment before I'd hit the water, I'd closed my nostrils, sealing them against an influx of water. Thanks to my easy descent and relatively slow heart rate, my lungs could hold out for a full couple dek before I'd need another breath—and I was an unexperienced Sunfilled. Over the many centuries of their dwelling on Oshal, the Starkissed had adapted more than any other clan to a dual existence in air and water. Kor could hold his breath for nearly a quarter deken, and that was without any practice. Starkissed fishers, hunters (distinguished from the fishers by their focus on defense, not provision), and members of the Waterguard—all multigenerational specialists who had deliberately furthered their adaptation with magic—could hold their breath for nearly a deken and skillfully maneuver in and fight at depths I dared not go.

Starkissed were also much more practiced at utilizing the air sacs all draká had distributed in their torsos; normally, those aided our buoyancy in air, giving a bit of natural help to the tremendous amount of magic that made our massive bulk flight capable. My control of my own sacs was almost entirely subconscious and much more adapted to air conditions; Starkissed had more refined and conscious control and used them to aid in their dives.

In the past couple generations, the most committed to that lifestyle had intentionally begun to develop gills, which had just become completely viable in a few drakón of my generation. Though outsiders had grumbled ever since the effort first became known, that success had sparked a full-blown debate that still raged about our identity as dramá and the morality of intentional, magical alteration of the forms the Tree had given us. Even though the Oshal Tree had given Her blessing from the start, some factions (the Traditionalists especially) thought the Starkissed were polluting their bloodline and had urged the Crown to act, lest other clans follow suit, and the Six Realms devolve into barbarous chaos. Avva had to veto more than one punitive measure against the Starkissed, including a few proposed trade sanctions and even a law against intermarriage.

I suspected it wouldn't be long before I would have to deal with the issue, and I was not looking forward to it—in good part because I wasn't sure where I stood on the matter at all. It didn't help that my primary adviser was a Starkissed. Kor was perfectly capable of objectivity (more so than most people, actually), but the Traditionalists would assume he would bias me, and whatever I did to appease them would likely be unsatisfactory.

For the moment, I pushed away thoughts of the controversy and focused on the present.

I both heard the muted thunder and felt the rush of water from three draká entering the surrounding ocean. The short strands of kelp below waved wildly in the roiling currents.

I and the other three rose to the surface, our full lungs and air sacs bringing us back up without effort. Yet another of our advantages in water: draká could rest on the surface more or less indefinitely, and we actually had to work to stay under. When my neck naturally rose high above the waves, I saw that Ordran, one other elite, and the Starkissed had followed me into the sea, and one elite remained circling above. Ordran must have told him to stay aloft as a scout.

Tread lightly, I told the ones in the water. *And don't touch the kelp.*

I didn't want to add the Rosin branch of the Conservation Guild to the list of all the others that I had aggravated over the years. It wasn't my fault that my job often seemed to come into conflict with theirs, but they still held it against me.

Although...one could reasonably argue that my berserk, wanton destruction in the Wirthen Desert of Romskal *was* my fault. Even though I remembered little of it.

I ducked my head back under and spotted the source of the white glow. Wedged into a small cavity at the top of one outcrop was a sealed crystal bottle with a crystal stopper glowing with a familiar white light. Another sign of either Sarah's willing participation or Kor's skill at manipulation. Given how he had tricked her into touching a doorgem on her first day in the Six Realms, it could have gone either way.

The bottle was placed very carefully: the stopper jutted just far enough above the crevice for the glow to be visible from above and the side, but the whole bottle was deep enough in the crevice that the chipin I had seen scatter as soon as I entered the water would not have been able to pull it out with their large pincers. And I was sure now that was exactly what they had been trying to do. The creatures were notorious for their fascination with shiny things, and their grottos could often be identified by their little hoards.

They would not like me coming in to take away their discovery. They were out of sight right now, but that would change once they figured out that was what I was doing—and saw me in amáform. I would have to make this quick if I was going to avoid a fight.

I could almost hear Kor chuckling at his cleverness. Clearly the chipin were supposed to represent the rothen that had come after Sarah and me on Yonvey when we went for the moongate. No one else would know that, but they would appreciate the added level of entertainment all the same. After all, why make this easy for me?

I swam as close as I dared to the outcrop. The waters were still shallow enough at this depth and the outcrop was large and tall enough that I couldn't fit over the top of it without hitting or standing on it in draká-form. Not a problem normally, but I didn't want to damage the rock, either—and especially not the bottle.

I raised my head above the water again and breathed normally as I changed back into amáform. I made things easier on myself and left my chest bare, only giving myself a pair of trousers. Although that, combined with this loose reenactment of that night we'd found the moongate, gave me an idea.

Using my half-form in this scenario would be excessive—like selecting a war hammer when your dueling partner was using a knife. I wasn't worried about the chipin, even if it came to a conflict, but now I was curious. I'd never tried my half-form underwater—I wondered if it would give me any advantages. Just being able to *see* might make it worth it.

But that was probably what Kor *wanted* me to do, and that irritated me. I could almost hear him egging me on.

Come on, Ben. Give them a show. Show them what you can do.

The practical, objective side of me knew that Kor wasn't just doing this to torture me—that he really did have a purpose for this search that was ultimately for my benefit. Was he getting some amusement out of it? Oh, absolutely. But my leftwing was clever enough to amuse himself *and* strengthen my position as King at the same time.

One of the hallmarks of a Royal's power was the half-form. Technically, most drakón were capable of it...for a second or two. Only Royals (and, secretly, the Tolsyon heir) could hold it for long enough to make any use of it. As such, it was the most flagrant and intimidating display of power I was capable of, and I'd used it as seldom as I could get away with.

In this scenario, however, there was no danger of me being misconstrued as a power-flexing bully; I had every excuse to say it had simply been the right tool for the job. It would certainly make the Starkissed storyteller's illustrations of this more interesting. It was, as far as I was aware, a unique use of the half-form, adding even more interest. For once, Starkissed would be delighted with me—and I could desperately use that goodwill.

I sighed as my pragmatism finally won out over my resentment and self-consciousness. Probably a sign of growing up. I knew what I would have chosen a year ago, and it would *not* have been this.

As I treaded water, I pulled the fire from my flameheart back into my blood, as I always did to change, except this time, I only let the change go so far. That was the hard part about the half-form: the transformation wanted to continue, like a candlewick wanted to burn through its course. Most people could either put the flame out or let it burn to the end. I could hold the flame in place, but even for me, that took constant, tremendous energy and effort.

Good thing it was full daylight now, and that noon still lay ahead.

When Sarah had asked to see my half-form, I had slowed down the process and even left out some aspects to not alarm her. Now, I didn't bother. With one exception, I let the change come as it would, and it was to a useful point in seconds.

Golden scales covered most of my body, thickening over vital organs in my torso, on top of my shoulders, and the fronts of my legs. My nails turned into claws on both my fingers and toes. Though my nose kept its shape, my normally above-average sense of smell increased twofold. My vision altered, changing to see the spectrum and details I only could as a drakón; I tested to make sure my second lid was there. Good. I'd need that.

Finally, three sets of golden horns grew from my head, one at the top, one at the upper back, and one just at the curve of my nape; each of them curled back and down, almost laying on top of each other, before spiking upward.

This was my first time with three sets, but I firmly suppressed the pang of grief. I didn't have the time, attention, or energy to spare for it now.

The one aspect of the change that I held back was my wings. I was afraid they would weigh me down and encumber me underwater, so I didn't let them get past stubs on my back. That would leave one of the most recognizable parts of half-form out of the illustrations, but the Starkissed could deal. I was giving them this much.

Even though the change only took moments, I didn't want to invite trouble, so the second I felt I had a firm grasp on the form, I took several deep breaths and dove back under the water.

As I'd hoped, my second lid helped focus and reshape my vision so that the water became clear and detailed. I swam downward, angling for the crystal bottle at least twenty feet below. The pressure built, but it was more manageable than it would have been in amáform, and the added strength helped make up for the spark I was using up at a dangerous rate. I was approaching the outcropping in moments, and my bodyguards swam wide circles around me, ready to intervene if necessary.

As predicted, chipin crawled out from their hidey-holes as they sensed me approaching. On average, they were about as long as one of my legs, with gray, segmented, insectoid bodies, long antennae, and probing mandibles. The only part I was mildly concerned about were their giant pinching claws, which they were raising toward me.

I mentally sighed.

I changed my hand just enough to bring out a stave. As I descended the last handful of erd, I used it to knock the closest chipin away with as much force as I could muster underwater.

I'm not here to hunt you, I told them, wishing they could understand. *I'm just here for the bottle.*

To them, though, that still amounted to a declaration of war. They'd found it, it was theirs, and now an extension of their selves. Threatening one of their treasures was threatening them.

Though my inner voice would impart no meaning to them, they sensed it for the challenge it was, just as if I had shouted the words instead. Chipin began swarming around the bottle in earnest, some trying once again to grab it to carry it away, while others waved their claws at me, snapping them menacingly. Unless I wanted to turn this into a slaughter, I was going to have to change tactics.

Thinking quickly, I put away my stave and brought out a gem instead—the biggest chunk of clear diamond that I had. With my blood so full of power right now, it began to absorb and glow from my effusions without me even doing anything.

The claws waving at me slowed...and the antennae sped up.

You want this? I asked them, holding it out from my body. I waved it from side to side, and their bodies followed. *You want* this?

Then I gave the gem an intentional burst of power, and it glowed like I held a sun in my hand.

The chipin were unusually still for a moment. Then they began swarming toward me.

I wound my arm back and threw the diamond from me—hopefully not so far that the chipin would lose track of it, but far enough to get them away. Almost as one, the swarm of a dozen or so chipin swam after the gem, claws snapping. Only one lingered over the bottle—the smallest one, only as long as my calf. There was something almost woebegone as it desperately grasped for the glowing stopper. I felt a bit of pity.

Sorry, I said as I knocked it away with my newly summoned stave. *I need her more than you do.*

But after I extracted the bottle from the crevice and began rising, I hesitated a moment, mentally sighed again, put away the stave, and tossed the small chipin a small, already charged gem. It had righted itself by that point and chased after the drifting gem, antennae quivering in what I interpreted as delight.

I smiled and swam hard for the surface, lungs burning. I'd carefully spaced out my exhales in small bubbles, but now I was aching to breathe in.

As I swam, though, a movement far to my right caught my eye—a great shadow in the distance, far beyond the ring my bodyguards were leisurely swimming around me. In my periphery, it was so massive, it took up most of the hundred or so feet of visual between the surface and the seafloor; the shadow hovered just beyond the sharp drop into the open ocean.

When I glanced again in that direction, though, there was nothing there—just clear waters as far as I could see.

I could have just imagined it. I could just be tired, or oxygen deprived. I could have just seen the momentary shadow of a cloud.

Yet I felt a chill crawl up my scale-covered spine. After eight years as Heir and a month and a half as King of Flame, I had instincts for danger as sharply honed as a blade, and I'd learned to trust them. When I didn't...people got hurt.

I surged for the surface. I didn't know what I had seen, and I wasn't entirely sure what to share at this point. But I knew one thing: I had to get myself and my people out of the water. As soon as possible.

I really hoped Sarah hadn't planned on going swimming.

CHAPTER THIRTY-NINE

FINDING

SARAH

I WOKE WITH MY side facing the stone wall of the bunk I was sleeping in, and for a moment, I hazily thought I was back in my hold, in the room I had slept in before giving that up to a sibling and moving to the special bedroom.

Then memory returned: Kor and Vadya's talk with me last night and my late-night walk with a handful of elites through the small underground, underwater tunnel to this shelter, where I could finally curl up and fall asleep.

I turned over with a groan and looked over the common room: the dramá version of a kitchenette, some tables and benches, more bunks, and a door leading to a privy.

It wasn't much, but it didn't need to be. I was told last night that it was meant to shelter the noble family in case of a disaster at Rosin. I'd also been told there was a concealed sea cave below us that allowed the family to either enter or escape by boat at night or draká by day, but to get here, we'd gone through the miles-long secret tunnel from Rosin so that the Devourer would hopefully not figure out where I was. Or, you know, give away the shelter's location.

Starkissed and their secrets. Half the elites they'd sent with me were Starkissed, and even those had to swear a blood oath to never reveal the tunnel or the shelter's location or existence. I'd been firmly warned to keep the secret as well, but either my rank or their uncertainty of how to safely administer a blood oath to me kept them from going to that extreme. Or, perhaps, they didn't want to risk my cooperation in this whole charade. Kor and Vadya had spent a long time getting me to agree, and only a very tempting offer had clinched it in the end.

Still, I couldn't help but feel another twinge of anxiety and guilt as my body gradually woke up. I felt like I had betrayed Ben's trust by leaving him without a word and being complicit in a ridiculous rite that I *knew* he would have much rather avoided.

But, in addition to the bribe, Kor had gone on at length about how important a successful search could be for Ben's self-esteem and public image.

"He can do this, Sarah," Kor said firmly. "This is a kind of challenge he can finally shine at in front of my clan, and he *needs* to shine for them. They need to see him being more than just a warrior and general. They need to see him being clever, agile, creative, and passionate—all qualities we admire, and all qualities he *has* but has so far been terrible at showing them. I've carefully calibrated each stage of the search to display just that, in ways that are natural for him. Yes, he'll grumble about it the whole way, but he can do this, and do it well. Please, give him this chance."

So, I did. What else could I have done? I wished we didn't have to back him into a corner for his own good, but I knew as well as Kor did what Ben would do if we tried talking to him about this first: even if we could convince him of all the benefits of a search, he would flatly refuse, simply because it meant separating me from him. He would say there were other ways to accomplish the same feats, together.

Yet Ben had to do this on his own. He couldn't rest on my prestige with the Starkissed; he had to build his own reputation with them, to show them what he was made of without me or his wings to help him.

And maybe he needed a reminder of that himself, too.

So, the burden of that separation fell to me. I could only hope that Ben wouldn't be too hurt or angry with me for it.

"Awake?" Petra asked me from where she sat on one bench, having noticed my eyes were open.

I groaned in answer, and she laughed. The other four elites scattered through the room glanced at me and smiled. Two were playing a game that looked a bit like chess but with gems for pieces, one was in the kitchenette cooking something, and another was sitting at a table by herself tending to her gear, just as Petra was.

"How's Ben doing?" I asked, pushing myself into a sitting position.

"Very well," Nevri, one of the Starkissed, said with a grin. She was also the oldest of the group; though I was still bad at guessing drakón ages, I would guess she was at least as old as Mom. She had assumed a matronly air with us all. "He's on the fifth challenge already. We were just talking about waking you up so you could eat something and we could get going."

They had kept me here thus far for my safety, but because every detail of the search was apparently being recorded for mass consumption, they had planned from the beginning to move me to a more suitable, publicly known location for Ben to finally "find" me.

As they were explaining things last night, I had to roll my eyes at their cheerful determination to pretend I could be lost to Ben—like a child insisting on playing hide and seek with an adult, fully knowing it would be no challenge for the latter. Even laying aside the fact that we could surge to each other as if we were gates, Ben was even better at pinpointing my location than I was at identifying his.

All I had right now was a gravitational pull going from my chest out into space, with only the direction and strength of the connection as my hints at where he was. Finding him would be a constant game of hot and cold, with frequent dead ends. Seldom was it possible to get somewhere by simply walking in a straight line toward it.

From what I had gathered, Ben could *see* me as a star in his mind—meaning, if he had a visual of the terrain or at least a map in his head, he could pinpoint where I was in relation to everything else and could then figure out the best way to get to me, which he had done many times ever since discovering he could. I suspected that he'd turned finding me into a sort of art form, and that he kept a closer eye on me than he let on.

I had no doubt that he had figured out exactly where I was by now, and the only reason he hadn't come to fetch me yet was because he was playing along.

Which...was surprising, to be honest. I'd half expected to wake up soon after dawn to him looming over me, scowling and saying he was taking me back, where we would have a *talk*.

Yet it was almost noon, I'd slept nearly my normal amount, and Ben was....

I blinked as my legs dangled over the edge of the bunk and I found the willpower to climb down. "Really? The fifth? Out of seven?"

"Yup," Petra said blithely.

"That's...fast, isn't it?"

I scrounged through my brain, trying to remember how long they told me to expect the search to take.

"Very fast," Yoshen, one of the only two males in our group, said as he set a plate of steaming food on the table. "Searches are designed to go on at least until sunset."

He was also a Starkissed, and at least in appearance, reminded me a lot of Kor with his dusky skin and short, curly midnight-blue hair. But unlike Kor, he had a short beard to match his hair, he was at least a decade older, and I knew by now that he was a lot less calculating and a lot more easygoing.

He gestured to the food with a flourish. "Your breakfast, O Queen."

But just as dramatic.

I huffed a laugh and turned around to climb down the ladder.

So...Ben was not only playing the game, he was excelling at it. I felt a flush of pride mixed with resignation. Kor had been right. As usual.

Although.... As I came back from the privy and sat down in front of my breakfast, a troubling thought occurred to me. There was such a thing as doing *too* well.

"Is it alright that Ben is getting through things so quickly?" I asked as I stabbed a fried vegetable and popped it into my mouth. After chewing and swallowing, I elaborated, "Is anyone accusing him of cheating?"

"Oh, some people are," Nevri said dismissively. "Usually the bitter ones who betted against him. But Kor was very careful in planning the trials. The Rosin grand tour committee vetted every one of them to ensure they passed a rubric they agreed on in advance."

Petra chimed in, counting off two fingers. "Kor and Yvera recused themselves from helping him altogether and testified under oath that they hadn't spoiled anything, and Ordran and the others guarding him have all sworn blood oaths against doing or saying anything beyond what's necessary to keep him safe."

Yoshen smirked as he cleaned up the kitchen. "So, there'll always be whiners, but these have no currents to carry them."

"And Lady Winthra has certified each passed trial as being legitimate," Kvina put in conclusively, moving a blue gem to an occupied square and making her opponent, Braven, scowl as she snatched his red one.

"What?" she said with a grin at him. "We need to wrap this up anyway, don't we?"

She also reminded me of Kor. Many of the Starkissed I'd seen had brown skin, which made sense given that most of their holds would be on islands, but there was a definite resemblance to him with Yoshen and Kvina, just as there was with Vadya and Fenra. It was that same dark blue in the eyes and hair, I had decided. Drakón soulcolors were supposed to be unique, but they seemed to be more similar the closer the relation. I'd seen the Starkissed blues range from Lady Winthra's cornflower to turquoise to indigo, but those four I had identified had a blue much closer to Kor's, a sapphire so dark it was almost black.

"Just once, I'd like to beat you at this," the Strongshield complained.

"Let me give you a friendly piece of advice," Nevri told him from across the room, smirking. She was an indigo, her drakón hair and eyes nearly purple. "Don't even try to beat a *tol'lon* at a game of wits. Give up now, while you still have some dignity."

"*Tol'lon*?" I repeated curiously. It translated in my head to *midnight*. The term sounded familiar for some reason.

"It's what the descendants of Lord Tolsyon call themselves," Nevri said easily. "Particularly the ones who keep his coloring."

Aaah. That explained a lot, actually.

I glanced between Yoshen and Kvina. "So, you two are related to Kor, too?"

"First cousin, once removed," Yoshen said with a wink.

Kvina grinned wickedly. "Second cousin."

I'd gathered that Kor had a rather large family—for a dramá, anyway—but just how many cousins did he have?

Or, perhaps a better question...why did I keep running into them? I knew Kor better than to think it was mere coincidence. Unfortunately...I also knew how little good it would do me to ask. Yet at the thought of a whole bloodline full of cunning, enigmatic *tol'lon* circling around me.... Well, it was a good thing that Kor had long since won my trust.

And yet, an anxious part of me whispered, *The same genes that made Kor, made Solim.*

As unfair as that thought might be, I couldn't entirely uproot the kernel of dread it planted. Not without understanding why the descendants of Lord Tolsyon appeared to be so interested in me.

THEY TOOK ME TO a grotto. Not the one underneath the shelter—one that was back on the main island. We had to hurry back down the secret tunnel, since Nevri got word just as we were leaving that Ben had found the sixth clue, and it would be a shame if he got to the last location before I did. Not to mention he might be frustrated or even alarmed if the seventh clue he received didn't seem to point him in the direction he knew I was in.

As I did my best to keep up with the power walking drakón, I wondered what Ben thought of seeing me move from one location to another. Hopefully he didn't think we were cheating.

I could see why the Starkissed thought the grotto had several advantages for a finale. First, it was near the entrance to the secret passage, so only minimal sneaking was required to smuggle me into it. Second, it was a much more dramatic setting.

Half of it was a gravelly stone cave floor, and the far half was seawater that glowed with distant sunlight and cast beautiful watery patterns onto the ceiling. The walkable portion was a kind of cultivated cave garden, complete with gravel paths that meandered between natural columns and giant glowing blue mushrooms, the biggest one coming up to my waist. A bioluminescent mold dotted the ceiling like a starry sky, and snow-white ivy crawled along the walls, adorned the columns, and spilled like a living curtain over the entrance.

"You should see it at night," Kvina said as I gaped. She winked at me. "It's quite romantic."

That was one word for this place. It was definitely a much more mysterious and theatrical end to Ben's search than a plain, one-room emergency bunker. State secrets aside, the bunker would have offended Starkissed sensibilities when this tale was told.

I was glad to have spent the night there rather than here, though.

Speaking of theatrics, the young Starkissed drakón led me to a higher rise in the above-water portion of the cavern, almost like a second level that overlooked everything. There she gave me a white suit coat to match my white two-piece outfit, except the coat had an elaborate train worthy of a bride. Then they had me sit on a bench while she and Nevri fussed over my hair and rearranged my train, almost as if arranging me for a photo shoot.

"Wait one second," I said with a laugh. "You're not actually expecting me to sit here like a prim princess and just wait for Ben to come to me, are you?"

They wouldn't have understood the term *princess* because they didn't have an equivalent in Drona, but I seemed to get my point across anyway. The women looked at each other, as if to say, *Here we go.* Then looked at me.

"Yes," Nevri answered innocently.

Before she could continue, I shook my head and said, "OK, first off, I don't think either Ben or I could keep a straight face. Second, it's not like the whole Starkissed clan is here to witness, so what does it matter?"

"We told you," Kvina said with a long-suffering expression. "All of this is being recorded to share with the others later."

"Yes, but not with *cameras*," I said, then hastily corrected, "I mean, nobody is speed painting portraits right now."

"On the contrary, Recorder Risha will do something much similar to that."

I blinked. "What?"

"Risha has been accompanying the King the entire day, witnessing the whole search," Nevri said. "She is a skilled lightteller and has an impeccable visual memory. Later this evening, she will recount all of it, using a crystal focus to display colorful light on a screen to depict each scene before our eyes."

I stared at her. Only now, the memory of the Moonfair pageant came back to me, with a light show of illustrations on the screen above the stage.

Flame help us, the Starkissed didn't have cameras, but they had figured out the next best thing.

Now I *really* understood why they had brought me here, and had me put on this elaborate white outfit with that impractical train, and why they were fussing so much with me now. This was the kind of set that a director would kill to have, and they were setting me up for the final shoot.

Kor. This was his doing. He had made it sound as if there would only be a verbal summary, an imaginative but purely oral retelling that would spare Ben and me from being "on stage." A visual retelling wasn't as bad as physically dragging us out in front of everyone, but it was far closer than I'd assumed. And Ben had been enduring that kind of scrutiny *the whole time*.

It could have been a simple misunderstanding—Kor not seeing that I wasn't comprehending the full picture—but I doubted that. He knew very well by now the kinds of things I did and did not know, and he could read me like I was an open, excruciatingly detailed book.

And there was that *look* that Nevri and Kvina had shared. As if Kor had warned them in advance that, at this point, I might start getting "difficult."

I was about ready to punch him—and thanks to all my training over the past month, I might make an impression this time.

I stood up at once, ruining their careful arrangement of my train. "No. No, absolutely not."

Nevri and Kvina looked alarmed.

"Queen—" Kvina began.

"I'm not going to pitch a fit and walk out that door," I said firmly. "I'm seeing this through."

I would not let Ben's sacrifice be for nothing.

"But I will not act out a scripted part in your drama, nor am I going to make Ben do the same. Not again. I'll finish this, but I'll finish this *my* way. *Our* way."

"Queen Sarah," Nevri said with a sigh, "the search represents the journey both of you have taken through life to find each other, and the end of the search represents the first time you meet."

Ridiculous, I thought, but I bit my tongue to keep the word from coming out. I had to tread carefully here. I had no right to trample over their traditions just because I didn't want to participate. For someone with a Starkissed's personality, it might be a fun, perhaps even moving experience, a true emotive rite of passage, a test of readiness before committing to something so much more binding.

Just because it was none of those things for Ben and me didn't mean I could tell them that the whole thing was a stupid idea.

Kvina chimed in. "Would you really rush to greet a complete stranger?"

"Ben wouldn't have gone through the search for a complete stranger," I snapped, refusing to embrace the metaphor. "In fact, he wouldn't have gone through it for anyone but *me*."

And only because I, not fully understanding what I was doing, gave him no choice. Not one that didn't involve an even greater spit in the Starkissed's collective faces.

"Exactly," Kvina said eagerly. "Because he's the Golden—"

Nevri shot her a warning look, and she cut off, looking sheepish at her slip. *Because he's the....*

I slapped a hand to my face with a groan. "The Golden Heir. And I'm the Moondaughter. *That's* what this is *really* about. Isn't it? You're using the search as an excuse to play out a *sequel*."

Because the pageant, at least, ended with the Golden Heir's search for the reincarnated Moondaughter, who died to save him and was reborn as a mortal.

I lowered my hands and glared at their carefully neutral expressions, which gave me all the confirmation I needed.

"Are you going to bring the Moonstar into this, or would that make it too obvious?" I drawled.

"Too obvious," Nevri said, unabashed. "The power of the story we are trying to weave is in its *subtlety*."

To me, this was about as subtle as a sledgehammer, but maybe it was only because I felt like I was being used as the hammer. At least she was being frank with me, now that I'd figured it out.

I sighed, folding my arms. "I'm *not* going to pretend I have no memory of Ben, if that's what you're wanting."

"You don't have to go to that extreme," Kvina said with a winning smile. "But a bit of hesitation...."

She trailed off as I glared at her.

Nevri sighed. "Queen Sarah, we have gone to all these lengths to cement your place within the Seven Realms. You have captured the hearts and imaginations of thousands, and right now your influence is burning like a blaze. But influence, like a fire, must be fed and tended, or it will go out. You will *need* that influence to carve a place for your people and rule in a way your conscience can sanction."

I looked away. That sounded too close to the argument Eskala had made to persuade me to reveal my identity to the Six Realms.

If you do not rule by baring your soul for them...you rule by wielding your fist. It's a hard, hard thing to do, to rule with vulnerability. But the alternative is even harder. And far crueler.

Sober now, Kvina said, "In order for the people to love you, they must know you. It's impossible for all of them to know you intimately, but we can help them feel like they do by telling them stories about you, stories that they'll love, and through them, love you."

I bit my lip. "But what if the stories are a lie?"

"Stories are always a lie," Nevri said with a smile and a twinkle in her indigo eyes. "But the best ones are beautiful lies that tell the truth, and far more plainly than true ones ever do."

When I just raised my eyebrow, she shook her head. "We're not trying to make you into something you're not, Sarah. We're trying to bring out the good qualities you both *have* but are too good at concealing."

I blinked at her. That echoed Kor's words about the benefits of the search, but he had made it seem like all the benefits were for Ben.

I sighed at myself. Of course Kor spun it that way. Because I would have only done it for Ben.

I couldn't believe I was doing this. But I settled my stance and looked at them both. "Alright. Maybe we should go over *exactly* what you had in mind, and then I'll decide what to do."

I would still do things my way. But maybe they could help me make *my* way work for all of us.

WE ENDED UP MEETING somewhere in the middle—somewhat literally. Instead of waiting dramatically at the back rise of the cave like some distant queen on her throne, I stood about thirty feet from the water's edge, where I was told Ben would emerge. (I had expected him to come through the ivy-covered entrance, just like we had, but I should have known better.)

I still wore the coat, and I still let them arrange my hair with braids, curls, and glowing diamond pins, and I allowed them to spread the train in a beautiful white circle around me. I was smug when even Kvina grudgingly admitted it looked a lot better that way. And I let them "disappear" into the shadows and behind the pillars of the garden. Ben and I wouldn't be left alone and unguarded, but that's what it could easily look like, with just a bit of artistic license.

I told them I would not follow their script. I was going to stand regally here for them at the start, but otherwise I was going to let things happen as they happened. When Ben came, I was going to be and do and say what he needed.

It was the least I could do for him after what I had put him through.

Just a minute or two after my guards made themselves scarce, I saw a familiar shape pass through the furthest, brightest part of the water, and I breathed a sigh of relief. Conversely, my heart began to pound. Even though *I* was glad to see Ben, he might not be so happy with me right now.

Ben broke the surface with a gasp, impatiently pulling the hair out of his face so he could see and breathe.

I couldn't help a chuckle, despite how much trouble I might be in right now—and how seriously the Starkissed would rather I treat this moment. Fortunately, I still didn't see this "recorder" in sight. "That's what hair ties are for, you know."

"Well, I didn't think about it," Ben grumbled as he swam his way to the stone lip nearest me.

Alas, a moment later, an unfamiliar blue-haired head broke the surface of the water. *She* had thought of a hair tie. She also seemed content to softly and expertly side-paddle to a different lip of the stone floor, all the while keeping a careful eye on the two of us. I was probably supposed to ignore her, just like you were never supposed to look at the camera—but a camera didn't catch you looking and wink at you.

Ben groaned as he pushed down on the stone lip with both hands to lift his body high enough to bring his knee up and climb up from there. "I think I've swum more today than I have in three years."

"Don't get out to the beach much?" I teased.

I was pushing my luck here, both with Ben and the recorder. Must have been the nerves. Plus, the way Ben's sopping wet shirt clung to his chest was very distracting. I was lucky he was wearing one at all, but that bit of cloth wasn't doing a whole lot of good right now.

"Do you think I've had the time?" Ben said incredulously as he wrung out his hair, which had darkened to the color of honey. Then shook his head like a dog.

There...might have been a few *practical* reasons for me keeping my distance at the start.

"Hang on," he said, turning his back to me. Then he peeled his shirt off.

Yup, practical reasons. This view of his broad shoulders, tightly muscled back, and trim waist wasn't much better than the front would have been. I quickly found a fascinating mushroom to stare at while Ben toweled himself off.

A minute later, out of the corner of my eye, I saw him turn back to me.

"It's safe to look now," he said with a chuckle, and for some reason, that made my cheeks heat again as I glanced back at him, even though he'd put on a fresh, dry shirt and had managed to get his pants to stop clinging to his legs.

It was something in the way he was smirking at me—a new burn in his golden eyes that told me he might have finally figured out why I became so discomfited when I saw him shirtless.

Well, it was only fair. I'd teased him, he could tease me. I'd gladly take teasing and smirking over the hurt or anger I'd been fearing.

But dang...I had never seen that glint of masculine confidence in Ben before, and that new look on him was doing all sorts of things to my insides that weren't helpful right now. It was a good thing I had already resolved not to follow a script, because the entire thing would have flown right out of my head.

I cleared my throat. "Ahem. Well. Congratulations. You found me."

His smirk died, and he approached me with a raised eyebrow. Silently, he said, *Later, in private, we're going to talk about this.*

I grimaced apologetically. *Understood. Sorry.*

He sighed, but when he reached me, he just scooped me up and crushed his lips to mine. I wouldn't have thought it possible, but the added spice of sun and salt on his skin took my normal intoxication with the taste of him to the next level. Ben, for his part, seemed perfectly willing to ignore our discreet audience and pending exposé and kissed me with a leisurely passion that set my already scrambled insides on fire.

I supposed we had to give them *something* to work with....

When his lips parted from mine, I only cracked open my eyes to meet his, which were half-closed as well.

"I missed you," he breathed.

I swallowed. "I missed you, too."

Even though, arguably, I'd had less time to do so, I still had. I had a surprisingly hard time falling asleep without the sound of his breathing nearby. I kept unconsciously reaching out for his pull and feeling it thinner than it should be. It was different somehow than all the nights we had been separated while we were on Romskal, maybe because that time it had been my choice, one I was having second thoughts about as I lay on my bunk.

He smiled slightly as he cocked his head and his eyes traced over me, drinking me in. Normally, I might have squirmed under that kind of look, especially with an audience, but maybe Ben wasn't the only one growing in confidence.

Instead, a smile of my own began tugging at my mouth.

Like what you see? I asked, raising my chin.

Mmm. Even Ben's silent voice was a wordless mental hum as he pulled me back in for another kiss, this one even longer. Even as slow as he took it, both of us were still breathless by the time he reluctantly parted and set me down.

That darn heartbinding couldn't come soon enough, and from Ben's half rueful, half burning expression, I knew he was thinking the same thing.

"Here," he said casually, bringing out a bottle and handing it to me.

It was the crystal bottle with the topper Kor had asked me to charge last night, still glowing brightly. Before, the bottle had been empty. Now it had something brown inside, and when I popped off the top, I saw it was an inch of sand.

I blinked up at Ben. "What's this for?"

He shrugged. "Beats me. The third clue was inside it, and the last clue said I was supposed to give it to you. I think, if I remember right, the searcher normally presents a gift to the one found, so maybe that's it—just a shiny present."

My eyes fell on the glowing white crystal topper, and my mind went back to my incredulous question about the Moonstar.

Subtle, Kor, I thought. *Real subtle.*

What? Ben asked, eyes narrowing as he studied my expression.

Later, I said, replacing the stopper and handing it back to him. "Hold this for me?"

If Kor wanted me to walk around with it, he would be disappointed.

"Sure," Ben said, taking the bottle and making it disappear. A bit more quickly than necessary. "Well, are you ready to go put an official stop to all of this?"

"What?" I asked, furrowing my brow. "This isn't it?"

Ben shook his head. "The search isn't over until I take you back to the King's Wing and you put the time candle out."

"What?" I said, my iceheart thumping in alarm. "The clock is still going? Why didn't you say so?"

I swept my train over my arm, turned on my heel, and began marching toward the exit.

Ben chuckled as he easily kept pace with me with those long legs of his. "Because I didn't care."

"You didn't care? Ben, you blazed through those trials for a reason."

How many hard-won seconds had our flirtations and leisurely kisses cost him? Why didn't he just grab my hand and go?

"Yes, and that reason was to get you back," he said, with a genuine casualness that made my iceheart pound for another reason. He held the ivy aside for me as I walked through, then followed.

This time, as he rejoined me, he took my hand and squeezed it three times, looking down at me. *I wasn't about to let them keep you locked up for longer than I could help. I came as soon as I could.*

I swallowed. All this time, I was worried about him—about how I might have hurt him, about how he was doing. And he was worried about me?

Did Kor really *get your consent?* Ben demanded, giving me a hard look that told me I'd better not lie to protect his leftwing. *Did he really explain this time?*

I finally understood. Last time, Kor had tricked me into participating, trapping me into the pageant with Ben. So, probably from the moment Ben discovered I was gone, he had been considering the possibility that the Starkissed had essentially *kidnapped* me.

Flame...no wonder he'd attacked those trials so determinedly.

Yet, if his gut had told him that was really what had happened, we wouldn't be here, having this discussion. He would have surged straight to me, and the "kidnappers," however well-intentioned they might have been, would have had a nasty surprise.

When Kor told him I was willing, Ben had grudgingly believed him and gone along with it, because he knew it wasn't worth causing an international incident over. But Ben was a worrier, and I doubt he'd been able to silence that one worry entirely, until now.

He'd broken *records*...to make sure I was alright. My chest clenched at the concern for just my mental wellbeing that implied.

I nodded, meeting his eyes so he would see the honesty there. *Mostly. He...obscured a few details. But I went with them willingly, and I never felt forced or frightened.*

Just exasperated, self-conscious, and resentful, but that was toward the end, and we'd worked it out. By the time I saw Kor again, I would be over it, and he wouldn't get that well-deserved punch. Probably why he had stayed away....

Ben snorted. *Well, obviously he didn't tell you about putting out the candle. What else?*

I looked at him sidelong as we reached the top of a long flight of stairs. *Didn't you want to wait until "later"?*

We still had company. Most of our guards and the recorder trailed us, and one of them led the way ahead. And now that we were out of the stairway, we'd reached a more populated level of the hold, with people passing by—and staring and whispering as they did so.

Ben schooled his expression into a more neutral mask, but he clenched my hand, and I knew him well enough to see the lingering tension. *I guess not, since it seems I can't wait. What didn't he tell you?*

I still hesitated. Ben would not like this anymore than I did. Less, even.

Sarah, Ben growled.

Making Ben wait wasn't a good idea, either. He would stew on it until he came up with something even worse.

Maybe I could satisfy him with just one of the two other things Kor had neglected to mention. *He didn't tell me that the Starkissed were going to put on a show. He made it seem like they'd just give an oral report or something. I should have known better.*

Ben huffed a dry laugh. *That explains a bit why you went along.*

I'm sorry, Ben. I really am. I didn't mean to put you through that level of public exposure. Are you...mad at me?

He glanced at me. *At you? What, no, of course not. You may have been more informed this time, but what else were you supposed to do? You're a victim of this as much as I am—again.*

He looked away, jaw set. *I am* mad, *but I'm mad at Kor, I'm mad at his clan, and I'm mad at myself.*

Yourself?

I was trying hard to ignore the stares and even claps and cheers we were gathering now. Ben seemed to do a much better job at it as he stared fixedly ahead and tried not to visibly glower.

I should have known better than you that something like this was coming. I should have protected you from them, but once again, I failed to do that. I'm the one who should be apologizing to you.

I sighed. *And what else were* you *supposed to do? We both did what we felt we had to, to do our duty, Ben. Maybe it's time we both grew up, realized that we can* do *this, and saw how much these people are trying to help us.*

He glanced at me and narrowed his eyes.

What? I asked wearily when he looked away and said nothing.

I'm going to ignore that sage advice for the moment, Ben said. *I want to stay mad and immature for a bit longer. Just long enough to get Kor to a dueling ring.*

I laughed quietly. *As if he'd let that happen.*

Come on, Ben wheedled. He'd recovered enough to wink at me. *You know you want to see it happen just as much as I do.*

I shuddered. *No, actually, I don't.*

Ben raised an eyebrow. *You don't think I can take him?*

I knew what the right answer was here. I struck a balance between assuaging his pride and being honest. *I'm sure you could, but at what cost? I hate to think what the two of you could do if you were* really *going at each other.*

The Golden King against the Tolsyon heir.... Even if Kor didn't use his ability to disappear into the ether.... They might just bring down the mountain.

Ben sighed. *Flame, I hate growing up. Life used to be so much simpler.*

When was your *life ever simple?* I teased gently, squeezing his hand.

Ben thought about that for a moment. Then grudgingly admitted, *Long before I was of age to challenge anyone to a duel.*

That's what I thought.

Chapter Forty

NEED

Koriben

That night, Sarah and I entered Lady Winthra's private box in Rosin's grandest theater, accompanied by a tumult of claps, cheers, and whistles. Sarah stood next to me with her hand on my arm as I raised my other hand to the crowd below and forced a smile in acknowledgement, and we both sat down in the seats of honor. Since tradition dictated that we be the last to arrive, Lady Winthra was already in her seat on my other side, and she waved at the stagemaster to signal they could begin.

The lights went out, and the musicians behind the screen played a vigorous, exciting melody—not composed for the occasion, thank Flame, just something the recorder thought appropriate, no doubt having worked out and rehearsed the entire production with them in advance. Her speed in getting this all ready for tonight grudgingly impressed me. She must not have had a moment's rest since before dawn.

I took a bit of satisfaction from that—the only bit I was probably going to get this evening. Now that I knew Sarah was safe and well, part of me regretted getting through the search so quickly. It meant that the Starkissed had even more time to pack in heartbinding rituals. The master of ceremonies was *thrilled*, and that was mildly frightening. It also meant that I had to sit through this torture *tonight* instead of tomorrow night.

All the respite I had received were the few deken between when we cleared the King's Wing of the day's spectators and when Sarah and I had to get ready and leave for the night's feast, which we had just come from. I spent a solid two deken of that precious time *sleeping*, and I worked with Kor for another two to take care of the Crown business that couldn't wait.

The only things that kept me civil with my leftwing were Sarah's warning and the fact that I would have twice as much work to do if I took him out. Kor, in turn, did his best not to radiate I-told-you-so smugness at what he considered a successful morning. Neither of us talked about it, and somehow we got through.

That had left me only *one* deken to relax with Sarah, and she was mostly in an overstimulated daze from a females-only thing that Vadya had dragged her off to while I was busy, and her only reply to my question about it was "lots of people, lots of gifts, very loud, very girly." She wouldn't even tell me what kind of gifts, and only when her cheeks started heating did I finally realize that I didn't want to know, so I shut up, and she was grateful. Almost as soon as she relaxed against me, she nodded off and didn't wake until Vadya came for her again.

I wished I could nod off right now. Being able to miss what was coming sounded downright blissful. Being able to sink through the floor would work, too.

Lights appeared on the screen, which took up the entire stage, forming into cohesive shapes and colors that the recorder was skillfully manipulating to tell the visual story of the search. No narration, thank Flame—just the musical accompaniment to fill the auditory void.

Sarah leaned forward in obvious interest. I wasn't sure whether to feel pleased or even more self-conscious about that, but I couldn't ask her to look away. This was partly for her benefit, after all. Everyone else who'd cared to stick around the King's Wing had seen at least parts of it and heard about others as word got around, and Sarah had been even less involved than most concealed partners, since she didn't even write the clues.

That was how the recording tradition got started: to show the one who had hidden just what the searcher had gone through to find them. It's just that most people *did* get a verbal retelling like Kor had tried to make Sarah think we would.

Lighttellers, especially of Recorder Risha's caliber, couldn't be enlisted for just anybody's betrothal search. Let alone a full theater and orchestra.

Lucky us.

Fields, Sarah muttered to me. *How did you figure that a small kelp forest was a fallow field?*

The clues were read at the start of the challenge, the only bit of narration for the whole production. Otherwise, what I was doing wouldn't make much sense—and everyone wouldn't be able to appreciate Sarah's (Kor's) cleverness.

I explained that there was usually a theme to the clues based on the couple's history, and she paid even closer attention, determined to figure it out. It didn't take her long after that hint. She let out a quiet, dry laugh while watching the vague, artistic depiction of me making my way through a dark tunnel deep within Rosin's abandoned mine with only shards of white light to point me in the right direction.

There was nothing particularly amusing about the scene, but it was several times removed from memory for her by this point, and Sarah's laugh was only the dry satisfaction of having figured out Kor's theme.

You chasing after me through an old rock wyrm tunnel in Romskal, Sarah said evenly. *It's the moongates.*

Yep, I said dryly. I was barely looking at the screen, for yet another reason now. Even two times removed, I didn't like thinking about that night—the time she truly *had* been taken from me, and I had spent agonizing dek thinking she was dead. I was once again in awe that Sarah could seem so calm about it. I had to focus hard on not clenching her hand like a vise.

So that's what Kor wanted me to charge all those crystals for, she said, and I glanced at her in time to see her rolling her eyes. *They were the closest thing he could get to my ice shards.*

Did he ask you to do them all last night?

No, actually, it was several nights ago. He said it was good magic practice. Same with the crystal bottle.

And you didn't think it strange that he collected them all at the end? I asked in amusement.

It sounded like they were Kor's crystals, but she'd done the work of filling them with power, which meant Kor couldn't just take them from her without her permission.

He said he wanted to study them, she said. *To see whether he could examine the differences in our energy wavelengths or some other nonsense.*

He probably did, too, I said wryly.

I know! Sarah said, gesturing subtly with her free hand. *That's the frustrating part. Most of the time, he's not even lying.*

I sighed. *Oh, I agree. You sure you don't want me to knock him around, just a bit?*

Her lips twitched as she glanced at me. *Honestly, yes, but I stand by what I said earlier: it's a bad idea. The two of you will either hold back and be dissatisfied or give it your all and break things. Lots of things.*

I sighed again and let her return her attention to the show.

A few dek later, partly to distract myself, I idly traced patterns with my thumbs on the back of Sarah's hand. She glanced at me and smiled.

Flame, she was beautiful. Even in the dim lighting, she was dazzling, with her hair braided back from her face and ears, white curls spilling wildly everywhere else, and the gossamer white and silver dress she had worn for tonight. Even her transformation and hard training over the past two months hadn't entirely taken away her soft, gentle lines and subtle curves. I found my eyes lingering on the lines of her delicate collarbones, heart-shaped face, and noble, dainty chin more than once.

What had I done to deserve her?

Which reminded me....

Tell me something, I said to her.

What? she asked, shifting away from her amused observation of me going through an obstacle course in one of Rosin's less-frequented halls. The Oshal moongate had been the least difficult for us to find, and Kor had taken some liberties in livening it up.

I tried to match the lighthearted turn in her mood in my tone. *Vadya said she and Kor bribed you to go along, and they wouldn't tell me with what. What in the Flame's name was that tempting to you?*

Oh, she said, cheeks heating. *It wasn't really about the bribe. I was already caving, and they just offered that to clinch it.*

But what was it? I was trying hard to keep my expression merely curious and my voice light, but the mystery had been eating away at me all day, and I was fit to bursting by this point.

It was more than the enigma. I felt like a failure as a betrothed that I didn't know what Sarah wanted that badly. I was painfully aware of how little I had given her, and how much I had taken from her forever. And how much she had given me: everything, and every day more. In my mind, if she wanted something, then it was my solemn duty and the duty of everyone she had helped and saved to give it to her.

Sarah examined me, her piercing silver eyes seeing more than I wanted, as usual. That probably made her decide to share, even though her cheeks stayed warm and her eyes darted away. *They...promised not to bother me with any more decisions about the heartbinding.*

My flameheart thudded. *What...decisions?*

She huffed quietly. *Oh, you know, the usual things a bride is apparently supposed to care about: colors and themes and table runners.*

I let myself relax, hoping she hadn't noticed my momentary tension. *Oh, you mean about planning the celebrations around it.*

Right, Sarah said, her exasperated tone unchanged, so perhaps I was in the clear. *They bugged me most nights while we were in Romskal. I tried to tell them I honestly didn't care, but they persisted, until finally last night they said they'd leave me out of it if I went along with the search.*

It was that important to you? I asked. I had settled back now, relieved to discover that I hadn't been drastically neglecting her needs.

Yes, Sarah grumbled. *I've got enough on my plate without planning a wedding on top of it. What do I know about weddings? I haven't even been to that many Earthren ones. I told Kor that if he wanted an Earthren's opinion, he could ask my mother. I feel a bit guilty about the Realms-shaking ramifications of pushing Mom and Kor to combine forces, but I'll still do it.*

You think your mother is like Kor? I asked in puzzlement.

I pictured Maria in my mind. In appearance, she was smaller than Sarah by at least half a foot, and with skin a couple shades darker, but otherwise she was much like an older version of Sarah. But from what I had seen of her personality, she was even gentler and more timid. Delicate in a way my *sera* wasn't—not fragile, just tender and sweet, like an easily bruised sava fruit. Emotional, too. In those senses, Sarah was much more like her taciturn father, Jake. If there was something about my eyes that still looked like my mother's, then Sarah's looked like her father's.

None of my impressions of Maria made her sound like the perfect coconspirator for my leftwing.

You haven't seen her in event-planning mode, Sarah said darkly. *The culture she comes from throws a* lot *of parties. Weddings, for her, are even worse. She drove us nearly insane for Michael's wedding, and he was the groom! I'm her first daughter to be engaged, and she's going ballistic. Every time she hears I'm calling someone back home, she bursts in and asks about the wed—er, heartbinding.*

I had gathered the English word "wedding" was the equivalent to the Drona "heartbinding," but I appreciated the confirmation.

She's driving me crazy. Sarah's voice then cheered a bit. *I don't know why I didn't think of putting the two of them together before. That's two birds with one stone.*

An odd idiom, but I thought I got the point. Besides, keeping up with Sarah's influx of emotive English wasn't the part that bothered me.

Sarah, you didn't tell me about any of this. If something was troubling you this badly, don't you think I'd want to know?

Sarah went silent for a moment, then said quietly, *I'm sorry. I didn't think about it that way. And really, it was mostly annoying in the moment, and then I'd get over it. By the time I saw you again, I was fine. I'm always happier when I'm with you.*

That last admission and her apology helped settle me again. I squeezed her hand three times. *I'm always happier with you, too. But I also want to be the person you come to with your problems and worries.*

Sarah squeezed back. *But* everyone *comes to you with their problems, Ben. That's what you do all day, and I see how it exhausts you. You don't need to hear me complain.*

I should have anticipated this. I'd learned within the first day after meeting Sarah that she tended to ignore her own needs in favor of those around her. But she had come a long way since then in asking for what she needed, and my vigilance had slipped. In all our conversations about her days and nights, I should have thought it strange that she never mentioned anything negative to me.

Knowing this was partly my fault, I kept my voice calm and kind. *Actually, yes, I do. Of all the people I want to help most, it's you, and you not giving me that chance bothers me. How are we supposed to be partners if we go to other people with our problems?*

Sarah sighed and said, *That makes sense. Sorry again.*

I wasn't looking for another apology. I just want to make sure you know you can talk to me, that I need you to talk to me. Let me decide if I've had all I can handle that day. At least ask.

Understood. Fortunately, she sounded amused, not offended.

I'm sorry for the lecture, I said ruefully. *I just want to save us problems over the horizon. Our jobs...they're the kind that will wear you to the bone if you let them, and that doesn't do anyone any good. Trust me, I've just been there, and it's...bad. We both—me included—have to be better at seeing to our own needs.*

Good, Sarah said. When I glanced at her, she had a smug smile on her face. *I'm glad that you know that about yourself, too.*

I smiled thinly. *I'm trying. But I give you permission to remind me.*

Oh, I will, she said, squeezing my hand three times. *Maybe between the two of us, we'll survive this.*

Flame, I hoped so.

AFTER SARAH AND I returned from the theater, I went to bed, but thoughts of the shadow I had seen in the water during the second trial had me tossing and turning on my pallet for several deken, replaying that moment and the events right after over and over in my head.

When I returned from the second trial, I walked back into the central court of the King's Wing with deliberate slowness to silently speak to Kor and Yvera about what I had seen. Neither of them doubted me for a moment; they knew me and trusted my instincts too well by now for that. In fact, Yvera was all for calling off the search for my safety and beginning a hunt immediately, and Kor—and, surprisingly, I—had to talk her down.

As sorely tempting as it was to end the search at that point, saving myself a bit of discomfort wasn't worth the repercussions. Calling it off so suddenly would have required a public explanation. The ones who believed me would panic, and the ones who didn't would think I was being duplicitous, and I would have an even greater uproar on my hands than if I had refused to take part from the beginning. I simply didn't have the proof or even a definitive idea of what I had seen, nothing that could justify halting the search.

So, while Kor and Yvera subtly alerted Lady Winthra, and she and her wings in turn alerted the Waterguard and took precautions, I went on with it. Fortunately, only one more trial had involved swimming, and that was right at the edge of Rosin Island—just a quick dive to get to the grotto where Sarah had been moved toward the end. (I'd been alarmed when I saw her star moving, but Ordran explained to me everything was fine and that moving her had been part of the plan all along.)

If I'd had to get in the water any more than that, Yvera might have been intractable. As it was, she added two more bodyguards to the three I already had, plus Risha. I was a bit surprised at her restraint in not assigning even more, but maybe she realized any more would raise questions we didn't want to answer. Perhaps the Flame had worked a miracle and a month and a half of being the *King's* rightwing had finally taught her the occasional need for discretion.

Every time I returned to the King's court, Yvera would give me an update on the security measures and the hunt, each time with nothing to report on the latter. I wasn't sure whether to be glad about that. On the one hand, the safety of my people and my reputation were at stake, yet on the other, I desperately wanted the danger to have gone away on its own.

I never could doubt there *had* been a danger. If anything, I became more certain the more I thought about it, until I was grimly sure that what I had felt was a warning from the Tree Herself.

The hunt went on until sunset, and no one caught a glimpse or sniff of the "shadow predator," as we'd begun calling it.

Kor protested that the adjective made the creature sound unsubstantiated and thus didn't help our case. Yet, if I had given the Starkissed a good impression in one measure, it was as a competent warrior. I'd been called many things by my detractors, but a coward wasn't one of them—and if someone had been tempted, then the thought of facing me in the ring to answer for that insult had probably silenced them. So, for now, my reputation with Lady Winthra, the Waterguard, and the hunters seemed to hold, but Kor was determined to make sure this incident did not erode it.

I said nothing as Kor and Yvera argued terminology, thinking to myself that "shadow predator" was more appropriate than either of my wings realized. I couldn't explain what I had seen or felt; I didn't have the words to describe how something could have seemed so monstrous and yet undefined, so imminently dangerous and yet not fully there. *Shadow* was the best word I could think of for it—save one.

Another word occurred to me as I finally had time to think and remember while I lay in the dark.

It couldn't have been.... I couldn't have seen.... Could I?

No. It was supposed to be impossible. The Devourer would have needed Royal blood to manifest in the Six Realms, and not just a few drops of blood—a body's worth. A life's worth.

But...how much would it need to be only partially there? To just...cast a shadow?

No, no—I couldn't think that way. That path was too dark and too terrifying to face. That path would drive me mad. Sarah was safe right now. She was *safe*.

And yet, my dream warning from the Tree kept coming back to me.

You have one moon, son of Flame.

One moon before...

The Devourer came back.

This time for my everything.

This time for Sarah.

And if I didn't....

She....

Gah! I sat up just for some movement and put my head in my hands, forcing myself to breathe slowly. I wasn't going to get any sleep like this. My flameheart was pulsing too rapidly, my head was spinning, and my chest felt like a vise.

Unfortunately, I knew what I needed, and I couldn't get it. The only thing that would calm me right now was holding Sarah—sensing in every way that she was safe and well.

At least for tonight.

Yet falling asleep with Sarah was *not* an option. Especially not with how desperate I was feeling right now. I couldn't trust myself to make rational decisions in this frame of mind, especially not about her.

Part of me was already wanting to grab her right that dek and bring her to the Rosin Tree for a secret heartbinding, but that was wrong in all the ways. That was me letting my fear of losing her take precedence over her happiness again. Sarah wouldn't understand why it was necessary unless I told her everything, and telling her *now*, just to get her to agree to do it now, might cause her the most pain I still had the power to inflict. She would probably do it, but she might never forgive me. She *shouldn't* forgive me.

I had to marry her right the first time. Properly, in every sense. Publicly, finally, traditionally, even extravagantly, if that's what it took to prove to her and the Seven Realms that I would put her happiness before everything.

Though the Tree hadn't told me to do it this way, now that I had committed to this course, I felt to my bones that it was the right one—right for Sarah, for her family, for me, for the Realms. I didn't need the Tree to tell me that.

That didn't make it easier to risk Sarah's life by waiting, especially on nights like this one.

I sighed and stared sightlessly out into the dark room. I pinched my nose, trying to ignore the headache I could feel building. Even so, I knew there was no point in lying back down—nothing would come of it.

I needed sleep. I needed Sarah. I would not get both...so I might as well go find Sarah.

I was pushing myself to my feet before I'd realized I'd even decided, and I had pulled a shirt on before I reached the door.

Fortunately, her star was close by, still in the King's suite—her study, if I had to guess. Sure enough, when I opened our bedroom door, I saw the brightest light coming from the open door of her study and heard her voice. Only when I was halfway across the central room did I realize she was reciting something: all the conjugations of the verb *say*.

"...serron, serrihn, serrahn...gah, serraht."

"Yes, that last one's an irregular," her language tutor said sympathetically.

What was her name? Alda? I hadn't met her yet, partly since, after joining our entourage, she kept later deken to accommodate her pupil. I had just heard about her and her lessons from Sarah.

I stopped, hesitating. My anxiety had lost its sharpest edge after I'd entered the dimly lit central room and heard Sarah, especially in the middle of something so ordinary. I hadn't realized she would be working with her tutor at this deken. Perhaps I could just sit here and listen, without interrupting, and Sarah would never have to know I was awake....

"If all of it were irregular, it would be easier," Sarah grumbled—in perfectly grammatical, only faintly accented Drona.

My lips flickered in an unconscious smile.

"True. But you almost had it!"

I warmed to this teacher, and I partly forgave Vadya for her part in the search this morning, just for finding Sarah someone who was kind and encouraging. Sarah needed at least *one* of the many people preparing her for her role to be just like that.

Silence fell, then Alda asked curiously, "Queen Sarah? What is it?"

"Could you wait for a moment?" Sarah asked, tone distant, as if her focus was abruptly elsewhere.

"Of course."

I heard a chair shift, and belatedly, I realized Sarah was coming to her door. I didn't have time to leave, so I stood in place, hopefully looking as if I had planned for her to notice me there all along.

Her face was only concerned, not surprised, when she came to the doorway of her study and saw me standing there. So, she *had* sensed me. I kept forgetting that, even though she experienced the connection differently, she still felt me somehow.

"Ben?" she asked quietly.

"I couldn't sleep." I shrugged, trying to seem casual. "Sorry, I didn't mean to interrupt anything. Go back to your lesson."

Sarah's eyes tightened. I knew I hadn't fooled her when she ignored my last statement and looked back into the room. "Miss Alda, could we...."

"Of course, we were almost done anyway. We can pick up again tomorrow."

I heard clicks and rustles of paper, and a moment later, an elderly amón woman emerged with a tablet and papers in her arm, dressed in Battleblood purple. I kept my face neutral, but inside, I felt a flicker of surprise.

A Battleblood linguist—and a gentle one at that. Interesting.

Her clan origin still showed itself in her dark hair sprinkled with gray that was pulled into a regimented bun, her olive skin, the disciplined set of her clothing, and her lithe body and supple movements that belied her age. Still, her brown eyes were warm when they met mine, not seeming to mind my intrusion in the slightest.

She nodded deeply to me in respect. "King Koriben."

I nodded back deferentially, a gesture of my thanks for her understanding. "Madam Alda, was it?"

"It was, and is, and as far as I am aware, will be tomorrow," she said, eyes twinkling.

"Ah," I said, forcing a smile to my lips. "A linguist indeed."

"I try not to disappoint," she said with a wink. She nodded again, this time placing her hand over her heart in a salute. "Warm hearth and safe sleep to you, O King."

"And to you," I said with another nod in return.

While she turned and left the suite, Sarah crossed the room and slipped her hand in mine. She gestured her head questioningly back to our bedroom. I sighed.

Even though the central room was vacant now, we never had the suite entirely to ourselves. Attendants were just down another hall; some of them were sleeping in small bunkrooms, and others—the ones on duty—were gathered in a common room that functioned as both a guard chamber and hangout area. No doubt through the many spells and sensor wards they could monitor from that room, they knew already that I was awake and speaking with Sarah, but since we didn't need anything from them, they stayed away. Yet that meant the only places we had true privacy were our bedroom and our studies, and even in those three rooms, there were various wards that would alert them to the possibility of danger.

Such extremes hadn't always been necessary or even standard. Avva often hadn't bothered—especially in Crownhold and in the earlier, safer years of his reign—and I had tolerated nothing of the kind during the first month of mine. But since Sarah returned, and especially since we began traveling together, I had given Yvera free rein to be as stringent and innovative as she liked, and she didn't need to be told twice.

Those measures didn't just stem from my protectiveness toward Sarah and Yvera's toward me. Everyone concerned with our security, from Kor to Alyish to Eskala, from Ordran to the lowest-ranking elite, from Vadya to the last carefully vetted attendant agreed that the two of us presented an unprecedented temptation to the Devourer: not just one but two young Monarchs, both of whom having defied the Devourer and survived. Those factors all combined into a potent motivation that we could not afford to underestimate.

If Sarah and I didn't want to be overheard, we had to leave this room. But though I felt steady and sure of myself again, our bedroom still felt wrong just for the symbolism of it. Besides, I was likely to get agitated again as soon as I began to tell Sarah what was keeping me up this late—and I knew she *would* insist on an honest answer. As she should. I couldn't lecture her about not coming to me with her problems and not come to her with mine.

At least this one.

Though my gut twisted with guilt about the other that I still would not tell her. Not yet.

I nodded toward her study. She lifted an eyebrow in surprise, but she led the way inside and shut the door behind us.

"There's something I have to tell you," I said with another sigh. "About something I saw earlier today. I may be wrong—Flame, I *pray* I'm wrong—but if I'm not...."

Sarah clenched my hand and led the way to the small sitting area in the corner of her study.

"Tell me."

CHAPTER FORTY-ONE

SHADOW

SARAH

SOON AFTER DAWN THE next morning, I was on Ben's back as he soared over the Rosin Archipelago, circling over a place where the continental shelf ended and plunged down into the depths of the seafloor. Ben said it was roughly where he had seen the shadowy something yesterday morning.

This morning, there was a giant tear in the outermost net of magic that normally kept large water-bound predators—consumed or otherwise—at bay.

That was why I was up here with Ben at this unholy hour—unholy for me, that is. The breach in the net was so urgent that someone had come into our room to wake Ben; as hard as the attendant and then Ben had been to try to not disturb me, I'd woken up too, and once awake, I had insisted on knowing what was going on and coming along, despite Ben's protests. Since there didn't seem to be any immediate danger, he didn't have much of a leg to stand on, and when he tried the sleep tack, I told him I wouldn't be getting any more, even if he left me. That finally made him give in.

Fortunately, he got past resignation and shifted into King mode as soon as we left our suite, and that meant making sure I understood what was going on right now.

See the frayed edges? Ben said to me.

They looked a bit like I might have expected from hearing about the net and its tear: a multitude of torn filaments that now undulated at the surface of the water at the top edges of the V-shaped cut. At least, I assumed the cut was something like a V, but I couldn't see much below the surface, especially not from this height and not with the blue draká swimming all around and through it. Those draká gave me the scale of the breach: at least three could comfortably swim abreast, meaning the cut was at least a couple hundred feet wide at the top.

I had not expected those filaments to be as thick as my torso; nor for the weave, if I was judging the intended shape correctly, to have been in triangles, and of the size that I could have easily fit through; nor for whatever fibers it was made of to look and shimmer much more like water than thread. In fact, the color of the filaments reminded me much of the color of the water, except dark as ocean depths nearest the torn tips, then lightening to the color of the surface water until I lost sight of the net altogether.

I see them, I answered.

That's bad, Ben said. *The net is only visible when it's damaged.*

So they know where to repair it? I asked, matching his businesslike tone.

Exactly.

Why make it invisible at all? To trap the predators?

No, the net is primarily meant to repel, not trap or kill. And it's good at it, despite being invisible. Trust me, if you were to go near it, you'd know what I mean. You'd know *it's there—and that's with you being identified as a friend. Nothing outside the spell's parameters—consumed or not—wants to go near that thing. If it tries anyway, it gets the shock of its life. And the Waterguard is alerted, so if it's daylight and the creature isn't dead from the shock, it's going to wish it was real soon.*

Then why? I asked, determined to understand. I wouldn't bother Ben if he were busy, but he'd already gotten his answers from the others and now he'd firmly told me it was my turn for questions. As long as I was here, he seemed equally determined to make the most of my loss of sleep.

They're the Starkissed, Ben said dryly. *I'll give you one guess.*

I only had to think for a moment. *Appearances.*

That's right. They also say something about "not wanting to disrupt the natural ecosystem," but the net was going to do that no matter what it was made of or made to look like, and either the ecosystem would adapt or it wouldn't. They made sure it adapted, centuries ago. No, it's about appearances. As long as you don't go near it, you can swim and fly about and pretend that there's nothing there but clear blue sea.

What is it made of? I asked curiously.

Magic.

I waited for Ben to go on, but he didn't.

I said, *Wait, that's it? Just pure...*magic?

Other than some crystalline anchors along the shelf's edge, yes. Just magic.

I stared. First down at the V, then around at the archipelago. *Wait. This net goes the entire way around these islands...and there's three of them? And they are almost entirely made of magic?*

That would have meant miles upon miles of sheer...power.

After only a couple months in the Seven Realms, I was by no means an arcane expert, but even I knew that represented a *staggering* amount of energy. More than I had thought the dramá could spare.

Yes, Ben said, voice grim. *Again...these are Starkissed. There's a reason I twist my tail in a knot trying to keep them happy, Sarah. No other clan could pull a magical feat like this off to begin with, let alone maintain it for over four centuries.*

For that reason alone, I was glad I came with Ben to see this. I didn't know if it had been one of his intentions all along, but if not, it should have been. This showed me in a way I couldn't have learned otherwise the magical might the Starkissed could bring to bear.

In that way, this net seemed a good representation of the Starkissed themselves. On the surface, they may look frivolous, extravagant, even childish, but if you looked beneath...you would find careful preparation, staggering power, and cunning brilliance. If you underestimated them, it was at your peril.

Flame and Ice help us all if they should ever go to the bad. Or even just get petty and human and decide to break off on their own.

Is that why they did this? I asked quietly.

Ben matched my tone, perhaps understanding what was going through my head right now. *I can't rule that out as a factor. There's never just one reason for the things they do. But I believe that, primarily, the answer is no. They did it to protect their own...and they're very good at doing that.*

They did it to protect their own....

Something about that statement struck a deeper chord with me than Ben had meant it to. But the connection didn't have time to fully form before Ben went on, his tone turning grudgingly admiring.

The almost purely magical nature of the net is why it's so effective. It's highly fluid and customizable, meaning that it's nondisruptive to benevolent marine life and dramá. Boats can sail through it and dramá can swim through it without a problem. Migrating creatures that use the islands as a stopping point come and go without harm. For over three centuries, almost nothing has been caught in it that wasn't dangerous. It's lethal to what it needs to kill, and it's harmless to what it doesn't.

In other words, it defied one of the fundamental laws of the universe: the more secure something was, the more inconvenient it had to be. This net tossed that rule out with the sharks and giant squids—or whatever heretofore unspecified "predators" it was keeping out.

The amount of magic it took to maintain it seemed a small price to pay, Ben said heavily. *It was the apex of our defensive capabilities. No storm could break it. No creature could damage it more than a small amount. The greatest damage came from simply running out of power, and that was only ever in small sections—the Starkissed were meticulous in caring for it. It was near infallible.*

Was.

I stared down at the hundreds-foot gap. And a tingle of warning heat went down my spine.

Ben, I said quietly. *What could do this?*

Ben didn't answer for a long moment. *Nothing we've ever dealt with before.*

Not for the first time, my mind went to Ben's revelation late last night.

I shivered, despite the warm sun and balmy breezes over this tropical paradise. It seemed impossible that darkness could be encroaching here. And yet....

Just as with the net, something might rest below the surface here that we would underestimate to our regret.

This is bad, isn't it? I asked.

That was why they'd *woken* Ben over this. That was why, even with no danger in sight, Ben had made me swear to surge straight into him the moment he told me to. Because the moment he had heard about the breach, he knew what it meant, and his mind had gone at once to the shadow, and what he feared it to be.

Well, Ben said wearily, *no consumed have been reported coming through the breach, and the predators they've found so far have been minor. We knew about the breach before anyone got into the water, and we were able to call the boats in quickly. So, right now...no. But I know what you mean, and the answer to that is...yes. Very bad.*

I reached as far as I could over the saddle to place my hand on one of his large golden scales. I didn't know if he could sense the touch through that hard, warm, polished surface, but maybe I did it to comfort myself more than him—to feel him there, warm, golden, strong.

Well, two minutely good things came of this, Ben said.

What? I asked hesitantly, not sure I wanted to know the answer.

First, everyone believes me now.

I sighed. *I never doubted you, Ben.*

I know. Nor did anyone who knows me. But now everyone is taking me seriously, down to my greatest detractors. Which leads to the second good thing.

And that is? I asked in weary amusement, seeing where this might be heading.

With forced cheer, Ben said, *We might get out of some Starkissed games.*

BEN'S SECOND STATEMENT TURNED out to be overly optimistic. Since there was no sign of the thing that had made the tear in the net and there was little Ben or I could do to help the Starkissed repair it, both Kor and Lady Winthra decided the best thing the Monarchs could do was keep up morale.

That meant the festivities were to proceed as planned.

Ben was annoyed but mostly resigned, as if he'd had little hope to begin with. But Yvera was livid, especially since the first thing on the agenda for the day was a hunt. Usually, they went out into the deep ocean to hunt a water predator—something called a kella—but considering the dawn's events, they were bringing in something they could chase on land across one of the larger islands of the archipelago. The catch: it was a *bachelor* hunt. Males only.

And not just that—only *Starkissed* males. This was, apparently, an initiation kind of ritual, no outsiders allowed.

"You cannot be serious!" Yvera was shouting from Ben's study as I beat a hasty retreat to my bedroom. Since the Starkissed hadn't planned anything for my morning, assuming I would be asleep, Kor told me to go back to bed. I doubted I would get any more rest, but I wasn't about to look a gift excuse in the mouth.

"I'm his rightwing!" Yvera raged.

In a way, I understood her emotional reaction. The last time she had let Ben keep her away on Oshal, Solim trapped and nearly sacrificed him. Now, not only could she not accompany him, only her male Starkissed elites could.

With both Solim and Kor as her primary examples of Starkissed males....

"And I'm his left!" Kor shouted back. "Yv, I swear on my life that I'll bring Ben back—"

"*You*?" Yvera said scathingly. "You're a—"

Whatever ignorant insult Yvera was going to hurl at Kor was cut off first by Ben closing his study door, then by me closing our bedroom door. Thank Flame for soundproofing charms. When the lock engaged, I sagged against the door in relief.

If only you knew, Yv, I thought.

How Kor could stand letting Yvera always underestimate him, I had no idea. Centuries-long secret or not, Kor surely had other ways to bring Yvera down a few pegs than revealing his pseudo-Royal status. I couldn't imagine that Kor's restraint had to do with mere benevolence; that degree of magnanimity wasn't in his character. Maybe it was that whole thing about not abusing his powers.

Then, as I dragged my feet with surprising sleepiness back to the bed, I thought, *If this grand tour drags on for much longer, those two are going to kill each other.*

THE HUNT WAS STILL going by the time I woke up, which was fine by the Starkissed, since they had another females-only activity planned for me: ritual bathing in yet another grotto, this one with a pool fed by a mix of a freshwater spring and saltwater from a source that, I was assured, was far too narrow for a predator to get through.

Vadya told me on the way there that this was yet another accommodation, but one planned much further in advance. Traditionally, they bathed in one of the archipelago's lagoons, consequently called the "Women's Lagoon," but the water there was warm, and sunbathing and other sunny, beachy activities featured prominently. Out of deference for my preference for the dark and cool, and Kor's thoughtful warning to Vadya that I sunburned, they'd chosen this grotto, and the participating women—Lady Winthra included—were surprisingly good sports about it.

In fact, with very little "ritual" about it, they stripped without hesitation and jumped into the cool water, squealing and fighting playfully with each other to warm up. I was much slower, since I still wasn't used to undressing in front of strangers, even if they were all women. I'd become somewhat inured with having attendants helping me dress all the time, but I knew most of them by name by now, whereas I knew only a sprinkle of these Starkissed women, and some of them only looked familiar because they had the *tol'lon* dark hair and eyes.

There are quite a few of them here, I realized as I pulled my shirt off. I counted dark heads and estimated that perhaps ten out of the fifty or so women here were *tol'lon*. A fifth. And that was only the drakón; who knew how many of those amón were Kor's relatives, too.

Contemplating how many of them were subtly gathering around me didn't make me feel any easier. I should have talked to Ben about this, but the concern kept slipping my mind when I was with him. Plus...he had such a bias against the Starkissed already. What if I was only letting his disgruntlement affect my judgment? Or if I, in turn, made his opinion worse—all for nothing?

"You can leave your underwear on, if you like," Vadya offered, standing next to me. *She* was already stripped, and very unconscious of the fact. Whichever Earthren had suggested that the cure for stage fright was to imagine everyone else in the room naked had obviously never been among the dramá.

She gestured to her large duffel. "I brought an extra pair for you, just in case."

"That wouldn't offend anyone?" I asked, trying to keep the hopefulness from my voice.

Vadya rolled her eyes. "Sarah, we're *here* because we're trying to make you comfortable."

If you'd wanted to make me comfortable, you would have left me out of it entirely, I thought, but I knew that was unfair. Vadya had made a good point: the Starkissed had been more than accommodating so far. The least I could do was continue to meet them halfway.

As I approached the water, the play fighting and splashing all stopped, and everyone turned to look at me with expressions of eagerness and mischief. I froze, like a rabbit whose scent had just been caught by a pack of foxes.

Maybe I shouldn't have taken so long to undress.

"Queen Sarah," Vadya said formally. Her face, when I glanced at her, was absurdly solemn. "Normally this duty is done by a mother, but as your chief of staff, the de facto planner of your heartbinding, and the woman you know best here, allow me to perform this simple, time-honored ritual to welcome you to the ranks of Starkissed women."

She paused, just long enough that I thought she was waiting for me to do or say something.

"What—"

She shoved me.

I fell, and the next thing I knew, my gaping mouth was flooded by brackish water.

I thrashed to the surface and coughed it up. The women crowded around me, cheering and laughing uproariously.

"Vadya!" I shouted as soon as I could, pounding the water with my fists.

She had already cannonballed into the water, complicating my recovery with her splash, and she now swam to me under the surface, which was illuminated by dozens of glowing blue pebbles that I had seen each of the women toss in before jumping in. Vadya glided to me with the ease of a mermaid and surfaced with a huge grin on her face.

"You called, my Queen?"

"You...." I growled inarticulately. Then, in a burst of petty aggression that I hadn't displayed toward anyone outside my family, I launched myself at her, and the two of us tumbled below the surface. Even underneath, I could hear the laughter and cheers egging us on. Something told me I had completed the "ritual" by doing pretty much the same thing all of them had done to their own mothers.

Far from further infuriating me, that made me feel...something warm. Like I was now a part of something.

A family.

THE STARKISSED WEREN'T FINISHED with me, of course. They somehow made a seat out of their arms while treading water and held me up while singing a song that, on the surface, sounded like a nursery rhyme, but I gathered enough innuendo that my cheeks were flaming by the time they dunked me back into the water to cool them off.

Then they had plenty of water games I had to participate in, until I finally had to beg for mercy to be allowed to crawl back onto the stone floor and collapse on a towel that Vadya had laid there for me. My muscles felt rubbery, my lungs ached, and my head felt waterlogged, and for a while I just closed my eyes and breathed, listening with surprising contentment to the sounds of an ongoing match of a version of water soccer.

Considering my epiphany from earlier, it took me longer than it should have, a couple minutes, to identify the feeling: it was like lounging back at a family reunion—that primordial satisfaction *Homo sapiens* felt at knowing one was surrounded by one's tribe. The illusion of safety that evoked was ridiculous, considering how, intellectually, I knew we weren't even the same species. Moreover, I was aware of how tricksy the Starkissed could be. Yet it was true. Something had just changed—or maybe something had changed a long time ago, and I'd only just let myself believe it.

I was now one of them. And that meant, no matter how they might trick or cajole me, they would defend me as fiercely as one of their own. Because that's what family did.

Vadya and Fenra collapsed on either side of me—casually, moaning to each other about being out of practice, but I couldn't keep a smile from tugging at my lips as I listened, still with my eyes closed. I knew they were there for me.

Then I felt something that shattered that illusion of safety like a baseball shot through a window.

A shadow, slithering through the darkness of my mind.

Ben said he saw his gates like mental constellations of stars. Well now, even with my eyes closed and my head turned away, I saw darkness. The corrupted kind, the kind that was a solemn mockery of what darkness was meant to be. Instead of potential, the promise of birth, this was the darkness that smothered and hungered. The darkness of ending.

It showed against *my* darkness like a shadow crossing the sun.

I bolted upright, so quickly my head spun.

"What—" Fenra began, tensing. As Vadya's drakón counterpart, I'd gathered that my safety fell under her portfolio. If Vadya was my substitute leftwing, Fenra was my right.

And yet there wasn't time to explain, let alone use her.

Before she could get another word out, I became a silver blur as I surged into the water, straight for the shadow. Only one glance had shown me what I'd already feared: it was nearest to Lady Winthra.

When I sliced through the water and into being again, it was only inches away from her back, fangs already bared.

I snatched it by the tail. Then I froze it solid.

With its body surrounded by water, that much was child's play. But the snake was more shadow than substance, and it writhed within its prison, threatening to break free. I surged back onto the stone, planting my feet firmly to keep from slipping as water cascaded off me in a rush. Everyone was still (as they could be, while treading water) and silent as I stood there grimly, dripping, holding the tail of the frozen shadow-snake as if it were a bat.

With a detached, calculating calm that was going to astound me later, I examined it, considering keeping it. We knew so little about what Ben had seen, and my gut told me that this snake was a sliver of the same. Yet it writhed harder inside the ice, straining to break through. To get to me, to get its original prey, or to get away, I didn't know. And I wasn't about to find out.

I looked at Fenra, my eyes hard and, I was fairly certain, glowing.

"When I release it, burn it. Immediately. Don't let a single particle of it escape. Do you understand?"

Fenra's eyes lost their glaze of shock and hardened to match mine, glowing with dark sapphire light. She stood, set her feet, and nodded, signaling her readiness.

"No," Lady Winthra said, climbing out of the water. Even naked and dripping, she stood tall and regal, more so than I had ever seen that tired, doting mother and mischievous lady to be. There was the same flint in her own eyes as there was in Fenra's, burning even more brightly with her cornflower blue.

"Allow me," she said, teeth bared in a ruthless, draconic smile.

I nodded, understanding. As the intended target, not only did she have the right to claim retribution, she *had* to in order to save face. To show her people, and the Devourer, that she was no helpless victim.

"Ready?"

"Ready," she purred.

I raised the snake-cicle over my head and brought it down into the wall of the grotto with all my might, shattering the ice. Not a second later, I surged clear, making way for the wall of bright blue fire that rushed forward, consuming the shadow before it had a chance to escape. My shoulders sagged when I felt the last particle of it disappear, and my crawling skin settled.

"It's gone," I told the Lady, who was still sending fire from her curled fingers as if she were a living blowtorch.

Only then did she let the fire die and the fountain of flame dry up, little tongues falling to the stone floor with a hiss as they met the puddle of water at her feet. In fact, the whole grotto was filled with steam now—not as suffocatingly as a sauna, but still enough to make me uncomfortable.

Lady Winthra looked at me. Her normal benign mask had not yet returned, and she studied me with a cool, calculating intelligence that sent a shiver down my spine.

"You may have just saved my life," she said.

I lifted my chin. "That's what a Starkissed does, right? We protect our own."

The Lady Starkissed slowly smiled, and the look in her eyes sent another shiver down my spine. Not in fear for myself. I was one of them now. But the look was an excellent reminder of why I should never do anything to jeopardize that status.

Flame help whoever crossed the Starkissed.

"Yes," she said, eyes like bright blue flints—ready to spark a war of retribution. "Yes, we do."

CHAPTER FORTY-TWO

GLIMMER

KORIBEN

"SARAH!" I CALLED THE moment I entered the King's suite.

"Here," she said, standing in the doorway of my study. She had been waiting for me.

I crossed the room to her in three strides and pulled her into a crushing hug, hard enough that I heard the huff of air leave her lungs. Yet she let me, knowing how much I needed this, and her arms wound around my neck.

"Flame, Sarah," I growled, not caring one wit about eavesdroppers or my wings behind me. Though I responded to Kor's nudge to step inside the room, allowing my wings in. I heard one of them shut the door.

"Sorry," Sarah said breathlessly. "I know I technically broke my three day promise. But...."

I sighed and slowly, reluctantly, set her down. "I wouldn't have wanted you to act any other way. Flame knows we can't afford to lose Lady Winthra right now."

Especially not in that way. No doubt the chaos that would have ensued had been the Devourer's intent, as all its other attacks had been: to damage the Crown's standing with the clans, to break our spirit and splinter us from the inside.

I shook off that thought. "And from what I heard, you had things well in hand."

I smiled thinly, trying to show that I was proud of her. Even if it felt like my flameheart was slowly being crushed by a vise, with each event like this tightening the screw.

Sarah nodded grimly. "I felt it as soon as it entered the cave, and my ice contained it easily. I just didn't want to risk it escaping, so Lady Winthra burned it."

"And that eliminated it?" Kor asked intently, coming into view at my left. "Entirely? You're certain?"

Sarah nodded firmly. "The fire burned it up, and the feeling left as soon as it was gone. I made sure."

"What *was* it?" Yvera growled, completing our defensive curve around Sarah at my right. I could see from the way she didn't meet Sarah's or my eyes that, mingling with her own fury at the danger Sarah had been in, she felt sheepish that she hadn't been there. She would have been forbidden, of course, not being Starkissed, but she hadn't fought for it like she had for me. She was still struggling to let me go and to stop resenting Sarah for taking me from her, but she'd come far enough to know in her heart that was wrong.

Not that she was going to admit it. This was about as far as Yvera ever came to apologizing: avoiding eye contact and expressing a modicum of concern. Preferably by being pointed toward someone she could pound until they were black and blue.

I didn't think she was going to get that chance this time.

Sarah glanced at the closed door in relief. This was why she had waited for me in here. At Lady Winthra's command, all the witnesses had been sworn to secrecy, and no word of the incident should have escaped. Lady Winthra had told Kor and me of it herself, and I'd told Yvera just now when she'd met me on the landing.

Sarah looked back up at me, eyes dark.

Have you told them?

Not yet, I said heavily. *You think this is related?*

I wasn't surprised—I'd come to the same conclusion. My flameheart still sunk from hearing Sarah's confirmation.

I know it is, Sarah said calmly. *I don't know how, but I know. Just like you did.*

"What now?" Yvera ground out, glancing between the two of us.

I took a deep breath and let it out slowly. "It was the Devourer."

"Well, obviously, but what did it use—"

"It didn't use anything, Yvera," I said, meeting her eyes. "That's just it. It's done using intermediaries. It *was* the Devourer."

She stared back at me as if she thought I'd finally lost it. Kor just studied me, his unreadable mask in place. Though I'd bet my best blade that he wasn't surprised.

Yvera snorted. "Impossible. It can't—"

"Can't?" I asked quietly. "Or simply hasn't?"

Silence fell for a moment. That reality sunk in so heavily, even Yvera had to face it: We simply didn't know.

I sighed, putting a hand on my neck. "I don't *think* it can fully manifest without Royal blood. Otherwise, it would have. I can think of no reason it would have held back if it could enter and devour us all. But what if it could still send...*something* through? A shadow, like I saw."

"Or a sliver, like I captured," Sarah said.

"Then why *hasn't* it before?" Yvera demanded.

"We don't know it hasn't," Kor said quietly. "We know it watches and listens somehow. Perhaps this is just the first time it has let someone see it at work."

"Why?"

"Because Ben and Sarah have foiled it one too many times. It is trying to frighten them."

"I always knew it was a bully," Sarah grumbled.

Kor smiled thinly. "And like all bullies, its increased aggression reveals one thing: it's getting desperate."

"Desperate?" I said skeptically.

Kor shrugged. "Or as close to it as it has ever felt. Call it bloodthirst, if you prefer, but it's getting hasty, sloppy. Perhaps it committed more to the Battle of the Solstice than we expected, counting on consuming the Six Realms to replenish itself. Not only did we not fall then, we are shoring ourselves up more quickly and thoroughly than it expected. Finally, its most powerful servant is potentially damaged. It has grossly miscalculated our ability to survive with both you and Sarah at our head. It needs a victory, and soon."

I felt an internal tremor, and I risked showing it by reaching out and grasping Sarah's hand tightly in mine. She squeezed back.

I'm not going anywhere, she told me.

That wasn't the part I was afraid of.

It needed a victory, and it needed to make an example of the one who denied it that victory thus far. I didn't need a Tree's warning to know what that meant.

It was coming for her.

Kor met my eyes. The faintest sheen glowed in his dark sapphires, telling me he knew it too.

"That's why it's started manifesting?" Sarah asked. "It's getting 'desperate'? How does that show desperation?"

Kor looked away from me, eyes dimming. "Granted, my logic is all based on the fact that we haven't caught it doing this before. That shows a change in tactics, which I am calling desperation. Because if it had that kind of advantage before, why not use it? Ben saw a shadow that seemed to take up the space from surface to seafloor. Something unprecedented sliced through our protective net like it was nothing. You encountered a sliver that could worm through the narrow passages through the rock to the cave—or had slithered unnoticed through the hold to get there."

My flameheart wrenched. *No.*

"No," Sarah said, but only in disagreement, not despair. "I felt it as soon as it emerged, and it emerged in the water, near Lady Winthra."

The vise in my chest loosened by a turn.

"Which makes sense," Kor said. "We have wards to prevent darkrifts and detect consumption everywhere, but less so in places we feel more secure, such as that cave. An oversight that I'm certain Yvera can work with Rightwing Mathya to rectify."

"That, I can do," Yvera said, folding her arms. I could already see her working out the task ahead in her mind. Having something concrete to do visibly calmed her. I could relate, but unfortunately, my skill set had yet to be useful to us here.

"But back to your question, and mine. Why not manifest before? It seems like a formidable and versatile tool, capable of sweeping force or precise control. And the answer to me seems obvious: manifestation must come with either a cost...or a risk. Perhaps even both."

"Such as?" I asked intently.

"I think you're right, Ben," Kor said. "I think that it really *must* need Royal blood to fully enter a world protected by a Tree, otherwise it would follow its nature and do so immediately. But to manifest partially? That might not cost it Royal blood, but probably something."

"Probably still something terrible," Sarah muttered.

"I won't argue with you there," Kor said. "So, that's the price. And the risk? I think Sarah demonstrated that beautifully today, with the help of the Lady."

"What?" Yvera demanded.

"Winthra burned it," Sarah said faintly, eyes distant. "If *that* was a sliver of the Devourer itself...she destroyed it."

Kor let that fact sink into the rest of our minds for a moment. The implication was nearly as staggering as facing the fact that it could manifest itself at all.

The Devourer had always been this great and terrible force, as unstoppable to a mere mortal as the rotation of the planets around each star. Our only hope of ever surviving was to keep it *out*, to pray it never gained the power to enter.

And yet, a drakón had just destroyed a piece of it.

"Flame, Kor," I breathed, running a hand through my hair.

"That is why I asked you if you were *sure* it was gone," Kor said to Sarah.

She thought for only a moment, then she nodded slowly. "I'm sure. I felt it...well, die isn't the right word, is it? It was only a sliver. Like saying a strand of hair can die. But I felt it...go. Not just somewhere else, but burn up. Removed from existence. I feel that's right, to my bones."

"Then what it truly risked and what we truly gained is something far greater," Kor said quietly. "*Knowledge.* It risked a piece of itself, but only a piece. I very much doubt we dealt it anything close to a harmful blow. Yet the destruction of that piece tells us that the Devourer isn't as infallible as it has always led us to believe. At the very least, when it is *partially* manifested, it can be contained. And it can be burned—to nothing. I think that is a weakness that the Devourer was very much hoping we would never discover."

I looked at Kor, flameheart sinking. "That's why it risked showing so much of itself to me. It was underwater."

He nodded grimly. "I believe so, yes. And probably why it risked striking at Lady Winthra, because it thought it could stay out of reach of flame. Once again, it underestimated Sarah."

Sarah grimaced. "Something tells me that's a trend that won't continue for much longer."

"Not after you helped destroy a piece of it, no," Kor said, eyes flicking to mine. "Before, you were just a nuisance and a potential source of Blood. Now, you've officially made yourself a threat."

"Ben too, right?" she said anxiously, glancing at me. "I mean, of the two of us, he's the one who can actually hurt it. And I suppose always could. But now it knows that *Ben* knows."

My mind hadn't yet gone that far, but I saw it as soon as she said it. Even though another drakón had destroyed its sliver, I was the King of *Flame*. In a battle against it, I would be at the front.

Great. As if I needed the target on my back to become even larger. If increasing my threat level in its mind lessened Sarah's, then I'd be fine with that, but the Tree's warning and my gut told me that wasn't the way it was going to work.

As Sarah had once memorably said, it was a torched coward. It wasn't going to face me head on, at my full strength. It was going to try to cripple me first.

And it knew exactly how to do that.

"There is that," Kor said grimly. "Before today, it would strike at you two indirectly, hopeful that it could still capture you and use your Blood. After all, it could have easily targeted Sarah today instead of Winthra. This might change that. It may calculate that taking one or both of you out is worth the loss of your Blood."

Yvera threw up her hands. "Fantastic. You sure you don't want to make my job any harder, Kor? Maybe throw in another invasion?"

You might not be as far off as you think, Yv, I thought grimly.

But those were thoughts for another time. If preparing for the last invasion had taught me anything, I had to focus on today's challenges, or I'd go mad thinking about tomorrow's.

And I had to have *some* faith that the Trees were preparing us today to face that tomorrow.

I took a deep breath. "So. What do we *do*? Right now?"

Kor sighed. "Well, as I said, Yvera can work with Mathya to shore up our defenses. We don't want a repeat of today's infiltration."

"No, we don't," I agreed, clenching Sarah's hand.

Kor shrugged wearily. "Other than that...frustratingly little. The Devourer's greatest advantage is the same as always: we can't take the battle *to* it. Even if we could, I doubt we'd be successful. I don't think even you and Sarah combined are enough to defeat it head on, on its own terms."

"No," Sarah said, clenching my hand in return. "I don't think we are. That doesn't feel right to me, in any case."

How far she had come in learning to trust her instincts—and in listening to and believing in her Tree. She probably put my faith to shame right now.

Kor grimaced. "Then all we can do is fortify, protect you two as best as we can, and react when it shows its hand. And..."

He hesitated, then groaned, as if hardly able to believe that he was the one suggesting this. "...pray."

UNFORTUNATELY, KOR WAS RIGHT. Yvera left immediately to speak to her Starkissed counterpart, but there was little the rest of us, even Kor, could do except pray. Especially since Sarah was almost immediately dragged away to get ready for the evening.

I wasn't in a good mood already, and that inanity finally gave me something to vent about.

"I don't see why it always takes them so long," I complained to Kor.

My leftwing smirked. "Art takes time, O King. And don't pretend you don't appreciate the results."

My face heated as I realized my tactical error in engaging on this topic with *Kor*, and I immediately tried evasion. "I don't appreciate it taking up a quarter or more of the time I normally have with Sarah."

The only reason that wasn't the case today was because Sarah had insisted on coming along to see the torn net.

Kor raised an eyebrow to show me he wasn't fooled. "Well, you can't have everything.... You could always take advantage of the time to do a little grooming yourself, you know. That beard of yours could use a trim."

I glared at him. "I trimmed it yesterday, and you know it."

I'd been careful to keep it from becoming "bushy," as Sarah called it, but it was finally filling and smoothing out enough that I wasn't scratching Sarah any longer when I kissed her, which was a relief. Besides, short, trim beards, as Kor frequently reminded me, were the fashion for our generation, so I'd always kept mine shorter than Avva's just to get my leftwing off my case. Same with my hair, which Kor always insisted on cutting when it got past my shoulders—or, last time, had an attendant do it. Lord Kolwin's long locks were the epitome of traditionalism. Which he still somehow wore well, torch him.

When Kor continued to examine my handiwork critically, I huffed and turned away to the stack of papers on my desk. "Quit it, Kor. Find a different way to compensate for your inability to grow a beard other than nitpicking mine."

Kor sighed. "It's such a shame. Even Rachel thinks I would look good in a goatee, you know."

"I do not need to know these sorts of things about you or her. I don't know why you keep insisting on telling me."

To distract myself, I picked up a report and tried to read.

"Have you ever thought that I'm doing you a favor?" Kor said, folding his arms and smirking as he leaned back against my desk. "Inoculating you, in a way? She's Sarah's sister, you know. You're going to have to interact with her regularly at some point."

No more than I can help, I thought.

Then what he'd said before fully sunk in, and I dropped the paper I'd picked up. "Wait, what? You told *Rachel* you're the Tolsyon heir?"

The only two people he had ever told outside his own clan were Sarah and me. Or so I thought. It was a politically complicated secret—one that I felt uneasy knowing someone like Rachel held. She was dangerous enough as it was.

"No, not yet," Kor said dryly. "So there's no need to blow a torch over it. But I might, sometime soon. It seems relevant to her decision making, don't you think?"

As if I could forget that was exactly why he told Sarah.

Then it hit me, and I pinched the bridge of my nose.

Rachel was the Heir of Ice. If she survived longer than Sarah, one day she would become Queen. And whoever became her consort....

I was an idiot. Of course, I didn't expect Kor to be this serious. He never had been before. Well...before Sarah.

I lowered my hand and looked at him warily. "Is that what this is about?"

Kor's eyes flashed, warning me to tread carefully. "What?"

I took a deep breath. "Kor, I'm asking this because she is, in fact, Sarah's sister, and because our relationship with her clan is so crucial. Are your motivations...personal...or political?"

Kor smiled thinly at my diplomatic wording. But because his eyes didn't flare again, and he didn't rip into me, I assumed that meant I'd passed.

"You, of all people, should know that those motives aren't mutually exclusive."

"Yes," I admitted. "But that also means I know which one makes one's potential partner the happiest."

Kor's lips twitched. "Rachel would be so touched to know your concern for her happiness."

"Well, as you said, she's Sarah's sister."

"Fortunately for all concerned, my motivations are the same as yours, Ben. Almost exactly the same, in fact. Personal, political, and, dare I say it...spiritual."

My eyebrow rose at that. "Really?"

Kor smiled. "I haven't told you all my clan's secrets. Nor do I have to. Suffice it to say that I'm doing my duty to my Tree. Same as you are."

I stared at him. I had never thought that he'd told me everything—this was Kor, after all. But for the first time, I had cause to wonder where my leftwing's true allegiance lay.

Just which Tree had Kor referred to? Flame...or Ice?

"How was the hunt?" Sarah asked conversationally.

We were walking arm in arm to the feast hall, with Kor and Yvera trailing behind us. Sarah looked resplendent, as always, this time in a diaphanous white and silver dress that would have done a cloud proud. Though, with Kor's teasing fresh in my mind, I tried to avoid looking at her too much, because when I did, my face heated.

"Barbarous," Kor jutted in before I could decide how to reply.

Sarah glanced back at him in surprise.

"What?" he said. I looked in time to see his shrug. "It was. Horrid tradition. I'd have avoided that one if we could have. But, alas, it's a favorite among the unrefined masses."

Sarah laughed. "What's got *you* so against it?"

"That, I cannot tell you. It's the *male* initiation, after all."

I laughed as quietly as I could, but my shoulders shook, and I could feel Kor's eyes on my back. When Sarah glanced at me, I said, *I'll tell you later.*

I saw nothing in the whole ordeal that was secret. It was just a hunt with unusually stringent rules: no magic, no armor, no weapons. Just teamwork and bare hands. That's why it had taken so long—and why Kor was being sore and secretive about it: he stood almost no chance of doing well. Unlike me. I'd done just fine. Especially since it had been on land, thank Flame for that. I was one of the best runners, and though I wasn't the one to kill the scaly urtha, I'd wrestled with it while a Waterguard elite did.

The feast passed uneventfully. When it drew to a close, a gentle chime sounded throughout the feast hall, and the chatter slowly faded as Lady

Winthra—seated at the high table between Sarah and me—stood, raising a hand.

"Friends and kindred, visitors and esteemed guests." At the last, she nodded to me and to Sarah before looking out over the hall again. "Thank you all for being here tonight. And, since you know I am no orator...."

She paused, grinning as a chuckle ran through the hall. "I will get right to it, the part you all have been waiting for...."

Ah, torch it, what now?

"Let the dancing begin!"

I blinked.

Cheers broke out everywhere. Musicians, who had been congregating on one of the balconies, took their cue and began playing a lively jig, calculated to get people moving, and the gathered feasters did not disappoint. Clearly, some people—usually young adults and older adolescents—had moderated their food intake in anticipation, because they leaped from their benches and rushed into the central rectangle, which had been left empty for that purpose.

The response was chaotic, colorful, and exuberant—and so completely Starkissed. The Sunfilled and mixed denizens of Crownhold liked a dance, too, but at least we waited until getting into another room first. The Starkissed didn't bother; tables were only being cleared and stowed as they were vacated.

I should have seen this coming. Starkissed dances were infamous. Dancing was obligatory most high days, and grand tour days fell under that category. Probably the only reason it hadn't featured in last night's celebrations was because of the search retelling, and I was certain that even then, dancing had been going on *somewhere*.

I wasn't sure how to feel about this now. I'd been bracing myself for more unpleasantness, and I was feeling the residual clench in my gut. But...I liked dancing. Didn't I? At least, I thought I did, but it had been so long.... I liked group dances, at least. The kind that didn't leave me with any one girl for too long, giving her no time to....

Wait.

I really was an idiot. Either that or I'd had too little sleep and too many problems on my mind lately. That's what Sarah would say.

Maybe it was time to forget a few of those problems. That was, if....

"Would you care to join them, King Koriben?" Winthra asked, eyes dancing wickedly.

I glanced around her at Sarah. She was looking at the whirling crowd with the grimness of a new, twelve-summer drakón who had just accepted a duel after only a few months of training and was determined to fight honorably or die trying.

She met my gaze and nodded.

You sure? I asked hesitantly. *We can just—*

No, Ben, this must be what I've been practicing for, she said, still with that grim determination. *Come on.*

As if afraid that she would lose her nerve, she stood abruptly, grabbed my hand, and began dragging me to the dance floor. That dragging was a familiar feeling for me; I was always self-conscious at first but usually let that go by the end of the first dance. The trick was getting me out there. Yet before, Yvera was usually the one doing the dragging, and that was, to me, like being dragged by a sister. I let her do it because I loved her, but not like that, and that interplay just added to the awkwardness until I could get away from her.

This felt familiar and yet completely different, like seeing the same place during the night, then during the day. I felt a thrill in my blood I hadn't felt before, pulsing to the rhythm of the drums and the thrum of the lute. I felt alive in a way I had no right to be, with the sun already having gone down, and I knew what the source was. I found myself clenching Sarah's hand in return, wishing this was a couple's dance instead, and loathing the moment I'd have to let that hand go.

Which I had to not a few moments later, because one of the young men grabbed Sarah's other hand and whirled her into the fray, with a flash of a wink at me.

Torch him!

Unfortunately, I didn't have time to track him or plot revenge, because in the next moment, a young woman grabbed my empty hand and pulled me in as well, and then it was either focus on the dance or bring everyone around me down.

I got Sarah back not a dek later, and by then, she was a different creature. Far from grim and uncertain, her silver eyes were bright and lips pulled into a wide smile. She laughed as we grabbed each other's forearms and spun around each other. I felt dizzy from more than just the rotation. I didn't think I had ever seen her this jubilantly, unabashedly happy. She looked into my eyes with a fearlessness so strong it was almost fierce.

I was utterly intoxicated.

And even more resentful when I had to pass her on a few moments later. Because the first dance ended less than a dek later, Sarah was too far from me for me to grab her before the next one began. At least it was another group dance—though the couple ones would start soon.

Fortunately, even the Starkissed seemed to have limits on their deviousness, because by the time the musicians strummed out the first one, Sarah was within arm's reach. I nearly laughed when I recognized the tune. How appropriate. It would be a crime if I didn't get Sarah for this one.

So, I snatched her from her last partner with an unapologetic smirk.

"Excuse me. I believe this dance is mine."

Ben? Sarah said laughingly, catching her breath. Apparently her practices hadn't taught her enough to anticipate what was coming from the intro alone. Perhaps because there was no noticeable change in tempo—this would be a lively one.

Brace yourself, I told her with a grin.

Then the first singer began his part of the duet, and Sarah's eyes widened in recognition. *Wait...isn't this—*

She cut off as I grabbed her hand and spun her. Just as I'd done the first and only time we had danced together like this before, back in the kitchen of her hold. I knew from her breathless laughter that she remembered, and her eyes were shining as she came back in.

Last time, she had known none of the steps and had stumbled trying to follow me. I hadn't minded in the slightest; I was the one who had sprung a dance on her, after all. I was only thrilled that she didn't just try but seemed to enjoy herself. It was the first moment I thought I might have a real chance with her.

This time had the same night-and-day difference: familiar, the same, and yet far more. The music pulsed through our blood like a living thing. The ephemeral layers of Sarah's dress floated around her like magic. And though Sarah still wasn't an expert in the steps, this time, she was fearless, throwing herself into the dance wholeheartedly. Even though this time we were in the middle of a crowd, she didn't seem to care. When we grabbed each other across the waists for another spin, her touch was bold and her eyes glowing, lighting a band of fire across my abdomen.

Flame, it was a very good thing we weren't dancing alone right now.

As it was, when the song came to an end with a final lift, I couldn't help crushing a quick kiss to her lips. That wasn't a part of the dance, of course, but it righted an injustice from the last time and thus was immensely satisfying.

I pulled away, grinning widely. That *should have been our first kiss.*

She laughed, leaning her forehead against mine. *Agree to disagree.*

Oh, come on. You can't possibly think—

"Alright, Ben, you can't keep Sarah to yourself the whole night," Kor teased, sidling up to us through the crowd. "The next one is about to begin. Put her down and give her to me or to someone else."

Argh. I knew he was right. Tonight—and the grand tour in general—was about sharing her with the Six Realms. Did it have to be *Kor*, though?

He'll behave, Sarah told me with a crooked grin. *Or I'll send an ice shard through his foot.*

I barked a laugh and set her down. "*Fine.* But I get the next one. Don't let anyone else snatch you up."

"I won't," she said with a mischievous look. "I'll find you, even if I have to surge to you to get away."

I laughed again, brushing her cheek. "I almost want to see that happen now."

Actually, there was no *almost* about it. I intensely wanted to see the shock on her would-be captor's face. Let that be a lesson to them all.

Sarah—this fiercely beautiful, brave being of light and joy—had chosen *me*.

Chapter Forty-Three

TEAR

Sarah

That night was one of the happiest of my life. I danced until I collapsed, and once I'd caught my breath and gulped some water, I danced again.

I didn't even mind when Ben and I had to finish off the night with a dance on our own, in the center of that empty floor. The Starkissed knew how to make every moment magic, and they pulled all the stops for that one. Like in a fairy tale, they dimmed all the lightgems until the only illumination came from a kaleidoscope of glowing spheres of light contributed by our audience and sent to hover around the two of us, leaving all the others in darkness. It felt like we were dancing in the stars.

That dance was the slowest of the night, the music the most exquisite. The notes of the flute soared through that hushed atmosphere, the strings plucked a mesmerizing harmony. Ben's black clothing mostly concealed his sweat, apart from the way the dress shirt now clung to his torso; he'd long ago abandoned his coat, but its absence suited both the moment and him. The steps were astonishingly familiar by now, the same as the first we'd danced together except slowed down to a tantalizing pace that built a slow burn inside me. The tempo left us plenty of time to look at each other, and after first glimpsing the burning gold of Ben's eyes, I found it hard to remember anything else, and even harder to look away.

If we were among the stars, then he was my sun, his touch my guide, and his pull—thrumming as strong as ever—my gravity. Those steps felt as natural and inevitable as the movements of the cosmos.

He had always been my sun—and was so now more than ever.

IN AN ODD REVERSAL of our energies, there was a spring in Ben's step as we made our way back to the King's wing, and I staggered along, almost drunk with exhaustion and with every step sending stabs of pain through my poor feet. I teased Ben that he'd stolen my nighttime energy to fuel his recovery, and when he realized I was probably right and became blushingly apologetic, I laughed and told him I was glad. He had needed that night.

We both had, but him even more than me. I didn't know why or how, but something inside him had healed. I could see it in his eyes, even when we parted ways—for once, with me going to bed before him. I offered to let him have the water-room and bedroom first, but he just chuckled and gently pushed me straight into Vadya's arms, saying that he was worried about me keeling over.

There might have been something to that concern, since Vadya had to wake me from my bath and lead me to bed. Ben was gone from the central room when we emerged, and his pull led to his study. The door was open, so I broke from Vadya and went to the threshold.

Ben looked up from his tablet and smiled at me. "Feel better?"

"Much," I said with a happy sigh. "Those bath salts work wonders."

As did having Fenra to heal my overtaxed muscles and blistering feet, but I wasn't going to mention that and risk making Ben feel guiltier than he already was.

I gave him a stern look. "You're not going to work for much longer, are you?"

"No, don't worry. I'll just finish reading this and then go to bed, I promise."

"Good." I hesitated, then impulsively, I said silently, *You could share the bed tonight.*

Ben's smile faded, and he leaned back, turning his stylus over in his fingers.

Just to sleep, I insisted. *You think I have the energy for anything else? And if I'm tired, Flame knows you could use a better night's sleep than you've been getting.*

He didn't deny it, but he looked away and down at his stylus, still slowly twirling it around.

I made my voice gentle. *Look, I'll probably be out before you even get there. You can decide what you're comfortable with; I'll understand either way. Just know the offer is there.*

He looked back at me, smiling thinly. *Thank you for making it.*

In that, I thought I had my answer.

And yet, maybe half an hour later, I rose from the oblivion of sleep to feel the covers shift. The unbelievably soft mattress absorbed movement, especially as far away as this newcomer was settling at the opposite side of the bed, but the sheets and blankets were another matter.

Before even my subconscious could worry, I smelled Ben's warm, pungent scent and remembered. With my back to him and my face partially pressed into the pillow, I risked a smile and drifted back under—and this time, deeply.

"BEN. BEN!"

Kor's voice was the next thing to break through.

"What?" Ben said thickly, and I felt the covers shift again. Perhaps from him sitting up.

What now? I thought with a groan. I sure hoped this wasn't what it was always going to be like sleeping with the King of Flame. It wouldn't stop me, but it would sure make life harder than I'd expected it to be. And I'd already figured it would be pretty dang hard.

"It's the nets," Kor said grimly, and I felt a chill of premonition enter my blood that had me pushing up a second later.

In the light of his floating sapphire orb, Kor looked haggard. He was fully dressed, and his current coherence attested that he had been awake at least a quarter hour. I wondered if he'd even gone to bed.

"What?" Ben said flatly. As I'd suspected, he was already propped up, and now he was throwing off the covers and sitting at the edge. I noticed he'd worn a shirt to bed.

Kor said, "The first wasn't fully restored before nightfall. Now it's in shambles again, and it's broken through the second."

Ben cursed. "Tell them I'm coming."

Kor nodded and rushed from the room. With Kor's orb gone, Ben slapped the lighting crystal, beginning the room's brightening sequence.

"What time is it?" I asked, then answered my question by tapping on my watch at my bedside table. "Still a couple deken before dawn, right?"

"Yes," Ben answered, standing. He went behind the privacy screen and began throwing his nighttime clothes over the top of it, probably changing into something more suitable for a crisis.

"Then what do they expect you to *do* about it?"

"This is bad, Sarah. The Devourer is essentially laying siege to Rosin. It could be going for the final net right now. Even if there isn't anything I can do right now, I need to be among them, and we need to be preparing."

I didn't ask for what.

"Then I'm coming," I said, pushing aside the covers and swinging my legs to the floor.

I expected Ben to protest, but there was only silence and the rustle of clothing. A few moments later, he stepped out from the screen and leaned against a wall to pull some boots on. Meanwhile, he looked at me, eyes hard and soulflaring in the still-dim light.

I knew what that look meant. He knew every argument I would use, and what was more, he knew he couldn't justify keeping me away from this. Not when this attack was happening at night. They could need me.

Perhaps he'd known that all along. After all, he had turned on the lights instead of pretending that I could fall back asleep.

"Meet me in my study," he said flatly, and he left the room.

"THE THIRD NET IS intact, my Lady," a guard reported.

It was just after dawn. Ben, Kor, Yvera, Lady Winthra, her wings, and I were all huddled in a loose circle in a large alcove in the enormous court off the main landing; here, the hold's guard and the Starkissed Waterguard had gathered, ready to fly out at a moment's notice with Ben at their head and me as their star.

We had prepared for the worst—a breach of the third net and a direct assault on the hold—but had waited to commit ourselves until we knew it was necessary. After all, this could be a trap to lure Ben and me out of the safety of the hold. With no dramá currently in danger outside the hold, the dramá risked far more by losing one of us through hasty action than they did by some caution.

So, we waited out the deken and a half until sunrise, all the while with lookouts and spells giving us a constant feed of information about what was happening outside. Above the surface of the water: very little. Below, it was a different story. Consumed sensor wards were going off the charts. Rosin hadn't seen this much activity since the Battle of the Solstice—and even then, the nets had not been breached. Now the underwater threat was closer than it had ever been since the nets' creation. I watched Ben, Winthra, and their rightwings pour over the readings that had been transferred with a touch to their tablets, quietly conferring to estimate the numbers and kinds of consumed we might be dealing with.

Yet nothing left the water, and with the final net still intact, nothing under the water could launch a direct assault on the hold. The situation was, in a nutshell, exactly as Ben had described it to me just after waking up. As soon as Kor had said the words, Ben had known what we were facing: a siege.

And a carefully planned one at that. Ben and Winthra agreed that the Devourer must have been gathering its forces in an intense effort over several days—far enough out to sea to get around the Rosin Tree's protections against darkrifts and to avoid detection. Even disruptions in migratory patterns or fishing hauls could have tipped the Starkissed off, hence another reason for the

Devourer to keep its forces in the relatively empty deep water, and another sign that it could have only been doing so for three days.

"Four at most," Rightwing Mathya said. "Or we would have noticed something, that's for certain—no matter how far out."

"Then it could have been planning this for far longer," Ben said grimly. "But its main effort began either just before or after Sarah and I arrived."

"So it seems," Mathya agreed. "Last night's breach was probably a test. Then it committed to the full assault this night."

"No," Kor said quietly. "This isn't the full assault."

We looked at him. His eyes were lowered wearily, his hair was unusually mussed. Yet he stood straight, and something that wasn't soulflare burned in his eyes. "It took most of the night deken to reach here, and at this rate, it won't breach the third net before dawn. It must have known that was the most likely outcome. This night was about moving into position. The full assault comes tonight."

Kor's correction might have offended any other clan's rightwing. Mathya only nodded in acknowledgement.

Now, more than ever, the deferential way the Starkissed treated Kor was coming to the surface. Everyone still reported to the Lady and her rightwing, and they gave out the orders, but when Kor spoke, every Starkissed leader listened.

"But we can deal with the ones it's sent before nightfall," Yvera protested. "Especially with the reinforcements that will come through the sungate."

"Yes, but that will leave us too busy to deal with the next wave," Kor said grimly. "Which will approach during the daylight now that secrecy is over and we're occupied here."

"How do you know another wave is coming?" Yvera demanded.

Kor shrugged wearily. "It's what I would do. Send in just enough consumed to keep us tied down during the day and prevent us from repairing the first and second net, then send in the main force for the crushing blow. It's the only thing that makes sense, if it wants to do more than make a statement."

Yvera opened her mouth, but Ben put a hand on her shoulder, and a silent conversation obviously ensued.

To me, Yvera had seemed to come a long way since becoming the rightwing of the King, but she still struggled to see the big picture. She was a lethal warrior, one of the best, but the tactics and leadership style that had served her well as the chief bodyguard of the Heir weren't serving her now as the foremost general of the Six Realms next to Ben. She had a long way to go to match Alyish's grasp of strategy.

But I assumed both Ben and Alyish were aware of that and were trying their best to bring her up to par. In the meantime, thank Flame Alyish was still partially in charge as Yvera's own rightwing. In the long run, I trusted in Ben's instincts and the judgment of the Tree in choosing Yvera, yet she didn't help her case when she insisted on making a leftwing show her up in martial acumen in front of the Starkissed leadership. Even I could see that what Kor was saying made too much sense.

Kor's words from yesterday came back to me. *It needs a victory, and soon.*

This was supposed to be its victory. First, try to scare Ben off with its shadow, or failing at that, discredit him. Then, take out the Starkissed leader, leaving a power vacuum with the Heir still a newly chosen boy. He had arrived with the Lady and stayed with us this whole time, and he listened with an intelligence and sobriety beyond his age, but I still doubted this twelve-year-old would have been able to lead his people through a crisis while reeling from his mother's assassination. And then, in the furor, the Devourer would have begun the siege that would breach the Starkissed capital.

It would be a smaller victory than the one it had planned for the Solstice, especially if Ben and I escaped, but the fall of Rosin and thus inevitably Oshal might start the avalanche to crush the rest of the Realms. Including mine. We were becoming more self-sufficient by the day, but we still depended on the dramá's support for our survival. Even if the Devourer still didn't know where in the vast universe to find us, my family would struggle without them.

And without me. Because if the Six Realms fell, I would as well. Not just because Ben would never abandon them, and I would never abandon him. Because I was their *Queen*, damn it. I was theirs, and they were mine.

They were all my family now—and family protected their own.

Not long after, somewhere outside that hold, the sun breached the horizon of the sea. Even if I didn't see a shift in all the dramá around me, I could feel it for myself. I was long past my peak, and I'd begun my true descent. Lady Winthra sent scouts out for a flyover, and one returned with the news.

Kor was right. The third net remained.

The Starkissed Lady, grim-faced, looked at her rightwing. "Begin the counterassault."

They had already decided on their course. Even knowing that more were probably coming, they had to address the threat closest to home first. They could not let the last net fall. Even during the daytime, that would be disastrous. I'd gleaned enough by now to know there were consumed out there big and nasty enough to cause tremors if they got close enough.

I tensed. It was time.

Mathya nodded, and she strode out into the court, giving orders right and left. Ben already had his assignment, so he took advantage of those few moments to duck in and kiss me.

Be safe. Come back, I said before we parted.

He pulled away, smiling faintly, and nodded. *I will. Remember, I'm not doing the dangerous part this time.*

It was true. My only scant comfort was that Ben would lead the aerial defense and assist in the water only as a last resort. That was the last bit of the Devourer's cleverness in this siege: Ben, the most powerful drakón of the Six Realms, was at a disadvantage in water combat. In fact, most all drakón were except the Starkissed Waterguard. That severely limited who they could call in for reinforcements: mainly just down to other members of the Waterguard that could be spared from other Oshal holds without tempting the Devourer to strike elsewhere.

Even Ben had been reduced to a symbol more than anything. He was there to show his solidarity but could do little else for them without risking himself more than was wise.

Essentially, the Starkissed were on their own. I found that unacceptable.

I'd tried to argue that Ben's relative safety meant that I should go with him, but Ben had vetoed that, and to my surprise, so had everyone else.

"No, Sarah," he said, unusually grim.

"Ben—"

"I'm being practical about this, trust me. You need to rest, because we'll be needing you by nightfall."

That shut my mouth. Things must truly be dire for Ben to admit that I needed to be sent into battle.

"Besides," Yvera said. "The risk isn't worth it."

When all of us looked at her, especially Ben, Kor, and me, she shrugged. "Ben, I can protect. And if I can't, he can surge to the sungate—it's right *there*, for Flame's sake. But add in Sarah? That increases the variables. Plus, this is the Devourer, right? Shouldn't we be avoiding exposing *both* our Monarchs at the same time?"

Ah, Yv, I thought with tired humor. *I didn't know you cared.*

But that had settled that. Ben was leaving to soar around, maybe fight. And I was staying. To "rest." And maybe fight later.

I watched him go with a heavy iceheart, the familiar dread beginning to build in my stomach.

"Come on," Kor told me wearily. "Let's get back to the King's Wing."

I felt a flicker of rebelliousness and thought for a second of insisting on staying where I was. But what would be the point of that? I would just be standing around uselessly, in public, for everyone to stare at, especially when the guard relinquished the court to the wakening denizens of Rosin. They had used the court as a staging area because nowhere else close to the main landing was big enough for everyone, but I could see the leaders packing up to shift command central elsewhere now that the counterassault was officially begun. So if I stayed, I wouldn't even be any closer to the center of things, and if I went with them, I would hardly be of use. If Ben needed me, I could surge to him, and I could help him better if I *rested*.

I resigned myself to the inevitable with a sigh and turned to follow Kor.

We walked in unusual silence for a few minutes, Kor lost in thought—and those thoughts weren't happy ones. I could relate.

"Did you even sleep last night?" I asked him.

"No."

No quip, no evasion, not even a smirk. Just a flat negative. Things truly were bad.

Why? I asked silently.

If you are asking whether I knew this would happen, the answer is no. But I should have.

Kor, I'm asking as a friend, I said sternly. *Anything that would keep you up all night concerns me—as a friend.*

He rolled his head to the side to finally grant me a smirk. But it was a weak effort. *I'm touched, truly.*

Fine, I said, shrugging. *Keep your secret. Just as long as my concern is noted.*

His smirk faded. *It's no secret.*

Want to talk about it? I asked.

He laughed hollowly. *I simply...couldn't sleep. Ironic, but true. The Devourer's ploys aside, everything was going well. Too well. I kept feeling like I was missing something. And here it was, staring me in the face. And yet I was too distracted and tired to see it.*

Kor, you know you're not infallible, right?

We'd been over this. But knowing Kor's arrogance, I wasn't surprised that he had forgotten.

Something this obvious shouldn't have escaped me, Kor growled, fists momentarily clenching at his sides.

You're the one who said we couldn't do anything but wait for the Devourer to show its hand. What could we have done if we had known?

Kor ran a hand through his curls. *Something! Something more than this! You see, this is exactly why I find it hard to trust Trees! She knew, She had to have known, and yet did She warn us? No!*

But She had—just enough. The epiphany blossomed inside me like an unfolding flower, one petal of understanding at a time.

If we knew, if we sent Ben and the others out into the deep water to head the consumed off, would that have been better?

Kor was silent for a few long moments. Finally, he grudgingly said, *Probably not. Much more could go wrong, that far out. Especially for Ben. Could be that the Devourer had a plan for just that contingency, and we wouldn't have liked the result.*

I felt a chill. *But if we had known, Ben would have felt obligated to bring the fight to them, anyway, wouldn't he?*

Kor's eyes flicked to mine, and he sighed. *Yes. Yes, he would have. If he didn't, he might have been accused of cowardice.*

Kor, when we were discussing what to do, I felt sick at the thought of going after the Devourer. Remember?

He didn't answer.

When I spoke the words, I felt to the core of my iceheart that they were true. *This was what was meant to happen, Kor. We were meant to make our stand here. And that means the Tree will see us through.*

Kor's lips flickered in the faintest of smiles. *When you say it like that, I can almost believe it. Almost.*

For a moment, I studied him. Not for the first time, I thought it strange that the Tree of Flame had chosen such a committed skeptic as Her Tolsyon heir. But then, I supposed, there was something earnest about Kor's very lack of faith, his constant questioning. It was authentic to him in a way that his forcing a simple, all-or-nothing faith like Ben's or a nuanced one like mine wouldn't be. Ultimately, after all his struggling, Kor still did Her will, doing the right things for the right reasons, and that must be what mattered to Her in the end.

It did mean that Kor caused himself a lot of needless suffering during the intervening struggle, such as last night. When he could have been taking that Tree-given opportunity to rest, instead he'd kept himself up the entire night thinking that everything depended on him. That detrimental combination of arrogance and mistrust was wearing him thin.

A lesson I could take to heart more myself. On the surface, I didn't have Kor's level of arrogance, but I had a growing confidence in my ability to shape events that could prove just as deceptive and dangerous. Hadn't I just stubbornly thought of waiting for Ben? As if just by standing there, I could somehow *will* events to take shape as I wanted them to—when I couldn't. I could rest and prepare...and trust. But that was all.

That wasn't fatalism. That wasn't giving up. That was seeing things clearly. That was...acceptance. Of the situation as it was, of my mortal limitations, and that, ultimately, what happened wasn't entirely dependent on me. By letting go of my struggle for control over things I really didn't have control over, I conserved my energy for what I *did*...and ultimately did my people the most good I could.

That acceptance was the first step in focusing on my part and giving up all the rest to someone I trusted knew far better than I did how to keep us all alive.

Easier thought than felt, of course. Even with that acceptance settling over me, my gut didn't entirely unclench. But I had hope now, and that made everything else bearable. I felt like I could breathe and think again.

What's going on in that mind of yours? Kor asked.

Only then did I realize I had been silent for a while. I hesitated, then I said, *I'm not sure it's something I can explain.*

At least, I thought it was something Kor had to figure out for himself. I didn't know what it would take for Kor to relinquish control and begin to trust. His brother's betrayal and his need to take up both the mantles of Tolsyon heir and leftwing of the Heir of Flame had fundamentally changed him. He had shaped himself into the man he was now out of a desperate fear that he was the only one who could figure out what must be done to save the Realms. He'd appeared to be right often enough to make that dangerous belief become nearly unshakeable.

Only once had I seen a crack in that belief, when he had admitted that he didn't—couldn't—have all the answers. Then he'd rebounded not a day later, as I'd known he would. If that crack was still there, he'd covered it up well.

Hmm, Kor said, eyeing me sidelong. *Interesting.*

What?

You don't normally keep secrets from me.

My cheeks heated, but I didn't know why. *Of course I—*

Kor grinned. *Or rather, I should say that you don't normally keep them well. But this one, I'm having a hard time guessing, and that intrigues me.*

I'm so glad I've made myself into a puzzle for your amusement, I said dryly.

At least his miasma of self-disgust appeared to be dissipating, so perhaps our talk and my distraction had done him some good after all. I supposed that made my discomfiture under his scrutiny worth it.

Speaking of things you normally tell me, though, Kor said innocently. *Did you and Ben enjoy yourselves last night?*

I knew he wasn't asking about the dance. As grim and worrying as the news of the net had been, a part of me had bemoaned the fact that *Kor* had been the one to burst in and see us sleeping in the same bed.

I gritted my teeth, my cheeks heating again. *I don't normally tell you these things, Kor. You force them out of me. Like now.*

Dare I take that as a yes? Kor said with a wicked grin.

Oh, yes, he was snapping out of it, at least for the moment. I was fairly sure torturing me like this was one of his favorite pastimes.

No! That's a definite no. We just slept, Kor. I knew Ben was tired, so I told him he could share the bed.

Kor laughed quietly. *Ah, Sarah. What did I tell you? Innocently seductive. You'll bring him around one of these days. If you ever want any tips, though....*

I gagged. *NO. Again, that's a definite no.*

Honestly, he was worse than Rachel. Maybe the two of them deserved each other, if they both wanted to live with their heads in the gutter.

Well, my offer, as a concerned friend, is there, Kor said with a wink.

Noted, I growled. *But I have plenty of females I can talk to, Kor. So thank you for your "concern," but no. Besides, I still have no intention of doing anything like that. Ben needs to do things this way, and I respect that.*

Hmm, Kor said. I glanced at him. I knew him well enough by now to know there was something a bit overdone about his casual air. *Any idea why that might be? Why he's gotten this notion in his head?*

No. And even if I did, it wouldn't be any of your business.

Kor raised an eyebrow at me and said nothing.

It isn't, I insisted. *There has to be some limit to your leftwing duties, and I draw the line there.*

Kor dropped the casual air. *This isn't me asking as a leftwing, or even as a friend. This is me, as a mortal during these dangerous times, being worried that there's something our King isn't telling any of us, even you. I know him, Sarah,* and I'm an outside observer. I see how he looks at you, and I'm not just talking about desire. He looks at you like he has good reason to think he is going to lose you. And I need to know why.*

I tried not to show the chill that sent through me. I shrugged. *That's the way Ben is. You know that. And you have to admit, I've given him a lot of cause for worry lately.*

Kor scowled at nothing. *This is different. You remember how I told you it would always be all or nothing with him?*

Yes, I said hesitantly. I wasn't sure I wanted Kor to continue. If I was being loyal, if I was determined to trust Ben no matter what, I would tell him to stop now.

Yet I didn't.

Not in time to stop Kor, at least. *Well, he still hasn't given you all. And yet he hasn't pushed you away again, either.*

He made a blood oath—

But why, *Sarah? You didn't see him before. And you didn't see the look on his face once he woke up. Or in the difference in him when he brought you back. In one night, no, one deken, he was three different people.* What did that Tree tell him?

I inhaled, realizing why Kor was bringing this up now. I hadn't distracted him at all. We had come full circle.

Kor clenched his fists and slowly released them. His voice was quiet. *And why hasn't he told any of us?*

Ah. There was the root problem. Kor had somehow gotten this far because he trusted Ben. It was that trust in Ben, as he perhaps trusted no one else, and Ben's simple faith in their Tree that in some convoluted way bolstered Kor's.

If Kor couldn't trust even Ben anymore....

That was the shaky cornerstone that could bring his world tumbling down.

I couldn't bear the sole responsibility of shoring it up. Nor did I think I should betray what little Ben had told me just because Kor thought he needed answers. Yet I wanted to help.

Wasn't there one thing Ben had told his wings about his dream? *He said...something about a danger to me. Didn't he?*

I had forgotten about that part, thinking the danger passed or too nebulous to dwell on. Kor hadn't.

Yes, and I think that *is the key,* Kor said in frustration. *And from the way he's watched you ever since, I don't think that danger is past. But that is the only detail he gave us. That's it. The only other bit I've been able to glean is that he told Rachel that the Tree commanded him not to push you away again. But how does that fit in with—*

"Wait, *what?*" I asked, startled into speaking out loud. Fortunately, we had entered the King's wing a couple minutes ago and were now walking down the hall to the King's suite. "When did you speak to *Rachel?*"

Kor only hesitated one beat. It could have been the pause to figure out where I was coming from. Or it could have been to come up with an excuse. "Oh, she told your father, and he mentioned it during one of our conversations."

I scrutinized Kor, but his face was the picture of innocence. Which may or may not have been genuine, since Kor put on an *act* of blamelessness even when he truly was. Perhaps for this very reason.

Well, I had one way of verifying his story this time. All I had to do was ask Dad. If I could remember to....

No, I'd remember. Even though I'd said to Rachel that I washed my hands of anything to do with the two of them, even though I'd just idly thought that maybe they deserved each other, the thought of Kor secretly joining forces with Rachel was too horrifying to forget. Or ignore.

Anyway, as I was saying, Kor said, giving me a wounded look for the interruption. By now we had entered the central room of the suite, and we came to a stop facing each other. *Those are the two details I have to work with: the Tree told Ben about some danger to you and said that he couldn't push you away. But there has to be more.*

What makes you think that?

I hoped no one monitoring us or passing through thought it odd that Kor and I were just standing there. I could have brought us into my office for some privacy, but I didn't think that was proper. As much as he some-times tried to act like it, Kor wasn't my leftwing. The two of us were known to be friends...but that made it even more important to set boundaries for appearance's sake. And...perhaps more than just appearances. So, I forced him to stand and speak to me silently in this public place, and he seemed to think there wasn't anything strange about it.

Though he gave me a long, evaluating look at my question. Finally, he said, *Sarah...I know this is hard to believe, but just before that dream, Ben didn't care an ashbucket what the Tree thought.*

I blinked at him. *You're kidding.*

I wish I was, Kor said grimly. *I told him that what he was doing in shutting you out put the renewed Covenants at risk, and you know what he said to me? "Well, then, the Trees can find some other torched idiot to renew them."*

I shook my head. *No. That...couldn't have been Ben.*

That's the whole point that I'm trying to make to you. He wasn't Ben. *And he certainly wasn't in any state to listen to the Tree, even if She appeared in that room and set his desk on fire. Yes, She probably told him those two things in his dream, but there had to have been* more. *At the very least, something to connect the two.*

To connect the two....

I narrowed my eyes. *Kor, are you saying...that the Tree ordered* him *to marry me?*

Kor folded his arms. *Or, more likely for his frame of mind back then, the Tree told him that if he didn't, you would die.*

I just looked at him. The implication of Ben being coerced into finally proposing to me did not offend me. I *knew*, to the core of my being, that Ben loved me, and that everything he had told me that night he offered me his earring was true. The fact that he had needed a bit of a push to claim some happiness...well, I'd already known that much. If that push had been more explicit than I'd assumed, that still wasn't a surprise, and I still wasn't offended. In a way, it explained quite a few things. I'd always known that something inside Ben would have to change for him to let me in.

But...why? I asked, puzzled.

Kor snorted. *Because a threat to you was probably the only thing that would break through his—*

No, I said, holding up a finger. *What circumstances would make that true? Why would I die if Ben didn't marry me?*

Kor looked away, for the first time seeming self-conscious. *Ah, well...it's more likely that you would die if you didn't marry the King of Flame. Specifically.*

I raised an eyebrow. *That's Ben, Kor.*

Yes, well...at that point, it would not have been Ben for much longer.

The way Kor still was not meeting my eyes finally made the connection for me. Ben had told me himself that he was close to losing the Tree's favor. And when he did, the crown would have gone to...

...Kor.

I put a hand to my forehead. It was too early in the morning for us to be getting into things like this. Why had I let Kor drag me into it?

This is about your theory, isn't it?

The Queen of Ice had to marry the King of Flame. The Tree never told Kavarian why, just that I did. But Kor, through some grand overarching theory that he *still* had not told me, suspected it was all tied up in the fate of the Realms. Meaning, if Ben hadn't changed his mind when the Tree gave Her ultimatum, then Kor would have had to dethrone him, and I, to save the Seven Realms—and thus my own life—would have had to marry Kor.

I didn't ask Kor if he would have done it. I didn't need to. Even if he hadn't explicitly offered himself to me as an alternative to Ben, he had already made it clear that he would do whatever it took to save the Six Realms.

Partly, Kor said. He had the grace to look uncomfortable. *But I don't think that's all of it. I used to, but...the longer Ben carries on like this, the more I think there must be more.*

What do you mean? What more could there be?

What more, indeed? Kor shrugged. *He's shown every sign of a change of heart. He proposed to you, and now he's putting up with a mild version of his hell to marry you. On the surface, it looks like he's all in now. And yet....*

I sighed heavily. *You know what I think? I think you are reading* way *too much into Ben's latest resolution.*

And that Kor's lack of sleep, paranoia, and brilliant mind had finally gotten the better of him. But I didn't say that out loud.

I kept my tone kind. *This is just Ben, being Ben, thinking he has to do things this way to atone for something. I tried to convince him that's unnecessary, that he's done enough, but I decided to just let this go. This isn't the sort of thing to rush into, anyway. We both need to be ready.*

Kor huffed and looked away. *Sarah, I saw the way he looked at you last night. This is something else.*

I shrugged wearily. *Alright, fine. Think that way if you like. I'm still not going to rush him, because that's wrong, and I see absolutely no reason I should. We're doing what the Tree asked, right? We're getting married.*

Eventually. Even though we hadn't been engaged that long, especially in Earthren terms, the night that Ben had proposed already seemed like an eternity ago, and our heartbinding felt like an eternity ahead.

One would think, Kor said, scowling at nothing again. *Yet I'm wondering if this grand tour was a good idea after all.*

I barked a laugh. *Well, that's quite the admission, coming from you. Need I remind you who insisted on this in the first place?*

No need, Kor growled. *I already told you I'm questioning my judgment in this.*

He was silent for a moment, but not long enough that I thought he was done. Abruptly, he looked back at me and said, *Sarah, if Ben asked you to agree to a secret heartbinding, what would you say?*

My eyebrows raised, but the question did not offend me. *You really think that will magically solve all our problems?*

It might solve at least one *of them,* Kor grumbled. *At the very least, it might give me some peace of mind. That would be no small thing at this point.*

I smiled. *Sorry, Kor. I love you as a friend, but I'm not going to ask Ben for a secret heartbinding just to give you a bit of "peace of mind."*

Kor threw up a hand in exasperation. *Oh, and I suppose your own fate isn't looming in your mind right now? This is about saving* your *life, after all.*

No, I said. Even I was surprised at my calm, though. *It's about the fate of the Realms, and my life is tied up in that. But I think my Tree would have said something to me by now if a secret wedding was necessary to save them.*

Kor put his head in his hands for a moment, then lowered them. When his eyes met mine again, they had a strange mixture of softness and hardness. *Sarah, you should know by now that just because the Realms might survive doesn't mean you will. Surely Kavarian taught you that.*

I flinched.

Do you finally get it now? Kor said. *Because I think Ben does. There are plenty of Tree-sanctioned ways in which this could end with the Realms intact and you dead. And I, for one...don't want to see that happen.*

I looked away from him, iceheart pulsing. His concern touched me, but it came far too close to opening a door I had long since closed. One that I had never wanted opened.

Agh, Sarah, I meant that as a friend, Kor said with a sigh. *I have torched few of those, and I can't afford to lose any of them.*

I chuckled, meeting his eyes again in relief.

Besides, Kor said, rolling his eyes. *Can you imagine what a mess Ben would be in? Not one I want to deal with.*

My smile faded. *True.*

Kor sobered as well. *So...will you just think about it?*

I hesitated, then sighed and nodded.

I still thought it was bizarre that my survival might depend on a heartbinding...but I had seen and even done many bizarre things over these past two months, starting with falling through my flash-frozen neighborhood creek to come here. Magic sometimes worked in mysterious ways, and the Trees even more so. But so far, neither Tree had steered us wrong. They only asked of us what was necessary, and even then, They always gave us a choice.

I could at least consider it, and I should have an answer ready in case Ben asked. Mom would kill me if she found out Ben and I had eloped, but there was no reason she should, if we still did the grand public wedding.

Assuming Kor was right about all of this...

...but he was seldom wrong.

Chapter Forty-Four

NEGOTIATION

Koriben

UNDER ANY OTHER CIRCUMSTANCE, watching the Waterguard at work would have been a fascinating experience. Normally, they were more than capable of handling any threat their holds faced, so I'd had the least amount of experience working with them of all the clan equivalents. As grim as the occasion was, I watched and learned with ever deepening respect—and a far greater understanding of why the Starkissed had changed themselves more than any of the others.

They moved through the water with an even greater grace than the best flyer could match. They were astonishingly fast, too, having altered their wings over the centuries to fold into themselves so tightly that they had very little drag. Their scales were also lighter and more flexible than other drakón's, and those things combined saved much of their strength to thrust through the water with their powerful limbs and tails and swerve with their supple bodies.

Observing them at work, I saw clearly why I might only get in the way if I were to join them.

Especially after blood clouded the water, as it did mere moments after the first member of the Waterguard speared into the ocean and "flew" through the innermost net. A sharp-toothed predator with a long neck and giant, paddle-like fins went for the drakón, but her comrades diving in right after her tore its exposed flank to shreds until finally severing that narrow neck from its much squatter body.

As more and more of the Waterguard plunged into the water just inside the third net and burst through it with lethal ferocity, that clear, beautiful water filled with scarlet blood and gray bodies, and I soon lost sight of attackers and defenders alike.

I would have been blind in that cloud, yet one more adaptation ensured that the waterguards were not. Their sense of smell was poor compared to the average drakón, but their *hearing* was far greater, and they had discovered a way to produce a kind of clicking in their throats that, I was told, reflected off their surroundings and back to them, giving them a mental map. That next-level hearing, combined with their heat sense, allowed them to "see" even in murky or dark water.

And so the fight raged on.

I kept a careful eye out for any clouds of blue blood, but we got through the first few deken without any injuries that were that severe. Injured drakón left and others replaced them, but for the most part, the only colors staining that water were red and the occasional nondraká purple, which I was told came from a kind of giant, leechlike sea worm.

I was assured that they bore no biological relation to wyrms.

The lingering integrity of the third net was crucial. It enabled drakón to reenter a safe zone at any point, to breathe, recover, or retreat where the consumed could only try to follow at their peril. In fact, waterguards often tried to push or lure them into the net; once the net incapacitated the consumed, finishing them was child's play. That zone also gave a space for the drakón to climb out of the water, take flight again, and dive back in with deadly momentum.

The importance of the net meant a solid quarter of the current active forces was dedicated to constantly circling the inner barrier, watching for the slightest sign of flagging power or torn ligaments and reinforcing or repairing as needed. Another quarter, or so I was told, was dedicated to repairing the second net, and another quarter to guard them as they did so. That left only one quarter of the current shift to circle the ring between the third and second nets, but considering how most of the consumed from this first wave were trapped between the two now that the breach in the second had been reclaimed and was now fiercely guarded, it appeared to be enough.

Had the Devourer been any mortal general fighting a mortal war, it would never have made such a move, knowing it would be sending this wave into a trap, and their losses would be absolute. But the Devourer was an immortal force of greed and hunger fighting an eon's-long battle and cared little for the loss of its slaves so long as it obtained the ultimate prize.

I could only hope that if we won this day, the Devourer would not have the sea-bound forces left to attempt another such siege for years to come.

Though I and the others of my elites circling above the archipelago monitored the horizon, no air-bound consumed ever appeared or approached. Either the Devourer was conserving what aerial attackers it had left or it had decided that we would eliminate them too easily for it to gain any benefit. I hoped it was both.

That meant, though, that I had a long few deken of lazy circling, especially after the water became opaque and the true battle concealed. Only the occasional report or explanation broke up the monotony. Still, since I was exerting myself so little, I insisted on waiting out three one-deken shifts before I received a message that sent my flameheart racing.

King Koriben, an unfamiliar voice sent to me. I identified it as coming from one of the drakón guards on the landing. A blue-uniformed amón stood next to her. *The Queen of Ice wishes to speak with you.*

Is she alright? I demanded.

A pause for the drakón to confer with the messenger, then she replied, *The Queen is well. There is just a matter she wishes to discuss concerning the defense.*

I hoped that didn't mean she was insisting on coming out with me already. She was supposed to be resting, for Flame's sake. It still wasn't even noon.

But I knew better than to torch the messenger, so I just said, *I'll be right down.*

Yv, I said to the violet draká at my right. *Sarah wants to talk. You coming or staying?*

Staying. Duh. I could hear the eye roll in her voice. *This is like watching moss grow, but it's better than listening to the two of you.*

That was what I had figured, but I knew she would be mad at me if I swerved off without telling her or giving her the option.

Have fun, I said dryly as I turned and broke away.

Wheeeeeee.

The utter deadness in her voice made me snort in amusement. To Yvera, the Devourer's greatest cruelty in all of this was in denying her any sport. That didn't mean she was going to leave, though. She'd rather sit in the stands, so to speak, than miss out on the action entirely.

I landed and changed quickly, transitioning back into the scale armor and tabard I had worn earlier, then strode over to the uniformed messenger. Because he had waited for me, I assumed he had something more to say, and I was right.

"If you will follow me, King Koriben," he said with a deferential nod. "The Queen is in one of the guardrooms."

"What's she doing there?" I asked in surprise as we began walking.

"She and Leftwing Korinth are meeting with several of our artificers."

Artificers? Last time Sarah was left alone with an artificer, she cocreated a new technology that was starting a quiet revolution in timekeeping. Adding Kor into the mix sounded even more ominous. What in the Flame's name were those two up to?

I didn't bother asking him more. Whatever they were doing, it wasn't something we should discuss out in the open, and the amón aide couldn't converse silently.

I followed him through the series of chambers located just inside the hold; they were meant as a guard post and barracks of sorts in case of an attack at the main landing. Now it was being appropriated as a command center for the counterassault.

I had to give it to the Starkissed: for not seeing much combat in their home Realm, they were well-prepared for a crisis. My estimation of Rightwing Mathya continued to rise. Part of it probably had to do with Starkissed serving in other Realms as members of the Warflight, but the development of and training in wartime protocols—not to mention gaining political buy-in—would have fallen on her shoulders.

The aide finally led me into a medium-sized meeting room. At least, that was what I assumed it had been at one point judging from all the chairs lining the walls, but someone had removed the table, and in its place was the dissected remainder of what looked like something between a spotlight and a telescope, but with a cylinder as big around as my waist and resting in a mount that would have been chest height to the average drakón.

I blinked as I stepped inside the room. "Is that...a lightburster?"

If so, that was about the last thing I might have expected Sarah, Kor, and the three artificers to be tinkering with right now. Did I need to downgrade my approval of Starkissed competence? I mean, I knew they liked their displays and all that, but was this *really* the time?

"It used to be," Kor grunted from his position under the cylinder. He appeared to be messing with something in the inner workings. "Over about four ild you think, Jake?"

Jake?

I followed Sarah's eyes and turned back to the wall I'd come through, and I saw to my surprise—and chagrin—that Sarah had covered much of it with her communication ice, and the wall up to the door was a floor-to-ceiling display of the library in Sarah's hold. Meaning I was unexpectedly face to face with my future father-in-law. While I was in full battle regalia. And his daughter was helping me fight off a siege.

Great.

Jake sighed, his arms folded. "It's so hard to say without being there. Speaking of which, though—Ben, it is good to see you."

He didn't look like he felt it was, but then, he almost always wore a mask as impenetrable as a Strongshield's, so he truly could. Or he could be inwardly seething at me. I just couldn't *know*.

Hopefully hiding my trepidation, I nodded respectfully. "It is good to see you too, sir."

He raised an eyebrow at that, which discomfited me further. What could I have done wrong *now*? Should I have echoed his greeting in English? Or—

He looked away from me and addressed my leftwing, distracting me from my doubts with the oddity of his request. "Kor, if you wouldn't mind handing your scale over to Ben?"

Kor was already clambering out from under the dismembered lightburster. "Of course," he said as he wiped his hands on his trousers.

He brought out one of his dark sapphire scales and handed it to me, already glowing with activation. In the ice wall, Jake held out an identical scale, which was now glowing as well. He tapped it, and his image appeared on the scale in my hands, and mine appeared in his. I was as familiar with call scales as I was with any tool, but the additional perspective of the ice wall was disconcerting.

Just what was this all for?

"Excellent," Jake said placidly. "Sarah, you can keep the ice going while I'm gone if you'd like. I imagine Ben and I won't be long. Ben, if you'll join me somewhere else, there's something I'd like to discuss with you, if I may."

I finally understood—this part, at least. Jake wanted to speak to me in private. But about *what*?

I darted a glance at Sarah, hoping she would give me some hint. But she just smiled. She obviously thought there wasn't anything to worry about. That didn't reassure me. She was Jake's daughter, and one thing I knew for certain about Jake's feelings was that he loved her deeply. I had no such protection. In fact, I was pretty sure that very fatherly love worked against me, especially on days like today.

Yet there was no getting around it. Jake had phrased his intention as a request, but I could hardly afford to deny it; that would just give him more cause to resent me. If he wanted a chance to finally tear into me, then perhaps that was for the best.

I steeled myself and nodded to him, hopefully still maintaining some level of outward composure. "Of course, sir. Just give me a moment."

I looked at the aide, who lingered in the corner. He was probably there to see that the people in this room got whatever they needed to continue this bizarre tinkering, which hinted that the project had at least Mathya's approval. I pushed aside that mystery for the moment. I had a much more immediate and ominous problem.

"Is there an unoccupied room nearby?" I asked him.

"Yes, King," he said, gesturing for me to follow him as he left the room.

I did so, holding the scale gingerly in one hand. I pointed its illuminated surface away from me for the moment, but from the side, I caught motion in its own display, reflecting Jake's own movement as he left the library.

The aide showed me to a storage room, little bigger than a closet. "Will this do?" he asked apologetically. "I could try to find something bigger...."

That would probably involve asking occupants to leave. I shook my head. "This is just fine, thank you."

"If that will be all...."

"Yes, you may return to your post. I can find my way back, thank you."

"You are welcome, King Koriben," he said with a nod, and he left, closing the door behind him.

I held the scale up. Jake was holding the scale casually, pointed at roughly a forty-five-degree angle toward the ground, but if I was judging correctly, he had passed into the room of ice. It had a name in English, but I didn't remember what it was. He came to a stop a moment later, and I heard the doors grinding shut behind him.

He brought the scale up, and his face came into view. "Ah, you're ready then?"

"Yes, sir."

Jake smiled thinly. "Should the King of Flame really be calling me 'sir'? Especially in public?"

I blinked, taken aback. "What else should I call you? Especially in public? I don't mean any disrespect. If there is some other address you would prefer—"

"I don't mean to confuse you," Jake said. "It is just, in my...former world, kings did not address inferiors as 'sir.' Or any of our linguistic equivalents."

I was baffled. "Sir, you're not my inferior. You're the highest-ranking member of a sovereign clan, save your Queen and Heir. What's more, you're my elder and the father of my betrothed. If I didn't give you that much deference, people would think I was crass and arrogant."

Plus, I didn't want to offend him more than I already had or inevitably still would. But was I somehow doing that, anyway? By *trying* to be polite?

He didn't look offended, though, merely mildly puzzled, and perhaps even interested. "You are the leader of six worlds, and yet, in order to be seen as a good one, you are expected to defer to others?"

I shifted, uncertain where this was going and struggling to explain. "I don't have to defer to them. There *is* an order to things, a chain of command. But everyone I have the authority to command still deserves my respect. I'm here to serve them, after all. Sometimes I serve them by directing them, sometimes by being their shield or their sword. Whatever they need—that's what I have to be. Even if it means laying down my life for them."

"Like your father did," Jake said quietly.

I flinched. I coped with my grief most of the time now, managing to not let it hinder me in what I had to do or poison every happy moment, but the pain of his absence was always there, in everything. No aspect of my life or character had gone without his warm, gentle touch, and thus, everything reminded me of him. As I trusted myself more and more after Sarah's return, I no longer made every single decision wondering what he would do, but it was a frequent concern.

I would have given my right hand to hear his voice again, telling me I was doing well, that he was proud of me. I would have given the other hand to feel his arms around me again.

I blinked back tears and cleared my throat. "Er, yes."

"I'm sorry," Jake murmured, and seemed to genuinely mean it. "I am simply trying to understand your culture. I do not think it is wrong. In fact, I think your attitude toward leadership is admirable—idealistic, even, so much so I find it difficult to believe that it is functioning in real life, at the highest levels of your society. Yet here you are. And I assume you learned it from someone who put it to the test for even longer."

He looked away, eyes growing distant for a moment. I was too dumbfounded to think of anything to say.

Surely I must have misunderstood. Jake hadn't just...*complimented* me? Had he?

Jake looked back at me, his eyes unusually gentle. That one look discomforted me more than any expression of anger would have.

With Avva's memory brought fresh to the surface, the look in Jake's eyes was far too familiar.

"Sarah always spoke highly of your father. Not for the first time, I find myself wishing I could have met him. He may have been just the leader I have been searching for my whole life and had despaired could actually exist."

I swallowed. "Sir, I can say with absolute certainty that he would have wanted to meet you as well...and that he would have thought highly of you in return."

Impulsively, I dared to add, "He loved Sarah, you know. Deeply."

He had no reason to believe me, and I feared I risked truly offending him this time. Yet something inside me had brought forth the words, more strongly than I thought it was wise to resist. It was as if I were delivering a message.

Then I realized why. They were exactly the words that Avva would have wanted to say himself.

Jake studied me for a long moment. Finally, he said quietly, "So Sarah said...and I believe both of you."

I let out a breath I hadn't realized I had been holding. I hoped he wouldn't notice.

He smiled thinly. "In any case, I am sorry for getting us sidetracked. You may call me 'sir' if you wish. Just don't be surprised if I find it amusing for a time."

I hesitated, then decided it was best to risk working this out now, in private, than to simply let it go on. "If you don't want me to be deferential, why do you act like it?"

Jake blinked slowly. "Excuse me?"

I chose my words with care, both to avoid offense and to articulate even to myself what it had been about Jake's attitude that had discomforted me from the start. Clearly there was a cultural difference at play here, so I couldn't take anything for granted.

"In front of the others, you called me Ben. Not even my full name, much less my title."

Jake blinked again. "I can see what you mean about the title. That was a little hypocritical of me, wasn't it? I'm clearly not used to interacting with royalty, of any kind. As for your nickname, I thought that was what you preferred. It's what Sarah and Kor always call you. I was trying to set you at ease."

He was...*what*?

I was stunned that had been his intention, not at how I could have so misread him. Considering the cultural differences, that now seemed inevitable.

"With all due respect, sir," I said, attempting a rueful smile through my shock. "Sarah and Kor are exceptions. Only peers call me 'Ben.' Especially since I became King. When I was Heir, elders always called me Koriben—Heir Koriben if they were feeling truly formal. Now they address me as 'King Koriben' or just 'King.'"

"Ah, I think I see," Jake mused. "I just insulted you, didn't I? Or belittled you."

I ran my free hand through my hair. "I'm trying to think how to explain. It wasn't just the nickname. It was your whole attitude, combined with it. That you were so informal in addressing me, yet formal in making a request—one that almost sounded like an order. I know it's probably just your way, but I misunderstood. I felt like a hatchling getting a scolding. And the last part is that you did it in front of the aide and artificers. It wouldn't have mattered if you'd talked to me that way in front of just Kor and Sarah...."

Coming from most anyone else, I wouldn't have taken it. I would have hardened and made it clear that I wasn't to be trifled with. I would have been a disaster as a King if I couldn't handle the occasional snub or challenge to my authority. But given how desperately I needed this man's good opinion, and my own good opinion of him, my instincts had instead turned to placation and uncertainty.

Jake chuckled dryly. "I see, I see. I truly was being hypocritical, wasn't I? I'm aware of how I sometimes come across, but I didn't realize I was making things worse, not better. I apologize, Ben. That wasn't my intention at all. Thank you for explaining it to me. I'll endeavor to not make the same mistake again, especially given the reason I wanted to speak with you."

"Which is?" I asked, too dumbfounded to protest his apology. It had just been a simple misunderstanding, and I couldn't understand where all his goodwill was coming from in the first place.

He paused one moment, either considering me or his words carefully. Perhaps both. "I...am requesting admittance for myself and my son, Michael, to your Realms."

"What?" This conversation wasn't going at all like I had expected. Every time I thought I'd found some footing, the terrain once again became uncertain. "Why?"

"First, because I would like to work on the lightburster project in person. I've given engineering advice over a long distance before, of course, but that was frustrating in normal circumstances." He sighed heavily. "Now, we're dealing with not just two different systems of measurement, two different languages, and two different cultures, but a different set of laws of the universe."

"No, Jake, I already swore I wouldn't close my gates to your clan again. By 'why,' I meant, why are you even asking?"

Jake smiled thinly. "Because it seemed like the right thing to do. I truly *am* trying to avoid giving offense. Besides, I believe we'll require your assistance in getting to where you are, won't we?"

"Yes, I guess you will. Are you sure you want to take the risk, though? Sarah's recovered from the fever and is hopefully at least somewhat immune now, but the rest of you...."

"Michael and I have been discussing this for some time. It isn't an impulsive decision, trust me." Jake gave the smallest of wry smiles. "Well, for me at least."

I chuckled. I'd gleaned enough of Michael's character to understand what he meant by that.

"And we discussed this with Sarah before you arrived. Our combined understanding is that the risk is low where you are now. And as you know, even if we catch the fever, Svyer has been making the cure in almost obscene amounts over here."

I did know that. Even if Svyer hadn't called me to talk about her efforts, in my spare time, I had picked up several crates full of the stuff that they had left outside the crowngate, and I had, in turn, left them outside the special entrance only Sarah or I could open, for others to pick up and distribute. Svyer wasn't our only producer of the cure, not by a longshot, but her work was the most potent, perhaps because of her infusion of the power of Ice, and so it went to the neediest.

"She will send us with plenty of it to save for our own use, should we need it," Jake continued. "It's a risk both Michael and I are willing to take, and we both think it is high time we did so. And that leads me to the other reasons for making my request, and these truly are things we need your permission for. We would like to join you in the battle tonight, and we would like to remain with your entourage until the heartbinding. We are Sarah's wings, and we think it is time we joined her as such."

Part of me flinched away from the idea of having Jake around constantly, much less him risking his life. But I still felt like I had no authority to refuse him. I had asked Sarah to stay at my side, so I could hardly deny her the presence of her own wings.

"Of course you may," I said, "It was never my idea for you both to stay away in the first place. I believe that was a command from your own Tree."

"True. And this morning, before we even heard of your siege, our Tree told Rachel that it was time for Michael and me to join you. Just the two of us, however. The others will only come for the heartbinding."

I nodded. That made sense. That would keep the most vulnerable the safest for the longest. The technical exception to that category was Rachel, especially if she had been training as hard as and possessed even close to Sarah's magical capacity. Yet she was the one we had to guard the most carefully. Because if anything happened to Sarah....

I could barely even think that way, but I had to, even in the most theoretical sense. We could not allow the Moontouched clan to become extinct again. For the survival of the Seven Realms, at least one of their Royals had to remain secure. Sarah was here by the command of her Tree, which meant Rachel was our failsafe.

As strange as that might be.

"Then, by all means, if it's a command from your Tree," I said with a wan smile. "I can hardly afford to aggravate Her any further."

Jake examined me again. "That's not the same thing as accepting our presence yourself, King Koriben. I made my requests as requests for a reason. As you've seen, I tend to...offend leaders, even when that is not my intention."

I could see why. Jake had a force of presence that affected even me, and I had grown up with Avva. Jake's was different, however. Whereas Avva was warm and fatherly if you were worthy or like a scorching sun if you weren't, Jake was unchanging, unreadable—as regal and implacable as a mountain. He exuded a centeredness that I envied and that the petty might mistake as indifference or even a challenge to authority.

Jake continued. "I have learned it is better to make sure as I can that there are no ill feelings. Resentment is...unproductive. And has cost my family no small amount of trouble in the past."

I burned to ask what he meant by that last bit, but I could tell from the set of his jaw that it was a topic he didn't want to explore with me, at least not right now. Besides, I apparently had some reassuring to do.

"I appreciate the gesture, and I give my permission and offer my assistance. But, sir, it would take quite a lot for you to make me resentful. I am too aware of what I owe you and your family. I know I...did not make the best impression on you all for a month, but even when I locked you out, it was never from resentment. Even then, I was aware every dek of every day what I owed your people."

I just wasn't always grateful that one of those things was my life.

"As glad as I am to hear that, I'm not looking for a sense of obligation, either," Jake said.

Was it this hard for Sarah to make sense of her father? Or was I just obtuse? "If I may be frank, sir, what are you looking for, then?"

Jake spoke slowly. "I am gauging your interest in a partnership. If this is to be an effective one, both parties must be on equal footing and have equal interest. Do you *want* us there, King Koriben? I know you want my daughter there...."

He smiled thinly, and I tried not to appear too self-conscious.

"But do you want me and Michael? Do you think you will gain something from our presence?"

I made myself think about that for a moment so he could see I was taking his question seriously. It was a surprisingly astute one, now that I understood it. He knew himself many ways he could be of use to us, but he wanted me to come to that conclusion for myself, before he committed any more members of his family to this situation.

Maybe he wouldn't have been so insistent on having me spell it out, except perhaps he had detected my initial hesitation when he made the request, that little flinch inside that I'd thought I'd hid. I might indeed have had a poor attitude about their presence that would have come out eventually and soured the crucial experiment. As I felt, my people might as well, sowing divisiveness further afield, until it could potentially undermine everything Sarah and I had worked so hard for.

He was right: respect for the Trees and a sense of obligation were not enough, not if we were going to make this work now and for generations. We both had to benefit and agree that's what we were doing from the start. There could be no room for resentment, at least in my flameheart.

I could learn a lot from Jake....

Which formed part of my answer.

"Yes," I said, with finality. "We'll gain many things, this modified lightburster, just to start with."

I didn't mention that I *still* didn't know what the purpose of that thing was, but I trusted that if first Sarah and now Jake were so interested in it, it was important.

"But you and Michael will also relieve a burden on my wings, who have been doing their best to serve as Sarah's as well. I know you have been assisting her from a distance, but Sarah will greatly appreciate having you closer at hand. And, crucially, Sarah will no longer be the only Moontouched we can rely on."

Flame, why didn't I think of that immediately?

I met Jake squarely in the eyes. "You said you are willing to participate in this hold's defense. You are not under my command, and I cannot ask you to take that risk. But if you are offering it of your own free will, then I will accept it gladly. How can I not, when you could be the difference that saves my people tonight?"

I paused for emphasis, then finished. "I say that's plenty to gain."

Jake nodded. "And what do you have to offer us?"

"What do you need?" I asked simply.

"You have satisfied our immediate needs for survival, and I think you will continue to do so regardless."

"Yes," I said firmly. "That's still paying the debt we owe you from before."

Jake nodded. "Then what we hope to gain from this partnership is a bit more nebulous than what we have to offer you."

"And that is?" I asked curiously.

Jake smiled faintly. "It is my understanding that one of the primary purposes of this grand tour is to show your people what their future Queen is made of. Well, seeing as your people aren't the only ones who will gain a Monarch, we want the same chance. Michael and I both, in our own ways, hope to discover whether you are a King worth following."

My flameheart thudded.

"Well...I'll just have to do my very best not to disappoint you."

Chapter Forty-Five

RELATIONS

Sarah

When Ben came back to the room, he first glanced at the wall where my ice had been.

I looked away from my "important" task of holding a giant lens for Kor while he and the artificers continued to tinker and told Ben, "Dad already came back a few minutes ago and said I could dismiss it. He's gone to go pack."

"Oh, good," Ben said, a bit too lightly as he crossed the room to me.

Something wrong? I asked.

It seems I owe you an apology, Ben said, giving me a crooked smile.

I sighed. *For what now?*

For not understanding how you could have been so nervous to talk to my father that first time.

I blinked at him, then laughed out loud, making the others glance at me reflexively. But I figured they were used to seeing silent conversations go on, because they didn't pay us any more mind than if I had been on the phone with someone.

Not for the first time, I wondered what kind of effect inner voices had had on the dramá's cultural development. Nothing too drastic, as far as I could tell. But then, human beings had used unfamiliar languages and secret means of communicating in front of others for ages, so perhaps we weren't that different after all. I supposed the dramá ability to understand any spoken language leveled the playing field a bit. If it hadn't been inner voices, it might have been sign language or something else.

Was it bad? I asked. *Dad said he just wanted to ask you if he could join us, now that the Tree gave permission. I figured you would say yes.*

I had trepidations, especially about Michael. But then, there was no other way to finally convince him, once and for all, that the dramá were our allies while he remained isolated from all but one of them. Hopefully Dad had convinced him to give them a chance.

Lesser concerns were about how the dynamics might change within our group. I hadn't realized I had become so comfortable with the way things were—and how much I liked my newfound independence. In a way...I had begun my own life, and I oversaw my own household now. It was just that my "house" was one in the loosest sense, and there were hundreds of people in it, all of them related to me in a more complex way than blood—and that was only counting our current entourage, let alone our subjects of the Seven Realms. But it still was like Ben and I had started our lives together, just like any couple. Except instead of worrying about things like mortgages and HOAs, we dealt with wyrm incursions and sieges. I liked to think we were doing pretty well figuring things out, all things considered.

Now I wasn't sure where my dad and brother fit into that anymore, and I'd puzzled on that while waiting for Ben to come and then speak with Dad. In that way, Michael would be the easier of the two. I'd already adjusted to a new status quo between us, first when he moved out and then when he started a family of his own. But Dad.... I was used to him being in charge.

Of course I did, Ben said, interrupting my renewed contemplation. *That doesn't mean speaking with him wasn't...interesting.*

In what way? I asked curiously.

Ben smiled ruefully. *Well, for one thing, I still can't figure out whether your father hates me.*

He doesn't hate you.

Ben raised an eyebrow. *He has every reason to.*

I looked away. My answer was quiet. *Dad...isn't like most people. He doesn't let emotion cloud his judgment. He understood, in a way no one else did, why you shut me out. He was the only one who listened to me and believed what I said.*

None of that says that he doesn't hate me, Sarah. Just that he doesn't let it dominate his decisions. And I've done very little since letting you back in except give him more cause.

I had no answer to that. I knew in my gut that Dad didn't *hate* Ben, but I had no way of proving it, and there were a range of negative emotions short of hate that Dad could still harbor toward Ben.

Would I have been brave enough to pursue a relationship with Ben if I'd suspected his father disliked me? If Kavarian hadn't *told* me he loved me, and more or less given me his blessing?

I winced. Maybe I needed to talk with Dad about this.

Kor had taken the lens from me at some point, leaving my hands free, so I took Ben's hand and squeezed it. *I'm sorry.*

He frowned. *You have nothing to apologize for, Sarah.*

Was Dad at least polite?

Painfully so, Ben said with a thin smile. *I assume he's usually that...formal.*

I grimaced. *Usually. Yes.*

Dad wasn't socially incompetent. He just...could not emote much. Mom always said it was because his father was Norwegian, and Dad was born in and spent the first eight years of his life in Norway, before his parents divorced and his British mother moved with him to the US. I'd met Gran enough times before she died to confirm that she wouldn't have been much of an ameliorating influence on her son's ability to show emotion. What had drawn Mom and Dad together, I would never know, but the two of them had always been determined to make it work, and so it had.

Even as self-aware as Dad was that his inscrutability made people from other cultures uncomfortable, he couldn't do much about his fundamental programing. He just tried to compensate in other ways.

I didn't know how to explain all of that to Ben, though.

It was like dealing with a Strongshield, Ben said, shaking his head and grinning. *Which I've done aplenty. Except I've never wanted a Strongshield's good opinion that badly before. It was mildly terrifying.*

I laughed ruefully. *He grew up in a culture that was like the Strongshield's, in some ways.*

Makes sense.

I squeezed his hand three times. Instead of apologizing again, which I knew he wouldn't accept, I opted for gratitude. *Thank you for doing that.*

Of course, Ben said, squeezing back the same number. He squared his shoulders and took a deep breath. *Well, you want to help me go get them? With your lashing, and Mathya's permission to use Rosin's internal daygate, we could bring them in with no one the wiser. And I think that's best.*

I sobered. Yes, if Dad and Michael were going to give us the edge we were hoping for tonight, it was best that no one but the defenders knew they were here.

Especially not the Devourer.

How do you feel about your father and brother fighting? Ben asked as we waited in front of the crowngate. I assumed he used his inner voice in case the door was already open on the other side. With the flames between us and the ice curtain, we couldn't tell.

Conflicted, I said, my gut clenching. *Part of me wants to shield them from it all. But the other part of me knows that's not realistic—or even fair to them. I can't be the only one allowed to risk my life, and I can't keep them from trying to protect me.*

Just as I couldn't keep Ben from doing the same.

Dad and Michael had been more than patient, all things considered. Yes, even Michael. He could have made a much bigger stink if he'd wanted. After all, nothing could have kept him from going through that crowngate now that it was open. He might not have been able to make it past the door at the end of the passage, but he could have caused a lot of problems for us by trying. Or gone on a hunger strike, or called me every day, or something. Yet, ultimately, he had deferred to my decisions. And, indirectly, our Tree's.

I can understand that, Ben said sympathetically. *Your plan is a good one, though.*

I'd explained it to him as we'd walked to find Mathya, finishing up as we waited here.

He continued, *Even if the modified lightbursters don't work like you intend, they should be out of danger.*

This time, I said heavily.

Ben lifted my chin to meet his eyes. *I'll do my best to keep them safe. As will anyone who is loyal to me. We know we can't afford to lose a single one of you.*

I swallowed. There were only twelve of us. That was a lot for a single family, even by Earthren standards. But still only twelve. And it seemed more depended on us by the day.

I was derailed for a moment as it occurred to me for the first time that we had no way to increase that number—no way to rebuild the Moontouched clan. Not unless dramá started volunteering, or the Tree of Ice provided us a way to leave Her Temple, which was deep underneath the ice pack of the most sparsely inhabited portion of Greenland, and we found Earthren willing to join us.

Or...we increased the slow, ol' fashioned way: reproduction. But the only partners that would be available to the rest of my siblings were....

Dramá.

I blinked, not sure how I felt about that. Of course, I was hardly one to talk, seeing as I was happily marrying their King. But I felt a twinge of guilt. Would my siblings blame me? Lizzy was only twelve, but she had already shown budding signs of genuine interest in the other gender; she was long past playing house and even squealing about cooties. Might she already resent me for taking away her chances with a human?

Rachel would have, for certain, except right now, she seemed content with the prospect of Kor. She had already figured out that this was the way things were going to be now, weeks before I had.

Of course, all I had cared about was Ben.

To me, he was just...Ben. His own thing. When I forced myself to think about our differences, I didn't feel like he was *in*human. He was more...*super*human. The parts of him that were different from me, I found incredible, not repulsive.

But would David, Lizzy, Noah, Jonah, Abby, and Tommie feel the same way? The latter four might not even think much of the difference, and in a way, that made me feel even more conflicted. David and Lizzy would know what they lost in leaving humanity behind; the littles probably never would. Was that even crueler?

Ben smiled and tapped my forehead. "Where has your mind wandered off to now?"

My face heated. "Um...."

Besides the awkwardness, would he find my troubled thoughts offensive? Would they make him doubt me? How to explain that the only thing I was mourning was their lack of choice? I'd had a choice, a real choice. They wouldn't.

Unless things changed....

Fortunately, Dad chose that moment to step through the fire, and Ben immediately settled into a more formal stance and expression.

Dad was too distracted by the transition to notice the change in him. He blinked, turned, looked back at the gate, and instinctively backed away from the tongues of flame. Michael passed through not a moment later, casting Ben a glare. He, too, however, glanced back behind him and then scooted away.

"It won't hurt you," I said with a smile. "Like I said."

I'd explained the crowngate to them before. To Dad in more detail than Michael, though; Michael's interest ended after he finally got that I truly couldn't make it functional again on my own.

"I know," Dad said, now cocking his head in curiosity. "Yet it feels so warm...."

Just as he reached his hand toward the flames, Mom stepped through. She caught his fingers with a wan smile.

"Mom!" I protested. "It's supposed to be just Dad and Michael."

There was no way in hell I was going to bring my tender-hearted mother into a war zone. It wasn't a females-shouldn't-fight thing. I would have welcomed Laura in a heartbeat if the Tree had included her with Dad and Michael; I'd like to see the Devourer try to intimidate my sister-in-law. No, this was a too-good-for-this-world-mother-who-can't-kill-a-spider thing.

"Good to see you, too, *mi hija*," Mom said dryly, pulling me in for a tight hug.

I held back a wince. Mom only slipped into Spanish around us when she was emotional; she could never explain to us or her own mother why she had never taught us her first language, especially given her career in linguistics. Maybe trying to reconcile those linguistic halves of herself was why she went into that field at all.

As I'd expected, tears were in her eyes when she pulled away; she kept her hands on my forearms. "Do you know how long it's been since I got to hug you? And then my baby just stands there, feet away from me, right when she's going off to war, *again*, and you expect me to just stay back?"

I tried not to shift. Well, when she put it like that.... Yeah, I should have seen this coming. "Mom, the brightfever...."

"Oh, Svyer's got more than enough of that cure stored up," Mom said dismissively, a stern look entering her watery eyes. "You can't keep using that as an excuse, *mi nena*. You should have come to visit a long time ago."

I knew any protests about how busy I'd been or how many life-threatening situations I'd had to endure would only keep digging a deeper pit for myself, at least in her mind. Mom could be as illogical as Dad was logical. Coming back to her should have come first, and that was that.

"Yes, Mom," I said meekly.

She narrowed her eyes and called my bluff. "So, when are you coming home, then?"

Was this how Michael had felt before, when Mom was always badgering *him*? When he would come over, why didn't he call her more, when would he send more pictures of her grandbaby...?

From the way Michael was smirking out of the corner of my eye, I thought so.

"I don't know," I said honestly. "I'm sorry, but I have other responsibilities that have to come first. But I promise to think about when. And I'll call you as soon as I can. Alright?"

She blinked rapidly, the tears finally spilling over. She pulled me in again and hugged me tight. "Oh, my little girl. You shouldn't have had to grow up so fast."

"What are you talking about?" Michael teased gently, putting a hand on her shoulder. "Sarah was born fifty, you know that."

I'd gotten an upgrade. Usually, it was thirty.

"I know," Mom said with another sniff.

She turned on Michael and hugged him tightly, even though I guessed from Michael's long-suffering expression that she'd gotten at least one in already. She wouldn't have been happy with the news that the two of them were leaving.

Mom let him go and gave Dad his turn. It was the kind of hug that had the rest of us looking away awkwardly, Ben just as much as Michael and me, if not more.

"What am I going to do without you?" Mom said wetly. She often said that, but this time there was a raw edge that made my iceheart clench.

"You will do just fine," Dad murmured. "As you always do. And I'll come back, as soon as I can."

Svyer stepped through the curtain of fire. I brightened and waved at her, and she winked at me, but she went straight for Mom.

"Maria," she said softly, then put a hand on her shoulder. "It's time to let them go. Rachel is waiting."

Waiting to close the doors, no doubt. And patience wasn't Rachel's strong suit. Much longer and she'd come marching through the gate herself, and she wouldn't be gentle as she dragged Mom back through.

"I know," Mom sighed, and she finally released Dad. The two women exchanged a look. I didn't know the exact meaning behind it, but it told me that Mom had already come to trust and rely on Svyer, and that made my iceheart lift.

I had known from the start that if anyone could win them over, it would have been Svyer. And if anyone could comfort Mom while her husband and firstborn were gone, and give her real hope that everything would be alright, it would be Svyer again.

At first, Mom let Svyer lead her back, but then she stopped and turned to Ben.

The most fire I'd ever seen entered Mom's eyes as she looked at him. "You take care of my family, young man. You understand?"

"I will, ma'am," Ben answered with dead seriousness. "With my life."

Michael snorted, making me bristle, but fortunately, Mom ignored him, as did everyone else.

Mom nodded, as imperious as any queen. "Good."

Then she walked back through the fire and ice, and Svyer, with one last smile at Ben and me, followed.

"Well," Ben said, breaking the silence. To Michael and Dad, he probably appeared relaxed. I knew better. "Are you ready to go?"

"Sure," Michael grunted, picking up his duffel again to sling it over his shoulder. Judging from the weight, I was certain it contained more than just clothing and toiletries.

"Allow me," Ben said, holding out his hand.

"No thanks," Michael said with a scowl and a step away.

Ben just lowered his hand without changing his expression. Though he raised it again to accept Dad's proffered bag and made it disappear with just the slightest shift of his fingers.

"Michael," I said, forcing myself to keep my voice even. "He's not offering just to be polite. It really is more practical for him to hold your stuff right now."

"I've got it," my brother said mulishly.

"But can you *hide* it? We're trying to conceal the fact that you and Dad are in the Six Realms for as long as we can—at least until tonight. That way, you give us the greatest advantage possible. That bag screams 'different.'"

It had far too many artificial materials, not to mention unfamiliar zippers and designs. It looked weird to *me* now.

Michael hesitated.

"How are you going to hide our hair and eyes?" Dad asked, merely curious.

"My leftwing will disguise you," Ben said. "The illusions won't hold up to scrutiny, but they will do for as long as it will take to get you to where you are going."

"And our clothes?" Michael demanded, gesturing to himself. Because of course he had worn a t-shirt, jeans, and sneakers. He glanced at Dad and scowled. "Or, my clothes."

Dad was wearing things from the hold's storage room: shoes, pants, belt, and shirt of natural materials. That *all* his clothing right now was dramá-make seemed deliberate, but most of my family had incorporated at least some dramá clothing from the storeroom into their wardrobes, just for some variety. Not Michael, though.

Ben raised an eyebrow and gave Michael a look that said, *What kind of amateur do you take me for?*

But he only said, "We have uniforms for you to wear. You'll be disguised as two of Sarah's elites."

"Her what?"

"My personal guard," I answered, as patiently as I could manage. I'd expected Michael's belligerent attitude, but the more it was directly targeted at Ben, the more it got under my skin, to a surprising degree.

"Oh," Michael said, looking a bit mollified. Of course, being a former police officer, that role would feel the most comfortable to him of any we could devise. I wondered if that was one reason Ben had chosen it. Though I carefully didn't mention to Michael that his disguise as one of my elites would be about as effective as Kor's illusions would be. There was no way he or Dad would pass as one under scrutiny. They walked, looked, and acted too differently—even Michael. I could see the difference now, from the cop who only saw occasional action to the battle-hardened elite soldier.

Ben held out his hand again. "I swear to not so much as touch the bag again until I hand it back to you."

"And you'll actually hand it back this time?"

I fisted my hands, nails biting into my palms. He might as well have *slapped* Ben with that callous reminder.

Easy, Sarah, Ben said with wry amusement. *I can handle this.*

Ben's expression did not change, and his eyes never left Michael's. "I will, this time."

Michael seemed surprised at that blatant acknowledgement of his failing to do so before. I didn't know if that's what finally convinced him, but after another moment, Michael handed his bag over. I noted in petty amusement that Ben handled the weighted bag much more lightly than Michael did—and the muscles in Michael's arm weren't puny.

Michael noticed too and scowled. Or maybe that was at watching the slight, momentary draconic shift in Ben's skin that made the bag vanish.

Much more of Michael's attitude, and I was going to punch him—and I might actually make it hurt now.

Ben could tell. He put his hand on my shoulder—ostensibly as a casual gesture, but I knew what the subtle pressure of his fingers meant: restraint.

"Ready?" he said with a smile at me, for once ignoring Michael's glare at the touch.

I sighed in acknowledgement of his message. I gestured to Dad and Michael. "Gather in. It's easier to do the lashing the closer we are together."

With it only barely past noon and lots of testing on the lightburster to go, every bit of energy counted.

Michael reluctantly stepped next to me, on the other side from Ben. Dad put himself between Michael and Ben in our loose huddle. We could have been closer, but I wasn't going to push them further right now. I'd pay the little extra in energy.

"Now, pay attention to what I'm doing, because you might be able to replicate it now," I told my two family members.

I'd described lashing to them before, with some emotional difficulty, because in the beginning, Michael had justifiably insisted I share every single thing I knew about what we could do. We'd never been able to reproduce the same effect, though. No one else except me seemed to be able to make the lashings, and even mine snapped the moment I surged, leaving the person behind. I never mentioned to them that my lashings were weaker with them than they had ever been with Ben, and I suspected my emotions were the reason; lashing reminded me too strongly of Ben. I wasn't being fair to my family, but I was eager for the experiment to fail so that Michael would leave it alone.

"What makes you think this time will be different?" Michael asked with a raised eyebrow.

"You'll see," I said. "Or rather, you won't see, but you know what I mean."

My brother rolled his eyes. "Just get on with it, Sarah."

There was only so long he could stand this close to Ben and not look at him. Ben was rather large, after all, even if he was out of his armor and in his regular black clothing right now.

I lashed us all together. Michael grunted—not from discomfort, but surprise. He *could* feel the difference between my lashings now and before. His eyes narrowed as he glanced at me, but before he could ask why I'd been holding out on them, I told Ben, "Ready."

"Brace yourselves," Ben told the other two. "This won't be uncomfortable, but it might be disorienting."

He could only promise the former now that he was King, but I didn't mention that.

"We're ready," Dad said.

Our surroundings shifted, and a split second later, we were standing in what I immediately dubbed the "portal room."

Lady Winthra, just like Lady Rowin, had a daygate in her wing, presumably for security and convenience. I never saw Lady Rowin's, but I assumed it was kept in some stark, dark, and triply bolted room that was barely more than a closet. Not so with Lady Winthra's.

The freestanding arch was placed in the center of a domed room. The ceiling was painted with a dark night sky covered in stars, "held up" by a ring of pillars around the edge. In between the pillars were murals that I assumed reflected bucolic scenes from each of the Six Realms, with the vast blue ocean of Oshal occupying the one directly across from us. Each mural was lent a bit of credence by veils of the clan colors over each, which obscured the artwork just enough to make you look twice to ascertain that what was beyond wasn't real. Plus, those veils waved in breezes of enigmatic origins. A ring of luxurious couches of blue silk cushions and marble construction went in a smaller circle around the room, a level up from the sunken circle we and the daygate were in. I smelled a soothing, citrusy incense, and, despite the warmth of the fire from the gate just behind us, the room felt fresh, cool, and mysterious.

Michael gawked. I had to elbow him to get him to shut his gaping mouth, since we were expected.

Lady Winthra and her wings rose from where they had sat at the highest couch: a little piece of the circle that almost seemed to have been broken off, pushed up to yet a higher level, and made the stairs leading up to go around. Now I realized what all this ostentation was for. If Lady Winthra was using the daygate herself, she could enjoy or ignore it. But if she were welcoming a Royal guest, well...the Royal could hardly complain at the grandeur of the reception area. But there was a bit of a message here, in both the splendor and the height difference: *You're in* my *Realm now.*

I knew from Ben's blandly polite expression that the message wasn't lost on him.

Except it might not have been meant for him this time, and this time might not have been about intimidation at all. Lady Winthra was dressed with unusual formality in grand blue silk robes and blue flowers woven into her light hair, but her face radiated genuine warmth as she looked down at my family members. And was that a hint of relief?

Kor stood on the ring just below her and came down the steps to greet us. He, too, had dressed up in fancy silks, his a dark sapphire embroidered and edged with gold.

"Greetings to you, Leftwing Jacob Lind, Rightwing Michael Lind of the Moontouched Clan. I, as you know, am Korinth Starkissed. As the leftwing of King Koriben Sunfilled, allow me to formally welcome you to the Six Realms."

You didn't mention you were planning a fancy welcome, I told Kor in amusement. His machinations weren't so bothersome when they weren't directed at me.

His lips pulled to the side in the most subtle of smirks. *You'll thank me later.*

Oh, from the look on Michael's face, I was ready to thank him now.

Dad stepped forward. One benefit of his composed exterior was that he looked as if he had expected all of this and did this sort of thing all the time. He nodded to Kor; thank goodness that at some point, I told him that dramá didn't bow, and he apparently remembered. Then again, Dad wasn't the bowing type, so maybe only his instincts were guiding him here. He had such a good memory, though, I doubted it.

"Thank you, Leftwing Korinth," Dad said in perfectly grammatical, if simple and heavily accented Drona. "It is good to be here."

Kor nodded and turned to the side. "Allow me to introduce you to the leadership of this Realm, Oshal. May I present the Lady Winthra, Leftwing Oran, and Rightwing Mathya of the Starkissed clan."

Kor gestured to each in turn.

Dad turned to Lady Winthra and nodded, more deeply this time. "Greetings, Lady Winthra. Flame watch over you and warm your hearth."

I quickly hid my surprise. *I* hadn't taught him that. Dad had been making good use of Svyer's lessons.

"And Ice watch over you, Leftwing Jacob," Winthra said with a twinkle in her eye as she descended the stairs. "Forgive me that I do not know what the proper thing is to say after that, since I am assuming you do not want Ice entering your hearth."

"No need," Dad said, smiling slightly, still speaking Drona. "We have not decided that part ourselves."

"Allow me then to welcome you to Oshal," she said with feeling. She reached with both her hands and grasped Dad's with one, and—much to Michael's shock—Michael's in the other. "The aid you both have offered my people in our deken of need will *not* be forgotten."

Dad switched to English. "Again, no need for thanks, Lady Winthra. We are only doing our duty to our Queen."

He hesitated only one beat. Hopefully the others would think it was for emphasis. "And our Tree."

Even if she suspected the truth, Winthra didn't seem to mind. "Then thanks be to our Trees—*both* of Them."

If your brother drops his mouth any further, a puka might fly in, Kor said in amusement—referring, I assumed, to one of the small, brightly colored birds that seemed to have adapted to life in the lofty upper regions of the hold, which was at least fifty feet above our heads. From the synthetic perches and nests up there, it seemed the Starkissed not just tolerated but welcomed the creatures. How the birds didn't leave poop everywhere, I had no idea; more Starkissed magic, probably. But I had to admit they were beautiful, and their songs were as melodious as wind chimes, adding a charming harmony to the boisterous cacophony below.

Michael, I silently groaned to my brother.

I know, I know, he muttered back, ducking his head once more.

I could hardly blame him. We were now walking through Rosin's primary market, which I was sure not even a grand bazaar on Earth could match for variety, richness, and general Starkissed flashiness. Magic shimmered around every corner, exotic scents hung in the air, silken blue streamers fluttered above in the drafts from the various brazier fires, and dramá of all clans thronged around us, examining, bargaining for, and hauling around the wares. Even during a siege, the Starkissed seemed to be doing brisk business. Then again, it wasn't the type of siege in which anyone was *really* trapped—not with the sungate still functioning.

Speaking of which, that was how Ben had avoided walking with us now. I attracted enough attention by myself; even if the hair wasn't a dead give-away, I had my white-and-silver uniformed elites surrounding me as part of the plan. Walking briskly with Ben somewhere would have attracted even more notice—and comment.

So, after Ben and I had agreed on our strategy for bringing in Dad and Michael unnoticed (at least mostly), I had made myself be seen walking into the Lady's Wing with Kor, so it looked like he and I were going there for a meeting with the Lady, while Ben surged to the daygate inside. Then he'd met us just outside the portal room (so when we had arrived was the first time I'd seen it), and Ben surged with me to the crowngate. Then, once he'd brought the four of us back to the daygate, Ben surged straight from the daygate to the Rosin sungate. When he walked out of it alone, people would think he had merely surged to Crownhold and back for a quick bit of in-person Crown business—not a huge surprise given the current crisis.

That formal greeting in the portal room hadn't been part of the original plan, but I should have known Kor would add in his own twist. And I had to admit it had a nice result so far. Michael was still dazed, and everything he'd seen since had only added to his shock. It was having a nicely humbling effect on him, taking away his hard edges. I could only hope it would last.

On the other hand, he was making his disguise even less believable than I'd anticipated. No elite would be gawking right now.

Fortunately, there was a ring of real elites around the three of us Linds, always at least partially shielding my father and brother from view. Dad's and Michael's illusionary brown hair and lack of scale armor, marking them as amón, made their inner position in the circle make sense to anyone who would glimpse them; any amón among my elites would still be deadly, but the drakón would form my first line of defense.

Somehow, we all made it back to the guard rooms without attracting too much attention. There, an artificer Dad had been working with before happily greeted him and eagerly whisked him away. Before Michael had too much time to stand around awkwardly, Mathya came out to meet him and asked if he would like to review the defense plan with her.

Michael flushed, looked away, and said, "I'm not sure I know enough to contribute."

Mathya just grinned. "Then it's a good time to learn, isn't it?"

Michael lifted his head in surprise, and then slowly smiled in return. "Well...I guess it is."

He and Mathya walked off, deep in conversation even before they were out of sight, leaving me with just Kor.

"Well...?" Kor said, arms folded and inclining his head toward me pointedly. "It's later, in case you haven't noticed."

I rolled my eyes, then smiled. "Thank you."

"You're welcome," Kor said smugly. "Although, to be honest, I didn't do it just for your brother's benefit. Winthra and the others would have been quite put out if we hadn't given them a chance to greet your wings properly. To have the entire first branch of the White Crown here in Rosin is too momentous an occasion to sweep under the rug. You don't know how long we've waited for this day."

About that.... I said slowly, wondering if this was finally the time to bring up the suspicion I was slowly putting into words. *Kor, why—*

"Ah, there you are," Ben said, coming out of another room with a smile. "Took you all long enough."

I smiled back. "Well, *some* of us had to walk all the way here. And through the crowds, no less."

Ben shuddered dramatically. "Glad I missed that part. I hate to think what the markets are like right now."

"As busy as they've ever been," Kor said cheerfully. "Rosin merchants will be making a tidy profit out of all of this."

"How does that work, exactly?" I asked skeptically.

Kor's eyes brightened. "Well, it has to do with mortal psychology in a crisis, and that the sungate is still open for people across the Realms to still pour in to buy what they *think* will be highly discounted, potentially endangered goods—"

"In other words," Ben said hastily, "economics."

Kor sighed. "It's a really good thing you have me to deal with fiscal and monetary policy."

"Yep," Ben said cheerfully. "It's one of the main reasons I keep you alive."

I grinned. "Don't you mean that's why you keep him *around*?"

"Ah, yes," Ben said. Unconvincingly. "That's what I meant."

"Right," Kor said as he folded his arms again, so dubious that both of us cracked and laughed.

Ben took my hand, looking hopeful. "I was thinking of heading back to the King's Wing for a nap. Want to come?"

I smiled up at him. "Ah, Ben. Voluntarily resting during a crisis? I'm proud of you."

Kor snorted. "Yvera and Mathya ganged up on you, didn't they? Told you that you couldn't go back out there, that you needed to rest up for tonight."

Ben looked away, red creeping over his face. "Maybe."

I only laughed. "Well, I still take listening to your rightwing as a sign of progress."

"Even when he's trying to turn it into time with you?" Kor said.

"Kor," Ben growled, the red spreading.

"Yes, even then," I said firmly.

After all, that was a form of resting for Ben.

"Sarah needs sleep too, I'm sure," Ben said, cooling a bit. He glanced at me speculatively. "You've gotten up deken before your normal time two days in a row now. When you got back this morning, how much did you sleep before you had your idea?"

"Um...."

Kor smirked. "None at all. She didn't even make it to her bedroom before she overheard Vadya sighing about what a *shame* it was that there wouldn't be a lightburst display tonight."

Kor had no sides, being equally willing to rat out both of us to each other.

"It *is* a bit of a shame," I said wistfully. "From what she described, it sounds beautiful."

Like fireworks, but even better.

However, I was also deliberately playing up the wistfulness to misdirect—but it was in vain.

Ben sighed. "Sarah...."

"Oh, don't worry, Ben," Kor said with a straight face. "I promised Sarah that we'd work them into the heartbinding celebrations somehow."

"Great, thanks, Kor," Ben said, rolling his eyes. He looked back at me. "Are you coming?"

There was more sternness and less hopefulness in his "offer" now, but I didn't mind. After all, I couldn't encourage him to rest without taking my own advice. Besides, he would be able to relax better with me there.

I gave a long-suffering sigh, though. "I suppose, for you, I will brave the crowds again."

"Oh, we don't have to do anything so odious as that," Ben said cheerfully. "I'll fly us down to the King's landing."

"Oh," I said, brightening. "Well, sure then. I don't think you need me here, do you, Kor? Now that Dad's here to help you with the fine-tuning and testing?"

Kor rubbed his chin. "Well, it always helps to have a greater pool of power to draw on...."

He laughed at Ben's death glare and flapped his hand as he turned away. "Go on, you two. Get some sleep while you can."

Or maybe talk about some secrets, hmm? Kor said to me as he walked away.

I suppressed a groan. Kor and his suggestions.

The problem was...he always made them stick.

Chapter Forty-Six

SECRET

Koriben

"I HAVE AN IDEA," Sarah declared grandly as she entered our room.

My flameheart pulsed in trepidation. Which I carefully tried to hide as I allowed the door to swing closed behind us. "And that is?"

She snatched one pillow off the bed and grabbed one of the spare blankets stowed in a cubby beneath and brought both toward my pallet.

"Sarah," I said sternly. "You're not sleeping on the—"

Just at that moment, she passed the pallet and tossed her pillow and blanket onto the nearest couch. Then she dragged the pallet over to the couch so that they were right next to each other.

"...couch?" Sarah said innocently as she kicked off her slippers, climbed onto it, and burrowed into her blanket. "Why not?"

I eyed the arrangement. We would be, essentially, sleeping next to each other. Close enough to talk and occasionally touch, but with just enough of a barrier against anything further.

I sighed and began crossing the room. "Alright, you win."

Sarah grinned. "That was easy."

I rolled my eyes. "The right strategy generally is. The trick usually is finding it."

"Well, the finding wasn't too hard once I thought about it," Sarah said contentedly as I sat down on the ground and pulled off my boots. "I wanted us to talk and rest at the same time, and looky here. Perfectly safe."

She was far too pleased with herself. I calculated rapidly, then decided the risk was worth it to take her down a notch.

I smiled. "Oh, so you don't mind if I get a bit more comfortable, then?"

Her face scrunched in confusion, then her eyes widened in alarm when I crossed my hands in front of me and pulled my shirt over my head.

"Ben!" she squeaked.

"What?" I asked innocently as I pulled the cloth away and tossed it aside. To my amusement, I saw she had actually brought her blanket up over her eyes, and now only her forehead and the white hair at the crown of her head showed. I was a bit flattered. This was an even better reaction than I'd expected.

She brought the blanket down a bit to peek, probably to see if the coast was clear, then brought it straight back up when she saw me only sitting there, grinning. Turned fully toward her.

"You've got to give me some warning before you do that!" she cried.

"I thought you said this was 'safe.'"

Personal amusement aside, that was the reason I'd justified doing this—to show her that this still wasn't foolproof. We couldn't afford to get cocky.

Well...I couldn't, anyway. So maybe I should stop torturing her. I laid down and pulled my blanket over me, only leaving my arms and shoulders bare as I turned on my side to face her.

"Alright, fine," Sarah grumbled. "You've made your point. Fire is never 'safe.' Now, are you going to cover that up, or what?"

"Already done," I said. "Should I be flattered or concerned that you compared me to fire?"

She brought the blanket down again cautiously, then lowered it the rest of the way when she saw the coast was clear. Then she scooted closer to the edge so that we could see each other. Her eyebrow raised. "I'll let you come to your own conclusions about that."

"That's dangerous," I teased. "Seeing how bad I am at reading these things."

"Oh, I think you're learning well enough," she grumbled.

I laughed quietly. Yes, I was learning. And that felt *good*.

Sarah sobered, glancing away. Something was clearly on her mind. My flameheart sank, all humor dying. She said she had wanted to talk. Had it been about something in particular? Something...bad?

"What is it?" I asked, trying to keep my voice even.

She grimaced. "I've been trying to think about how to bring this up more gradually, but I can't. So, I'm just going to have out with it, if that's alright."

My flameheart pounded. "Alright...go ahead."

What was the worst she could say, if she was still willing to drag my pallet over to sleep next to her, and be so flustered by seeing me without a shirt that she hid under a blanket? Those weren't the actions of someone about to break off a betrothal. So, anything less than that, I could handle. Right?

Sarah still didn't meet my eyes. "Kor...has a theory."

I blinked. Was this about the siege? Or the Devourer's plans more generally? If so, why would he have talked with Sarah about it and not me?

Unworthy spike of jealousy aside, I could think of only one *logical* reason: Kor's theory was so terrible, he wanted Sarah to broach it with me instead of him, thinking she could reason with and reassure me better.

My flameheart pulsed even faster. "About what?"

She took a deep breath and finally looked me in the eye. "About what the Tree actually said to you, in your dream. Right before you let me in."

About....

I froze.

"He thinks," Sarah said slowly, "that the Tree told you that if you didn't marry me, I would die."

Oh.

Well.

That was....

Torch it, that wasn't *exactly* right, but it was far, far too close for comfort. Kor was a genius, hellfrosts take him.

When I remained silent, Sarah continued. "I haven't asked you for specifics about your dream because I figured if any of it were my business, you would tell me." She raised an eyebrow. "So...now's your chance, Ben. Have anything to tell me?"

I inwardly squirmed with guilt, but she was right. My time was up. If I didn't tell her *now*...she would never forgive me.

I couldn't meet her eyes, though. I tensed, bracing myself. "If there were some truth to that theory...how would you feel about it?"

"Amused."

I blinked in shock, and my eyes met hers. She was smiling.

Smiling.

"What?" I said blankly. It was a good thing I was already lying down, because if I'd been standing, I would have had to immediately sit.

I felt almost as floored as when I'd discovered Sarah and I had accidentally renewed the First Covenant.

She rolled her eyes. "Ben, I've had a long time to reconcile myself to the fact that both our Trees, your father, Eskala, Kor, and, heck, half the Six Realms expected us to marry. And I chose you anyway. Because I loved you. I chose you anyway, *knowing* how hard it would be for you to finally let me love you. Did you honestly expect me to be offended by the Tree coming to you and saying you'd better get a move on?"

I chose my words with care. More because my head was spinning so badly I'd otherwise spout pure nonsense than because I was still afraid of her reactions. "I thought you would doubt.... I'd hurt you so badly, I didn't want to make you think I was only doing it because...."

Sarah smiled sadly and reached to brush her fingers down the side of my face. Her touch, cool and gentle as snowflakes on my skin, made my skin burn more than it had any right to.

"Ben, I never would have thought that you were only marrying me because the Tree told you to. I always understood that you would need...some kind of catalyst, something to finally let you give yourself permission to be happy. But from the moment I figured out you loved me, I have never doubted you. I still don't understand what finally made the difference for you, but I know you proposed to me because you love me."

She grinned. "And, yes, because you don't want me to die. But that's also because you love me."

Well, hellfrost. Now I was feeling lighter and heavier, freer and more wretched, hotter and colder than ever. Because she was too good, far too good.

And I still hadn't even told her the truth.

"What is it?" she asked, her fingers still lingering on my face as she looked deeply into my eyes. Those silvers pierced me to my center.

It was time to stop being a coward. It was time to risk it all and finally *trust* her. Or I didn't deserve her.

I took a deep breath and captured her hand, holding it in mine. I held our joined hands in front of my face and studied them, as if I could find the right words to say written there.

Maybe the perfect words didn't exist. Maybe I just had to come out and say it, like she had.

"What if...Kor wasn't *exactly* right?"

"What?" Sarah said curiously, leaning a bit more forward. "What *did* the Tree say, then?"

My face burned. "Remember, the Tree said this. *Not me.* I don't understand it. I really, truly don't. It wasn't my idea. At all."

"I get it, Ben. This comes from Her. I won't judge you for it."

I was certain my face was on fire now. Too late, I wished I was across the room from her. "You're going to be sorely tempted to, trust me. So, try to remember that."

"Go ahead." She squeezed my hand three times.

I took a deep, deep breath. Yet, the coward I still was, I closed my eyes. "She said that your life was in danger, yes. The Devourer would come after you, seeking revenge. And it would find you. One month from that day."

I listened, but Sarah's breath was still even, and her hand in mine still relaxed.

How could she always be so *calm* in moments like this?

"Go on," she murmured. "What else?"

"She said there would be nothing I could do to hide you, nothing I could do to protect you. It was a battle you would have to face on your own."

"That must have been hard for you to hear," Sarah said softly, clenching my hand.

I groaned as I relived the moment, even more easily with my eyes closed. "You have no idea."

"What then? Did she say how I could defeat it? Or at least survive?"

I took another deep breath. "Yes—to survive. But you're not going to like it."

"I gathered that part. But remember, I promise not to judge you for what She said. Now, what is it?"

"She said the *only* chance you would have...was if you were with child.... My...child."

I braced myself.

Silence.

I cracked my eyes open, unable to bear the suspense any longer. Sarah's lips were pressed thin, her eyes were wide, and she was shaking slightly. I started pushing myself up, wondering what was wrong.

Then a giggle finally escaped. She flipped onto her belly and pressed her face into her pillow, using it to smother her convulsions.

She was *laughing*.

"Sarah!" Just moments before, I had thought my face couldn't get any hotter. Now, I discovered I was mistaken.

"Sorry, sorry," she said, gasping as she pushed herself up onto her elbows for some air. She wiped the corners of her eyes. "Oh, gosh. Sorry. Just...oh, man, of *all the things*—I wasn't expecting *that*. But I guess I should have. It all makes so much freaking *sense* now."

"*How*? How can you make sense out of such a nonsensical...."

I didn't even have words.

"Oh, not *that*," Sarah said with another giggle. And a hiccup. "Not Her. *You*. Everything to do with you suddenly all makes sense. *That's* why you never told me. *That's* why you've been acting this way. And *that's* why you won't sleep with me, isn't it? It's because the Tree told you to...to...."

It was my turn to turn onto my belly and hide my face in my pillow. Except I wasn't laughing. I would very much have preferred being able to sink beneath the stone floor.

Especially when Sarah spoke again, voice strained from trying to stay in control. "So, let me get this straight. The Tree came to you in a dream, gave you a sound scolding, and then told you that you had one month to get me pregnant, or else the Devourer would finish me off. Have I got that?"

"Yes," I said into my pillow, so the sound was greatly muffled—and I hadn't said it loudly to begin with. Sarah might have only heard an unintelligible sound of confirmation.

"I have to hand it to you, Ben. That...that's some dream."

"Yes," I said again, still muffled.

And she still didn't even know the other part of it. But that part really *was* meant just for me, so I didn't feel the slightest bit guilty for not telling her about it. Not only did I not have adequate words to describe it, it wouldn't mean the same thing to anyone else. Even Sarah.

"Oh, gosh," Sarah said, taking a deep breath to recover. "You know, I'm quite touched, Ben. It must have been hard to wait all this time, knowing my life was riding on this."

I finally risked turning my head to the side to look at her. "Why do you think I did it that way? I'd hurt you so badly that the only way I figured I could make up for it was to put your happiness before everything."

"And here I laughed at you," she said, shaking her head with a sad smile. "I'm sorry. Really, I truly am. I blame hysteria. You made me fear it was going to be much worse than that."

"You're not mad?" I asked, blinking. "At *all*?"

She paused thoughtfully. "Well, I might have been, if you'd handled things differently. If you'd been selfish and pushed. But you didn't. You did the exact opposite. Figures."

She shook her head at me fondly. "I wish you would have *told* me upfront, but...."

She blinked. "Oh, gosh, now that I think about it, I can understand why you didn't. Especially not in the beginning. We were only just getting our footing again, for Pete's sake. Yes, we got engaged in one day, but I still would *not* have been ready to talk about children."

She mused for a moment, then said, "To be honest...I might have done the same thing you did. I don't think you made a mistake, Ben. I think you did the best thing you could have done, given the circumstances. So...no, I'm not mad. Not at all."

I just stared at her, dumbfounded. It was a good thing we'd had this conversation while I was lying down.

"Now, how I feel about what the Tree said...." Sarah shook her head in bafflement. "That's a different story. How on earth does that even make sense? How does me being *pregnant* make the slightest difference in my survival in a fight with the Devourer?"

I turned onto my side again. "I don't know. You think I haven't asked myself the same question a million times by now? But...but I know that was a real dream, Sarah. I can remember every single moment. Better than I can remember anything, actually. I know the Tree was really speaking to me, and I know that's what She said. She left me no doubt."

"I believe you," Sarah said firmly, glancing back at me and smiling. "I believe you. I do. And I believe Her. Flame knows I've learned to trust what the Trees tell us is necessary by now."

She shook her head. "I just...don't understand. And I'd really prefer to, before I make a decision as big as that."

"I can only think of one reason," I said slowly.

"What?" Sarah asked curiously.

I sat up slowly. It seemed the kind of thing I shouldn't say lying down for some reason. Fortunately, Sarah seemed to be over the shock of my bare chest, but she *did* seem to fix her gaze on mine.

But this was actually part of what I was trying to show her.

I gestured to myself. "Kings are...visually impressive. Larger. Stronger. More intimidating. But everyone with sense knows that *Queens* are the most powerful."

"Why's that?" Sarah said in surprise.

Had no one mentioned this to her yet? She was a Queen, after all.

That someone should probably have been me. I was sheepish at my neglect at not doing so before now. It had been a while since I'd had to feel guilty about botching some explanation to her, but the feeling came back like an old, familiar friend—the kind you would rather stay far away.

I shrugged. "We don't know exactly. The Tree hasn't told us why She seems to give Queens a greater portion of Her power. So, people have come up with lots of reasons. Some say that it's *because* they are smaller—the same power, in a more compact package. Other people say it's because Queens are female, like the Tree Herself. Once, when I was a lot younger, I asked the High Priestess if that was true."

Sarah smiled, as if she were trying to imagine that conversation. "What did she say?"

"Well, first she laughed at me," I said wryly. It seemed to be a common theme with the women in my life.

Sarah looked chagrined. "Sorry. Again."

I huffed a laugh of my own as I ran a hand through my hair. "I'll take laughter over anger from you, especially when it comes to this. Anyway, after that, she said that she didn't know either. But if I wanted her *opinion*, then she said that I was right, but only partially. She said that the Tree's most defining characteristic isn't that She's female."

I paused, letting Sarah think that through for a moment. Her brow scrunched. "Well, no.... She's immortal, powerful, omniscient...."

I smiled. "I said some of the same things. But she just shook her head at me and said that wasn't it, either."

"Most defining...."

Her eyes widened, and she propped herself up onto her elbow. Her white hair spilled over her in a tantalizing wave, but I kept my hands on my knees.

"She's not just female," Sarah said quietly. "She's a Mother."

"Yes," I said simply. I *thought* she might get it on her own, even though I hadn't. But then, she had a bit of an advantage over me there.

"That's why she thought Queens are more powerful," Sarah murmured, her silver eyes distant. "Because they have the same potential. They can be mothers."

"Yes," I said again. I shrugged helplessly. "I don't know, Sarah. I really don't. But that's the only thing I can think of that makes even a tiny bit of sense."

She mused, "That maybe, just maybe, I'm not as powerful as I can be. As I *need* to be. Not until I become a mother."

"Maybe," I echoed, feeling a clench in my gut—the same dark, helpless dread I always felt when I contemplated the Tree's warning that there was nothing I could do to protect her. Except....

She sunk back down onto her back with a loud exhale and stared at the ceiling. "I don't know, Ben. This is all just so...."

"I know," I said, swallowing.

"It's a big decision, you know?" she said soberly, still looking up. "And I don't want it to be just because I don't want to die. How do you think that would make the child feel, learning that? That I only had them so that they could save my life."

"I know," I repeated.

"And then there's the fact that I know I'm going into danger, and I'd be knowingly putting that child *in* danger."

"I know."

She glanced to the side and smiled at me weakly. "You've thought all the same things, and then some. Haven't you?"

"Yes," I said heavily.

She reached out, and I took her hand again, clenching it in mine.

"How have you borne it, all on your own?"

I smiled thinly. "Not well. I didn't expect it to take this long. Much longer and I might have gone mad."

"Would you still not have told me?" she asked, eyes piercing into me. "Even after the heartbinding and we...."

I hesitated. "I...don't know."

Then I took a deep breath and forced myself to be honest. "I thought...about...not. Not telling you. I thought maybe I should just take all the guilt on myself, spare you from it."

Sarah's lips pulled into a ghost of a smile. "*That* would have been your mistake. Then, I would have been mad at you."

"But by then, you would have been alive," I whispered, clenching her hand tightly. "In that scenario."

And I would infinitely prefer her mad at me and alive than...not.

"True," she said, looking up at the ceiling.

Silence fell for a few moments as she became lost in sober thoughts.

I let go of her hand and put my face in both of mine. "Agh, Sarah. You have no idea how much this has been killing me. For the Tree to ask us—*me*—for something like this...after everything...."

I heard a rustle, and I lowered my hands to see her sit up, mirroring my cross-legged position on the couch. She was looking at me with an expression so compassionate it hurt me.

"I'm sorry. I didn't even think. I was so wrapped up thinking about myself that I didn't.... This...probably hits a nerve. Doesn't it?"

I swallowed, realizing she'd seen it.

"Yes," I rasped, curling my hands into fists. "It's the same thing again. *Again*. And I swore to myself never again. That's what renewing the Covenants was supposed to be about. That *my child* would not have to go through the same thing I did."

That my wife....

And yet...despite everything...I'd fallen into the same pattern. I'd let myself love, and so deeply that would I pay any price to keep her. Even if that meant perpetuating the cycle.

Did that finally make me a monster?

Sarah's voice and eyes were gentle. "Except the child isn't supposed to claim my life, Ben. They're supposed to save it."

I wanted to say that didn't matter. But I knew that wasn't true. Of course it *mattered*. That crucial difference was the only reason I was contemplating going through with it. That didn't make me feel any less....

"You're not a monster, Ben."

I started guiltily and looked up at her. Was mind reading one of her new powers? No, that couldn't be right, or she'd have figured out all this a long time ago.

"I know that face," she said with a crooked smile. "That's your I'm-a-terrible-person-who-doesn't-deserve-to-breathe-air-let-alone-be-happy face. You've been much better about that lately. Don't start spiraling on me again now."

"Sorry," I said, feeling surprisingly sheepish. And...relieved. Calling me out on my nonsense oddly...helped.

"Just to reiterate," Sarah said, holding up a finger. "You are not a monster for the decision your parents made to have you. And you are not a monster for contemplating having a child now. Got that?"

"Yes." Harder to feel than to say, but not...that much harder.

Maybe I really was getting better.

"I emphasize *contemplating* because, well...." Sarah sighed. "Dire warnings aside, I don't think either of us is quite ready to commit yet."

"True," I said heavily.

"And we should *be* committed," Sarah said, eyes distant again. "That's the only thing that will make it right. No wishy-washiness. No accidents. No secrets."

I spread my hands and shook my head. "That's it. I'm clean out of secrets. I swear."

"Good," she said with a tired smile as she sank back down. "Because I think that's all the energy I have for them. At least for today."

"You think you're going to be able to sleep after that?"

"Yes," she said, and as if as proof, she yawned. "Emotions are exhausting, don't you think? So is contemplating life-altering decisions. I think we've had enough of both for one afternoon."

I sighed. "I agree. And yet..."

She turned her head to look at me, face tightening. "I need time, Ben. I know we don't have much of it. But you've had longer to think about this than I have, and you've...grown up thinking a bit differently than I have about marriage and children. In my culture, both decisions are expected to take months or years...at least, if you're being responsible."

I rubbed the space between my eyebrows, where I could feel a headache building. "I...understand. I do. And it's not like I ever thought...."

I looked away, then said quietly, "By the time most of my peers began thinking of the kind of life they would like to have one day, I had already decided that...I would never have a child."

Sarah smiled faintly. "Sometimes I forget I turned your world upside down nearly as much as you did mine."

I laughed tiredly. "That's one way of putting it."

I fiddled with the edge of my blanket. "I know I should have told you all of this earlier...."

"Maybe, maybe not. I don't know if earlier would have done more harm than good, Ben. In a way, I've had a chance to think about it in more natural ways first." She sighed and looked at the ceiling again. "Now, I simply have a deadline."

"Regardless, though I'm not trying to rush you...." I took a deep breath. "Bear in mind that the decision has to come much sooner than the end of the month. We can't know how long it would take...after you're decided. Remember, my people aren't particularly...."

She smiled thinly. "I believe the word you're looking for is 'fertile,' Ben."

Torch it, when was my face going to get a proper chance to cool? "Well, you know how long it took my parents to have *me*."

"Sixty years, wasn't it?"

I shook my head grimly. "That was after Avva became King—which was over forty years after their marriage."

Sarah blinked slowly. "A century...."

"If...the Tree asked us to do this within a month, then it's possible." I shrugged wearily. "She told me to trust Her, and I do. But from the start, I knew it would be a miracle. That's the only reason I had the courage to wait. Though I was truly hoping it wouldn't take this torched long before our heartbinding."

"Does that mean you can wait one more day?" she asked. "I am getting the sense that I need to talk to my Tree, and I'd like to do that in person. Which means after...tonight."

And whatever came of it.

"Of course," I said, smiling thinly. "You have all the facts and my thoughts now, I think. You take however long you need. And..."

My smile faded, and my flameheart pulsed. "And...I will accept whatever you decide."

That was the true price of placing her happiness above everything. The price I'd always known, from the first moment I chose to let her back into my life, that I might have to pay. And yet I'd still made that choice.

Because it was the only one with a *chance* for *my* happiness. It flickered now in the distance, like a far-off candle on a dark, moonless, misty night. Yet it was enough to keep me going—for now.

Sarah reached out and grasped my hand again. "I don't want to die, Ben," she whispered.

I just squeezed her hand, my throat too tight to speak, and my thoughts too heavy even to convey silently.

I sensed the caveat there, before she said it.

"But...I want to do this for the right reasons."

"I know," I rasped.

I didn't ask her if she was willing to choose death instead. I knew my *sera* too well for that.

The candle flame flickered, but I kept pressing through the dark.

CHAPTER FORTY-SEVEN

SIEGE

SARAH

"READY FOR THIS, SIS?" Michael asked me, grinning.

I glanced at him sidelong as I fiddled with one strap of my arm shield.

Both of us were dressed in our Moontouched armor: white skintight jumpsuits underneath clear plates of a resin-like material that was lighter, harder, and cooler than it had any right to be, with silver tabards emblazoned with white trees and gun holsters over that. We still didn't know what the plates were made of, but we'd found out at the Battle of the Solstice at least one thing they were good for: amplifying our light.

A benefit which hopefully wouldn't be necessary in Michael's case. As it was, he was wearing a cloak right now to hide his set, which would be a dead giveaway.

It was strange that his illusionary brown hair and eyes looked wrong to me now.

"You look way too cheerful to be gearing up for a battle," I said dryly.

Michael shrugged. "Chalk it up to naivety. It's my first one."

I carefully didn't mention that his cheer might also have something to do with the fact that he would hopefully not be seeing any direct action. Saying so would only remind him that I *would*.

He looked over the crowd gathering in the court. "To be honest, this feels like a tournament to me right now."

Michael's extracurriculars had always been a martial art of some kind. Wrestling, karate, ROTC, you name it—if it meant he could hit or shoot something, he was all over it. Mom and Dad had no idea how he came from their pacifist genes, but since he never seemed to want to use his powers for evil, and he was willing to pay for his classes and gear with his own income, they let him be, so long as he didn't bring a gun home. We'd always assumed he'd enlist the day he could, but to our surprise, he opted for law enforcement. I'd been too relieved at the time to ask him why.

Now I wondered.

"Michael, why didn't you go into the military?"

He glanced at me in surprise, then frowned. As he thought, his hand rested on his gun in its holster, and his fingers drummed against it.

"You wanted to be an Army ranger, didn't you?" I pressed.

For as long as I could remember growing up with him, Army posters and paraphernalia had always covered whatever space he'd called his own. For a straight semester his senior year, he wore almost nothing except black and gold. And then he'd just...stopped. In a single day, all those posters and knickknacks were gone, thrown into a box and shoved into a corner of the closet he and David shared until Mom finally dropped it into Michael's arms when he got his own place.

"Yes," he said flatly.

"So...."

"So, I don't know," he said finally. His mouth twisted, as if the words tasted sour. "It didn't feel right. Every time I thought of signing up...I just couldn't do it."

Someone as cerebral as Dad would have needed a reason; he would have needed to be shown why, in detail. That was why the Tree had gone to such lengths to convince Dad of the reality of the danger to his family and Earth before I even found my way back to them.

Michael, however, always followed his instincts. That trait could be a weakness sometimes, but in this case, it had meant that he had been able to throw away his lifelong dream because of nothing more than a gut feeling. And, since his gut had been right, I thought I knew where that feeling had come from.

He scowled and looked to the side. "I felt like a coward."

I raised an eyebrow. "Michael, you are many things, but you are *not* a coward."

He folded his arms. "Then why, Sarah?"

I thought I knew now, but I was pretty sure he wasn't going to like the answer, so I made my voice gentle. "Has it occurred to you that if you had, you likely wouldn't have been able to come with us when we left for Greenland? That you wouldn't have even been anywhere close to home while I was gone or when I got back?"

He blinked. Then his face twisted again, but before he could say how he felt about that theory, Dad, Mathya, and Ben joined us. Even Dad was in armor, again beneath a cloak. I had only seen him in his set once before, when Michael had made him try it on to make sure it fit. I had been truly disturbed to see my *father*—my scholarly, down-to-earth, formerly pacifist dad—look so warlike. Combined with his otherworldly white hair and silver eyes, he had almost frightened me. I was relieved for the cloak right now; to see what lay beneath would hammer in the reality of tonight in a way nothing else could.

The worlds were truly in danger if Dad had become a warrior.

"Are you ready, Rightwing Michael?" Mathya asked.

Michael straightened. Somehow, over the course of their half-day working together, Mathya had earned Michael's unquestioning respect. Even though he technically outranked her, he nodded to her with the deference he normally gave his chief.

"Ready."

"Excellent. Then please follow this aide, who will take you to your post." She gestured to a blue-uniformed amón man standing next to her. "Flame and Ice watch over you."

"And you," Michael said. He gave me a parting smile and followed the man, but he couldn't help one last silent quip to me.

You know I'll be watching. So that big guy better take care of you, or he's answering to me.

I didn't bother gracing that with a response.

"Leftwing Jacob," Mathya said, turning to Dad and gesturing to another aide. "Worran will lead you to your own post when you are ready. Flame and Ice watch over you."

"Thank you, Rightwing Mathya," Dad said formally.

While Mathya walked away, he came to stand in front of me and look me in the eye.

I was grateful he didn't ask me the same question Michael had: if I was ready. The answer to my physical preparedness was self-evident, and Dad could read my mental readiness for himself in my eyes.

He nodded slowly. "Be careful," he said quietly.

I swallowed. "You too."

He smiled thinly. "I will hardly be in as much danger as you will be."

"Unless something happens to me," I said as evenly as I could.

That was the real reason Dad and Michael were in armor: in case they needed to be called out there to provide the energy only a full Moontouched could.

"Which won't happen," Ben said flatly.

"Right," I agreed, for Ben's benefit.

I believed that, intellectually and in the deepness inside me that was my connection to my Tree, but it was the organs all in between that wouldn't be quieted so easily. Plus, once again, my period was horribly timed. At least Ben's healing energy was unconsciously staving off my normal cramps and lethargy. Sadly, it didn't seem to be helping my emotions as much.

It was the mortal part of me that Dad saw in my eyes, mixed in with that faith.

Dad nodded again, as if in agreement with our words, but I knew it was because of what he saw. I didn't know if my fear comforted him. It was healthy, in a way. It meant I wasn't a fool. It meant I *would* be careful.

He leaned in and kissed my forehead briefly. "I love you, Sarah," he said, his words hardly above a whisper. In the court's hubbub, they wouldn't have been audible to anyone but Ben. He could have spoken them silently if he'd wanted absolute privacy, but he didn't.

I swallowed again, eyes stinging. "I love you too, Dad."

He took a step back. He hesitated one moment, then said, "Ice go with you."

A tear spilled over and onto my cheek. "And you."

Dad looked at Ben. I thought he was going to say something like Michael had, except a bit more polite, but he just said, "Flame go with you, King Koriben."

"And Ice with you," Ben said, carefully hiding surprise.

Dad nodded, then looked to his assigned aide, and the two of them began walking, in the opposite direction that Michael had gone.

As I watched him go, Ben put his hand on my shoulder.

"It's almost sunset, isn't it?" I asked. Needlessly. Even though I wasn't wearing my watch, I knew by now what this point in my waxing power meant. This was the tipping of the scales. When Ben's sovereignty ended.

And mine began.

"Yes," Ben answered.

Just like we had that morning, we had all gathered in the court just off the main landing.

The second wave of consumed were already within sight, but they were traveling slowly, no doubt timing their arrival for dark. Their numbers were hard to determine given the distance and varying sizes, but Mathya's analysts estimated there were twice as many of them now as there were before—perhaps in the thousands.

Our numbers had swelled as well, members of the Waterguard and Warflight pouring in from across Rosin and the Six Realms. Some of them were already out there, shoring up the nets as best they could and ready for the first round of the night. The first wave had been defeated hours before, letting the Starkissed turn their full attention and bolstered ranks to mending the nets with record speed. Both breaches had been closed. Not to full strength—that wasn't possible in the time we had—but we hoped it would be enough.

Without saying so, we all knew that tonight would determine Rosin's fate, one way or another. We had seen a similar scenario play out at the Battle of the Solstice. The ferocity of the Waterguard in defending their home wasn't the question; it was whether they could outlast the consumed hoards the Devourer had gathered against them.

Except this time, there were two crucial differences: First, the Devourer could not open any darkrifts within miles of the Rosin Tree, not so soon after Kavarian's sacrifice had strengthened Her borders across all Six Realms. Second, the defenders had not just one but three Moontouched to help them survive the night.

Although we were hoping the Devourer had not figured that last one out.

It knew about me, and it would plan for my appearance. Yet even Ben knew there was no way to keep me safely inside. The defenders needed my power too badly. They needed their drakáforms to defend the nets, or their nets would once again fall, and this time, even the third—exposing Rosin to direct assault.

That's why the Warflight was here: to protect me, so I could give power to the Waterguard, so they could protect us all—and hopefully Dad and Michael could give us the edge we needed to win.

Ben looked at me. His gaze wasn't as piercing as Dad's, but it didn't have to be. He knew me in ways now that no one else in my family did...or could.

His hand on my shoulder slid up to my throat, and he bent down and kissed me, his mouth slow yet demanding. In words he couldn't speak, that kiss ordered me to be safe, to be careful, to be well. It told me he loved me.

"I will," I whispered when we parted. "And I love you too."

"And this time, for Flame's sake—*stay with me*," he growled.

I just smiled thinly. He knew as well as I did that I had to follow my instincts, just like last time. He huffed as he straightened, but that amounted to surrendering.

"It's time," he said, now fully the King.

WE CIRCLED ROSIN AS the dying sun gradually bled into the ocean.

Like parasites sensing the coming weakness in the world, the waters beyond the first net churned, thousands of shapes faintly disturbing its surface with fins, tails, and the occasional head. Every prehistoric oceanic nightmare I had ever learned of or imagined awaited in those waters, anticipating when their frenzy would begin. The blue-scaled Waterguard swam on the other side of the net, staring death in its very jaws and, with typical Starkissed cheek, taunted it to come any closer. They had already scattered the shallow depths all around the archipelago with enormous, brightly lit crystals that illuminated the waters, leaving the monsters with no shadows to hide in.

This second consumed wave had come with flyers, and those flew in a much more distant circle beyond the last of the swimmers, just far enough that it wasn't wise to commit our air forces to an attack at this time. Part of the Warflight flew in circles above the swimmers, ready to defend when the moment came; the other part surrounded Ben and me in a meticulously coordinated cloud of wings, tails, and scales.

All of this made Rosin the epicenter of a circling, living storm. All the many rings were locked in a tenuous stalemate as the world held its breath, waiting for when the board would reset, and we would find out if the White Queen would be enough to save the children of the day from those of the night.

I had never deliberately tried to sustain this many drakón, let alone with just lightform. This was over triple the numbers I'd supported on the Yonvey hunt, and some of them would be perhaps a couple miles out to sea and underwater. All the defenders had been warned that their power could fade with the sun, just as it did on any other night; that was why they held back—to see if my radiance would be enough. And if not, to retract our sphere of defense until it was. Even if that meant abandoning the nets to the onslaught.

The consumed also waited, presumably for the same reason as the Devourer delayed to see what the rules would be before it finally committed its pawns to the game.

Although its swimmers gathered in greater numbers near where the first breach had been, making the Devourer's first move clear: it would attempt to batter its way through the weakened points to regain the ground it had won over the past two nights as quickly as possible, so that it could spend the maximum time tearing through the final net and breaking down Rosin itself.

As we had prepared for that worst outcome, children, the elderly, and anyone who wished to flee through the sungate had been given the chance to do so over the course of the afternoon, carefully dispersed across Oshal and the Six Realms to not overwhelm their hosts or create a tempting target for the Devourer elsewhere. Just in case, every hold across those Realms was now on high alert, prepared as they could be for a siege of their own.

Again, I marveled at dramá unity; they could bicker over small things all day long, but when push came to shove, they closed ranks across the Six Realms and shoved back.

Maybe it had to do with centuries of banding together in tightknit communities for survival, tempering their passionate, independent draká natures into a remarkable weaving of individualistic and collectivistic mindsets. Maybe it was their combination of dispersed and centralized governance, the former giving them enough autonomy for self-governance, the latter giving them order and unity to tackle the challenges they could face only together.

I suspected, though, that none of those things would be possible without the foundation laid by their Tree. None of those ideas were new; the best-intentioned humans had been trying to make them work on Earth for thousands of years. Yet ultimately, the flaws of mortality inevitably led to corruption of those ideals and the collapse of the system itself. Without a constant purifying and stabilizing influence, no society could last.

By all rights, the dramá civilization should have fallen apart centuries ago. There was no way that a government even partially formed by extraordinarily long-lived Monarchs and Nobles should have been able to function so well and so fairly. Even if those Tree-appointed leaders were limited by a system of more democratic checks and balances that I was only just beginning to learn about, the leaders wielded tremendous *literal* power and thus should have torn themselves apart from ambition or collapsed from beneath from revolution after only a few generations.

Yet those leaders were carefully chosen and given their authority by a Tree, an immortal of unimaginable power and wisdom who loved them as Her own children. Which meant She wasn't above reprimanding those leaders and stripping them of that authority if they continued to lead themselves down the path of destruction. Yet, though Her influence began at the top, none of it would work if everyone, at every level, didn't in some way connect with the Tree and respect Her will. Otherwise, the people could lead themselves to destruction as surely as their leaders could.

As I sat on Ben's back, circling it all from high in the air, the epiphany hit me like a battering ram.

It was the Tree. She was a part of it, at every level, and in every person, otherwise it would never have worked. She didn't make them all the same. None of the leaders I had met were the same; in fact, each was vastly different, leading vastly different societies. And yet She connected them all, every branch and root, into one great forest with one overriding purpose: survival. She not only encouraged diversity, She turned it into strength, every difference being necessary for the continuation of life itself. Like an expert gardener, She nudged and nurtured, encouraged and chastised, all to ensure the survival of the *worlds*, making them work as one giant, symbiotic, living thing.

I had always been told that the only way to protect a world from the Devourer was for that world to have a Tree.

But that isn't enough, I realized, staring down at Rosin, where, somewhere inside that island mountain, Oshal's Tree rested. *It isn't enough for Her to be inside a world. She has to be inside each one of us. In our very hearts, purifying us with its every beat. Because if She didn't....*

Before the final, terrible truth could hit me, the last golden rays of the sun bled out and disappeared into the horizon, plunging the world into deadly twilight.

Now, Ben said to me urgently.

I threw all other thoughts aside and focused on our immediate survival...

...which all hinged on how brightly I could shine.

I threw open all the doors of my power. I wasn't at full strength yet, and I had to sustain my light over perhaps hours, so I had to moderate the flow. Yet I also exposed it all, as if I had been a candle concealed within a closed lantern, and now not only were all the shutters open, the lantern itself had exploded outward, and the candle had turned into a torch.

I glowed so brightly, I couldn't look at myself. I radiated power so thickly it streamed off me in wisps out into the air in every direction for at least five feet around me. Draká swerved away from me momentarily, as if something inside me truly had exploded, sending energetic shrapnel everywhere.

The golden dragon beneath me raised his head and roared, bellowing a challenge to the darkening air.

The next battle for our survival had begun.

EVERYTHING BEGAN HAPPENING ALL at once.

Later, I was told that the consumed charged the first net, particularly at the location of the last breach, and the Starkissed Waterguard rushed through to its defense, skillfully darting in and out of the weave to avoid becoming overwhelmed by the masses teeming up against it at every depth. Other members of the guard simply circled, continually sending power into the net to shore up any weakness. The Warflight circling above torched whatever monster was foolish enough to come close enough to the surface; the flames that skimmed the water sent up clouds of steam like bursts of geysers, and soon the air was saturated with moisture. Then the flyers rushed in.

At the time, all I knew was that Ben almost immediately began swerving and spinning, turning my world into a dizzying kaleidoscope of darkening blue sky, glowing blue ocean, shadowy rocky mountain, golden scales, and searing fire. And that was only when I could glimpse anything through my off-gassing vapors of light. The sights were too distracting and nauseating for me to focus on. Mostly, I just leaned into Ben, clung as tightly as I could to his saddle, gritted my teeth, and closed my eyes.

And focused on my radiance.

I was pushing myself dangerously far, approaching the threshold of my starform as closely as I dared. It was a very delicate balancing act, a constant struggle to exert just the right amount of power. If I slipped into starform, I would burn out within minutes, and that would be deadly for everyone. Yet if I didn't push myself, if I stayed in the lowest, most effortless levels of my lightform, I knew it wouldn't be enough to give light to everyone who needed it.

Is this working? I asked Ben. Even speaking mentally, it felt like I was doing it through teeth gritted in concentration.

Yes, Ben answered curtly.

Really? I said, a bit stunned. My control slipped and drifted even brighter until I reined myself back in. *At the furthest reaches?*

Yes, Ben repeated. His tone left no room for wonder, questioning, or pride in that unexpected achievement. With a mind honed by years of battle, he was only laser focused on what was immediately necessary. *Can you sustain this? Or should I call them in closer?*

We'd been over this. I did them no favors by pushing myself too hard in the beginning and then abruptly retracting, leaving the outer defenders stranded and our generals scrambling. We had to find the distance I could *sustain*—and make our stand there.

I thought hard for one moment. I was hardly aware of anything anymore except that focus. I was only vaguely aware anymore of moving with Ben, of the feel of the saddle grips in my fingers, of the air rushing around me, of the bursts of heat from draká flame, of the g-forces that should have been tossing me to and fro, if I had been any more corporal. All those sensations felt distant, removed—evidence of how dangerously close to starform I was, when I would lose them entirely.

Yet I still *could* feel. I was still walking the line in front of that threshold. I felt like I had a grip on the power now. It was like the wheel of a car constantly buffeted by high winds, but I could hold it. If I focused, I could stay in the lines. I had enough focus and gas in the tank for at least a few hours, and my power would only increase with time.

I could ride out the storm.

Yes, I told Ben.

Are you sure?

I didn't mind that he was double checking. Not only were hundreds of lives at stake right now, but the tiniest sliver of his normal self also came out in his voice, worrying that I was pushing myself too hard.

I made my inner voice certain. *Yes.*

Alright. I'll let Mathya know. Tell me the moment you feel yourself weaken.

I will.

He left it at that, having no other time to spare for even me. He had to trust me with all our lives. Just as I was now trusting him with mine.

Chapter Forty-Eight

WEAPONS

Koriben

SARAH WAS A MIRACLE. Even Mathya was surprised when I let her know that all our forces could remain where they were. We'd placed them at the outermost edges, fully expecting to draw them in bit by bit until we found our ground. Instead, there they stayed.

Aside from the third of the Warflight that swarmed around Sarah and me. Those drakón fiercely drove off the darkness that would dare swallow our star. Here finally was the reason the Devourer had heretofore not sent flyers against us: it had saved them for the true assault, when it knew it would have its best chance to get to Sarah.

The consumed intent was clear, from the fixation in their glittering eyes to their suicidal charges to dive into our midst. I was also there, of course, but I was a much tougher target, either to grab or to bleed. Besides, taking me out would be a blow, but Sarah was the lynchpin around which our entire nighttime defense depended.

Or so we'd led them to believe.

And would for a while longer. Now wasn't the time to play our hand. Sarah had enough energy to support us on her own, and we had things under control for the moment. Besides, the Warflight was too closely engaged with the enemy for our new weapons to be effective. For now, we would continue to fight the old-fashioned way, with tooth, claw, and flame, tearing our foes to shreds or burning them to ash and letting the pieces fall to the ruined paradise of Rosin.

If we held, then paradise would recover. If the Devourer got its minions to the Oshal Tree, it never would. So I spared no thought for the destruction I was causing, either by covering the mountain in blood and ash or by occasionally knocking over a structure or setting off a rockslide in my pursuit of my prey and my twists to elude any who approached Sarah.

I kept a portion of my attention always fixed on her, making sure her star had not moved from its position on my back. I would let no one take her from me again.

Plus, I needed to be aware of her presence for purely practical reasons, such as twisting her away from draká fire or the stray wing or tail or making sure she didn't inhale too much smoke. I couldn't give my all to the fight as I normally would, not with such a vulnerable element between my shoulder blades. Yvera and Kor, flying at my flanks, knew this and compensated with their own ferocity. Even Kor exhibited a savagery that I would have found amusing in another circumstance, considering his protests about the barbarism of our hunt the day before.

Ben, Yvera snarled, *veer left.*

I did without question, even though that led me into the mountainside. I felt the heat of distant draká flame roll across my back as I thrust my legs out and hit the rocky slopes on all fours, then pushed back off with a force that made the rock crumble beneath me, causing another slide. At least that positioned me to grab an arrel in my jaws and bite down, feeling the stone body crack satisfyingly before I tossed it away, sending the pieces flying.

I had to admit, I had a particular grudge against arrel now.

Sometime later, Mathya informed me, *They've broken through the first net.*

Her voice was calm. We'd planned for this, after all. But....

So soon? I asked in concern. It could only be a deken after sunset, at most.

I spat a ball of flame at a trio of vulture-like volpan ahead of me to buy myself some time and swiveled my head in that direction. I could see the roiling water at the breach.

This will work in our favor, I think, Mathya said distractedly. No doubt she had many other things to focus on than updating me, so I was surprised she'd done so herself in the first place. Of course, maybe she'd anticipated my questions and wanted to address them personally. *It's committed more of its forces to the breach than we expected. Hoping for a swift victory, perhaps.*

Leading them into our trap?

Let's pray it holds, she said with grim humor.

Oh, I prayed. This could be just what we needed to turn the tide in our favor. Was it too much to hope that the Devourer could at last have turned reckless in its greed? It would have been smarter for it to wear us down gradually, assuming it had the forces to do so. That was the sure and steady way to victory against us, the way that it came so close to winning at the Solstice. But then, perhaps this attack had originated from just that sort of recklessness from the start.

Or perhaps it no longer had the forces to outlast us.

Flame, I prayed that was true.

Though I felt a flicker of a premonition, a subconscious knowledge that began forming in the back of my mind. Something that told me a desperate Devourer was not a good thing.

I didn't have time to decipher it, because some harpies were swerving for Sarah, and I had to swerve in turn to avoid them and give Kor an opening to torch them. Though whenever I had a chance, I kept an eye on the sea.

Out there, the consumed poured through the opening in the first net and spilled recklessly onto the next like sand slipping through parted fingers, forming a new mound of bodies against the next barrier. And moving among them, a darkness slithered.

As soon as I saw it, a chill went through my blood. *Mathya, it's out there! A shadow of it is out there!*

I hear, Mathya said sharply.

But I passed on the message too late. A waterguard began convulsing in the water, the shadow slipping away from them like an assassin in the dark, and in the chaos of their comrades rushing to the aid of the fallen, the shadow rushed the second net.

And was repulsed, the net lighting up like icy fire. The darkness recoiled, its inky tendrils lashing back in surprise.

This was no weakened section of the net; in fact, it was untouched, and heavily reinforced. Last night, the Devourer had sliced through the second net straight ahead of the tear through the first, making its intent clear: it was going to try to cut through all three in a straight line the very next night. Well, we knew we couldn't entirely repair either net to its former levels in one day, so we had deliberately left the first repair weak to encourage the Devourer to go through with its plan, and we had *turned* the second net. Very, very carefully, the Waterguard disguising their shifting of the anchors as their normal patrol movements, but now the weakened portion was a quarter way around the ring.

The Devourer's plan to batter its way immediately through both nets had failed. Now a large portion of its forces had died throwing themselves against an intact, reinforced barrier, and it didn't know where the weak portion was. For all it perhaps knew, we may have miraculously repaired it completely.

Yet that failure made it dangerous.

The inky blackness spread itself in menacing rage, then launched itself at the nearest drakón, sending the guard into convulsions with gut-wrenching speed, then launched itself at the next, then the next. The Warflight, circling above, could do nothing as their jets of flame didn't penetrate deeply enough.

Get everyone out! I shouted at Mathya. Probably needlessly. She surely knew the situation better than I did from what glimpses I could glean through my own struggles.

Yet those were my people down there, dying—while there was nothing I could do to help them, and nothing they could do to defend themselves. They couldn't so much as touch the shadow, I could see that; one drakón foolishly tried cutting through it with their claws and only fell to convulsions themselves. With a drakón's greatest weapon, fire, rendered useless, the Devourer thought it could strike with impunity.

Thank Flame it was wrong.

As soon as the Waterguard scattered, clearing the area around the shadow, a bolt of pure light burst from the northern point of Rosin—so bright it seared my vision with its path—shot through the air, and cannoned into the sea, sending up sprays of water astonishingly full of shards of ice. Through the spray and churned up water, I didn't catch whether the meteor of light had struck the shadow, but a second later, I felt—yes, *felt*—a mental screech that had me roaring in echoes of agony.

Ben, Sarah gasped, her power flaring momentarily. *What was that?*

The Devourer, I said, gritting my teeth. *Brace yourself, you may feel it again. Whatever you do, don't stop—*

Just then, another ball of light seared across the sky, this one coming from the opposite direction, from the south, and struck the water. By now, almost the entire Waterguard had retreated behind the second net, leaving the consumed free to spill around the ring between the first two barriers, where they continued to probe, trying to find the weakness. Except their search in one direction was suddenly brought to a halt by the burst of light and ice, and the waters around the impact zone filled with blood.

Another burst coming in from the north, crashing into the consumed that were flowing the opposite direction around the ring. Another from the south, this one striking for the shadow, which again let out a mind-shattering scream. Fortunately, I was better prepared this time, and even better, I seemed to be the only one so affected. No one else joined in my roar, and Yvera's voice in my mind was urgent but free of pain.

Ben, what's wrong?

The Devourer, I said, flames instinctively rising in my throat and licking at my teeth. *I think it's trying to make Sarah and me feel its pain.*

And it was doing a torched good job of it. Though I didn't mention that.

Mental silence followed for a moment, even as the bursts continued pounding into the consumed line with lightning-fast strikes and tremendous sprays, and the Warflight continued to swarm around us, compensating for my lack of focus.

Then Yvera said in a dumbfounded voice, *We're* hurting *the* Devourer?

It would seem so, Kor said grimly, having been included in our communication. *Or the shadow of it that it sent, at least.*

The number of air attackers had thinned at last, giving us moments to ponder and eye the modified lightbursts laying waste to the consumed ranks. I scanned the water urgently, trying to find the shadow, but I couldn't see it.

Well, Kor said mildly. *I would call our experiment a success, wouldn't you?*

What did you call those things? Yvera said, trying to sound casual and failing.

Sarah named them, since it was her idea. She called them "lightcannons."

A combination of our word for *light*, coming from *lightburster*, and an English word, "cannon," being an Earthren weapon. An old one, Sarah had said, not even in use anymore as far as she was aware, though she said the same fundamental principle had led to a far more lethal set of modern weaponry. Well, if this was based on an *old* weapon...a chill went through my blood as I thought of what the new ones could do.

Sarah had once said that her kind could level cities. I'd believed her then, but now...I had something more than belief. I was staring the evidence in the face. *Now* I understood her fear that my wings and I would be discovered and hunted while we traveled through her world, and her absolute certainty that if that were to happen, there would be nothing we could do to escape.

It was a very good thing that the two Moontouched wielding those lightcannons were on our side.

Even as my emotions processed that fact, I divided most of my attention between the fight still going on around us and watching the water for the shadow. I still couldn't see it, and that disturbed me deeply. Had it fled? That seemed too much to hope—

Like a black version of our own lightbursts, darkness shot out of the water in a stream and flew swiftly as an arrow but as large and devastating as a battering ram straight at me.

No.

Straight at the shining star at my back.

NO! I roared with my mind and my throat, but it was coming at me from the side, and I didn't have time to twist away, and couldn't blast it effectively with my flame, though I tried.

I didn't even have time to warn Sarah to surge into me before—

Light.

An explosion...of light.

Then pain, screeching in my mind and slicing into my body.

Then nothing.

Chapter Forty-Nine

INSTINCTS

Sarah

NO! BEN ROARED, AND I snapped my eyes open to see why.

Only to be blinded by an explosion of light that threw Ben—*Ben,* my golden behemoth—back. Instead of heat, I felt a wave of cold wash over me. Only pure instinct made me activate my arm shield in time to save myself from being peppered with shards of ice.

And then, before I could even comprehend what had happened, we were falling. Ben's wings were shredded, but even worse, he had gone completely limp, and we were now tumbling through the air.

"BEN!" I screamed with both my voices, grasping forward uselessly to touch him.

No response.

No, not again.

Not *again*!

I surged into his heart just before we hit the water. That second instinctual action again probably saved my life, since I had slipped on my hold of my lightform and become corporal enough to have been devastated by the impact. But I was only thinking of Ben, desperate to do the only thing I could think of to save him.

My consciousness...changed. The only part of *me* that remained was a bodiless, senseless sentience of the vaguest sort. But unlike when I was in starform, I felt enmeshed in something far greater than myself, surrounded by comforting warmth. The faintest of memories of when this had happened last time came to me, and the contrast was terrifying. Last time, I had still been connected to Ben's emotions and most subconscious thoughts.

This time, I felt nothing.

Nothing.

I lingered in the frantic hope that my power would bring him back to consciousness, but nothing happened. I retained enough other memories of the most recent past to know that was a terrible thing.

A deadly thing.

No! I sobbed with all that remained of me, and I surged back out of him.

Sure enough, I emerged underwater, and in front of me, I saw a water-blurred golden dragon settle onto the shallow sea floor, like a downed ship, sails torn to shreds and streaming golden blood.

Memories poured into my restored self with horrifying clarity, especially of the last time something like this had happened.

Unlike the last time, if he didn't wake up soon, he may never.

But what could I do?

I surged to his head, ignoring the water pressure that doubled around me, instinctively flaring my lightform both to reduce my corporality and hopefully lend Ben some strength.

But what I saw there nearly stopped my iceheart.

A giant spear of ice had pierced Ben's half-closed serpentine eye, which now streamed with golden blood.

NO.

No, no, no.

No, it couldn't be.

He wasn't dead! I could feel him, his pull, it was still there!

I heard a thunder as something enormous entered the water behind me, but I didn't care what it was, even when the wave from it rocked me. I just surged back to him, placing my hand on the shard.

Did I dare remove it? Would that only hasten his death?

Why, oh why, had they filled me with such useless knowledge, and yet I *still* didn't know how to save a life?

Dispel it, child, a voice whispered inside me.

I didn't hesitate. Whatever a Tree said, you do.

Or disaster followed.

I grasped what I could of the shard—it was too large for me to wrap my fingers around—and I willed it to nothing but water, which flowed away under my hand. Golden blood now gushed around me in a cloud, hot on my skin.

I didn't know how long I had been underwater. My lungs, even as semi-corporal as they were, screamed for air. But I ignored the sensations. Ben was still dying.

Sarah, move! Yvera snarled. *Go! We have to get him to the surface!*

There was no time and no way to do that safely. I knew that without being told.

Bring him in, the voice whispered. *We will guide him to you, but you must pull.*

So, I grasped for Ben's pull, ignoring my terror at how weak it was, and I pulled back.

I had once longed to be able to wrap myself around Ben, to cradle his heart in mine to shelter it from all further harm...and that was exactly what I did now. Ben's colossal bulk disappeared as his golden essence glided into my heart with the gentleness of a dove.

Ben? Yvera choked.

Then I burst with the light of a sun.

A constellation of stars appeared in my mind. I instinctively chose the nearest viable one and pulled us to it, knowing every drop of Ben's power that I spent was more precious than his blood.

I emerged hundreds of miles away, where the last fading rays of sunlight were dipping below the horizon of Oshal once again.

My legs folded under me, and I collapsed, sopping wet, onto the flat stone in front of the dying sungate. Golden light spilled from me and reformed Ben on the ground, but this time in his amáform. He sprawled on his back, his eye still gushing blood even through the now-closed lid, like macabre golden tears.

So not healed yet, if at all.

How his wounds could transfer, even to a different place and in a different state of being, I didn't stop to wonder. It was all impossible anyway, so why bother? Especially when he was dying.

Dying, but not dead yet, even though he should be. So I wasn't going to question why.

Still following my instincts, I slammed my hands into his too-still chest with a burst of power, and he heaved, water bubbling up through his mouth. I pushed him onto his side with all my might and he instinctively threw up an arm to brace himself, coughing up water and more blood.

I blearily blinked up at the people rushing toward us, my sight strangely hazy and unable to make them out. The light seemed to be fading unusually fast....

"Healer," I croaked. "Ben...."

Then, as Ben unconsciously took from me the power he needed to stay alive, everything plunged into darkness.

I WOKE TO DARKNESS as well. Before I could panic, I felt a familiar warmth and smell enveloping me. I recognized that shoulder my head lay on, and that chest that my arm sprawled so casually across.

Even though this time, that chest was bare.

I stiffened, but Ben didn't react. His breath was deep—unusually deep, actually. Something about that rhythm, without his usual light snoring, struck a familiar chord.

Alarmed, I rose and began hurriedly slapping around to find the lighting gem. That none of my shifting around woke Ben gave me my confirmation even before I finally found the gem and the lights began their brightening sequence.

Sure enough, Ben lay far too still and straight on the bed.

What had Kor called it? "Magically enhanced deep sleep"?

Well, I still called it a coma. And the reason for that coma became clear from the web of bandages plastered over his left eye.

I stilled as I hovered over him, then reached to touch his left cheekbone. My hand shook slightly.

He was alive.... But how much of him was left with me?

CHAPTER FIFTY

PURPOSE

SARAH

"ALRIGHT, SARAH," EDRIK SAID soothingly the next morning. He withdrew his hand from Ben's forehead and looked at me. "He's waking up now. He might even be able to hear you. Try talking to him."

"Thank you," I said fervently.

Of all the healers to have taken over Ben's primary care, I was glad it was Edrik. I'd liked the handsome, kindly Peacegrowth healer from the moment I'd met him, back when I was briefly disguised as one of his assistants. Now he was again the head healer of our entourage, which made it convenient for him to spend time with his new wife, Fenra. I would have never put the two of them together to begin with, but surprisingly, they seemed to fit like two pieces of a puzzle, or yin and yang in perfect balance.

Edrik had one of those confident yet calming presences that made you feel as if everything was going to be OK, and that was exactly what I had needed when he had walked into our room just after dawn—the soonest he could get to Olsdak with the timing of the sungates.

Yes, of all the places in Oshal I could have taken us, I had brought Ben and me to Olsdak, the cultural center of Oshal and host hold of the Moonfair. So, the King's suite I had woken up in had been familiar—if with another occupant who hadn't shared my room and especially not my bed last time.

I sat against the headboard of that bed right next to Ben, my legs tucked underneath me.

Yvera and Ordran were standing on the side of the bed closest to me. Technically, Yvera should have remained at Rosin to help with the cleanup efforts and care for her people there, just as Kor had, but no one was stupid enough to keep her away. Alyish just came from Crownhold to take over, and Yvera was through the sungate the second it opened, before even Edrik.

Fenra had come with her husband, ostensibly to oversee the small staff of volunteers from our entourage who had come to serve us here for however long we needed to stay. She was elsewhere right now, doing her thing.

Dad had come, too—I assumed to be there for me. He sat unobtrusively on one couch in the corner of the room, present if I needed him, but currently giving me—and Ben—space. We had enough people surrounding the bed right now.

Eskala sat next to Dad, and they were conversing in respectfully muted tones about something on his tablet. To my knowledge, this was the first time the two leftwings had ever met, let alone spoken, but they acted with the familiarity and comfortableness of old friends. Given how long it usually took for Dad to open up to someone, that was enough to make my eyebrows raise in surprise every time I glanced at them.

I knew why Eskala had come, even though she never said—it was for Ben. He had us all worried for a bit.

Standing next to Edrik on Ben's side of the bed was another healer that had come at dawn, this time all the way from Crownhold. She was an eye specialist, and though the Olsdak healers had made Ben stable, they had left the final delicate healing of his eye to her, which was why I had woken up to see him with bandages. Not only was Ben their King, they relied on him for their defense; they weren't about to leave his eyesight to chance.

Standing next to *her* was a third healer and second specialist from Crownhold, this one for the brain. His introduction had made me nervous, but he assured me that from everything he had heard, he fully expected his visit to be merely a formality. Yet the possibility of brain damage was yet another reason Ben had been put into a magically induced coma.

Until now.

Now, with Ben's eye healed and mind declared undamaged, he could wake up.

I took a deep breath, said a prayer, and touched the side of his face. "Ben? Ben, can you hear me?"

Silently, I added, *I love you, my sun. More than you will ever know.*

Ben's eyes moved under his lids, and his breath quickened. He shifted, and his eyes cracked open. I leaned over him.

"I'm here, Ben."

Both golden eyes fixed on me, and when they widened, I saw they were perfect—perfectly clear, perfectly cognizant, perfectly Ben.

I let out a breath that I felt like I had been holding ever since I had woken up—no, since he fell.

"Sarah," he gasped, and in the next instant, I was being crushed into him. His arms wrapped around me like they were never going to let me go...and I had no problem with that plan.

"Are you alright?" he demanded. His warm healing energy began pouring into me to check, and I laughed at the irony.

"Ben, I'm *fine*. Not a scratch. You're the one who gave all of us a scare."

"What? Why...." He pushed me away enough to look at my face, and that was when he seemed to notice there were other people in the room. Red began creeping up his neck. "Hang on...."

I shifted up and off him, and he propped himself up on his elbows. "What's all this for?" he said with a nervous grin. "I'm not dying, am I?"

"Definitely not," Edrik said with a reassuring smile.

"But you *were*," Yvera grumbled.

Ben looked at his foster sister and blinked. Yvera wasn't one to exaggerate. "What?"

I thought it appropriate that I answer this one, so I said quietly, "A light-cannon blast took out the Devourer's shadow that went after us. Unfortunately...you were so close to it...that you took a lot of damage."

"Ah," Ben said carefully, sitting up slowly. He glanced at the healers arrayed at his side of the bed and said, "Just how much damage?"

"We're told that your wings were no longer flight capable," Edrik said, glancing first at me, then Yvera. We were the primary witnesses. Then back at me. "And that you took a shard of ice to the eye."

I was the only one to have seen that—and even I shouldn't have seen it clearly, considering I had been deeper underwater than I had ever ventured before. At night. In battle-disturbed waters.

I used all those reasons as excuses, both to myself and to the others, to explain away the impossible: how Ben could have survived that kind of damage. Yet I knew I had seen what I had seen. My brightness had provided illumination, and my eyes had seen more clearly than they'd had any right to. Far more clearly than I liked. Yet, if they hadn't, would Ben be alive right now?

"To my...eye?" Ben said, gaze distant. His hand hesitantly reached up toward his left eye. Perhaps now the faint memory of the moment he'd briefly been conscious while he was coughing up seawater was coming back to him.

"It's fine," I said with a hopefully comforting smile. I took that hand and squeezed it. "You're good as new."

"I can certify that," the eye healer said with a crooked smile. "That's why I'm standing around here still, after all."

Ben looked at her. "And you are...?"

She nodded. "Healer Tirna Brightflare, King Koriben. Eye specialist. The Olsdak healers did an admirable job stabilizing your condition, and I finished the healing of your eye."

Ben looked at me sidelong. "*Olsdak*?"

I gave him a rueful smile and a shrug, and said, "I'll explain later."

AND SO I DID, after the specialists had done their last tests, everyone saw for themselves that Ben was fine, and Edrik kicked them out. Edrik didn't even give them an excuse; he just told them to go and spread the good word, and when he finally got the last one to leave, he closed the door after him with a wink at me.

Perhaps something of Fenra had rubbed off on him. Or maybe his playful bent had just been more deeply concealed.

Ben lay back down, and to my surprise, he pulled me with him. I certainly wasn't going to protest. So, while we cuddled (with covers between us), I told him everything, from start to finish, including the pieces I'd learned later, such as the fact that Michael had been the one to make the shot that had nearly killed him.

I still felt a jumble of emotions about that. I didn't blame Michael—he had been trying to save us both, and far worse would have happened to us if the Devourer's shadow had reached us. If anything, I blamed myself. The light-cannons had been my idea to begin with, an idea which had created something so dangerous, they nearly took Ben from me. On the other hand, they had saved many lives and were a part of saving Oshal itself, and the Seven Realms in turn.

Even now, I trembled a bit from the overwhelming relief that Ben hadn't paid the price for that victory. That he was not just alive but *restored*.

He was quiet for a bit after I was done. His fingers didn't stop rubbing soothing circles into my back, for which I was more grateful than I could say. His constant, reassuring touch was one of the few things that had kept me going through the explanation.

Finally, he met my eyes. "I scared you, didn't I?"

"You don't know how much," I whispered.

That seemed to confirm something to him, and he studied me for a moment. "You just told me what you told everyone else, didn't you? But there's more."

I looked away. "Well...I didn't tell everyone else about the Tree bits...."

I'd let them assume Ben had consciously surged into me.

Ben lifted my chin and waited until I met his eyes again. He searched them, and then he nodded to himself. "I should be dead, shouldn't I?"

I swallowed and didn't answer.

He continued calmly. "Sarah, I've dealt with death and killing enough to know this much. That specialist was wrong, wasn't he? That shard went into my brain. It had to have. It should have killed me, instantly."

"You weren't dead," I rasped, eyes stinging. "You *weren't*. I could feel your pull still."

Ben smiled softly. His hand left my chin to stroke the side of my face, brushing my hair back.

"Only you would have known that, my star," he said. "If anyone else—Yvera, Kor—had seen me like that, they would have thought I was dead. Anyone else would have given up."

"No, they wouldn't," I whispered. "Not on you."

His smile faded. "Maybe not, since I'm the King. And Yvera *was* involved. She would have known I was probably dead, but she's good at ignoring reality when she wants to. But see, Sarah, anything anyone else might have done would only have finished me off. You're the reason I'm alive."

"And the Trees."

Somehow, miraculously, They had kept that shard, which from all that I had seen *must* have pierced into his brain, from killing him, or damaging him beyond repair. How, I did not know. By holding his spirit within his body after it should have departed, long enough for his healing power to begin to work? By healing him Themselves? By melting that shard before it went too deep? We could ask, but we may never get the answer, and I was not about to question Them for it.

He sighed and nodded, echoing my thoughts. "And the Trees. They're probably the reason that shard didn't kill me in the first place. It seems that, for some strange reason, They're willing to keep me alive. Can't imagine why, with how poor a servant I've been lately."

I felt a flare of temper. "Maybe you're not as bad a servant as you think."

Ben looked down, and he withdrew his hand. "I still haven't gone to see Her. You realize that? Not once. Not since She confirmed me as Her King that first day.... Avva would be ashamed of me."

I cupped his cheek. "I don't think that's true."

When Ben opened his mouth to protest, I said, "How often did he visit the Tree after your mother died?"

Ben's mouth slowly closed. He was silent for a long moment. "I...I don't know. I don't remember."

"Grief does things to people, Ben," I murmured. "Even people as good as your father. And I think the Trees understand that. They want us to love, after all. And to love is to someday grieve."

As I'd nearly had to.

I thanked the Trees with all the fervor of my soul that They had spared me that. This time, at least. But that miracle gave me hope for our future. Perhaps we were meant to survive this, after all.

Ben's face softened and his eyes became distant, so I let that sink in for a few moments before speaking again.

"You know what I think?" I said.

Ben still didn't meet my eyes, but his lips twitched. "I don't, but please tell me."

"I think you need to ask Her for yourself."

His eyes darted to mine, then away. I thought he was going to deny it, then his expression firmed. "You're right. It's...time. Past time, but it will only get worse the longer I delay it."

I smiled. "I think you might be surprised."

He sighed and looked at me, smiling softly. "If only I could see myself the way you see me, Sarah."

"Hmm," I said with mock thoughtfulness. "Though I definitely agree you need some more self-compassion, I don't think you should see yourself *exactly* the way I do."

From his grin, he seemed to know where this was going, but he asked anyway. "And why's that?"

I smirked. "Because then you'd be in love with yourself, and that wouldn't do."

Ben laughed. He cupped the back of my neck in his hand and brought me in for a kiss. Even though he was trying to keep things tame, I couldn't seem to help myself and snuggled closer, hands sliding to his bare shoulders. He stiffened, then rolled away from me and onto his back with a groan.

"You know what *I* think?" he said, staring at the ceiling.

"What?" I asked, face heating.

He looked back at me with his own smirk. "I think we *both* need to talk to our Trees. As soon as possible."

I blinked, then remembered my own reason for wanting to talk to mine. And my face heated even more.

I cleared my throat. "Agreed."

WHEN BEN DETERMINED SOMETHING needed to happen, he made it happen.

He didn't allow himself any more time to rest. Right after that, he got up, saying he'd no doubt had enough sleep by now, and that he was certain he was needed back in Rosin. He told me to stay and rest if that was what I wanted, but I wasn't about to be left behind. So back we went, just like that.

I was seeing why people kept putting Ben into a coma.

Rosin had seen better times, but the damage that I saw as Ben and I circled above wasn't bad as I feared, and cleanup efforts were already well underway. There wasn't much they could do about the scorch marks and murky waters, but the corpses had already been cleared from the land and the sea, crews were clearing debris, and some craftspeople were already at work repairing structures.

When Kor greeted us at the King's landing, the leftwing was scowling. "Ben, you're doing a terrible job at looking like you just nearly died."

"I thought that was precisely the point," Ben said briskly as he continued his way inside.

"There's a delicate balance," Kor said as he strode to keep up, and I half jogged, "between a show of strength and a show of sacrifice. And you are utterly failing at it."

"Well, tough, Kor, because I'm torched certain my life wasn't spared for the sake of your narratives. My people here just survived a siege. There's work to be done."

Kor cast a glance back at me in exasperation.

You know you're relieved he's back, I said with a thin smile.

Yes, Kor snapped. *So I can strangle him myself.*

Fortunately, he refrained. As always.

My morning then took a sobering turn. Remembering Kolwin's lessons, I spent the first couple of hours with the wounded and families of the fallen. There weren't many dead, thanks to our strategies and lightcannons, but any was still too many.

I struggled to keep myself afloat amid their pain and my guilt that I did not have to share it, but none of the families expressed any bitterness. One mother, after hugging me in gratitude, asked about my betrothed in concern, and one brother clasped my hand and, even through tears in his eyes, thanked Flame that at least the King still lived. That knowledge seemed to give them hope, as if more people than just me saw it as a sign of better days to come. And even though my words, especially in Drona, could have scarcely been adequate to comfort them, each of them seemed to draw comfort from my attempt.

Meanwhile, Ben got a full briefing on the battle, including the part he was in and especially the part after. From the summary an Olsdak healer gave me when I woke up, it sounded like the sudden loss of my power wasn't catastrophic. The burst Ben and I gave just before I surged us away held the drakón over until Michael was rushed out to replace me.

The defense radius had to decrease because he had less power to give, but with the Devourer's shadow gone, the consumed became disorganized, and the Waterguard were once again able to fight as normal, supported by meticulously timed and coordinated bursts from Dad at the remaining lightcannon. The fight was essentially over within the next half hour.

After his briefing, Ben went out on one of the many patrols that were searching for any more traces of consumed hordes, but they found nothing. That conclusion, and an assurance that the Rosin Tree gave to Lady Winthra, meant the siege was officially over.

Then I helped Lady Winthra greet the returning refugees as they came through the sungate.

The children and adults needed very different forms of comfort. The youngest ones were overexcited from an adventure they had little understood the gravity of, and they wanted to chatter to and especially touch me. I think not even one of them called me by name or title; to them, I was "Moondaughter," and that was it.

The teens tried to appear calm even through an underlying tension, but even they craned their necks to catch glimpses of me as they passed, and the more confident or adventurous still came up to meet me. The adults were mostly noncombatant amón, many of whom I presumed had left to take care of the ones younger and older than them. They were generally too busy doing so to cast more than a wan smile or curious look my way, but I still noticed how their walk tended to be lighter afterward.

Or maybe they were just glad to be home.

Finally, the older the dramá were, the more they approached me with childlike frankness, caring little for social conventions in the face of a chance to meet me. In their eyes, more than any of the others, I saw the centuries of waiting for the Moontouched's return, and the hope that the fulfillment of their faith gave them.

Are you ever going to tell me? I asked the Lady during one rare reprieve. *The big secret?*

She smiled at me. *My dear Queen...we already have. It's on the lips of every child who greets you.*

More than just me being the Moondaughter, I said with a sigh. *There's more, isn't there?*

What more do you need to know? she said, her tone making the words a statement, not a question.

I knew then that I wasn't going to get anything else out of her.

After the main bulk of the refugees had returned, I went back down to the King's wing, and after confirming with Vadya that there wasn't anything requiring immediate attention, I collapsed into my bed and took a long, blessed nap.

IT SEEMED THE STARKISSED had cheated Ben's three-day limit and gotten another day and night from us, but Ben didn't seem to resent that fact. The feast that night was a special one. For once, Ben and I got to sit at one of the lower tables while the families of the fallen sat at the higher. There were speeches and sad songs, but overall, the mood was surprisingly light. In fact, to my shock, dancing started up after all the eating, speechmaking, and singing were over. When I looked at Ben, he shrugged.

"This is the way we remember our dead," Kor said quietly from where he sat across the table from me. "By celebrating the life they gave us, and the blessed rest they've gained in return."

"Do you believe that?" I asked him quietly. When he looked at me, I said, "In life after death, I mean?"

Kor threaded his fingers on the table and examined them for a long moment. "The Tree says there is. And I haven't yet found a reason to disbelieve Her. Though I admit, I've tried."

"Why?" Ben asked quietly. Not because he seemed surprised or offended, rather because that seemed to be what Kor needed him to ask.

Kor looked over his shoulder at the dancers for a moment, then looked back at us. "Has it ever occurred to you, Ben, that what the Tree stands for is contradictory? She claims to be our protector, the guardian of life. And yet, to those who mourn, She says that the next world is a better one, one of light and peace—a world that, if we could catch a glimpse of it, we would gladly give up our lives now to obtain it. What is this life all for, if the next is the only one worth having? What is She protecting us from?"

Ben thought for a few long moments before answering. "I wouldn't say the next life isn't the only one worth having." He clenched my hand under the table as he said so.

Kor raised an eyebrow. "*You*? I seem to recall that only seventeen days ago, you were questioning why you were born."

I stilled, but Ben's expression didn't change. "I was. And I was wrong."

"What changed?" Kor said intently, as if the answer mattered to him—deeply and personally. "And don't just say it was Sarah."

"It wasn't. First, I had to realize...that I was still worthy of life." He took a deep breath. "And not just life, but happiness."

"And what finally convinced you of that?" Kor murmured.

I realized now what Kor was looking for: the contents of Ben's dream. But he wasn't just being his normal, nosy self. He truly seemed to *need* to understand. I was starting to have an inkling why.

"Forgiveness," Ben said simply. "And love."

"From *whom*?" Kor seemed to be trying to contain his frustration but was failing.

Ben smiled slightly and shrugged. "Everyone."

Kor glared at Ben as if he were struggling to feel much goodwill toward him right now.

Ben sighed. "To go back to your first point, Kor.... If there is in fact a purpose to our existence, and that purpose, as She says, is to have joy...I think there's a kind of happiness we can only get in *this* life—perhaps *because* it is so precious. Because we have to reach for it."

I hopefully hid my start, but Ben's phrasing struck a chord with me. His own father had told me to reach for happiness, when I was at my most uncertain of being worthy of it.

But Ben wasn't finished, though his voice grew quieter. "I don't think happiness is a gift that we can be given. Otherwise, I believe the Tree would give it to us. Like any mother, the only thing She can do is give us life—a chance to *learn* happiness. To *choose* it."

He glanced soberly over Kor's shoulder at the dancers. "And, sometimes, to fight for it."

He clenched my hand again.

"If only it were that simple," Kor said with a thin smile.

"Oh, it's not easy," Ben said with an answering smile. "Trust me, it's not. But simple...? I think so. At least, it is for me."

He turned his smile to me. "Speaking of which—Sarah, would you like to dance with me?"

I smiled back, so full of every kind of emotion that I needed some outlet before I burst. "I thought you would never ask."

CONTINUE THE ADVENTURE...

DRAGON'S HOPE

Ready for the next one? Scan the code to find where you can get *Dragon's Hope*.

ABOUT THE AUTHOR

Leah E. Welker graduated from Brigham Young University (Provo) in 2016 with a degree in English language and a minor in editing. She then edited for seven years and pivoted to writing in 2023. She is based in the DC area, where she lives with family and her rescue Australian shepherd, Wes.

You can connect with her at

https://www.leahewelker.com

Subscribe to her newsletter for updates, cover reveals, dog pics, and more:

https://www.leahewelker.com/follow

www.ingramcontent.com/pod-product-compliance
Lightning Source LLC
Chambersburg PA
CBHW060208030726
47499CB00004B/960